Also by Joel Shepherd

Crossover
A Cassandra Kresnov Novel

Breakaway
A Cassandra Kresnov Novel

Killswitch
A Cassandra Kresnov Novel

A TRIAL OF BLOOD & STEEL

Sasha

JOEL SHEPHERD

an imprint of **Prometheus Books**
Amherst, NY

Published 2009 by Pyr®, an imprint of Prometheus Books

Inquiries should be addressed to
Pyr
59 John Glenn Drive
Amherst, New York 14228–2119
VOICE: 716–691–0133, ext. 210
FAX: 716–691–0137
WWW.PYRSF.COM

13 12 11 10 09   5 4 3 2 1

Library of Congress Cataloging-in-Publication Data

Shepherd, Joel.
    Sasha / Joel Shepherd.
        p. cm. — (a trial of blood and steel ; bk. 1)
    Originally published: Australia and New Zealand : Hachette Livre Australia Pty Ltd.,
2007.
    ISBN 978–1–59102–787–4 (pbk. : alk. paper)
    I. Title.

PR9619.4.S54S37 2009
823'.92—dc22

2009022251

Printed in the United States on acid-free paper

❧ RHODIA ❧

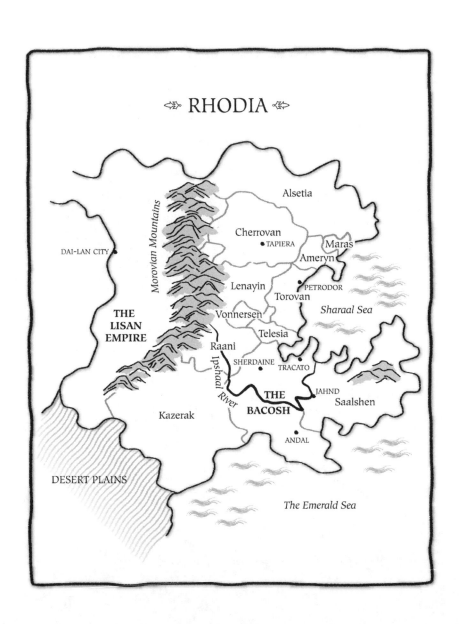

⊰⊱ LENAYIN PROVINCES ⊰⊱

Cherrovan

Udalyn Valley

• HALLERYN

Banneryd

Hadryn

Yumynis
River

Ranash

• RALYMER

YMOTH •

Taneryn

• PERYS

Fyden

• BAERLYN

CRYLISS •

Mt. Tvay

Valhanan

Tyree

• ALGERY

Yethulyn

•

KALTHYN

• BAEN TAR
Baen-Tar

Torovan

Neysh

Rayen

Isfayen

Vonnersen

Blood & Steel Characters

Lenayin

Valhanan

Sasha . . . . former Princess of Lenayin
Kessligh Cronenverdt . . . . warrior, former Commander of Armies
Peg . . . . Sasha's horse
Terjellyn . . . . Kessligh's horse
Teriyan . . . . leather worker
Lynette . . . . Teriyan's daughter
Jaegar . . . . headman of Baerlyn town
Andreyis . . . . Sasha's friend
Lord Kumaryn Tathys . . . . . . Great Lord of Valhanan
Tarynt . . . . councilman of Yule village

Tyree

Jaryd Nyvar . . . . heir to Great Lordship of Tyree
Lord Aystin Nyvar . . . . Jaryd's father, Great Lord of Tyree
Captain Tyrun . . . . Commander of Tyree's Falcon Guard
Lieutenant Reynan Pelyn . . . . Falcon Guardsman
Lord Tymeth Pelyn . . . . Tyree noble
Sergeant Garys . . . . Falcon Guardsman
Tarryn . . . . Jaryd's younger brother
Wyndal . . . . Jaryd's brother
Lord Redyk . . . . Tyree noble
Lord Paramys . . . . Tyree noble

Lord Arastyn . . . . Tyree noble
Galyndry . . . . Jaryd's sister
Pyter Pelyn . . . . nephew of Lord Pelyn
Rhyst Angyvar . . . . Tyree noble youth

Baen-Tar

Damon . . . . Prince of Lenayin
Torvaal Lenayin . . . . King of Lenayin
Krystoff . . . . Prince of Lenayin, *deceased*
Koenyg . . . . Prince of Lenayin, heir to the throne
Wylfred . . . . Prince of Lenayin
Wyna Telgar . . . . Koenyg's wife
Sofy . . . . Princess of Lenayin
Marya . . . . Princess of Lenayin, married in Torovan
Petryna . . . . Princess of Lenayin, married
Alythia . . . . Princess of Lenayin
Myklas . . . . Prince of Lenayin
Queen Shenai . . . . Queen of Lenayin, *deceased*
Anyse . . . . Sofy's maid
Archbishop Dalryn . . . . Lenay archbishop

Hadryn

Lord Rashyd Telgar . . . . Great Lord of Hadryn, *deceased*
Lord Usyn Telgar . . . . Rashyd Telgar's son, Great Lord of Hadryn
Farys Varan . . . . Hadryn noble
Lord Udys Varan . . . . Hadryn noble
Heryd Ansyn . . . . Hadryn noble
Martyn Ansyn . . . . Hadryn noble

Taneryn

Lord Krayliss . . . . Great Lord of Taneryn
Captain Akryd . . . . Taneryn soldier

Udalyn

Daryd Yuvenar . . . . Udalyn boy
Rysha . . . . Daryd's younger sister
Essey . . . . Udalyn horse
Chief Askar . . . . Udalyn chief

Banneryd

Captain Tyrblanc . . . . Banneryd Black Storm captain
Lord Cyan . . . . Great Lord of Banneryd
Corporal Veln . . . . Black Storm soldier

Isfayen

Lord Faras . . . . Great Lord of Isfayen

Neysh

Lord Aynsfar . . . . Neysh noble, *deceased*
Lord Parabys . . . . Great Lord of Neysh

Ranash

Lord Rydysh . . . . Great Lord of Ranash

Bacosh

Duke Stefhan . . . . Larosan duke
Master Piet . . . . Larosan bard

Saalshen

Rhillian . . . . serrin leader in Petrodor
Aisha . . . . female serrin
Errollyn . . . . male serrin, archer
Terel . . . . male serrin
Tassi . . . . female serrin

Others

Jurellyn . . . . senior Lenay scout
Aiden . . . . Nasi-Keth from Petrodor, Kessligh's friend

Historical Figures

Hyathon the Warrior . . . . Goeren-yai mythical hero
Markield . . . . Cherrovan warlord
Leyvaan of Rhodaan . . . . Leyvaan the Fool, King of Bacosh
Tharyn Askar . . . . great Udalyn chieftain
Essyn Telgar . . . . Hadryn chief
Soros Lenayin . . . . former king, head of Liberation army of old
Chayden Lenayin . . . . former king, Soros's son
Tullamayne . . . . Goeren-yai storyteller

One

SASHA CIRCLED, a light shift and slide of soft boots on compacted earth. The point of her wooden stanch marked the circle's centre, effortlessly extended from her two-fisted grip. Opposite, Teriyan the leather worker matched her motion, stanch likewise unwavering, bare arms knotted with hard muscle. Sasha's eyes beheld his form without true focus. She watched his centre, not the face, nor the feet, nor especially the wooden training blade in his strong, calloused hands.

An intricate tattoo of flowing black lines rippled upon Teriyan's bicep as his arm flexed. Thick red hair stirred in a gust of wind, tangled where it fell long and partly braided down his back. High above, an eagle called, launched to flight from the row of pines on the northern ridge overlooking the Baerlyn valley of central Valhanan province. The westerly sun was fading above the ridge, settling among the pines, casting long, looming shadows. The valley's entire length was alive with golden light, gleaming off the wood-shingled roofs of the houses that lined the central road, and brightening the green pastures to either side. Nearby, several young horses frolicked, an exuberance of hooves and gleaming manes and tails. From a nearby circle, there came an eruption of yells above the repeated clash of wooden blades. Then a striking thud, and a pause for breath.

Of all of this, Sasha was aware. And when Teriyan's lunging attack came, she deflected and countered with two fast, slashing strokes, and smacked her old friend hard across the belly.

Teriyan cursed, good-naturedly, and readjusted the protective banda that laced firmly about his torso. "What'd I do?" he asked, with the air of a man long since resigned to his fate.

Sasha shrugged, backing away with a light, balanced poise. "You attacked," she said simply.

"Girl's gettin' cute," Geldon remarked from amidst the circle of onlookers. Sasha flashed Geldon a grin, twirling her stanch through a series of rapid circles, moving little more than her wrists.

"Always been cute, baker-man," she said playfully. Guffaws from the crowd, numbering perhaps twenty on this late afternoon session. Strong men all, with braided hair and calloused hands. Many ears bore the rings of Goeren-yai manhood, and many faces the dark ink patterns of the wakening and the spirit world. Lenay warriors all, as fierce and proud as all the lowlands tales, a sight to strike terror into the hearts of any who had cause to fear. And yet they stood, and watched with great curiosity, as a lithe, cocky, short-haired girl in weave pants and a sheepskin jacket dismantled the formidable swordwork of one of their best, with little more to show for the effort than sweat.

Teriyan exhaled hard, and repeated his previous move, frowning with consideration. "Bugger it," he said finally. "That's as good an opening stroke as anyone's got. If someone has a better suggestion, I'm all ears."

"Improve," Tyal remarked.

"Kessligh says the low forehand is a more effective opener than the high," Sasha interrupted as Teriyan gave Tyal a warning stare. "For a man your size, anyhow."

"Ah," Teriyan made a mock dismissive gesture, "that Kessligh, what would he know about honest swordwork? You and him can stick to your sneaky svaalverd. Leave the real fighting to us, girlie."

"Look, do you want to know how I do it, or not?" Sasha asked in exasperation. There weren't many men in Lenayin who would dare call her "girlie." Teriyan was one. Kessligh Cronenverdt, the greatest swordsman in Lenayin and her tutor in far more than just swordwork for the past twelve years, was another.

Teriyan just looked at her, a reluctant smile creeping across a rugged face.

A bell clanged from the centre of town, midway up the valley. Stanches lowered, and all commotion about the training yard ceased as men turned to look, and listen. Again the bell, echoing off the steep valley sides, and then again, as someone got a good rhythm on the pulley rope.

"Rack your weapons!" yelled Byorn, the training hall proprietor, above the sudden commotion as men ran, boots thundering up the steps from the outside yard to the open, broad floorboards of the inner hall. "No haste in this hall, respect the circles!"

Despite the haste, men did keep to the dirt paths between tachadar circles, careful not to disturb the carefully laid stones, nor the sanctity of the space within. Sasha moved with less haste than some, seeing little point in elbowing through the crush of young men taking the lead. She walked instead with Teriyan and Geldon, up the dividing steps and into the high-ceilinged interior, unlacing her banda, and taking time to select her real weapons from the wooden rack where she'd hung them earlier. With weapons, Kessligh had instructed her often, one never rushed.

Most men did not own horses and began running up the trail toward the main road. Sasha fetched Peg from his field beside the training hall, used a stone paddock wall to mount, and galloped him in their wake . . . but before she could go racing to the lead, she spotted a familiar bay mare coming up the road to the training hall, a slim, red-haired girl upon her back, waving one-handed for Sasha's attention.

Sasha brought Peg to a halt, and waited. Lynette arrived with a thunder of swirling dust and flying hair, eyes wide within a freckled, pale face. She was panting and the mare—Chersey—was sweating profusely. Maybe enough for a seven-fold ride at speed, Sasha reckoned with a measuring eye, knowing Chersey's abilities every bit as well as Peg's.

"Sasha," Lynette gasped, "it's Damon. Damon's here."

Sasha frowned. "Damon came to Baerlyn? With what?"

"I thi . . . think it's the Falcon Guard." She brushed a ragged handful of curling red hair from her face as a gust of valley wind caught it. Her long dress was pulled well above her knees, with most unladylike decorum, exposing a pair of coarse-weave riding pants beneath. And leather boots in the stirrups. "I'm not sure . . . I was taking Chersey for a ride out past Spearman's Ridge when I saw them coming, so I turned around and came back as fast as I could . . . They had the banners out, Sasha, it was full armour and full colours! They looked magnificent!"

Sasha's frown grew deeper. The Falcon Guard had been lately posted in Baen-Tar. "You didn't speak to them? You don't know why they're here?"

Lynette shook her head. "No, I came straight back and told Jaegar, and he sent someone to ring the bell, and then I came looking for you . . ."

"Damn it. Lynie, I want you to go and get Kessligh—he went to buy some chickens."

"He'll hear the bell ringing, surely?" Lynette asked in confusion, as more men mounted nearby, and went galloping up the road.

"Kessligh takes his chickens very seriously," Sasha said wryly. "Just try and hurry him along a bit."

"I'll try," said Lynette doubtfully. Sasha kicked Peg with her heels, and went racing up the road as Lynette pulled Chersey about in a circle and followed as best she could. A short way along, Sasha came across Teriyan, Geldon and several others, running at a steady pace. She pulled Peg to a trot alongside and extended an inviting hand to Teriyan.

"Come on," she said, "council heads should get there first."

"Leave it, girl," Teriyan answered without breaking stride. "I still got some pride left, you know." Sasha scowled. Lynette went racing past on Chersey. "Hey, where'd you send my girl off to?"

"Ask her yourself, if you ever catch her," Sasha snorted, and galloped once more up the road.

The road wove between paddock fences and low stone walls, catching the full face of the sun before it vanished behind the ridge.

She was gaining fast on two men ahead as she reached the main Baerlyn road. Upon the wooden verandahs flanking the road, Baerlyn folk had gathered—mothers with their children, elderly folk in light cloaks or knitted shawls, and the men now walking or running along the road's broad edge, keeping the middle clear for horses. Peg loved a target, and passed the leading horses in a thunder of hooves.

The road wound past Geldon's bakery, then past the trading houses and side alleys leading to warehouses, and the workshops of jewellers, potters, furniture makers and Teriyan's own leather shop.

Up ahead she saw a gathering of horses and dismounted men in armour blocking the road, milling before the stone facade of the Steltsyn Star, Baerlyn's only inn. Heraldsmen held banners, gusting now in the light valley wind, indicating that Damon was still in the vicinity.

Sasha pulled up beside several men from the training hall and surveyed the scene. There appeared to be an effort underway to lead the regiment's horses down the Star's side lane, to the stables and paddocks that stretched to the southeastern valley wall at the rear. Her searching eyes found Jaegar, Baerlyn's headman, upon the Star's verandah gesticulating in earnest discussion, then waving a thick, tattooed arm across the semi-organised mass of waiting men and horses. He spoke with Damon—tall, darkly handsome and notable by his purple and green riding cloak, the gold clasp at his neck, and the gleaming silver pommel of his sword at one hip. Now twenty-three summers, by her reckoning, and seeming tired and dishevelled from his ride. All the men held a respectful distance, except the Falcon guard captain and a young man in lordly clothes, eagerly surveying the conversation, whom Sasha did not recognise.

Then the guard captain turned upon the step and shouted above the snort and stamp of hooves, the jangle of armour and the busy discussions of men, "In units down the lane! The stables are already half full, fill them as you can, then fill the barn—it should take another ten! The rest, there's three more properties behind the inn toward the valley side, there should be enough room in those barns, if not, move down and knock on the next door. Be polite, I want not a hay bale disturbed without permission, nor a chicken's feather plucked, nor a sow's tail pulled. I'll not have the good folk of Valhanan saying the Falcon Guard make poor guests! Tend to your mounts, then gather back here for a good hot meal on the king's own coin!"

That got a rousing cheer from all present.

"Men of Baerlyn!" bellowed Jaegar, with a barrel-chested volume that surpassed even the captain. He was a stocky man of middling height but with massively broad shoulders. The angling light appeared to catch only one side of his face, leaving the other darkly ominous . . . except that the darker side was facing the light. Upon closer inspection, the spirit-mask of Goeren-yai manhood revealed its finer intricacies of weaving curls, waves and flourishes. Sunlight glinted on the many rings in his ears, and upon the silver chain about his broad, sculpted neck. His long hair, parted cleanly down the middle, bound down the centre of his back in a single, leather-tied braid.

"Those with space available indoors, please find a sergeant or corporal and say so!" Jaegar continued. "There's no need for any more than the horse tenders to spend a night in the cold! Illys, we'd welcome some music inside tonight!" There was a cheer from the Baerlyn townfolk who had encircled the Falcon Guard, in all curiosity and eagerness to help.

"And Upwyld with the ale!" yelled someone from the periphery. "Don't forget the ale!" And that got an enormous cheer from everyone, soldiers and locals alike.

Jaegar held both calloused hands skyward to quieten the racket, and then bellowed, "It is the honour of Baerlyn to receive this most welcome visitation! Three cheers for the Falcon Guard!"

"Hoorah!" yelled the Baerlyners. "Hoorah! Hoorah!"

"Three cheers for Master Jaryd!" with an indication to the young man beside them on the verandah. Again the cheers. The young man held up a hand with a cheerful grin. Something about the glamorous cut of his clothes, and the self-assured smile on his lips, made Sasha's breath catch in her throat. The Falcon Guard were all from neighbouring Tyree province of central Lenayin. He must be one of Great Lord Aystin Nyvar of Tyree's sons. Not Jaryd *Nyvar*? Surely the spirits would not be so cruel to her? "And three cheers for Prince Damon!" And those three cheers, to Sasha's mild surprise, were loudest of all. Damon, she noted, glanced down at his riding boots and looked uncomfortable. She repressed an exasperated smile. Same old Damon.

"Three cheers for Baerlyn!" yelled the captain, and the soldiers answered back in kind. "Let's move!"

With little more fuss, the soldiers began filing down the Star's cobbled side lane. Sasha finally completed her rough headcount, and arrived at perhaps eighty men and horses, their numbers clustering a good way up the road past the inn. The strength of standing companies varied from province to province—in the north, the great armoured cavalry companies numbered closer to a thousand each. The Falcon Guard company, by her reckoning, should have about five hundred at full strength. Perhaps this contingent had left in a hurry and the others were following.

She left Peg in the care of a farmer she knew well. Damon and the young Tyree lordling stood in continued conversation with Jaegar, now joined by another two Baerlyn councilmen, similarly tattooed and ringed as Jaegar. Sasha eyed that contrast as she approached unseen, slipping between soldier-led horses—the Baerlyn men rough and hardy Goeren-yai warriors. And Damon tall, clipped and elegantly attired, a Verenthane medallion—the eight-pointed star—prominently suspended on a chain about his neck.

Rural Goeren-yai and city Verenthanes. The old Lenayin, and the new. The Goeren-yai believed in the ancient spirits of Lenay hills, the Verenthane in the foreign, lowlands gods. Sasha was born Verenthane, but lived amongst Goeren-yai . . . and was raised by Kessligh as Nasi-Keth, the followers of the teachings of far-off Saalshen. She sometimes wondered if she'd done something to offend some gods or spirits in a previous life to have deserved such a complicated fate. She often thought things would be so much simpler if she could just choose one or the other . . . or the third. But no matter which she chose, her choice would offend countless powerful people.

Sasha thrust the doubts aside, cleared the gathering about the steps, and trotted briskly up. Damon saw her at the last moment and straightened stiffly. Nearby commotion abruptly slowed, and conversation paused, as people turned to look.

"Damon," said Sasha, managing a half-genuine smile as Jaegar quickly made way for her atop the steps.

"Sashandra," Damon replied, similarly ill-at-ease. And then, with meaningful emphasis, "Sister." And spread his arms to embrace her. Sasha returned the hug, the first time she had embraced her brother in nearly a year, by her immediate reckoning. From about the verandah, and upon the road, there was applause and some cheering. Beneath Damon's riding clothes, Sasha felt the hard weight of chainmail, which was sometimes decorative custom for a travelling prince, and sometimes not. This, she guessed from the size of the company, was not. They released each other, and Damon put both gloved hands upon her shoulders and looked at her.

"You're looking well," he remarked.

Liar, Sasha thought. Little though she'd seen him of late, she knew well his true opinion of her appearance these days. In Baen-Tar, the seat of Lenay kings, the ladies all wore dresses, and hair so long you could trip on it. Some of her wry amusement must have shown on her face, for Damon barely repressed a smile of his own.

"You too," Sasha replied, and meant it. "What brings you to my humble town?"

"Well," said the young prince with a hard sigh. "Therein lies the tale."

"We're still not clear exactly what happened," Damon said to the table, his voice raised to carry above the mealtime clamour. Changed into a clean shirt beneath a patterned leather vest, covered again by the riding cloak in regal purple and green, he looked to Sasha's eyes far more comfortable now than in the armour. His fingers toyed absently with the wine cup. "We only received word that Great Lord Rashyd Telgar is dead, and that Great Lord Krayliss is responsible."

Sasha stared sullenly at the open fire upon the centre of the Star's main floor. Flames blazed within the stone-lined pit as several kitchen hands hurried about and rotated the three sizzling spits. Men clustered at long tables between ceiling supports as Baerlyn youngsters served as waiters, hurrying back and forth with laden plates and mugs of ale.

Voices roared in conversation, and heat radiated from the fire, as music and the smell of good food filled the confined air beneath the Star's low ceiling.

"You're sure it was Krayliss that killed Rashyd?" Jaegar pressed from his seat alongside Captain Tyrun, commander of the Falcon Guard. Tyrun and Sasha were sitting on either side of Damon at the head of the table. On Sasha's left sat Teriyan, widely regarded as Jaegar's right-hand man in Baerlyn, due mostly to his swordsmanship and exploits in battle. The young Master Jaryd completed the group, ignoring the breathless stares that the serving girls sent his way. At the end of the table, a chair for Kessligh sat empty. If Damon were offended at his absence, he didn't show it. Probably he knew that Kessligh was Kessligh, and did as he pleased.

"I'm not sure of anything," Damon replied to Jaegar, somewhat testily, but recovered from his outburst no sooner than it had begun. Same old Damon indeed, Sasha noted sourly. Damon took a breath. "I only know what word reached us in Baen-Tar. The messenger said his lord was dead and that revenge must follow. Against Krayliss."

Damon took another bite of his roast, then cleaned up the remains of his vegetable raal with a piece of bread. The table exchanged sombre glances, an oasis of silence amongst the raucous din. Sasha met no one's gaze and simply stared at the central fire. Lord Rashyd was dead, and Hadryn province, the greatest of Lenayin's three northern provinces, was now without its leader. And now the Falcon Guard were riding from Baen-Tar to take revenge on Lord Krayliss of neighbouring Taneryn province. It seemed that the age-old conflict between Hadryn and Taneryn had flared once more, with all the ancient, treacherous history that entailed. Sasha did not trust herself to speak, lest some slip of caution unleash the seething in her gut.

Lenayin had ten provinces—eleven, if one counted the city lands of royal Baen-Tar. A century earlier the Liberation had permanently established long-disputed borders and created a class of nobility to rule over them. In all of the provinces save one, the nobility were Verenthane. The one exception, of course, was Taneryn. Lord Krayliss was the only Goeren-yai great lord in Lenayin. No surprise then that the Hadryn–Taneryn border remained the most troubled in Lenayin. To all the many causes for countless centuries of war between the Hadryn and Taneryn, the Liberation had added religion.

As grand as the Liberation had been, not all the Lenay peoples had shared in its benefits. For the Udalyn peoples, the Liberation had proven a disaster. Today, they lived trapped in their valley within the boundaries of Hadryn, holding fiercely to the old ways, despite the Hadryn's attempts to convert them or kill them. The Taneryn considered them heroes. The Hadryn, heretics. It remained perhaps the most emotive of unresolved conflicts in Lenayin. For Goeren-yai across Lenayin, the Udalyn represented antiquity, the old ways from before the Liberation, too strong to die, too proud to give up the fight. If the Udalyn were somehow involved in this latest calamity, Sasha reckoned, then matters could become very grim indeed.

"Rashyd's men were on manoeuvre, we heard," said Captain Tyrun, downing his mouthful with a gulp of wine. Tyrun had a lean, angular face, like the falcon from which his unit took its name. His nose was large, his moustache broad and drooping. Less well clipped, Sasha noted with reluctant curiosity, than most Verenthane officers, although his face bore no sign of the ink quill, nor his ears of rings or other, pagan decoration. Most likely he was no Goeren-yai, although if he wore a Verenthane medallion, it lay hidden beneath his tunic. "It seems he was killed within Taneryn borders. What he was doing there, if he was there, we don't know."

"Making nuisance, most likely," Teriyan remarked around a mouthful. "Hadryn's claimed the western parts of Taneryn for centuries, damn Rashyd's been angling for a war since his father died."

"Words were exchanged," Tyrun continued, ignoring the dark look that Damon fixed on Teriyan. "A fight ensued between Rashyd's men and Krayliss's. Some were killed on both sides. And Krayliss killed Rashyd personally, with clear intent. So the messenger said."

"He might not have seen it all," Jaegar cautioned.

Or might be lying through his teeth to protect the honour of his ass of a lord, Sasha thought to herself. Still, she forced herself to remain silent. It would not befit anyone to be speaking ill of Lord Rashyd so soon after his death.

The calamity was beyond her immediate comprehension. No one in these parts liked Lord Rashyd Telgar, with his arrogant, northern ways and strict Verenthane codes. But for Krayliss to kill him . . . There were some who'd said that Lord Rashyd sat at the king's right hand. And others who'd said that the king, at Lord Rashyd's . . .

Tyrun heard Jaegar's caution and shrugged. "As you say," he said. "We have yet to discover what happened. But Krayliss has taxed the king's tolerance for a long time now, and there comes a time when even our tolerant king must put his foot down. In this, we are the heel of his boot."

"Our king," said Master Jaryd, somewhat tersely, "is vastly long on tolerance. He is a merciful man, a man of the gods, for surely they favour him. My father says that Lord Krayliss has preyed upon this mercy as a spoilt child preys upon the tolerance of a doting parent. Like the spoilt child, Krayliss deserves a spanking. With His Highness the Prince's blessing, I intend to administer it personally."

Jaryd downed a mouthful of ale with a flourish, lounging in his chair as an athletic man might, who wished others to observe the fact. Sasha observed him with a dark curiosity, having never seen this particular young noble face-to-face before. Jaryd Nyvar was a name known the length and breadth of Lenayin, and even those like Sasha who tried to avoid the endless gossip of Verenthane nobility knew something of his exploits. At no more than twenty-one summers, Jaryd Nyvar was the heir of Tyree. His mother was a cousin to Sasha's father—King Torvaal Lenayin—which made her and Jaryd related, she supposed. It was hardly uncommon amongst Lenay nobility—she was probably related to far more arrogant young puss-heads than Jaryd Nyvar. But it made her uneasy, all the same.

Every year at one of the great tournaments, Jaryd Nyvar would win personal honours of swordwork or horsemanship. His flamboyance was famous, his dancing reputedly excellent, and it was said he made grand gestures to the ladies before every bout. Sasha had heard it said jokingly that Jaryd's swordwork was so excellent because he'd spent most of his days beating off hordes of girls, and their mothers, with a stick.

Looking at him now, she grudgingly conceded the stories of his appearance were not too farfetched. He *was* very pretty, with light brown hair worn somewhat longer than most Verenthanes, just above the collar at the back, and large, dark brown eyes that promised fire and mischief in equal measure.

She had not heard of his command posting to the Falcon Guards. Perhaps his father grew tired of his pointless gallivanting and thought to put his skills to some decent, disciplined use. And his father, they said, was dying. Perhaps that added to the urgency.

"The Falcon Guard was posted to Baen-Tar for the summer?" Teriyan asked Jaryd.

"The latter half of the summer, aye," Jaryd agreed. He took a grape from the table and tossed it easily into his mouth. "We trained with the Royal Guard and others . . . gave them a right spanking too, I might add. Right, Captain?"

"Aye, M'Lord," Captain Tyrun agreed easily. "That we did."

"I've served in both Hadryn and Taneryn," Teriyan said, chewing on a slice of roast meat. "That entire border's full of armed men waiting for an incident. I wonder if the Falcon Guard will be enough. You're damn good, sure, but eighty men can't be everywhere at once. If this gets serious, there'll be hundreds runnin' around like headless chickens. Thousands, maybe."

"Three more companies are several days behind us," Damon said. "Each of those is promised at closer to their full strength—five hundred men in total. Most of the Falcon Guard were on manoeuvre about Baen-Tar. That's another hundred. We left in too much haste for anything more."

"We'd have gathered a Valhanan company on the way through," Captain Tyrun added, "but there's none standing ready at present. We did think it common sense to gather Yuan Kessligh on the way through, however. If he's willing."

He glanced toward the empty chair. Sasha shrugged. "I can't speak for him," she said. "But I'd be surprised if he weren't."

Jaryd slapped the table with one hand, delighted. "Wonderful!" he exclaimed. "To ride with Yuan Kessligh! I've dreamed of that since I was a lad—smiting evildoers at Kessligh's side! That fool Krayliss won't know what hit him."

"Krayliss is the evildoer?" Sasha asked, implacably cool. "We have yet to establish what occurred surrounding Lord Rashyd's death. Until such a time as we know for sure, Lord Krayliss deserves the benefit of any doubt, surely? Or has my father's law changed so drastically when I wasn't watching?"

Jaryd smiled broadly, in the manner of a masterful warrior challenged to a duel by a raggedy little farmer's girl with a stick. "M'Lady," he said, with a respectful, mirthful nod, "surely you know what Lord Krayliss is like? The man is a bigot, a . . . a rogue, a thief—a vain, strutting, pompous fool who is a blight upon the good nobility of Lenayin! And now, apparently, a murderer, though this will surely surprise no one who knows his type."

"I've met Lord Krayliss, Master Jaryd. Have you?" Jaryd gazed at her, his smile slowly slipping. "I've met Lord Rashyd too. And strangely, I find your description could just as readily describe him as the other."

"I too have met Lord Rashyd, several times," Jaryd said coolly. Sasha wondered if he'd ever conversed with a young woman on a matter that did not involve her giggling shyly with starry eyes. "He is . . . or rather was . . . a hard man, at times confrontingly so. But at least he was not a . . . a shaggy-headed, mindless, chest-thumping . . ." he waved a hand, searching for a new, derogatory adjective.

"Pagan?" Sasha suggested.

Jaryd just looked at her for a moment, realisation dawning in his eyes. Sasha shifted her gaze to Jaegar, beneath meaningful, raised eyebrows. Jaegar coughed, and sipped at his drink. From this angle, the spirit-mask on the left side of his face was not fully visible, but gold glinted from his ear, and upon his fingers. The long braid, also, was like nothing a respectable Verenthane would ever stoop to wear.

Anger flared in the future Great Lord of Tyree's eyes. "You put words in my mouth, M'Lady," he said accusingly. "I meant no such thing!"

"You young Verenthane lords put words in your own mouths," Sasha retorted, "and scarcely a thought before putting them there. Remember whose guest you are. They're *far* too polite to say so. I'm not."

"Shut up, both of you!" Damon snapped before Jaryd could reply. The young man fumed at her, all trace of cool demeanour vanished. Sasha stared back, dark eyes smouldering. "Please excuse my sister, Master Jaryd," said Damon, with forced calm. "Her tempers are famous."

"And her allegiances," Jaryd muttered.

"Oh pray do tell us all what that means?" Sasha exclaimed, as Damon rolled his eyes in frustration.

"I have many Goeren-yai friends, M'Lady," Jaryd said, levelling a finger at her for emphasis. "None of them admire Lord Krayliss even a jot. You, on the other hand, seem all too pleased to rush to his defence."

"I've heard those stories too," said Sasha. "The Hadryn and their cronies have never been friends to either me or Kessligh. They accuse me of sedition, of plotting against my father." She put both hands upon the table with firm purpose. "Are *you* accusing me of sedition, Master Jaryd?"

Jaryd blinked. Sedition, of course, was punished by death, with no exceptions. A person so accused, without reasonable proof, had obvious grounds for an honour duel. Those, also, ended in death. With very few exceptions. Jaryd started to smile once more, disbelievingly. No man about the table seemed to share his humour. Jaryd Nyvar, tournament champion of Lenayin, seemed barely to notice.

"No," he said, offhandedly, with an exasperated raise of his eyes to the ceiling, as though he felt his dignity severely pained to have to tolerate such dreadfully silly people. Fool, Sasha thought darkly. "Of course not. Your tempers delude you, M'Lady. I have nothing but admiration for so great a Verenthane beauty as your own."

"Tell me, young Master Jaryd," said Teriyan, leaning forward with evident amusement, chewing on some bread. "Have you ever sparred against a warrior trained in the svaalverd?"

"As a matter of fact, no," Jaryd said mildly. "The only two people so trained in Lenayin, I believe, are Kessligh Cronenverdt and his uma. And the visiting serrin, of course, but they never enter a swordwork contest, even though I have often seen them at tournaments."

"And have you ever wondered why the serrin don't enter swordwork contests?" Teriyan pressed.

Jaryd smirked. "Perhaps they are afraid."

"Not afraid, young Master," said Teriyan. "Just polite."

Damon strode angrily along the upper corridor, the Star's old floorboards creaking underfoot, as the sounds of merriment continued from below. Sasha followed, conscious that her own footsteps made far less noise than her brother's, and that their respective weights were only half the reason why. When they reached his room, Damon ushered Sasha inside, closed the door and threw on the latch.

It was a good room, as Lenay accommodation went. Four times larger than most of the Star's rooms, its floorboards covered with a deer hide rug, and small windows inlaid across the stone walls. Against the inner wall, two large beds, with tall posts and soft mattresses beneath piles of furs and fine, lowlands linen. Between the two beds, a fireplace, crackling merrily, and a small pile of firewood in the wicker basket alongside.

"Why do you have to go and do that?" Damon demanded at her back. Sasha walked to the space between the two beds, where heat from the fire provided some comfort.

"Go and do what?" she retorted.

"And this!" Damon exclaimed, striding over, reaching with one hand toward the tri-braid upon the side of her head . . . Sasha ducked away, scowling at him. "What in the nine hells is that?"

"It's a tri-braid, Damon. One braid for each of the three spirit levels. Don't they even teach basic Goeren-yai lore in Baen-Tar any more?"

"Why, Sasha?" Damon demanded, angrily. "Why wear it?"

"Because I'm Lenay!" Sasha shot back. "What are you?"

"Cut it off. Right now."

Sasha folded her arms in disbelief. "Make me!" she exclaimed. Arisen from the dinner table, there was a sword at her back now, and more weapons besides. Damon, unlike Master Jaryd, knew better.

"Good gods, Sasha," he exclaimed, with a sharp inhaling of breath. He put both hands to his head, fingers laced within his thick dark hair, looking as he would never wittingly appear before his men—utterly at a loss. "A year since I've seen you. A full year. I was almost looking forward to seeing you again . . . almost! Can you believe that? And this is the welcome I get!"

Sasha just stared at him, sullenly. Her temper slowly cooling as she gazed up at her brother. Not all the Lenayin line were blessed with height—she was proof enough of that. But Damon was. A moderately tall young man, with a build that spoke more of speed and balance than brute strength. He would be very handsome indeed, she thought, if not for the occasionally petulant curl of his lip and the faintly childish whine in his tone whenever he felt events going against him.

He was the middle child of ten royal siblings, of whom nine now survived. With Krystoff dead, Koenyg was heir. Wylfred would be next, had he not found religion and committed to the Verenthane order instead, with their father's blessing. Then came Damon. Second in line now and struggling so very hard beneath the burden of expectation that came of one martyred brother who was already legend, and an overbearing stonehead of a surviving elder brother.

"I'm not a Verenthane, Damon," Sasha told him, firmly. "I'll never be a Verenthane. You could cut my braid, stick me in a dress and feed me holy fables until my mind dissolves from the sheer boredom, and I'll still not be a Verenthane."

"Well that's all fine, Sasha," Damon said, exasperated. "You're not a Verenthane. Good for you. But you have a commitment to our father, and that commitment includes *not* making overt statements of loyalty toward the Goeren-yai."

"Why the hells not?" Sasha fumed. "Goeren-yai are more than half of Lenayin last I looked! It's only you lordly types that converted, and the cities and bigger towns . . . most of Lenayin is just like this, Damon! Small villages and towns filled with decent, hard-working folk who ask nothing more than good rulers and the right to continue being who they are without some shaven-headed, black-robed idiot strolling into their lives and demanding their fealty."

"Sasha, your last name is Lenayin!" Damon paused, to let the impact of that sink in. Wiser than to rise to her provocations. That was new. "The family of Lenayin is Verenthane! It has been for a century, since the Liberation! Now, whether your arrangement with Kessligh means that your title is officially "Princess" or not, your family name remains Lenayin! And while that continues to be so, you shall not, under any circumstances, break with the continuity of the line of Lenayin!"

Sasha waved both hands in disgust and strode across the floor to lean against a window rim. Looking northeast up the valley, small lights burned from the windows of the houses that lined the road, then the dark, ragged edge of the upper treeline, separating the land from the vast expanse of stars. Hyathon the Warrior sat low on the horizon, and Sasha's eye traced the bright stars of shoulder, elbow and sword pommel raised in mid-stroke.

"Sasha." Damon strolled to her previous spot, blocking the fire's warmth. "Master Jaryd speaks the truth. There have been rumours, since the call to Rathynal, of Krayliss courting your approval . . ."

"The nobility talks, Damon," Sasha retorted, breath frosting upon the cold, dark glass. "Rumour is the obsession of the ruling class, everyone always talks of this or that development, who is in favour with whom, and never a care for the concerns of the people. That's all it is—talk."

"Just who do you think you are, Sasha?" Damon said in exasperation. "A champion of the common people? Because I will tell you this, little sister— it's precisely that kind of talk that breeds rumours. Krayliss and his kind cannot be dismissed so easily, they *do* have a strong following amongst some of the people . . ."

"Vastly overstated," Sasha countered, rounding on him. She folded her arms and leaned her backside against the stone windowsill. "The ruling Verenthanes simply don't understand their own people, Damon. And do you know why that is? It's because there are so *few* Goeren-yai among the ruling classes. Krayliss is the only provincial lord, and he's a maniac!"

"A maniac who claims ancestry with the line of Udalyn," Damon said sharply. "You of all people should know what the Udalyn mean to Goeren-yai all across Lenayin. Such appeals cannot be taken lightly."

"I of all people *do* know," Sasha said darkly. "You're only quoting what Koenyg told you. And he knows *nothing*."

Damon broke off his reply as the door rattled, held fast against the latch. Then an impatient hammering. Damon looked at first indignant, wondering who would dare such impetuosity against Lenay royalty. Then realisation, and he strode rapidly to the door, flung off the latch and stepped back for it to open. Kessligh entered, holding a wicker cage occupied by three flapping, clucking chickens.

"Ah good," said the greatest swordsman in Lenayin, noticing the fire. He carried the cage across the creaking floor with barely a glance to Damon or Sasha, and placed the cage between the two beds. The chickens flapped, then settled. "These lowland reds don't like the cold so much. Makes for bad eggs."

And he appeared to notice Damon for the first time, as the young prince relatched the door and came across with an extended hand. Kessligh shook it, forearm to forearm in the Lenay fashion. Damon had half a head on Kessligh and nearly thirty years of youth. Yet somehow, in Kessligh's presence, he seemed to shrink in stature.

"Yuan Kessligh," Damon said, with great deference. "Yuan," Sasha reflected, watching them from her windowsill. The only formal title Kessligh still retained, and that merely denoting a great warrior. An old Lenay tradition it was, now reserved for those distinguished by long service in battle, be they Verenthane or Goeren-yai. It remained one of those traditions that bound the dual faiths of Lenayin together, rather than pulled them apart. But Kessligh, of course, was neither Goeren-yai nor Verenthane. "An honour to see you once more."

"Likewise, young Damon," Kessligh replied, his tone strong with that familiar Kessligh-edge. Sharp and cutting, in a way that long years in the service of refined Lenay lords had never entirely dulled. Hard brown eyes bore into Damon's own, beneath a fringe of untidy, greying hair. "And are you the hunter, this time? Or merely the shepherd, tending to errant sheep?" With a cryptic glance across at Sasha.

Sasha made a face, far less impressed by the gravitas of the former Lenay Commander of Armies than most.

"Oh, well . . ." Damon cleared his throat. "You have heard, then? About Lord Rashyd?"

"I was just talking downstairs," Kessligh said calmly. "Catching up with old friends, learning the news, such as it is. So Master Jaryd will live to see past dawn, I take it?"

Damon blinked, looking most uncertain. Which was often the way, for those confronted with Kessligh's sharp irreverence on matters that most considered important.

"It appears that way," Damon said, with a further uncertain glance at Sasha. Sasha watched, mercilessly curious. "Please, won't you sit? I'll have someone bring up some tea."

"Already done," said Kessligh, "but thank you." And he sat, with no further ado, cross-legged on the further bed, with the chickens murmuring and clucking to themselves on the floor below.

Sasha considered the study in profiles as Damon undid his sword belt and made to sit on the bed opposite. Damon's face, evidently anxious, his features soft and not entirely pronounced. And Kessligh's, rugged and lined with years, with a beakish nose, a sharp chin and hard, searching eyes. Like a work of carving, expertly done yet never entirely completed. He sat straight-backed on the bed, legs tucked tightly beneath, with the poise of a man half his years. It was a posture that wasted not a muscle or sinew, an efficiency born of lifelong discipline and devotion to detail. And his sword was worn not at the hip, as with most fighting men of Lenayin, but clipped to the bandolier on his back, as with all fighters of the svaalverd style.

Damon sat with less poise than Sasha's teacher—or uman, in the Saalsi tongue of the serrin—placing a foot on the bed frame and pulling up one knee. At his feet, the chickens clucked and fluttered at the further disturbance. Damon looked at the chickens. And at Kessligh. Struggling to think of something to say. Sasha tried to keep an uncharitable smile in check.

"These are good chickens?" he managed finally. Sasha coughed, a barely restrained splutter. Damon shot her a dark look.

"Well I'm trying to broaden the breeding range," Kessligh replied serenely. "These are *kersan ross*, from the lowlands. The eggs have an interesting flavour, much better for making light pastries."

"You traded for these?" Damon asked, attempting interest, to his credit. It was Lenay custom that no serious talk could begin before the tea arrived. Poor Damon was horrible at small talk.

"A local farmer placed an order through his connections," Kessligh replied. "A wonderful trading system we now have with the Torovans. Place an order with the right people and a Torovan convoy will deliver in two or three months. They're becoming quite popular."

"As with all things Torovan," Sasha remarked. Damon frowned at her. Kessligh simply smiled.

"Ah," he said. "Thus speaks she of the Nasi-Keth. She who fights with Saalshen style, loves Vonnersen spices in all her foods, washes regularly with the imported oils of coastal Maras, lives off the wealth from the Torovan love of Lenay-bred horses, speaks two foreign tongues, and has been known to down entire tankards of ale with visiting serrin travellers while playing Ameryn games of chance. But no lover of foreigners she."

Kessligh's sharp eyes fixed upon her, sardonically. Sasha held her tongue, eyebrows raised in a manner that invited praise for doing so. There had been times in the past when she had not been so disciplined. He grunted, in mild amusement. Then came a knocking on the door, which Sasha answered and found the tea delivered on a tray.

She set the tray on a footstool for Kessligh to prepare, then settled into a reclining chair with a sigh of aching muscles.

Damon accepted his tea with evident discomfort. Prince or not, few Lenays felt comfortable having Kessligh serve them tea. But that had not stopped Kessligh from cooking for entire tables of Baerlyn folk when suitable occasions arose. Sasha had always found it curious, this yawning gulf between the popular Lenay notion of Kessligh the vanquishing war hero, and her familiar, homespun reality. Kessligh the son of poor dock workers in lowlands Petrodor, trading capital of Torovan, for whom Lenay was a second (or third) language, still spoken with a tinge of broad, lowlander vowels that others remarked upon, but Sasha had long since ceased to notice. Kessligh the Nasi-Keth—a serrin cult (or movement, Kessligh insisted) whose presence had long been prominent amongst the impoverished peoples of Petrodor. Kessligh, serrin-friend, with old ties and allegiances that even three decades of life and fame in Lenayin had not managed to erase.

Kessligh considered Sasha's evident weariness with amusement, sipping at his tea. "Did Teriyan wear you out?" he asked.

"More demonstrations," Sasha replied wryly, stretching out legs and a free arm, arching her back like a cat. Her left shoulder ached from a recent strain. It seemed to have altered the balance of her grip, for the tendon of her left thumb now throbbed in sympathy where her grip upon the stanch had somehow tightened, unconsciously. The knuckles on her right hand were bruised where a stanch had caught her, and several more impacts ached about her ribs, causing a wince if one were pressed unexpectedly. The front of her right ankle remained tender from where she'd turned it several days ago, during one of Kessligh's footwork exercises. And those were just the pains she was most aware of. All in all, just another day for the uma of Kessligh Cronenverdt. "They all want to see svaalverd, so I show them svaalverd. And rather than learning, they then spend the whole time complaining that it's impossible."

Kessligh shook his head. "Svaalverd is taught from the cradle or not at all," he said. "Best they learn little. It makes an ill fit with traditional Lenay techniques. Men who try both get their footing confused and trip themselves up."

"We could try teaching the kids," said Sasha, sipping her own tea. "Before Jaegar and others get their hooks into them."

"The culture here is set," Kessligh replied. "I'm loath to tamper with it. Tradition has its own strength, and its own life. And I fear I've caused enough damage to Lenay custom already." Meaningfully.

Sasha snorted. "Well I *would* be a good little farm wench, but it's difficult to fight in dresses, and impossible to ride . . ."

"You could have kept your hair long," Kessligh suggested.

"And worn a man's braid?" With a glance at Damon, who listened and watched with great intrigue. The former Lenay Princess and the former Lenay Commander of Armies. To many in Lenayin, it still seemed an outrageously unlikely pairing. Many rumoured as to its true nature. "I couldn't wear it loose like the women because then it would get in the way, but I can't wear a braid like a man because then I'm not allowed to be a woman at all. The only option left was to cut it short as some of the serrin girls wear it. I don't do *everything* just to be difficult, you know, I did actually put some thought into it."

"The evidence of *that* doesn't equal your conclusion," Kessligh remarked with amusement.

Sasha gave Damon an exasperated look. "This is what passes for entertainment in the great mind of Kessligh Cronenverdt," she told him. "Belittling me in front of others."

"What's not entertaining about it?" Damon said warily. Sasha made a face at him.

"I assume you've made comment on Sasha's new appendage?" Kessligh continued wryly, with a nod at her tri-braid. "She insists it's all the fashion. Myself, I wonder why she can't hold to Torovan jewellery and knee-high boots like good, proper Lenay children."

Sasha grinned. Damon blinked, and sipped his tea to cover the silence as he tried to figure out what to say. "You approve?" he said finally.

Kessligh made an expansive shrug. "Approve, disapprove . . ." He held a hand in Sasha's direction. "Behold, young Damon, a twenty-year-old female. In the face of such as this, of what consequence is it for me to approve or disapprove?"

Damon shrugged, faintly. "Most Lenay families are less accommodating. Tradition, as you say." Sasha raised an eyebrow. It was more confrontational than she'd expected from Damon.

"This is my uma," Kessligh replied calmly. "I am her uman. In the ways of the serrin, and thus the ways of the Nasi-Keth, it is not for uman to dictate paths to their uma. She will go her own way, and find her own path. Should she have chosen study and herbal lore instead of swordwork and soldiery, that would also have been her choice . . . although a somewhat poorer teacher I would have made, no doubt.

"So she feels a common cause with the Goeren-yai of Lenayin." He shrugged. "Hardly surprising, having lived amongst them for twelve of her twenty years. The mistake you all make, be you Verenthanes or romantics like Krayliss, is to think of her as anything other than my uma. What she does, and what she chooses to wear in her hair, she does as uma to me. This is a separate thing from politics. Quite frankly, it does not concern you. Nor should it concern our king."

"Our king concerns himself with many things," Damon said mildly.

"Not this," said Kessligh. "He owes me too much. And King Torvaal always repays his debts." Damon gazed down at his tea cup. "Baerlyn is not the most direct line from Baen-Tar to Taneryn. What purpose does this detour serve?"

Damon glanced up. "Your assistance," he said plainly. "You are as greatly respected in Taneryn as here. My father feels, and I agree, that your presence in Taneryn would calm the mood of the people."

"The king's justice must be the king's," Kessligh replied, a hard stare unfixing upon the young prince's face. "I cannot take his place. Such a role is more yours than mine."

"We have concern about the people of Hadryn taking matters into their own hands," said Damon. "Lenayin has been mercifully free of civil strife over the last century. The king would not see such old history repeated. Your presence would be valued."

"I claim no special powers over the hard men of Hadryn," said Kessligh, with a shake of his head. "The north has never loved me. During the Great War, my successes stole much thunder from the northern lords, and now Lenay history records that forces under my command saved them from certain defeat. That could have been acceptable, were I Verenthane, or a northerner. But I'm afraid the north views Goeren-yai and Nasi-Keth as cut from the same cloth—irredeemably pagan and godless. I do not see what comfort my presence there could bring."

"But you will come?" Damon persisted.

Kessligh sipped his tea, his eyes not leaving Damon's. "Should my Lord King command it," he said, in measured tones. "Of course, you understand that Sasha must therefore accompany me?"

Damon blinked at him. And glanced across at Sasha. "These events make for great uncertainty. I had thought for her to remain in Baerlyn, with a complement of Falcon Guard for protection."

"You'd *what*?" Sasha asked, with no diplomacy at all.

Kessligh held up a hand, and she held her tongue, fuming. He unfolded his legs, in one lithe move, and leaned forward to pour some more tea from the earthen-glaze teapot. "She's safer at my side," he said. And gazed closely at Damon. "And her continued presence here, away from me, would only create an inviting target, wouldn't you say? In these uncertain times, it's best to be sure."

Two

"I'M SAFER AT YOUR SIDE?" Sasha whispered incredulously, as she walked with Kessligh out through the inn's rear exit, and into the paved courtyard at the back. "What am I, some Baen-Tar noble wench to be protected at every turn?"

The night chill was sharp, breath frosting before her lips as she spoke. The remains of a declining fire burned within the courtyard, surrounded by a great many men, with a cup in hand, or placed somewhere nearby. Kessligh walked so as to keep well clear of the fire's light, and together they passed unnoticed in the dark.

"Damon's not here for me, Sasha," Kessligh said grimly, hands in the pockets of his jacket as he strode. "He's here for you."

"For me? He doesn't even want me along . . ."

"Damn it, pay attention," Kessligh rebuked her, with more than a trace of irritation. "Haven't you grasped it yet? Despite everything I've been telling you, with your friends and drinking sessions, and that new growth sprouting from the side of your head? Krayliss is making his move, Sasha. It's a desperate, stupid, foolish move, but no more so than one might have expected from Krayliss. He threatens martyrdom. If we're all not extremely careful, he might just get it."

Sasha frowned. She didn't like it when Kessligh got like this. He made everything seem so complicated. Why couldn't he just accept what she was, and how she felt? Why couldn't everyone? "Krayliss . . ." and she shook her head, trying to clear her mind. "Krayliss can't use me as a figurehead." Trying to be rational. "I'm a woman, he'd never accept a woman as his symbol of Goeren-yai revival . . ."

"You're worse than a woman," Kessligh cut in, "you're Nasi-Keth. Krayliss hates all foreigners, Sasha—that means me, the lowlanders and the serrin equally, he makes no distinction. But you're the closest thing to a genuine Goeren-yai within the royal line that he's got, and he might just be desperate enough. Have you seen the condition of the Falcon Guard's horses? Damon made the ride from Baen-Tar *fast.* He came to secure you, to make sure Krayliss couldn't reach you first. That's the doing of your father's advisors. Your father has little enough fear of you. They have plenty."

"My father's advisors now include Wyna Telgar," Sasha muttered. "To hear Sofy tell of it, anyhow. I'm sure my eldest brother's wife would not have been pleased to hear that her father is dead. I wonder why Koenyg did not come himself, with that dragon breathing fire down his neck."

"Prince Koenyg is a stickler for the rules," Kessligh said grimly. "Rathynal approaches and the heir should not go gallivanting off to the provinces to bash some lordly heads together. That's what junior princes are for."

Lamps lit the stables ahead where several guardsmen were talking with local Baerlyn men, some of them regular stablehands. Several lads carried heavy blankets, or lugged saddlebags, or shifted loads of hay. The air smelled of hay, manure and horses—to Sasha's nose, a most familiar and agreeable odour, tinged with the sweetness of burning lamp oil.

"It's the Rathynal, isn't it?" Sasha said, arms wrapped about herself, only partly to repress the shivers brought on by the cold air. "That's why everyone's so jumpy."

"There's a lot to be jumpy about," said Kessligh, raising a hand in answer to the horsemen's respectful hails. "Such a large meeting can only reopen old wounds. Especially with foreign lowlanders invited. There's war in the offing, Sasha. Us old warhorses can smell it in the air. Damn right we're jumpy. You should be too."

"There won't be a war," Sasha said, with forced certainty as they walked down the long line of stables. "I just can't imagine we'll get involved in some stupid war in the Bacosh. It's all too far away."

"It's nearer than Saalshen," Kessligh said grimly. "And serrin come here all the time. Be careful of Master Jaryd—I know you derive great joy from boxing the ears of stuck-up young idiots like him, and I sympathise. But Rathynal is a time for all the great lords to make great decisions, and this Rathynal shall be greater than most. Lord Krayliss is a huge obstacle in such meetings—so long as he continues to sow division, Lenayin shall be forever divided, and the Verenthane nobility will never have its way on any great issue. Lord Krayliss delights in twisting the knife and ruining their grand plans at the most inopportune moments.

"Whether you like it or not, Verenthane nobility hear the rumours connecting you to the Goeren-yai, and to Krayliss, and they worry. In Lord Aystin's eyes, there may not be very much difference between you and Krayliss at all, and so I'd be surprised if his heir Jaryd feels differently. You can be certain Lord Rashyd and the northerners are not the only Lenay lords who would love to see Krayliss deposed and the entire ruling line of Taneryn replaced with a good Verenthane family. It would not surprise me to find that whatever incident has occurred, it was cooked up by Lord Rashyd with support from other Lenay lords, possibly including Great Lord Aystin Nyvar of Tyree himself."

"You're telling me that the gallant and dashing Master Jaryd Nyvar may wish to plant a knife in my back?" Sasha suggested with some incredulity.

"I'm telling you to be careful. Verenthanes frequently claim that all the old blood feuds and bickering disappeared with the Liberation and the coming of Verenthaneism—don't believe it. It's still there, just hiding. It's sneaking self-interest disguised beneath a cloak of smiling Verenthane brotherhood, and that makes it even more dangerous than when it was out in the open, as in older times . . . or more dangerous, at least, if you are its target. Trust me—I was born in Petrodor, and I've seen it. In such disputes of power, it's always the knife you *can't* see that kills you."

"I'd prefer the old days," Sasha snorted. "At least then rival chieftains killed their opponents face to face."

"Don't be stupid," Kessligh said shortly. "A thousand corpses honourably killed is no improvement on a handful of victims strangled in the night."

Terjellyn hung his head over the stable door, having heard them coming. Kessligh gave him an affectionate rub as a stable boy hovered, awaiting anything Baerlyn's two most famous residents might require.

"You'll be with Jaegar all night?" Sasha asked. The unhappiness must have shown in her voice, for Kessligh gave her a sardonic look.

"I think you can handle your brother for one night," he remarked. "It would be nice if I could discuss Baerlyn's affairs with Jaegar before we ride. We might be gone several weeks." Terjellyn nudged at his shoulder. The big chestnut stallion was a direct descendant of Tamaryn, Kessligh's mount during the great Cherrovan War thirty years gone. He'd ridden Tamaryn all the way from Petrodor, a mere sergeant among the Torovan volunteer brigades that had flooded into Lenayin following the invasion of the Cherrovan warlord Markield. The Liberation seventy years gone, the Archbishop of Torovan had not wished to see the thriving "Verenthane Kingdom" of Lenayin lost to a raging barbarian mob and had commanded Torovan believers to ride west on a holy war. Kessligh, however, had not ridden for faith.

Tamaryn had then borne him through the better part of an entire year's fighting, in the wooded valleys and mountains of Lenayin, during which Kessligh had risen to lieutenant, then captain, and then Commander of Armies for all Lenayin, and inflicted a thrashing upon the Cherrovan from which they had not recovered to this very day. Ever since, Kessligh had never had a primary ride that was not a descendant of Tamaryn—Terjellyn's great-grandfather. It was the only superstition Sasha had ever known him to concede.

"Be nice to Damon. Try not to provoke him too much."

Sasha stared elsewhere as Kessligh opened the stable door, and gave Terjellyn a once-over before mounting bareback. The big stallion, a more mature and refined gentleman than her Peg, walked calmly into the courtyard.

"We'll be off before dawn," Kessligh told her from the height of his mount. "We'll go home first, get the gear, then rejoin the column on the way to Taneryn." Sasha nodded, arms folded against the cold. "What's your problem?"

"What'll happen to Krayliss?" she asked.

"You care that much?"

"About the fate of the Goeren-yai?" Sasha shot back. "How could I not?"

Kessligh exhaled hard, glancing elsewhere with a frown.

"I don't know what to tell you," he said finally. "You chose this path for yourself . . ."

"I did not," Sasha retorted, sullenly. "It chose me."

"You are still your father's daughter, Sasha. Whatever new role and title you bear now." His eyes refixed upon her with narrowed intent. "None of us can escape the accidents of our birth so easily."

"That's not what you told Damon back there. What was all that about me being your uma, and nothing more should matter?"

"One side of an argument," Kessligh said calmly. "I'm sure Damon can provide the other side himself."

"You should have chosen another uma. One without the family baggage."

Kessligh's lean, wry features thinned with a faint smile. "I don't recall that I did choose you. In that, you chose me."

Sasha gazed up at him. Kessligh's expression, alive with the dancing shadows of lamplight, was almost affectionate.

"Don't sleep in," he warned her. "And for the gods' own sakes, stay away from that rye beer. It's murder." And he nudged Terjellyn with his heels, clattering off up the dark, cobbled path to the courtyard, and the laughing merriment of men.

Sleep did not come easy. For a long time, Sasha lay beneath the heavy covers and gazed at the ceiling. The room glowed with the orange embers from the fire. From the second bed, furthest from the door, she could hear little sound from Damon's bed.

She would have preferred her own, separate room, as was the usual arrangement when she had cause to stay overnight at the Star. But Damon having acquired the lordly quarters, form dictated that one royal should not sleep in lesser accommodation than the other. Such an occurrence might spread rumours of a division.

Sasha hated it all. Hated the gossip and sideways looks, hated the out-of-towners who stared and whispered, hated the northerners who sneered and made smirking comments amongst themselves. Had always hated it, in all her living memory. And her memory, Kessligh had frequently noted with something less than pleasure, was vast. She recalled the echoing stone halls of Baen-Tar Palace all too well, with their expensive tapestries and paintings. Recalled well the texture of the grass in the little courtyards between buildings where she had sat for lessons on a sunny day, and found far greater interest in the beetles and flower gardens than in classical texts or Torovan history . . . to say nothing of scripture, or embroidery.

Recalled the look her instructors, servants and various assorted minders had given her, the "Sashandra-always-in-trouble" look, that expected bad behaviour and was frequently presented with such. She'd never understood those rules. Should a deep cushion mattress *not* be used for jumping? And what on earth was wrong with throwing scraps of food to the pigeons that sat upon her bedroom window ledge? And running in hallways, what possible harm could it cause?

"Unladylike," had been the routine answer. And undignified, for a princess of Lenayin. "Then I don't want to be a princess of Lenayin!" had been her typically untactful, six-year-old reply. They'd locked her in her room and given her a composition assignment to fill the time. She recalled even now the blank page of paper sheaf, and the little, sharp-tipped quill that looked like it had once been a waterbird feather.

Was that natural? To recall the experiences of a six-year-old with such detailed clarity? Kessligh had said, only half-seriously, that it stopped her from growing up, so tightly did she clutch to the memories of her past. Sasha had answered that on the contrary, it spurred her to leave that time even further behind. But now, lying in the warm, orange glow of the Star's lordly quarters, she wondered.

She recalled throwing the sheaf of papers out the window, scattering pigeons from the ledge, and papers all over the gardens below. Not being able to do what one chose had seemed a great injustice. Her minders had concluded that she was spoiled, and had determined to make life more difficult, removing more privileges, and increasing the severity of punishments. That had only made her angry. The next time she'd thrown something out of the window, it had been heavy, and she hadn't opened the window first.

Damon, of course, had since challenged her recollections of those times. It had not been all her minders' fault, he'd proclaimed, upon her first visit back to Baen-Tar in four years, at the ripe old age of twelve. He'd been fifteen, somewhat gangling and with two left feet—not an uncommon condition for boys, Kessligh had assured her, and one reason why girls were easier to train. She'd been born wild, Damon had insisted. Wild like a bobcat, breaking things and biting people from the moment she'd learned how to walk. They'd only been trying to stop her from killing someone—most likely herself. And all of it had been no one's fault but her own.

Twelve-year-old Sasha had punched him in the nose.

Whatever the cause of the madness, Krystoff had been the cure. Krystoff, the heir to the throne of Lenayin, with his flowing black hair, his easy laugh, and his rakish, good-humoured charm. Eleven years her senior, the second eldest after Marya, who was now safely married to the ruling family of Petrodor. Sasha suffered a flash of very early memory . . . hiding behind a hay bale in a barn, watching Kessligh and Krystoff sparring with furious intensity.

Gods she must have been young. She tried to recall the dress—her memory of dresses was particularly excellent, much the same way as a long-time prisoner must surely recall various types of shackles and chains. The frilly, tight-stitched petticoats? Yes, it must have been, she remembered yanking at them beneath her pleated, little girl's dress, trying to stop them from tugging as she crouched. She'd been five, then, that night in the barn . . . and it had been night, hadn't it? Yes, she recalled the flickering lamplight and the musty smell of burning oil behind the familiar odour of hay.

But there hadn't been any fire damage to the northern wall in that memory. She'd nearly burned it all down at the beginning of her sixth year, when she'd been caught sneaking and forcibly removed. She'd grabbed and thrown a bale hook in her fury as they'd carried her away, striking a nearby lamp and sending hay bales up in roaring flames. Serrin oil, she'd later learned—long-lasting, but very flammable.

Kessligh had seen that throw, however, and been impressed. That had been about the time Krystoff had begun to take pity on her, taking an interest in one of his sisters at an age when the others, save for Marya, might as well have been invisible. She recalled him entering her room the day following the fire, an athletic and well-built seventeen, and surely the strongest, most handsome man in all Baen-Tar to her worshipful eyes. She'd been crying. He'd asked her why. And she'd explained that she was to be kept under lock and key for a week. No sunlight, save what fell naturally through her bedroom window. No natural things, save the pigeons that squabbled and made silly sounds on her window ledge. No grassy courtyards. No running, and definitely no chance to sneak to the creaky old barn in the old castle and watch the Lenayin Commander of Armies attempt to whip her eldest brother into a respectable heir and Nasi-Keth uma.

Krystoff had melted. And suddenly, in the following days, she was free. He'd promised her that if she just behaved herself, she could come and watch him train that night. She'd been courteous and attentive all through that day, and had performed all her required tasks without so much as fidgeting. Her minders had been incredulous. And Krystoff, true to his word, had found her a nice, high hay bale to sit on and watch proceedings in the barn that evening after dinner . . . for Krystoff trained twice a day, she'd been amazed to learn, and did many other exercises in between. He was going to be not only heir of Lenayin, but Nasi-Keth, like Kessligh. She had not, of course, grasped anything of the broader significance of this historic fact, nor the disquiet it had surely caused amongst devout Verenthanes everywhere, despite assurances that in Petrodor, most Nasi-Keth were also Verenthanes, and found no conflict between the two. All Sasha had known was that it seemed awfully exciting.

Kessligh, with curious humour, had even shown her some basic footwork when big brother Krystoff had needed a rest. She'd gotten it first go, slippered feet dancing on the dust and loose straw. Krystoff had encouraged her with typically infectious enthusiasm. They'd found her a broomstick, broken the end off and she'd used it for a practice stanch. She'd managed the basic taka-dan first time also—some of which had come from spying, and some from simple inspiration. She'd even gotten the tricky wrist angle, and how it shifted with different footing. Krystoff had been excited enough to pick her up and spin her about, where another man might have felt slighted, upstaged by his little sister with a broomstick. Very few pupils ever simply "got" the svaalverd first time, not even serrin. Kessligh had just watched, his expression unreadable.

From then on, within the privacy of the barn at evenings, there'd been instruction for Sasha also. Lessons and exercises, too, for her to perform in her room in early mornings, before the servants arrived to fill her morning bath, and dress her in their latest torture contraption, and brush her long, flowing hair. She'd kept that half a broomstick beneath her mattress, and when it was found and confiscated, she'd used the fire poker in her room instead. Those exercises had been her wonderful secret—something her minders could never take away—and she'd practised every time she'd found a private moment. Her minders did not approve of Krystoff's increasingly active role in her life, despite her improved behaviour. With improved behaviour had come high spirits, and a happy, rambunctious little Sashandra Lenayin had been every bit the challenge that a sullen, moody one had presented.

They'd been kindred spirits, she and Krystoff. She recalled helping him to raid the kitchens when soldiers just arrived from impromptu exercises were hungry and unhappy at being told to wait until mealtime. Recalled Krystoff flustering the chief cook, and sweet-talking the giggling, blushing kitchen maids, while Sasha had stood on a chair, and loaded loaves of bread and bowls of soup onto trays for the queuing soldiers, who'd grinned at her and ruffled her hair.

Another time, he'd somehow talked the proprietor of the training hall into admitting her—Krystoff had been said to own the knack of talking fish out of water, or chickens into flight. (Or virtuous Verenthane maidens into his bedchambers, many had also said, when they thought she couldn't hear.) There she'd watched athletic Lenay warriors drenched in sweat, pounding each other's defences with utmost confidence and swagger . . . until they'd come up against Krystoff's svaalverd, and found it like trying to swat a fly from the air with a wheelwright's hammer.

Yet another time, rather naively, he'd introduced her to horses, and his little sister had fallen in love for a second time. Little Sashandra would abandon classes to go wandering around the stables, watching the stable boys and pestering the trainers for desperately coveted knowledge. And when the Royal Guards put on a formation display for a visiting foreign lord . . . well, no locks nor bars nor solid stone walls could hold her.

Those had been the best days, when her newfound confidence had blossomed, and with it, her first true sense of self. She'd even made peace with her other brothers and sisters . . . or no, she reflected now as she gazed at the ceiling—maybe not peace. More like a truce. An uneasy and often hostile one, with occasional breaches caused by either party, but usually resolved in short order.

Given nine headstrong siblings, that had been no mean achievement. Other than Krystoff, Marya—the eldest—had been her best friend, and her marriage and departure for Petrodor had been a sad day indeed. Koenyg, then second in line for the throne behind Krystoff, had long been jealous of his elder brother's carefree popularity, and had spent much of his life attempting to become everything that Krystoff was not—disciplined, calm and sober. Her sister Petryna, now married to the heir of Lenayin's Yethulyn province, had been studious and sensible, and no lover of outrageous antics. Wylfred had preferred his own company and spent much of his free time in temple with his books. And then there was Damon, only a boy himself in all her

Baen-Tar memories, and oh so self-conscious and awkward in the presence of his overbearing, talented elder brothers. And Alythia, the glamorous one, who loved everything princessly that Sasha hated, and loved even more to demonstrate that fact to the world.

And then, of course, there were her two younger siblings, Sofy and Myklas . . . and her eyes widened. She had not asked anything about Sofy! Gods and spirits, how could she be so forgetful? She rolled her head upon the pillow and cast a glance across at Damon, apparently asleep beneath the covers. But there might be no time tomorrow, she reasoned.

"Damon," she called across the beds. "Damon. Are you awake?"

"If I said no, would you leave me alone?" came Damon's reply, muffled in the pillows. Sasha wasn't fooled—he couldn't sleep either. No wonder, given how heavily the weight of command usually sat upon his shoulders.

"How is Sofy?" Sasha asked him. "In all this fuss about Krayliss, I forgot to ask."

"Like Sofy," Damon retorted.

"Is she enjoying her studies?" Sasha pressed determinedly. Damon wasn't going to get off that easily. "She seemed happy in her last letter, but I sometimes wonder if she tells me everything."

"Sofy's always happy," Damon muttered. As if there were something vaguely offensive about that. "She asks about you a lot."

"Does she?"

"Oh yes. Every time a noble traveller arrives in court, having passed within scent of Valhanan, she never fails to corner him and ask for news of you."

Sasha smiled. "But she's well? Her last letter spoke of Alythia's wedding. She seemed very excited."

"Not nearly as excited as Alythia," said Damon. And rolled onto his back, appearing to abandon hope of sleep, at least for the moment. "But yes, Sofy is helping with the preparations. Alythia scolds her, and tries to be upset at her interference . . . she was unhappy with Sofy's suggestions for the ordering of vows and ceremonies, thinking that she knows best in everything. But of course, on reflection, she agreed that Sofy's ideas were best. As always."

For all Sasha's differences with Damon, they shared a common affection for their younger sister Sofy. It was mostly thanks to Sofy's mediation that Damon and Sasha had arrived at their present truce. Sasha was yet to be convinced of Sofy's faith in Damon, but she had conceded that her previous, less flattering impressions of him had been wide of the mark. But then, that was Sofy, always intervening, always drawing compromise from the most hardened of opinions.

"And the holy fathers are pleased with the wedding preparations?" Sasha asked, having heard a little of that controversy.

"It's ridiculous," Damon sighed. "Father Wynal now protests that the arrangements are not in full accordance with the scripture, but Alythia protests that she wants a traditional Lenay wedding like Marya and Petryna had . . ."

"Marya and Petryna's weddings were anything *but* traditional," Sasha snorted.

"Well, they had the fire and the dancing with hand painting . . ."

"That's *hanei*, Damon," Sasha corrected. "And the fire is *tempyr*, the purifier, the door between states of being. It symbolises a couple's transition into married life, the *athelyn*, the destruction of the old, making way for the new. It's the foundation of the Goeren-yai view of the universe."

"Sounds serrin," Damon remarked, with less interest than Sasha might have hoped. The ignorance of so many Verenthanes toward the old ways disgusted her. They had been their ways too, a hundred years before.

"Serrin and Goeren-yai belief has much in common," Sasha agreed, keeping her temper in check. Outbursts and lectures would serve no good purpose, she told herself firmly. "It's one reason the Goeren-yai and serrin have had such good relations for so long."

"Anyhow," Damon said dismissively. "Alythia thinks it's pretty, and the hand painting—the *hanei*—is. And so much more glamorous than a traditional Verenthane wedding."

"I'm glad I'm not the only one who thinks so," Sasha said sourly. "Verenthanes have to be the most morbid bunch, Damon. I hear in some parts of the Bacosh and the rest of the lowlands, women aren't even allowed to *dance*. Can you imagine?"

"I can't imagine," Damon admitted, frowning at the ceiling. "But then, being a Verenthane means different things from one land to another. Lenayin will always be Lenayin. That is one thing Goeren-yai and Verenthane shall always have in common in this land. I think I shall always have more in common with a Lenay Goeren-yai than with a lowlands Verenthane."

"We'll see if you still believe in Lenay brotherhood should you have the misfortune to encounter Family Telgar on this ride," Sasha said darkly.

"The men of the north are brave," Damon said shortly. "I won't prejudge them."

"It's not their bravery I question," said Sasha. "It's their humanity."

Damon made an annoyed face, looking across the space between their beds. "Seriously, Sasha, need you always pick a fight? You of all people who can afford it *least*. I'm well aware what you think of the Verenthane north, you don't need to hurl it at me at every opportunity. I can form my own opinions."

Sasha bit her tongue with difficulty. "And how is Myklas?" she asked, determined to prove to herself that she *could* simply move on and not spill blood upon the floor. Kessligh would be proud.

"Well," said Damon, with a note to his voice that suggested he too was surprised at the ease of his victory. "He'll become a fine swordsman. He's better than I was, at his age. Better than Koenyg, maybe. It's certainly not from hard work. It must be talent."

"Some things can't be taught," said Sasha, putting a hand behind her head upon the pillow. The air was cold upon her arm, whatever her under-shirt and the fading warmth of the fire's embers. But beneath the heavy weight of skins and blankets, the warmth was delicious.

Damon gave her a long, curious glance, the fireplace illuminating one half of his face upon the pillows. "I heard that you fought," he said. "Last summer, when the Cherrovan pressed Hadryn hard. I heard tell of some stories. Deeds of yours."

"All lies."

"The stories were greatly in your favour," Damon added.

"Then they were all true," Sasha corrected, with a faint smile. The incursion had been, for the most part, yet another ridiculous waste of Cherrovan life. A new chieftain had required a blooding, the story went. And a blooding he had received, most of it his own. Surely the Cherrovan had not been so stupid during the centuries when they had ruled Lenayin and all the mountain kingdoms as their own.

"I had doubted your abilities, once," said Damon. "Even with Kessligh as your uman . . . I'd thought he'd only chosen you for other purposes. But the men bearing these stories are honest. It seems I was mistaken. And I apologise."

Sasha gazed across at him with great surprise. And smiled. Sofy had always told her to try being nice to Damon, rather than arguing with him all the time. Good things will come of it, she'd insisted. And once again, it seemed, her little sister was right. "Apology accepted," she said graciously. "You're not the only man to make such a judgment. There are thousands who believe such, up in the north."

Damon snorted. Then, "Has Kessligh told you of your standard? One story came from a man who was himself a master swordsman. He said he'd never seen anything like it."

Sasha sighed. "Praise from Kessligh is rare. He hates complacency."

"Can you best him sparring?"

"Sometimes. Maybe one round in three. More on good days, less on others." But Damon looked *very* impressed. Besting Kessligh at all was said to be a worthy achievement. Most men would have been happy with one round in ten. But then, for those who did not fight with the svaalverd, it was no fair contest.

"I still don't see how it's possible," Damon said, with a faint shake of his head. "For a woman. I have bested three Cherrovan warriors in combat. Combat is exhausting, for the fittest, strongest men."

Never "frightening," Sasha reflected. No Lenay man would ever admit so. "Yes, but you waste strength when you fight," she told him. "*Hathaal*, serrin call it. There's no direct translation in Lenay . . . energy, perhaps. Or maybe a life force, though serrin have too many names for that to count. A symmetry. A power derived from form, not bulk. The straight, sturdy tree is more *hathaal* than the crooked one, even if they are both as tall. You are stronger than me. But using svaalverd, I am more *hathaal*. And you cannot touch me."

Damon snorted. "So confident are you. We've never sparred."

"Tomorrow, perhaps?" Sasha said mildly.

"We ride first thing in the morning."

"Convenient."

"You know much of serrin lore," Damon remarked, ignoring her barbs.

"Of course. I am Nasi-Keth."

"Do you love the serrin?"

Sasha frowned. Footsteps creaked in the corridor outside, the last of the revellers coming upstairs to their beds. The dying fire managed one last, feeble pop. "I've yet to meet a bad or unpleasant one," she said after a moment.

"That doesn't answer my question."

And it was not, Sasha knew, such an innocent question. There was war afoot between the Bacosh and neighbouring Saalshen. Visiting merchants fuelled a wildfire of rumour, serrin travellers had been rare of late, and Kessligh's mood grim. She didn't like to think on it. There had been bad news from the Bacosh before—for many, many centuries, in fact, one endless succession of terrible internal wars over power, prestige and matters of faith. Those had come and gone. Surely these latest rumblings would follow.

"The serrin are a good and decent people," she answered. "Much of their lore, skills and trades has improved human lives beyond measure, from irrigation to building to medicines and midwifery . . . sometimes I wonder how we ever managed without them. Anyone who would make war on them will not gain my sympathy."

"They live on lands that are not theirs," Damon responded flatly. "Many include Verenthane holy sites. Sites of the birth of Verenthaneism itself. The Bacosh are the eldest and most powerful of Verenthane peoples, they'll not let the matter rest." Sasha rolled beneath her covers to fix her brother with an alarmed gaze.

"What have you heard?" she asked accusingly. Damon shrugged, his mood sombre.

"There is much anger. Talk of the Verenthane brotherhood uniting to take back the holy lands."

In all recent history, the Bacosh had only been united once. The man who accomplished it, Leyvaan of Rhodaan, had named himself king, and repaid the serrin who'd assisted his rise with invasion and slaughter. The serrin response had been devastating, crushing Leyvaan and his armies, and taking the three nearest Bacosh provinces for themselves. That had been two centuries ago, and today, the so-called "Saalshen Bacosh" remained in serrin hands. Many in the priesthood called those lands holy, and wanted them back, out of the clutches of godless, pagan serrin.

"Such talk has existed since Leyvaan the Fool created the whole mess in the first place," Sasha retorted. "The Saalshen Bacosh is a happy place. The only unhappy people are those outsiders who resent that fact. Besides, there is no Verenthane brotherhood. It's a myth."

"Even so," Damon said tiredly. "People talk, is all. Perhaps it will fade, I hope so. We have enough troubles in Lenayin without lowlands concerns thrust upon us also."

"Hear hear," Sasha murmured. But Kessligh's words remained with her: "War is in the air. Us old warhorses can smell it."

"You're not going to ask after Father's well-being also?" Damon queried into that silence.

"No," said Sasha. And tucked her warm, heavy blankets more firmly down about her neck. "Father has advisors enough to see to that already."

Three

JARYD NYVAR RODE at the head of the Falcon Guards as the road wound uphill from Baerlyn, with Prince Damon at his left stirrup. The morning dawned bright and clear across rugged hillsides of thick forest and sparkling dew. Cold air nipped at his cheeks, and the steaming breath of horse and men mingled about the column, so that it moved along the road like some great, puffing beast. The land in these parts was as beautiful as Jaryd's native Tyree. Birds sang in the trees, and on the way out of town, a pair of handsome deer had startled across the road.

At the distance of perhaps one fold from Baerlyn, they encountered a pair of riders waiting for them on the road beside a narrow trail through the trees. Kessligh Cronenverdt and his brat uman. That trail, then, would lead to their horse ranch in the wilds. Prince Damon acknowledged them with a wave, which both returned. They fell into line several places further back, in plain cloaks to ward the morning chill, their back-worn swords invisible beneath those folds. An unremarkable and plain-looking pair they seemed, amidst a column of Tyree green and gold, gleaming silver helms and polished boots. Unremarkable, that was, but for their horses—both stallions, one light bay, the girl's a charcoal black, and both beautiful to behold.

It was a reminder of Cronenverdt's past service, of the debt owed to him by the king. Jaryd had heard the mutterings of his father's men, that Cronenverdt was little more than a hired sword who had commanded from the king a steep ransom for his services. Jaryd thought it somewhat rich for wealthy nobles to accuse Kessligh of being a mercenary considering the plainness of the man living out here in the wilds with his uma. Cronenverdt could have commanded a far larger sum and lived in a grand holding, with lands and gardens and prospective wives clamouring for his hand. Instead, when Prince Krystoff had met an unfortunate end, he'd left the king's service and asked for nothing more than a grief-stricken, impossible brat of a princess to replace the uma he'd lost, and some horses.

Jaryd thought it far more likely that his fellow nobility were jealous of the man, partly for his accomplishments, and partly for the way in which he showed up their expensive tastes. It was surely not unreasonable that a man who had freely *given* his services, instead of being born into the obligation of service, should receive some gift in return? How to criticise such a man, who did not play by the rules that others understood? No wonder he made so many enemies amongst the ruling classes.

After a while riding along the forested hillside, Prince Damon fell back in the column to talk with Kessligh. Lieutenant Reynan took his place at Jaryd's side.

"The brat was up before dawn," said the lieutenant, rubbing sleepy eyes beneath his helm. "I'd thought to follow her, but that horse of hers is fast and doesn't mind a nighttime torch. Mine gets all flighty near a flame."

Jaryd frowned at him. Lieutenant Reynan Pelyn was the brother of Lord Tymeth Pelyn, head of one of the twenty-three noble families of Tyree, and close allies of Family Nyvar. He was a big man, with a round head, small eyes, and a barely discernible chin. He had not served with the Falcon Guards for long—barely a year, in fact, just a short time longer than Jaryd had been in command. Jaryd did not think that the men were particularly fond of him.

"You'd follow her to her home?" Jaryd asked. He kept his voice low, and there was little chance of anyone overhearing above the stamp of hooves and jangling harnesses.

Reynan shrugged. "Lord Tymeth told me to keep a close watch on her at all times. I'm keeping a close watch."

"So much effort for one girl," Jaryd mused. "One might think your brother actually believes the tales the Goeren-yai tell about her swordwork."

"It's not her sword that's the bother," Reynan said darkly. "That little bitch causes enough trouble with the Goeren-yai as is, and the king's gone too teary-eyed since Prince Krystoff's death to do anything about it."

"Do about it?" said Jaryd. "Lieutenant, who said anything about doing something about it?"

"My Lord brother said to keep a close eye on her," Reynan said stubbornly, "and that's what I'll do. Make sure she doesn't cause any trouble."

"She's just a girl," Jaryd said shortly. "How much trouble can she cause?" And why, he thought, be so much more worried about her than about Cronenverdt? Cronenverdt held the real power, surely. The brat was just a distraction. A distraction for Cronenverdt himself, some said, in a meaningful way. A plaything for a man who'd developed strange tastes in sword-wielding women while amongst the serrin and Nasi-Keth of Petrodor. Some claimed he wished to sire a son from her, who might then claim the throne. Surely the nobles of Tyree did not believe such nonsense? There were so many before her in the line of succession, after all . . .

Reynan gave his commander one of those weary, superior, adult looks that Jaryd disliked so much. "Never you mind, Master Jaryd," he said tiredly. "You just concern yourself with the road ahead, and leave the other business to me. Just remember to call on me if you need any advice—you're a fine warrior, Master, but older heads have ridden this road before."

"I have plenty of advice from Captain Tyrun," Jaryd replied, annoyed by the older man's patronising tone. "He's ridden these roads far more often than you."

Reynan's face hardened. "Master Jaryd," he said in a low, harsh voice, "that man is not noble born. He's a peasant, little better than a pagan . . ."

"Captain Tyrun is a true Verenthane and a veteran warrior!" Jaryd retorted in rising temper. "He rose from lowly status because he was the best, as is the tradition in the Guard! Do you question that tradition, *Lieutenant* Reynan?"

Reynan's jaw clenched. So *that* was the sore spot, and the reason why the other men disliked him. A lieutenant, after just one year. True, Jaryd was in command after a shorter period, but he was heir to all Tyree, and made no bones that Captain Tyrun remained in true command.

"No," Reynan bit out. "I would merely advise, Master Jaryd, that you give some serious thought to where your future interests lie, for yourself and for Tyree."

It was midday before the column took its first rest, the men dismounting upon a broad, open shoulder of the Ryshaard River. Kessligh and Sasha found a large rock in the river shallows and spread out their food, whilst Peg and Terjellyn remained on the shore with a handler. Horses splashed in the shallows nearby, drinking deep, and men gathered to share rations.

Across the wide, wild bend of river, cliffs rose near vertical in a broken, granite wall. Atop the cliff, trees lined the high ridge. Above those, an eagle circled. Sasha shaded her eyes against the bright sun as she ate, gazing upward.

"Oh look!" she exclaimed. "That's a silvertip. She must have a nest up there somewhere. There must be good fishing in the river."

"How do you know it's a she?"

"I don't. But Lenay men have this silly habit of assuming every dangerous animal is a he, when in fact the females are usually more dangerous."

High above, the eagle cried. Across the riverbank, men were gazing skyward, and pointing. Goeren-yai men in particular had a love of wild things, and birds of prey had a special place in their hearts. "Do silvertip eagles have a legend to go with them?" Kessligh asked wryly.

Sasha frowned as she thought about it, watching the eagle's circling flight. "Not that I can recall. Although it is said that a white-headed eagle swooped down to carry Hyathon the Warrior away from the fire mountain to escape the dark spirits. But white-headed eagles are much bigger than silvertips."

"All nonsense," Kessligh pronounced, and took a bite of his roll.

"Why?" Sasha demanded. "Just because it's not what *you* believe?"

"Sasha," Kessligh said around his mouthful, "if you'd seen as many people killed as I have, all because one of them believes this thing and the other believes this other thing, you wouldn't think it was all so harmless. Tales and legends are fun, but *beliefs*, Sasha. Beliefs are dangerous. Be very careful what you believe in, for beliefs are far more dangerous than swords."

"And you believe in the Nasi-Keth," Sasha retorted. "That makes you just as dangerous and misguided, doesn't it?"

Kessligh nodded, vigorously. "Aye. But the Nasi-Keth take their learnings from the serrin, and the serrin simply don't think like us. They don't believe in truth. They don't believe in anything they can't prove, and they won't construct these elaborate fantasies with which to advance their own power and kill each other. That's the whole point of the Nasi-Keth, Sasha— it's an attempt to help humans to think rationally. And that's difficult, I know, because humans are fundamentally irrational. But it's worth a try, don't you think?"

"Hmmph," said Sasha, chewing her own mouthful. "What's rational?"

"Exactly the question the serrin ask each other constantly."

"And what's irrational about the Goeren-yai beliefs?" Sasha continued. "It's rational, surely, that people survive as well as they can? Goeren-yai legends tell us much about these lands, and the animals, and the ways people can live and survive well out here. And the serrin have come here for centuries—*they* find Goeren-yai culture fascinating! So why should you, who takes his inspiration from the serrin, be so dismissive?"

"I'm not dismissive of the process, Sasha, just the conclusions. I'm dismissive of any culture that thinks it knows everything."

"The Goeren-yai don't . . . !"

Kessligh cut her off with a raised hand. "I'm dismissive of any person who lives his or her life like a frog down a well—all it knows is that well, and those walls, with no interest in what lies outside. I'm trying to make you think, Sasha. That's all I've ever tried to do. That's all the Nasi-Keth as a whole have ever tried to do. To make people think before they commit some terrible evil in the name of their various truths, if it is at all possible that they might be wrong."

"Aye," Sasha replied, "well maybe that's the difference between me and you. You lead with your head, I lead with my heart."

"Hearts can be rational too," said Kessligh. "They just need a little training." Sasha knew better than to try and get the last word in. "How was Damon last night?" he asked then, changing the subject.

"Nervous," she said. "He slept a while, I think. His temper's short, but that's normal. Best not to push him."

"With any luck, he won't make me. He's second from the throne, in truth. It's best he learned to deal with these kinds of things on his own."

Sasha stifled a laugh behind her hand. "Damon. King!" She swallowed a mouthful, shaking her head in disbelief. "I can't imagine it."

"Men have similar difficulty picturing you as my uma," Kessligh replied, unmoved by her humour. His eyes flicked toward the riverbank. Sasha looked, and saw Master Jaryd Nyvar talking animatedly with a corporal. Their conversation was about swordplay by the look of their moving hands.

Sasha snorted. "Only because those men have never thought women good for anything but babies and housework."

"What's wrong with babies and housework?" Kessligh said with a faint smile.

Sasha shrugged expansively. It was pointless to get annoyed. Kessligh simply liked contradicting her.

Kessligh swallowed his mouthful. "Before I came to Lenayin, I hadn't thought women good for much but babies and housework."

Sasha frowned at him. "Oh come on! There are serrin everywhere in Petrodor! What about all of these wonderful serrin women you keep talking about, the ones you studied with as a Nasi-Keth uma yourself?"

"Serrin women, exactly," said Kessligh around another bite. "Petrodor has a very conservative branch of Verenthane belief where women are concerned. My mother died when I was young and from then on the Nasi-Keth were my family. I saw many serrin women, but the human women I knew were very fixed in their notion of what a real woman was. Even when I rode to Lenayin for the war, I didn't see Lenay women as much different. It's only when I met you that I truly realised that a human woman might be born with the aptitude to be my uma."

Sasha smiled. "Well at least I know what kind of behaviour impresses the great Kessligh Cronenverdt—bratish, noisy and overactive. I could revert, if you like?"

"Revert?" Kessligh asked in mock surprise. Sasha kicked him lightly on his boot and scowled. "My point," Kessligh continued, "is that people never know what they shall be, and how they shall respond, until the moment of testing arrives. I can assure you that very few of my Nasi-Keth elders and peers suspected that I could rise to such heights from my beginnings. As a student I was quiet, uncooperative and solitary. I loved serrin teachings because they seemed to me to offer the best solution I'd yet seen to all humanity's obvious ills.

"But I was always frustrated that neither my uman nor my other tutors seemed to grasp the implications of those teachings fully. And so I enjoyed the company of the serrin more than humans. Serrin never judge. Through them I learned to see the world as it is, and myself as I am, rather than what I might want or expect them both to be. Which is how I recognised your talents, while other men would not. I realised I was wrong about human women. Many men cannot admit this about themselves.

"Always be aware that you may be wrong, Sasha—about anything and everything. I rose to Commander of Armies during the Great War simply because I learned from my mistakes, and the mistakes of others, and when something did not work, I stopped doing it and did something else. Many commanders did not, due to pride or stubbornness, and killed not only themselves, but many good men as well. The unquestioned belief in one's own supremacy and righteousness is the surest road to ruin yet devised by man. Avoid it at all costs."

Sasha listened sombrely, chewing the last of her lunch as the river bubbled about their rock. Kessligh did not lecture often, yet she was not surprised that he chose to do so now. A Hadryn–Taneryn conflict was surely the most serious calamity she had yet ridden into. An uman's role was to teach, and to prepare his uma for trials to come.

"Why have the Nasi-Keth not spread more through Lenayin?" Sasha asked suddenly. "I mean . . . you led Lenayin to victory over Chieftain Markield, you risked your life and became a Lenay legend—all because you *volunteered* to come from Petrodor. The popularity of the Nasi-Keth and the serrin was surely never so high in Lenayin as then. And yet there are so few other Nasi-Keth here."

Kessligh nodded slowly, as if faintly surprised at the question. "Your father tried," he said. "He believes in providence, in signs from the gods. When Markield was beaten, your father saw that the gods favoured the Nasi-Keth, and thus surely they favoured the teachings of Saalshen. That was a time when the king was least persuaded by the northern fanatics, since the north had failed to defeat the invasion without help as they'd insisted they would, and had protested my ascension to commander at every turn. Trade with Saalshen improved dramatically, and many senior serrin were invited to visit the capital. And, of course, he declared that Krystoff would be my uma, binding the kingdom and the Nasi-Keth inextricably together.

"But the response of the Verenthanes was not good, especially in the north. And precious few Nasi-Keth from Petrodor have felt inspired to follow me to the highlands." He shrugged. "Perhaps it would have been different had Krystoff lived. Then Lenayin would have had a king both Verenthane and Nasi-Keth, as are so many in Petrodor."

"And we have the Hadryn to thank that it didn't happen," Sasha muttered.

Kessligh fixed her with a hard stare. "Sasha. What happened to Krystoff is old history. It hurt me as much as it hurt you. But we're riding into this mess now on the king's business, and the king must be impartial. If you feel that will be a problem for you, best that you tell me now."

"They killed him," Sasha said darkly. "Not by their own hands, but nearly."

"I know," said Kessligh. "It changes nothing."

"And who are you to be accusing me of partisan loyalties?" Sasha retorted. "Saalshen is losing credit fast with Father, and doubtless the Nasi-Keth with them. And now you come on this ride claiming to act in Father's interests?"

"I have always been your father's servant," Kessligh said flatly. "I've fought in his service since I rode to Lenayin thirty years ago."

"And should Father act against the Nasi-Keth?" Sasha persisted. "What then?"

"Then," said Kessligh, "I shall cross that bridge when I come to it."

Four

CAMPFIRES LIT SMALL CIRCLES OF LIGHT in the forest, a leaping dance of tree trunks and long, flickering shadows. Men gathered about their fires and cooked, while others tended to horses, or mended worn gear. There was cloud overhead, the wind was gentle from the south, and Sasha knew it would not grow so cold tonight. But she missed the stars, her one great consolation for nights upon the road.

"There is dispute over Lord Krayliss's ancestry," Damon said as the regal party ate. Sasha wolfed her meal with her usual appetite—roasted meat on skewers, and a vegetable raal Kessligh had whipped up. Damon, however, seemed to pick at his food. "I've heard it claimed that he's not actually Udalyn at all."

To Sasha's surprise, he looked directly at her. As if she, above all others present, would be likely to know. Well, perhaps she would. "His grandmother," she managed about a hot mouthful, seated upon her saddle with a tin plate balanced in her lap. "So it's said. But the maternal grandmother, not the paternal."

Damon frowned. "That's important?"

"In the old ways, power passes through the paternal line. A maternal grandmother is the weakest claim to ancestry. But then, some have accused Krayliss of overstatement." To her left, Captain Tyrun repressed a humourless laugh. From across the fire, Jaryd frowned at her above the flames.

"How important is it?" Damon asked bluntly. "To be Udalyn?"

"For Krayliss?" Sasha raised her eyebrows. "Very. Spirits know he gains precious little credit among the Goeren-yai from anything else."

"To claim ancestry to the chieftain of a dying clan who were once in league with the Cherrovan?" Damon looked dubious.

Sasha could not resist a glance around to see who else might overhear. But the neighbouring fireplace conversations were too distant, and too jovial, for that to be likely. "People in these parts see it differently," she said warningly.

Damon made a dismissive gesture. "I'll never understand it," he said darkly. "This obsession with the Udalyn. They've barely emerged from their valley for a century, have been little good to anyone, yet Goeren-yai the length and breadth of Lenayin worship their name." He took a reluctant bite of his meat.

Sasha glanced at Kessligh, seated to her right. He gazed into the flames as he ate. His eyes were unfocused, as if he saw the ghosts of past memories dancing amongst the coals. "Best perhaps that you tell your brother that story," he said then, distantly. "We ride squarely into this matter, much unresolved. Best that he understands."

Sasha nodded. "I agree. But I think one here might tell it better than I." She looked across to Captain Tyrun.

Tyrun looked surprised. "Me, M'Lady? I'm Verenthane, I claim no great wisdom here."

"Today at the talleryn stones of Spearman's Ridge," Sasha said, "you showed respect for the dead. You rode toward the sun, so as not to cast your shadow upon the roadside stones. And you gave the spirit sign." Tyrun nodded slowly, with new respect in his eyes. "The tolerance of Tyree Verenthanes is well known."

"Aye, M'Lady," said Tyrun, nodding slowly. "I might know a little. Men of Tyree sit often and speak of honour and war. To speak of such matters with Goeren-yai anywhere is to speak of the Udalyn."

Damon, Sasha thought, looked a little uncomfortable. Well that he should, she thought sourly. To display such ignorance was to admit that he had never sat and talked with Goeren-yai warriors before. So much for the high esteem of Family Lenayin for the ancient ways.

"Prior to the Liberation," Tyrun began, "there were two clans dominating the province that is now Hadryn. The Udalyn occupied the east, and the Hadryn the west. They were similar, yet different enough to provoke a hostility many centuries old. Intermarriage between the two was punished by the death of both parents and offspring. The bloodlines were kept pure. Northerners have always believed in purity—once as Goeren-yai, and now as Verenthanes.

"Understand, my Prince, that the north was once the bedrock of Goeren-yai belief. Many of the great Lenay heroes of old were from the north, men of a steel forged in battles against the eternal Cherrovan foe, between rival clans, and with the harsh terrain and climate.

But the Cherrovan warlords were strong, often destroying entire Lenay villages. Tharyn Askar, the great Udalyn Chieftain, compromised with the Cherrovan in his lands, so that his people could grow healthy and strong, and not drained by constant minor uprisings and reprisals. He desired liberation from the Cherrovan also, but knew that the Udalyn had not yet the strength.

"He might not have had to compromise if the Hadryn hadn't remained more interested in waging war on the Udalyn than the Cherrovan," Sasha added, sipping water from her tin cup. "As men tell the story in Baerlyn, Tharyn tried to join with the Hadryn against the Cherrovan and sent his son as a symbol of trust to the Hadryn chieftain Essyn Telgar, who's reputed to have been just as thickheaded as the present line of Telgars. Essyn had him tortured and disembowelled alive. The Hadryn claim to have been key in uniting Lenayin during the Liberation, yet in truth, they prevented its arrival for generations."

"Aye," said Tyrun. "They tell it much the same in Tyree. Anyhow, my Prince . . . there had been a prophecy for generations in the north. It was said that a great leader of Lenayin would ride from the south, bearing supernatural powers, and would smite the Cherrovan from the face of the world. When Soros Lenayin arrived at the head of his army of free Lenay clans and lowlands crusaders . . ." here he glanced at Kessligh, who snorted, "the north joined his cause in force, forgot their petty disputes and rallied beneath the star of Verenthane.

"The Udalyn fought valiantly, yet Essyn Telgar was clever. He decreed that all the Hadryn should convert to Verenthaneism, as did most of the north, as they believed the Verenthane gods had fulfilled their prophecy and were just and true. But the Udalyn, having the deep roots of their homeland valley to sustain their traditions through even the hardest times, refused. Soros Lenayin rewarded Essyn Telgar with Lordship of all Hadryn, and asked that the Udalyn swear fealty to him. Tharyn refused, for his people would never have listened had he agreed.

"What followed was a slaughter." Tyrun paused for a moment, gazing into the flames. About the blazing fire, none spoke. From a neighbouring fire, men's laughter carried high on the cool night air. "The united Verenthanes of the north fell upon the Udalyn, for Essyn poisoned the minds of all the north against them, calling them traitors, friends of the Cherrovan and enemies of the new light of salvation. There were no prisoners taken, nor offered conversions accepted. There was only murder—of men, women and children. I am a proud Verenthane, my Prince. I believe that the star of Verenthane has been a blessing of unity and peace upon this land. But truly, the fate of the Udalyn, I believe, was surely Verenthane's darkest hour."

Damon met the captain's sombre gaze across the fire. Sasha could read his expression well enough to see that he had not heard this history told with such confidence by a Verenthane man. Most Verenthanes denied the accusations of Hadryn atrocities against the Udalyn, and many blamed the Udalyn for bringing their decline upon themselves.

"Finally, all that was left of the Udalyn was their ancestral valley," Tyrun continued. "Here, versions of the story differ. Some say that King Soros intervened and gave the Udalyn one last chance to convert, or face annihilation. Others say that he did nothing. Yet others defend King Soros, saying that his army was weary and he had not yet been crowned king, so he had no means with which to stop the slaughter. But whatever the truth, the Udalyn did not convert, and the united Verenthane north pressed the attack into the valley.

"The Udalyn were outnumbered twenty to one, at best. But within the valley's narrow confines, their defences gained hope. Over many days and nights, the Udalyn made a fighting retreat up the length of their valley, and their enemies paid a high price for every stride advanced. Finally, the morale of the Verenthane north began to wane, for the Udalyn slew five and more attackers for every loss, so great was their desire to survive as a people and pass on their traditions to the next generation.

"Essyn Telgar saw his glorious victory slipping away, as his men refused to advance further. He rode out before the Udalyn and offered that they could convert to Verenthaneism and save their lives. In reply, the Udalyn charged, full of fury and vengeance. They crashed into an army that was still ten times their number and split them down the centre. Tharyn Askar himself, it is told, carved his way through ten of Essyn's personal guard and family to slay Essyn Telgar by his own hand, before falling dead from wounds. The remaining Verenthanes broke and ran, and the Udalyn survived—the last, small pocket of Goeren-yai defiance in a Verenthane sea.

"Several times in the years to follow, successive Lords of Hadryn attempted to rid their land of their ancient enemy. Each time, though greatly outnumbered, the Udalyn were victorious. Then Chayden Lenayin came to the throne—your esteemed grandfather, Prince Damon, M'Lady Sashandra. He saw how the fate of the Udalyn had aroused the passions of all Lenay Goeren-yai, and forbid the Telgars of Hadryn to attack the Udalyn again. Since that time, the Hadryn have left the Valley of the Udalyn largely alone under King's orders—a policy continued to this day by your father, my Prince, M'Lady. And I pray that it shall always be such."

Sasha took a skewer of cooking meat from the fire by its wood handle and gave it to Tyrun—reward for a tale well told. Tyrun gave a small smile of thanks.

"And now Lord Krayliss attempts to play the Udalyn card once more," Damon said. His own food remained largely untouched upon his plate. "Why? What is to gain?"

"The Udalyn are the one issue," Sasha replied, "the one singular thing, upon which all Goeren-yai can agree. They are heroes. They are the very symbol of Goeren-yai pride, courage and the will to survive in the face of advancing foreign religions. Krayliss claims to represent the old ways, and the Udalyn fly that banner far better than he. He dreams of an age long past, before the coming of Verenthanes, when Lenayin was wild and free."

"And a bloody, barbarian rabble," said Kessligh, with his usual diplomacy. Sasha knew well enough what Kessligh thought of such romanticism . . . and of her own undeniable attraction to it.

She shrugged, too wise by now to respond with temper. "Aye," she said. "Krayliss would bring back those days if he could, the good and the bad. But most Goeren-yai are too smart for that. Lowlands trade is prosperous and many have benefited. So long as Baen-Tar does not attempt to convert them by force or coercion, they care not if the towns all pray to lowlands gods. And so Krayliss grows desperate. He needs the Udalyn. He is the last remaining Goeren-yai lord—although he would style himself as chieftain—and he claims blood ties to Tharyn Askar himself. On such credit does he ask the Goeren-yai of all Lenayin to love him."

"And now there comes talk of lowlands war," said Kessligh. There was a note to his voice, and his expression, that Sasha did not like. It suggested a certain exasperation. A dark, brooding disgust. Well . . . she was disgusted too, by fools like the Rashyds and Kraylisses alike. Yet she doubted if that were the only target of Kessligh's distaste. "To reclaim Verenthane holy lands in the Bacosh, no less. As well invade the moon to reclaim its silver. Bacosh, Torovan, it's all lowlands—Verenthane—and a world away. Folks here aren't interested. And Krayliss seeks an advantage."

Damon seemed about to reply, but Sasha cut him off. "It's worse than that," she said with force, somewhat annoyed with her uman for oversimplifying. "Don't you see? Krayliss seeks to turn the entire province of Taneryn down the path of the Udalyn before them. He's killed the Great Lord of Hadryn, that much seems clear. Just as Tharyn Askar, his ancestor, killed Essyn Telgar a century before. He tries to relive old Goeren-yai glories."

"Taneryn is a province unto itself," Damon replied, frowning. "The Valley of the Udalyn is entirely within the borders of Hadryn province. Few from outside have even met one of the Udalyn."

Sasha shrugged. "That only makes the Udalyn legend grow stronger. Damon, Hadryn is powerful. All the northern Verenthane provinces are. Endless battles against Cherrovan incursions, and favourable taxation from Baen-Tar, have made them so. Few other provinces can match them for sheer force of arms, least of all quiet, rustic Taneryn. Most Taneryns know this. For all their bravery, they're not stupid. They won't follow Krayliss to pointless suicide against the armoured cavalry of the north, all for naught but the greater glory of Krayliss himself. They see Krayliss for what he is—a vain, pompous fool, who offers them nothing but rhetoric, poverty and an early grave.

"But that does not mean they will like father's lowlands war any better. And it does not mean they will like having Krayliss removed and a friendly, Verenthane lord appointed by Baen-Tar. Krayliss is a fool, but he is the only Goeren-yai great lord. A people can become desperate, feeling that no one listens to their concerns; that there are none to represent them in the halls of power. If Krayliss gains martyrdom, he could be far more popular in death than he ever managed in life."

Damon gazed into the fire, considering that. To her left, Sasha saw that Captain Tyrun was considering her with narrowed eyes. Studying her, as if measuring her for something. She found it strangely disconcerting and returned tentative attention to her food. Jaryd said nothing. He seemed little interested in any matter that did not involve tournaments or gossip and offered no opinions.

"Thank you," Damon said then. "To both of you." Looking at Sasha, and then at Tyrun. "I shall think on this."

Kessligh stabbed at the fire once more, raising another cloud of swirling sparks. His expression boded nothing good.

The following morning, the column passed a simple marker indicating the border between Valhanan and Taneryn. The morning was an overcast grey, and a cold wind accompanied the cloud moving in from the east. The road crested a new ridge, ever higher than the last, and Sasha gained her first clear view of the Marashyn Ranges, spreading their dark, jagged line across the rumpled horizon from north to northeast.

The land swelled more steeply here than in Valhanan, with great, dramatic thrusts of hillsides, crowned with sharp ridges, and broken with erupting outcrops of dark stone.

The road to Garallyn, the Taneryn capital, was eerily free of travellers. Occasionally at a clearing in the trees there would appear a wooden farmhouse, crossed by fences of wood or stone. But there was no sign of the occupants and all windows and doors remained tightly shut. Returning scouts reported no sign of activity anywhere . . . until one man came galloping breathlessly along the road and reported the horror that had befallen Perys.

The column made good time then, leaving the road for a horse trail along an undulating, forested hillside. Sasha rode at Kessligh's rear, heart thumping unpleasantly, in a manner that had little to do with exertion. Perys was the southernmost Taneryn town bordering Hadryn. There were men of Hadryn on the border who had claimed these lands for centuries. And now, it seemed that old dispute had been consumed by something greater.

The horse trail climbed for some considerable distance, affording the occasional glimpse of valleys and vast hillsides through the trees. Then the ground became level and the trees abruptly ceased, the entire column emerging upon the fringe of traditional Perys farmland. The fields lay wide on an open hillside as the column descended a road that wound between stone paddock walls and small barns. Gates were broken open and livestock roamed free along paths. Smoke rose from the smouldering ruins of several farmhouses.

Sasha stared at the nearest pile of ashen debris and saw hoof marks where brown earth tore through the lush green grass. Horsemen had done this.

Sasha tore her gaze away, allowing Peg an easy rein as she stared downslope. She'd travelled to Taneryn before, but never to Perys, so close to the Hadryn border. It should have been beautiful—the open hillside was vast, divided into lush pasture, dotted with farmsteads and orchard groves, and roamed by livestock. Below, the hillside narrowed to form a long, shoulder ridge with a lovely collection of rustic, wooden buildings—Perys village— occupying the uphill half of the shoulder. Beyond that ridge lay a steep gorge with forested slopes, rugged and beautiful.

There was smoke rising from the village, black and sinister. It scarred the view, a single, dark smudge toward the west, and Hadryn. Now, as the trail cleared an orchard, a new hillside presented a scene that chilled Sasha's heart.

Scattered across a neighbouring field were motionless shapes on the grass. Many carcasses, their blood staining the grass. Sheep, she realised with relief as the column thundered closer, the forward guard displaying the royal banners and the banner of Tyree for all to see. Suddenly Kessligh was pointing off to the left, where something darted behind one low wall, men across the column pulling swords or readying crossbows upon their saddle horns. And then something else became visible behind the near paddock wall that had Damon raising a gloved fist in the air and Captain Tyrun yelling for a halt.

They reined up, as the cry and signal passed back along the line of horsemen, horses tossing and snorting impatiently as one of the forward guard dismounted, weapon drawn, and ran for a look at the bundled rags mostly hidden behind the trailside wall. Whatever he saw caused him to raise one hand and make the Verenthane holy gesture upon throat, heart and lips. Impatient, and trusting Peg's abilities, Sasha urged him into a little jump across a runoff trench, and onto the ledge alongside the stone wall.

Lying in a row upon the far side were ten corpses, bloodied and broken. Men, mostly, Sasha saw past the horror. Several looked very young. And at least two, upon closer inspection, appeared to be women. Sasha stared, as Peg fretted and fought at the reins, smelling blood and knowing what might likely follow. Kessligh swung off Terjellyn's back, leaving his halter in the care of Captain Tyrun, and jogged across to look, gesturing irritably at Sasha to clear her beast away from the wall.

She did so, and suddenly there were cries from behind the wall of an adjoining paddock—villagers were emerging, wrapped in ragged cloaks and shawls. They had seen the banners and were crying for the king. Most appeared to be women, with some children in tow, grieving and wretched. Amidst the foreign sounds of local Taasti, the wails and tears, Sasha heard the only words from the locals that mattered—"Telgar," "Hadryn" and "Verenthane."

Sasha caught a glimpse of Master Jaryd's expression, hard with disbelief, muttering something now to Captain Tyrun. Jaryd couldn't believe Verenthanes had done this. For a brief moment, she almost felt sorry for him.

Kessligh stood atop the stone wall by the bodies, looking down at the gruesome wounds, then glancing about the surrounding farmland. Eyes narrowed, as if piecing together the previous day's events in his mind. Then he gazed down toward the little town of Perys below, as village folk wailed and sobbed about his feet.

One of the women noticed him and stared upward with wide, tear-streaked eyes. She gasped and exclaimed something in loud, frantic Taasti. Others came crowding, some exclaiming, others falling to a knee before the vanquisher of the Cherrovan.

"Lenay!" Kessligh demanded. "Who speaks Lenay?"

An old man came forward, his face hidden in bedraggled beard, hunched shoulders wrapped in a shawl. Halting conversation followed, punctuated with gesticulations and pointing. Several villagers clustered about Sasha as she sat astride, one work-worn woman trying to touch her boot, murmuring something Sasha couldn't understand.

Damon came alongside, watching with a concerned frown. "What do they say?" he asked, nodding at the other villagers.

"I don't speak Taasti," Sasha said shortly, straining her ears to overhear Kessligh's conversation. She did not wish to look down at the woman by her boot, head wrapped in a scarf, her eyes lined with hard work, age, and more fears than any city-bred nobility could possibly understand. Such reverence made her uncomfortable.

"I heard mention of the 'Great Spirit,'" Damon pressed, his eyes now suspicious. "What is that?"

Sasha shot him a look of disbelief. Damon understood some Taasti? "Kessligh saved these people from the Cherrovan thirty years ago," she replied. "The legend of the Great Spirit changes from region to region, but it's common among all Goeren-yai. People here think the Great Spirit was Kessligh's spirit guide. Some people call it the Synnich."

"And what do you think?" Damon asked pointedly.

"I think it's a nice legend," Sasha said blandly, tired of feeling as though she were on trial all the time.

"You don't believe in the spirits?"

"I didn't say that."

"You only know that you don't believe in the gods?"

"I said I don't follow them," Sasha replied with a dark, sideways look. "Whether I believe in them is irrelevant."

"Not to father it isn't."

"Aye," Sasha muttered, "well he's not here, is he?"

Kessligh jumped from the wall and swung back into his saddle. "Hadryn did this," he said to Damon without preamble. "They're still in the town. They don't appear to be expecting trouble from this direction, doubtless they have the northward approaches covered. I advise we make them pay for the oversight."

Damon swore beneath his breath, staring away across the rolling, descending hillside, as if searching for inspiration. Villagers crowded about Terjellyn, some sobbing, some pleading. Others approached Peg, Sasha keeping him steady with a shortened length of rein as he started and tossed his head nervously.

"I'll vouch with your father for the necessity," said Kessligh, his tone hard.

Damon gave him a hard look. "I'm not concerned with that!" With enough temper to assure Sasha that he truly meant it. "But it will be Verenthanes attacking Verenthanes. There will be repercussions."

"This is a land grab," Kessligh said firmly. "It's against the king's law. If Hadryn nobility have a problem with Taneryn nobility, it should remain limited to that. This is opportunism—murder—and illegal by your father's own decree. It doesn't get any easier than this."

Decisions, he meant. Judgments. When to fight, and when to kill. The daily bread of princes and kings. Sasha wondered darkly if Damon would have quite so many doubts if the men to be fought were Goeren-yai.

"Damn it," Damon muttered and reined his horse about, signalling to Jaryd and Captain Tyrun. The commands went out from the sergeants, forming companies.

Kessligh pulled Terjellyn as close to Peg's side as possible, considering the villagers. "We'll run the left flank behind Sergeant Garys," he told her. "Remember you're not armoured, we're running reserve for the front line."

Sasha nodded, gazing out across the farmland, wondering at the footing and the line. She looked down at the woman by her boot. "Please, mother," she said, in kindness laced with desperation, "the soldiers are moving. Please move back or you'll be trampled." She leaned down to grasp the woman's hand, gently. The return grasp was hard, work-hardened fingers clutching like claws.

"I know you, Synnich-ahn," said the woman, in hoarse, broken Lenay. Her eyes were bloodshot red and her earrings were curling, metal spirals that might denote a spirit talker. Unusual, for a woman. Sasha stared, as her heart skipped a beat. "The line is unbroken, Synnich-ahn. What was once the father's shall pass to the daughter. The time has come."

The woman moved back with the others, as horses jostled past and large portions of the column broke in different directions, spilling through the shattered gates into broad fields to the left and right. Kessligh took off downslope and Sasha followed, galloping along the winding trail until there was another gate in the left wall, and they turned sharply through it. The open field stretched before them, sloping rightwards, as Sergeant Garys's contingent ran along the upper slope to their left. Kessligh allowed Sasha to pull alongside at a gentle canter, sword out.

He pointed his sword, indicating the vast sweep of hillside before them. "What do you see?"

"No space for a wide line," Sasha replied, standing half upright in the stirrups for a better look, the wind tossing at her tri-braid. "Best to keep them in small groups, perhaps five apiece, following two routes of approach."

"Why not more?" Kessligh asked, voice raised above the thunder of hooves.

"There are only so many good approaches through broken terrain. Also ambush spots are limited on the way in, we only need so many vantage points."

Kessligh nodded. "Also, see the way the paddock walls follow the contours of the land?" He swept his sword across a forward arc . . . and Sasha noticed that indeed, the stone walls did hold to the higher ridges and climbed the steeper folds at right angles. Which was one of those things that Kessligh called the difference between knowledge and wisdom—of course she'd always *known* the farmers constructed their walls as such, she'd simply never thought of the military implications. Most wisdom, Kessligh insisted, was comprised of things that most people already knew, but simply hadn't understood in all its implications. "Trust the farmers, they know the land better than we. Follow the walls, use them as a guide to the land. And see this shallow depression downslope? If we follow it further leftwards instead of the direct route to town, we'll have cover for longer and gain some surprise."

"Might they already have seen us?" Sasha asked.

"Perhaps . . . but I suspect they'll be watching north for Taneryn reinforcements, not south. These are Hadryn villagers, I'm moderately sure, not company soldiers."

A low stone wall approached, Peg and Terjellyn jumping it comfortably. "You think they've claimed this land for Hadryn?" Sasha asked.

"I think they've been awaiting an opportunity for a long time," Kessligh said darkly. "As for what they've actually proclaimed . . . we'll know when we're down there."

"Who's in charge now with Lord Rashyd dead? Usyn?" Kessligh nodded. Usyn Telgar was heir to the Hadryn Great Lordship and not much older than herself. "You think Usyn ordered this?"

"I think he'll deny it. But so much in the Hadryn–Taneryn conflict just happens by mutual consent of all involved."

Leftwards, Sergeant Garys's contingent of perhaps thirty horses came to a halt upon an open, sloping field and began forming up. Sasha and Kessligh reined upslope, angling past a broad shelf of dark rock that thrust from the green field, forming a minor cliff below which numerous sheep were grazing.

"Back there," said Kessligh. "That woman called you the Synnich."

"It was Synnich-ahn," Sasha corrected. "Across all the northern tongues, the "ahn" infers a guide."

"They used to call me that."

"They still do. But I'm your uma. It seems it's fallen to me."

Kessligh looked displeased. "You shouldn't fool around with prophecies, Sasha. This kind of superstitious nonsense can get you into deep trouble."

Sasha stared at him, aghast. "How is this my fault? What possible say can I have over what people may choose to believe?"

"You've become a symbol to the Goeren-yai, Sasha. You of all people should know how long they've wished for a royal Goeren-yai—"

"I'm Nasi-Keth, I can't speak for them!" Sasha cut him off, angrily.

"And as Nasi-Keth," Kessligh replied, "you should remember that you are bound to the Nasi-Keth as much as to anyone in Lenayin."

Sasha snorted in disbelief. "Why is it that as soon as anyone important says anything nice to the Goeren-yai, all the Verenthanes are up in arms!"

"Because it is the nature of power to be nervous," Kessligh said grimly. They reached the next low wall, and cleared it together. "And because the ruling class are all Verenthanes and know only too well what a Goeren-yai uprising could mean for them all."

"How could anyone *possibly* be stupid enough to think I would be interested in that?" Sasha demanded.

"Because the more powerful men are, the stupider they become. Lord Krayliss threatens exactly that. And rumours now place you at his side. As I predicted, if you recall."

"I can't control what people say about me!" Sasha snapped. "I am who I am!"

Kessligh did not reply. Up ahead, every man was watching as they rode forward. Sasha could see the confidence in their eyes, and their posture in the saddle, to see the great man approach. Many had no doubt grown up with their ears filled with stories of the great Kessligh Cronenverdt. To ride into conflict of any in the company of the great Kessligh was an honour above nearly all else.

A cheer went up as Kessligh and Sasha approached, and Sasha decided to pull Peg back a length and allow all attention to fall upon her uman. Kessligh waved his sword in reply. Surely these men weren't to know how much Kessligh hated all the adulation. Not that he ever let it show—he respected the pride of Lenay warriors far too much. Let them have their hero, and cheer when they wanted to cheer. Kessligh had more important things to worry about.

"We'll take the rear," Kessligh announced to the group, meaning himself and Sasha, "like the pair of unarmoured cowards we are." A roar of laughter. "We'll be crossing the road to Hadryn on this side, and the guardpost there. If they've got archers, remember—don't charge, flank. That's what cavalry's for. Get behind them and kill them, no need to give them easy shots. If they look undecided, demand they surrender and save yourself the trouble. It'd be lovely if they all surrendered immediately, but I don't expect it. As flankers, we have the perimeter, Prince Damon shall lead the main force into the town. He's relying on us to keep his flanks and rear secure from counterattack. Let's not let him down. Sergeant Garys has the lead."

Another cheer went up. From back at the road, an answering cheer, no doubt in reply to a similar speech from Captain Tyrun. The right flank would be led by a lieutenant whose name Sasha hadn't yet learned. Kessligh had said that Damon would lead the central attack, Sasha reflected as they moved aside for the formation to come past. Flattery of the prince before the men— technically Damon *was* leading the central charge, but he would be several rows deep from the front, surrounded by his little contingent of Royal Guard.

To her faint surprise, she felt the first, genuine stab of worry. Concern for Damon, no less. And reprimanded herself a moment later—Damon was a fine horseman and swordsman . . . for a non-svaalverd fighter, anyhow. No effort in training was spared for a Prince of Lenayin. And he was the best protected soldier in the formation; not easily distinguishable from a regular soldier in his dress—he would be fine.

"You," said Kessligh, pointing to Terjellyn's rear, "stay right here, the whole time. You're good on your feet, but cavalry's a whole different world. Know your limitations. And his." With a sharp gesture to Peg.

"I know," she told him, meeting his stern gaze as calmly as possible. "I won't do anything stupid. I promise."

"First time for everything, I suppose." But his crooked smile held a hint of real affection. Sasha felt her heart swell. He reached out and they tapped fists. From Kessligh, a rare gesture indeed. It almost worried her, that he should choose this moment for such a gesture.

A yell then from the centre, and across the rolling hill, the central formation moved off downslope, three lines of horsemen following the road and two additional lines to either side. Sergeant Garys waved a fist and the left flank moved forward at a canter. As the last of them passed Sasha and Kessligh's position, they tapped heels and followed.

The low wall they'd jumped on the way up presented the first obstacle—armoured Lenay horsemen regularly practised on obstacles twice as high, and cleared it comfortably. The pace accelerated to a fast canter, each of the two lines' leaders scanning intently ahead, selecting their line across the undulating downward slope, over walls, past orchards, farmhouses, barns and clusters of livestock, planning ahead and predicting events. The leader of the rightward column had another man at his side, holding formation with his leader, but glancing continually across at the central formation as they came down the winding road, making sure this flank did not outpace, nor were left behind.

The rear had a certain freedom, Sasha saw, realising now the other reason why Kessligh preferred it, apart from his and her lack of armour. She could see everything without bothering about formations—the central column upon the right, weaving and splitting to pass about another burned farmhouse, the broken, rocky ridge over to the far left where the open farmland appeared to stop, and all the sweeping contours in between. The pace accelerated once more, and she took the liberty of galloping off to Kessligh's side, to gain some space.

The hillside was flatter for a moment, then fell away more steeply and she had a brief, fantastic view of the town of Perys, nestled upon its protruding ridge below. As they drew closer, some of the smoke in town appeared to be accompanied by flames.

The horses in front leaped another wall, then descended the steeper slope beyond . . . the wall rushed up, Sasha counting Peg's strides and judging distances by reflex, then sailing precisely over, touching with barely an impact as the slope fell away. They plunged at rapid speed as the whole front accelerated, Peg stretching out and threatening to gain on the riders ahead. Sasha wove him off to one side, then back again, and liked the way the vantage changed at that speed, as the wind stung at her eyes and clods of earth from the racing horsemen in front spun and fell to all sides like rain.

They raced into the depression Kessligh had indicated earlier, Perys out of view behind the intervening ridge, then rounded the ridge's end. Over and across a slanting rise in the land, then, hurdling another wall and skirting the smouldering remains of a farmhouse, a rush of ashen smell upon the wind. Suddenly to the right the road was visible once more, and upon it the central formation, which had skirted the cliff's other end.

She saw the other horseman before anyone—a startled figure racing from behind the cover of an orchard—and yelled warning. More yells went up from the front as he was joined by a second, racing downslope at full speed. Suddenly Kessligh was peeling off, selecting a path to the right of the orchard strip. A farmer's hut lay in ruins behind the orchard wall and then Kessligh's arm was indicating another line to the right, a stream, Sasha saw, cutting downslope and through the orchard.

Kessligh jumped, and then she did, past the ashen ruin and angling right to take the stream directly . . . and Sasha caught a glimpse from the corner of her eye—bodies upon the ground, human and livestock, slaughtered together. Peg leapt the stream, then skirted the orchard's right flank, low fruit trees whipping past her, Sasha drawing her blade for the first time and holding it low to the right, ready for surprises. The orchard passed with no sign of further hidden riders as they leapt the end wall and continued across an open field, panicked sheep scattering before them in waves.

Ahead, several guardsmen were closing on the two escaping riders. Peg and Terjellyn hit their full stride for the first time, closing the gap and hurtling down the slope. Another cry rang high upon the wind ahead above the thunder of pounding hooves.

"Murdering thieves! Murdering thieves!" A pursuing soldier aimed a crossbow upon his saddlehorn. A jolt, and one of the thieves faltered, clutching awkwardly at the reins. Then fell, rolling and crashing at bone-breaking speeds. The soldier's companion was gaining on the second man, sword raised, but at the last moment, the remaining thief evaded him and the guardsman and his formation charged on, having no time to stop and deal with stragglers.

Except that now, Kessligh angled directly toward the thief, weapon raised with obvious intent. Sasha fell back and moved across, ready to intercept any obvious escape route. The rider swung from the saddle, clutching stirrup and rein to use his horse as a shield. Kessligh and Sasha flashed by him, one to either side, Sasha sparing a disgusted glance over her shoulder as the man regained the saddle and spurred his mount uphill, making no attempt to follow.

She and Kessligh leaped a wall, skirted a rising mound of rock, then crested another slight rise as suddenly Perys appeared directly before and below. Three groups of horsemen now rushed downslope upon that central, converging ridge. The downhill road linked with another from the left that ran off toward Hadryn, along the shoulder of the gorge. Through that junction ran a stone wall no higher than the others, and a simple guardpost with a hut and a small barn for horses. Squinting through the wind, Sasha could see figures manning that post and several spots along the wall, plus several tethered horses. Above the thunder of hooves, there came the sound of a bell tolling.

The Falcon Guard raced the final length of slope, weapons brandished and banners flying. From the town, well behind the stone wall, there emerged a number of horsemen coming out to greet them. Sasha saw the guardpost archers fire, and abandoned any last hope of a rapid surrender as a leading guardsman's horse went down in a horrid tangle of animal and human limbs. There came an answering roar from the Falcon Guards, and then they were plunging over the wall, the archers ducking for shelter as the central formation continued across open ground to the town and the emerging riders.

She missed that first clash, however, as Kessligh swung wide right, then back left to jump the wall at a close angle. Sasha followed a width wider for cover, and saw Terjellyn fairly trample one runner into the ground, Kessligh reversing for a neat backhand cut to fell a second as he ran. And then he was riding up along the wall, flushing men from their hiding crouches even as a number of Sergeant Garys's group came circling back. Several reloading archers leaped the wall to escape Kessligh's blade, another freed his horse and leapt astride just in time to be cut from the saddle at Kessligh's passing.

They swerved to miss the guardhouse and barn; the remaining, tethered horses scampering in fear, another man throwing himself clear in time to avoid Terjellyn's pounding hooves only to find himself in Sasha's path—Peg had no respect for human-sized obstructions when his blood was up, and she barely felt the bump as Peg smashed him spinning aside. Then some of Sergeant Garys's men were in amongst it, riding down foot soldiers and sweeping both sides of the wall.

Sasha lost Kessligh momentarily in a confusion of riders, struggling for control with a double-reined grip in her left hand—Peg saw a gap almost before she did and went through it with little urging, into open ground before the town. Riders wheeled ahead, more of the flanking formation dealing with those the central formation had bypassed. Weapons slashed and cut, outnumbered defenders trying desperately to survive through manoeuvre and defence . . . several horses with empty saddles, a pair of guardsmen collided, a crash of horses and a catapulting rider, Sasha reining aside that collision and searching in vain for Kessligh . . .

A snarling rider in northern dark greys came at her from the right and she dug in her heels, Peg's acceleration leaving the rider's swing far short. She dodged again as another two men locked in jostling combat threatened to hit her, then slashed hard at a wild stroke from her side—it jolted her arm and she spurred Peg on, emerging from that little knot to find open ground to Perys in front, and the tail end of a horse she fancied was Terjellyn disappearing fast into its main street. She spurred after him, flexing her aching arm and risking a glance behind to see if she were pursued. Having cleared the wall of opponents, guardsmen were now heading for the fight in strength—soon the odds for the defenders would be overwhelming.

Peg raced across the undulating final stretch, frothing and blowing hard, Sasha wriggling the fingers on her gloved right hand, as the index finger had gone suddenly numb. She hadn't performed that parry well at all. Kessligh was right, cavalry fighting was not ideal for a svaalverd fighter—balance in the saddle was not always simple, and fared far better with two hands than one. Deprived of her technique, the strength of Lenay fighting men became formidable. That last man had struck *hard*.

Then Peg's hooves were pounding upon the packed earth road, ramshackle houses to either side, their doors smashed in. Further ahead, several dwellings were reduced to smouldering ashes. Beyond that, something large still burned. She raced by several bodies in the road, recently slashed and weapons at their side, blood pooling upon the dirt. Ahead, the road opened into what appeared to be a central village courtyard. Within, fighting raged, horses trampling in circles and swords clashing. There was no sign of villagers anywhere.

She burst into the courtyard and saw the main source of smoke—the roof of the broad, wooden training hall, which dominated the centre of the square, was on fire. Guardsmen seemed to have mostly won the fight against opposing cavalry as many Hadryn bodies lay sprawled about the square. Numerous guardsmen had dismounted to give chase into broken doorways, or across the debris of previously destroyed buildings. She noticed guardsmen clustered upon the front verandah of the training hall, hammering at the door with their sword hilts. One gave a harsh command to others, who went racing about to the building's other side, searching for entrances. From inside, she could hear the shrill cries of women.

Sasha spurred Peg forward while sheathing her sword. She leaped from the saddle, running across the stones and onto the verandah. "Someone give me a lift!" she yelled at the men hammering at the door, which appeared to be firmly locked. They spun . . . and to her surprise, the leader was Jaryd, his young face streaked with sweat beneath his helm. "Get me onto the roof! I can get in from there!"

"The damn roof's on fire, fool!" Jaryd yelled back as his men continued hammering.

"I know! I spend a lot more time in these buildings than you do, just trust me!"

Jaryd swore and ran to her side, hands clasped together for a cradle. Sasha stuck her foot in it, grasped the support pillar for balance and shoved upwards. Jaryd lifted at the same time, with a great heave, and she caught the verandah roof with both hands. She got an arm over, braced an elbow and scampered with both feet upon the pillar . . . it propelled her over the edge and onto the wooden shingles. She rolled upright, immediately feeling the heat of the flames that roared and surged upon the right side of the roof, threatening to cave it in.

Sasha ran up the increasing incline, aiming booted feet for the nails, knowing that a misstep could break straight through (she'd done it before, playing games on various roofs as a girl). She manoeuvred around the forward triangle panel and rolled onto the upper rooftop from there. Moved along a little way, then simply started kicking with a heel at a likely spot. A wooden shingle broke, and she kicked several more, clearing a space of exposed beams through which dark smoke poured out. One of the big Lenay soldiers might have struggled to fit through it, but Sasha quickly knelt, got both feet in, took her weight on her arms and lowered herself through with a handhold reversal, gasping a deep, final breath as she went.

Smoke within the enclosed ceiling space made breath and sight impossible. She screwed her eyes shut, held her breath, and felt about upon the straw ceiling matting for an edge. Pulled it up and threw it aside, drew her sword and plunged it point first through the light planks below. Stabbed repeatedly, then got her gloved hands into the broken gaps in the wood and pulled. They broke easily. Sasha threw them away, sheathed her sword as the lack of air began to burn at her lungs, stuck her head out of the gap below and saw the broad, open space of the training hall divided by multiple tachadar circles amidst numerous wooden ceiling supports. There were more horizontal beams below, and she grasped the edges of her hole, thrust her body out and half-somersaulted upon that grip, legs swinging and catching a beam. She grabbed onto it, swinging upside down by hands and knees, and overarmed to the ceiling pillar, sucking air thinly as the smoke clustered about the ceiling. She grabbed the pillar and slid down the smooth hewn sides to the ground, gasping a deep breath as the air cleared near the bottom.

A crowd of villagers were clustered at either end around the huge doors, which appeared to have been barred and padlocked. "Padlocked from the inside, but not the outside?" was her immediate thought. "How did the person with the key get out?" A crash from the middle of the hall interrupted that thought as ceiling beams collapsed in a clatter of flames, charcoal and sparks. The low ceiling of smoke was growing lower, the visibility already terrible, blocking light from the small windows high in the walls. A hammering sounded above the screams and crackling of the fire—someone trying to hack through a wall with axe or sword. Neither would work, these walls were vertyn hardwood, four times the weight of regular pine and just as many times the strength.

"Stand aside!" she yelled to the villagers. "Get aside, give some room!" They turned in astonishment and pulled others aside who had not heard, clothing held to their mouths, eyes wide with panic. Sasha redrew her sword and examined the padlock, a big, heavy, iron contraption, no doubt imported from the lowlands where such things were commonly engineered. She pointed to the nearest woman. "Hold this lock! Like this. Keep this side facing up! Don't worry, you'll keep your fingers!"

The woman grasped it in fear, held as instructed, and shut her eyes. About her, Sasha was aware, there were children crying. She took stance, trying to relax her shoulders . . . without a clean breath to take, it wasn't easy. But then, for her, swinging a sword was easier than breathing, and serrin steel was far tougher than iron. The lock broke with a ringing clash and Sasha tore the lock aside, villagers crowding to lift the heavy bar across the door and crash it to the ground. Pressure from inside and out sent it rolling aside and villagers poured out, clutching children and coughing for air.

Sasha remembered the group at the other end and turned back to stare desperately through the smoke . . . but already they were coming, skirting the flames.

"That's all of them?" Sasha yelled as they came. "No others?"

"That's all!" answered an elderly, coughing man. "They locked us in here, threatened to kill a child on the outside if we did not throw the key out . . . we . . . we didn't know the roof was afire until . . ."

"Tell me later!" She ushered him out, onto the verandah, to find that most of the others had already been escorted across the square to the neighbouring inn. She moved down the stairs and across the square at the old man's side, several women hastening to help.

Halfway across, and a thunder of hooves and motion took her attention left . . . a horseman came to a skittering pause, several men on foot behind, weapons in hand and assuredly Hadryn from their dark grey cloaks. Their heads were bare, hair closely cropped in the Verenthane way, nearly bare at the back and sides in the northern style. Gleaming star symbols hung prominently about their necks.

"It *is* the Cronenverdt bitch!" yelled the horseman to the others, their eyes wild with the fury of recent combat, sweaty, dirt-stained and, in several cases, bloody. "We may have lost Perys, but this trophy shall be ours!"

"Run!" Sasha yelled at the straggling villagers, who ran for the inn. The horseman spurred his mount, pounding straight for her. Sasha switched her sword to her left hand, and waited. For a charging warhorse, it seemed to be approaching very slowly. Everything did. The Hadryn's face was contorted with rage and the lust of revenge. And Sasha felt a wave of hatred, calm and smooth, like fire in her veins.

She rolled aside at the last moment, the rider's sword flashing empty air, performed a simple roll to one knee, a hand to the knife at her belt, and threw. The knife struck the passing rider in the side and he clutched at it with a cry.

The first of the foot soldiers reached her at full pelt and unloaded with a huge swing fit to cleave her in two . . . Sasha sidestepped with a neatly angled, swinging deflection, and slashed him open from behind as he skidded by. The second swung high, low and sideways, Sasha fading smoothly before each, feet and hands shifting in unison. A third came at her flank with a ready blow, and Sasha reversed the parry into a swivelling footing-change that took half a length from the new attacker before he realised he was in range. Her swing cleft head from shoulders, before reversing in turn to slash at her original opponent, low backhand to high overhead . . . his footing entangled as his defence struggled to make that difficult transition, his guard faltering, and Sasha split him across the middle with a vicious cut. A fourth charged with a roar, a huge man with bare biceps rippling beneath his sleeveless tunic . . . Sasha saw the basic pattern of his attack before perhaps even he did, and simply invited the right-quarter cross that she knew would follow the half-step fake and thrust. Deflected it straight past its target as he overbalanced, her blade circling in that singular, foot-sliding movement to remove arm and head in quick, precise succession.

Silence, then. She stood amidst the gruesome, human carnage she had wrought, and looked about. She felt amazingly calm. Sound seemed to come at her as though from underwater. Colours appeared strange, almost tactile. The black smoke roiling above seemed impossibly black, and ominous. The blood that spurted and flooded about her boots was the deepest, reddest of reds she'd ever seen. She swung slowly in her stance, a sliding pivot in the centre of the dirt courtyard between neighbouring buildings and the burning hall. Behind, guardsmen were staring at her. Blades limp at their sides, paused as if halted in midrush, having come to her aid but finding themselves far too late for assistance.

Jaryd Nyvar was at their head, staring as if he'd seen a ghost. Sasha took a long, slow breath and stepped carefully past the ruined corpses, her boots already splattered red with blood. Jaryd made the Verenthane holy sign repeatedly. A Verenthane guardsman did likewise. Another made the spirit sign, then another. Further along, a guardsman had removed the rider she had knifed from his mount. He sat upon the dirt now, clutching the knife wound in his side, guarded at blade point. The wound, she noted coldly, appeared several finger-breadths away from his heart. More throwing practice was in order, it seemed.

"Your Highness . . ." Jaryd said hoarsely as she passed, eyes filled with utter disbelief. "I . . . please, Your Highness . . ."

From the verandah of the inn, a crowd of villagers stared and gasped amongst themselves.

"Synnich-ahn," she heard the reverent, frightened murmur. "Synnich-ahn." With wonder.

She paused before the fallen rider. He stared up at her from within a grimacing, battle-stained face. Hatred and fear battled for supremacy in his eyes. Sasha met his gaze directly with a stare of utter contempt.

"Where are your gods now?" she said.

Five

THE COLUMN RODE FROM PERYS in the early afternoon, short five of their number. Two were dead, and another three bore wounds too severe for them to continue. All remained in Perys, confident of the goodwill and care of their hosts. Thirty-one to three. It was, Sasha reflected, an abject lesson in the importance of basic tactics.

She was almost surprised at herself for finding the time to think on such things through the turmoil and heartbreak of the scene at Perys. But above the suffering, and any simple human compassion, there was strategy. Such was the lesson that Kessligh had driven into her—that the lives of soldiers, and indeed the lives of an entire people, would in times of war become dependent upon something so simple as a commander's decisions and deployments. If Kessligh and Captain Tyrun had not been so competent many more families of Tyree would have been mourning the loss of a son, brother or father at Perys.

They left their Hadryn prisoners within the care of a Verenthane monastery along the valley from Perys. Leaving them in Perys, to the tender mercies of the townsfolk whose families they had slaughtered, was out of the question.

Sasha gazed along the old monastery walls as she rode beside them, turning back in her saddle to contemplate the single spire that thrust skyward above a magnificent sprawl of Lenay hillside. With its small, arched windows placed high in the walls, the monastery seemed as much to shun its beautiful surroundings as to revel in them. The Goeren-yai in her soul rebelled at the feel of it—dark, worn stone, unsmiling and welcomeless.

"How long has it been here, do you think?" she asked Kessligh, as they rode two abreast behind Damon and Captain Tyrun, the forward guard in full armour and banners ahead of them. Not that the banners could be seen for any distance through the thick pine forest . . . but then, there was always the prospect of ambush from Taneryns thinking them a Hadryn column, or vice-versa.

"Torovans have been coming here for centuries," Kessligh replied, eyeing the monastery's dark walls with an unreadable eye. "Verenthaneism moved from the Bacosh into Torovan perhaps six hundred years ago. There was a century then, before the Cherrovan Empire, when Lenayin was wide open to Torovan missionaries. Goeren-yai didn't take any more kindly to attempted conversions then than they do now . . . but if these foreigners wanted to spend the effort hewing stone and living alone in the wilderness, well, they weren't bothering anyone. I'd guess this one is somewhere between five and six hundred years old."

Sasha nodded—it had that look to it, of age and constant use. "Damon," she thought to call forward. Damon glanced over his shoulder, turning in the saddle in order to see her past the obscuring helm. "How old a building? Did you see the foundation stone above the door?"

"The year 309, it said," Damon answered, and Sasha pursed her lips. Five hundred and forty-eight years old, then—it being the year 857 by the Verenthane calendar, since the gods had presented Saint Tristan with the Scrolls of Ulessis, in the Bacosh province of Enora. The number meant something to Verenthanes. To Goeren-yai, it provided merely a convenient yardstick against which to measure time.

"The Cherrovan didn't mind these monasteries?"

"No," said Kessligh. "Cherrovan weren't bothered by much, back then. Or at least, they didn't find a few monks in the wilderness threatening."

"There's an old ruin off the road to Cryliss," Sasha countered. "The stones are blackened, it looks as if it might have been put to fire a long time ago."

"Yes, but that's Valhanan. There are no monasteries around Valhanan or Tyree. Or much of central Lenayin, for that matter."

"Why?"

"Because the good, tolerant folk of Valhanan burnt them all down and put the inhabitants to the sword, of course." Sasha gave him a frowning look, questioning his sincerity. Kessligh shrugged. "Good people can have bad histories, Sasha. And bad people can have good moments too in their past. Not everything the Cherrovan did in their occupation was bad either . . . a lot of very good, enlightened Cherrovan formed allegiances with Lenays, and worked with them for the common good. The Udalyn especially met and worked with many such. I met some, in the war—Cherrovans who had married into Udalyn families and ended up fighting their own people for the liberation of Lenayin. I don't doubt their descendants are still alive in the Valley of the Udalyn, those that survived. All forgotten today, of course."

"I thought an enlightened Cherrovan was a contradiction in terms," Sasha remarked.

"I asked a serrin about that once, when I was young and naive. She was well-versed in Lenay history, her uman had taught her the accumulated tales of more generations of Lenays than any Lenay human could possibly hold in his head. I asked her if, from the serrin point of view spanning countless centuries, the Cherrovan were a particularly bad or barbaric people. She was quite surprised at the impetuosity of the question, coming from a Lenay . . . or at least an adopted Lenay. "Young man," she said, "I believe the Lenay expression is that your implication is like the pot calling the pan black. Over the span of the last thousand years, Sasha, the most barbaric, bloodthirsty warmongers in all of Rhodia were the Lenays. That's one reason the Torovans are so keen on recruiting us to fight in the Bacosh—they hope that the simple fear of a Lenay army in the lowlands will frighten the Saalshen Bacosh into conceding ground without a fight. They tell tales of Lenay warriors in Petrodor that would make your blood run cold. The Lenay 'enlightenment,' such as it is, is a very recent phenomenon, I assure you."

"Do you think the coming of Verenthanes with Grandfather Soros made Lenayin a better place?" Sasha asked sombrely.

"A central authority in Baen-Tar made Lenayin a better place," Kessligh replied with surety. "This conflict between Taneryn and Hadryn may be contained because of what we are doing right now—companies in the service of your father riding to put a stop to it. In previous centuries, that didn't happen. Lenayin is a nation now, not just a squabbling rabble. And Verenthaneism is the glue that holds the provinces to your father's will."

"So you think Verenthaneism *has* made us better?"

"I didn't say that. Glue is glue. Verenthaneism serves its purpose where fractious ancient beliefs and loyalties could not. It makes Lenayin one. But any other glue may have served as well."

There was nothing quite so lonely, Sasha thought, as sitting watch at camp after a battle. The log beneath her was hard, the air far colder than a summer night had any right to be, and there was no light but the brilliance of a billion stars. From about the camp came the sound of men snoring, or a horse snorting. Alone in the dark, a watchman's thoughts were his only company. And his memories.

A twig snapped. Sasha stared into the darkness, hands grasping the sword by her side. A rustle of pine needles. "M'Lady Sashandra? Are you there?"

Jaryd's voice. She could see him now, very faintly, a shadow in the blackness. She wondered if he would go away if she remained silent. "I'm here," she said instead. "Sitting down, on the log."

The shadow approached. She did not know why she'd invited him over—like most Verenthane nobles, Jaryd Nyvar was a pain in the neck. Perhaps, she thought wryly, she was just as much the fool as those idiot noble girls who giggled and whispered at the tournaments. Sitting alone on guard watch, even a demon of Loth might be welcome company if his eyes were handsome and his shoulders manly.

The log shifted as Jaryd settled beside her, wrapped tightly like her beneath cloak and blankets. "I couldn't sleep," he explained. He spoke in little more than a whisper, but in the vast, empty silence, it seemed as loud as a yell. "Damn but it's cold!"

"Northerly wind and no clouds," Sasha replied, standard knowledge for any Lenay who lived in the wilds. "Westerlies can be even worse, the wind comes straight off the mountains. Some Goeren-yai say unseasonal weather means the spirits are disturbed."

Jaryd hissed through his teeth, rubbing hands together beneath his cloak and blanket. "Well, the stars are beautiful," he admitted. "Don't the Goeren-yai believe that stars are lucky?"

Sadly, it was too dark for Sasha to see either his handsome eyes or manly shoulders. This conversation, then, would rest entirely upon the strength of his personality. She nearly laughed. "Aye," she agreed.

"Did you make a wish?"

"No."

"Then what were you thinking of?" Jaryd pressed.

Sasha sighed. "My mother," she said quietly.

"Ah, Queen Shenai." As if he'd known her personally. Jaryd was perhaps only a year older than Sasha—he couldn't have been more than six when the queen had died, in childbirth to Sasha's youngest sibling Myklas. Sasha nearly snorted. "She was very beautiful. My father says she was a wonderful queen."

"I knew her only a little," Sasha admitted.

"I can recall the days of mourning," Jaryd continued, very much in love with the sound of his own whisper. "My family all wore black for seven days. My mother also died young, in childbirth. So sad a thing . . . and yet so noble, to die whilst giving life. A far more Verenthane end, I fear, than most warriors shall meet—dying whilst taking life."

"Perhaps if the priests would allow Verenthane women to use the serrin's white powder," Sasha remarked, "all these women needn't die young at all."

Though his face remained unseen, Sasha could sense Jaryd's consternation. "But it is against the gods' will!"

"It's against the priests' will," Sasha retorted. "Serrin women can fight, play music, make arts, conduct trade . . . all the things that men do. It's far easier when you're not pregnant all the time, I gather. I wonder what amazing things Lenay women would discover they could do if given the opportunity."

"M'Lady . . ." said Jaryd, appearing to fight down an amazed smile, "what is a woman, if not the opposite to a man?"

"Should a woman then not walk?" Sasha replied. "Not breathe? Not talk and think? You do all of these things, yet you are a man, so surely I cannot be a woman, because I do them too. I think, Master Jaryd, that the only state in which a woman can meet the Verenthane ideal and not mimic any of your manly deeds is in death."

Jaryd shook his head. "You truly are a strange girl. The serrin spread strange notions from Saalshen."

"Do they frighten you?"

"Frighten? M'Lady, I assure you . . . I do not frighten easily."

"Yet you disapprove of me. Why? Why wish me to be something else, unless you feel threatened?"

Jaryd did not reply immediately. Somewhere in the forest, an owl hooted. "I was raised to be a good Verenthane," he said then. He sounded troubled. "Yesterday, at Perys, I saw you do things with a blade that . . . that I had not thought possible for a woman. Barely possible for most men, in fact. I admit, I am confused. I would like to think that had it been me in your place, I would have acquitted myself as well. I am one of the best swordsmen in Lenayin, I know this with all my heart . . . and yet the artistry with which those men died was . . . truly amazing."

Spirits help him, Sasha thought, he was trying. What he admitted was surely no easy thing. "The serrin know many ancient arts," Sasha told him, somewhat more gently. "The svaalverd is not invulnerable by any means, but when taught by the very best to a capable pupil . . . well, I have options in a fight that my opponents do not."

"I said your ways do not frighten me, and I mean it," Jaryd said determinedly. "I am a swordsman, I can only admire such talent, however unexpected. But I should warn you, M'Lady . . . I know others who feel differently."

"I know . . ." Sasha began, but Jaryd had not finished.

"Noble men," he said, "my relations amongst them. They have long resented Kessligh's influence with the king. And they speak ill of serrin and Nasi-Keth alike."

"Kessligh has little enough influence with the king these days," said Sasha. "And noble Verenthanes have always resented or disliked me for one reason or another. But thank you for the warning. Is there some particular reason I should be worried?"

Jaryd's silence did not help her nerves. Events were in motion, and clearly the lords saw an impending war as an opportunity for self-advancement. War against the serrin would sever all the king's remaining ties with Kessligh and the Nasi-Keth. If it was a chance to get rid of him, then it was surely a chance to get rid of her. She recalled Kessligh's grim warning at the Steltsyn Star, and suffered a shiver that had nothing to do with the chill night air.

"A part of me looks forward to this war," Jaryd said. "The holy war to reclaim the Saalshen Bacosh from the serrin. You would feel differently, I suppose?"

"Saalshen took that land because they were attacked," Sasha replied. "They never started the conflict, they only finished it. The Saalshen Bacosh is formidable because it is defended by armies of humans *and* serrin. Most humans seem happy there, and they fight ferociously to defend their lands from the so-called liberators. If Lenayin went, we'd be just another bloody invader. Is that what you want?"

"Those lands are holy," Jaryd countered, though he sounded less than certain. "I am Verenthane, and the places where the faith was born are occupied by those who do not belong. Any young man wishing for adventure would welcome the chance to ride on such a crusade. And many Goeren-yai I've spoken to said they would welcome a great war, Lenayin has always been a land of warriors, but the Liberation brought peace. Too much peace for many, I think."

"Serrin did not travel as much to western provinces like Isfayen," said Sasha. "Goeren-yai to the west may have no trouble fighting serrin, but the story is different here." She paused. "But you said only a part of you. What of the other part?"

Jaryd sighed. "I've never been interested in the things that my father and uncles love. Wealth and power, more lands, more taxes. They complain endlessly that the nobility has little true power and that the king saves all the authority for himself, and they expect me to be equally outraged . . ."

He shook his head, gazing into the dark. "And now my father is dying. He sent me to the Falcon Guards when he found out. He said I might learn something. I have the Great Lordship of Tyree waiting for me and . . . and I can't find it within myself to care."

Sasha stared at him in astonishment. She hadn't suspected that at all. "You and your father aren't on good terms?" she guessed.

"Never," Jaryd said darkly. "I try to feel sad for him, truly I do. But it's difficult." From somewhere distant, there came the mournful howl of a wolf.

Another answered. Some people disliked the sound. Sasha had always loved it. Such a cold and desolate beauty.

"I know the feeling," Sasha said quietly.

Jaryd glanced at her. "The king seems . . . distant. Though it is said he became far more so, after Prince Krystoff died. He loved Prince Krystoff dearly, as did you."

"He loved his heir," Sasha muttered. "All kings must love their heir, the same way a priest must love his robe, or a princess must love her father. It's an obligation, nothing more."

"He retreated into temple after Prince Krystoff's funeral and rarely comes out to this day," Jaryd objected. "The first place my father would visit if I died would be the stable, to reclaim my horse."

"My father desires the faith of the gods above all else," said Sasha. "It is said he loved my mother, but I don't know how anyone could prove it. He's a humourless, uncaring statue of a man, and for the life of me I couldn't describe to you his smile, for I've never seen it, before Krystoff died or after. He prays for Krystoff because he thought the gods had slapped him in the face by taking Krystoff from him. *That* upset him; Krystoff himself he barely knew."

"Do you see him often?" Jaryd asked. He sounded a little surprised . . . but only that she was telling him this at all, she reckoned.

"A perfunctory meeting when I travel to Baen-Tar. Nothing more."

"Fathers," Jaryd said distastefully.

"Fathers," Sasha agreed.

They sat together in the cold for a while and listened to the vast silence. The wolves were quiet once more. Jaryd then seemed to smile in the dark. Then repressed a laugh. Sasha stared at him, wondering what could possibly be so funny.

"It's just . . . you mentioned the serrin," Jaryd said eventually, with restrained mirth, "and I always think of this when anyone mentions . . ."

"What?" Sasha said impatiently.

"My little brother Tarryn," said Jaryd. "Such a cheerful little fellow. He liked to stride about everywhere with this big, wooden sword that tripped him when he marched or turned. One time when he was around four my sisters thought it would be grand for him to lead a ceremonial presentation for a visiting serrin scholar. So we're all sitting down in the grand hall, with banners on the wall and tables loaded with food . . . and in comes little Tarryn, all dressed in these . . . this little tailored collar and vest and golden buttons . . . all bold and beaming at everyone, just a wonderful, cheerful little boy . . . and he comes down these grand steps before the crowd, with everyone admiring, and he's loving the attention so much that he catches the heel of his shiny new boots on the last step and falls *smack* right on his face on the floor."

Jaryd nearly doubled over with laughter, trying desperately to keep from waking anyone. Sasha's first thought was that it was a very mean thing to find so amusing. Then she remembered a time when her favourite dog had gotten loose, jumped on Alythia and knocked her face first into a waiting row of pastries. And suddenly, she was doubled over in near hysterics.

After a while of laughing through his nose, Jaryd straightened and tried again. "And . . . Tarryn started to cry, while me and my other brother Wyndal are falling out of our chairs laughing, and our . . . our sisters are glaring at us. And Father just . . . just sighs and puts his head in his hand." He took a deep breath and tried to recover himself. "But the serrin scholar was nice, he got up and went to Tarryn, picked him up, sat him on the edge of the table and suddenly it didn't matter any more. Serrin don't get ruffled very often, do they? I still remember that man, he was . . . he was nice."

Sasha rearranged her blanket and cloak, and wiped tears from her eyes. It was like this, sometimes, after a fight. The smallest thing set off the wildest emotional responses. But she greatly preferred this train of thought to those previous.

"Where is Tarryn now?" she asked.

"He's at Baen-Tar," said Jaryd. "He's eleven now, Father sent him for a bit of sophisticated education. He has some cousins there . . . it's been nice, the past few months, being posted to Baen-Tar with the Falcon Guard. I could see him nearly every day."

"I put a lizard in Alythia's bed, once," said Sasha, aware as she said it that it might not be proper to share such things with Jaryd . . . but her mouth was away now, and when that happened, her mind had a struggle to catch up.

Jaryd blinked at her, his disbelief clear despite the blackness. "You . . . in *Princess Alythia's* bed?" Sasha nodded, biting her lip. "Why?"

"She's my sister, I don't need a reason why," Sasha retorted. "She was being a pain. Besides, it was Krystoff's idea."

"What happened?"

"We hid around a corner near her chambers . . . we had to shoo a guard away, he just shook his head and smiled, we were always pulling pranks. Then we heard a loud scream and Alythia came running out in her night gown. She knew who did it, she's a pain but she's not stupid.

"But she killed the lizard. She threw it at us, all dead and limp. I was upset, I yelled at Krystoff and went off to cry in my room. Krystoff came up and made silly jokes until I forgave him."

"Over a lizard?" asked Jaryd.

"I've always loved animals. Horses, dogs, lizards, birds, bats. Some of my best friends have been animals. They're always honest and they never betray you."

"True," Jaryd agreed. "The first thing my horse master told me—it's never the horse's fault. If he makes a mistake, it's the rider's fault for not communicating properly."

"I agree. I've often thought that if more rulers went about their rule as they're taught to go about their riding, most lands would be far better places."

There was another silence, longer than the last. "Well, M'Lady," Jaryd said eventually, "I must admit, you're nothing like the person that I'd thought you were. It seems that I've been told lies about you."

Sasha gave a silent laugh. "And you're not so bad yourself, for a self-important, preening Verenthane noble," she replied.

"I'll admit to preening," Jaryd suggested, "if you'll admit to a sharp tongue."

"Admit? How could I deny it?"

Jaryd smiled. "It must be near time for your watch to end. Say . . . it's a cold night. Two bodies are warmer than one, and there's plenty of room in my bedroll . . ."

"Oh no," Sasha laughed, "you'll not find me quite that easy a mark, Master Jaryd. I've admitted that I no longer wish to break your skull with a blunt stick, but the distance from there to where you're suggesting is a long one indeed."

"A pity," Jaryd sighed, utterly unperturbed. "The short hair is an acquired taste, but I think I was beginning to acquire it . . ."

"Truly." She was amused, in spite of her better judgment.

"It does rather draw attention to your lovely eyes, I feel."

"It's dark. I can barely see you, how can you possibly notice my lovely eyes?"

"How could I not? And truly, you must be built like a rock to produce the swordwork you showed in Perys with such speed and balance . . ."

Ah, so that was it. "I'm sorry, Jaryd," Sasha told him, smiling, "if you wish to indulge that particular curiosity, I'm sure you could ask a visiting serrin lady very nicely and she'd be happy to indulge, as serrin often will. I'm sure she'll show you all of her muscles in all the most interesting places."

Spirits help her, she thought later as she lay snuggled in her own bedroll, she was almost tempted. Unlike Verenthane ladies, Goeren-yai had little worry about using the serrin's white powder, so pregnancy was no issue. She always carried a little on such rides, not in the expectation of an amorous encounter, but as a final guard against the unpleasant prospect of being taken prisoner. She had no illusions about the superior morality or sexual virtue of women—Verenthanes might believe that, and Goeren-yai to a lesser extent, but the serrin placed the concept somewhere between amusing and ridiculous, and in this, Sasha took her teachings firmly from the Nasi-Keth.

But it was a pricklish thing, for her. Serrin might leap from bed to bed with carefree abandon, but she could not. She was human, after all, and lust alone (for her at least) was not quite enough. Besides which, there were enough unpleasant rumours about her dubious morality already in circulation throughout Lenayin—she had no wish to add to the lies with facts. If she was going to risk such a thing, then the man would have to be damned impressive to make it worth her while. Jaryd might well be a decent man, and was certainly a handsome one, but that was still somewhere short of her requirements.

The following morning, the farmhouses upon the trail were all deserted, livestock let out to graze on the thickest pasture in the hopes that the troubles would pass them over. The trail descended along a broken, jagged cleft in the hills, toward a lake below. It shone vast and silver beneath the overcast sky, like flashes of precious metal through the pines. Beyond the far, northern shore rose genuine mountains, whose highest peaks bore white caps of snow.

Part way down the slope toward the lake, the column encountered the senior scout Jurellyn, scanning the clear view of the lakeside below.

"Vassyl," he said as Sasha, Kessligh, Damon, Captain Tyrun and Jaryd gathered about. Jurellyn's finger indicated the near side of the lake, mostly obscured by trees. "They're under attack, almost certainly. One of my lads is down closer, he heard trumpets and massed horse. The town's not afire though, so the defenders may yet hold the day."

"This trail is guarded?" Damon asked, frowning as he considered the scene. Sasha doubted he was admiring the beauty of the alpine lake, nor the majesty of the mountains beyond.

"Aye," said Jurellyn. He was chewing on a grass stem, Sasha saw. His manner, as roughened and weathered as his face and hair, was as informal as she'd ever seen a common man dare with royalty. Lenayin was full of such men—foresters, hunters, wild men, as they were commonly known. Some were recruited to arms, as scouts. The basic notions of civilisation, like manners, were often strange to them. Wise commanders tolerated the indifference, and reaped the benefits. "No knowing by who. I'd guess perhaps the locals, knowing this terrain better." He removed the grass stem, and spat.

"I'll tell you this—there's not much room for massed cavalry down there on the lakeside. It's not a walled town, but they've got archers. It might not matter."

Kessligh pursed his lips as he considered. "You're right, old friend," he said. "That's a narrow lakeside bank, just a few fields and farm walls. Vassyl blocks the way around the lake entirely for cavalry. Attacking Hadryn might try to sneak some infantry around along the high slope, but that'll leave them isolated against Taneryn cavalry between Vassyl and the pass yonder."

His finger drew across to the right, where Sasha's eyes followed the lake's distant shore beneath the mountains. There was the back route to Halleryn. It ended beneath the tallest peak opposite—Mount Halleryn. Directly below, she could clearly make out the dark cluster that was Halleryn town. And if she was not imagining things, she thought she could make out a dark smudge within that open, green valley. Those would be soldiers. An army, encamped before Halleryn's walls.

"The Hadryn have no business even *being* in Taneryn," Sasha muttered. "It's an invasion."

"Usyn Telgar may claim good cause," said Damon. Sasha stared at him. "His father was murdered. He may claim justice."

"This," Sasha retorted, "is not justice."

"We don't know what this is, just yet," Damon replied, his expression dark. There was greater force and certainty in his manner than Sasha had expected. "We shall go down and find out. We shall enforce a truce and interrogate the commanders."

"We are but eighty men, Highness," Captain Tyrun reminded him.

"Not once the other companies arrive."

"They may be days." Tyrun's manner was calm, merely reminding his prince of the facts, not advocating or arguing.

"Then we shan't tell them that," Damon said simply. "Shall we?"

He looked around, seeking disagreement, and appeared mildly surprised when he did not find any.

The descent through the forested lower slopes was guarded, for the column heard many strange calls echoing off the hills as they descended. But with the banners prominently displayed, there came no attack. Finally the trail emerged from the thick trees above the town of Vassyl. The surrounding grassy fields were thick with the last of the summer flowers and the town's shingled roofs and decorative trimmings looked pretty indeed before the vast, flat span of the lake.

Spoiling the tranquil scene were the dark, motionless forms lying on the fields closer to the town. Here at the treeline, Sasha knew, they were already within range of high if inaccurate longbow fire.

Guardsmen were pointing westward along the lakeshore, just beyond arrowshot from the town. A cluster of soldiers and horses was visible there, encamped within the narrow space of open land between the lake and the steep rise of the forested slope. One rider was now galloping forth, bearing a banner on which there flapped a white flag.

"I advise we come closer before he arrives, my Prince," Kessligh called to Damon. "I should like a look at the town."

Damon nodded and they continued forward, the rear sections of the column galloping to draw up the flanks as they cleared the treeline. Sasha saw an arrow protruding from the ground nearby, half buried at a steep angle. Then, from the town, there came a second rider, also bearing a pole with a white flag. He jumped the low surrounding wall and spurred toward them.

Sasha could see now that the tight cluster of buildings was no accident of planning—the narrow streets would weave between such buildings, providing no easy avenues for galloping horsemen and plenty of cover for defending archers. There were men standing on some of the roofs, leaning on railings that seemed designed for the purpose, while others stood along the low stone wall that ringed the town. Lenay soldiers did not typically favour archery, but for the defence of Vassyl, it seemed the logical method—northern cavalry armour was rarely more than leather on chain, which would blunt longbow fire, but not stop it. And horses, of course, were not armoured at all. And now, as the column drew closer, they passed the first fallen body—a horse, sprawled upon its side, an arrow shaft through its neck. Sasha noted its side continued to rise and fall.

"Damn," she muttered and swung in her saddle to call to the nearest man behind . . . but he had already spotted the animal's plight, and swung off from the column whilst drawing his sword. Sasha averted her eyes from what followed—she'd seen enough killing of late. Besides, there were dead men lying up ahead, and more fallen horses. These men did not wear the dark grey of the Hadryn militia at Perys, but rather the black and silver of Hadryn line troops.

"The Hadryn Shields," Kessligh noted as they passed one man, sightless eyes gazing at the sky, a shaft effortlessly puncturing his mailed chest. His surcoat bore the emblem of a silver shield upon black. "Excellent soldiers. Some of Lenayin's best, not like those idiot militia. Their commanders can sometimes let them down, however."

The man galloping from the town reached the column's head first, and the forward guard parted to let him through, hands warily on their weapons. Damon halted and Kessligh rode to his left side, Captain Tyrun to the right, as the forward guard held the man's back, and Damon's small Royal Guard contingent clustered close behind. Sasha kept herself in reserve at Kessligh's rear, with Jaryd for company.

"My Prince," said the rider, with an accent that was somewhat northern, but mostly familiar. He bowed in the saddle, long, braided hair falling about his face. When he straightened, Sasha saw that his face bore tattoo markings, and his ears shone with many rings. "Good that you have come. The Hadryn make war on us, my Prince. This is an invasion, as surely you can see. We defend the rear way to Halleryn and we have not yet let them pass. But the northern clans are more numerous than we, and we fear that a reinforcement may see our number overwhelmed. You must put an end to this aggression, my Prince."

"What the prince must and must not do," Captain Tyrun said sharply, "is for the prince to decide." The Goeren-yai rider simply looked at him, head high and eyes proud. The men of these regions were deferential to royalty, but only from politeness . . . and when they found some personal benefit in it.

"Lord Krayliss holds Halleryn?" Damon asked the rider.

"Aye, my Prince. And Lord Usyn Telgar puts Halleryn to siege even now. They have heavy cavalry that Taneryn cannot match in the open. We can only defend what is ours and hope for justice from Baen-Tar."

"And how did Rashyd Telgar die?"

"Some Hadryn priests came to Gessyl, not five folds over yonder," pointing west toward the Hadryn border. "They disrupted the people's livelihoods, angered the spirits and offended the honour of the women." Sasha frowned at that. Most Goeren-yai women, though not fighters, could look after their own honour. "They were driven from Gessyl, but invented stories of their mistreatment and of pagan insults to the Verenthane gods. Both Lord Rashyd and Lord Krayliss heard this and rode to Gessyl. Lord Rashyd was upon Taneryn land, my Prince. He invaded our territory, he insulted the people and caused mortal offence to Lord Krayliss. A great lord need not suffer such insults upon his own land. The fight was for honour and my Lord Krayliss proved the most honourable."

A new thunder of hooves approached and the Hadryn rider was admitted into the circle before Damon, Kessligh and Tyrun.

"My Prince," said the Hadryn man, all in black and silver, with the leather and chain of the vaunted Hadryn Shields cavalry. He bowed in the saddle. "Well that you have come. Have you more forces on the way?"

"Many," Damon said flatly. "They arrive shortly. Explain your presence on Taneryn land."

"The matter is simple, my Prince," said the Hadryn cavalryman. "My Great Lord Rashyd Telgar was murdered at the hand of Lord Krayliss of Taneryn. By your father's law, my Prince, the now Great Lord Usyn Telgar, son of Rashyd, may seek revenge. Lord Krayliss has refused to yield to the demands of manly honour. Thus, we seek it from him by other means."

As Sasha understood it, Usyn Telgar could seek revenge as a son, and as a man. But to do so in the capacity of provincial great lord, by risking all-out war, undermined the authority of the king in Baen-Tar. Here, at this moment, Damon represented the king's authority, but was he prepared to use it.

"How dare you murdering thieves speak of honour . . ." the Taneryn man growled, but Damon held a clenched, gloved fist in the air.

"Insults and posturing shall do nothing to sway my favour," he said with a dark glare at the Goeren-yai. "I assure you."

"My Prince," said the Hadryn Shield, "these animals do not even allow us a pause within which to reclaim our dead and wounded. We fear some of our wounded may even have been murdered as they lay . . ."

"We did no such thing!" the Taneryn shot back, eyes hard with fury. "We gathered the wounded and are tending to them with the best of our care, as the customs dictate. Should the invaders decide to withdraw their presence, we shall return those men to their comrades."

"The men of Hadryn shall tolerate no hostage threats!"

"Enough!" Damon barked. The two men subsided to a simmering, furious silence. The Hadryn was well armoured, armed and elegantly presented astride his huge lowlands charger; whilst the Taneryn was a roughened, rural image in long braids, tattered skins and leathers astride his wiry, half-breed dussieh pony. It turned Sasha's blood cold to see them as such, these two halves of Lenayin, Verenthane and Goeren-yai, with such murderous hatred between them. Pray that it did not spread. Pray to the gods or spirits; whoever would listen.

"My Prince," said the Hadryn, after a lingering, boiling silence. "At least, if we are not granted a truce, if your own men could retrieve our fallen comrades? It should not befit anyone's honour to leave them lying here."

"The soldiers of Baen-Tar," Damon said coldly, "are not here to sweep up after your conflicts." The Hadryn man paled in silent anger. "Soldier," Damon continued, turning his gaze upon the Taneryn, "upon my request, will you grant a truce for this purpose?"

The Taneryn thought about it for a moment. There was a command in Damon's tone that Sasha had never heard before. A newfound confidence?

No. More likely simple fury, Sasha thought. It seemed to affect the Taneryn, for he nodded. "No more than five horses may come," he said.

"Upon your honour," Damon insisted.

"Upon my honour, we shall not fire."

"Go," said Damon, "carry the message. We shall ride to Halleryn."

"My Prince," protested the Taneryn, "if you would ride the back route along our side of the lake, we can offer you a safe journey to Halleryn . . ."

"I shall talk with the new Great Lord of Hadryn first," Damon said firmly. "He is the one claiming grievance, after all. Have no fear, I shall interview Lord Krayliss in his turn. You are both dismissed."

The two men bowed low in their saddles, then reined their mounts about and set off galloping toward their respective camps. The forward guard reformed ahead and Damon pressed after them. Kessligh held to Damon's side and Sasha took the opportunity to move abreast herself and listen to their conversation, above the clustered noise of hooves, jangling harnesses and equipment.

"Well done," Kessligh said simply, and Sasha could hear real approval in his voice. From Kessligh, that was rare. Damon seemed to ride a little taller in the saddle, but his expression remained dark.

"I hate these fools," he muttered in reply. "Gods how I hate them, Verenthane and Goeren-yai alike. So ready to split each other's skulls with their petty squabbling. I've half a mind to let them at it."

"In such conflicts," Kessligh said calmly, "it's always the villagers that suffer most."

Damon let out a sharp breath. "I know. I'm just . . . angry." He shook his head, as if to clear it, and gazed out upon the lake. The mountains on the far side made a perfect reflection on the water and it seemed to calm his nerves. "So we shall have at it with young Usyn. I hear he's as much a pain as his father. Sofy says she'd heard he once challenged a courtier to an honour duel for making fun of a new shirt he'd worn. The courtier was found hanging in his bedchambers the following morning, too frightened to partake. Apparently his swordsmanship was nothing close to Usyn's, and everyone knew it."

"It's well known they don't fight fair in Hadryn," Sasha remarked sourly.

"Oh aye," remarked Captain Tyrun from the far side of their four-abreast line, "he's a wonderful young fellow, Usyn. Brash, vain and immature. To be expected, if you knew his father."

"But not stupid," Kessligh said calmly, "never think that. His father was smart as all hells."

"What do you suggest, Yuan Kessligh?" Damon asked.

"I have no suggestions," Kessligh said mildly. "I have every confidence in you, my Prince."

And Damon, Sasha noticed, seemed most unhappy with that vote of confidence.

They rode past the Hadryn lines as preparations were being made to send five riders back to Vassyl for bodies. There were some light tents erected and some heavy skins unfurled on the ground for men to sleep under. Perhaps a hundred men, Sasha reckoned—not enough against the several score archers Vassyl looked to have. Probably Usyn Telgar was keeping most of his cavalry at the walls of Halleryn, to prevent any breakout, and lacked enough strength as yet to send more about the lake. Equally probable that some hot-headed Hadryn Shields commander on this side of the lake had become impatient with waiting, and attempted to take Vassyl with single-handed glory . . . and predictable consequences. With Vassyl fallen, the rear route into Halleryn would be cut, and any potential Taneryn reinforcement with it. Also, Sasha guessed, it would open a second front against Halleryn's walls.

Many of the Hadryn men had paused in their routine of tending horses, food and weapons to gaze sullenly at the passing Tyree column. There was little affection in their manner and, above the pounding of hooves, Sasha fancied she heard several cries in a northern tongue . . . "Go home!" seemed the gist of it. She wondered if the men of Tyree could not be equally justified in yelling the same thing back.

The ride about the lake was not so long, for the trail across the mountains' feet was well maintained, with little stone and wood bridges to cross the streams that descended from the peaks; sheer rock faces thrusting clear of the tree-covered lower slopes.

Eventually, the column passed the last of the mountains and rode from the patchy tree cover into the open, grassy basin of a valley. Directly opposite, upon the lakeshore, loomed Mount Halleryn, with Halleryn town nestled on its lower slope, one wall facing directly onto the water. Encamped about the feet of the Halleryn walls, visible only in patches past intervening clumps of pine and valley floor boulders, was an army. Damon urged the column into a final gallop, and they thundered in formation across waving grasslands and flowers until they could see a line of tents, carts and emerging soldiers ahead. Tent formations were widely spread, suggesting that the Hadryn were present in less strength than they would have liked. Men tended horses, or performed various duties about camp, or sword drills and other exercise on the grass. Sasha guessed that they only appeared spread out because the valley was so wide. There were several thousand men here, at least.

A small group of riders headed out to greet them and directed them to the lakeshore, where the command was given to dismount. A soldier came forward to collect the horses and a Hadryn Shields captain, in sweeping black and silver cloak and red helmet plume, beckoned them toward the several large tents that had been pitched directly upon the last of the valley's grass, before the broken stones of the lakeshore.

"Is it wise for her to come?" Damon asked Kessligh, with a dubious glance at Sasha. Sasha held her tongue.

"The authority of Baen-Tar is absolute," Kessligh replied. "Make no concessions. If I come, she comes. Do you wish me present?"

Damon nodded, brusquely. "Let's go." He removed his helm as they walked, running a gloved hand over flattened hair. Captain Tyrun and Jaryd remained behind, organising horse care and feed. Sasha stretched as she walked, saddlesore and weary.

Rather than entering either of the large, lakeside tents, the Shields captain led them across the grass beyond. On the right, men were washing clothes and gathering water from the lake. One soldier passed, laden with ten bulging skins, and granting even Damon no more than a curious glance.

Several men, Sasha saw, were squatted naked in the chill waters, scrubbing themselves. Damon shot her a concerned glance. Sasha snorted. As if she hadn't seen *that* before.

Ahead, then, Sasha could see a lone figure on the open, grassy plain. A light breeze caught at his black and silver cloak, revealing a firm, resolute stance as he contemplated the walls of Halleryn before him. They were of old, dark stone, perhaps as tall as five men, with battlements on top. It was not an enormous fortress, but Mount Halleryn blocked assault from one side and the lake from another. A tributary stream from Mount Halleryn had been diverted to run before the walls, spanned by a bridge where it ran into the lake. Over the bridge a trail climbed to the wall's gate—a big metal grille, as tall as two men. No more than a third of the town's wall was suitable for assault and the rear, lakeside trail would require an impossible attack in single file.

The man did not turn around as Damon, Kessligh and Sasha approached. The Hadryn Shields captain halted at his side and saluted.

"My Lord," he said, "Prince Damon, Kessligh Cronenverdt and Sashandra Lenayin." No "Princess" or "Highness" from this man. Not even, she suspected, a "M'Lady."

Usyn Telgar did not turn to greet them. His hands appeared to be folded upon something before his waist. His sword, Sasha guessed, considering that his scabbard was empty. And her heart beat a little faster, recognising the significance of that gesture. "So Prince Damon," Usyn said then. A young man's voice, cold and bleak. "I heard that you were coming. With eighty men."

"Shortly, more than a thousand," Damon said curtly.

Usyn nodded slowly to himself, considering. Still he did not turn around. "And a girl," he added, with dry irony. His tone did not work Sasha's temper as another man's might. That was hot temper. This anger she felt was cold, dark and menacing. She could enjoy hot anger—the exhilarating burst of temper and retaliation. Of cold anger, there was nothing pleasant to be said.

"You have ordered Hadryn forces onto Taneryn lands," Damon said, ignoring the remark. "State your business here."

Usyn finally turned. It was a pale, youthful face, framed with the close-trimmed, dark hair of a devout northern Verenthane. An eight-pointed star lay prominently upon his leather vest, and his belt held gold-handled knives and a large, engraved horn. They were the clothes of a soldier in the field, yet to Sasha's eye they seemed too well polished to be the kit of an honest soldier.

"You would command *me*, my Prince?" Usyn said coldly. "When Baen-Tar has ignored this Taneryn rabble for so long? Has let them breed upon our borders like rats? Many times we warned of this development and Baen-Tar, in all its wisdom, chose not to act. And now you would seek to impose command? Your timing is lacking, sir."

"Baen-Tar has always commanded here," Damon replied. "Baen-Tar always shall. State your business upon Taneryn lands. I won't ask again."

Usyn glared, his nostrils flaring. He hooked both thumbs into his belt, his sword quivering behind him, impaled in the soft, grassy earth. No doubt Usyn had thrust his blade into the turf upon first arrival at the walls of Halleryn. It was an old Lenay custom for a man with a grievance to do so before the home of another, the blade remaining until the matter was settled. Some such of the old ways survived even in the north, even as the northerners denied any connection to Goeren-yai. It was "Lenay tradition," they claimed. Sasha remained unimpressed; the Goeren-yai *were* Lenay tradition.

"The townsfolk of Gessyl mistreated some travelling brothers," said Usyn. "My father rode to their rescue, as the townsfolk knew he would. It was a trap, my Prince. Lord Krayliss lured him there, with the express intent to commit murder.

"There was talk of insurrection in Gessyl. Townsfolk were agitated about the coming Rathynal, there were claims that they would be made to fight for a lowlands, Verenthane cause. They spoke ill words of the king, my Prince. They spoke of a Verenthane plot against the Goeren-yai. Lord Krayliss led them in this treason. Rocks were thrown. My father charged the crowd to scatter them, but made no attempt to swing on them, merely to prevent them from throwing, as is his right and privilege. Lord Krayliss, also mounted, charged my father from his blind side and killed him with a stroke. I was there. I saw it happen. Any man who claims it different is a liar."

"What of Gessyl now?" Damon asked, his expression dark.

"My men have occupied it and rounded up the most prominent trouble-makers . . ."

"You shall send a message immediately for them to desist," Damon said sharply. "Your grievance is with Lord Krayliss. You have no cause against the village folk of Taneryn."

The young Telgar appeared to bite back something unpleasant. "My Prince," he said then, with heavy irony, "if family Lenayin will not enforce its will against acts of subversion aimed at Baen-Tar, then perhaps you should allow us to—"

"I passed through Perys on the way here," Damon cut in, with every sign of losing his temper completely. "I saw two score and more innocent villagers slaughtered by raiding Hadryn men . . ."

"With respect, my Prince, my people have been receiving trouble from raiding Taneryn villagers for months. If you have only just arrived, how can you possibly know who is guilty and who . . ."

"Enough, I say!" Sasha had never seen Damon so angry. "You shall not attempt to justify what I saw there! Did you send them?" For the first time, Usyn's confidence appeared to slip, just a little. "Answer the question!"

"I did not!" A sullen look crept over the lordling's face. Suddenly, he looked no more than a pouting, temperamental seventeen. "The villagers of Hadryn can organise their own defence! If you have a problem with that, deal with it yourself!"

"We dealt with it," Damon said darkly. "We dealt them thirty dead and more. More shall follow, Hadryn or Taneryn, for any who commit wanton murder in the name of ancient feuds!"

"My father was murdered by this heathen animal!" Usyn yelled, eyes wide with indignant fury. "The father-in-law of Prince Koenyg, who is *also* my brother! If the authority of Baen-Tar does not defend my right to justice, then what in all the hells' good is it for!"

There was a silence, then, upon the grassy plain by the wide, cold lake-side. Sasha felt rather than heard the gathering presence behind, the creak of a leather belt, a faint rustle of clothing, the compression of grass beneath heavy boots. Damon stared at the younger man, anger duelling with a rare distaste that seemed to sit like acid upon his tongue. The younger, paler man glared back, breath coming hard, his manner that of one accustomed to sudden fits of temper.

"Family Lenayin would be *nothing* without the north!" Usyn hissed. "The king owes his throne to our unwavering support! Your father knows this, Princeling! Well that you should learn it too! Well that you should know with whom your true loyalties lie!" This last with a harsh glare at Kessligh, acknowledging his presence for the first time. The eyes remained upon him for one hard-breathing moment, wild and white about the rims. Then to Sasha, also for the first time, with an even greater hatred than before.

"I serve the king," Kessligh said simply.

"You serve only yourself!" Usyn spat. "Yourself, your whore and your godless serrin friends! Your power in Baen-Tar grows weak, old man! The king no longer listens to you and your kind! You may have those idiots in Valhanan fooled, but you've never fooled the men of the north—we know what you are!"

"Sure you do," Kessligh said with an utterly unpleasant smile. "I'm the reason you're not speaking Cherrovan."

Usyn's hand went to his belt knife, and Kessligh's to his own in a blur of motion. And Usyn's eyes went wider still, face draining of any remaining blood, as if realising, with sudden terror, what his temper had nearly brought him to.

Kessligh's smile grew wider. Sasha had seen him hit crawling insects on a tree trunk from ten paces with that knife.

She decided it was a good time to swing on her heel and check the scene behind. Sure enough, there were upward of thirty Hadryn men standing there, and more gathering behind. Some in a state of partial dress, others fully armed and armoured. Strong men and tall, as with the soldiers of all standing companies; their pale skin untouched by any ink quill, their hair trimmed short, sometimes even shaved. Their eyes were hard and their manner unwelcoming. Behind them, she glimpsed members of Damon's Royal Guard contingent hovering by the lakeside tents with evident alarm.

"Forget the knife," Kessligh told Usyn then. With all the ease and assurance that one might expect from the greatest soldier in Lenayin. "If what you say of your father's death is true, your case seems good. Baen-Tar's justice serves here. Whatever disagreements exist, you shall find justice in Prince Damon, where it is warranted. Only remember this, young lord. Do not try us and do not test our patience. All the north should know very well what *I* am capable of."

And he bowed, all good form and politeness. Sasha swung back long enough to do likewise. Damon did not bow. He would nod, affirmingly, if Usyn bowed first. But Usyn simply stared, wild-eyed and hateful. And so Damon swung on his heel and walked, Kessligh and Sasha at his sides.

The Hadryn men stood back just enough to let them through, but not enough for comfort or respect. Sasha walked with her right thumb hooked into her belt beside the knife there, ready for the fast thrust of a close quarters attack. A man bumped her arm, not moving aside quite in time. She could feel the eyes upon her, roaming over her body. But the Royal Guard were close ahead now as they emerged from the crowd.

"That little fool's a real worry," Kessligh muttered as soon as they were out of earshot. "His loss has made him unstable."

"I think he was expecting Koenyg," Damon said darkly. "Given that it's Koenyg's father-in-law who's been killed. I warned Koenyg that Usyn would take it amiss, but he insisted he was too busy with Rathynal approaching. Wyna was distraught."

"Poor girl," Sasha said sarcastically. "Meeting Usyn, I suddenly see the family resemblance. The whole Telgar family's unstable. I'm so thrilled to be related I could vomit."

"And I'm sure your graceful presence shall do wonders for Usyn's stability," Kessligh remarked.

"You didn't help," Sasha retorted, determined to get some payback for all the times he'd accused *her* of provocation.

"I thought it best to scare him a little," Kessligh replied, the familiar, hard edge to his tone. "He's a bundle of raw impulses right now, most of them aggressive. I appealed to the only raw impulse that might give him pause."

"What if he thinks you're bluffing?" Damon asked, casting a wary glance across as they walked.

"I don't bluff," Kessligh said grimly.

Damon glanced at Sasha. Sasha shrugged. "He doesn't bluff," she admitted. "Feints and misleads from time to time, but never bluffs."

"There's eighty of us threatening to take on several thousand of them," Damon retorted. "What is that if not a bluff?"

"Suicide?" Sasha suggested, raising an eyebrow at Kessligh.

Kessligh shook his head. "It's a start," he said.

Six

E VENING, AND THE SETTING OF THE SUN behind the mountains transformed the overcast sky to a deep, ominous red. The lake seemed ablaze as they walked along its bank, headed for the walled town of Halleryn. The mountains behind cast all the land and lake into shadow, the sun long since set behind its rugged peak. The colour was mesmerising, and reminded Sasha of tales told in the Steltsyn Star, of dark spirits with eyes the colour of fire . . . and she made the spirit sign to her forehead; an unthought, reflex gesture.

"Stop that," Kessligh said with irritation at her side. Of all the dinner party, he alone had eyes more for the town walls ahead than for the ill-omened sky. "I told you, the colour is caused when the lowering sun strikes the underside of the clouds instead of the top. And it looks so bright because we're in the mountain's shadow, and it's reflecting off the lake. It's very beautiful, but I tell you there's nothing otherworldly about it."

"This is a demon sky," Jaryd disagreed, staring upward as he walked. "Father Urys in Algery used to tell me about this when I was a lad—sometimes at evenings, when the sun god slips into his netherworld, there opens a space between Loth and our world. This is all the power of Loth spilling free, and demons with it . . . there's bad things afoot this night, I can feel it."

"Aye," Kessligh said sourly, "and if you lot don't cut the superstitious rubbish, I'll be one of them."

They crossed the bridge above the small stream, the torches held by the Royal Guardsmen to the front and rear gusting trails of flame. Ahead, the walls of Halleryn were alive with torchlight and whipping, wind-blown banners. Their party's own banners, held aloft by the two guardsmen not wielding torches, fluttered and snapped above their heads. In the light from the battlements, Sasha could see the dark shapes of archers watching their approach.

On the far side of the bridge, she risked a glance back across the river. The Hadryn camp stretched wide among the scattered trees and farmhouses of the valley, the blaze of many fires aflicker in the cold wind. Another five hundred men had arrived that afternoon, mostly militia from Hadryn villages, without the heavy armour and equipment of the Hadryn Shields, but formidable soldiers all the same. Word was that there were another thousand infantry afoot, but delayed without the speed of cavalry. Sasha eyed the movement atop the torch-lit walls ahead. She greatly doubted the forces within would match what was building outside.

"Usyn will have enough forces before the walls to contain any breakout by tomorrow," she said to Kessligh, folding her arms tightly within her cloak to guard against the freezing wind. "He'll then divert forces about the lake, and Vassyl will fall. Halleryn's forces will be trapped, and then a real siege."

"We can't let it come to that," Kessligh replied, eyes also scanning the battlements. His mood was the darkest Sasha had seen on this trip. "A siege will drag into Rathynal. Such is precisely what your father would wish avoided."

Some horsemen were approaching along the lakeside road ahead, the back way from Vassyl, moving for the gates. The tall, metal grille stood open, but was doubtless manned to slam shut at a moment's notice. In the gathering gloom, the horsemen looked to be Taneryn militia, long braids blowing in the wind. Behind them came several horse-drawn carts, laden with what Sasha guessed would be fresh food. So long as Halleryn held the back road around the lake, food supplies would stay fresh. So long as they kept the Hadryn on the other side of the stream, fresh water could be collected from the lake. But if Usyn decided to press forward in force, neither could be guaranteed.

"What's wrong?" she asked Kessligh then, into that solemn, wind-swept silence. The blood red sky was fading now, deepening to the colour of coals in a dying fire, once the most brilliant heat had paled.

"I remember this place," Kessligh said heavily. "Thirty years ago. The walls had not held the Cherrovan then. We took it back after they'd held the place for a week. Inside the walls we found . . ." and he grimaced, unwilling to complete the sentence. He gazed away across the rumpled, darkening surface of the lake. Sasha stared at him for a moment. Kessligh rarely displayed such emotion recounting his time in the Great War. The spirits of this place must surely have been unsettled, for all the blood that had been spilt here.

She made the spirit sign again, unable to stop herself. This time, Kessligh did not appear to notice.

Halleryn's gate loomed ahead, alive with burning torches within the archway.

"Who approaches?" came a cry from the battlements, and they halted on the road.

"Prince Damon Lenayin!" a Royal Guardsman yelled up, with extra volume to be heard above the loud flapping of green and black Taneryn banners overhead. "Yuan Kessligh Cronenverdt! M'Lady Sashandra Lenayin! Master Jaryd Nyvar of Tyree!"

Along the walls to either side, many faces peered down, some leaning out for a better view. It was one of the more dramatic announcements any arrival could have declared. A formality, of course, as they'd been invited.

"The Great Lord Krayliss of Taneryn grants you welcome!" came the call down from the battlements. "Pass within and be at peace, for you are within the protection and hospitality of the Great Lord of Taneryn!"

They passed beneath the portcullis into Halleryn town itself. The main street ahead was lined with buildings of stone base with wooden walls and rooftops, as was the fashion of northern towns. A soldier of obvious Goeren-yai appearance arrived before them and beckoned them to follow. The road was cobbled, rare for a Lenay town, but then, stonework was the tradition in these parts. And there were drains, Sasha saw as they walked, leading to what she presumed were underground outflows. God forbid they led into the pristine lake. She couldn't imagine any Goeren-yai township allowing that. More likely a river inflow washed it someplace outside the walls to be buried or composted for farm use . . . another serrin innovation that the Goeren-yai had adopted many centuries ago.

The streets of Halleryn were mostly empty and unlit by any street lamp or torch. Sasha could not help but think the town dank and gloomy, with nary a tree to break the monotony of stone and cobbles. The central road sloped upward until it opened on a broad, paved courtyard busy with soldiers. New arrivals were dismounting and leading their horses to the stables on the right. Men gathered in the courtyard about makeshift ovens and the smell of cooking wafted in the air.

Attention turned as the royal party crossed the courtyard, some men coming to their feet, more from curiosity than respect. Here too, there was little warmth to greet a prince and, in several quarters, even some coarse laughter at a whispered joke. Then, halfway across, there came a new murmur sweeping through those watching . . . "Cronenverdt! Cronenverdt!" . . . and suddenly all men were standing and pressing forward to watch, open-mouthed and incredulous.

Overlooking the courtyard was a tall keep of stone walls and overlooking arches. The keep's grand wooden doors were thrust aside by a pair of guards as the royal party approached, and they entered a stone hallway lined with old, faded tapestries and alive with the dancing flame of ensconced torches. Their guide led them up a broad stone staircase to the left, where they found themselves emerging from the floor of a great clansman's hall.

All was stone, but for the tall windows in the walls. Central pillars made rows to either side of the very long, central table, laid for serving. Light came from flaming torches mounted to the ceiling pillars, and a grand, carved chair dominated the table's far end. About the pillars, standing with swords at the hip and mugs in their hands, were numerous Goeren-yai warriors of Taneryn—long-haired, tattooed, beringed and proud. All paused in conversation now and turned to look as the Royal Guard extinguished their torches and parted to present their four charges.

Damon walked forward, surveying the array of hard faces that confronted him. Sasha remained at Kessligh's side . . . and realised that Damon, to the best of her knowledge, had never met Lord Krayliss and did not know what he looked like. She scanned the faces herself, searching.

"This is a meeting of war!" announced one man, tall and broad with long hair flowing, a strong moustache trimmed in two lines on either side of his mouth. His hard eyes were fixed upon Sasha with evident anger. "There has never been a woman present at a Goeren-yai council of war, and there never shall be!"

Sasha glared in return. Kessligh hooked a thumb into his belt and repressed a grimace that was somewhere between a wince and a sarcastic smile. "Looks like dinner to me," he remarked.

"Yuan Kessligh," growled the man. "You walk into this hall with more honour, and soaked in the blood of more enemies, than might any man in Lenayin. Do not tarnish that honour, sir, by betraying the honour of Taneryn and its chosen men."

Kessligh strolled forward to Damon's side, and then a step beyond, gazing about at the gathering as he might typically consider a strange clutch of chickens—with thoughtful, off-handed curiosity. To Sasha, his manner and poise seemed nothing but familiar. And yet the armed and braided strongmen of Taneryn seemed to flinch backward—not in steps taken, but in posture, a slight lowering of the eyes here, a defensive folding of the arms there. Kessligh stood no taller than most, and somewhat slimmer than some, his unkempt hair streaked with grey, his person lacking any martial adornment save the blade at his back. And yet somehow, before warriors, nobles and a prince, he dominated the room.

"Your name, sir?" Kessligh asked the angered man, as calmly as ever.

"Yuan Cassyl Rathan of Dessyd village," the man replied, with a proud lift of his chin.

"A first thing, Yuan Cassyl." Meeting the man's gaze with a firm stare. "My honour is mine. Not yours. It is mine to do with as I wish. Your preferences mean nothing to me. Likewise your honour is yours. My actions have no bearing upon it. Only you can gain honour, Yuan Cassyl. Or lose it, by your deeds."

There was a brief pause, to allow for a collective rumble of approval to follow, with some nodding of heads. For a great warrior to talk of such a thing as honour, before such a gathering, at such a time, was a serious matter indeed. At such times, men of great import listened hard.

"A second thing—you claim that your honour depends upon adherence to certain ancient traditions. I don't care." An utter hush had filled the hall, broken only by the faint, rippling sound of flaming torches above. "I cannot afford to care. I am Nasi-Keth. Your ways are not my ways. I respect them nonetheless. Thirty years ago, the men of this place swore a similar, undying respect to me and my ways, however strange they found them. My ways include an uma—a student, if you will—who remains by my side to learn as best I can teach. I would never require you to change your ways, Yuan Cassyl of Dessyd village, were you to enter my house and my hospitality. It would be dishonourable of me. And yet now, you ask me to be like you—Goeren-yai, which I am not."

"A rider came today from Perys," came a new voice, deep and powerful. "He witnessed the great deeds there of our guests and the warriors of Tyree, against the bloody-handed Hadryn. He also claimed that the uma of Yuan Kessligh was there possessed by the Synnich, and in such a state slew nine Hadryn warriors by her own hand and tasted their blood."

There was a flurry of spirit signs across the hall and a murmuring of oaths. Then the speaker emerged from behind a stone pillar. He bore a thick, wild mane of dark hair and a vast, bushy black beard. Grim, dark eyes peered from a profusion of strong yet intricate tattoos that masked the left side of his face. A long, single tri-braid fell clear from the rest, to lie upon the right of his jaw. He walked slowly forward in heavy boots and a leather vest beneath a cloak of green and black Taneryn colours. Lord Krayliss of Taneryn, the sole Goeren-yai great lord of Lenayin.

"The spirit men all agree there have been omens," Krayliss continued, his eyes still fixed on Kessligh. The sword that swung from his hip was a monster, although to judge from the breadth of the man's shoulders, Sasha reckoned it might be about the correct size for him. "The sky tonight was red, foretelling of much blood to be shed . . . or of the coming of a great power. Perhaps that is you, Yuan Kessligh? Or your uma?"

"I am not a man to judge such things, Lord Krayliss," Kessligh replied, shrewdly. "If you wish a recounting, best that you ask her yourself."

Krayliss stopped at the forefront of his gathering, assorted village headmen and respected warriors from across Taneryn. Followers of Krayliss, at least. Not all the men of Taneryn could be described as such. But some, facing Hadryn aggression, might rally to his side nonetheless.

"Yuan Cassyl makes a fair observation," he rumbled, meaty thumbs tucked into his broad leather belt. "Women are not welcome at Goeren-yai councils of war. It is not our way."

"If my ways are not welcome here," said Kessligh, "then I shall leave. Do you revoke your previous invitation?" Their stares locked. A contest of wills, the stubborn versus the disciplined. The blunt instrument versus the sharp. A lord never revoked an invitation. Kessligh had drawn the line, somewhat closer to Lord Krayliss's toes than most men would dare.

"Girl!" Krayliss barked then, with a wry twist of his lips. "Come forward! Step where we can see you!"

Sasha cast her cloak away from her left shoulder, exposing the hilt of her sword, and moved quietly to Kessligh's side. It was an effort not to meet Krayliss's eyes, but she kept her gaze demurely on his broad chest, as a good Goeren-yai maiden should among such mighty warriors. Surrounding her, some men stared in displeasure. Others with intent curiosity. And some with mouths smirking in imitation of their lord, as if thinking the matter some huge jest.

"So . . ." rumbled Krayliss, raking her from head to toe with his gaze. "The girl who was once a princess. Some men still call you that, do they not?"

"The men of Lenayin shall do as they will, my Lord," Sasha replied, provoking some laughter at that truism. "It is no longer my title, I ceased to be princess when I left Baen-Tar."

"The bonds of blood are deeper than mere titles, girl," said Krayliss. Some of the smirking ceased at that utterance. The lord's eyes bore deeper. Sasha's instinct was to meet challenge with challenge. The effort to keep her eyes lowered was enough to bring sweat to her brow. "These tales from Perys. The rider who gave them was young and with little hair between his legs . . . much like our Master Jaryd here."

A roar of laughter from the gathered men. Sasha repressed a retort with difficulty. Sometimes, in her love of the Goeren-yai, she forgot why she disliked Lord Krayliss so greatly. Now she remembered.

"I did not slay nine men," she said tightly.

"Ha," said one village headman, contemptuously, "as I said. Just as I said."

"I slew four."

Deathly silence across the hall. "You witnessed this deed?" Krayliss asked Kessligh.

"Not I," said Kessligh. "I saw the bodies in the aftermath."

"I saw it!" called Jaryd to the group, proudly. "I was not ten paces from the last when he fell! All four fell so fast and so close that I had barely yelled warning of the first, when the last had fallen upon his corpse! It was a masterful display and I pity those who were not there to see it! Even as Verenthane, I swear I could see the mark of your spirits in the strokes of her blade!"

Sasha swore beneath her breath, through clenched teeth. Stupid, ignorant, macho young fool. Oh how she was going to kick his backside when they were outside once more . . .

"You make great claims, young Master," growled Krayliss, with considerable displeasure. "What does a Verenthane know of such things? On what authority does a follower of the lowlands order claim knowledge of the ancient spirits?"

"I was there, my Lord," Jaryd retorted with all too little fear. Did he know who he faced? Challenging Lord Krayliss within his own hall was not the same as defeating wooden swords at tournaments. In these parts, men fought to kill, not for games. "I have eyes. I tell you only what I saw."

"Even if true, it proves nothing!" retorted another man, from the far side of the long table. "The spirits are not guides for women! They never have been!"

"Spirits alone were never mentioned," said another, low and soft, as if fearing the presence of unspoken, unseen power. "Only the Synnich was mentioned."

There was about the room another flurry of spirit signs and the muttering of oaths. In some faces now, there was real fear. Krayliss surveyed the commotion with a dark, furrowed stare.

"I don't believe her!" pronounced another. "The men of Hadryn are bastards, yet their swordsmanship is unquestioned! Perhaps only the smallest handful of men could defeat so many! No woman has such skill with a blade to take four in the manner described! Only a woman of Saalshen could manage such a feat, and a great one at that!"

"Exactly!" retorted another. "A serrin woman could manage such a feat because the serrin walk with the spirits!"

An uproar followed, men shouting argument and counterargument at close, heated range. In several quarters, pushing broke out, quickly separated by cooler heads before it could escalate. To Sasha's left, Damon was staring about in disbelief. To her right, Kessligh simply folded his arms and waited, as many times he had waited for a much younger Sashandra Lenayin to cease her raging tempers before insisting just as firmly upon the very thing that had caused them. Sasha simply watched Lord Krayliss, unafraid now of meeting his gaze. Krayliss stared back, unmoved within the commotion.

Perhaps he expected her gaze to drop. Anger burned in Sasha's stare. A warning, when the others were not looking. And it was Krayliss's eyes that widened, in surprise and anger, from the power of that meeting.

"Enough!" he yelled, a broad fist held high, and the clamour eased as quickly as it had begun. "Such debates should wait for a later hour," he said darkly. "We have other business to attend to. Prince Damon rides to serve the justice of Baen-Tar. Little enough hope do we of the Goeren-yai have in the justice of Verenthane kings . . ."

It was said with great sarcasm and brought a harsh laugh from many of those surrounding.

"He comes to us with a mind full of questions!" Krayliss announced, in louder, defiantly jovial tones. "He wishes to know the cause of our old friend Lord Rashyd's death, and the reason his son stands upon our gate with his blade in the turf, stamping his little temper tantrum now that papa is no longer about to spank his skinny backside!"

Another laugh from the men and some mugs were raised in salute. Krayliss turned to Damon with defiant confidence. "Yes, I slew Lord Rashyd! His priests came to harass the Gessyl townsfolk and I rode to see them off! Rashyd crossed our border uninvited and confronted us! He spurred his horse against my people and I slew him for his insolence! And what, Prince of Lenayin, shall you do about it?"

"Take you to Baen-Tar for a judgment at the king's pleasure," Damon replied. Sasha blinked at Damon, unable to believe she'd heard such a decisive statement, so coolly delivered, in the face of such defiance. For a moment, the entire hall seemed hushed with similar surprise.

Krayliss threw back his head and laughed. "The young prince has some balls after all!" he roared, to an eruption of laughter that shook the ceiling. "And how do you propose to achieve this monumental feat, young Lenayin?"

"I shall await the arrival of my line companies," Damon said icily, "and we shall join forces with the Hadryn. Should you refuse to comply with my order, we shall kill you all."

Another silence followed. Sasha's stomach tried rapidly to tie itself in knots, to her great displeasure. There was a fine line, where most men of her experience were concerned, between balls and stupidity. Only Kessligh could be reliably expected to find that precarious balance with consistency.

"My father's law is quite clear," Damon continued. "Lord Rashyd deserved a censure for his conduct. He did not deserve death. Your punishment can only be decided by the king himself, upon a full presentation of the facts. My task, I see now, is to take you there within the custody of the crown. Should you refuse, your life is forfeit. I therefore suggest, Lord of Taneryn, that you do not refuse. For the sake of your people."

Lord Krayliss's already vast girth seemed to swell even larger with rage. "And from what time have the Verenthanes of Baen-Tar cared for the people of Taneryn?" he snarled, bushy eyebrows and beard seeming to bristle like a great wild animal. "Even now the king calls a great Rathynal, to force his tame Verenthane lords to approve his decision to march to war in the lowlands! A war in the Bacosh, with whom we have no interest whatsoever! A war for Verenthane causes and the profit of lowlands merchants! With such do the Verenthanes of the towns and cities seek to protect their ill-gotten wealth and prestige—with the blood of poor Goeren-yai farmers who have no interest in your foreign causes and false titles!

"Who but me will speak for the Goeren-yai? Who but me is left to speak?" He roared to the assembled men. "It was royal Verenthanes like this one who appointed only Verenthane lords to the provinces! It was they who belittled us, scattered us, patronised and left us to our fates at the hands of Hadryn tyrants! Of all the Udalyn descendants, I am the greatest of rank and the greatest of honour! Who but me will speak for the true, the ancient, the rightful people of Lenayin!"

The roar that followed paled all those previous, a deafening thunder that threatened to split Sasha's ears. There followed the heavy, rhythmic stamping of boots on flagstones, accompanied by the hard clapping of hands. Krayliss surveyed his new commotion, wiping his beard of the spittle that now hung there, residue of his outburst. Pride burned in his eyes, vain and spiteful. This was a man, Sasha saw only too well, who was prepared to die for his cause. No matter how many others he took with him to his pyre.

"Entertaining," Sasha remarked as they walked from beneath the gates of Halleryn. "Nothing like a bit of open hostility to develop the appetite."

"I've had worse meals," Damon muttered, tugging on his riding gloves for warmth.

"When?" Sasha asked, pulling her cloak more firmly about her.

"Anytime someone thinks it a grand idea to get me together with Maryd Banys of Ranash, and her mother."

Sasha frowned at that. The sound of the wind above the vast, moonless dark of the lake held an eerie power. Yet, for all the frozen chill of the open night, it was a relief indeed to be free of that hall and the dark stares and muttered, suspicious conversation about the long table. "Maryd is the eldest daughter?" she asked.

Damon grunted in reply.

"I've made her acquaintance," Jaryd remarked helpfully. He'd been attempting to appear untroubled all night but, to Sasha's eye, he looked unsettled. For a young man previously uninterested in the lordly affairs of Lenayin, such encounters were surely a lot to digest. "She's very pretty, think you not, Prince Damon?"

"Aye, she's pretty," Damon muttered. "The wits of a chicken and the charm of a leech, but she's pretty. Dinner with Krayliss was a pleasant affair compared to that." Sasha shot Kessligh a glance and could have sworn she saw him smile.

"So Father wishes you to marry a Ranash girl?" Sasha questioned further, with considerable distaste. "A northerner?"

"Koenyg's idea," Damon said, gazing off across the dark lake as the road approached the shore.

"Two northern sisters-in-law," Sasha said with displeasure. "I'm not sure I could stand it. Wyna Telgar is enough."

"Poor girl," Damon retorted. "You wouldn't have to share her bed for the rest of your life, you've nothing to complain about."

"I think we must be talking of two different Maryd Banyses," Jaryd said quizzically. "The girl I mean is sweet-faced, black-haired with blue eyes and a full bosom . . ."

"And what interesting topics have you discussed with her, Master Jaryd?" Damon asked. "Have you spent more than a heartbeat in her presence? Or merely admired her bosom from afar?"

"It's a very nice bosom, Your Highness."

"Master Jaryd never met a bosom with which he couldn't hold a conversation," said Sasha with a sideways glance.

Jaryd grinned. "Yours is disappointingly quiet."

"You just haven't asked it the right questions." Jaryd laughed. "These treaties of marriage are ludicrous," Sasha continued. "Ranash will obey the throne simply because their lord's daughter shares a prince's bed? Hadryn's behaviour has barely changed since Koenyg married Wyna . . . and little Dany now gives them a Hadryn in the line of succession."

"The other lords will not be happy if I marry another northern girl," said Damon. Her brother's eyes were joyless in the wind-blown torchlight. Damon the petulant, he'd been called before. Lately, however, he'd been Damon the grim. "This line of princes was going to be a rich vein to be mined, but Krystoff died and Wylfred now thinks to take the holy vows, and suddenly, with Koenyg wedded, five available princes are only two. It's just me and Myklas left, and I fear the competition will be fierce."

"It's the creeping feudalisation of Lenayin," said Kessligh.

Jaryd frowned. "The what?"

"Before King Soros," said Kessligh, "there were no lords and titles, just chieftains, clans and regional allegiances that split into warfare as often as they came together. But Soros didn't only bring the gods from the lowlands, he also brought nobility, land titles and all the rest. He thought he was bringing civilisation to the barbarians. Lowlands civilisation. Now, the lords see that their powers do not match those of their lowlands cousins and they push for more. In the name of civilisation, of course."

"It'll never work," Sasha said firmly. "Lord Aynsfar of Neysh tried it just a few years ago, brought a hundred hire-swords from the lowlands and declared himself ruler of his 'ancestral lands.' But Goeren-yai came from near and far, killed his hire-swords and took his head. No man or woman of Lenayin will be anyone's serf—it might be the lowlands way, but not here."

"You're talking of the murder of Lord Aynsfar!" Jaryd realised, suddenly aghast. "How can you . . . how can you approve of that barbarity? They tied him down and took his limbs one joint at a time until . . ."

"I heard it was a swift blow to the neck," Sasha interrupted, turning to walk backward on the undulating grass, facing him. "I also heard that he was warned repeatedly, but gave only threats in return. Do the lowlands ways appeal to you, Jaryd? Would you like to inherit lands for your family? Allow minor lords to levy the royal tax instead of the king?"

Jaryd gave a protesting smile, but Damon's eyes were now on him as well, and curious. "I . . . I hadn't given it that much thought . . . but, I mean, what's the harm? Lowlands customs work very well and . . ."

"In the lowlands they work well," said Damon.

"No harm?" Sasha added, incredulously. "Would *you* like to be ruled by a succession of lords, ladies and knights even before we get to Baen-Tar royalty? It was a great enough feat to get ordinary Lenays to swear allegiance to one king in Baen-Tar, you'd add all these other fools on top of that and expect them to accept it?"

"But . . ." Jaryd was flustered now. Sasha doubted he'd ever been challenged to justify his own privilege before in his life. "But the noble families already have authority over their regions . . ."

"Horse shit," said Sasha. "The nobles derive their authority from the king and from each other, and that's only if they pray to the lowlands gods and have loads and loads of money to begin with. No one ever asked the rural folk, Jaryd. In their eyes, the nobility is just another strange little clan, all interbred and foreign, and nothing to do with their daily lives.

"They pay taxes to the king because he's the king, and the small tax to the provincial lords because they're the king's men, and because it occasionally does some good with roads and irrigation channels and bridges and the like. The rest of them are just dogs around the dinner table as far as the villagers are concerned, whining for scraps."

"But a noble lord offers protection to his people with his forces!" Jaryd protested.

"In the Bacosh, they use armies paid for by the peasants' coin to murder and terrorise them," Sasha said firmly, still walking backward. "In the Bacosh, the ordinary folk have neither the weapons nor the skills to fight back. Lenayin is *vastly* different. They don't *need* your protection, Jaryd, and they certainly don't want it, and they'll fight you tooth and nail if you try to impose it upon them."

She nearly spoiled her speech by tripping on uneven ground, stumbling to recover her balance. "Just . . . please," she added, skipping sideways, "as a favour to me, look about you on this ride. Talk to your low-ranked men. Insist they be honest with you. It's not only sad that you should misunderstand your own people, it's dangerous."

They crossed the wooden bridge once more, the Hadryn camp laid before them, a flickering line of campfires and shadowy activity.

"My Lords," said one of the Royal Guards as they approached the main line of tents, drawing their attention forward. Rising from the light of a large campfire were a small cluster of well-dressed Hadryn men, buckles and clasps gleaming in the firelight. They strode forward, a wall of weaponry and self-importance.

"Did your negotiations go well, Prince Damon?" came the loud voice of Usyn Telgar. Some of his men laughed with ugly humour. "Negotiation," in the northern tongues, had never been an honourable word. It reeked of compromise and cowardice. The Royal Guard stopped and parted, Damon coming forward to confront the young Telgar directly.

"Well enough," Damon said. "Did you wish to raise some matter with me?"

"Your *sister*," said another man, with great sarcasm, "appears to claim the title of saviour of the Goeren-yai!" The new speaker was dressed in the travelling finery of northern nobility, short-haired with a little, trimmed goatee. He'd been drinking, Sasha judged. They all had. "A message arrived from Perys just now, apparently she inflicted great carnage there in the name of pagan spirits! These claims are an insult and, in the name of the devout House of Varan, I demand an apology!"

"You'll get nothing," Damon replied. "My sister is not responsible for the claims others make. I suggest, Master Farys Varan, that you do not raise your voice in her direction again."

"Pah!" Farys spat, with a blaze of anger. "She ceased to be a Verenthane princess when she left Baen-Tar! You have no brotherly claim on her honour, Prince of Baen-Tar! These pagan lies dishonour the names of brave Hadryn warriors who die for the honour of their gods! Do not defend her, sir! She comes here upon our lands and she has the temerity to claim victories over Verenthane warriors after joining forces with barbarian scum to celebrate their deaths!"

"*Your* lands, Master Farys?" Damon replied, darkly furious. "We stand upon the lands of Taneryn. Do you claim them?"

Sasha's gaze ran along the line of Hadryn faces. All, clearly, were of noble Hadryn families. Their ages varied, from hot-headed youngsters, to cold-eyed, calculating elders. Sasha wondered, her heart assuming a familiar, unpleasant rhythm, if they'd put Master Farys up to it. There were an increasing number of armed men gathering behind to watch.

"We claim no lands," Usyn Telgar said coldly, his face strained as though withholding some great outburst. "We claim only the satisfaction of avenging our lord . . ."

"I claim more!" shouted Master Farys, stepping forward to thrust an accusing finger past Damon's shoulder at Sasha . . . and Sasha noted the silver-haired man at Farys's side give a cold, satisfied smile at the outburst. Farys's eyes were blazing, his face flushed red. "I demand an apology from this false princess! The honour of Hadryn has been slighted! If it were not enough that the god-fearing men of Lenayin had to suffer the insult of a cow-ardly, woman-chasing, pagan-loving fool of an heir named Krystoff for so long, is it now our fate that we must suffer his sister's—"

Sasha snapped and abruptly strode forward with a hand moving to her shoulder. Kessligh grabbed her arm, but she smacked it away with her other hand, spinning clear to draw her blade as weapons rang clear in the night air all around. Before any could move to strike, Sasha drew back her arm and hurled the sword point first into the turf before Master Farys's feet. All froze, staring at the quivering blade.

"This dawn, Master Farys," Sasha said icily, "I challenge you to defend your honour."

For a long moment, there was only the shuddering whistle of the wind and the flapping of banners. Then Farys laughed, high and slightly hyster-ical. "You challenge me to a duel?" Disbelievingly. "I cannot fight a *woman*!"

"Then you are a coward!" Sasha snarled.

Farys turned pure white, his newly drawn blade trembling within his hands. "I should strike you down where you stand, whore!"

"With your guards and friends to back your flanks?" Sasha said contemptuously. "Need you so much assistance to defeat a single girl?" Farys's mouth worked open and closed in soundless fury. "No answer? Will you not accept? Snivelling, whining, bed-wetting coward?"

Farys's clenched teeth parted and he let out a great, shuddering roar . . . yet did not advance. Sasha knew, from the darting eyes of the Hadryn before her, that Kessligh was close at her back, blade at the ready. That alone would make even the bravest, angriest, drunkest warrior think twice.

"I accept!" Farys bit out, hoarse with effort. "Tomorrow at dawn, the lies and myths of the Goeren-yai princess die!"

The silver-haired man at Farys's shoulder placed a hand upon the younger man's arm, lowering his weapon with a final look of cold satisfaction. Farys's trembling hand lowered and he thrust past his companions toward the camp-fire. All about, there came the sound of sliding steel as blades retreated into sheaths, the line of Hadryn nobility fading back, their departing expressions both angry and smug.

"Sasha?" Damon said cautiously, stepping forward to stand at her side as she retrieved her sword from the turf, and wiped dirt from the end. "Sasha, what did you just do?"

"I defended Krystoff's honour," Sasha said shortly. Her heart was beating hard, but not with the fevered thumping of fear or excitement. This was colder, more calculating. Damon just stared at her, greatly pained. And it occurred to Sasha then, with only a mild surprise, that he feared for her life.

"Sasha, that was Farys Varan, son of Udys Varan! He's . . . he's known by all to be one of Hadryn's finest swordsmen . . ."

"Forget it," Kessligh said grimly, taking a place at Sasha's side, eyeing the retreating Hadryn with calculation. "Farys's a corpse. It's what happens after he's dead that worries me."

Sasha could hear the hard displeasure in his voice. She didn't care. When the fury caught her like this, she rarely did.

Camp that night was an abandoned barn on the valley floor. Sasha sat on a hay bale, her back to one corner of the barn's outer wall, where it would shelter her from the wind. On the grass nearby, there were many sheep huddled—Sasha knew only because of the occasional, restless bleating, their woolly shapes mostly invisible in the darkness. She gazed at the stars for a long, long time, thinking of many things, yet of nothing in particular. Sleep seemed far away.

A dark shadow approached soundlessly to her left, from over by the barn's mouth. There was just enough light for her to make out Kessligh's familiar outline, even wrapped in heavy cloak and blanket. He settled onto the hay bale at her side without a word. For a while they sat together, uman and uma, and gazed at the stars.

"It's past time for my watch," Kessligh said then.

"I won't sleep," Sasha replied. "I might as well take another watch if I'm to stay awake."

"The surest way not to sleep is not to try," Kessligh remarked. "Meditate. I slept well enough during the war in full knowledge that I would fight the next day. You should manage."

"Probably." Somehow, she just couldn't manage the energy for one of their customary arguments of technique and method.

"Sasha," Kessligh said then, with the note of a man about to begin something . . .

"I don't know what else I could have done," Sasha cut him off, tiredly. "There are lines to be drawn. In this land, respect is everything, and to tolerate such disrespect is to invite our enemies to attack us. Master Farys crossed the line. The north cannot be allowed to think their Lenay enemies will not fight back, otherwise they will continue to push and push, and soon every group in the land that does not agree with their bigoted ways will find themselves under attack."

"I agree," said Kessligh. Sasha turned her head against the wooden barn wall and gazed at the dark outline of his face. "I blame myself, in part. But the way of the uman is not the way of a parent. I cannot dictate your path to you, I can only help you to find your own.

"And I have seen this coming for a long time. I've warned you, haven't I?" Glancing across at her, a faint motion in the dark. "I warned you of consequences should you continue your attraction to the Goeren-yai so openly. I told you the offence it would cause, here in the north in particular. But perhaps, like so many things, it was meant to be."

Sasha frowned. "That doesn't sound like serrin philosophy. That sounds fatalistic."

Kessligh shrugged. "I am human, after all. But then it is serrin philosophy, too. Life is a battle, Sasha. All existence is in conflict. We fight the elements, we fight our consciences, we fight the limitations and eventual mortality of our bodies. All things happen by conflict, of one sort or another. The serrin have long recognised this fact. Once, long ago, they fought amongst themselves as we did. But then, having accepted the inescapable reality of conflict, they set themselves toward finding ways of living with it and negating its worst consequences."

He sighed, softly, and resettled his shoulders against the hard barn wall, seeking better posture. "It was always going to be trouble, Sasha. Choosing you for my uma." Sasha's eyes strained to make out his expression. "I knew it then, and I know it now. But I could make no other choice. I knew the choice would cause conflict, but sometimes, a forest fire brings new life, and from bloodshed can spring renewal. Such matters are not always ours to decide."

"Renewal," Sasha murmured. "That's a Goeren-yai philosophy."

"Warlike cultures always believe in renewal," Kessligh replied. "They have to." And then, before she could respond . . . "Sasha, I'm not happy that you chose a fight. I sympathise with your reasons, but you are far too important to be risking yourself in such a way. Important to your role as uma, and important to me personally.

"However, what's done is done. And I know you, Sasha. You cannot sleep because you feel compassion. Even for a thug like Farys Varan, you feel compassion because you know your skills utterly outclass his. I know because I've faced the same. When your opponent has so little chance, it feels like murder, and then you must face your conscience."

He reached from beneath his blanket and clasped her shoulder with one firm, sword-hardened hand. "Feel no pity for him, Sasha. Only you can cause your defeat tomorrow morning. As skilled as you are, any hesitation, any indecision against a man of his talents will surely cost your life. As long as you remain *hathaal*, he cannot touch you. But *hathaal* requires total concentration and technical perfection. In that way, he actually has more leeway for error than you. He fights with strength and strength is always strong, even when imperfectly applied. For svaalverd, strength comes from the application itself. Should the application fail, you shall lose not only technique, but strength as well."

"I know," Sasha murmured. "I know that. The edge is fine, even against my opponents in the Baerlyn training hall. At my best, even the best of them is no chance against me. When I fight distracted, or without full concentration, I come home black and blue. But . . ." and she took a deep, shuddering lungful of cold air, ". . . you know my moods. I cannot sustain one emotion for any long period. And now, as much as I hated Farys at the time, and still hate him now . . . it is difficult to sustain. That's all."

"You hold the Hadryn responsible for Krystoff's death," Kessligh reminded her.

Sasha nodded. "I do," she murmured. "But it was not by their own hands. It was not by Farys's hand." A flash of memory . . . a priest at the door to the tuition room. Musical lessons—the piccolo pipe, no less. A grave, sombre man, kneeling at Sasha's side. Dawning trepidation and terror. "They misinformed him as to the size of the Cherrovan raiding party. They knew he would charge in and be defeated by superior numbers. Once, I thought I could kill every man in Hadryn for that treachery. But now . . ." She broke off, unable to finish the sentence. A lump grew in her throat. For a moment, there was only the silence of the vast, cold night.

"Perhaps I don't love him enough," Sasha whispered. The piccolo pipe, falling to the floor. Breaking. "He was my only true friend. He had faith in me when no one else would. I dreamed of duelling with Hadryn men for vengeance for many years. I should not be having these doubts. If I'd truly loved Krystoff, I'd kill Farys and dance on his corpse."

"Dreaming is easy," said Kessligh. "Killing is hard."

"It shouldn't be," Sasha said. "Not if you believe in the cause." She gazed at her uman, her eyes hurting. "How did you do it? You've killed so many. How do you do it, and not doubt?"

"I always doubt," Kessligh replied, with as close as Sasha had ever heard him come to a gentle tone. "When you cease to doubt, you are lost. But the world is as it is, Sasha. One cannot find peace without accepting that. People die and people kill, and even if we are all flawed people, we cannot achieve anything good if we allow our enemies to defeat us. We must survive, Sasha. You must survive. Now, by your own choice, you must kill to survive. And you shall."

Sasha gazed at the mist upon the lake as she walked behind her honour guard, six men of the Falcon Guards who had volunteered for the duty. The eastern hills formed a dark, rugged line against the pale sky. High above, sunlight caught distant wisps of cloud and turned them brilliant yellow against the blue. The grass beneath her boots was damp, a not-quite frost that lay across the valley plain and gave the huddled white sheep something to drink with their morning feed.

Her honour guard were leading her toward the bridge where the tachadar circle had been formed upon the Halleryn side of the river. The town walls rose close and the gathering by the stream was well within arrowshot, yet all present were safe from Taneryn archers. No Goeren-yai archer would ever disrupt the solemnity of such proceedings. Along the walls, Sasha could see the dark shapes of many men gathered anywhere they could find a vantage. The Hadryn, it was plain, expected the Goeren-yai princess to die this morning. And they wanted the Taneryn to see it happen, firsthand and personal.

She followed her honour guard across the bridge and up the grassy bank toward the gathering ahead. The men of her honour guard were all in the full armour and colours of the Falcon Guard, save for their helms. Long, braided hair hung free on the shoulders of the three Goeren-yai, who marched with the slow, arrogant swagger of Goeren-yai manhood, a hand clasped to the hilt of each sword and threat in every step. The three Verenthane soldiers walked in a line behind their comrades, with no less intimidating a posture for all their lack of swagger. Three of each, Goeren-yai and Verenthane together. It was a clear and defiant symbol. No doubt the Hadryn, and the Taneryn onlookers from the walls, would notice.

Behind, at a suitable distance, followed Damon, Kessligh, Jaryd, Lieutenant Reynan and the six Royal Guardsmen. Captain Tyrun had remained behind with his troops, as at least one senior officer was required to do. It was unclear why Lieutenant Reynan had come, except that his family connection to Lord Jaryd gave him some influence. Alone of the Tyree men, he seemed vastly displeased by proceedings and wore a scowl beneath his helm. Perhaps he hoped she would lose.

Ahead, a party of Hadryn nobles had gathered about the far, northern side of the tachadar circle, some house guards and regular troops amongst them. Perhaps twenty men, Sasha counted as they approached. On the far bank, a great many soldiers were now gathering, their officers attempting to form them into orderly lines, so as not to present disarray in view of the walls of Halleryn. As Sasha's party strode closer, there came some yells from the walls to the right. Encouragement, Sasha realised, although she did not pay attention to the words. The uma of Kessligh was going to fight the Hadryn in honourable combat. Whatever trouble Lord Krayliss had with Kessligh's uma, it evidently did not extend to all the soldiers of Taneryn.

Answering yells came back from the troops across the river and suddenly the still, sombre morning erupted into raucous cheering, one side against the other. Sasha let it wash over her, her breathing calm as Kessligh's training had taught, her pulse level and controlled. Her eyes remained fixed on the gathering ahead and the man in shiny, polished brown leathers beneath a flowing black cloak, standing upon the edge of the circle with his blade unsheathed, point down on the turf.

The honour guard reached the circle's edge and parted. Sasha took her place, the toes of her boots on the small stones that defined the rim, and the yelling grew even louder. A horn blew from the wall to her right and then there came the thundering roll of a hide drum as many hundreds of Goeren-yai men tried to equal the racket of thrice that number from across the river. From across the circle, Master Farys Varan was staring at her, eyes blazing with all the fire such a reception would breed within the heart of any Lenay warrior. Sasha felt a tingling down her spine and then elsewhere as the sensation spread. Little sleep though she'd had, she could not remember ever having felt more awake. Colours, sounds and smells assaulted her senses. She took a deep breath of the chill morning air and surveyed the circle.

It was wide, perhaps eight armspans in diameter, with room enough about the perimeter for at least thirty men to stand shoulder to shoulder. The silver-haired man of the previous evening was now removing Farys's cloak from his shoulders and folding it ceremoniously. One of Sasha's honour guard did likewise for her and her limbs welcomed the chill air. Another man, a Verenthane, presented her sword in its scabbard—a Goeren-yai tradition, performed by this Verenthane soldier at his own insistence. He had been present when she had slain those four at Perys, Sasha knew. She drew the blade clear, leaving the soldier with the scabbard, and stepped into the circle.

The yells, horns and drumbeats faded, then ceased completely. Once again, silence ruled the valley. That abrupt transition gave Sasha a worse chill than the last, and her breathing threatened to quicken as her heart skipped a beat. Focus, she reprimanded herself, testing the feel of the blade in one, thin-gloved hand. Do not think. Be.

Behind and in front, men of both parties moved about the circle, finding space for a clear vantage. One of them, in flowing black robes, stepped into the circle and walked to the centre. A priest, Sasha registered. Of course the armies of Hadryn would bring their holy men with them. Reaching the centre, he produced a small book and began reading. Across the northern side of the circle, men bowed their heads in prayer. Some of the southern side did also.

The priest completed his incantation and holy signs were made upon heart and lips. The silver-haired man who had taken Farys's cloak met her gaze by chance and smiled a smug, contemptuous little smile. These were the men who killed Krystoff. The hatred flared, a rising sea of molten fire. Focus, she forced herself with effort. Anger can work for you. Don't drown in it.

The priest walked to Farys, who sank to one knee, the sword held point down before him. The priest blessed him with obvious reverence. Then turned in a swirl of black robes and considered Sasha darkly as Farys rose at his back. Dark smiles spread across the gathering behind to see the priest's manner. Then he walked toward her. But Sasha did not kneel.

"Child, do not be foolish!" the priest whispered in harsh temper as an angry murmur spread across the circle's northern side. "You must make your peace with the gods, for your father's sake!"

Sasha met his stare with an intensity that made the priest's eyes widen.

And he blessed himself in recoiling reflex. "Why?" she asked him. "I won't be the one meeting them today."

The priest blessed her hurriedly as she remained standing, then departed in haste. The silver-haired man then stepped into the circle as angry ripples continued amongst the Hadryn. "Let the record state," he cried to all those watching, "that Master Farys Varan, son of Lord Udys Varan, has been challenged to this duel by the uma of Kessligh Cronenverdt! Let it also state that this challenge was only accepted following the most grievous provocation and insult to Master Farys's honour! The uma of Kessligh Cronenverdt presumes to wield the authority of a man! If a man she thinks herself to be, then let her be treated as one!"

The silver-haired man glared proudly across all gathered. Then, with a spiteful, final stare at Sasha, he turned and departed. Farys advanced, proud in his stride, broad shoulders set. Imparting upon the occasion all the honour and dignity he could muster for the ritual slaying of an impetuous girl. But he would do this all the same, for the purposes of his masters, who had surely put him up to it. Kill the Goeren-yai princess. Discredit the hated Kessligh Cronenverdt. Show the pagan fools the sum total of all their hopes and prophecies. And show to all Lenayin that the tales of serrin martial prowess were nothing more than superstitious fables, to pave the way for the holy war to come.

Sasha found that she could not move. Her booted feet remained anchored, her previous calm slipping as the blood began to pound in her ears. She would kill this man to suit her purposes. He was ignorant. He did not know what he faced. Suddenly, she saw before her not a hated northerner, a peddler of spite and bigotry, but just a man, the same as any other. He had a father and a mother, and more family besides. He seemed to have perhaps thirty summers, and so probably he had a wife and children, also. Surely there were many who loved him. She had killed men before in battle, who were trying to kill her at the time. This was . . . something completely different.

Krystoff's coffin, open before the altar of the Saint Ambellion Temple. She had worn a white dress and held a white lily in her hands. Remembered numbness. A black, all-encompassing grief. She had wanted the service to be grand, to do justice to the great, gaping void that had opened in her world. To do justice to Krystoff. To the way he had made her feel when he smiled at her, or laughed at her humour, or hugged her and made her feel warm and loved as no one else in that grey, formal world had ever made her feel.

The funeral had failed miserably to do any of that. She had concluded in her grief and despair that everything was fake and nothing that she knew was worth keeping. She had smashed things and attacked her minders; refused to eat for days on end. That day at the funeral, even more than the day she had learned of Krystoff's death, she had truly become an unbeliever. All of their rules, all the ceremony, all the fancy clothes and pompous manners, and her father's strict and formal habits . . . it was all a great, stupid fraud. She'd always suspected it. That day, she'd had proof.

Something now drew her gaze down to both lightly gloved hands, grasped in a tight, unthinking grip about the hilt of her sword. Strong hands, calloused in all the right places. She'd worked hard and gleefully on those callouses when Kessligh had first brought her to Baerlyn. Her hands then had been the hands of a little girl—soft and pale. Kessligh had given her the hard, capable hands of a warrior and she loved him for that. But for all his lessons, his relentless training, high standards and cryptic wisdom, the lore of the Nasi-Keth alone could not give those hands the strength they required for the task at hand. The Nasi-Keth were an idea to her. A wonderful idea, full of promise and the prospect of a brighter future for all. But that idea remained in the future, beyond the reach of the present.

And her present . . . she took a deep, cold breath as it came to her, slowly, yet with the building force of revelation. Her present had been stories from old Cranyk before the fireplace of his old, creaking house near the training hall—tales of great deeds and heroic warriors, of pride and honour, and all the things that made life worth living. Her present was an evening at the Steltsyn Star with music and dance, and friends, and laughing so hard that she nearly cried. Her present was the tradition of the Wakening, the wise scolding of the women, the worship of the spirits that dwelled in all living things and that overpowering, timeless bond with the natural world.

Those things had been her present since the time she had arrived from Baen-Tar. Lost and disconnected from the world, the wisdom and humour of the Goeren-yai had come to make her feel whole again. They had reassured her that life was indeed a great and noble thing, and well worth treating as such. Kessligh had given her the hands of a warrior and the mind of a thinker . . . yet it was the Goeren-yai who had relit the fire in her heart. She took another deep breath, shoulders heaving, poised within the tachadar circle with a serrin blade in her hands. The confusion lifted and suddenly all was clear. She was Goeren-yai. And it was simple.

She moved forward, barely aware that they were her steps, like paws upon the wet, morning grass. Her vision seemed to burn unnaturally sharp and she could almost count the bristles on Farys's broad chin. She may have never done this before, but the Goeren-yai had practised its like for as long as there had been people in Lenayin. She stood upon the sacred ground of countless previous battles, watched by the eyes of countless reincarnated souls. The cycle was never ending and this moment was nothing so rare and precious as she had imagined. It was merely her turn, that was all, and the surge of ancient fury lit a fire in her veins.

Her blade moved to the starting pose with barely a thought. The posture felt a model of muscular perfection, the feet spread to shoulder width, the knees slightly bent, poised with a coiled, motionless power. Her grip on the sword had never felt so firm and secure. Her breathing came calm and impossibly, deadeningly slow. Her heart barely seemed to beat at all. The world felt so calm. So still. She savoured the moment. She did not want it to end.

Farys moved. A shift in footwork brought his blade slashing for her neck. It seemed only natural that her own posture should shift in turn, a foot sliding back as the hands came up, an intersection of steel at the shoulders, a brace of perfect power through arms, back and legs. Farys's blade deflected effortlessly by, glancing from her swinging edge like a skate on ice. She could perhaps have finished it then with his guard exposed in the follow-through, the commonest form of death for regular fighters against the svaalverd . . . yet the perfection was lacking and the feet could not quite position for the stroke the hands desired.

He recovered fast and pressed the attack. This time, there were no enormous follow-throughs, as if someone had thought to coach him what not to do. Sasha retreated, a step to each stroke as their facing shifted, countering one, and another, and then another in a clever, deceptive combination that swung at the last moment to an unexpected, high-quarter slash from an interrupted backswing. But it was the simplest, most beautiful thing in the world to shift her guard from low to high, switching the retreating foot to rear and rotating that defence into a fast, offensive cut.

Farys survived only with a desperate, downward slam of his blade, but his left foot failed the transition, and so she swung to that side instead. His frantic parry barely made it in time, and his balance not at all as he stumbled back a step . . . and that necessary movement opened the way for the most exquisite shift of balance to her forward pivot foot, as the blade circled to his low, right quarter and slashed him cleanly open from right hip to left shoulder.

Farys stumbled back, slowly collapsing as his eyes stared in disbelief. Blood spurted in a horrid flood, drenching vest and legs, and he crumpled in a motionless heap on the grass. Sasha held that posture, blade held high in final flourish, arm perfectly extended from the shoulder, feet at the precise position and angle. It was the most beautiful thing she had ever done, that killing stroke. So perfect. So supreme. She gazed up at the lethal, gleaming edge, almost bloodless with the speed of her strike, and marvelled at her own magnificence.

Of the horrified gasps, cries and then yells from the Hadryn surrounding, she was only dimly aware. Of the sudden roar from the Halleryn walls, beyond the silent pause that followed Farys's fall, even less so. Except that suddenly, there was a sound of rumpling cloth, a cloak thrown back and a high, metallic slide of a small blade leaving its sheath.

A desperate yell came from the perimeter's friendly side and she spun, aware only of an onrushing threat, her blade slashing to meet it . . . and struck the knife from midair, sending it spinning into the nearby turf. The thrower himself was felled a moment later, clutching another knife in his neck, and then there were men breaking the circle on all sides in a flurry of dropping cloaks and flashing blades.

Before she could think to find her target, Kessligh was beside her, dropping one onrushing man with a single stroke of such simplicity, it took her breath away. Another, too, came at him, Kessligh simply stepped inside the swing, cutting him down as a gardener might slash a weed.

Amidst the confusion, someone slashed from her left . . . Sasha ducked, but already that body was falling, cut down by Jaryd, his eyes wide with fury. Then, as abruptly as it had begun, it all stopped. An entire line of Hadryn lords and men, behind the two Kessligh had felled, were now all wavering, staring with fearful, furious stares at Kessligh. Falcon and Royal Guards alike had closed at Sasha's sides, weapons ready and eager.

"Honour has been satisfied," Kessligh told them all. His voice was hard, yet calmer than Sasha had heard in many a training session. "The result is clear. Take your losses and leave. Be thankful I ignore the cowardly knife and do not challenge each of you to mortal combat, one at a time, for your complicity."

Sasha had never seen any array of faces more furious, and more hateful, than those of the Hadryn lords confronting them. Nor, she thought, more scared. They drew back, gathering the bodies of their fallen as they went. Sasha looked over her left shoulder to where Jaryd still stood above the body of the man he'd killed. It was a long way back to have been a Hadryn man . . . and she realised with shock that the dead man was a Falcon Guard.

Another guardsman knelt to remove the fallen man's helmet . . . it had a lieutenant's crest and came off to reveal the heavy, round face of Lieutenant Reynan. There was blood in his mouth and his eyes were sightless. Jaryd stood above him, his sword bloody, breath coming in great gasps. The kneeling guardsman stared up in disbelief.

"What did you do?" he said in horror, a hand creeping to the pommel of his sword.

"No," said another, stepping forward. "I saw it. Reynan would have struck M'Lady Sashandra from behind. He meant to kill her in the confusion."

Sasha stared at Jaryd. Reynan Pelyn had been brother to Lord Tymeth Pelyn, from one of the most powerful noble families of Tyree.

"I'd thought his manner odd last night and this morning," Jaryd said hoarsely, as Kessligh and Damon pushed in to see. His eyes met Sasha's. "I asked him what troubled him and he muttered something about 'that brat' ruining everything. He never liked you, M'Lady, I thought he was just . . . just making talk. I was wary, but I never thought he'd . . ."

"Treachery," said a guardsman—a Verenthane. "Unbefitting of a Tyree man or a Verenthane. He got what he deserved."

"Even that horsefly Farys has more honour," his Goeren-yai comrade agreed. "At least he gave his challenge to her face, not her back."

"Coward," agreed a third.

They withdrew from the circle, leaving their former lieutenant alone on the ground, gazing sightlessly at the grey morning sky. Sasha felt light-headed and shorter, somehow, her posture no longer quite so perfect, all colours and sounds no longer so sharp.

"You saved my life," she said to Jaryd, determinedly focused on keeping her balance as they walked. She'd seen an honour duel once before where the victor's legs had folded beneath him in the midst of his victory celebration. Now, she knew why.

"I would have done so even were you my enemy," Jaryd muttered. His normally confident, carefree expression was darkened with fury. "Some things cannot be tolerated, even from family allies."

"Even so," Sasha added, determined to give further thanks, but Jaryd cut her off.

"Damn fool, I should have known!" he snarled. "They were plotting, damn them. Now there'll be Loth's ransom to pay."

The chanting from the Halleryn walls continued, accompanied now by multiple drums, and the piercing shrill of reed pipes. Sasha pushed free of her surrounding company and walked across the open grass before the walls. The cheer erupted louder to a full-fledged roar. She could see a crowd of men atop the walls, fists and swords held aloft. The Goeren-yai. Saluting her as passionately as they'd ever saluted anyone. The tears in her eyes spilled and ran down her cheeks.

She placed the sword down and held both arms aloft, palms outward, then lowered them slowly, requesting silence. Slowly, the volume declined. And then, finally, the morning still returned. An eerie, unreal hush, after the din that had been. Sasha pressed both palms together before her forehead and bowed in thanks and respect. Such triumphalism was not what the situation needed; it had cost far too much already.

A horn sounded by Halleryn's main gate, announcing an imminent departure. The royal party waited and the Hadryn moved their bodies to the stream, where someone had brought a raft to save them the humiliation of the long walk back. Upon the far bank, Hadryn soldiers milled in shock and anger. Even at a glance, Sasha could see much gesticulation, rude hand gestures and raised voices. She hoped that the Falcon Guard, back at their camp, were prepared for any eventuality.

Then, from the main gate, a grand, chestnut warhorse clattered onto the road and turned along the wall toward them. Two more riders flanked their leader, Taneryn banners flying, and Sasha recognised Lord Krayliss astride the leading horse, riding square-shouldered and proud as his men watched on from their wall-top positions.

The riders left the road and approached across the grass, halting before the royal party. Krayliss swung his heavy weight from the saddle, rearranging his cloak about the enormous sword at his hip. His dark eyes peered from beneath thick black brows, his expression unreadable behind the profuse black beard. He inclined his head to Damon and then again, more deeply, to Kessligh at Damon's right hand. He had watched proceedings from the wall, it was very clear. Sasha was only a little surprised when the gaze then swung and fixed upon her.

Lord Krayliss strode toward her, a hand upon the massive hilt of his sword, and knelt to one knee, his head bowed. Sasha blinked. *That* was unexpected. It brought her no joy, and even less when Krayliss lifted his gaze and beheld her from that position. There was calculation in his eyes. This was a display for his men. A cold dread replaced the general unease in the pit of her stomach. This just got worse and worse.

"Princess Sashandra!" he announced, in a loud, ponderous tone. That bass voice would surely carry to the nearest positions atop the nearby walls. "I had doubted, but today we have seen for our own eyes. The Synnich is your guide. You are the one who has been chosen. Forgive my shortsightedness."

"I do not claim the guidance," Sasha said softly. "I have not been chosen for anything."

"I concede to the authority of the Synnich!" Krayliss announced, ignoring her statement entirely. "I shall leave this place and ride to Baen-Tar where I shall await the judgment of the king on this dispute! The armies of the king shall remain behind, and see that the Hadryn are escorted from the lands of Taneryn! They state that their quarrel is with me alone, not with Taneryn, and so we shall see them prove it! I shall do all of this on one condition! That the Princess Sashandra Lenayin shall give me her word, the word of one guided by the Synnich itself, that she shall ensure all fairness and impartiality upon my trial before the king, and that she shall guarantee that the good people of Taneryn are not made to suffer at anyone's hand! I ask the Princess of Lenayin, does she grant me her word?"

Sasha took a deep breath. The lake beyond the Halleryn walls was serenely beautiful as yellow flushed the eastern sky atop the hills. Above, the looming presence of Mount Halleryn looked down. The chill air smelled sharp and fresh.

"I give my word," she said with as firm a voice as she could muster. Whatever Krayliss's intentions, she knew that she had no choice. To end it here, to separate the warring sides before the bloodshed could escalate into terrible proportions . . . surely it was worth her word? What was a simple word against the lives of hundreds? Perhaps thousands?

And yet she knew with dread certainty, as Krayliss grasped her hand in his and placed it to his lips, that that word would cost her. In Lenayin, the price of honour was never slight.

Krayliss regained his feet and turned to Damon and Kessligh. "I shall make preparations to ride immediately. What are your plans?"

"I shall await the arrival of further forces," Damon announced. "They should arrive shortly. That will free myself and a suitable escort to ride with you back to Baen-Tar. After witnessing your departure, the Hadryn forces have no reason to remain on Taneryn lands. The royal forces will supervise their departure. Master Jaryd and Captain Tyrun of the Falcon Guard shall command that effort."

"Acceptable," Krayliss said shortly. "Yuan Kessligh?"

"My uma and I shall attend Rathynal in Baen-Tar," said Kessligh. "First, we shall return to Baerlyn. I am expecting an important visitor."

Sasha shot Kessligh a look. It was the first she'd heard of any visitor. She didn't like the sound of that at all.

"I have your uma's word, Yuan Kessligh," Krayliss rumbled warningly. "I expect her presence at my hearing."

"And you shall have it, Lord Krayliss," Kessligh replied. "She shall be at Baen-Tar before the beginning of Rathynal. It shall be understood by all that no hearing should begin before her arrival. On that, you have *my* word."

$\mathcal{S}$even

$\mathcal{S}$OFY STRODE QUICKLY down the stone corridor to the king's chambers, her maid Anyse at her side. "Oh, I hope I'm not late," she worried, brushing hastily at her hair. "Is my hair tangled?"

"It's lovely, Highness," said Anyse, always diplomatic. "Just . . . here." She pulled a brush from an apron pocket and Sofy stood still long enough for her to pull the brush through quickly. It caught several times.

"Oh damn," Sofy fretted, "it's been doing that a lot lately, hasn't it?"

"Not at all, Highness. You have the loveliest hair in Baen-Tar, but it's no wonder you get tangles when you never slow down."

"Slow down?" Sofy exclaimed. "Alythia's wedding is less than a month away, Rathynal will be here shortly and every provincial lord and his entourage will be arriving, all demanding entertainments, decorative quarters—and gods forbid anyone should find themselves bored or in disagreement with my program . . . oh hells, how did I end up with so many responsibilities?"

Anyse fought back a smile. "You volunteered," she said succinctly.

Sofy gazed at her in despair. "I did, didn't I? Heavens, I'm such a fool."

"Nonsense, you're simply too kindhearted and intelligent for your own good, that's all."

Sofy brushed her long hair with a hand, then grasped Anyse by the arm and pulled her on down the hall. "I wonder what father wants me for. Perhaps I'll be able to get out of it soon, then I can get back to rehearsal . . . oh! Could you rush back and tell Alythia I'll be late? She insists she needs my help to decorate her wedding shawl . . . my fingers will be raw to the bone from needlework at the end of this, I'm sure of it!"

"I'll tell her, Highness," Anyse reassured her. "And your gown for the banquet tonight? Shall you leave some time for a fitting?"

"Oh drat!" Sofy said crossly, drawing an amused looked from a tall Royal Guardsman as he stood at attention. "I knew I'd forgotten something . . . look, could you just arrange the green and blue one with the curl pattern? I'd thought since it is a foreign reception and green and blue is not so far from Lenay purple and green, is it?"

"Quite adequate, Highness."

"And stop calling me that!"

"In the royal quarters, certainly not, Highness."

They stopped before the grand twin doors to the king's chambers, panelled white and inlaid with gold, unlike the plain dark wood of most of the Baen-Tar Palace. Sofy took a deep breath, wondering at her nerves. It had been days since she'd last seen her father, or Koenyg, for that matter. Lately, they'd both been spending much time in closed chambers with advisors and, some said, the holy fathers of the Saint Ambellion Temple. There was serious trouble in the north with that prize fool Lord Krayliss, they said, and now, a foreign delegation had arrived. She had far too much on her plate to be concerned about the issues that troubled the family's menfolk, but meeting her father was never a lighthearted affair.

Anyse adjusted the silver Verenthane star against her princess's chest. "There. Your Highness is looking forward to M'Lady Sashandra's visit for Rathynal?"

Sofy grinned at her and spun a pirouette. "Sasha's coming to stay!" she sang happily. "I hope she stays a week! No, I hope she stays a year! Maybe I'll . . ." and she slapped a hand to her mouth, horrified. "Oh no, where are my wits? I'm late already!"

She readjusted her hair and dress in a hurry, with Anyse's mirthful help. Took another deep breath, made a face at Anyse when the older woman could barely refrain from laughing at her overexcitable charge, and pushed through the wide white doors.

The doors opened onto the reception, a grand, rectangular room of dark stone and decorative wall hangings. Upon the wide carpet stood many men, sipping from glasses whilst immersed in conversation, as musicians played the reed pipe and guitar in one corner. Sofy blinked in astonishment—many of them were clearly not Lenay men, for no Lenay man, Goeren-yai or Verenthane, would have been caught dead in the outfits they were wearing. Their boots were high and polished, their leggings tight and their beaded tunics were fitted tight about the torso, yet flared puffily at the shoulders. Cuffs enveloped their hands in explosions of embroidered white lace, offsetting the predominance of darker, richer colours. Many men had curls in their hair and the hint of perfume scented the air, stronger than Sofy's own. They stood in conversation with various palace officials and some officers.

Then she saw Koenyg, excusing himself from one conversation and striding to her side. His calm expression darkened to a scowl when no one could see. "Where have you been?" whispered the heir of Lenayin. Sofy's elder brother was a broad, solid man, with none of the lean elegance of his foreign guests. His wide-sleeved jacket was made of luxuriantly soft skins with a leather tunic beneath, displaying none of the decoration of the foreigners. But then, it had never been the way of Lenay men to preen and prance like mating birds.

"What do you mean 'where have I been'?" Sofy retorted. "Have you any idea how busy I am?"

"Practising ceremonies and embroidering costumes does not constitute busy," Koenyg answered, presenting his right arm for her to take. Sofy did so, quickly replacing a scowl of irritation with a friendly smile for the guests. Koenyg walked her to the edge of the carpet and all the men stopped talking to look at her. Something in the foreigners' eyes made her uncomfortable. Not that their gaze was rude—they were far too cultured and dignified for that—but it was . . . judgmental, somehow.

Koenyg stopped and, to Sofy's surprise, all the foreign men gave a round of polite applause. Sofy smiled, because it was funny, and . . . well, every girl liked to be praised, even with such strange, foreign customs. She curtsied. And continued to feel uncomfortable, whatever the well-practised charm of her smile.

"Sister," said Koenyg, with polite formality, "please allow me to introduce Duke Stefhan of the Bacosh province of Larosa." Indicating a man before her who seemed to stand a little straighter than the others. Sofy curtsied, grateful of the chance to lower her eyes and smother an abrupt surge of distaste. Larosa! She'd heard tales of the Larosa, some of them from Sasha. Larosa was the most powerful of the Bacosh provinces and most of the Bacosh spoke the Larosan tongue, or were influenced by their culture. Larosa had led numerous wars against the Saalshen Bacosh over the past two centuries and had been defeated each time. She had heard what the Larosa had done to captured full or half-caste serrin, with or without the excuse of war, and her blood ran cold at the thought.

"Duke Stefhan, here is my youngest sister, the Princess Sofy Lenayin." Sofy extended her hand and the duke took it lightly. He wore more rings than Sofy even owned, let alone wore.

"Utterly charmed," said the duke, with a strange accent that was itself rather charming, and pressed her hand to his lips. The duke had a goatee and dark hair in curls down to his shoulders. A handsome man, Sofy thought, in perhaps his mid-forties . . . with a funny nose, bulging at the tip. "Your Highness, you are even more beautiful than all the tales I have heard. My companion Master Piet is a skilled bard, I must have him write a song for you so men can sing of your beauty all through Larosa and all across the great Bacosh lands."

"Indeed," said another man—Master Piet, it seemed. "You set me an easy task, my Duke. Before such a beauty, words and song cannot but leap to my lips."

Against all her better judgment, Sofy found herself blushing. "My Duke, Master, you flatter me."

The duke's eyes widened. "Flatter? No, no, Your Highness, you must not think so!" The accent, Sofy thought, really *was* very nice. All the sounds were soft and all the hard Lenay vowels seemed to flow together with velvet ease. "I have found, in my travels through your beautiful kingdom, that all the mountain women are full of vigour! Perhaps it is the mountain air, or the wonderful water. But you, my Princess, you have a rosy glow to your cheek, and a gleam in your eye, that is unsurpassed. Unsurpassed. And I would be honoured if you would accompany me to the dinner tonight."

Sofy blinked and looked at Koenyg. The dinner . . . of course. The banquet, rather, to welcome the arrival of this foreign delegation—the Larosa. They had come for Rathynal, the great meeting of Lenay clans. And Koenyg wanted her to be the duke's escort? Well, that was hardly surprising—she was the one who usually got stuck with that kind of thing. The one who actually liked talking to strange foreigners, or anyone, for that matter.

"Would that interfere so terribly with your busy plans?" Koenyg asked her. Men laughed to hear that touch of dry irony—a brother's exasperation with feminine obsessions. Especially amusing from blunt, pragmatic Koenyg.

"Of course not!" Sofy retorted and favoured the duke with a smile. Perhaps it wouldn't be so bad after all. The duke seemed nice and lowlanders certainly knew how to outshine Lenay men with charm. Besides which, there were so many beautiful crafts, songs and paintings she'd seen from the Bacosh provinces; surely the duke was a cultured man and they could talk of such things. Sofy loved the arts above all else . . . and as for Sasha's tales about the Larosa, well, Sasha certainly *was* prone to exaggeration. "I would be delighted to accompany you to the banquet tonight, Duke Stefhan," she said.

"Such a treat is more than I deserve," replied the duke with a sincere smile. "Please, allow me to introduce the men of my companionship."

"Of course, that would be lovely . . ." Before her brother could turn away and leave her with the duke, she quickly whispered. "Where is father? I'd thought he would be here?"

"Father is meeting," Koenyg said vaguely. "He'll be at the banquet."

"Meeting with who?" Sofy wondered, as the Duke led her first to Master Piet, who also kissed her hand. Everyone seemed to be in meetings, at the moment. All these comings and goings were too much to keep track of. She only hoped that Sasha would come sooner rather than later. Sasha helped things to make sense. And, as much as she enjoyed the flattery of the Larosa men, it was a little annoying to be treated so condescendingly. Not only like a girl, but like a child. Just let them try and do that to Sasha!

"My Lord?" The squire hovered at Usyn's elbow. "My Lord, please come inside. You'll catch cold. Breakfast will be ready soon."

Lord Usyn Telgar stood atop a rocky vantage on the Helmar Pass, and watched the first light of dawn break over the Aryn Valley. A day's ride north from Halleryn. A day's humiliation. He stood in nothing but his loose pants, boots and undershirt, wrapped in a heavy cloak. His breath frosted before his lips, and the snowline of these first, low mountains of the Marashyn Range began just a short climb up the nearest, rocky slope. Yet he welcomed the cold chill of pain and, through sheer determination, willed his knees not to tremble. It was a small victory, perhaps . . . but of late, it was the only victory Family Telgar had.

"Call me when breakfast is prepared," Usyn told the squire.

"But my Lord . . ." Usyn turned a cold, blue-eyed stare on the young man. The squire paled and swallowed hard. "Yes, my Lord," he bowed and hurried back toward the tents. From behind, and across the length of the pass, the camp was stirring. Horses snorted in the cold and men chipped at ice puddles for cooking water, or chopped dead wood from the straggly pines.

The dawn was so beautiful. A strip of golden light upon the rugged horizon, fading to yellow, then through all shades of blue and then black in the higher sky. Above, the brighter stars yet shone, glorious in their final moments. Yet the young Lord of Hadryn felt no pleasure in the coming of such wondrous light. The gods mocked him with their grandeur. He had failed, and yet the sun still rose, as if all were right with the world. The gods were infallible. His Verenthane star felt heavy upon his chest. For the first time in his life, he doubted his right to wear it.

The squire returned a short while later with news of breakfast and Usyn turned back toward his tent. Within, Udys Varan sat on a tent stool, hands wrapped about a hot mug of tea, and stared into the central fire. Smoke thickened the air, escaping through a small hole above the centre pole. Several other lords also sat, drinking tea or eating the first strips of bacon that the servant provided. Usyn took his place, received his plate from the squire without a word, and brooded.

From across the fire, Udys Varan looked up. His hair gleamed white in the firelight, his eyes cold. Usyn's father's wisest companion and confidant in matters of war and power. And his most powerful rival. "And what are your plans this fine, cold morning, young Telgar?"

There was a note of dark sarcasm to the old campaigner's voice. A note of accusation. Of disrespect. Usyn struggled to keep a check on the temper that seethed in his gut. "I am Great Lord, Lord Udys," he said coldly. "My age is none of your concern."

"Yet you fail to answer the question," Udys replied. "Have you a plan? Or do you intend to attend the king's great Rathynal as though nothing has happened, like a whipped dog with its tail between its legs?"

"It's not my fault your son was killed," Usyn bit out. "I recall it was your idea to challenge the Cronenverdt bitch in the first place."

"My son," Udys said with blazing eyes and hardening tone, "is but a sign of our predicament! I grieve not only for my son, young Lord of Hadryn, I grieve for Hadryn itself!"

"It's not my fault!" Usyn shouted, rising from his stool. "Not *one* of you predicted that Lord Krayliss would cast himself upon the king's mercy, you all swore to me that he would fight to the death!"

"It is *our* fault!" Udys replied, also rising. "We should have known better than to entrust a pup like you to go charging into Taneryn to avenge your father . . ."

"Enough!" shouted Yuan Heryd, rising as well. He was a big, wide-faced man. Lord of the northern fortress town of Wayn, directly on the Cherrovan border. "This bickering shall achieve nothing. My Lord, please sit. Yuan Udys, please. You have lost your son, yet Lord Usyn has lost his father. Any more arguing and we shall start killing ourselves, and that shall only make our enemies laugh all the harder!"

Varan nodded, coolly enough, and reclaimed his seat. Gestured for Usyn to retake his, with no small irony. Usyn stood for a moment, trembling. His temper seethed, desiring escape, yet no convenient target presented itself. Family Varan were one of Hadryn's oldest and wealthiest. They had many claims to the Great Lordship of Hadryn and there had been blood feuds in the past between Telgars and Varans . . . all buried now, within the common unity of the Verenthane brotherhood. Usyn was young, yet he knew that Udys Varan had many supporters amongst the other Hadryn nobles. Given his chance, Udys would make his move and claim Hadryn Great Lordship for himself.

Usyn took a deep, shaking breath. Then he sat, fighting to keep his breathing even. This was intolerable. Never in all his life had he felt so trapped, so humiliated, so . . . small. He was Great Lord of Hadryn. Long had he dreamed of the moment when his father's title would be his. But not like this. Not like this.

Breakfast was eaten in merciful silence. The coming sunlight coloured the walls of the tent increasingly bright. From about the camp, the sounds of activity increased. Finally, Lord Udys spoke.

"Our predicament is not unique," he said, wiping the last grease from his plate with a piece of bread. "For as long as the descendants of the Udalyn continue to raise the flag across the border in Taneryn, these troubles will continue. They shall trouble *your* sons, too, my Lord," with a meaningful glance at Usyn, "and most likely our grandsons and great-grandsons as well. The Udalyn are their inspiration, and our never-ending shame. The Udalyn have survived us for a century, hidden in their valley. We claim to be the greatest of the northern powers and yet we have failed to destroy them. That failure invites others to attack us in the Udalyn's name."

"This was our best chance," Yuan Heryd said sombrely. "The death of our lord gave us rights under the crown law. It is the first time we have had the chance to get that bastard Krayliss's head on a pike. Now, he's run cowering to the king for protection." He shrugged, always pragmatic. Yuan Heryd had that reputation. "We tried. At least he may lose some credibility amongst his own people. He is belittled. We have achieved at least that much . . . and who knows? The king's law may see his head on a pike yet."

"The satisfaction shall not be quite the same," Usyn said icily. It was difficult to speak of such things so calmly as Yuan Heryd. But his father had respected the man. He would try, whatever the effort. "Sometimes I wonder whether our support for the crown law is worth all the trouble it gives us."

"Young Lord," said Yuan Varan, leaning forward on his stool, with meaning, "disabuse yourself of such notions. There are only three provinces of Lenayin that follow the true, chosen path of Verenthane. The other eight are weak; their Verenthane nobility lacks the courage to whip their local pagans into shape. In those eight, the pagans remain a majority. We cannot control them on our own. We control them through the king; for the king, though flawed, is a true Verenthane. Such are the unpleasant compromises of power, young Lord. Your father knew it and you should learn it also."

"That wonderful king," Usyn said sarcastically, "has spent the better part of my life gallivanting with pagans and serrin demons from Saalshen."

"The better part of your life, yes," agreed Udys. "You have barely nineteen summers, my Lord. An eyeblink in the passage of power. For a moment, the king favoured the serrin. That was the doing of Cronenverdt—that man has caused more damage to Lenayin than any other in our history. He claimed credit for great victories against Markield, and the king, believing in omens, foolishly believed that the Nasi-Keth and their serrin puppet masters were responsible.

"But now, Cronenverdt's influence is fading. He tried to mould the king's heir into his own image, but failed. The second heir, gods be praised, is a true Verenthane, and the north holds his favour. His wife—your dear sister Wyna, my Lord—is the Lenay queen-in-waiting and has already borne us a Hadryn heir to the Verenthane throne. The king now reads new omens, most especially in the birth of his heir's son, and favours the north once more.

"Soon, the war shall come and we shall march to the Bacosh to reclaim the holy lands from the serrin demons. The Verenthane gods shall become strong as they have never been strong before, and with their strength, ours shall increase. We shall strengthen ties with our lowlands cousins in the Larosa and the free Bacosh, for they are the ones who truly know how a pagan should be treated. That shall put some backbone into our southern Verenthanes, at last.

"Soon, young Lord, there shall be none but Verenthanes as far as the eye can see and the serrin demons shall be wiped from the earth. But it takes patience, my Lord. I may not live to see that day. Even you may not. But it will come, and our everlasting glory shall be all the greater for our part."

"You speak fine words, Yuan Udys," said Usyn. "But our concerns are more immediate. You tell me that the Taneryn problem will remain for generations, but I cannot now assault Taneryn with Lord Krayliss under the king's protection, for the king's law forbids it! What is the central rule from Baen-Tar truly worth to us if it does not allow us to deal firmly with that which threatens us?"

"My Lord," said Varan, shaking his head with impatience, "you did not listen. Taneryn is little enough problem. They are poor, and weak, and led by fools. They trade little, grow poor crops and gain little in wealth and power.

"The true problem, my Lord, are the Udalyn. As long as we allow them to resist us, we invite all our enemies to attack us. And our chance to finally end this problem is now."

Usyn stared at him. About the campfire, all men did. Usyn frowned. "But the king's law prevents us from attacking the Udalyn just as it prevents us from attacking the Taneryn without just . . ."

"No!" said Udys, triumphantly. "The crown law was written by King Soros a hundred years ago. It recognised the boundaries between provinces as immutable, and a lord's rights within those boundaries as sacrosanct. The king's historical protection of the Udalyn Valley is an *understanding*, my Lord, not a law. A verbal understanding between King Chayden, Soros's son, and the pagans. It is nowhere in the writings, and had I a copy of the document here before me, I could show you."

"But . . . but . . ." Usyn rolled his eyes in exasperation. "What does it matter? Previous lords of Hadryn have tried to end the Udalyn, but each time the king stopped them! The pagans have spies within our borders and the Udalyn always summon help! We shall have yet another royal army descending upon our heads before we can breach the Udalyn's wall. And if they trap us within the valley, we are finished!"

"My Lord," said Udys, very intently. His eyes drew them all in, conspiratorially. "Some of us, from all three northern provinces, have been in contact with Prince Koenyg. He wishes for the Bacosh war most strongly. Yet he knows that the war shall be unpopular amongst the pagans. He needs us, my Lord, and the king also needs us. There shall be no war without our support or else the holy lands in the Bacosh shall remain occupied by the serrin demons and there shall be no allegiance with the great power of a united Verenthane Bacosh.

"Prince Koenyg is a strategist and holds his father's favour. He needs us so much, he has made it known that he will not stop us from any pursuit *not explicitly forbidden by the king's written law.*"

There was a silence within the tent. Usyn felt hope flare, hot and bright. A hope for success. A hope for glory. For the rise to the Great Lordship of Hadryn that he had always dreamed of. A chance to be worthy of his great, departed father.

Udys saw the look upon his lord's face and gave a tight, hard smile. He knew. "My Lord," he said quietly, "I pray of you. Let us remove this weeping sore from the honour of Hadryn once and for all."

Sasha sat on her chair in the Steltsyn Star, a mug of ale in her hand, and gazed at the blazing coals of the central firepit. About her, the merriment of mealtime continued with music and laughter. She had recited her telling of the ride to Halleryn, which had been met with much applause and shouts of approval from a room crowded full of long-haired, tattooed and ringed Goeren-yai men. But now, while they caroused, she only felt like sitting near the glowing warmth of the fire, and watching the ripple of red and orange across the surface of coals.

Soon, Teriyan dragged a chair and sat beside her, with a head toss to keep his long red hair clear of the chair back. "So Kessligh's got a visitor?" he said. His tone suggested he'd had several ales already . . . but Teriyan was one man Sasha knew could hold his drink.

She nodded, taking an absent sip. It was her first, and only, ale of the night. Kessligh didn't like her drinking the stuff at all, but she liked to be sociable . . . more than she liked the taste, in truth.

"His name's Aiden," Sasha replied, somewhat sourly. "He rode all the way from Petrodor, just to talk to Kessligh."

"About what, do you know?"

Sasha shrugged. "Nasi-Keth business, I guess. I was booted out of the house before I could hear."

"Could you be a little more enthusiastic?" Teriyan suggested, taking another pull at his ale. "You'll be heading to Rathynal soon, you'll get to see your Sofy again." Sasha smiled. "Aha, I thought that would do it. Cheer up, kid, you look like Lynie did when her pet rat died."

"Lynie had a pet rat?"

"She did until the dog ate it. She nearly killed the poor mutt, never seen a boarhound so frightened." Sasha grinned, well able to imagine that. "But then she teamed up with you and your horses, hasn't looked at a rat since."

"I think it's a Goeren-yai thing," said Sasha. From the other side of the room, there came a roar of triumph—some of the men were playing a game with knives and a throwing board. Another night, and another mood, she might have joined them.

Spirits, she'd loved it when she'd first come to Baerlyn. There were animals here. Kessligh had brought six classy mares with him, gifts from the king's stables, and her new life meant being around them *all day*. Every morning when she'd awoken within the timber walls of her new home, the horses were waiting for her. And there were the dogs, the two cows, birds in the trees, deer in the woods, the occasional bear, big and small wildcats, and wolves howling at the moon.

Well, she'd not loved it *entirely* at first. Kessligh had been a hard taskmaster. There were no more servants prying into her life, which was wonderful . . . but also, there had been no one to make her bed, prepare her meals, set the fire, fetch water, chop wood and all the other small tasks that took her away from her precious horses and important svaalverd work.

There'd also been Kessligh's training. She'd thought it would be fun, at first, for she'd loved training on her own or with Kessligh and Krystoff in the privacy of the empty stables in Baen-Tar. But Kessligh's new routines were far more advanced than the little exercises he'd suggested in Baen-Tar. These included painful stretches every morning and evening, long runs up the hill behind the ranch, and endless, tedious sessions of repeating the same, basic swing over and over and over again.

Soon enough, the little loud-mouth brat princess had begun whining and complaining about her aching shoulders, her blistered hands and the sheer, mind-numbing boredom of not getting to do any *real* fighting. And she'd been tired all the time, and sometimes ill, and winter had been well on its way. Kessligh had explained, time after time, the necessity of learning the svaalverd's most basic forms until they became as second nature as walking and breathing. But her tantrums had grown worse, especially in the freezing downpours and howling gales of autumn.

After one particularly hysterical tantrum, Kessligh had dragged her from her room where she'd flung herself on her bed, and sat her down before the fireplace. He'd explained to her, in a very serious way, that if she no longer wished to be his uma, she could always return to Baen-Tar and become a proper princess again. She'd wear dresses, learn manners and etiquette, and practise needlework instead of svaalverd. There'd be no more pain, no more exercises and stretches, no more bruises, strains and blisters. But there'd also be no more horses, no more wide open spaces, no more hiding on the forest ledge along the hillside to spy on the wolfcubs playing before their den. No more spear fishing in the little stream at the bottom of the hill, or swimming in the waterhole beneath the little falls on a warm summer's day. No more crackling log fires in the evenings, and the cabin filled with the sweet smell of burning old pine, a book of serrin poetry on her lap as she slowly unravelled the beautiful triple and quadruple meanings of the Saalsi tongue.

That had been her last great tantrum. Oh, she'd had more minor ones since—far too many to count, in fact. But she'd stretched, and run, and done push-ups and sit-ups until her arms, legs and stomach ached all over, and she would stagger about the stables like a cripple.

Then, one day in midwinter, with the snows piled high on the ground and the trees all gleaming with icicles, Kessligh had taken her down to Baerlyn for a special occasion. It had been Midwinter's Day, her very first in Baerlyn. The locals had gathered for a great feast outdoors, as the weather had been chilled but fine. There had been fires for warmth, and music, dancing and laughter. Everyone was there, men, women and children, and Sasha had been amazed to see that they paid no greater respect or homage to the village councilmen than they did to a poor pig farmer, or to Denys the simpleton, who spoke funny, and laughed far too much, but was never teased for it. Some had even dared jokes at Kessligh's expense—they'd only gotten a smile from him, but a smile was as good as a belly laugh from Kessligh Cronenverdt.

There'd followed contests of swordwork, including limited-contact contests for the children. Sasha had swung her child's stanch through those same old boring, predictable strokes Kessligh had spent so much time drilling her on . . . and to her amazement, the boys contesting her would meet no firm contact with their wooden blades, and lose their balance, or expose their defences, or fall flat on their backsides as their footing entangled. Not always, of course—often it hadn't worked, and she'd get a belting for her faults. But if she did it just right, and concentrated as hard as she could . . . well, the boys had protested, fumed and sulked, but they could not deny her ability. Some of them had simply shown respect, including some of the older men who'd ruffled her hair and told her she was good. It had given her a feeling she'd never known she'd craved so badly until that moment. Pride, and belonging. In that moment, it had truly dawned on her that she could never go back to the life she'd once had. She was no longer a princess of Lenayin. She was Sashandra Lenayin, uma to Kessligh Cronenverdt, of the Nasi-Keth.

She'd never complained of Kessligh's training techniques since. Slowly the exercises had become less painful, the runs less exhausting, and the blisters had grown over with hard callouses. Lynette had become a permanent feature at the stables, and then Andreyis. She'd begun to know the townsfolk and their children better. She had had fights and made friends, had played seek and chase along the dusty lanes and been scolded by the women for riding one horse or another too fast through the town. She'd been born in Baen-Tar, in the great royal palace of Lenayin, but this, Baerlyn, village of Valhanan province, was her home.

Jaegar dragged a chair across to sit opposite, his back to the fire and a plate of roast meat and vegetable raal on his lap. "Greetings all," he said, "sorry I missed the tale. Upwyld filled me in. Most impressive."

"And where were you?" Teriyan challenged his village headman and good friend. "When our girl was standing on the table, pouring out her latest great glory to we mere mortals?"

"Rony has a light fever," Jaegar explained, utterly unruffled, taking a big mouthful. "Took her to see Cranyk. He gave her some foul-smelling serrin stuff. Rony wouldn't eat it. From there, it became a grand battle."

Sasha and Teriyan grinned. Rony was Jaegar's youngest daughter, now four years old. Jaegar had four girls, no boys, and contempt for anyone who thought that made him unlucky.

"Who won?" Sasha asked.

"Well I'd like to claim a great victory over the forces of darkness," Jaegar admitted, taking his cup from the floor to wash down a mouthful, "but in truth, it was a brutal, bloody draw. Rony suffered a spanking, but Sharyn now has to devise a way to bake a flatbread with the damn stuff inside it, so Rony can eat it without noticing the taste."

"Sweet spirits," Teriyan groaned, a hand to his face with the agonised expression of a father who sympathised.

"The most devious and stubborn of adversaries, little girls," Sasha said knowingly.

Jaegar nodded, eating hungrily. "The very worst."

Sasha rode back to the house with a lit torch in one hand. Chersey did not mind the flame, nor the ghostly shadows that it cast across trail and trees. Sasha rode at a fast canter, partly because the distance was short and Chersey knew the road well, and partly because she'd learned to be cautious of possible ambush, even here so close to town. One did not become uma to Kessligh of the Nasi-Keth without learning to be careful.

She was greeted upon the open lower slope by a raucous barking of dogs from the verandah. Light glowed in the house's windows, spilling across the verandah where it raised on stilts above the gentle slope. She rounded the huge vertyn tree, and the chicken run and wide vegetable garden that it sheltered, and continued upslope to the stables. Once in her stall, she gave Chersey a rub in case of sweat that might chill, made certain she had feed and drink for the night, and fastened the heavy blanket over the mare's broad back and about the sides.

Then she checked on each of the sixteen long faces that peered over their respective stall doors at her, having no doubt of Kessligh, Andreyis and Lynette's care, but always wishing to check for herself. Her horses were her life, at least as much as her swordwork. She fussed over them for a while by the light of an oil lamp, more for the pleasure of their company than because they required the attention. Then she made her way down the long, dark slope toward the dim light of the house ahead, with nothing to guide her steps in the pitch, silent blackness than memory of the grassy ground.

Kaif and Keef greeted her on the rear verandah, taking time from crunching a huge bone to sniff at her with wagging, shaggy tails. The open kitchen was warm, with evidence of a recently prepared meal on the bench. Beyond the partition, Kessligh sat with his Nasi-Keth guest, Aiden, before the open fire of the main room, sipping tea.

"Evening!" said Aiden brightly, rising from his chair. "Did you have a good time?" He had a round, cheerful face and a flat mop of black hair. His build seemed verging on fat, yet there was a poise to him, and a balance, that perhaps only a fellow swordsman would notice.

"A wonderful time, thank you," said Sasha, kneeling by the fire to warm the kettle on the stand above the flames. "Please sit, we Lenays aren't much on formality."

Aiden sat, with a beaming smile. His accent was very broad and his manners very Torovan, Sasha thought.

"I was telling Kessligh," said Aiden, as Sasha walked to close the main room shutters that Kessligh had left open to give her some light to ride home to, "that in Petrodor, there are few inns with women. Petrodor is very conservative place, yes? Very Verenthane. No women drinking, no women dancing . . ."

Sasha finished the second shutter's latch, and noted the several large books lying beside Kessligh's comfortable chair. Serrin books, she recognised them. She wondered what he and Aiden had been discussing all evening.

"Very few women here either," Sasha replied, standing before the fire. Kessligh's expression remained distant, barely listening. Something about it made her uncomfortable. "Mostly the women are stuck at home, cooking and caring for the children. I have to admit, I don't know many of them half as well as I should. And have precious little to discuss with them when I do get a chance to talk. Our lives are just so different. At least with the men, I can talk horses and swordwork."

"Very few women in the Nasi-Keth too," Aiden added, watching her curiously. "Yuan Kessligh is great visionary. No Petrodor women achieve your success. Not all serrin teachings taken so seriously by humans, yes?"

Sasha snorted. "He's a great visionary?" Half serious, half joking. "What about me? I did it, not him."

Aiden laughed. "True, true," he conceded, cheerfully.

"Besides, how much vision does it take to tell the difference between a woman and a lump of coal?" With a sideways glance at Kessligh.

Aiden shrugged, broadly. "In Petrodor, I think maybe a lot," he said.

Kessligh usually rose to that bait. Tonight, he barely noticed. Sasha looked at him, uneasily. "So what did you two spend all evening talking about?"

Aiden's good cheer faded. He looked at Kessligh, waiting for him to speak. Sasha had often wondered what Kessligh was to those Nasi-Keth in Petrodor with whom he corresponded. What was he to Aiden? A leader? An inspiration? A "great visionary"? His achievements in Lenayin had certainly made him a significant figure for Nasi-Keth everywhere. But he'd been gone for thirty years, and lived so far away . . .

"Aiden brings news from Petrodor," Kessligh said. "Saalshen's representative there, Rhillian, is making waves. I've spoken to you of her before."

Sasha frowned. "I remember. Isn't she Saalshen's second in command in Petrodor?"

"Serrin concepts of rank are not easily translated," Kessligh replied. "There is no rank, only *ra'shi*. Respect. One earns *ra'shi* through deeds and experience, so it's not always easy to tell who's truly in charge. Rhillian's *ra'shi* grows powerful across all Saalshen, not just Petrodor."

The kettle began to boil. Sasha knelt and put two teaspoons of ground tea leaves into the teapot where it sat beside the fireplace. "So what did Rhillian do?" she asked, taking the tea cloth so that the kettle's handle did not burn her fingers, and pouring. "She's been agitating for Saalshen to get tough, hasn't she?"

Kessligh looked at Aiden, inviting him to speak. "The holy brotherhood are saying she attacked the archbishop and tried to steal the Shereldin Star," said Aiden.

Sasha stared at him. "The Archbishop of Petrodor?" she asked.

Aiden nodded. "It is nonsense of course—if she attacked the archbishop, he would be dead. Everyone knows this, yet no one likes to say it. No one will admit the true power of Saalshen in Petrodor, and that no one is safe from the serrin, if the serrin don't want you safe, yes?"

"But . . . the Shereldin Star?" Sasha remembered the kettle in her hand, and put it down before the fireplace. "Isn't that that stupid artefact all the Verenthanes rave about?"

"The holiest relic of Verenthanes," Aiden said solemnly. And Sasha realised in a flash that Aiden, like most of the Petrodor Nasi-Keth, was most likely Verenthane. She'd probably offended him, she thought, and chided herself for not minding her tongue. Kessligh had renounced all other faiths in the pursuit of serrin teachings. But for most lowlanders, faith was not so easily cast aside. "I have spoken with serrin, they say Rhillian did not want the star. I think they tell truth, here. We think Rhillian only means to warn the archbishop. Some things the serrin will not take lying down."

"And what was the archbishop doing with the Shereldin Star? Isn't that . . ." and she paused, and something cold and worrisome occurred to her. "Isn't that in the possession of the Larosa?"

Again, Aiden nodded, sombrely. "It was. The Larosa have had many wars against the Saalshen Bacosh. They want the Verenthane holy lands back. They want to unite the Bacosh under a single king and throw the serrin out. They swore, two centuries ago, that the Shereldin Star would one day be returned to the holy lands, but only when the serrin are gone.

"The Larosa give the archbishop the star so that all Torovan will unite beneath him and fight with the Larosa."

"And now the Larosa are here!" Sasha exclaimed. Her heart thumped unpleasantly in her chest. "Someone at the inn said a large group just arrived in Baen-Tar!"

"The last piece in the puzzle," Kessligh said tiredly. "The armies of the Saalshen Bacosh are formidable. All the remaining Bacosh provinces are uniting under the Larosa. But it's not enough. A Torovan army is useful for numbers, but Torovans have never been noted fighters. What the Larosa want from the archbishop is the loyalty of the Petrodor families, and all their money. Petrodor might not be much in a fight, but they can pay for a huge army, Sasha, of far more than just Torovans. The archbishop will convince them to pay, for the sake of their souls.

"Still, even Torovan and Larosan armies together are insufficient. They need Lenayin. And by the looks of things, they're going to get Lenayin."

"And I've just been sitting in a large room filled with Goeren-yai warriors who have always insisted that they'll never fight against the serrin!" Sasha replied. "Not even should the king command it!"

She could feel the pieces of the puzzle clicking together. Suddenly, it was all making sense . . . and what she saw frightened her. All because some stupid Verenthanes couldn't stand the serrin living on what had once been human lands. Now, their intolerance threatened Lenayin with civil uprising and disaster.

"*Now* you see the scale of it," said Kessligh, with tired exasperation. "Now you see what I've been telling you all these years. These foreign matters, these things you dismiss as unimportant, can rise up and destroy your world, Sasha. It is all connected. Your father now seeks to align Lenayin with what he sees as the destiny of the Verenthanes. That means supporting their war."

"Well then we have to stop him!" Sasha exclaimed. "You . . . you still have influence left with father, you were his Commander of Armies for eighteen years, for heavens' sake! He listened to you! This Rathynal, we must ride to Baen-Tar and convince him not to join the Larosa!"

"I'm not riding to Baen-Tar," said Kessligh. "I'll be riding to Petrodor." Sasha simply stared at him. She could not think of anything to say. "The game has changed, Sasha. Lenayin will march to war, it can't be stopped. What *can* be saved is the Nasi-Keth. Aiden brings news that the factions have split. Some favour Rhillian; others disagree and seek a path separate from Rhillian's influence.

"Petrodor is the key to stopping this war, Sasha. Without Petrodor's wealth, the war will not happen. And the Nasi-Keth are the key to Petrodor—united, they are the only power in Petrodor capable of restraining the families. I cannot allow them to become divided. They need me now. I cannot wait, or things will be worse."

Sasha continued staring. She felt as if the very ground had disappeared from under her. Her ears could not believe what they were hearing. "And what about Lenayin?" she breathed, incredulously. "Do all your loyalties to Lenayin just . . . disappear?"

Kessligh frowned, his jaw tightening. "I have given thirty years of my life to Lenayin. I swore allegiance to your father, yet I never claimed to be anything other than what I am—Nasi-Keth. I cannot ignore that calling any more than your father can ignore the callings of the Verenthane holy fathers from Petrodor. And I won't."

Tears sprang to Sasha's eyes. Kessligh was Lenay. Of foreign origin, surely . . . but in many ways, he *was* Lenayin. The greatest Lenay warrior. And she, his uma. Now, he was casting it all aside, as one might throw aside a peel once the fruit was eaten. She couldn't believe it.

Kessligh sat forward on his chair, his expression intense. "Sasha, think!" he demanded. "Of all the serrin teachings I've told you, of all the things you know! Broaden your vision, Sasha! The important thing is to stop this damned war from happening! I can do that! In Petrodor!"

"If civil war takes Lenayin," Sasha said with difficulty, "countless lives will be lost. Towns like Baerlyn will be destroyed, perhaps Baerlyn itself, and all its people killed. I know enough Lenay history to know what our civil wars look like. You would just abandon them to this fate?"

"Damn fool, you're not listening to me . . ."

"It'll be too late!" Sasha yelled at him, coming abruptly to her feet. "You go off to play your power games in the alleys of Petrodor . . . there's trouble brewing here now! You may save the serrin, and you may save the Nasi-Keth, but Lenayin shall be ashes! What were your last thirty years here *for*, if you just run away when Lenayin needs you most? What were your last twelve years with *me* for?"

"You are my uma," Kessligh said simply. The firelight cast his features into rumpled, hard-edged shadow, an animation they could never acquire on their own. "You must come with me to Petrodor."

Sasha felt something snap. This betrayal was too much. She could have struck him. "Damned if I will!" she yelled. "I promised Krayliss I'd be at Rathynal, and I won't give him free rein in Baen-Tar to cause trouble without me! You go to Petrodor! You go there, and you rot there, with your beloved Nasi-Keth! Me, I'm Lenay, and I'll *never* abandon my people! Never!"

Eight

"BUT DARYD!" RYSHA COMPLAINED. "Mama said we're not allowed beyond the trees!"

Daryd ignored her, as was an elder brother's right, his eyes searching through the forest. Essey's breath plumed in white clouds, brilliant in the golden sunshine that fell through the treetops. Sunlight gleamed on wet trunks and undergrowth, low and bright in the early morning. To the right through the trees rose the Aralya Range—Hadryn lands, and a barrier before the lands of Valhanan. Essey found her way easily enough, nimble hooves picking through the bracken.

"Daryd!" Rysha protested from her seat at his back. "We'll get in trouble!"

"We've picked all the good stuff from the treeline," Daryd replied. "There'll be more growing along the river."

"But we'll get lost!"

"How can we get lost?" Daryd asked in exasperation. "The river's just over on the left, the mountains are on the right, how can anyone get lost?"

He'd been feeling very confident of late, ever since he'd bested Salyl Wyden in the Hemys Festival contest. Salyl Wyden had twelve summers and was a bully. He, Daryd, had only ten summers, but he was good with a stanch. The best his age in all Udalyn, his father claimed, with obvious pride. It made Daryd's chest swell to think on it. Perhaps at the Festival of Rass, he could prove it. The Udalyn Valley was long, and many families lived there. Rass was a bigger festival than Hemys and all the valley would attend. Then, surely, he could prove his father's claims. Until then, he would settle for being the best his age in the town of Ymoth beyond the valley mouth. Better than the bully Salyl Wyden, anyhow.

"But Daryd," Rysha resumed after a thinking pause. Daryd rolled his eyes. "The Hadryn live this way. I don't want to meet any Hadryn."

"Look Rysha, I *told* you. Up ahead is Lake Tullamayne. Lake Tullamayne lies right up against the Aralya Range. There's no way around it on this side. We have scouts there who spy on the Hadryn in case they come across the fields on the other side of the river. They'd have told us if there were Hadryn here, and there aren't. Okay?"

He had his hunting knife at his side and, for a ten-year-old boy, that was as good as a short sword. Essey was his father's horse, but now that he was ten, Daryd's father allowed him to take her over the southern and eastern fields, looking for the various mushrooms and herbs his mother and aunts used in their cooking and medicines. There were farmers all across the fields who would keep an eye on a boy on his horse, so it was not really as dangerous as Daryd liked to imagine. But riding now into the forest toward the lake that marked the eastern-most boundary of Udalyn lands, he could almost imagine himself a full-fledged warrior, riding proudly upon his steed, his braids flowing down his back and his face bearing the ink marks of Udalyn manhood.

"Oh look!" said Rysha then, removing one hand from his sides to point. "Butter flowers! Look how big they are . . . Daryd, I want to pick some, then I can take them home to Mama!"

"We're looking for much more important stuff than butter flowers," Daryd told her sternly. If only Mama hadn't insisted that he take Rysha with him this morning! He could hardly feel like a true Udalyn warrior with his seven-year-old sister clinging to the back of his saddle, complaining all the way.

"I want to pick some flowers!" Rysha insisted, indignantly. "If you're going to go into the forest, I'm going to pick some flowers! Or I'll tell Papa where you went!"

Daryd scowled. "You're such a pain, Rysha."

"You're a pain!"

The forest and the undergrowth became thicker, so Daryd steered toward the river. Soon enough, the great Yumynis appeared through the trees, wide and broken with rocks, its level low in the late summer.

Daryd rode along the grassy verge above the riverbank. Below, where erosion bit into the earth, a gravelly, rocky bank ran perhaps fifteen strides until the water's edge. Daryd made the spirit sign to his forehead and, behind him, Rysha did the same. The Yumynis was the lifeblood of the Udalyn. It had sustained them in the Catastrophe, a century before, when the Hadryn had tried to kill them all, and nearly succeeded. It had sustained them in the century since, locked in their valley, surrounded by the vilest of enemies. And it would sustain them in the future, as the Udalyn rebuilt their numbers and their weapons, working for the day when all that had been taken from them would be theirs once more. The great spirit of the Yumynis had given birth to the Udalyn countless centuries before, and now it kept them alive in all their struggles.

Soon Daryd found a grassy meadow and dismounted. While Essey grazed happily upon the grass, her tail swishing, Daryd and Rysha looked for herbs and mushrooms. Which was not such an unmanly thing, he assured himself as he peered beneath a large, mossy log for flashes of telltale colour. The wise ones of Saalshen loved herbs and mushrooms also, it was told, and made magical potions from them. The wise ones had not visited the Udalyn since the Catastrophe, but many stories were told of them still. And their disciple, Yuan Kessligh Cronenverdt, *had* come to the valley, when he was liberating all the north from the Cherrovan warlord Markield—Daryd's grandfather had told him that story many, many times. Kessligh Cronenverdt fought just like the wise ones, and he was the greatest warrior in all Lenayin. He'd even trained one of the princesses of Lenayin to fight like them too, it was said.

Soon, Daryd's hessian bag held a small weight of herbs and fungi. Absorbed in his searching, he suddenly realised that he did not know where Rysha was. He was about to call, but stopped himself. Not that the forest was unsafe—he'd told Rysha the truth about that—but if he was going to become a great warrior, he needed to learn to think like one.

Feeling pleased with himself for thinking of it, Daryd retraced his steps on sodden undergrowth and mossy roots toward the meadow, where he had last seen Rysha. Rysha could be annoying, but she wasn't stupid. She knew not to wander and was usually far more cautious than Daryd was. Even so, Daryd moved at a crouch, scanning through the trees as he'd seen his father and uncles do on a hunt, a hand on the hilt of his knife.

The forest grew lighter as he approached the meadow . . . and then, he could hear a new sound, above the calling of birds, and the gentle rushing of the river. A deep, distant sound. Like thunder, only steady, not rising or falling. Daryd had never heard anything like it before in his life.

Still creeping, he made his way to the edge of the meadow and peered out. Essey's head was raised, no longer chewing on the grass. Her ears were pricked, her attention turned toward the river. Beyond the fringe of trees where the meadow opened onto the riverbank, Daryd saw a dark mass moving. Atop the dark mass, sunlight glinted on metal. Occasionally a banner rose, flying as it moved. Horses, he realised in shock. The dark mass was hundreds of horses. And the thunder noise was the sound of all their hooves.

"Daryd!" hissed a voice behind him, and he spun in shock, fumbling for his knife. Rysha stood there, her light brown hair now decorated with a bright yellow butter flower. Daryd's heart restarted, his knees threatened to give way. His fumbling hand had not found the hilt of his knife at all, much to his frustration.

"What?" he demanded angrily. Her big eyes stared across the meadow.

"It's the Hadryn!" she whispered, as if fearful they would overhear. "The Hadryn have come!"

Daryd stared across at the far bank. And then he realised . . . "Essey!"

He ran onto the meadow, grabbed the horse's reins and led her back to the trees, hoping none of the riders would see her through that brief gap in the trees. The Hadryn were headed toward Ymoth. Toward home. Toward Papa, Mama and all the family.

"Quick!" he said to Rysha, "get up!" For once she didn't complain, and he helped her astride before following. "We have to warn Ymoth! That's the entire Hadryn army!" Even now, the column of horses was continuing to pass and showed no sign of stopping. Not hundreds. Thousands.

He urged Essey forward through the trees, but the undergrowth here was thicker than nearer the fields. Immediately, his path was blocked by a large fallen log and he had to go around, only to find that way partially blocked as well. Nimble-footed though she was, Essey made little progress as bushes caught at her legs and roots caused her to stumble. Across the river, the Hadryn were moving far, far faster.

"We're too slow!" he told Rysha desperately, ducking a low branch that clawed at his hair. "We have to ride along the riverbank!"

"But they'll see us!" Rysha protested, her voice filled with fear.

"We have to warn Mama and Papa!" said Daryd. "We have to go faster!" He turned Essey toward the river and the mare wove, stumbled and bounded her way between the trees as best she could. Finally the undergrowth thinned and Essey cleared the last, twisted trees upon the riverbank. The sight took Daryd's breath away. Across the fields on the far side of the Yumynis, a single, endless column of armoured men on horseback was moving at a canter. Even from the far bank of the wide river, the roar of hooves made a sound so loud it was frightening. Banners flew at even spacings along the column, flying colours and symbols that were foreign. Many of the riders were wearing black, a Verenthane colour. Daryd knew little of the Verenthanes, except that some were good, some were bad, and the Hadryn were worst.

He kicked his heels to Essey's sides and she broke into her fastest gallop along the uneven riverbank grass. Rysha clutched him tightly from behind, her face pressed against his back—she had never liked it when he went this fast and the riverbank was not as flat as he would have liked. Essey raced up and down the bumps, at frightening speed, and Daryd simply tried to stay straight in the saddle, unable to crouch as much as he'd like lest he give Rysha nothing to hold onto.

Above the thunder of Essey's hooves, he heard a distant shout, then another. He risked a glance across the river and saw a rider separating from the column, galloping to match him along the opposing bank. That man was looking straight at him, from a hundred strides away, and fear knotted in Daryd's stomach. The Hadryn wore a mail shirt with a coloured vest and jacket over the top, and his head was covered by a pointy steel helm. An arm was waved and another rider joined the first, together they tore ahead along the opposite riverbank. It startled Daryd to see how fast they were—Essey was running at full gallop, yet the two Hadryn horses gained a big lead in no time, disappearing now behind some poplars growing in lines along the riverbank.

Then they reappeared again, leaping down from the high bank to the gravelly riverside and cantering to the water. Daryd's heart nearly stopped again as he realised the horses were going to cross the river. The water level was low this time of year and, for the big horses the Hadryn used, it probably wouldn't be difficult. It hadn't occurred to him. Terror flooded his veins and he cursed himself bitterly—not so much for himself, but for Rysha. He should never have taken a risk with her life. His first and most important role as a big brother was to protect her, and he'd failed, miserably.

The Hadryn horses slowed as they splashed in the shallows, then slowed some more as the water deepened. Essey galloped past them, and then the forest was ending and the wide, open fields of Ymoth's outer lands spread green and shining before them. Ahead a distance was farmer Vayen's cottage, nestled amidst the poplars along the riverbank. Daryd galloped that way, through the open gate of the empty field nearest the forest, casting desperate glances over his shoulder at the pursuers. Both Hadryn horses were swimming now, passing the river's midway point. They were rapidly being left behind. Daryd felt a surge of hope. Maybe they still had a chance.

The next field was filled with sheep, the gates in its low fenceline shut. "Hold on!" he yelled to Rysha and thumped his heels to Essey's sides as he aimed her straight for the low, wooden fence. Essey leaped and then grounded on the far side, quickly regathering her momentum. Sheep scattered in a white, woolly tide. Farmer Vayen's cottage was closer now. Beyond, the Yumynis swept about in a vast, right-hand turn to the north, toward the Udalyn Valley mouth. Just beyond that river bend, invisible now behind the poplars, lay Ymoth, at the base of foothills that rose into mountains beyond. It was still a long way.

Essey cleared the next fence too, and Daryd took another look over his shoulder. The two horses were bounding up the riverbank behind, galloping in his wake. Those men were heavy and armoured, but Essey was carrying two. The terror, momentarily subsided, resurfaced with a vengeance.

Ahead, farmer Vayen came running from his cottage, his hair flowing out behind and a big sword grasped in both hands. "Ride children!" he roared at them, waving a big hand. "Ride fast! Don't look back!"

Daryd rode, tearing past the cottage into which he had been invited for lunch on numerous occasions and wondering where Mrs. Vayen and the children were. He sped through the next open gate and took another look back—Farmer Vayen stood on open ground before his cottage, blade raised with muscled arms, as the two Hadryn horses thundered straight for him. Their riders' swords were unsheathed, gleaming in the bright morning sun.

He had to leap another fence then and when next he looked about, both riders were still coming and Farmer Vayen was nowhere to be seen. The riders were closing fast and Daryd realised that he had no chance of getting even close to Ymoth before they caught him.

He turned Essey left, away from the river and toward the treeline about the base of the Aralya Range. The rolling farmland climbed gently and Essey's gallop seemed to slow just a little. Daryd kicked her desperately, looking about to find that both Hadryn horses had cut across the corner of his sharp turn, and were now halving the previous distance. Another mistake. But he hadn't had a choice.

The high ridge of the Aralya Range loomed far above, like an enormous, sheer rock wall. The paddock slope became steeper and the treeline closer. Another glance behind and he could see the foam about the Hadryn horses' mouths and the red decorations hanging from their bridles. Closer and closer they pounded. Rysha's grip was painfully tight.

Essey managed a final burst of speed and then they tore amongst the trees—they were pines here, not the broadleaf of the riverbank. There was space between the trunks and Daryd wove Essey between them. Trunks flashed past at dangerous speed, Essey slowing somewhat, but the big Hadryn horses slowed more.

Suddenly the forest floor surged up in a sheer rock wall and Daryd turned Essey to the right, galloping that way and hoping it too would not be blocked . . . a Hadryn cut past behind and Daryd saw the man's determined face, his jaw set beneath his helm, sword in hand and fighting the reins one-handed.

The bigger horses seemed to have trouble changing direction amongst the trees, however, and Essey surged ahead, just missed colliding with a pine . . . and then there was a line of thick broadleaf ahead, and undergrowth, where a stream fell from the Aralya mountain face. Daryd plunged into it, undergrowth tearing at Essey's legs, branches whipping at his face. It opened suddenly into the stream, into which Essey splashed, then bounded up the far side. The undergrowth there was impenetrable and so Daryd reined her downslope, searching for a way through . . . and suddenly there was a Hadryn rider crashing across the stream in front of him, moving to cut him off. The second rider had flanked him, he realised in shock. The oldest manoeuvre of horseback warfare. He'd fancied himself an Udalyn warrior, but in truth, it seemed that he was just a boy after all.

Behind him, the first rider was now crashing onto the far streambank, cutting him off completely. Something hissed through the air, then a thud . . . the first rider screamed, then cursed. Daryd stared and saw the man had been struck by an arrow in the shoulder and was struggling to stay ahorse. Then there was another horse emerging from the treeline directly behind Daryd and Rysha, its rider wielding a bow.

The second Hadryn charged along the streambank and the new rider cast the bow aside, charging past Daryd and Rysha whilst pulling his sword. Essey reared in fright, then Rysha screamed and fell from the saddle.

"Rysha!" Daryd cried as the two riders collided with yells and clashing steel, horses shrieking and stamping . . . but Daryd cared only for Rysha, leaping from Essey's back and slithering down the streambank where she'd rolled. A horse fell and rolled in the stream with a huge splash and a man emerged soaked from the water alongside—his hair was longish, Daryd saw, and he wore no colours or mail. His horse bounded clear of the stream—a smaller horse, like Essey—and the Hadryn, still astride, descended the sloping bank with weapon raised.

The fallen man pulled a knife and threw, which the Hadryn swatted with a mailed arm . . . but the big horse reared and the fallen man sprang forward and thrust for the Hadryn's leg. The Hadryn yelled with a yank on the reins, causing the big horse to twist, then slip and fall. It slid heavily into the water, scrambling once more to its feet as its rider staggered upright in its wake.

The other man was on him before he could recover, steel rang loud and clear from one blow, then another. The Hadryn slipped, defended another blow, then reversed with a surge of raw power—his attacker parried but lost balance from the sheer force, falling half in the water and losing his blade. But he was up before the Hadryn could finish him, grabbing the Hadryn's sword arm and grappling. Both men fell wrestling into the water, splashing and flailing, with grunting, frantic desperation.

Daryd clutched to Rysha, the two of them watching on the streambank in mesmerised horror as the two men tried to kill each other. The Hadryn seemed to be stronger and held the other man under water, his teeth bared in a furious snarl. The other man struggled, splashed, then struck the Hadryn's wounded leg. The Hadryn screamed, but did not relent his grip. Was struck again, which loosened a hand enough for the other man to grab and bite. Again the Hadryn screamed, and the man beneath him struck him in the face and rolled him over, searching the stream bed with another hand. He found a rock, raised and struck with it—again and again, as the Hadryn tried to defend himself.

Rysha sobbed and buried her face into Daryd's chest. The Hadryn's helm was missing, and the mail hood provided some protection, but the man with the rock was relentless. He continued to strike with terrible fury, until the Hadryn's struggles ceased. Then he stood up, shoulders heaving, and searched the shallows until he found his blade. That done, he stood over the fallen man's body, raised the blade with its point down and plunged it through the protective mail. And twisted, horribly.

Daryd's stomach turned and he lunged for the stream to vomit. He was still there, on hands and knees, when the bedraggled, bloodstained victor splashed upstream past him, his blade in hand. Daryd watched, knowing he shouldn't, but unable to tear his eyes away. The man arrived at where the second Hadryn now lay on the streambank, clutching helplessly at the shaft beneath his inner collar-bone. The fear in the wounded Hadryn man's eyes twisted Daryd's stomach once more and he vomited again. He looked up, just in time to see the victor yank off the Hadryn's protective mail hood and cut his throat.

Then he walked to the Hadryn's horse, which was standing fearfully nearby, and extended a hand, speaking softly. Soon he was stroking its nose, and it seemed noticeably calmer. He led the horse downstream, where it drank while the man crossed the stream to recover his bow. Finally, he walked to where the two muddy, wet and terrified Udalyn children huddled together by the streamside.

Daryd got to his feet, stood before Rysha and put a hand on his knife, warningly. This man was clearly not Hadryn, but he did not look Udalyn, either— his face bore no markings and his wet hair, while shoulder length, was not long enough for a braid. The man had rugged, weathered features and his wet clothes were the leathers and rough cloth that a woodsman might wear.

He crouched on one knee, disregarding Daryd's warning stance. "Udalyn?" he asked, pointing at Daryd. His accent was very strong. Daryd had never met a non-Udalyn before in his life. He nodded, warily. "My Edu . . ." the man made a face. "Very bad. Little Edu. Understand?"

Again, Daryd nodded. His mouth tasted of vomit and his head spun. But he was determined not to faint. That would be a final humiliation, before this strange, foreign warrior who had defeated two Hadryn cavalry before his very eyes. "I understand," he said warily. "Who are you?"

Inexplicably, the man's rugged features split in a hard smile. As if the very sound of Daryd's speech had caused him pleasure. His eyes, hard and merciless the moment before, now narrowed with a look of wonder. "Udalyn," he murmured. And something else, in a foreign tongue, with a faint shake of his head. "My name Jurellyn," he said then, very carefully. "Prince Damon *efryn sy. Rels en* Prince Damon Lenayin. Understand?"

The foreign words must have been Lenay, Daryd guessed. Lenay was spoken in the middle provinces, he'd heard . . . although in the last century, it had spread elsewhere and become Lenayin's major tongue. But in the Valley of the Udalyn, it remained as strange and foreign as the many tongues of the wise ones of Saalshen.

"Prince Damon Lenayin sent you?" Daryd guessed.

The man, Jurellyn, nodded vigorously. Then clicked his fingers as a word occurred to him. "Scout," he said. "Me scout. Prince Damon's army. Scout Hadryn." Pointing at the fallen men. "I scout Hadryn." Pointing to his eyes. "See Hadryn. Tell Prince Damon. Hadryn go Ymoth. Fight Ymoth. Understand?"

Ymoth. Abruptly, Daryd recalled his original mission. His family were in Ymoth. The Hadryn were here to kill. He had just seen killing, for the first time, with his own eyes. The thought of that happening to his family filled him with a terror that made any fear for his own life seem like nothing.

"My family live in Ymoth!" he told the man, desperately. "My mother and father, my brothers . . . I have to warn them!"

Jurellyn shook his head, firmly. "Hadryn, Udalyn, fight," he said, smacking fist into open palm. "You go Ymoth, you die. Understand?" Daryd stared at him. Tears spilled down his cheeks. Jurellyn put a firm hand on his shoulder. "You go Baen-Tar. You see Prince Damon. You see King Torvaal. You scout. You . . . you tell him, what you see. Then, you save father, you save mother, you save brother. Understand?"

The king would send an army, he meant. Daryd's eyes widened in hope. He recalled what the adults had always said—that the Hadryn would never dare attack so long as the king forbade it. Ever since King Chayden, the Lenay kings had forbidden it. Daryd did not understand what had changed that the Hadryn now dared the present king's wrath. But if he could meet with the king . . . if he could tell him what was happening here today . . .

"I'll go!" he said firmly. "I'll meet with the king! But I don't know the way . . . will you take me there?"

Jurellyn smiled a hard smile. "My friend. My friend . . . take?" Daryd nodded. "My friend take you, see King Torvaal. Good man. Brave Udalyn."

Daryd felt his chest swell at that. The foreign warrior thought him brave . . . and thought the Udalyn brave. The foreigners still told stories about the bravery of the Udalyn, as he'd heard some in Ymoth say. Surely the king would listen. Surely no one could just stand by and let the Udalyn be slaughtered once more.

"Ow!" Sasha exclaimed, somewhat after the fact, as she prodded the new bruise on her bicep. Andreyis backed off, stanch twirling, looking very pleased with himself. Sasha gave him this morning's customary dark stare and he sobered a little. She windmilled her arm, fast, to keep it loose. "Don't get too pleased with yourself," she told him. "I hate fighting with this stupid style."

"But I'm getting better, right?" Andreyis insisted. "That was a good strike!"

Sasha wondered if he truly appreciated how difficult it was for her to fight in a traditional Lenay style. But the Wakening would be barely a moon from now—the end of summer, the traditional time for the ceremony of manhood—and Andreyis needed the practice. Even with the handicap of her gender, there were things she could teach him in this style that the Baerlyn menfolk could not show him in the training hall.

They stood on the bare ground beneath the old vertyn tree, near the top fence of Kessligh's vegetable garden. The horses grazed across the vast upper slope enclosure, their coats gleaming in the sun. Kessligh had gone to town, taking Aiden with him. Sasha had not been unhappy to see them go.

"You're planting the front foot too soon on the second transition," she told Andreyis, trying her best to ignore both the bruises and her bad mood, for Andreyis's sake. All young Goeren-yai males eagerly anticipated the Wakening. Andreyis's technique was good, but his recent growth spurt had impeded his footwork, and thus his timing. She refused to let him fail. "See here . . . the arms follow the feet, Andrey." She took the stance, holding her arms clear, and danced the several fast steps of the racha-dan, without moving her arms. "It's like drums in a folk tune—your footing gives you the rhythm that everything else should follow. This lead foot is too fast," and she stamped that foot to demonstrate, "the swing and plant should be simultaneous."

"I got you, didn't I?"

"I can't defend in this style, Andrey," she told him, with barely restrained temper. "I'm not strong enough." One thing Andreyis *did* have going for him lately was his reach. She could barely believe how tall he'd become, still recalling the awkward, nervous boy she'd wrestled with, climbed trees with and defended imaginary castles with against equally imaginary hordes of bloodthirsty Cherrovan warriors. Now, the top of her head came barely to his shoulder, and the swing of his arms, though lacking the power of a grown man, generated considerable speed with stanch or sword. "Now, are you going to listen to me, or am I just wasting my time?"

Andreyis must have seen the dark look in her eyes for he held up both hands, defensively. "I'm listening. Show me again?"

She took him through all of the fundamental taka-dans, which were not so different in basic strokes to svaalverd taka-dans, truly. And she acquired several more bruises along the way, for Andreyis knew better than to pull his strokes—if he acquired that bad habit before the headmen at the ceremony, he'd remain a boy for one more, humiliating year, and have his hair cut short once more. Mostly, she concentrated on footwork, which was the one thing svaalverd and Lenay styles had in common. Except that the serrin understood balance and momentum with far greater sophistication. Sometimes, svaalverd knowledge *could* assist a non-svaalverd fighter, whatever Kessligh's doubts. She'd seen it herself, in Andreyis's improvements.

And saw it again now, as he smacked her stanch back to a hard blow against her right thigh. Andreyis grinned outright. Sasha scowled at him, rubbing her leg. "It wasn't that good," she told him. "Your elbow lost extension again, you'd have so much more power if you could keep the lead arm straight."

Andreyis slung the stanch over his shoulder and gave her an exasperated look. "You just can't stand to admit when someone's beaten you," he told her.

"Oh you think that, do you?" Sasha said loudly.

"You've always been like that!" Andreyis retorted. "Like that time I beat you racing up the road from town and you insisted Peg had a cold? Or the time I beat you at the knife throw and, of course, you just *happened* to have a sore elbow? Or that time . . ."

"Okay then, let's try that again," Sasha told him, resuming her fighting stance. Andreyis followed, eyes hard with concentration, lips pressed thin. "This time, I get to fight *my* way. Ready? Go."

Andreyis paused a few moments, poised on the balls of his feet, awaiting the right moment. Then he attacked. Sasha met his lead overhead with a firm blade—it jarred her arms, but when she knew it was coming, she *did* have the strength for it. Then she stopped being polite, swung an angular intercept to the strike that followed, deflecting Andreyis away from whatever he'd intended next, and left him open for her counterslash that smacked into his ribs beneath his right arm.

Andreyis staggered sideways at the force of it, dropping his stanch and holding his chest. "I've told you before," Sasha said firmly, as he doubled over, winded, "you can't make training personal, Andrey. It can't be about ego and pride, it has to be about improving your technique. Now if you'll just get this stupid notion that you can beat me at svaalverd out of your head, then maybe we can get back to fixing your footwork, yes?"

Andreyis did not reply, still doubled over. Sasha's temper fled, replaced by concern. The sound her stanch had made against his banda came again to memory . . . How could she have been so stupid? She hadn't needed to hit him that hard!

"Andrey!" She dropped her stanch and grabbed him, carefully. "Oh spirits, Andrey! Spirits, I'm so stupid . . . I'm sorry, Andrey, I wasn't thinking. Are you okay?"

Andreyis took a deep breath and winced, holding his side. "I think you cracked a rib," he said in a small voice.

Sasha swore, loudly. "Look . . . just sit down. Damn it, I'm such a fool! Come on, sit. Here." She helped him down and began unstrapping his banda. Andreyis tried not to breathe deeply, or move. She lifted the padding away. "If you can lift your arm at all, I'll get your shirt off," she told him anxiously. "Can you do that?"

"Don't bother," Andreyis said, in a small, muffled voice.

"Don't bother?" She stared at him, aghast. "Andrey, I have to look. I can see if it's broken, then . . . then maybe Kessligh will have something to help it heal . . . Spirits, why am I such an idiot? Just before the Wakening too! What was I . . ."

And then she saw the grin on Andreyis's face and the reason his voice had been muffled. He was trying to stop from laughing. She stared at him, dumbfounded. Something bubbled up inside, half fury, half laughter. "You! You . . ." She turned about, fetched up her stanch and thought about removing his head with it. Andreyis put both arms over his head, shaking uncontrollably, but not with fear.

She threw the stanch down, hard. "You utter bastard!" she shouted at him. "I thought I'd really hurt you!"

"You did!" Andreyis retorted, now indignant despite his laughter. "It hurt like hell! Serves you right, hot-tempered wench!"

Sasha cuffed at the top of his head, but missed on purpose. And found herself laughing. "Oh thank the gods," she sighed, and sat heavily beside him.

Andreyis made the spirit sign, with his left hand. "Don't say that," he said. "Not in the circle." Not that there *was* a proper tachadar circle beneath the vertyn tree, but one did not praise lowlands gods within them, lest the spirits be offended . . .

"Old habit," said Sasha.

Andreyis winced again as he took a deep breath. "I still don't know how you do that. I was almost overpowering you for a while there, and then you just . . ."

"Technique is more powerful than muscle," Sasha said simply. "If my technique is superior, my strength of muscle is irrelevant. Even Jaegar can't touch the svaalverd."

Andreyis frowned. "So no non-svaalverd fighter even has a chance? Then how did the Saalshen Bacosh armies even take *any* losses in all those wars the Larosa launched against them?"

Sasha shook her head. "That's a different kind of fighting. The Bacosh wars are all armour and shields, huge formations of men with no room to swing. I wouldn't last a heartbeat in that kind of fight. You'd do better than me, probably. The Saalshen Bacosh armies are so formidable because they combine the best of human tactics and mass formations with serrin fighting technique and serrin steel and craftsmanship in weapons and armour."

Andreyis just looked at her. It was a face that might have been handsome, were it not so familiar. Despite his eighteen summers, and the new strength of his jaw and brow, she could not help but notice the boyish ears that stuck out, or the reluctant nose. With his dark hair and funny dark eyes, he continued to look . . . well, puppyish. Sadly, many other girls in Baerlyn seemed to think the same. Those girls only flirted and giggled with the rough-and-tumble lads, and regarded a quiet, awkward, thoughtful boy like Andreyis with cool disdain or worse.

"Are you going to Petrodor with Kessligh?" he asked finally.

Sasha stared at him, incredulously. "And abandon Lenayin? What does Krayliss do when he arrives in Baen-Tar and discovers I'm not there? At least if I'm there, I can . . . I don't know. Try to keep him under control somehow. The man's only a hairsbreadth away from open treason."

Andreyis stared at his boots. "I don't understand," he said quietly. "I don't understand why Kessligh would leave."

"That makes two of us," Sasha said darkly.

"Is there . . . is there something in the Nasi-Keth beliefs that . . . I mean . . ." He seemed at a loss for words. Sasha knew how he felt. "So much of what the serrin think is so strange and . . . I don't know, maybe he has his reasons. Reasons we can't understand."

"I'm Nasi-Keth," Sasha retorted, "and I don't understand."

"Aye, but you're not *really* Nasi-Keth." Sasha frowned at him. Andreyis blinked. "Well, you *are* Nasi-Keth, but . . . but you're Goeren-yai first, aren't you?"

"The serrin don't think like that, Andrey. They can be many things at once, not like humans who can only be one thing at a time. The Nasi-Keth aren't a religion, they're just a collection of ideas and none of them are exclusive of other ideas. So most of the Petrodor Nasi-Keth are Verenthanes too—they practise serrin teachings, yet they pray to the Verenthane gods and hold temple communion like any Verenthane. So there's no reason a Goeren-yai can't follow serrin teachings . . . hells, a lot of Goeren-yai already do, sort of. Serrin have been coming here for centuries, they've left a lot of knowledge behind.

"But serrin don't have a religion. They don't believe just one thing. They . . ." Damn, she'd tried to explain this to various Baerlyners before, but it was difficult. Now, it seemed important to try . . . for herself, as much as Andreyis. "They have a way of thinking; they try to be rational. It's not that they don't believe in anything, they do . . . but that's the problem, they believe in *everything*. They don't go around saying this is impossible or that's impossible, like humans do. They accept everyone's beliefs because they know they can't disprove them. And anything you can't disprove is possible, right?"

Andreyis frowned for a moment, thinking that over. Proof. No Goeren-yai, and no Verenthane, ever thought of proof. The spirits, or the gods, didn't need to be *proven*, they just were.

"So if Kessligh's just being rational," Andreyis ventured, "maybe . . . maybe he's right to go to Petrodor. Maybe he's just smarter than us, maybe he can see things we can't."

"Aye," said Sasha, nodding. There was a slow-burning fury inside, now that the shock had worn off. And it was building. "He's being a general. In the Great War he had to make nasty decisions—liberate some towns, leave others to die; keep some men in reserve, send others to die. Nasi-Keth teachings make him good at that. He's a rational commander. He didn't believe he was going to win a battle because the stars were in alignment, or because the priest gave him a holy blessing—he knew that it was up to him, and him alone, and he didn't just leave it to faith. That's why he won all the time.

"He did that with me, too. He wouldn't say nice things when I might want them said. He wouldn't comfort me, or give any real affection. He wanted me to be strong enough to take care of myself. It's all a part of the pattern, Andrey. He's so damn sensible and intelligent it makes me want to throw up."

"But . . ." Andreyis's gaze now was worried. "But if he's thinking like a general, then surely . . . surely he's going to do the right thing in the end, no matter what we might think of it now . . ."

"Don't you get it, Andrey?" Sasha snapped at him. "Don't you understand? All that man ever cared about was the Nasi-Keth and the serrin. He said as much himself. He never renounced those loyalties to my father and, my father was such a soft-headed fool, he never demanded it. He's not interested in saving *us*, he's only interested in saving *them*! And now he's been to Halleryn, he's seen what Krayliss is up to, and he's decided we're all a lost cause and he'll go running off to Petrodor to take care of what's truly important to him!"

Sasha got to her feet and snatched up her stanch from the dirt. "Lenayin made him a hero, it gave him all this status with the Nasi-Keth, and now he's got it, he's finished with us. Well, he may be a great general, and he may be smart and rational, but he's got no heart and no soul! Damned if I'll end up like him. I'd rather stay here and die for something I believe in."

Sasha was forking hay in the barn behind the stables when there came a new thunder of hooves from outside. At first, she barely noticed—Andreyis had been practising his cavalry moves on the white-socked mare, Rassy, and this sounded like just another pass. Then the hooves came again, only this time she could hear two horses, one lighter than the other.

She looked down from her high bale as a little dussieh rode straight into the barn, ridden by a smallish Goeren-yai man she did not recognise. Andreyis arrived as well and dismounted at the barn's entrance.

"M'Lady Sashandra!" said the man, sighting her above him. "M'Lady, I come from Cryliss! Lord Kumaryn rides to Baerlyn with the Valhanan Black Wolves and more! He means to apprehend you and Yuan Kessligh on charge of murder!"

Sasha frowned at him.

"Murder?" she said incredulously. "Whose murder?"

"M'Lady, I'm not certain, but I think it was a man of the Falcon Guard. A lieutenant, I believe."

Lieutenant Reynan Pelyn. Sasha swore in disbelief. Tyree was Valhanan's close neighbour and the nobility of both provinces were close; there were many marriages and relations between the two. Family Pelyn was an important family in the heirarchy of Tyree nobility and it would be no surprise if there were close relations to Family Tathys, of which Lord Kumaryn Tathys of Valhanan was head.

But Lord Kumaryn thought to pin that death on *her*? Had someone lied to protect Jaryd? Or had Jaryd betrayed her? Or was Kumaryn simply determined to rid his province of Valhanan's most troublesome twosome? He had some balls, if that were the case. Balls, or rocks in his head.

She stabbed her pitchfork into the hay bale. "How long until they get here?" she asked.

"They departed at dawn," said the Cryliss man. "I left before dawn, my horse is fast over distances. I'd guess they might be here a hand before sundown." The man's pony was lathered white with sweat and breathing hard. "I gave word to several villages along the way, some pledged to send help. Four other riders from Cryliss set out in other directions, it remains to be seen if the help they send arrives in time."

"We'd best ride back and tell the town!" said Andreyis from the doorway, a little breathlessly. "There's no way we'll let him take you for something you didn't do! Besides, he's got no rights over Baerlyn; Baerlyn only answers to the king!"

Sasha let out a short breath. "I'll ride back," she replied. "I want you and Lynette to stay here . . ."

"No!" Andreyis was indignant. "No way! My town is threatened, you're not going to stop me from defending my people and my family!"

Sasha jumped down to a lower bale, then onto the floor. "Andrey . . . someone has to stay here," she said, taking up her bandoleer with scabbard attached, and clipping it to her belt. "If it's not you, it'll have to be someone else—we can't make a defensive line forward of the ranch, we'll have to leave it open to them. Those Cryliss bastards have never liked me or Kessligh, they might just take the opportunity to steal a few horses or damage the house, if there's no one here to see it. You'll be safe enough, they'll never hurt children—"

"I'm not a child!" Andreyis retorted.

"Andrey . . ." Sasha sighed, positioning the bandoleer comfortably over her shoulder, where the skin was tough beneath its familiar weight, "the mark of a Lenay man is that he defends what's his. This ranch is yours, Andrey, as much as it is mine or Kessligh's. Don't you want to defend it?"

Andreyis looked uncomfortable. "Of course I do, but my family . . ."

"You think you can do a better job of defending the village than the older men? Would it be a sensible allocation of resources to send one of the more experienced warriors here to watch the horses, while you take his place on the line? Would that make Baerlyn safer?" Andreyis looked at the ground. Sasha gathered up the armfuls of hay she'd pitched and began dumping them into the barrow. "Your time will come, just be patient. Besides, it'll be just you against an army. Sounds like much more fun, wouldn't you say?"

"Me and Lynette," Andreyis retorted. "She could scratch them to death."

But he seemed mollified as Sasha wheeled the barrow to the stables. She explained the situation to a wide-eyed Lynette, who had been taking her turn at stablework, and gathered Peg from his grassy field for the ride into town. Lynette helped the Cryliss rider to water and feed, and rubbed down his horse—the dussieh was clearly tired. Sasha suggested he should leave the little mare to rest and borrow one of her own horses instead.

The Cryliss rider politely refused. "She'll be good in just a little while," he insisted, giving the pony's jaw an affectionate rub as she chewed contentedly on some hay. "She'll run all day on a cup of water and a handful of grass, then do it all again the next. No offence, M'Lady, but I wouldn't trade her for ten of your big brutes, no matter what the lowlanders pay for them."

Great Lord Kumaryn arrived at Baerlyn as the late afternoon sun hung low over the valley. His host numbered perhaps three hundred, Sasha reckoned, a great, snaking line of thundering hooves and glinting helms. Banners with the stallion on the red and gold of Valhanan flew to the forefront, alongside the howling black wolf on blue of the Black Wolves. The column came across the uphill paddocks beyond the upper treeline, threading between boulders that loomed from the green grass and glowed a dull, iron grey in the light from the lowering sun.

Baerlyn's defensive line spread wide across the uphill end of the Baerlyn Valley, concentrated here before the upslope buildings. All the village's men stood, or sat ahorse, weapons unsheathed and gripped with the casual ease that a smithy might grasp his hammer. Some stood across the fences to either side of the main road, in paddocks emptied of livestock, before rickety wooden barns, shacks, and a pigsty, keeping the line straight. Sasha sat behind the main line on Peg, with Kessligh astride Terjellyn at her side.

Further to the left, the exposed fields about the valley's small stream held the majority of gathered horsemen, warding a flanking move. Amongst them were many men from Yule, perhaps five folds distance to the south, who had arrived just a few moments before.

They conceded Kumaryn the high ground above the valley's end; should an attack come, they would fall back into the village, where the buildings and lanes would remove much of the cavalry's advantage, and strategically placed ropes, pikes and spears would avail the local swordsmen of a surprise. As would some of the more assertive Baerlyn women who had taken up Sasha's suggestion some years ago and learned archery. They waited now by the windows of their houses, ready to put arrows into any passing attacker.

Lord Kumaryn did not line his army across the open ground atop the slope into Baerlyn—such a move would have been almost a declaration of war. Instead, the head of the column approached between wooden fences that hemmed in the leading horses, just as the defenders had intended. Lord Kumaryn wanted to talk, Sasha reckoned . . . at least for a while. A gaunt-faced man with a large, pinched nose and a white beard held up his hand. The three hundred horse column came to a stop in clouds of sunlit dust. A young man in lordly clothes rode forward. In one hand, he carried the banner of Family Tathys—a stone tower pierced by a lightning strike.

Verenthane lords and their family emblems, Sasha thought sourly, watching him. Pompous fools. Fancy parading it around lowlands style, as if the very presence of that bloodline should cause men to fall to one knee in reverence.

"Greetings men of Baerlyn!" the young man cried, his voice high and clear. A squire, Sasha recalled such banner carriers were called amongst the lordly classes. Another stupid, imported lowlands word. Goeren-yai and the rural folk of Lenayin were not yet educated in such civilised terminology. Sasha hoped fervently that they would never need to be. "My Great Lord Kumaryn Tathys of Valhanan bids you greetings!"

"Aye, hello!" called one of the Baerlyn men cheerfully, to a roar of laughter from the rest.

The squire swallowed nervously. "As Great Lord of Valhanan, Great Lord Kumaryn has ridden today to Baerlyn to claim his right under law! It has recently come to my Lord's attention that upon the recent ride of the Tyree Falcon Guard into the province of Taneryn . . ."

"Where's your balls, lad?" yelled another man. Sasha thought it sounded suspiciously like Teriyan. More laughter.

"He left them in Cryliss, by the sound of it!" yelled another.

"Nay, Kumaryn borrowed them!" Raucous howls. This, Sasha thought with a sigh, was quite certainly Teriyan. "Be fair, Kumaryn! Give the lad his balls back, we know you've got no need of them!"

"Into the province of Taneryn," the squire continued, his high voice wavering. Sasha almost felt sorry for him. "There the Great Lord Kumaryn's dearest relative, the Lieutenant Reynan Pelyn, of the noble Tyree family of Pelyn, and family to Great Lord Kumaryn through his marriage to his sister's cousin . . ." Groans of derision from the Baerlyners. ". . . met his end in highly suspicious circumstances! Word from truth-loving men has placed the blame for this callous murder upon the person of Sashandra Lenayin . . ."

"Fuck off, you two-bit fool!" came a yell with precious little humour in it.

"Nay!" came Teriyan's loud reply. "Even for a fool, he's not worth one-and-five!"

Behind the squire, at the head of Kumaryn's column, Sasha noted many men who had ridden forward to hear. Some were officers of the Black Wolves, others were noble Verenthanes, well dressed and well-groomed atop their large horses. Several others were Goeren-yai—Cryliss had some Goeren-yai, Sasha knew, largely about the city perimeter. A few Cryliss Goeren-yai were wealthy merchants and traders like their Verenthane comrades, though none had yet accepted a title. Most refused nobility as a concept. Swordwork and honour, not wealth and titles, made the measure of a Goeren-yai man. And Sasha knew some Verenthanes who felt the same.

"And so," the squire resumed, now utterly flustered, "Great Lord Kumaryn demands by the powers of law vested in him that the Lady Sashandra be handed over to his custody at once, for a trial by the procedures laid out within the king's law!"

The squire finished and backed up his horse. Ironical applause followed him. "Well done, lad!" someone shouted. "Fucking incomprehensible, but well done!"

Jaegar walked forward from the line. Like many in Lenayin, he disdained horses when there was a chance to fight on foot. In rugged, forested Lenayin, that was often. His leather jerkin had no sleeves and he wielded the massive blade in his hand as if it were a twig.

"Lord Kumaryn!" he shouted, in a deep, yet eloquent voice. "I'm very sorry that you've come all this way for nothing! Baerlyn swears its allegiance to the king in Baen-Tar, not to you! You have no authority to apprehend or administer a trial against any man, woman or child of Baerlyn in the name of justice! Justice belongs to the king, not to provincial lords! Goodbye!"

The gaunt-faced, white-bearded man rode forward atop a dappled, grey-white mare. His cloak was red and gold, and he wore a blue shirt and leather vest over chain. Sasha saw the sweat on his brow. He had to have at least fifty summers . . . didn't the heat bother him? She swatted at a fly . . . up here about the pig and sheep enclosures, the flies bred something fierce in summer.

"Master Jaegar, I presume?" Kumaryn called down from his horse.

"Yuan Jaegar," Baerlyn's headman corrected. He planted his swordtip on the road and folded his hands atop the hilt, feet set wide. Kumaryn's blue eyes were cold with disdain and his nose was wrinkled.

"You forget yourself, Yuan Jaegar," said Kumaryn. He did not speak loudly enough. Further along the line, men were straining to hear. "I am Great Lord of Valhanan. That title was granted to Family Tathys a hundred and three years ago by King Soros and has carried on to me from my father and grandfather before me. I rule Valhanan, Yuan Jaegar. Best that you recall."

"No, you *tax* Valhanan!" Teriyan retorted from behind. "In these parts, we call someone who takes money whilst giving nothing in return a thief!"

A cheer went up. Jaegar held up a hand and the men quieted. "The king's law is quite explicit," he said, very reasonably. "A provincial lord may levy a property tax, and no more, for the upkeep of provincial affairs. A provincial lord will deal with such local matters of law and order that do not concern the king . . ."

Some of the mounted nobles were laughing. "You think to lecture *me* on the king's law?" said Kumaryn, smiling coldly.

"No, well, I thought there might be some disagreement," Jaegar said conversationally, "so I brought along a copy." He waved to Teriyan, who stepped from the line with a scroll in one hand and sword in the other. The nobles' smiles faded. Teriyan unravelled the scroll for Jaegar to read from. "Aye, here it is. The rights and responsibilities of the office of provincial lordship."

"Aye, that'd be you then, wouldn't it?" Teriyan suggested to Kumaryn with an insolent grin. Kumaryn glared, fingering the hilt of his sword.

"The law of Lenayin shall be administered by the king," Jaegar continued, reading easily from the scroll. Some of the nobles looked astonished. No doubt many had presumed that *all* Goeren-yai were illiterate. "On matters pertaining to the provincial lord's peace, said lord shall be considered an officer of the king, for the purpose of justice. Provincial affairs beneath the king's consideration shall include common theft, rape, affairs of marriage and all pertaining rights and properties, matters pertaining to contests of honour, disputes of land and boundaries . . ."

"Where does the scroll come from?" one of Kumaryn's party said suspiciously.

"A copy," Jaegar said mildly. "Those among us learned in writing do make copies of such things and distribute them among the villages. You never know when they'll come in handy."

"You can read Torovan?" another asked, with equal suspicion.

"It's a translation," Jaegar admitted.

It was said that King Soros had barely spoken any Lenay when he had arrived in Lenayin all those years ago, Sasha knew. Raised in Petrodor from childhood, having been smuggled from Cherrovan-occupied Lenayin, he'd known mostly Torovan, and most official documents of the period remained in Torovan even now.

"Enough of this nonsense!" Kumaryn barked. His face was reddish now, partly from temper, and partly, Sasha suspected, from the heat. "You defy your lawful lord! The girl Sashandra is accused before the law! If you resist my lawful request, I shall take her by force and have Baerlyn declared a village of traitors!"

"If there is an accusation," Jaegar retorted, his tone hardening, "then the law explicitly states that she is answerable to the king, and the king alone. You are the king's *officer*, my Lord. A servant. And the accused, may I remind you, is the king's *daughter* . . ."

"A title she renounced twelve years ago when she abandoned him to the service of that foreign cult!" Kumaryn glared straight at her for the first time, over the heads of armed Baerlyn men. "You shall yield, or you shall face the consequences!"

"Got a lot of gall, doesn't he?" Sasha suggested to Kessligh. Kumaryn was the greatest fool in Lenayin if he thought this pathetic bluff was going to work. Kessligh, however, looked grim.

"Hey look!" came a shout from a Baerlyn man. "There's Master Wensyl, he brews the finest ale in Cryliss! What are you doing with these damn fools, Wensyl?"

Wensyl, a Verenthane noble, looked uncomfortable.

"Have you nothing to say for yourself?" Kumaryn shouted at Sasha. "Will you not spare the lives of your so-called friends? Or shall you hide behind them like a coward?"

"I am a villager of Baerlyn, Lord Kumaryn," Sasha replied calmly. "I obey my village council, like any villager. Should they wish me to leave with you, I would do so. However, I've heard opposite sentiment put to me, very strongly." She shrugged. "It's out of my hands."

A Goeren-yai man jostled his horse to the fore of Kumaryn's party. "I've heard enough!" he announced. He wore the good clothes of a wealthy city man, yet his bald head wore long hair at the back and his ears were adorned with rings. "This is the stupidest excuse to slaughter an entire village I've yet heard! If there's fighting, I'm on *their* side!"

He nudged heels to his horse and rode through the Baerlyn lines to raucous cheers, yells and raised blades.

"Anadrys Denaryn!" yelled a noble at Kumaryn's side, levelling a blade at him. "You are a traitor to your lord!"

But more Goeren-yai city men were pushing down the column and crossing into the Baerlyn lines, some waving cheerfully to their new friends as they came. Jeers and catcalls accompanied the cheering as Kumaryn, his noble friends and officers fumed.

"I said I'd come to help in the fight!" the man named Anadrys yelled back at Kumaryn across the gap. "I didn't say on which side!"

"Come on, Wensyl!" the man who had shouted out to him before was yelling above the noise. "The man's an ass! You don't want to fight for him. Come over this side!"

"He's Great Lord of Valhanan!" Wensyl protested, almost apologetically.

"So what? Does he own your honour, or do you!"

Wensyl grimaced, rode across to the man in question and dismounted. Kumaryn's comrades yelled at him to come back, but Wensyl was now engaged in a heated debate with his Baerlyn friend and several others. A pair of Baerlyn men approached Kumaryn, whose companions raised weapons in threat, but a Black Wolves sergeant intervened, and that began a new argument. More men crossed the line, weapons gesticulating dangerously, and suddenly the grim face-off had degenerated into a milling, chaotic debate between sometime friends, trading partners and tournament contestants, as men found others they knew on both sides.

Sasha found herself grinning. It was approaching a farce. She knew what the lowlanders would say if they could see this. "Lenay rabble." Ill-disciplined, chaotic and leaderless. Uncivilised. Barbarian. All were quite possibly true. And Sasha had rarely felt any more proud of the fact than today.

Some dried horse manure sailed dangerously close to Kumaryn's head, but it was impossible to tell who'd thrown it. Sasha saw Geldon climb onto an adjoining fence and call to someone in the column he recognised, followed by handshakes and greetings—Geldon supplied bread to Cryliss and bought grain from them, Sasha guessed this was one of his partners. Anadrys and the other Goeren-yai who'd come over were calling to Verenthane friends still in the column, some of them in the Black Wolves.

The men of the Black Wolves now appeared confused, looking to their lord for direction. Their disquiet was obvious—such companies had been used by lord or king to hit rebellious villages before, but this was different. No Lenay man liked to be seen as another's vassal. No Lenay warrior was obliged to follow a dishonourable command, whatever their oaths. Some more manure actually hit one of Kumaryn's nobles. Kumaryn signalled furiously for a withdrawal and the long column began a slow reverse, leaving many of their number behind to continue the debate.

"So much for that," Sasha said cheerfully to Kessligh, watching them leave. Kumaryn now seemed in furious argument with the Black Wolves captain. If the Wolves refused to fight, that was the end of it.

"Nothing to be pleased about," Kessligh said grimly. "The nobility becomes ambitious. They're flexing their muscles, demonstrating their power to the king."

"And failing," Sasha retorted, steadying Peg's impatient head toss. "There's not enough of them in Valhanan, just the big towns and Cryliss. Rural folk outnumber them by a lot, their power is less than they think."

Jaegar and Teriyan came back to Sasha and Kessligh, who dismounted to meet them. A councilman from Yule joined them—Tarynt, a small, older man with a bushy beard that tried desperately to make him look larger, and failed.

"Thank you for that," Sasha said, knowing as she spoke that it was unnecessary. "I'm grateful."

"Would have done it even if you were guilty," Jaegar said with a shrug, swiping at a fly. "He's got no right, and he knows it. We let him do this, it's a whole slippery slope from there. He'll not get a warrior nor a horse nor a mangy chicken from us."

"Just when did the lords of Valhanan start fighting the Tyree nobility's wars?" Tarynt asked with concern.

Jaegar took a swig of his small water skin and spat. "Kumaryn over-reached this time. He was never very bright. Hopefully he'll get the message now."

"He wasn't sending a message to the villages," Kessligh said grimly. "He was sending a message to the king. They all were. They've had a taste of power now and they want more."

"Aye," said Teriyan, "it's the grand crusade to civilise Lenayin. First it's the lowlands gods, then it's land-owning lords, peasants and feuding armies, and soon one day no one will remember what it ever meant to be Goeren-yai and free." Teriyan was always the educated one, Sasha reflected. The one who knew far more than his wisecracks and bragging let on.

"Over my dead body," Jaegar said simply.

"All of theirs too," Teriyan agreed.

"*Did* you kill this . . . this lieutenant person?" Tarynt asked Sasha curiously. The men of Yule had rushed to help at a moment's notice. Evidently they had not heard all the circumstances when they came.

"Lieutenant Reynan?" said Sasha. "No. It was Jaryd Nyvar. Reynan was trying to kill me from behind. Jaryd saved my life."

"Nyvar!" Tarynt pursed his lips into a whistle. Even village Goeren-yai knew and respected that name. Tournaments were not combat . . . but then, it was far more to respect a man for success in tournaments than success in titles or wealth. "Spirits, that's a mess. Isn't he a relation, or . . . ?"

"Of Reynan, aye," said Jaegar, nodding. "No doubt some quick wit saw a chance to pin it on Sasha before anyone could say otherwise. Perhaps they reckon Jaryd will comply and deny it was him."

"Aye, his papa will twist his arm to that," Teriyan agreed.

"They lack numbers, but the lordly classes make up for it in unity," Kessligh said grimly. "Goeren-yai disunity, now, they're relying on. Why aren't Sedyn or Dayen villages here? They're closer than Yule."

"Small matter of ancient bloodfeud with Sedyn," said Jaegar uncomfortably, glancing over his shoulder. The Cryliss column appeared to be forming a line on the upper slopes near the trees, but there was nothing of orderliness about it. "Dayen . . . well, they're nearer Cryliss than we are. Plenty of folk make good money from the wealthy families, don't want to upset them much."

"Makes sense," Tarynt said cheerfully. "Us in Yule, we've not a bean between us!" He cackled.

Kessligh, Sasha saw, was looking straight at her. She knew that look. "What?" she bristled.

"They want you dead, Sasha," he said flatly. "They need the Goeren-yai divided, as Goeren-yai always are. They want to make Lenayin into a model of lowlands civilisation, with vastly increased powers, lands and wealth for themselves. To do that, they wish all obstacles removed. They think Lord Krayliss might unify the Goeren-yai, so they want him dead. And now there's you, with all the rumours . . ."

"Bugger the rumours!" Sasha said hotly. "I'm not *doing* anything! I'm just . . . here!"

"Exactly. They'd like you elsewhere."

"And you'd oblige them?" she asked incredulously. "Send me running off to Petrodor with you like a coward because some fancy-dress noble threatened me?"

Jaegar and Tarynt looked uncomfortable, as in the manner of men who'd stumbled into a private family spat. Teriyan watched curiously.

"No," Kessligh said tightly, with as dark a scowl as Sasha had ever seen. "The choice is yours. It's always been yours. Go get yourself killed, I won't stop you." He strode and leaped into Terjellyn's saddle, spurring his way through the Baerlyn line and up the road in the wake of the retreating column.

"He's impossible," Sasha muttered, hands on hips.

Teriyan opened his mouth to remark, but Jaegar cut him off. "He's right about it being dangerous for you, Sasha. With a war coming, the Verenthanes think their time has come. Your father might wish to protect you, but no power in Lenayin is absolute—it's a great balancing act—and if the lords all find you a menace, even King Torvaal can't protect you. Today is just the first strike of many."

All because the stupid Larosa in far-away Bacosh couldn't stand to live side by side with the serrin. A dull panic settled in Sasha's gut. It wasn't fair. Baerlyn was her home. It scared her, all this talk of leaving. She looked at Jaegar desperately. At Teriyan, taller, and with a concerned frown.

"What do you think I should do?" she asked them.

Jaegar sighed and scratched at his scalp. "I can only really give you counsel where the affairs of Baerlyn are concerned, Sasha. It's not my place to be giving instructions to the king's daughter . . ."

"I'm not asking for instructions, damn it! Just . . ." she turned away in exasperation, "just a little advice! I can't ask Kessligh, he's stubborn as a mule for all the Nasi-Keth's talk of open-mindedness—he either tells me what I don't want to hear, or tells me an uman can't dictate the uma's path."

"You are Nasi-Keth, aren't you?" Jaegar asked.

Sasha felt uncertain. She shouldn't, she knew. Kessligh had devoted twelve years of his life to her. But now, he asked for things from her that she did not know if she was prepared to give. "Yes," she said quietly.

Jaegar shrugged, broadly. "We are Goeren-yai, Sasha. We believe in following a path. Your path is with the Nasi-Keth. Perhaps you should go with your uman."

Sasha stared at him. "And abandon the Goeren-yai?"

"Are *you* our saviour?" Jaegar asked, with an eyebrow raised.

Sasha blinked. "I never said . . . I mean, I never thought . . ."

"Then why stay?"

"You don't want me to?" A lump threatened to grow in her throat.

Jaegar sighed. "It's not about what I want, Sasha. I am headman. I am also umchyl, the spirit talker. I help to find the path desired by the spirits. Especially in the young in the Wakening ceremony and beyond. The path does not care what I want. The path is yours, and only you can decide if you shall take it."

"*I* care!" Sasha protested. "If you don't think I can help, if you don't think I'll bring any more than just trouble, then I'll leave! I don't want to bring those bastards down on Baerlyn again, I just wish someone would . . . would have the balls to tell me . . . to tell me . . ." She gave up in exasperation and turned to leave before the building desperate emotion escaped her control.

Teriyan caught her arm, hard. "I'll tell you," he said firmly. "I don't claim to be some spirit-talking wise man like my friend here . . ." Jaegar smiled, faintly. "But I think you should stay. This, this nonsense . . ." he waved a hand toward the disorganised rabble of Cryliss warriors across the upper slopes, ". . . it's been coming for a hundred years. No offence to your great-grandfather, Sasha, but let's be honest—King Soros was raised a Torovan, he'd barely known Lenayin. He did a great thing ridding us of the Cherrovan, but he had no real idea what to do with Lenayin itself except to try and remake it in the image of the lowlands.

"So he turns all his most loyal chieftains and clans into noble families as reward for service, but only then discovers the Goeren-yai and the villages won't stand for it, so he waters down the nobles' powers to avoid civil war. The nobility bought it then because it seemed better than nothing, and they thought they'd try to increase their powers by stealth . . . but a century later and they're growing impatient. King Soros *promised* them they'd be full-fledged noble lords like in the Bacosh, not limp-dick puppets.

"We can't let them win, Sasha. You matter to the Goeren-yai. Damn it, Kumaryn's *right* to worry about you, far more than he is to worry about that buffoon Krayliss. Of all the royal children of Baen-Tar, you're the *first* who truly loved the Goeren-yai. It means a lot to people, Sasha."

"The second," Sasha said quietly. "Krystoff loved the Goeren-yai too."

"Aye, that he did," Teriyan agreed. "But Prince Krystoff lived in Baen-Tar and only knew us as soldiers he served with and servant girls working in the palace. You live *here*. The spirits are bound to the land, Sasha. They live in the rocks in the hills, and the trees of the forest, and the dirt beneath your feet. You're the first of all Lenay royalty to be here, and to feel it. I'm not itching to lead some damn rebellion, Sasha . . . but damn it, you know what the stakes are in this. We need all the help we can get. And if men get desperate enough that Krayliss looks like the only alternative . . . then spirits save us."

Tears prickled in Sasha's eyes. She took a deep breath, pig-smelling air and all. "Thank you," she said. "I'll help. I have to talk to my father. Once upon a time, men say he used to listen to reason. Perhaps he still will."

"That damn Archbishop Dalryn jerks your father's strings now," Tarynt muttered. "Him and your big brother Koenyg."

"Then we'll just have to see what we can do about that," Sasha replied, with firming resolve. "Shan't we?"

Nine

SOFY STOOD AT THE EDGE of the stable's mustering yard, watching the milling chaos of horses and soldiers in the blazing torchlight, as frenzied shadows splashed across neighbouring buildings and the towering inner stone wall of Baen-Tar City. Anyse was at her side, trying to hold a spare cloak over her princess's head and ward off the light, chill rain. Sofy recognised Damon, surrounded by Royal Guardsmen, their gold and red distinct amidst the green of the Falcon Guard.

As he dismounted, stablehands rushing to take his horse, she caught sight of a second group of very different riders. They wore the dark skins and leathers of the Goeren-yai, their hair long and wild, some with rings in their ears that glinted in the torchlight. The banner carried by one was their only identification—green with three diagonal black stripes. Taneryn. One man in particular was giving orders—a huge man in a big fur coat with a bushy beard to match.

Anyse's arms were clearly tiring. "Oh Anyse," Sofy scolded her, "it's barely raining!"

"Your Highness will catch a chill," Anyse said stubbornly.

"You're getting wet, you should be more worried for yourself."

"Goeren-yai don't catch chills," Anyse replied. "Only stubborn princesses who should have more sense than to venture out on stormy nights."

Then Damon was approaching, his mud-spattered boots splashing in puddles. In his full colours, armour and sword, Sofy barely recognised him . . . until he pulled off his helm, revealing a face tired and wet with rain, his dark hair plastered flat to his head. He saw Sofy and managed a weary smile.

Sofy refrained with difficulty from hugging him, settling instead for a sisterly kiss on both his cheeks. "Walk with me," he told her. "I must present Lord Krayliss immediately to father. No doubt there are things to be said."

"Lord Krayliss!" Sofy gasped, hurrying to walk at his side. "So that's who that big man with the beard is!"

Anyse gave up trying to cover Sofy's head, walking instead at her heels alongside a Royal Guardsman who took Damon's helm for him.

"What happened?" Sofy asked Damon as they followed the torchbearers toward Soros Square. "Why is Krayliss here? Did he come willingly? I haven't been able to discover a thing lately; it's been so frustrating!"

Damon smiled faintly. "Sasha fought a duel against Farys Varan, son of Udys Varan."

Sofy stared at him, aghast. "A duel! Is she . . . ?"

"Our sister is well," Damon pronounced, with more than an edge of tension. "Farys is not." Sofy clasped a hand to her chest with a gasp of relief. "Krayliss apparently took this as a sign from the spirits . . . one in particular he called the Synnich. He now claims Sasha is guided by the Synnich and has placed himself under the protection of her word. Otherwise, I'm sure he and Lord Usyn would be fighting to the death right about now."

"A duel!" Sofy exclaimed once more, in disbelief. Past that announcement, she'd heard very little Damon said. "What was Sasha doing fighting a duel? You swore to me you'd look after her!"

"Sofy," said her brother with exasperation, "one does not 'look after' Sasha, any more than one 'looks after' a wild animal. She does what she does, and the best any in her vicinity can hope is to remain alive at the end of it." And to Sofy's continuing, accusatory stare, he added, "Farys insulted Krystoff's memory. It was calculated, I'm sure his elders put him up to it."

"Oh dear lords," Sofy exclaimed. And shook her head in despair. "Old family history. I swear nothing causes more catastrophes in this kingdom than old family history. Shall we ever be free of it?"

"Twelve years is not old history, Sofy," Damon said sombrely. "I remember Krystoff well." Sofy gazed at him. He seemed more serious, somehow, than when he had left. More adult. The look in his eyes was the look of a young man concerned with matters far greater than himself. Prior to this ride, there had not been so many of those.

"What is it, Damon?" Sofy asked him. "What happened out there?"

Damon sighed and shook his head. "I'll tell you later," he said.

The road opened onto Soros Square, a vast expanse of stone paving centred by the Verenthane Angel of Mercy. On the left were grand stone buildings fronting the square with ornate facades, pillars, arches and windows. To the right, the great front gate, open to the traffic of early evening and surrounded by many guards who warmed themselves near the blazing fires beyond the wall.

"Sasha sends her love," Damon added.

"She is coming to Rathynal?" Sofy asked.

"She'd better," Damon said darkly. "Krayliss will make a fuss if she doesn't."

"And Kessligh?"

"That was the impression." Sofy was glad to hear that . . . and yet nervous, too. There were probably only three men she'd known in her life whom she'd never been able to charm: Her father, Koenyg and Yuan Kessligh Cronenverdt. He loved Sasha, that was clear to her, even if Sasha was sometimes uncertain, and the relationship they shared was utterly remarkable in its unlikeliness. And yet, somehow, when he looked at Sofy, she felt it was as if he saw straight through her and was considering the texture of her bones.

"Oh well," she sighed, trying to get her thoughts back into order. "More people. I swear I'll go crazy trying to remember them all."

"I doubt Kessligh will be attending the events you're organising," Damon reassured her.

"No?" Sofy said, with a sudden, humorous inspiration. "You're certain he wouldn't like a formal dance? Perhaps a tour of the artworks? Or maybe some flower arrangements? Arrangements are all the fashion in Petrodor now, it's becoming quite an art."

"I'm sure all the *important* people will have far more important matters to attend to," Damon retorted. Sofy scowled at that. "Particularly Kessligh."

"Not true!" said Sofy, skipping sideways to jab a delighted finger at him. "Kessligh *loves* gardening, Sasha's told me all about his precious vegetable patch! She says he even grows ythala flowers in rows between the vegetables because they're good for the soil!"

Damon sighed and swiped at his flattened hair, now a little damp in the light rain. "Nasi-Keth are strange," he said with a shrug. "I know *Sasha* doesn't have much time for flower arrangements."

"I don't know about that! Sasha loves all wild things."

"Exactly. She wouldn't understand why you need to cut its head off to make it look pretty. And I'd agree with her."

"Well, at least it wasn't the two of *you* who fought the duel," Sofy said with a meaningful sideways look. "It sounds like you have finally become at least civil with each other." Damon nodded glumly, but his attention was wandering. They passed the square's central statue, the angel's wings and outstretched arms making a ghostly silhouette against the gloomy sky. Ahead, the spires of the Saint Ambellion Temple soared into the night. "Damon, what's wrong? Why are you so brooding?"

Damon's jaw tightened as he walked. "I sent a scout from the Falcon Guard to follow the Hadryn," he said in a low voice. "Several scouts, actually. They volunteered. I was worried our wise Lord Usyn might do something stupid."

"Like?"

"Attack the Udalyn," Damon said grimly. "Every bit of Goeren-yai trouble the Hadryn get from Krayliss, they conveniently blame on the Udalyn. It's as good an excuse as they've had in decades. And with father's mind as it is lately, I don't know if he'll stop them."

Sofy did not pretend to understand everything about *those* old troubles . . . except that the Hadryn had wanted to destroy the Udalyn since long before there was ever a Lenay king. But she did understand some of Damon's responsibilities on rides to troublesome provinces beneath the king's banner. "Are you allowed to send scouts across the Hadryn border?" she asked anxiously.

"They're scouts," Damon said shortly. "Wild men of Lenayin. They go where they please . . . and, like I said, they volunteered."

Sofy guessed that the answer to her question, therefore, was "no." She gave her brother a long, misgiving look. "I hope you know what you're doing," she said quietly.

Damon sighed. "Me too."

The procession passed the wide steps leading up to the doors of the great temple. The Royal Palace loomed opposite, its many tall windows ablaze with light, guards waiting at the doors to the Grand Hall entrance. They crossed the road from the temple to the palace and climbed the wet stairs, Damon recalling his manners to offer an arm to his sister, approaching those doors.

Through the grand foyer, with tile-patterned floors and busts of family-long-dead, then into the hall proper. The ceiling arched high overhead, beneath which four enormous chandeliers hung suspended along the hall's length. The procession's footsteps echoed in the vast space. Groundsmen extinguished their torches and departed, replaced by the senior hall master of the hour, leading the way with brown robes and a formal stride. Large paintings and tapestries looked down from the high walls. Ahead, servants scurried, preparing to open the doors to the throne hall.

"Are you invited?" Damon asked, as Sofy showed no sign of stopping.

"Assuredly," Sofy said sweetly. And it was Damon's turn to fix *her* with a wary glance. A princess at the king's formal business? Surely not. But Damon said nothing.

The servants hauled the doors open with a squeal of weight-bearing hinges. Damon and Sofy walked the throne hall together, its many tall columns forming a row down the central aisle toward the raised dais and its throne. Along that length, many Royal Guards stood to attention . . . and Sofy wondered if it were merely her imagination, or whether those guards truly were as attentive and edgy as they appeared. Certainly there were a lot of them and their hands seemed uncommonly near their weapons, resting upon the hilt of a sword or with thumbs tucked into a belt.

The king stood at the foot of the three-step dais, in close conversation with Koenyg and Father Dalryn—the Archbishop of Lenayin. The king wore his customary formal black robes with golden trim. Koenyg wore similar, only with a greater prominence of leather as one might expect of a Lenay warrior. All looked up at Damon and Sofy's approach, and the procession that trailed them.

At the last moment, Sofy disengaged Damon's arm and stood demurely to one side. Koenyg did likewise, giving her a displeased, "What are you doing here?" stare that Sofy ignored. The king took a pace forward and extended his black-gloved hand. Damon dropped to one knee, took the hand and kissed it. Then stood and embraced his father, to one side and then the other. From the sides of the dais, and from behind the rows of columns and guards, well-dressed nobility looked on, their expressions both grim and anxious. Lord Krayliss was not the first of the provincial lords to arrive in Baen-Tar for Rathynal, and Baen-Tar was becoming crowded with important lords and ladies from all over Lenayin.

"My son," said King Torvaal, his hands on Damon's shoulders. His face, with its dark, close-trimmed beard, remained as impassive as his formal black robes. Verenthane black, like those of the archbishop. The colour of purity. "News precedes you of a crisis averted at Halleryn. Yet details are lacking."

"Aye, my Lord," said Damon. His expression, Sofy saw, was guarded. He rarely wore that expression with her. She would spot it and suspect him of concealment. She wondered if their father would. No, she decided sadly, that was unlikely. But Koenyg might. "Lord Krayliss has cast himself upon your justice, and has accompanied me to Baen-Tar. He awaits your audience even now."

A crease divided King Torvaal's dark brows, ever so faintly. "And how did this come to pass?"

Damon explained. Torvaal listened, with the same faint, dark frown. Sofy felt her heart beating faster.

"The girl had no right to submit to those demands on my behalf," Torvaal said when Damon had finished. His tone was firm, yet devoid of obvious emotion. As usual. "She serves the Nasi-Keth. Her privileges as a daughter of Lenayin were renounced twelve years ago. The king is not bound by her word."

Damon's jaw seemed to tighten, just a little. "She saved lives, my Lord," he replied. "Lord Krayliss admitted to killing Lord Rashyd, though he claims just cause. As such, his was the wrong deed under the king's law, and Lord Usyn Telgar was merely reacting to that wrong deed. Lord Krayliss defied my original demand that he submit to your justice. To enforce your law, my Lord, I saw that I had two options—to join with the Hadryn armies and defeat him by force of arms, or to agree to the terms provided by M'Lady

Sashandra. An assault would have cost hundreds of lives on both sides, and perhaps sparked a broader conflict between Taneryn and Hadryn that could have cost thousands. I deemed the second option more sensible . . . with your blessing, my Lord."

Koenyg, Sofy saw, appeared somewhat annoyed, although he hid it well. Their father's expression remained unchanged. He considered his son with thoughtful dark eyes, within a face that might have been handsome if it had just once shown the faintest hint of levity. And that thought gave Sofy a familiar, melancholy sadness.

Torvaal nodded. "You did well, my son," he said, and Damon seemed to relax a little. "I will see Lord Krayliss now."

Koenyg made a gesture to the guards at the end of the hall and, once again, the doors squealed slowly open. Damon and Sofy moved to Koenyg's side as Torvaal ascended the three steps and sat in the simple, wood-carved throne. At the hall's end, a new procession appeared. These men did not walk with the refinement and dignity of Verenthane nobility. They swaggered, with heavy, muscular steps, swords swinging against their legs. Their hair was long, tied with apparently random braids. Gold glinted around necks and along ears and, despite the uniform glow of many lamps, it seemed somehow that the light only came from their right, for all the men's left profiles appeared cast dark into shadow.

At their head strode a huge bear of a man, abristle with wild hair and beard, and a sword so enormous its leather binder squealed as it swung from his belt. His girth was greater than two Damons, Sofy reckoned with amazement, and Damon was a skinny lad no longer. His clothes were all leathers and skins, and his boots were patterned with intricate, beautiful stitching. Only when he and his men drew closer could Sofy see the equally intricate tattoos across the left side of their faces. Not all Goeren-yai men wore the tattoos, Sasha had told her. Those who did began to add the first strands after the Wakening, the Goeren-yai ceremony of manhood.

The Taneryn contingent halted before the dais, staring about them insolently. There were perhaps twenty men in all, Sofy reckoned. She realised then why the guards had seemed on edge. Disquiet spread throughout the hall, a disbelieving, angry murmur. It grew louder when Lord Krayliss took a step forward and stared directly at the king with no sign of obeisance.

"Kneel before the king!" Koenyg demanded. King Torvaal's expression remained impassive. Krayliss's stare turned to Koenyg . . . Two dark, burning eyes within a bristling mass of dark hair. The fur coat over his huge shoulders added to the bear-like effect. To the right side of his face lay a long, winding braid, composed of three separate strands bound together.

"Ha!" Krayliss laughed, his voice like a heavy drum at festival. "The king's heir defends his father's honour!" Within that mass of beard, his lips appeared to twist in humour. "That is good! Honour should be defended at all costs! Only know this, king's heir—not all men of Lenayin follow the path of honour quite so rigorously as others."

Lord Krayliss knelt before the dais, and his contingent did likewise. His eyes, however, did not lower. Around him, the angry murmuring continued. Sofy found herself wondering at his accent—it was not unlike the northern accents she had heard, from men of Hadryn, Banneryd and Ranash. In Lenayin, one could never avoid the question of languages when determining a man's loyalties. Some said that the sooner all peoples abandoned their mother tongues and spoke only Lenay, the better. But what would that cost the kingdom, to lose so much of their ancient ways forever? Men like Krayliss would never stand for it. And, quite possibly, women like Sasha too.

"Lord Krayliss," said the king from his throne. Sofy noted Duke Stefhan and several of his Larosa contingent watching from between the columns. She wondered what they would make of this very Lenay scene. "My son informs me that you have ridden to Baen-Tar to place yourself within the protection, and the justice, of the king's law. Is this correct?"

"No," Krayliss said proudly, looking his king firmly in the eye. Another angry muttering from the crowd. "I am here on behalf of my people. The ancient people, the last of the true Lenays. It is we who are here to judge your law, King Torvaal. We shall judge it and we shall see if we find it worthy."

The king raised a hand to forestall the angry words from the crowd. His manner was calm. "And what expectations do you hold, Lord Krayliss, of my justice?"

Krayliss smiled a dark, unpleasant smile. "We in Taneryn have had a hundred years experience of the Verenthane kings, King Torvaal. A hundred years of Hadryn attacks. A hundred years of Verenthane cronies and syco-phants raised to the nobility of every lordship of Lenayin, to the point where I stand before you as the last remaining Goeren-yai chieftain in Lenayin. I shan't hold my breath for your justice."

"If you have not cast yourself upon the king's justice," Koenyg said loudly from Damon's side, "then Lord Usyn Telgar's claims of vengeance still stand. Are you within the king's justice, Lord Krayliss, or are you not?"

"Aye, you'd like that, wouldn't you?" Krayliss growled at Koenyg. "An outright invasion of Taneryn by the bloody-handed Hadryn to remove this mischievous Lord Krayliss once and for all? Behold, the heir Prince Koenyg! Not as talented as the great, departed Prince Krystoff, nor half as pretty I might add, but a great friend to the Goeren-yai of Lenayin is he!" His men laughed with raucous, ugly humour. Koenyg fumed. "March us all off to kill serrin babies in the lowlands, he would! Make us abandon our farms and our families for a good year or more so the Cherrovan can come raiding and the Hadryn can rape our women and steal our livestock with none of us here to do a damn thing about it!"

"That's enough from you!" shouted one noble from the crowd, as others yelled their disapproval, and suddenly the guards were more concerned with containing the observers than guarding the Taneryn. "Respect the king!" shouted another. Krayliss stood unmoved before the dais and gazed proudly about at the commotion he had caused. From his throne, Torvaal simply watched. The noise began to die, but Krayliss wasn't finished.

"Oh, you think I'm joking, don't you?" he boomed to the hall at large, sweeping them with his shaggy-browed stare. "You think I'm just giving the prince a jab or two? Then what by the spirits is *he* doing here?" Krayliss levelled a thick finger at Duke Stefhan. "Yes, you, you perfumed, limp-wristed *wystych*!"

Sofy's eyes widened. Sasha had told her that word—it was common to old Valhanan Lerei such as was still spoken in the valleys near Baerlyn and to the Taasti language of Taneryn. It meant sexual self-gratification, Sasha had said. Between friends, it was a joke. In the royal courts of Baen-Tar, it was dangerous provocation.

"Behold," Krayliss continued with glee, "a duke of Larosa—the most defeated Bacosh province of the last two centuries! The greatest losers in all Bacosh history!" At the duke's side, several of his men looked on with puzzled concern. Those, Sofy reckoned, could not penetrate Krayliss's thick accent . . . and just as well. The duke simply stared, dark and cautious beneath his fringe of curls. "Here in Baen-Tar for Rathynal! Fancy that! Recruiting willing fodder for your armies, are you, Master Duke? Please tell us all, what is the good Prince Koenyg's going price for the life of a poor Goeren-yai farmer these days? Three pieces of copper? Four?"

"We in the provinces are not stupid. We know that the king's favour has swung with each heir. Prince Krystoff trained to be Nasi-Keth and loved the Goeren-yai, and so while he lived the king did also . . . until of course the northerners conspired to have Prince Krystoff killed in combat with the Cherrovan. All so that the good, devout, Verenthane Prince Koenyg could take his place! And now they get their reward! Don't they, *Master* Koenyg?"

Deathly silence. Sofy could hear the shock. Could feel it emanating from the very stones. She had expected another uproar, but there was nothing. The typical Lenay response to such dastardly accusations was anger. But this . . . this felt more like fear. Was that it? Were all these Verenthane nobles actually *scared* of Lord Krayliss now that he had vastly, *enormously* overstepped the mark of no return? Or were they only scared of what he could unleash upon them, and upon the entire kingdom? Sasha had said often that the Goeren-yai would never follow him . . . but what if she was wrong?

Sofy found herself staring at a Royal Guardsman standing alongside Duke Stefhan, his eyes wary, a hand on the hilt of his sword. That man, too, wore the tattoos on the left side of his face and long, braided hair spilled from beneath his gleaming helm. So did nearly half the Royal Guard. What would happen to all the powerful people in this room if the Goeren-yai rose up in open rebellion? If the Royal Guard were split down the centre? If all the provincial armies divided along the lines of their faith?

Suddenly, she could feel the fear herself. Sasha had said this, too. Had said how crazy it was for there to be so few Goeren-yai left in the seats of power. Surely there was need for a calming, moderate voice to counter Lord Krayliss's provocations. But who? Aside from Krayliss, there were no Goeren-yai leaders left. The trappings of noble power were too Verenthane, and far too foreign, for the Goeren-yai's liking. It wasn't the lifestyle that they knew, or wanted.

Suddenly, Sofy realised what it was that Sasha had found so frustrating all these years. The Verenthane nobility had taken advantage of the Goeren-yai's naive, rustic good faith. Distributing all the seats of power beneath the new, central throne amongst like-minded Verenthanes had been simple and convenient—the Goeren-yai had not complained and it meant that Veren-thanes would not have to deal with their rural cousins' exasperating, uncivilised, pagan traditions. It had been so easy, and so rational, at the time. Only now, when the normally disinterested Goeren-yai showed the first signs of real anger with the throne in a century, did the price of those actions come sharply into the light. Now, the Goeren-yai looked for leadership . . . and found only Lord Krayliss.

Dear gods, Sofy thought to herself. No wonder many of the initially out-raged Verenthane nobles now looked a little pale. Krayliss was picking a fight. Now, they wondered if they dared to accept.

"Lord Krayliss," said the king, into that silence. "You have ridden to Baen-Tar to submit yourself to my justice. Yet you make grave accusations against the throne and against the throne's friends. How are we to believe that your intentions are just as you say?"

"The king's justice has a champion in the eyes of the Goeren-yai," Krayliss rumbled. "Her name is Sashandra Lenayin. Her uman is perhaps the greatest warrior Lenayin has ever known. In the eyes of my people, her uman's path was guided by the great Synnich, the most powerful spirit of these lands. Now, we have seen with our own eyes that the Synnich guides the path of Sashandra Lenayin also. I submit to your justice, King Torvaal, on the condition that Sashandra Lenayin shall attend the proceedings and shall speak only the truth on my behalf. It is on her credit, in my eyes, that your justice rests. Nothing more do I ask."

"Sashandra Lenayin," said the king, "bears neither rank nor privilege within the king's law." Sofy could have sworn she saw Lord Krayliss's eyes gleam, ever so faintly, as if sensing an opportunity. "But," the king continued, "for the purposes of that ride, she was beneath the authority of Kessligh Cronenverdt, who was in turn beneath the authority of my son Damon. Your claim is valid, Lord Krayliss. When she arrives, Sashandra Lenayin shall speak for you."

"My king is wise," said Krayliss, with a slight, almost mocking bow of the head. "May my king sit upon the throne for many, many years to come."

Jaryd Nyvar entered his father's guest chambers on the uppermost floor of the Baen-Tar palace and found all the lords of Tyree waiting for him. Lord Redyk, of vast girth and white whiskers, standing by the blazing fireplace with a cup of wine in hand, as usual. Lord Paramys, slim shouldered and poker straight, his long black beard almost reaching his navel. Lord Arastyn, to whose son Jaryd's younger sister Galyndry was due to be wed within the year—a handsome man with a big jaw and heavy features, yet clever eyes. Jaryd's gaze settled upon Lord Tymeth Pelyn, a wide, bald man with three chins and ill-fitting robes that struggled yet failed to hide his dimensions. Lieutenant Reynan Pelyn had been his brother. Lord Tymeth's eyes fixed upon the heir of Tyree as he walked across the flagstone floor, unblinking and unreadable.

There were fifteen lords in all, Jaryd counted, out of twenty-three in all Tyree . . . but some were more important than others, and possibly not all had travelled to Baen-Tar for Rathynal. It was disconcerting to have left Baen-Tar in normality, with his family far away, and then to return three weeks later and find all these grand figures of Tyree nobility gathered and waiting for him. Jaryd's father sat on a chair before his bed, attired in a cloak of Tyree velvet green. His thin face was drawn and sweat beaded upon his pallid forehead. White hair hung limp around his face and there was a cup in his listless hand. His eyes barely seemed to register his son's approach.

"Father," said Jaryd, and bent to embrace him, then kissed him on both cheeks. It was shocking to recall that his father had only forty-three summers;

Jaryd had seen sixty-year-olds with greater vigour. The air was overly warm and smelled sweet, almost sickly. "You summoned me."

"My son," said the Great Lord of Nyvar, his voice hoarse. "You return with Lord Krayliss in custody."

"You sound displeased," Jaryd observed. Wasn't that just like his father, to disparage every achievement with which he was even remotely involved? He had led the Falcon Guard, Tyree's finest company, into battle to restore the king's peace and his father remained unimpressed.

"You needn't have brought all of him back," said Lord Redyk, stroking his whiskers. "Just his head, lad."

"It wasn't my decision," Jaryd said shortly. "Prince Damon was in command."

"Oh aye," said Lord Paramys, his blue eyes cold. "And Kessligh Cronenverdt was only along to pick flowers from the roadside. Where is the great Nasi-Keth, anyhow?"

"With his uma in Baerlyn, I believe," said Jaryd. He hooked a hand into his belt near the sword pommel, his weather-stained cloak tossed back from one shoulder. It made him look good and he knew it.

"Prince Koenyg erred in sending Prince Damon," Lord Redyk growled in distaste. "He should have gone himself. Prince Damon lacks steel, no wonder he did not stand up to Cronenverdt. Now things are worse."

"We rode to restore the king's peace," Jaryd replied with a frown. "Peace was achieved, at a minimal cost, and now Great Lord Krayliss shall face the king's justice. How do you accuse Prince Damon of any fault?"

Lord Redyk's expression became faintly incredulous. "Any fault? Are you mad, boy? At this Rathynal, we push for power. For a full hundred years since the Liberation we have waited for the king to grant us the powers that King Soros promised our forefathers, but he has never seen sufficient reason to do so. Now, the king needs us for his lowlands war. He will grant us what we want, or else his conquering army shall be comprised of Royal Guards and kitchen hands.

"The great lords must present the king with a united face at this Rathynal to demand noble rights . . . and yet you bring Lord Krayliss, the very face of disunity, back into our midst? Are you mad?"

That was twice that rhetorical question had been asked. Jaryd bristled. "And that's your only concern about Lord Krayliss?" he asked coldly. "What about the Goeren-yai? You want to kill the last remaining Goeren-yai great lord, from the only province in Lenayin without a ruling Verenthane nobility, and you're not worried about the anger it may cause the rural folk?"

"Pah!" Lord Redyk waved a dismissive hand. "The pagans nearly came to blows just pitching their tents outside the Baen-Tar walls, arguing over the best camp sites. They're the last of our concerns—half of them want to kill Lord Krayliss as much as we do.

"They won't mind him dead, but they *will* mind him if he shames them! You know what the pagans are like, always falling over each other to make grand gestures of heroism, waving their cocks for all to see. Krayliss will defy us in our demands to the king, you watch. He'll refuse to partake in the low-lands war and he'll shame the other pagans into doing the same . . ."

"I disagree," said Lord Arastyn, mildly, from Jaryd's other side. Jaryd suspected that Arastyn, unlike Redyk, was still on his first cup of wine. In his other hand, he held an ornate warhorn—one of the chambers' decorative arte-facts. He had been considering it, offhandedly, while the others talked. "The pagans want war. Perhaps the Taneryn do not, nor the easterners, for the serrin have long travelled to those parts and are admired there. But the west and the south have had less contact and see little of Cherrovan incursions in the north. These are warlike people, yet for a century there's been little but peace, save the usual, stupid honour squabbles between villages. Left alone, Goeren-yai will fight themselves. Those folk in the south and west want a glorious war to relive the tales of their ancestors. And to them, Lord Krayliss is as much a foreigner as the serrin."

Jaryd knew that his father thought highly of Lord Arastyn. It was one reason why he'd promised Galyndry to his son. His family had been loyal, too. That was the other reason.

"The south and the west, perhaps!" Lord Redyk retorted. "But Tyree is neither south nor west, Lord Arastyn! Hellfire and floods take the south and west, the one place where Krayliss *does* have an influence is right under our bloody noses! And in Valhanan, where that bloody Nasi-Keth and his wild bitch hold sway, and in Taneryn with Lord Krayliss himself! And I tell you, in some places they may hate Krayliss enough to want to kill him, but if he stands up against a lowlands war, then none of them will suffer to be seen as a lapdog to Verenthane lords. I know these people, I tell you, and that's how they think!"

"If only our good friend Great Lord Kumaryn would have had the balls to move against Cronenverdt and his bitch earlier," Lord Paramys muttered. "If she joins with Lord Krayliss, *then* there'll be trouble. Did you hear him call her the Synnich? What the hells is a Synnich, anyhow?"

Jaryd listened to them argue, but his thoughts were wandering. He thought of the girl, with her short hair, lively eyes and, it could not be denied, firm buttocks. As pretty as her sisters, when one learned to disregard the unwomanly presentation. And crazy as a fevered mule. But then, who amongst these men present, who called her names and wished for her downfall, could match her with a sword or on a horse?

Jaryd Nyvar did not know much about a lot of things, but he knew honour. His father thought him a simpleton, and had often wondered aloud what he'd done to so displease the gods that they would give him a dunce for an heir. Jaryd had never excelled in studies. Written words still troubled him, and numbers moreso. An heir to the Great Lordship of Tyree would need such skills, he was often told. He was clever with a sword, a genius on a horse, and had surprised even himself with his gifts as an artist. The latter skill he'd been too embarrassed to practise, lest the other noble boys laugh at such girlish pursuits . . . but his tutors had noticed. He was obviously intelligent, they said. He was just lazy. He was not applying himself hard enough. His head was so full of horses, swordwork and pretty girls that he had lost all sense of priorities.

He'd become so tired of hearing those accusations that he'd decided he might as well make them true. At least that way he'd have a little fun.

He'd discovered soon enough that the commonfolk didn't care whether he could recite Torovan poets or make sense of the taxman's books. To them, he was a hero, something he'd enjoyed vastly more than being a dunce. Noble boys were more wary, aware of his father's concerns, which were therefore also their fathers' concerns. Some of them had teased him about his lack of scholarly skill, for which Jaryd had mercilessly tormented them in the practice yard or on the lagand field. They hadn't liked that, but Jaryd hadn't cared. He was heir to the Great Lordship of Tyree and could best them at all the things that should *truly* matter of a young Lenay man. What were they going to do about it?

"My brother is dead," said Lord Tymeth, which stopped all conversation immediately. "I wish to know how it happened."

Jaryd turned to face him. Pelyn were a powerful family with a large holding in western Tyree and access to lands that could become a large source of revenue should the lords get their wish and force the king to allow them to tax such lands.

Oddly, Jaryd found himself recalling the girl's scolding about lands and taxes. And of the death of Lord Aynsfar of Neysh, in the south, after he had tried to impose such taxation without the king's leave. Were they all fools to be standing here in Baen-Tar, with not a Goeren-yai in sight save the serving maids, and pretend that they had nothing to fear from the followers of the ancient ways?

The cold accusation in Lord Tymeth's eyes added to Jaryd's discomfort. This was all wrong. He'd thought the girl a fraud, but in truth, she was a formidable warrior. He'd thought his father's goals just and fair, yet he'd seen now how fiercely the Goeren-yai loved their freedom and he doubted they'd just lie back and accept a new set of local, tax-raising rulers any more than they'd tolerated Lord Aynsfar. He'd always thought his noble peers basically honourable, with a few notable exceptions . . . but he'd seen Lieutenant Reynan Pelyn attempting to put a blade in the girl's back, when honour should have compelled him to rush to her defence, whatever their differences.

Lord Tymeth stared, yet Jaryd could not feel any shame at what he'd done. He was not a brilliant man, perhaps, but he was honourable. Honourable behaviour, with the stanch, blade and lagand hook, had brought him the only true happiness he'd ever known. His honour was something right and something pure, and something his, that no teasing from his peers or contempt from his elders could ever destroy.

"I killed your brother, Lord Tymeth," he said, with as much firm disdain as he could muster. "Sashandra Lenayin won a duel against Farys Varan of Hadryn, one of the north's best swordsmen. The Hadryn proved dishonourable and attacked her following a fair victory. I moved to defend the victor, with the rest of the Falcon Guard, and in the ensuing confusion, I saw Lieutenant Reynan attempt to shove his blade into Sashandra Lenayin's spine, with clear intent. Thankfully, I was there to save Tyree from this blight on its honour."

There was no sound in the palace guest chambers but the crackling of the fire. They had already heard, Jaryd saw.

Some men stared in open hostility. Others looked at each other, as if wondering what now might happen. Lord Redyk wore a dark frown. Lord Arastyn, a serious contemplation. Great Lord Aystin Nyvar wore no discernible expression at all. He had barely reacted. He just sat in his chair, looking pale and ill.

Jaryd felt a great surge of frustration that, once again, he should be blamed for something that was most certainly not his fault. "Which one of you ordered it?" he demanded, scanning the lords of Tyree with his eyes. "Which one of you ordered something so dishonourable? I can understand a man deciding that Tyree would be better off with Sashandra Lenayin dead, but to do so by such a method? I should kill the man who ordered the deed for he deserves death far more than even Lieutenant Reynan."

His father cleared his throat. "That would be me," he said. Jaryd stared, his breath caught in his throat. His father looked up and met his gaze properly for the first time. A dry, humourless smile tugged at thin, pale lips. "It's no surprise I should deserve death. The gods give all men what they deserve."

"Boy always did have more wind than wits," Lord Paramys muttered. No one leapt to Jaryd's defence.

"Why?" Jaryd asked, in bafflement.

"Tyree would be better off with her dead," his father rasped, "you said it yourself. A man might decide that. A man did. Many men. Any one who might unite the Goeren-yai is a threat. The moment for Lenayin's nobility has come. We can afford no division and no obstacles. Krayliss is one obstacle. Kessligh Cronenverdt is less so, for he was always more Nasi-Keth than Goeren-yai, but his bitch is not. A royal Goeren-yai was always the dream of many. Best that it does not happen."

"You never told me!" Jaryd bristled. "You never trusted me with your plans! Why?"

"Why?" His father snorted a laugh, as equally humourless as the smile. "Look at you. You think this piteous whining surprises me? I did not tell you because I know my son. I know my son better than I wish to."

"My honour displeases you?"

"Honour is the last refuge of a fool!" his father snarled. "Honour is the excuse for traitors to betray and for cowards to take heel! This is honour!" He jabbed one bony forefinger at the men surrounding. "Your family! Your class! Your faith! These things make you honourable, no more! If you do not understand that, then your honour is no more than ashes in your mouth, and blood on your hands."

"I will challenge, my Lord," Lord Tymeth said coldly. "I have no wish to, but my brother has been slain. Family honour, my Lord."

"Indeed," said Great Lord Aystin Nyvar, coldly. "But a challenge can be averted. I have had word from our friend the Great Lord Kumaryn of Valhanan. He has heard Sashandra Lenayin is responsible for this death, not my son. I see no need to disabuse him of the notion."

"It makes no difference," Lord Tymeth replied. "I know the truth, and the truth cannot be . . ."

"It makes all the difference!" Lord Aystin snapped. "Have you heard nothing that has been said? We must present a united front to the king! Honour is to be found in advancing our cause, not squabbling amongst ourselves like . . ."

"I shall not allow my brother's murderer to escape justice!" Lord Tymeth retorted, his jowls reddening with rage.

"If it's justice you want, Tymeth," Lord Arastyn said calmly, "then you'd best keep your mouth shut. Master Jaryd was within the king's justice, your brother was not."

Lord Tymeth stared at him, too furious to speak.

"Who's going to challenge me?" Jaryd said angrily. "You, Lord Tymeth? You're almost too fat to walk, let alone fight. What would you do, sit on me?"

"I challenge on behalf of my nephew Pyter!" Tymeth yelled. "He's equal a swordsman to you and only too eager to see your head on a pike, I assure you, Master Jaryd!"

"Enough!" Great Lord Aystin yelled, struggling from his seat. "Enough with this . . ." and he broke into a fit of coughing. Men came to his sides, holding his arms to keep him from falling. Jaryd watched as coughs racked his father's frail body. He did not feel much emotion beside anger. The coughing passed, leaving Great Lord Aystin limp in his chair like an empty shell. "There shall be no challenge," he rasped, weakly. "Sashandra Lenayin shall bear this accusation. My son shall vouch for the truth of it."

He looked up, his sunken eyes watery and pale.

"You want me to lie?" Jaryd asked incredulously.

His father wiped his lips with a bony hand. "Bright as a bonfire, this lad."

"The Falcon Guard were there too! You can't get all of them to lie! Soldiers spread gossip worse than housewives!"

"Boy's got a point," said Lord Arastyn.

Great Lord Aystin waved his hand. "Gossip, there's always gossip. Gossip also says that Prince Krystoff never died, that he turned into a great grey wolf and can still be heard near the Hadryn border, howling at the moon. It's what *we* say that matters; the king can't act on gossip. Sashandra Lenayin killed Reynan Pelyn. Didn't she, my son?"

Ten

UPON THE LATE AFTERNOON RIDE out to Spearman's Ridge, a sharp wind began from the north and cloud formed, as if out of nowhere, rolling in a dark, swirling mass above the hills. Riding homeward at a moderate gallop, Sasha fancied the air smelled of rain, cold and gusting, as the trees shifted and groaned uneasily in the thunder of her passing.

Returning home, she unsaddled and washed down the colt, arranging feed and checking all over. She then saddled a filly, and was riding it past the house in the darkening, blustery afternoon, when she saw Kessligh leaning upon the fence about the vegetable patch. She steered past the vertyn tree toward him.

"Where is Aiden?" she asked.

"Walking. His legs needed stretching."

"If I'm to make Rathynal, I must leave tomorrow," Sasha said shortly. "You'll be leaving too?"

Kessligh said nothing. He looked at her, with wry consideration. Then . . . "Be quick with the ride, we've some exercises before sundown and it's about to pour."

"She needs a good gallop," Sasha said darkly, patting the filly's neck as the young horse fretted and tossed, smelling the rain in the air. "Are you leaving for Petrodor?"

"Quick, I say," Kessligh said, with a hard edge to his eye. "You're underdone yourself."

Sasha glared. "Fine," she snapped, and kicked with her heels. The filly shot off across the lower slope with a startled snort, straight for the path to the road.

The rain began even as she reached the foot of Spearman's Ridge, light specks of moisture that stung in her eyes as she turned back for home. The filly's condition seemed good and so she held to a fast gallop for a long stretch up the winding incline she had come. The rain grew heavier, stinging her face, and she held a careful line through the fast corners, knowing well where the road could become treacherous for the unwary. Soon she was partly drenched, and rivulets of water ran across the road in little streams.

The road remained rough where Kumaryn's force had ridden, hundreds of hooves churning the surface. They had camped last night upon the fields above Baerlyn and then departed the following morning. Lord Kumaryn, she suspected, would head straight for Baen-Tar—already the other lords would have gathered for feasting, games and celebrations before the serious business began. She had little interest in arriving so early herself. Some more time with Sofy would be nice. The extended company of so many nobles and lords would not be.

Predictably, the rain stopped. Sasha wasn't fooled—approaching northerly weather in Lenayin was always as such, first some showers, then a break, and then a torrential downpour to send even the snails scurrying for cover.

She returned the second horse with due attention to its condition, then descended from the stables to find Kessligh waiting with a pair of stanches, his own banda padding already strapped to his torso and thighs.

"High defence," he told her as she strapped on the banda. There was an unusual urgency to his manner and a grimness beyond even his usual, hard discipline. "You jarred your arm defending from your horse at Perys—that's partly balance and partly upper body strength. A girl needs to work on it extra hard."

Sasha shook her head impatiently as she tightened the straps. "It was bad balance, I wasn't set . . ."

"Sasha," Kessligh said firmly, "strength is the foundation. *Hathaal* is not all of svaalverd, even the greatest serrin female fighters could not escape strength . . . *elsa'as hathaal*, strength within form. Lenay men waste time building power for power's sake . . . a svaalverd fighter must build strength and flexibility as the *demarath alas'an hathaal*."

Sasha fed the torso straps about her back. "I'm as strong as I need to be for what I need . . ."

"Speak Saalsi," Kessligh instructed. "You're tripping your tongue already."

Sasha took a deep breath, trying to order her thoughts. "I have sufficient power across the dimensions," she said . . . or thought that she said. So many words in Saalsi had multiple translations depending on context. "I cannot master all things simultaneously . . . I need to focus my training or . . ."

"Focus is manifold," Kessligh replied, in far more fluent and commanding Saalsi. "You separate the inseparable. All is one. I have only ever taught you one thing. Draw it into your centre. Find the symmetry. You'll find that each new thing I teach is not truly new, only a variation of that one thing which you already know."

Sasha frowned as she finished her straps. Gave a yank of hard leather upon the cold, wet shirt beneath. Confusion aside, Saalsi described the svaalverd far better than Lenay ever could . . . or Torovan, for that matter. A word could be one thing, or it could be another, with a subtle shift of contextual grammar . . . just as a svaalverd stroke could be many things, either offensive or defensive, depending on the slightest slide of a foot, or the angle of a wrist to the hilt and blade. Saalsi forced her to think, to consider every word. Sometimes she thought that was also Kessligh's intention.

They began with a series of high offensive combinations, Kessligh attacking with rare speed and fury. Sasha defended each with a rapid retreat and flashing stanch, occasionally feinting or misdirecting to a sidestep for the offensive counter . . . yet rarely, today, did her counterattacks find success. Always Kessligh's strokes found the limits of her high arm extension, straining her shoulders as her arms struggled to hold their form above her head. Once, she simply lost the grip with a hard impact, the stanch snapping back to clip her skull as she ducked. Another blow caught her a glancing strike on the forearm as she hissed in pain and clutched at the bruise. The next time an attack came from that quarter, she was ready with a hard slash and counter . . . yet Kessligh's own reverse caught her hard across the middle with a lightning *thud!* upon the banda that drove breath from her lungs.

"You overcompensate," he told her in hard, calm Saalsi. Wind whipped the untidy hair about his brow, as wild as the rugged lines of his face. "You know that's your weakness. You overcompensate and leave your opposing quarter unguarded. A good fighter or a lucky fighter may find that opening and split you. If you were less lazy on the arm strength, you'd be better."

Sasha breathed hard, regaining her composure as she leaned upon her stanch. "If I build too much shoulder strength," she said through gritted teeth, "I get stiff. Stiffness is the surest way to limit my extension . . ."

"*Bhareth'tei*, not *bhareth'as*," Kessligh said. "You're implying the theoretical, this is practical." Sasha rolled her eyes in exasperation. "Combat is the place where the unlikely becomes probable," he continued. "You do not think your weakness great, yet I exploit it even now. Few soldiers ever see the stroke that kills them. Once more."

The resulting session gave her a whole new set of bruises and the very nasty suspicion that Kessligh had been going easy on her, even during her better bouts against him in the past. Certainly he'd warned her of the need to improve her high extension for a long time, but she could not recall him having exploited it so ruthlessly before. And she'd thought she'd been approaching his standard. It was time, it seemed, to think again. Like on so many things, of late.

Finally her late swing barely intercepted a slashing cut that collected her arm and cracked the left side of her head. She stumbled to one knee, clutching a hand over her ear, as her head rang like the inside of a great temple bell. Kessligh, crouching opposite, held her shoulder to be sure of her balance. When she did not fall, he stared into her eyes, drawing her attention.

"Sasha. Sasha, are you well? Focus on me." She tried, though it hurt. She brought the hand away from her ear and looked at it. There was blood on her fingers, though not much. A small cut. Kessligh's perfunctory glance proved as much. "Slow and sloppy, that's what happens when your shoulders get tired so quickly. Watch my fingertip."

She focused on it, as he moved it closer, then further back, then side to side. Her bruise throbbed in a familiar, straight line where the stanch had struck. High defence was difficult to practise without helms. Sometimes, they'd used them . . . but svaalverd fighters rarely wore such restrictive armour in combat. Mostly, they were careful and knew each other's capabilities well enough to avoid injury. Mostly.

"Stand up." She did, and found her balance was good. In fact, there was little, if any, dizziness. It just hurt. Kessligh saw as much, grimly. "You always had a thick skull," he said. "Now run. To the ridge and back."

Sasha glared at him. "In a moment."

"In combat, there are no moments to choose. Now."

Sasha seriously considered hitting him. It wasn't the first time. Then, as now, she refrained . . . if for no other reason than she was highly unlikely to connect. And fist fighting was one thing she could never afford to do with bigger, stronger men. Kessligh's expression was utterly unsympathetic.

"Fine," she snarled, turning away to unstrap her banda. Once done, she flung it away and set off running gingerly across the slope as the wind howled across the open, wet grass, and the horses snorted and galloped nervously within the enclosure.

The rain began before she'd even reached the steepest part of the ridge path. Trees shrieked in protest as the wind roared and water fell in great, enveloping sheets that quickly drenched what little of her clothing was not already wet. Sasha gritted her teeth and slogged slowly up the steepening path, feet quickly soaking within her boots, avoiding the slippery rocks and mud. Her head ached with each struggling step, her vision blurred with pouring water, and she cursed Kessligh with every gasping breath.

The rock atop the ridge was shining wet beneath blasting, sideways sheets of rain. Sasha paused a moment upon the edge of the hilltop clearing, gasping for air . . . and could not help but marvel at the raw power of the storm, the trees bending and thrashing like wild things, the howling roar of rain and wind that obliterated all view of the surrounding hills. There was a loud crack as a branch broke. Then a sudden boom and rumble of thunder that made her jump and sent a new chill through her soaked, cold limbs . . .

She made a fast spirit sign to her forehead and turned back the way she'd come. Despite the blinding rain and slippery path, she knew this trail well. She descended fast, taking her weight upon each pounding, downward impact with practised skill. A brilliant blue flash lit up all the blackened sky, followed by a booming, bass rumble that nearly stood her hair on end. She increased her pace as the path dropped yet more steeply, hurdling one intervening outcrop with a downward rush . . .

Her ankle twisted in a flash of pain, and suddenly she was falling, crashing and rolling downslope, a tangle of sliding earth and mud, her leg hit a tree, spinning her about as the ground fell from under her . . . and she crashed painfully into a harsh tangle of bushes. For a moment, she just breathed and hoped she hadn't hurt anything worse than her ankle. Unfolding herself one limb at a time from the bushes, it didn't seem so.

Cold, muddy, bruised, drenched and with a throbbing head, she was now in quite possibly the foulest mood she could recall since her worst childhood tempers in Baen-Tar. Some achievement. Thunder boomed and rumbled in nearby displeasure. She hauled herself gingerly to her feet and hissed in pain at the weight on her right ankle. So now she could barely walk. Just wonderful.

Limping down the slippery path took an age. Moving slowly, and trusting one foot with all her weight, she had to search for secure footing as water poured down the path and any smooth surface became treacherous. Twice, she slipped again, once sliding several strides on her backside, accumulating yet more bruises. Finally, at the bottom of the steepest slope, the rain and wind eased somewhat . . . but she was now shivering with cold.

Worse, her excellently crafted boot had ceased to fit her right foot snugly and now every step was agony. Sasha sat down to remove it and found the ankle swollen and ugly. Limping onward, her bare foot quickly chilled in the mud and water.

The hillside was darkening fast as she emerged from the ridgetop treeline onto the vast, grassy shoulder, the blackened sky quickly losing whatever daylight it had retained. Here on the southern slope, the northerly wind merely gusted and swirled. The house itself remained distant yet, a small shape in the gathering gloom beneath the spidery vertyn tree. There seemed to be a light at the rear and one at the stables. Kessligh, she hoped, had taken in the horses.

Then there came the unmistakable shape of a galloping horse and rider along the lower fence. It rounded the corner post and came straight for her. Sasha recognised the horse—Terjellyn, with his familiar, elegant gait. She did not stop limping.

Kessligh reined Terjellyn to a halt before her. "Bad?" he asked her from that height, eyeing her limp and the boot in her hand. Sasha kept moving, ignoring both horse and rider. Kessligh held a hand down to her. "Come on, get up." And stared in blank disbelief as Sasha continued limping straight past him, eyes fixed on the distant house with grim determination.

For a moment, Kessligh sat in his saddle and watched her. Sasha thought he might simply ride back and leave her to finish the journey alone. She didn't care. Strangely, at that moment, she didn't care about anything. Movement behind her, then, as Terjellyn trotted easily to her side.

"Sasha, you'll make the ankle worse." A calm, matter-of-fact statement. No alarm. No concern. Sasha felt a spark of fury. She limped on, relishing the pain each cold, shivering step caused. "With treatment, it might only trouble you for a few days. But if you keep walking on it, that could be longer. If you need to fight, you won't be able to."

Always the practical concern. Always worried about her "role" as his uma. Always interested in what she could do for him, no concern for what she wanted herself. She kept limping. She'd reach the house herself if it were cause for amputation.

"Sasha, don't be a damn fool." With tired irritation, now. No anger. He didn't care enough to be angry. She was just another strategic exercise to him. A project for his beloved Nasi-Keth. "Sasha? I'm warning you, get up on the damn horse. I don't have time for this childish nonsense."

She limped onward. Behind, there came a light thud as Kessligh leaped from the saddle. Footsteps approached, then a hand grasped her shoulder, hard, pulling her about with precious little concern for the ankle. Pain stabbed, and Sasha swung at him in blind fury . . . and struck a glancing blow to his head as he ducked, grabbing that arm. She tried to rip her arm clear, lashing with her left fist, which caught him squarely in the mouth. He spun back, still grabbing her arm, twisting it as she was yanked off her feet, scrambling to her knees then as Kessligh wrenched that arm behind her, trying to immobilise the other arm now.

Sasha's left hand had found the knife in her belt before she could think, pulling it free . . . but Kessligh abandoned her right arm to take the left instead. She tried to slash clear, but a sudden twist and pressure on her elbow threw her face down on the grass and rolling onto her back, the left arm now painfully beneath her and Kessligh's own knife at her chest in lightning, dangerous reflex. Sasha stopped struggling, her uman's knee in her stomach, knife blade hovering with a clear, obvious line to her throat. There was blood on his lower lip, which was cut and appearing to swell. His eyes were dark and dangerous in the cold, windswept gloom.

"Go on and do it!" Sasha yelled at his face. "Go on and waste the last twelve years of your life! Serve you bloody well right, that would!"

Kessligh blinked at her, shock rapidly replacing deadly instinct. He threw the knife away, as if suddenly discovering it were a poisonous snake. Took a deep, gasping breath, and another. It was a look Sasha had never seen before. Fear. The sight of it gave her a surge of vicious satisfaction. Kessligh released her and moved back, still kneeling.

"Some uman you turned out to be!" Sasha snarled at him, retrieving her arm from behind and struggling to a seat. Still the knife was in her hand. "The first one gets killed when you're not looking and then you nearly do the second yourself!"

Anger blazed in Kessligh's eyes. "Sasha . . . you stupid, contemptible idiot!" He was *really* angry now. She liked this much better. "*Never* draw a blade on me! I've warned you many times, never surprise me like that! I have no safe reflexes, Sasha! They're all dangerous! All of them!"

"You're never to blame for anything, are you?" Sasha retorted, far, far beyond any semblance of self-control. "Godsdamn it, you're always accusing *me* of immaturity. I have twenty summers and I *know* I'm not perfect! When's it going to dawn on *you*, Master Swordsman?"

Kessligh stared at her, incredulously. "What in the nine hells are you . . . ?"

"You've never thought about anyone but yourself in your whole blasted life, have you? You didn't ride out from Petrodor all those years ago to save the poor, suffering Lenay people—you did it for yourself! Yourself and your own stupid, blind conviction that your view of the world is all powerful!

"You didn't save Lenayin because it was the right thing to do! You wanted payment! And you took it! First you took my brother, the person I loved most in all the world, and then when it got him killed, it's suddenly my turn!"

"Don't you *ever* suggest I never cared for Krystoff!" It was as close as Kessligh had ever come to genuinely yelling at her. "I loved him like a son!"

"And why is it that you never had your own real sons? Why not inflict this destiny upon your own flesh and blood? Why do it to someone else's?"

"Because it's not the Nasi-Keth way!" He stared at her, kneeling on the lower slope, seeming torn between anger and consternation. Then he put both hands to his hair, as if to tear out several great handfuls. "Gods blast it, Sasha, what do you *want*? I gave you the life you wanted, didn't I? You were *miserable* in Baen-Tar, you swore *anything* would be better than that life! Deny to me that you don't love it here?"

"I never thought I was a pawn in one of your damn power games!" she yelled at him. "You never told me it was all a set-up!"

"I've tried to tell you so many times," Kessligh continued, with increasing forcefulness, "there's no easy choices in life! Your father is king and he suffers for it daily! Damon is a prince, yet he fears the weight of that responsibility! I chose the Nasi-Keth, for they seemed to offer the best chance of escape from the many hardships and terrors of human life.

"And you . . . you had the choice between a princess of Lenayin, or uma to a senior Nasi-Keth. You chose me. And I put it to you, my uma, that you have had precious little cause for complaint until now. Damon has suffered far worse than you—all your siblings have. Royalty has its responsibilities and hardships, but you . . . you were born for this—running about in the wilds, rearing horses and learning svaalverd. It's in your blood; you'd choose this life whether I was your uman or not. Did you seriously think it would go on being perfect forever? There's always a trade, Sasha. Always. Not even you can escape it."

"You lied to me!" Sasha yelled at him. It wasn't fair that he should start making sense, now of all times. He couldn't be right. She wouldn't let him. "You never told me what it was all about! I didn't volunteer for your blasted war!"

"You did," said Kessligh. Rain plastered hair to his brow. Blood trickled a slim rivulet to the point of his jaw. His eyes were as grim and as penetrating as Sasha had ever seen them. "If you think hard, you'll even recall the day."

Sasha stared at him. Recalling, suddenly, the eyes of Master Daran, fixed upon her with a similar, grim contemplation. She'd been curled on her bed in her Baen-Tar chambers. The Master himself had attended her chambers, after she'd attacked the maid posted there previously with a knitting needle and drawn blood. Stray shards of glass had crunched beneath his foot, where the remnants of the fitting mirror had escaped the maids' brooms. Several other items of her chambers' furnishings had disappeared after she'd smashed them, or tried to. She'd been restrained, and slapped, and forcefed her dinner until most of it had ended on her face, in her hair or up her nose.

Eventually all the fury, and all the urge to break and to smash and to vent her despair upon any person or object within reach, had dissipated, and left her drained, weak and vacant. Krystoff was dead, and her life was over. And so she had sat on her bed, watched over by Master Daran, the senior court official in whose meticulous hands had rested the education and deportment of all the royal siblings. Master Daran had brought in his notes and papers, and had worked at her desk with a scribble of ink and quill, positioned precisely between bed and door. Occasionally he had glanced her way, to find she had not moved. Occasionally he had tried to talk, and to reason, to no result.

Then, Kessligh had entered. Sasha recalled her mild surprise. She could not recall Kessligh ever having entered her chambers before. He was a god-like figure of the barracks and the training hall, he did not belong in such mundane places as little girls' bedrooms. He had asked Master Daran to leave them. Then he'd taken the chair Master Daran had been sitting on and carried it to her bedside, all resplendent in uniform purple and green, with squeaking leather boots and a cloak that was almost a cape.

He'd sat upon the edge of the chair and leaned forward, with elbows on knees. His expression had been very sombre and very subdued. Sasha remembered the wash of relief that it had been Kessligh who'd come and not one of the others. Not one of the stupid jesters with their silly shoes and sillier hats, with bells and whistles and stupid tricks to try and cheer her up. Not one of the matrons, with their commanding, "motherly" presence, to which she was somehow supposed to respond in some fit of feminine empathy. And certainly not big brother Koenyg, who had never particularly liked Krystoff, and could certainly never replace him. She'd looked at his rough, uncompromising face, and had known that, unlike the others, he would always take her seriously. Here was a man who would never lie to her. Would never baby her and coddle her with soft lies and half-truths. Here was a man to whom her slim, remaining sanity could cling to.

"I offered to take you as my uma that day," Kessligh said, above the hissing rain and distant, rumbling thunder. "I told you what that would mean. I said that you would become Nasi-Keth and that your future would belong to them. And when you agreed too hastily, I left you to think about it for seven days. On each day, I explained it to you again. I *told* you, Sasha. And you agreed. Had you stayed where you were, I think it quite likely you would have given up hope and died."

"I didn't . . ." There were tears in her eyes. Suddenly, she was back in her room in Baen-Tar and could feel the leaden, oppressive weight of dark stone all about. The grief and despair were as fresh as before in overwhelming intensity. "I didn't think I'd have to kill people! I didn't think so many people would hate me!"

Kessligh leaned forward intently, his expression incredulous. "Sasha, you picked that fight against the Hadryn all by yourself! I warned you what would happen! *Now* you decide you don't like the taste of blood? What's the matter with you? What do you really *want*, Sasha? All the rest of this is manure. What do you *want*?"

Sasha's face contorted in grief. "Why are you leaving me?" she barely managed to sob, as composure left her completely. "I can't do this alone. I can't abandon the Goeren-yai. And now you're going to leave me, and I can't do this on my own . . ."

Emotion struggled to find purchase in Kessligh's eyes. He grabbed her and hugged her close as she sobbed upon his shoulder in the pouring rain upon the sodden, darkening hillside.

"There's a war coming, Sasha," he murmured in her ear as she clung to him, desperately. "The Nasi-Keth must be strong, for only we can find a middle way between two opposing sides. Yet the Nasi-Keth in Petrodor are divided and weak. I must return to them. And one day soon, you must join me there, for I cannot do what needs to be done without you.

"And yet, when I took you as my uma, I swore that I would give you the freedom to walk your own path." He released her and took her face in both hands, to stare firmly into her tear-blurred eyes. "Walk the path, Sasha. Go to Baen-Tar. Reason with your father and brother. Save that idiot Krayliss's neck, if you can.

"When the Nasi-Keth spread out from the Bacosh hundreds of years ago, they thought to bring their enlightenment to all human lands, not by force but by reason. I knew that when I took Krystoff as uma, and I knew it when I took you. Don't be angry with me. I love Lenayin. I owe much to Lenayin. When I rode here from Petrodor as a young man, I swore that I was doing it not so that Lenayin could serve the Nasi-Keth, but so that the Nasi-Keth could serve Lenayin.

"I have taught you as best I can, Sasha. You have surpassed my wildest hopes." Sasha could only stare, disbelief joining grief upon her face. "I have given so much to Lenayin, but now, I find I have no more left to give. But you do. Whatever you set your mind to, you can achieve. It is your gift. Be very careful what you set your mind to, for not all achievements are great. But know also that you make me proud beyond words."

Sasha embraced him again, and sobbed some more. Kessligh held her. They were cold, and wet, and shivering in the gathering darkness. And yet, despite the fear and grief, Sasha knew that she had not been betrayed. That, for the moment, was enough.

They had been riding for three days and Daryd did not know where they were. The scout that the man Jurellyn had sent to guide them rode ahead, keeping to small horse trails that sometimes seemed to vanish in the undergrowth. It was raining now, a steady, miserable downpour, and in places the mud sucked at Essey's hooves like a live thing. It was lucky, Daryd thought, that he always rode prepared, even about the fields of Ymoth. Otherwise, he wouldn't have brought his and Rysha's cloaks, which now kept the worst of the rain and chills off their heads. But Mama always warned them of how fast the weather could change and he never rode out without a cloak in the saddlebag.

Thoughts of his parents made him more miserable still. He did not know if they or his brothers and sisters were still alive. The wet saddle was chafing his thighs and his back was sore, but he dared not complain. Behind him, Rysha was no doubt suffering even worse—she was a good enough rider, but not as good as him. Also, she wore a dress, which had to be pulled up for her to sit properly astride. Her legs had been chilled, until the scout had given her a spare pair of his own pants to wear under her dress. She rode with them now all bunched up, her feet lost in the long, trailing pant legs as she clung to Daryd's back.

The scout's name was too difficult for him and Rysha to pronounce, so they just called him the scout. Daryd thought he might be from Tyree, but he wasn't certain. The scout had led them over the Aralya Range, which had been exhausting and treacherous. Always the scout had seemed nervous on that path and several times had led them off the trail to hide in the forest as riders had passed going the other way. The scout seemed to have very good eyesight and had ridden ahead of them a lot to make sure they weren't surprised. Now that they were down on the flat once more, he stayed close and made sure they didn't get lost on the narrow trails. Or maybe they were lost, Daryd thought. The scout didn't appear to be lost, though. He always seemed to know which way to go.

"Daryd, I'm hungry." Daryd reached into his pocket and pulled out a handful of berries the scout had given them. He gave them to Rysha.

"Here, be careful. Don't drop any." She didn't. They had better food, for proper meals, but these were good for snacks, and the scout was good at finding them growing wild. The forest here was thick and, despite his wet clothes and aching muscles, Daryd thought it very beautiful, even in the rain. The pine trees seemed to be taller here and the spirits that lived in such trees would be great and majestic. He wondered if the trees would keep getting taller all the way to Baen-Tar. Maybe they'd be so tall in Baen-Tar, he'd barely be able to see their tops.

The berries tasted funny, but Rysha ate without complaint. Rysha had barely complained all trip, not even when the rain had started and her legs had chilled. Daryd had been amazed, and still was. She used to complain about *everything*. She'd slept against his side on the hard ground at camp and had sometimes squirmed and whimpered in her sleep. But, come the next morning, she'd risen bleary eyed, eaten breakfast and even insisted on helping Daryd to saddle and feed Essey. It had been enough to freeze all of Daryd's own complaints on his lips. If Rysha was not complaining, certainly *he* was not allowed to.

"Daryd," she said after a while, as the rain was easing. "Why are we going to Baen-Tar?"

"To meet King Torvaal," Daryd explained. "King Torvaal can send armies to fight the Hadryn."

"But what about Lord Krayliss? Auntie Sedy says Lord Krayliss is Lord of Taneryn and that he's our friend."

"Papa says Lord Krayliss is just a big bag of wind," Daryd replied. "Lord Krayliss says he's a relative of the Udalyn, but he doesn't do anything. Papa says he's not really interested in helping us, he just says that he is, so that people will like him."

"But why doesn't he do anything? If he was really a relative, he'd help us."

"Taneryn's a different province, Rysha. They speak Taasti, there . . . and a few other things I can't remember. They worship the spirits differently. Papa says they don't really know very much about the Udalyn. They haven't really seen us for a hundred years. And Taneryn's not very powerful, and not very rich, not like the Hadryn. So Lord Krayliss just makes a lot of noise, but he couldn't really help us if he wanted to."

"What language does the king speak?" Rysha asked, as Daryd ducked a low, wet branch.

"Lenay. Everyone around the middle of Lenayin speaks Lenay, like the scout."

"It sounds funny."

Daryd smiled. It felt good to smile. He'd barely smiled in three days. "Probably we sound funny to them, too."

"*You* sound funny," Rysha retorted. "I don't." Then, "Is the king a Verenthane?"

"All the big nobles and royals are Verenthanes," said Daryd. "Taneryn's the only province where they're not."

"I don't like Verenthanes."

"How do you know that?" Daryd challenged. "You've never met any Verenthanes."

"The Hadryn are Verenthanes," Rysha objected. "They call us nasty names because we're not Verenthanes too, I heard Auntie Sedy say so."

"The Hadryn don't count," Daryd said firmly. "Even lots of other Lenay Verenthanes don't like the Hadryn." A thought occurred to him. "I think the scout might be a Verenthane."

"Do you think?" Rysha sounded unhappy at the prospect.

"Well, I can't tell if he's Goeren-yai. So he might be Verenthane. Why don't we try and ask him?"

"No, Daryd, *dooon't*," Rysha complained. Finally, a real Rysha whine. Daryd grinned.

"Papa says King Torvaal's a good man," said Daryd, changing the subject. "He's done nice things for the Goeren-yai before. I'm sure he'll help us, if we ask him."

They ate a lunch of bread and dried meat by a small stream that rushed and gurgled from the recent rain. The birds were different here, Daryd noted. Little blue and black bobtails flittered and chirped around the streamside bushes. Yellow flower birds snapped at insects above the rushing water. Some small, plain brown birds with long beaks pecked at things on the water surface near the streamside, where the flow was not as fast. The only birds Daryd recognised were the black and green wood ducks that swam further downstream, where a big, rotting log had formed a still pool behind a dam.

The scout saw him watching the birds and tried to name them for him. Daryd managed some of the names, but others he couldn't pronounce. The scout had perhaps thirty summers, Daryd reckoned—not as old as Jurellyn had been. He was quite clean for a scout or woodsman, too, with short hair and well-mended clothes. He washed every morning and after meals, and even put some funny-smelling paste on his teeth after dinner. The more Daryd thought about it, the more he thought the scout was probably a Verenthane. He'd heard that Verenthanes liked to keep clean, and this man had no rings, braids or tattoos whatsoever.

At midafternoon, the scout took them off the narrow trail and into the forest. They stopped behind some undergrowth where the scout gestured for the children to stay with the horses and be quiet. He then disappeared down a shallow hill. Daryd stood guard while Rysha supervised the horses as they grazed on some wild grass. It felt different, to put a hand on his knife hilt and pretend to be a real warrior. He'd seen real warriors fight now, and he'd seen them die. He'd always been frustrated by childhood, but now he found himself longing for that childish innocence. Back then, he could be a real warrior any time he liked, just by imagining. Now, no matter how hard he pretended, he remained just a little boy far from home, cold, lonely and frightened.

It was not long before the scout came quickly back up the hill, but now he had some men with him. These certainly *were* Goeren-yai men, all five of them, with long hair, earrings and the left side of their faces covered by the spirit-mask. They stared at Daryd and Rysha as they approached, like men creeping up on some rare and magical animal. They spoke amongst each other, with wonder in their voices, and Daryd heard the word "Udalyn," over and over. The strange men made him anxious, but the scout seemed to trust them.

"Friend," the scout said in Edu—the one Edu word he'd been quick to learn. Pointing to the five Goeren-yai men. "Friend."

Daryd nodded, warily. There must have been a village nearby, he realised. Just out of sight beyond the trees. The villagers had the look of men who worked hard, with worn clothes and hardened hands. Two of them were very big and the others, although middle size, all looked strong, even the older ones. All wore swords at their hips and knives in their belts.

"*Eyastan*," said one man, extending a hand to Daryd, a friendly smile parting his bushy beard. "*Eyastan*, Yuan Udalyn."

A greeting, Daryd reckoned. "*Eyastan*," he replied and clasped the other man's forearm. The man's smile grew to a grin. Each of the men said hello in that way. One of them seemed to ask for the Edu word for hello and repeated it over and over delightedly when Daryd told him. With Rysha they did not exchange the warrior clasp, of course, but rather shook her hand gently and patted her on the head. Rysha stood close to Daryd's side, anxious and shy.

The villagers gave them good, fresh fruit and some delicious fresh bread. The children ate and the adults began jabbering in their strange, foreign tongue, with many gestures toward the children. After a while, one went running back to the village.

"Daryd, what are they doing?"

"I don't know," said Daryd, watching the men's expressions and gestures intently. Every now and then he heard a word that sounded familiar, but he didn't know if that was because it was the same word, or just a coincidence. "These are Goeren-yai men, they'll be friendly."

He realised that he didn't even know what province they were in. Valhanan? Or was it Tyree? One of the two, he decided. Lenay was spoken here, but these men probably spoke a native tongue as well. He wished again that he could speak another language. Everyone else in Lenayin seemed to be able to.

Soon the man who had run off came back with five women. The women greeted them with as much wonder as the men and considerably more fuss. They all had long hair, a mixture of braids, loose locks and some beads and ribbons. Their dresses were coarse weave, sewn together with some light, tanned skins—without the decorative embroidery and beading he was accustomed to seeing on his mother and aunts.

The women made a particular fuss over Rysha, which Rysha seemed to find much less intimidating than she'd found the men. One woman produced a pair of child's pants and Rysha was ushered away to the privacy of some bushes to pull them on.

An older woman remained behind to look at Daryd with a beady eye, and talk with the men. Her hair was long and grey, with an important-looking topknot, and she walked with a decorated staff. The men were very polite with her. Daryd reckoned she might be a spirit talker, as the staff decorations held elements of all the spirit levels—feathers of birds from the sky, rocks from the earth, smooth pebbles shaped by water, and beads of polished wood or nuts from trees. When she hobbled close to peer at him, Daryd bowed low. And when he straightened, everyone looked pleased, so he knew it had been the right thing to do.

When Rysha returned, wearing her new pants under her dress, a new argument ensued. Some of the women seemed quite adamant about something. The men seemed more doubtful. The spirit talker just watched and listened.

Finally, one of the women turned to Rysha and smiled in that way adults did when trying to explain something to children. Daryd felt immediately suspicious. "*Endrynet chyl,*" she said sweetly. And pointed back down the slope, to where the village was surely located. "*Karamyt tervyst'al. Selysh.*"

The woman mimed putting her head down on some pillows, palms pressed together, hands to one cheek.

"Daryd, what's she saying?" Rysha sounded nervous.

"Maybe she thinks we should have a rest," Daryd said dubiously. But the woman was only looking at Rysha, not Daryd. "We must ride," Daryd said loudly, and pointed on in the direction they'd been travelling. "Baen-Tar. We must ride to Baen-Tar. King Torvaal."

They seemed to understand that, at least, for worried looks were exchanged. The woman tried again with a longer sentence, yet no more comprehensible. Her entreaty was all the more gentle and heartfelt, and again, directed only at Rysha.

"I think she thinks we should rest," Rysha said uncertainly. "I am very sleepy."

"We've no time, Rysha." Daryd's frustration mounted. "All the Udalyn will have gone behind the wall, but the wall won't last forever if the Hadryn attack properly! I heard Papa say so. We have to get the king to send help!"

The woman seemed to take Rysha's uncertainty for a good sign and took her by the hand. "*Endrynet chyl. Amath ul lysh to wayalesh tai.*" She pulled Rysha gently forward, away from Daryd.

"No," said Daryd, his alarm rising. And then he realised what she was suggesting. "No!" he shouted, a hand on the hilt of his knife. "No, you let her go! You let her go right now!"

The woman said something in alarm, a plea for the others to reason with him, while pulling Rysha onward. Rysha pulled back, frozen with fear. Daryd pulled out his knife and pointed it at the woman, his hand shaking.

"She's my sister!" he shouted. "She belongs with me! You can't have her. Let her go!"

There followed a lot of shouting, with the woman protesting, backed by several other women. Finally the bushy-bearded man intervened, impatiently removing the woman's hand from Rysha's. Rysha ran back to Daryd and clutched his arm instead. The woman looked upset, both hands to her mouth. The bushy-bearded man was saying something forcefully to the woman, in which the word "Udalyn" featured prominently. Goeren-yai men seemed to have a high opinion of the Udalyn. The threat apparently over, Daryd sheathed his knife before anyone could notice how much his hand was shaking.

"Daryd, what's going on?" Rysha asked shakily, still clutching his arm.

"Don't be scared, Rysha. I think she just thought it would be safer for you to stay here in the village with her. She was trying to protect you, I think. Mothers are like that."

"She's not my mother!" Rysha protested, upset. "I've *got* a mother!"

"I know, Rysha."

"I want to stay with you! Daryd, don't let them take me away!"

"I won't, Rysha. Shush, everything's all right." But everything was not all right, because the quaver in Rysha's voice when she said the word "mother" caused his own throat to tighten and his lip to tremble. He swallowed it, violently.

The villagers brought yet more food and some fodder to give the horses a break from wild grass. Extra fodder was packed into saddlebags and the spirit talker made an appeal to the local spirits . . . presumably to watch over them, Daryd thought. The woman who had tried to take Rysha still looked upset. Daryd suddenly found himself wondering what his own mother would be feeling. Her son and her little girl would be missing. Perhaps she'd fear they were dead, killed by the Hadryn. Suddenly, he thought he understood.

He walked to the woman and reached for her hand. She took it. "My sister," he said helplessly, pointing to Rysha as she stood by Essey, waiting to mount. "I can't leave my sister. She's all I have." He pointed to his heart. The woman's eyes filled with tears and she bent, and kissed him on both cheeks. That was when he knew for sure that the Udalyn were not the only people who loved their family. He could only hope that King Torvaal felt the same.

Eleven

DAMON MADE HIS WAY toward the lagand field. Downslope, the great tent city spread across the paddocks like a forest of pointy white mushrooms on a green hillside. Flags flew above each provincial contingent, colourful banners against a summer blue sky. The air was warm, the breeze welcome, and the hills beneath the walls of Baen-Tar were alive with colour and life. It was a wide rectangle of hillside, by no means an even surface, but the slope was overall quite gentle. Talleryn posts marked the goals, one pair at each end, with horses thundering across the intervening space, weaving and crossing in pursuit of the ball. The scaffolding caught Damon's eye—an amazing work of woodcraft, erected in just six days by Goeren-yai craftsmen. He guessed it might hold as many as six hundred people on its rowed benches.

Colours draped across different sections marked out the seats where each province's nobles would sit. The royal box was central, draped in green and purple, and flanked by several Royal Guardsmen. Serving maids made their way up and down the steps with platters of wine and food, and more crowds gathered about the firepits erected behind the scaffold, where kitchen staff served snacks and drinks, and prepared whole legs of lamb and beef for roasted lunch to come.

A pair of red flags marked the entry point for competitors, where the surrounding spectators kept clear. Damon recognised Jaryd amongst the gathered horsemen and cantered that way. Tyree men greeted him—perhaps half the Tyree team were from the Falcon Guard, including Sergeant Garys, a stout Goeren-yai man whom he knew and respected. The other half of the fourteen-men side were Tyree nobility.

"Wonderful morning for a contest," Jaryd remarked as Damon dismounted alongside. Damon had contested with the Tyree team for four days now and, somewhere along the line, "Your Highness" had vanished from Jaryd's vocabulary. Damon cared not at all. "We have Banneryd this morning, half of them are heavy cavalry. We'll have some bruises this evening."

A handler tended Damon's horse while another handed him his bundle of equipment. Damon strapped on the metal forearm guards, gazing across the field at the game in progress. "Fyden plays Taneryn," he observed, recognising the colours. "What score?" There was a scoring platform up on the scaffold, but he could not see it from this angle.

"Taneryn by eight to four, I believe. It's a long match." Disparagingly. "Perhaps they should play hourglass rules or else we'll be here till lunchtime." Under royal rules the game did not stop until one team scored ten goals.

Jaryd seemed grimmer this morning. He tightened his forearm strap now, his helm under one arm. Not quite as tall as Damon in his riding boots, but more broadly and powerfully built. Sofy had told Damon of some of the rumours circulating, that Jaryd was on the outs with his father, and there had been threats and insults traded. Jaryd Nyvar's once shiny reputation had been tarnished. Apparently, when questioned on the death of Lieutenant Reynan, he'd not been saying what some others had been wanting to hear. Damon looked across at one man in particular—Pyter Pelyn, amidst a cluster of young noble friends. Pyter had been Lieutenant Reynan Pelyn's cousin. The last four days of contest, he and Jaryd had barely spoken a word to each other.

Damon completed a count of the assembled riders, as groups of giggling noble girls gathered nearby, pointing and whispering. "We're a rider short," he realised.

"Danyth's shoulder came up sore from yesterday's fall," said Jaryd. He swiped with his hook, a shiny, curved length of wood as long as his forearm, with a wide blade like a shovel, and a long, sharp edge at the end. No question about it, Damon thought—Jaryd was angry this morning. He wondered what had happened. "I found a replacement."

"No shortage of those," said Damon. To represent one's province in a great Rathynal tournament was an honour indeed. Although, it was the tradition in such tournaments that the princes of Baen-Tar would not take one side, but rather would spread their number across the various teams of cenayin. To be royalty was to take no side. Damon was pleased to know that he, at least, had qualified on merit—he did not feel any awe of the Tyree men he rode with, except perhaps Jaryd. "Who'd you get?"

"Over there," said Jaryd, pointing toward the cluster of replacement horses, chewing and drinking from temporary mangers and water troughs. Damon looked, and saw two people astride the same horse. The first was Sofy, laughing with delight as the rider behind guided her hands on the reins and indicated when to apply the heels with a tap on the leg. Most unbecoming of a Verenthane princess, Sofy's dress was pulled up nearly to her knees and folks in the surrounding crowd were staring. Surely that could not be a man behind? Archbishop Dalryn would have his head . . .

The horse turned and Damon saw short dark hair, a lithe figure in pants and jacket, with a blade strapped diagonally to her back. He gave Jaryd a disbelieving look. Jaryd snorted and tightened his glove.

Sasha had arrived yesterday afternoon, accompanied by two male friends from Baerlyn, itself something of a minor scandal. Koenyg was unhappy that one was Teriyan, who Damon recalled from his stay in Baerlyn as a smart-mouth. The other was a gangly lad who had worked the ranch with Sasha for years.

Kessligh was not with her, and that too had sent the rumourmongers scurrying like rats in a granary. Sasha said he'd gone to Petrodor, but rumours suggested he was either dead, in hiding, riding north to do battle with the Hadryn single-handedly, or that he and Sasha had had a lover's tiff and he'd abandoned her. Some suggested she was with child and he'd left for Petrodor because his task was done. And other rumours as well, too stupid to mention.

Damon had found last night's family dinner a chore. Alythia had sent icy barbs Sasha's way and Sasha had replied with hot ones. Koenyg had asked suspicious questions of Kessligh and this Teriyan Tremel. Father had said little—a dark, sombre sentinel at the end of the table—while Wylfred had attempted to explain to Sasha why it was not proper for a young Verenthane lady to travel alone with two male companions. Only Myklas had seemed to enjoy it, the way any sixteen-year-old boy might enjoy watching dogs fight, or a carriage load of history scholars falling off a cliff.

If a strong family was the core foundation of virtue, as the Verenthanes insisted, then Damon reckoned his family's house might have all the godly virtue of a Petrodor brothel.

"I realise this is a stupid question," Damon remarked, turning to Jaryd, "but is that wise?"

Jaryd shrugged. "As the only Nasi-Keth present, she is officially the Nasi-Keth's representative in this Rathynal. Form dictates one person from each represented party should be invited to participate in the tournament."

"And that answers my question how?"

Jaryd scowled. "I had a bad opinion of her myself, once. Then I saw her swordwork with my own eyes and I came to know her at least a little, person to person. She forced me to reconsider. The audience here today is a little larger, but she deserves the chance to do the same."

Sasha had torn strips off many a young man's pride in junior lagand tournaments across the years, in Damon's memory, and people had not loved her any more for it. But the look in Jaryd's eyes suggested he was not to be argued with. As team captain, he could pick whomever he wished.

A rising gasp came from the crowd, then a roar as the Taneryn scored.

Damon wondered if Lord Krayliss himself was playing. Sasha and Sofy's horse came trotting over and Sasha leaped off, then helped Sofy from the saddle.

"You'd best prepare, M'Lady," Jaryd told Sasha, pointing to her bundled gear. "One more score and we're on."

"Do you always tuck your pants into your socks?" Sofy asked the young champion, with mild curiosity.

Jaryd looked down, confusedly. "The . . . I mean, a man's pants can become entangled in the stirrups, Your Highness. Or worse, in your opponent's stirrups, or their spurs if they wear them." He managed a mischievous smile. "A man's pants have been known to come clean off, in such an encounter."

"I should not want to see *that!*" Sofy remarked, in a tone that suggested much the opposite. "Sasha, why did you not inform me as to this most unexpected aspect of lagand before?"

"Because it's such a boring, bloodthirsty activity," Sasha replied, fastening armguards over her shirt sleeves. "You said so yourself."

"Well, perhaps one could learn to appreciate it better," Sofy said mildly, with a mischievous glance at Jaryd. "If one were educated properly."

"It's just a bunch of sweaty men on horses whacking each other with sticks," Damon said dryly. Sofy had never liked lagand. Her tastes were more refined. "Why are you boring yourself with us savages, don't you have a poetry recital to attend? A Larosan ode to how we are all but smelly undergarments dangling from the tree of life?"

Sofy scowled at him. "Sarcasm is the surest sign of savagery, dear brother," she said disdainfully. "I wish to see my sister ride, is that so uncommon?"

A tangled melee of horse came thundering by, punctuated by the yells and grunting exertion of men. Past the waiting riders, Damon caught a glimpse of wild-haired Goeren-yai men of Taneryn astride their little dussieh, their lagand hooks flailing.

"Here," said Sasha, handing Sofy her sword in its scabbard. "There's no swords allowed on the field. *Don't* hand it to a guard to mind, I'd rather you kept it yourself. In hand."

"Is it valuable?" Sofy asked dubiously, taking the scabbard with careful hands.

"It's Saalshen-forged and at least five hundred years old," Sasha told her. "Probably it could buy every horse on the field today."

Sofy pulled the blade a short way from its sheath. "Five hundred years? It looks so new!"

"Careful! Don't play with it. And for spirits' sake don't try the edge, you'll lose a finger."

"Okay, okay!" Sofy slapped the hilt back into the scabbard. "I'll be watching from the box. I made Myklas promise he'd sit with me for a while . . . he's playing later today for Baen-Tar against Isfayen, his friend Master Serys invited him."

"He's been playing for Baen-Tar province with Serys for the past four days," Damon told her.

"Well, I didn't know, okay?" Sofy pouted. "I've had other things to do. Anyhow, Myklas said he'd explain the rules to me."

"Rules, Your Highness?" Jaryd asked with a mischievous glint.

"Oh, Master Jaryd!" Sofy scolded. "Noblemen are such savages!"

"And noblewomen find it so distressing," said Jaryd, with a glance toward the clustered, whispering girls nearby.

Sofy looked amused. "Best that you tighten your belt, Heir of Tyree. I'd hate to see a young man lose his pants before such an admiring crowd." She gave Sasha and Damon each a kiss on the cheek and departed in a swirl of skirts. A pair of Royal Guardsmen followed and the crowd parted before them.

"Am I mistaken," Jaryd said uncertainly, "or was the princess flirting with me just now?"

"A princess of Lenayin does not flirt," said Damon. "Everyone knows that."

"I've heard it said that a princess of Lenayin does not fart, either," Sasha said cheerfully, pulling on her heavy gloves. "But I happen to know differently."

"Master Jaryd!" came a new, angry voice. Damon turned to find Pyter Pelyn pushing past the jostle of horses. "This is Danyth's replacement?" He pointed his lagand hook at Sasha.

"You have a problem with that?" Jaryd asked.

"You insult me, and you insult my family's honour! I'll not ride with this . . ."

"Half the Falcon Guard know what truly happened to your cousin!" Jaryd retorted. "If you'd ask them, you'd discover the truth, but no, you insist on preferring my father's lies because it suits your purposes!"

"My father also says that Sashandra Lenayin killed cousin Reynan!" Pyter snarled. "Do you call *him* a liar too?"

"Your father was not there! Neither was mine. I killed your cousin, Pyter. I killed him with my own blade as he attempted to kill Sashandra from behind like a coward! Sergeant Garys was there, he can vouch it true!"

He pointed to the sergeant, a short, thick-built man with a bushy beard and tattoos on his forehead. Sergeant Garys looked at the ground. "Aye," he said reluctantly. "On my honour, you killed him, Master Jaryd. And it was well done."

"It's a conspiracy!" Pyter fumed. There were friends at his back, now—fellow nobles all. The Falcon Guardsmen, Damon noted, gathered more to Jaryd's side. "Family Nyvar have never liked Family Pelyn, you fear us a threat to the great lordship!"

"I'd have more fear of a sick goat," said Jaryd.

"Enough!" Damon shouted, stepping between them. "This is the grandest tournament of the year! Tyree's honour is at stake. The team is chosen and we shall compete! This bickering achieves nothing."

Pyter glared at him, as if weighing the consequences of an insult to a prince's face. Then he spat and stalked back to his horse, his friends following.

Damon turned on Jaryd. "What's got into you today?" he demanded. "Are you determined to start a fight? We're at more risk now from those fools on the field than we are from the Banneryd."

Jaryd snorted and turned back to his horse, unanswering. "No matter, Your Highness," said Sergeant Garys, watching Pyter's departure with a dark stare, "we'll watch that one for you. He'll not cause any accidents without befalling one himself, I'll promise that." Several guardsmen growled agreement. The Falcon Guard were mostly *not* nobility. Even the Verenthanes among them were not overly fond of the likes of Pyter Pelyn. They had, however, appeared to come to a liking for Jaryd Nyvar.

Damon turned to Sasha. She appeared not at all perturbed by the argument, stretching her arms behind her back, gloved fingers interlaced. "It's going to get rough out there," Damon ventured.

"Good," said Sasha.

"Look, matters would be vastly improved if you just declined to take part . . ."

"Give in to those lying thieves, you mean?"

All the rationalisations, all the possible defences for Tyree's nobility flew through Damon's mind. But it was all manure and he knew it. "Yes," he said instead, with mounting exasperation. "Give in, Sasha. Just this once."

"No," said Sasha. "That's where it starts."

"Where what starts?"

"If you don't know that," Sasha snorted, "then you're the biggest fool here." And she also attended to her horse.

Taneryn scored a winning goal and paraded around the field in ferocious, fist-waving celebration. Then a herald on a white horse galloped onto the field and announced the next two sides. Damon put heels to his horse and the Team of Tyree galloped onto the field. Banneryd came out opposite, fourteen big men on big horses, holding a perfect line. Cavalry men of the Banneryd

Black Storm, as grim-faced and strong-muscled a selection of Lenay soldiery as one was ever likely to see. At their head rode Captain Tyrblanc, with a big square beard and a close-shaved scalp. He rode with a hand on one hip, straight-backed in the saddle despite his wide girth, and with barely a glance at his opposition.

Only as they drew closer did Damon recognise the man who rode second, with a Banneryd black and blue shirt and saddlecloth. It was Koenyg, as broad and strong as any of the cavalry, astride his favourite chestnut stallion.

The adjudicator waited astride his white horse with a ballskin dangling from his hook. He dropped it as the two teams lined up opposite each other, and Jaryd and the Banneryd captain dismounted to inspect it. The ball was a folded bundle of skins wrapped with twine and leather strips, about the size of a man's chest. Jaryd dug his hook into the folds and lifted, then tried the same with a hook through the outer straps and twine. Tyrblanc did the same, and both seemed satisfied. They clasped forearm to forearm, but if words were exchanged between them, Damon could not hear. Tyrblanc was the larger, and by far the more ferocious looking, but skill in lopping heads was not necessarily the same as skill in hauling the ball.

The teams then lined up abreast, facing the scaffold seating. Archbishop Dalryn stood in his robes before the royal box and proclaimed the gods' blessing upon proceedings. As that lineup dispersed, the Tyree Goeren-yai performed a chant in a tongue Damon did not recognise. The captains returned to the centre circle with several others, and the rest found their starting positions across the field.

Damon found himself starting next to Koenyg. His big brother smiled at him, the dark, knowing smile that only an older brother could manage, foreboding of future torments and humiliations.

"I'd thought you were busy?" Damon suggested, as their horses jostled and snorted, eager to be underway.

"Not too busy to teach my little brother a lesson or two in horsemanship," Prince Koenyg replied. Damon sat taller than Koenyg in the saddle, yet he knew better than to take comfort in that. Koenyg was all muscle and determination. He was Commander of Armies now, Kessligh's old title, besides his usual responsibilities as the heir—defence of the realm primary amongst them. The king made broad decisions, but where force and strategy were in question, it was up to Koenyg to turn those decisions into action. Such responsibilities were the apprenticeship that would prepare an heir for the task of kingship. There were those, however, who suggested that the king had delegated too much.

"What's she doing here?" Koenyg asked, nodding to Sasha on the far side of the field.

"Her name's Sasha," Damon said sourly. "You might recall her—little terror in a dress, always yelling?"

Koenyg gave him a whack across the stomach with the back of his hook, none too gently either. "This will be trouble for Family Nyvar," he remarked.

Damon refrained from hitting him back. It was perhaps not a great idea to hit the heir in front of more than one thousand people. "You don't sound surprised."

Koenyg gave him a sideways look as his horse danced and tried to rear. Koenyg knew everything that went on within palace walls, and many things beyond, that look said. If Jaryd had had a fight with his father, the heir of Lenayin would know.

Koenyg smiled. "You should have declared Krayliss in breach at Halleryn," he said offhandedly. "If you'd killed him there, we wouldn't have this trouble here."

"It would have cost lives," Damon retorted.

"It may now cost more lives. You've heard Lord Kumaryn tried to arrest Sasha in Baerlyn?"

"I heard."

"The great lords are relatively powerless, Damon, all save the northern three, and perhaps Krayliss. Their power comes from having their people united beneath their leadership. The others like Kumaryn are largely ignored by their own people. They insist the king needs them, but in truth it's the north we need. The north is strong, we must keep them on our side."

"At the cost of justice?" Damon retorted.

"Most likely we'll have to kill Krayliss anyway," said Koenyg. "Here or there, what's the difference?"

"Sasha didn't leave much choice," Damon replied. "Krayliss threw himself upon the king's mercy after her duel, I could hardly refuse."

"Sasha has a habit of siding with troublemakers," said Koenyg. "Best that you wise up to it, brother."

Damon snorted. "I'll not lick the north's boots just because it's convenient."

Koenyg turned a hard gaze upon him. A strong, broad face, more rounded than Damon's or Sofy's. More like Sasha, Damon thought, and their departed mother. "You will if I tell you to," Koenyg said darkly.

Damon could not think of a reply. Then the adjudicator saved him the trouble and yelled for a start.

Tyrblanc drove his horse straight at Jaryd, and Jaryd's mount shied aside. Other horses rushed the circle, but the Banneryd were better coordinated, using their horses to block while one rider leaned low from his saddle and hammered the ball with his hook. That rider wove past intercepting Tyree horses, dragging the weight on one arm and steering with the other, then a skilful switch of hands as Sergeant Garys came thundering up on his right, and hauled the heavy ball across the saddle to the protected side.

Garys ducked a forearm blow aimed at his head, jostling the Banneryd's horse, steering him away from the goals toward the outer wing as a massed thunder of horses pursued. Damon galloped to the defence, between the ball and the goals. Another Banneryd horse blocked Garys's, which reared alarmingly, and the ball carrier galloped free down the flank, to the cheers of slightly nervous spectators on the perimeter, who were pleased to see the action come close, but were making to scatter even now.

Banneryd riders formed a blocking perimeter for their man, harassing those who tried to intercept, but already a Tyree horse was coming at him from the right, and another, unnoticed, had somehow come ahead to stand unattended on the perimeter line. As the ball carrier's attention switched to his new assailant, the unnoticed rider dug in heels and accelerated up the line. The ball carrier saw, too late, and tried to switch the ball, but the charging rider leaned left-handed from the saddle as the horses slashed past in opposite directions, and smacked ball on hook so hard it tore the Banneryd's hook from his hand.

Damon was already racing in pursuit to assist, weaving past the mass of confused riders, who tried to change direction or figure out what had happened . . . and there ahead was Sasha, racing at top speed astride a middle-sized dun mare, her left arm low and behind her with the weight of the ball on her hook. She galloped right past the noses of the Taneryn contingent on the sidelines, who roared and cheered as if she were one of their very own.

Ahead, two Banneryd riders came across from deep defence to block her way . . . where were the Tyree forward blockers, Damon wondered? Then he saw them, holding back and making no attempt to make a path for Sasha. One of them was Pyter Pelyn.

Sasha swung the ball across her saddle to the right, pulled hard left, swinging her horse across and exposing her right side . . . a Banneryd rider held back, turning in a circle in case she reversed and tried to flank him. Sasha held her line, heading for the second Banneryd rider, then tried to dive between him and his comrade. It was suicide, and they converged on her, but Sasha threw a glance over her shoulder to Damon, took both hands off the reins and threw the ball two-handed off to her left.

It hit and rolled, catching both Banneryd riders wrong-footed. Damon accelerated straight for it and leaned low from his saddle to swing. He felt the hook catch, and the weight on his arm . . . and nearly slipped, his heart racing as he suddenly noticed the speed at which the grass flew past.

One Banneryd rider was on him before he could properly reseat, as Sasha blocked the other with dangerous force, deflecting one blow with her arm-guard, and returning a hard one of her own to the cavalryman's middle. Damon swung the ball across his saddle to the left hand, fending with his right, but the Banneryd's pressure was hard, forcing him across the face of the goals. Now behind, the great mass of riders was catching him. In a moment, he knew he'd be swamped.

The weight on his left arm suddenly disappeared and he turned in astonishment to see Jaryd dropping back from his left. Where the hells had he come from? The ball neatly stolen, Jaryd reined back behind Damon and tore for the goals. Two Banneryd pursuers arrived from behind, one chasing on each side. Jaryd swung the ball to his left side and, as the rider on that side tried to snatch it, he swung it back straight into the right-side man's face.

That man flailed and nearly fell, his horse falling back. Jaryd swung into a controlled collision with the other horse, gaining space and ducking a forearm swing, and then Sasha was there to backhand the Banneryd's shoulder with the back of her hook. A last Banneryd rider came in front, looking left and then right over his shoulder to try and block . . . but Jaryd feinted three, four, five times until the other man went the wrong way, and with an explosive burst of speed, he shot past, reversed the ball to the protected side and galloped across the line between the talleryn posts.

"M'Lady!" he called to Sasha as they cantered three abreast back to the centre circle. "That was a lovely steal! My compliments!"

"Says he who only beat four defenders across the line!" Sasha replied happily. She rode lighter in the saddle than most men, Damon noted, and she moved in the stirrups with almost acrobatic confidence when contesting the ball. Her eyes shone with an enthusiasm that seemed to light her up from head to toe. There were those, like Alythia, who insisted that Sasha's only motivation in being what she was, was to spite her family and peers. Damon had thought something like it himself, once . . . but seeing her now, he realised that Sasha could no more help being what she was than Alythia could, or Sofy, or Koenyg. This was where she belonged. To deny her that, because it offended Verenthane sensibilities, seemed suddenly ludicrous.

Damon saw Pyter Pelyn ahead and accelerated to intercept him.

"You ride for Tyree," he told Pyter harshly, coming alongside. "When your fellow rider needs a block to reach the goals, you provide it. Understand?"

"That rabid bitch is no Tyree comrade of mine," Pyter snarled.

"That rabid bitch is a hundredfold the rider you'll ever be!" Damon snapped. "And better yet, that rabid bitch is my sister. You call her that again, I'll mistake your head for the ball."

The following round was messier, the Banneryd continuing their formation tactics to better effect. The pack rumbled forward, men wheeling, yelling and hacking, as the northerners relentlessly pushed to the goals. A Tyree rider was unhorsed, but climbed back into the saddle apparently none the worse. Another took a side hook to the face and bled from the nose. Jaryd blocked Captain Tyrblanc in a rearing, lashing collision, and Tyrblanc retaliated with a sharp-ended hook to Jaryd's side. Jaryd's quilted tunic seemed to take the blow well, but it was illegal all the same, and Damon spared a moment's respite to glare at the adjudicator cantering nearby on his white horse, a red flag in one hand but not raised.

Things degenerated into a wild melee, men leaning from their saddles, jostling for position, gaining the ball briefly only to have it torn from their hook. One of the Falcon Guardsmen was jostled by Pyter Pelyn, nearly lost his seat, and then did so as a northerner hooked his stirrup. He crashed down and curled up, arms over his head as hooves stamped and thrashed all about. Again the adjudicator saw nothing. Koenyg then won free, with two Banneryd men for battering rams, and completed a weaving run toward the goals, avoiding attempted interceptions with tremendous skill until he flashed between the posts.

The next several rounds were all to the northerners' advantage as they scored four more times without reply. Many of the side's Tyree nobles engaged willingly enough on their own, but refused to lend assistance to Jaryd, Sasha or even Damon when they received the ball. Horses were changed, as the starting mounts began to gasp and froth. In the midst of one round, the ball flew to pieces as the twining leather snapped, and play paused for a new one to come from the sidelines.

When Jaryd returned to the centre circle following the next Banneryd score, he was fuming mad. "You're all honourless cowards!" he shouted at Pyter and his noble companions. "You wear the green of Tyree as if it were something to wipe your arses on! Fight for your honour, you motherless bastards, or by the gods I'll see your family banners thrown into the shit as carpets for the pigs through the rest of this Rathynal!"

The outburst, Damon observed, was not well received.

The following round was a series of slashing runs by one side and then the other, with the horses finding room to run as the play became more spread out. Damon had one good run himself past the cheering scaffold before getting cornered against the perimeter line and losing possession. Pyter Pelyn tried to hook the ball but missed, and two riders from opposing sides and directions came straight at each other, each rider leaning low on one stirrup with hooks ready. With typical Lenay stubbornness, neither gave way, and they collided above the ball with a violent tangle of limbs.

Garys hooked the ball, but was hacked on the arm by Koenyg, and lost it again. A Tyree man took a hard block from Tyrblanc, giving Koenyg time to wheel about, but then Sasha careened across his front, spinning her mount across the ball's rolling path, and somehow using her horse's momentum to lean low and wide and rip the ball away from Koenyg's reach. She continued the spin, reversed the ball, and shot off, dodging one northerner and then another, Koenyg cursing in close pursuit.

Suddenly Jaryd was there, blocking the heir to the Lenay throne with a vigour some men might not have dared. "Go Sasha!" Damon heard him yelling, as he followed in pursuit, and another rider came flying toward Jaryd from the side. It looked like an intercept, even though Jaryd did not have the ball . . . and Damon saw with a sudden chill through the sweaty heat that the interceptor was Pyter Pelyn.

"Jaryd, to your right!" Damon yelled. Jaryd swung about, raising an arm to block. Pyter's hook caught him about the shoulder and yanked him from the saddle. Jaryd fell with all the graceless horror of a man deliberately unhorsed, slammed hard into the turf and rolled repeatedly. Then he stopped, and did not move.

Damon swore, reined up alongside and dismounted, fearing the worst— many men had died on the lagand field, or become cripples for life. "Jaryd!" He knelt at the lordling's side and listened against his lips . . . Jaryd was breathing, so that was a start. Then his eyelids fluttered and his legs moved. That was even better. About them, other horses had stopped, the game apparently suspended. Except for one horse, that he could hear galloping hard . . . yells of warning and anticipation came from the crowd.

Damon looked up to see Sasha tearing directly toward Pyter Pelyn. She'd seen it. That wasn't good. She hit him with a back hook to the face, which sent him reeling from the saddle. That wasn't good either. Then Pyter's noble friends were after her, hooks raised with clear intent. Falcon Guardsmen set off in pursuit and a brawl erupted, horses jostling and men swinging. Three more nobles were quickly unhorsed—the Tyree nobility might have been a dab hand at lagand, but against Falcon Guardsmen they were little match in a fight.

Jaryd struggled to sit upright, wincing in pain. He tried to put weight upon his left arm and bit back a scream. Damon supported his weight, as Koenyg dismounted alongside. Nearby, the fight was breaking up. The adjudicator raised his red flag at Sasha. Sasha threw her hook at him, and would have dragged him physically from his horse had not a Guardsman intervened.

"I think it's broken," Damon said wearily to Koenyg, feeling gently at Jaryd's arm.

"It's not," Jaryd said fervently. "I've broken bones before, this isn't as bad." And nearly screamed again when he tried to move it.

"It's broken, you fool," Koenyg told him, kneeling alongside. "The way you came off, you're lucky it's not your neck." Damon could understand Jaryd's reluctance to admit it. Many breaks reset cleanly, with good medicine, splints, binding and sometimes some skilled knifework. But some did not, and men would carry those deformed limbs to their grave.

"That shit pile Pyter," Jaryd muttered, his face pale with pain. "I'll duel him. Maybe he'll find some honour with a sword in his gut."

"With that arm?" Koenyg snorted. Some more horses were riding now from the perimeter, no doubt with a healer astride, someone who knew how to move a man with broken bones.

"When I've recovered then," Jaryd insisted. "I'll kill him, you watch."

"The road you've travelled," Koenyg said sharply, "you won't live that long. Take some advice from someone in a position to know, lad. You may not care for your own neck, but if you've any concern for your family, you'll apologise to Master Pyter and never talk to my wild sister again."

"She's the one coming to my defence," Jaryd retorted, breathlessly. "You're telling me these . . . these honourless cowards are my true friends, and those who risk their own necks to ride at my side are my enemies?"

Koenyg shook his head in disgust and rose to his feet. "If you don't know the answer to that question, Heir of Nyvar," he said sourly, "then I fear for not only your future, but your family's."

The morning was overcast, with a blustery wind that blew grey, misting swirls along the valley's upper slopes. Lord Usyn Telgar, a man of the cold northern heights, did not mind the chill. He sipped hot tea from his tin cup, wrapped in his warmest fur cloak, and observed a sight of pure wonder.

Ten catapults. Great, ungainly wooden contraptions, never before used in Lenay wars. The horses that had hauled them up the length of the valley now grazed somewhere behind the tent forest on the grassy slopes beside the Yumynis River. The catapults now sat in a line across grassy fields on this, the eastern side of the river, swarmed about with labouring men.

Facing the contraptions, a vast, dark stone wall spanned the width of the valley. It stood perhaps the height of five men—too tall for the ladders. More than half of the Hadryn army were cavalry, and not equipped for such obstacles. Thick buttresses reinforced the wall at even intervals, and two huge wooden doors with welded metal binding stood thirty strides from the river's edge on this eastern side. Beneath the wall, the river surged with a roar of foam and spray—the Udalyn had diverted the mighty Yumynis to flow through a narrow channel, above which spanned the wall's arch. It was more ingenuity than Usyn had expected of the pagans. But it would not help them.

A nearby catapult groaned and strained as men hauled the two great wheel spokes, winding the rope tighter and tighter. Two men carried a heavy rock between them, muscles straining, and placed it into the sling. The release mechanism was checked and men moved away to a safer distance. An officer yelled the order and the firing rope was pulled—the catapult's safety catch released and the rope unwound with a squealing rush, hauling the long arm and sling skyward. Crack! The arm pulled up short, lurching the entire contraption nearly enough to topple it, and the huge rock continued onward, hurtling high and long toward the wall. A distant thud, as it shuddered the great wall doors, adding yet another white, splintered mark in its surface, before joining the growing pile on the earth before the doors.

A man arrived to stand at Usyn's side, a steaming cup in his hand. It was Yuan Heryd, similarly rugged against the cold, with the look of a man newly woken. Heryd had led much of the advance up the valley's length and was surely tired. It had taken a full day longer to sweep to the valley's end than Heryd had expected. Udalyn defences had been surprisingly sophisticated. The valley had many roads and trails that meandered along its steep sides, each successively higher than the last, as the slopes rose up from the broad valley floor. These were well forested, and dotted with cultivated fields, farm-houses, retaining walls, fences and watercourses.

The Udalyn had used all, in their defences. Major forces moving along the flat valley floor had confronted defended barricades blocking the best routes. Even when breached, a straight drive up the valley floor risked a flanking ambush from the height of a neighbouring slope. The valley slopes had had to be cleared at an equal pace, but that going proved even slower, as riders advancing along narrow, winding roads were shot with arrows, pelted with rocks from higher vantages, or unexpectedly ambushed by suicidally brave pagans leaping from cover to hack at horse and rider with indiscriminate abandon.

So ferocious had been their defences that, at times, Usyn had wondered if the Udalyn had made the worst miscalculation of all, and had tried to win the battle outright. The combined Hadryn companies and militia were not the untested rabble of a century ago—trade and exchanges with their lowlands Verenthane brothers had improved the quality of Hadryn horses, weapons, armour, tactics and fighting skills considerably. The Udalyn had discovered this to their loss, with barely a mailshirt or a crossbow between them. Hundreds had fallen, their bodies strewn across the roads and barricades of their precious valley.

But their sacrifice had served its purpose, as the valley cottages and farms had been emptied of both people and livestock by the time the Hadryn army had arrived. All now sheltered behind this, the great Udalyn wall, at the far northern end of the valley. Great walls of sheer rock loomed at the valley's end beyond the wall, broken only by the plummeting roar of the Yumynis Falls. The Udalyn were trapped in there. Getting them out was just a matter of time.

There was a squeal and crack as another catapult fired. "A glorious sight, is it not?" Usyn said to Heryd, his eyes tracking the rock's flight through the air. Thud.

Heryd nodded. "Aye, my Lord. Do you know your father's price for them?"

"Fifteen pieces each," Usyn said smugly. "Made and transported from Larosa itself. The Bacosh are truly masters of war. It would be a grand thing to campaign there."

"Aye, it would, for such a holy cause." Heryd's lips pursed, considering the great doors. "The pagans build well. Doubtless those doors have been reinforced behind. We may splinter the timbers, yet not break through. Worse, we litter our approach with rocks. Men may trample each other in a crush, assaulting such a space under archer fire."

Usyn stared at the doors, now clearly weakening beneath the catapults' combined assault. He had not considered Heryd's concerns. It angered him. "Why did you not say so earlier?" he said harshly.

"My apologies, my Lord," said Heryd. "I was sleeping. The terrain was difficult, I lost a hundred plus men."

"We are thousands!" Usyn said angrily. "Our friends from Banneryd are riding to assist us in Taneryn, once here they can relieve our forces from Ymoth instead, and then we shall be more. This battle must be won before the southern pagans realise what is happening! I cannot tolerate further delays!"

"Aye, M'Lord," Heryd agreed. He pointed to a spot further along the wall. "I suggest we divert half the catapults and begin a new point of entry. The stone wall shall take longer, but to guarantee a successful assault, I would like another entry point at least, perhaps two."

Usyn considered, broodingly. Udys Varan continued to speak ill words of him with the captains and nobles, he was certain of it. The Hadryn Shields were sworn by oath to family Telgar, but their captain was a cousin to the

Varans. The bulk of the army were militia, and no less capable for that, as in most of Lenayin . . . but their allegiances were divided amongst the noble families and their respective towns and regions. He had cousins and uncles amongst those serving, yet they afforded him little comfort. Some spoke angry words of Udys Varan and implied the new Lord of Hadryn weak in not dealing with him more sternly. But the soldiers respected the seasoned Udys, clearly more than the untested heir of Telgar. Usyn felt trapped, and increasingly resentful.

"Deploy the catapults as you see fit," he said finally. "Should we not also breach the wall on the west of the river?"

"No, M'Lord," said Heryd. "That would force us to divide our forces to either bank, and the pagans have destroyed the last bridge. The Udalyn have no point of exit on that side, let's keep them bottled up and not expose ourselves to a flanking assault."

"As you will," said Usyn, shortly. Heryd sipped at his tea, unruffled by his lord's tempers. Usyn regarded him for a moment. Yuan Heryd Ansyn. Family Ansyn had long been allies of the Telgars. Usyn's mother had been an Ansyn, the sister of Heryd's father. Some suggested Heryd's daughter for a match with Usyn. Usyn disliked the notion—the girl was pallid and spotty. But he wondered what her father thought. "Some of the men say that I am too young to command this effort," he said now.

Heryd swallowed his tea and shrugged. "None can choose the time of their father's passing," he said. "Family Telgar have ruled Hadryn since the Liberation. The turn was always yours, my Lord."

"Our ascension was challenged by some," Usyn said darkly. "Many Varans feel the great lordship was rightfully theirs and that King Soros made a mistake to grant it to us."

"Not I, my Lord," said Heryd, fixing him with a pale blue gaze. A big man, with blond hair beneath his helm and a heavy, honest face. "Family Ansyn has been an ally to Family Telgar since before the Liberation, and always shall be."

"And Family Varan?" Usyn asked bluntly.

"Family Telgar won the great lordship through valour in battle," Heryd replied. "Your ancestors slew many of the Cherrovan, and then many more of the traitorous pagans in the cleansing to follow. Clearly your blood was chosen by the gods to rule. None in Hadryn dispute it. Prove yourself now, my Lord, and remind them of that choice. The gods' will cannot so easily be undone."

Another catapult shot clattered and whistled. Heryd finished his tea, bowed and departed. Usyn watched him go, his fingers clenched tightly about his cup. Victory in battle, the cornerstone of all honour. He'd show that fool Varan. He'd show him the true meaning of victory.

A new presence arrived at his left elbow and he turned to find Father Celys in black robes with his staff in hand.

"My Lord," said Celys with a bow, a bald man with a thin grey beard. "My Lord, I wondered if I could have a word?"

"Of course, Father," said Usyn, turning to face him with as much lordly dignity as he could muster. He liked this part—the part where men he had known his whole life, and who had never shown him the respect he deserved, now suddenly had to bow before him and lower their eyes. "How can I help you?"

"Well, my Lord . . . there is the matter of the pagans' bodies. It is the custom of the order that even an enemy should receive a proper burial . . ."

"These are not merely enemies, Father," Usyn said coldly. "These are pagans. They spit on the rightful gods, as their ancestors spat on them during the Liberation and assisted their enemies. Their souls now descend to the fires of Loth to burn for eternity, and I say good riddance. Burn the bodies. And do it before the walls, so the rest of them can see."

Father Celys took a deep breath and swallowed hard. "Aye, M'Lord." Usyn regarded him disdainfully. His father had suspected Father Celys of defective moral character for a long time. The Bishop of Hadryn had always been more interested in converting pagans than killing them. "However, if it pleases my Lord, I would request permission to entreaty the pagans behind the wall to save their souls by conversion."

Usyn snorted. "That is your right, Father—souls are a bishop's prerogative just as lives are a lord's."

"And should they agree, M'Lord . . . would you consider a surrender?"

Usyn glared at him, lips pressed thin. His temper boiled. "We hold the Hadryn's most ancient enemies by the throat and you would beg for mercy on their behalf?"

Father Celys ducked his head. "No, M'Lord. But . . . but one would like to make contingencies, for future plans. When the walls are breached, M'Lord, there will be many more bodies to dispose of, and their souls too will be in question . . ."

"Burn them," Usyn said coldly. "Burn them all."

"Aye, M'Lord. And the prisoners, M'Lord? What of them?"

Usyn raised a thin eyebrow. "Prisoners?"

"The women and children, M'Lord." Looking up at Usyn hopefully, from beneath lowered brows. "When the holy armies reached Torovan from the Bacosh five centuries ago, they did report a great success at persuasive conversions with the women, without their menfolk there to protect them. The pagan womenfolk are good workers, we could . . ."

"There shall be no prisoners, Father Celys," said Usyn Telgar, Lord of Hadryn. "This valley is lacking in firewood, I would guess. Best that you make plans to collect some."

Twelve

SASHA WOKE EARLY THE NEXT MORNING, and did her exercises on the floor of Sofy's chambers while her sister slept on, peaceful in the wash of morning sunlight through the windows. The taka-dans woke her, however.

"I'd never thought something so deadly could look so beautiful," Sofy said from her pillows as Sasha lowered her blade. Sofy gazed with amazement. Sasha performed the last third of the defensive elia-dan, the silver blade flashing in the sunlight, finding the perfect form of foot, wrist and shoulder. Then sheathed the sword over her shoulder in one, smooth motion.

"*Da'el she'hiel alas themashel*," Sasha told her.

"Is that Saalsi?" Sofy asked, enchanted. "What does it mean?"

"Literally, 'the beauty of danger' . . . only that doesn't translate well, does it? Most Saalsi doesn't. It basically means that all dangerous things are beautiful. But serrin words rarely state things so directly."

"Oh, I'd love to learn Saalsi," Sofy sighed, rubbing her eyes. She yawned. "Are you going for a run?"

"Always," said Sasha, stretching her thighs. "Want to come?"

"You're crazy!" Sofy laughed. "What would people think?"

"I don't know. What would people think?"

"A princess of Lenayin does not run," Sofy said primly. And yawned again. "Especially not so early."

"Thank the spirits for that, then," Sasha said cheerfully. "I'd hate to be mistaken for something I'm not."

She collected Teriyan and Andreyis from their chambers in the southern guest quarters and walked with them along the grand halls, alongside balconies overlooking the southern courtyards and gardens. Groundsmen trimmed the bushes and swept the paths, and servants scurried about their early morning duties. Few of the guesting nobility had risen.

Their morning run took them on the road circuit within the city walls. Sasha pointed out the Soros Library, the Royal Guard barracks and the merchants' square, now filling with traders unloading carts of fruit and vegetables, bags of grain and racks of fowl or fish. Many of the traders were Goeren-yai and gave a cheer as they saw her pass. Sasha waved cheerfully in return.

Their run completed, she sparred with Teriyan and Andreyis in the great training hall beside the Royal Guard barracks. By now the hall was filling with soldiers, and some nobles, and the trio met with men of the Falcon Guard, who greeted them warmly. The ensuing session was lively, yet Sasha refrained from making too much of a scene. Some Verenthane soldiers, and a few nobles, gave her dark looks across the floor.

"Word is the Kradyc family's right mad with you, M'Lady," said one man-at-arms as he recovered his breathing, rubbing the bruise on his side.

"Kradyc?" Sasha asked him, lowering her stanch to a ready posture. A true svaalverd fighter was never truly resting, and the blade was always ready.

"The Ranash family. Their uncle was the adjudicator you near pulled from his horse yesterday."

"Oh, the lagand match." She shrugged and twirled her stanch. "The adjudicator was Ranash? No wonder he wouldn't give us a call."

"Master Pyter Pelyn means to take the field without us," said the grizzled corporal nearby, leaning on his stanch. He had a scar across one cheek that took half an ear and the upper side of his jaw, turning his speech to a mumble. "No Falcon Guard'll ride with the fool, not after what he did to Master Jaryd. Tyree will miss the title matches for sure."

"First time in three Rathynals," the man-at-arms sighed. "Probably Taneryn will win now, that'll make Lord Krayliss real happy."

"Is Krayliss competing?" Andreyis asked.

"No," said the corporal, "not before his trial. Might I ask when the trial is, M'Lady?"

"No idea," said Sasha, in all honesty. No one had told her. She suspected controversy on the question of Lord Krayliss's trial. Krayliss was full of bluster and determined to pick a fight. Should the trial be closed from public view to deprive Krayliss of a podium for his grievances? Or would a closed trial make the king and his lordships appear weak?

"Any idea of where the new Lord Telgar might be, M'Lady?" the corporal pressed, raising his lock-jawed mumble to carry above the yells and clashing wood of the hall. "Given neither he nor the Hadryn have come for Rathynal?"

"I don't know why you ask me," Sasha said a little testily. "No one tells me anything around here."

"Something about you being the king's daughter," Teriyan said sarcastically.

"Am I really?" Sasha gave Teriyan a warning look.

"Is it true the Hadryn are going after the Udalyn Valley?" the man-at-arms wanted to know.

"That's just a rumour, lad," the corporal said gruffly. "We shouldn't be bothering M'Lady Sashandra with rumours. Besides, Lord Usyn wouldn't dare. I'm no Goeren-yai, but I serve with plenty, and they'd never stand for it." He gave Teriyan a wizened stare.

Teriyan shrugged broadly. "We'd have to make a unified stand to stop it," he said. "Just in my part of Valhanan alone, we've got villages that have barely spoken or traded with each other for centuries, and others that still skirmish to this day, despite the king's law forbidding it. How is that rabble going to stop the lordships from doing anything?"

"You sound just like a Verenthane bigot!" Andreyis retorted angrily.

"I'm Goeren-yai, I'm allowed to," said Teriyan, putting his stanch across his broad shoulders and hooking his arms onto the ends. "I just speak the truth, lad. To find the solution, first we must recognise the problem. Otherwise we're like a man with a broken leg who refuses splints or crutches to save his pride and ends up a cripple for life." He glanced at Sasha. "That's what Kessligh always said, anyway."

"Kessligh said a lot of things," Sasha said quietly.

"Aye," said Teriyan, "he always told a person what he thought, whether it was what they wanted to hear or not. I always liked that about him. He wasn't always right, but he always tried to make a person think. Lots of Goeren-yai never liked what he had to say about them—folks never do like being told their own worst flaws, most especially when they're true. But being scared to face the truth is cowardice, I reckon. And no Goeren-yai likes a coward."

Sasha left Teriyan and Andreyis to their sparring and headed back to merchant's square—Andreyis needed as much practice as possible, and she herself found sparring against non-svaalverd fighters only so helpful. It exercised her eye, reflexes and muscles, but she knew she'd achieve more for her technique by practising taka-dans alone.

As she walked along a cobbled road through morning crowds, she thought on what Teriyan had said. "To find the solution, first we must recognise the problem." It was Nasi-Keth thinking, through and through. Teriyan was a well-read man, and had accumulated many books, a rare thing for a rural Goeren-yai. He was also one of the proudest Goeren-yai she'd ever met. Surely he was angry, and frustrated, to be saying such things at such a time. Sasha knew he had friends about the land, contacts with whom he kept in touch, as Kessligh did with his Nasi-Keth friends in Petrodor. He would be talking now with Goeren-yai soldiers and others attending Rathynal, with all these events and rumours afoot. Suddenly she was worried for him. She hoped he wouldn't do anything stupid, or get drunk and start a fight with that big, loud mouth of his.

She headed to the Garrison Barracks, where Jaryd was quartered with the Falcon Guard. It was a broad, grey stone building with several wings about a central courtyard, all teeming with Falcon Guardsmen and men of the Black Hammers of southern Rayen province.

All the provincial companies of Lenayin were required to serve six months garrison duty in Baen-Tar at one time or other . . . all save the northern companies, who were on constant watch against the Cherrovan threat and could not be spared. Such rotations helped the unity of Lenayin, it was said. What was not said (or at least not as often) was that it also under-lined how little true power the Lenay king held. The Royal Guard were his— nearly a thousand men, drawn from all over Lenayin. But they were rarely used away from Baen-Tar, lest the capital be left undefended. The Lenay throne, ultimately, had only as much power and protection as the great lords wished it to have. The great lords allowed the king to rule because the arch-bishop said the king was the gods' chosen representative in Lenayin and, more to the point, because it was better to tolerate a king in Baen-Tar than the awful, bloody squabble that would surely erupt if he were removed and the provinces fought for power amongst themselves as they once had.

Even Sasha, uninterested in the affairs of nobility as she typically was, could see that it was an imperfect arrangement at best. Such were the compro-mises that her great-grandfather Soros had been forced to make in order to sell the fractious peoples of Lenayin on the new, central power of Baen-Tar. So far, successive Lenayin kings had refrained from spending any more of the royal tax revenue on building royal armies—King Soros had known that a powerful king with enormous armies would have been opposed tooth and nail by the provinces *whatever* their newfound Verenthane fervour. The alternative would have been for the great lords to raise those royal taxes themselves . . . but con-sidering the purposes to which they would wish to put such taxes, there was no way the Goeren-yai were about to wear *that*, either. And so, what remained was a shaky agreement between the great lords and the king that if the provinces did not cause trouble, the king would not raise armies, and would instead continue to spend the royal tax on things the people needed . . . or at least were thought to need, on the rare occasion they were actually asked.

That shaky arrangement, Sasha could see more clearly of late than ever, was now being tested. It had lasted roughly a century now, a period of unprecedented peace and stability in Lenayin. Kessligh, for one, had voiced amazement that it had even lasted that long. A great wind, he'd said, would break a brittle tree. And at some point, the king would have to decide whether his own relative powerlessness was a worthwhile price to pay for stability . . .

A Falcon Guardsman admitted her to the commander's chambers with a friendly greeting, and she found Jaryd seated upright in his wide bed, dressed in a plain shirt with the sheets pulled to his middle, his left arm in a sling across the chest. A boy of perhaps ten, with sandy hair and freckles, sat on Jaryd's bedside, talking animatedly.

"M'Lady Sashandra!" Jaryd exclaimed cheerfully as Sasha entered. "Have you met my little brother Tarryn?"

"I have not had the honour," said Sasha. The boy twisted about to stare at her. "Master Tarryn, I'm very pleased to meet you. I hope you're better at staying on your horse than your brother."

Jaryd laughed.

"He was knocked off!" Tarryn said indignantly. "Pyter Pelyn did it, he never plays fair. I was just telling Jaryd, Pyter Pelyn's son Garret cheats at four-sticks! He's in some of my classes here, I never liked him."

"I'm not surprised," said Sasha and bounced onto the end of Jaryd's bed. Tarryn stared at that most unladylike act. "How's the arm?" she asked Jaryd, kneeling.

"It's not so bad," said Jaryd. His face was pale and his brown hair hung lank and unwashed, but the confidence in his tone made Sasha believe it. "The healer says it's just a small break of the forearm, he didn't need to use the knife. He bound it and put in splints for support, but it should heal clean in less than a month. The elbow and shoulder are all swollen, but that should heal too, he said."

"That's wonderful!" Sasha exclaimed with feeling. "The way you came off, I was certain you'd smashed something good!"

"He says it doesn't hurt," Tarryn said eagerly, with a mischievous smile. "He always says it doesn't hurt. He fell down some stairs once and split his head open, there was blood everywhere. Our house healer had to clean the wound with boiled wine, and Jaryd said that didn't hurt either."

"Nothing hurts after you faint," Sasha said wryly. There was a wine pitcher on the bedside table and a bowl of something that smelled strongly of crushed herbs. Sasha knew well that even with such remedies, Jaryd's arm would hurt like hell. But few Lenay men would show pain in a woman's vicinity . . . and even less so to a younger brother.

"I never did," Jaryd said mildly. "This is my third break, I've never yet fainted."

"You're pretty," said Tarryn.

Sasha blinked at him in surprise. And grinned. "Thank you very much!"

"Fenyl Harys said you were really ugly," Tarryn continued. "He said you were an ogre, and that you had a moustache and warts."

"I shaved off the moustache just this morning," Sasha admitted.

"You did not!" Tarryn laughed. "Are you really as good a fighter as Kessligh Cronenverdt?"

"Who said I was?"

"Jaryd," said Tarryn. "He said you were the best fighter he'd ever seen." Sasha raised an eyebrow at Jaryd, who shrugged.

"But Jaryd's never seen Kessligh fight," Sasha told Tarryn. "Not really. Kessligh's better than me, but I'm close." Close . . . well, that was maybe stretching things a bit, but she wasn't about to throw away her good reputation entirely.

Sasha sat on the bed and talked with Jaryd and Tarryn for a while. Jaryd seemed pleased of the company and Sasha wondered if he'd had any other visitors, besides his guardsmen. Tarryn and the Great Lord of Nyvar were the only members of Jaryd's immediate family presently in Baen-Tar, Sasha had gathered, but for Rathynal there were cousins, uncles, aunts, nieces and family allies aplenty. Tyree was a prominent province and Jaryd was possibly just a few months from the great lordship. There should have been a queue of well-wishers, friends and assorted sycophants crowding about the bed. Instead, the broad flagstone floor remained sparse and empty.

The hour bell rang to ten from the courtyard and Jaryd firmly informed Tarryn that he'd best attend to his studies. "I wish our sisters were more like you," Tarryn told Sasha as he reluctantly got up to leave. "You're fun. They're never fun."

"I'm sure your sisters are wonderful," Sasha said diplomatically, but crawled on the bed to give him a big kiss on the cheek anyway. Tarryn squirmed, and grinned, and ran off to his lessons with a wave. "He's a darling!" Sasha exclaimed once he'd left.

"Ladies have been known to think so of all the men in my family," Jaryd said mildly.

Sasha grinned and leaped across to sit beside him propped on the remaining pillows. "Even with your arm in a sling, you'll still have a try, will you?"

"A true man of Tyree never rests."

"Someone would catch us," she suggested.

"Not if we were fast."

"Are you always?"

Jaryd grinned. "Not always, M'Lady."

Sasha laughed. "I'm not 'M'Lady,' I'm Sasha."

"Sasha," said Jaryd, thoughtfully.

"Were you not offered chambers in the palace?" Sasha asked. "It's customary even for soldiers to take adjoining chambers at the palace when their families visit. For important nobility, anyhow."

"My place is with my men," Jaryd said flatly.

"I doubt your father would agree," Sasha ventured.

Jaryd snorted. "My father doubts I can make an adequate Great Lord of Tyree. He gave me command of the Falcon Guard so that I might learn better. Well, I'm certainly learning. I'm learning a great many things."

"Such as?"

"Who my friends are," Jaryd said angrily. "There are men my own age, whom I grew up with and learned to spar and ride with, all here for Rathynal and yet they've barely even said hello. They have no honour, any of them."

Sasha took a deep breath. "Jaryd . . . I admire your conviction, but . . . isn't it a little foolhardy to be picking a fight with your own father? And with all the assorted nobility of Tyree? You're going to rule these people one day, you'll need their support . . ."

"When I rule," Jaryd said stubbornly, "I'll rule in my own way, according to the values I've learned. Maybe they'll learn to like it—it can't be good having no honour in your life. Besides, you'd rather I lied, and said *you'd* killed that bastard Reynan?"

"I can take care of myself," Sasha said shortly.

"In a fair fight, I've no doubt," Jaryd agreed. "But you saw Pyter Pelyn on the lagand field. These people don't fight fair, M'Lady . . . I mean Sasha. That's what it means to have no honour. When I'm Great Lord, that's the first thing I'll teach them."

It was nearing midday when she emerged from Jaryd's chambers. She had not walked ten strides around a corner when a man in a pale green, lordly shirt emerged from a doorway ahead, a sword swinging at his hip. Clearly a nobleman. She glanced over her shoulder and found another man of similar appearance walking behind her. Damn.

More men emerged from the open doorway the first man had come from. One was tall with a gaunt, bony face and silver hair. He wore a cloak of red and gold—pure vanity, Sasha thought, for the air was not cool. That man had five companions all nobly attired, with swords at their sides.

Sasha stopped, her heart beating faster. Her right hand flexed, unconsciously rehearsing the fast reach to the hilt above her left shoulder. "Lord Kumaryn," she said, attempting pleasantry. "Have you been waiting here for me all this time?" Some spy must have seen her heading to Jaryd's chambers. The Falcon Guard may have liked Jaryd, but they remained a company of Tyree and there were bound to be some spies reporting to the lords. But Kumaryn came *himself*?

"Did you have a pleasant meeting with your new lover?" Kumaryn asked. His voice was hoarse and reedy. His blue eyes were hard with malice. There were great lords in Lenayin whom Sasha did not like, yet could not help but respect. Kumaryn was not one of them. The man was petty and vain.

Sasha smiled. "You'd like to think so, wouldn't you? Scared I'll wed him and raise heirs of Tyree as Nasi-Keth?"

Kumaryn scowled. "You'd never dare! The lords of Tyree would never stand for it!" He thought I was being serious, Sasha realised in disbelief.

"Jaryd Nyvar would be foolish to do so, my Lord," said a smooth voice at Kumaryn's side. "With this one, he'd have to always wonder if the child was truly his. I hear she's had half the men in Baerlyn, and some of the women too."

The speaker was a man of short stature. He had perhaps thirty summers, with a round face and short hair. The Verenthane star hanging from his neck was twice the size of his compatriots." That, plus his northern accent, made Sasha fairly certain of his origin.

"Please, Master Stranger," she said reasonably, "it's impolite to insult someone without first offering your name. How else will I know whom I kill?"

"If you wish to challenge," the northerner said with a smile, "then you may challenge Yuan Martyn Ansyn. I and my sword shall be waiting for you."

"Martyn Ansyn." Sasha's eyes narrowed. "Heryd Ansyn's brother, yes?"

"The very one."

Family Ansyn were Family Telgar's oldest allies in Hadryn. There was much shared blood between them, and Lord Heryd was said to have been the old Great Lord Telgar's closest friend.

"So the lords of Hadryn and Valhanan lock arms at last," said Sasha, surveying the group before her. There were two men behind her—seven in all, including Kumaryn and Martyn. More Hadryn than Valhanan, to judge from the cut of their hair and the prominence of Verenthane symbols. And too many, even for her. "What message do you have for me that it takes seven of you hiding outside the door like common cutthroats to deliver it?"

"A reminder," Kumaryn said coldly. "There are more of us than of you."

Sasha laughed. "My Great Lord, you've learned to count! Your wet nurse will be so proud!"

"It's not *our* ability with numbers that was in question," Yuan Martyn replied before Kumaryn could bristle his outrage. "You don't have your pagan rabble to defend you here."

"You threaten like a coward," Sasha retorted, her temper slipping. "If you were brave, you'd challenge. My family won't take kindly to my murder beneath their protection."

"Oh aye," Martyn said with a cool smile, "Prince Koenyg loves you well, I hear. The king has not called you 'daughter' for twelve years. The king no longer favours your pagan ways, nor your devil friends from Saalshen. You have few enough friends in Baen-Tar, girl."

"I'm going to go and have a pleasant lunch with my sister," Sasha said impatiently. "For the last time, say what you will and begone."

"The trial of Lord Krayliss," said Lord Kumaryn. "It will be soon."

Sasha rolled her eyes. "You know, the last time we met, you were trying to arrest me for something you knew damn well I didn't do. Was this what that was about? You were trying to keep me from Lord Krayliss's trial and, since that didn't work, you now resort to threats?"

"The king wants Lord Krayliss dead," Kumaryn continued, his bony cheeks reddening. "Prince Koenyg wants him dead. Every sane man and woman in Lenayin sees him for the rabble-rousing troublemaker he is, and . . ."

"All the nobility, you mean," Sasha interrupted. "The only sane men and women in Lenayin." Mockingly. "What'll you do once he's gone? Have the king appoint some friendly Verenthane lord to the great lordship?"

"Such would be a great boon to the people of Taneryn," Martyn said softly.

"Did you ask them?" Sasha retorted. "I'm no friend of Lord Krayliss, but I'll not deny him a fair trial to help you fulfil your grand vision of a holy, Verenthane Lenayin with not a pagan lord in sight. You forget who the people of Lenayin truly are, so little you see of them in your Verenthane cities and castles. Best that you remember soon, or one day they'll walk into your cities and castles all together and remind you."

Kumaryn's nostrils flared. "Now who would be making the threats, girl?"

"Not a threat, Lord Kumaryn," Sasha said coldly. "Just seeing if you truly can count after all. They look so little from your castle towers, don't they? All the commonfolk? And so few. Like all the little streams in the hills after a winter's rain. It's only when you see them reach the valley bottom and come together that you realise what a flood looks like."

"The little pretend princess thinks the Goeren-yai all love her," Yuan Martyn said softly. His manner was all light-tongued menace, beside Kumaryn's blunt bluster. Sasha had no doubts which man was the more dangerous of the two. This was Princess Wyna's man, and Princess Wyna shared not only Koenyg's attention, but also his bed. Lord Kumaryn had no such advantage. "There are thousands of Goeren-yai soldiers camped before the walls for Rathynal. I hear they could barely agree on where to pitch their tents. Upslope was more fortuitous, I hear, and downslope potentially an ill omen. It nearly came to blows. Such a rabble could no more unite against the true lords of Lenayin than they united against the Cherrovan Empire. It took a lowlands Verenthane to save Lenayin from its disgrace. There is no such hero to ride to your rescue this time, little pretend princess."

"And it took a lowlands Nasi-Keth to come and rescue the Verenthanes when the Cherrovan came back seventy years later," Sasha retorted. Yuan Martyn's eyes flashed with anger. "Why go to such lengths to remove Lord Krayliss? If you're so unconcerned about the Goeren-yai?"

Yuan Martyn smiled. "Someone must save Lenayin from herself. The gods' work is never easy, but it is rewarding. The gods are merciful, but their wrath is harsh upon all who would obstruct the righteous path. Remember, little pretend princess. Never forget."

Sasha was almost surprised when the Verenthane Royal Guardsmen at Koenyg's door let her in with barely a query. Koenyg's chambers were large, with a main room here and a dining room beyond, half hidden behind curtain drapes. Memories hit her with a rush, hard and unwelcome. These had been Krystoff's chambers. They'd seemed lighter then, somehow. The sun had always been shining through the far windows, in those memories, and gleaming golden upon the dining table. Now, the stone walls seemed darker, more foreboding.

She passed the curtain drapes and found Koenyg seated with Archbishop Dalryn at the near end of the long dining table, each with a drink in hand. Both men rose upon her entry. "Sister," Koenyg said blandly. "What a lovely surprise. What can I . . . ?"

"Did you send your wife's Hadryn lapdog after me?" Sasha demanded angrily. "Or did she send him herself?"

Koenyg gazed at her for a long moment, the flexing of his free hand the only sign of a reaction. "You should refer to your brother's wife as either Princess Wyna, or sister," said Archbishop Dalryn into that silence. "Your own title is no longer 'princess,' and such informality is unbecoming."

"Was I talking to you?" Sasha snapped at the holiest Verenthane in Lenayin. The archbishop reddened. He was, in Sasha's opinion, an utterly unremarkable man. He had a longish face, with a pointy jaw, a bloated nose and loose skin sagging from his cheeks. His hair was dark streaked with grey, and curly—an unusual trait in Lenayin. It was usually hidden beneath his tall archbishop's hat, which now sat upon the dining table. Now it stuck up in fuzzy curls. Like an old feather duster, Sasha thought.

"What happened?" Koenyg asked simply, sipping his wine. Or Sasha assumed it was wine, the archbishop's tastes were well known.

"Martyn Ansyn told me not to support Lord Krayliss come his trial, or I'd suffer for it. When *is* Lord Krayliss's trial anyway, Koenyg? Have you decided? Or does it depend entirely on what I plan to say in his defence?"

"Your brother should be addressed as *Prince* Koenyg," the archbishop persisted, "or as *brother*. From your mouth in particular, such informality is . . ."

"From my mouth in particular?" Sasha leaned on a chairback, and glared at him. "And how would you like me to address *you*, Dalryn? As the rural folk of Lenayin do? The Holy Brewery, perhaps? The Listing Bishop? Father Red Nose?"

"You *dare* say such things in this place!" the archbishop fumed. His horrified stare fixed on Koenyg, but Koenyg only watched, wearily.

"In this place more than any other!" Sasha retorted. "This is *my* brother, in the chambers that once belonged to my dearest friend, and I've far more claim to the sanctity of this place than you ever will. If you don't like it, get lost."

"Sasha, this is my invited guest." Very little ever penetrated Koenyg's rock-like calm. He seemed no more alarmed by his sister's outburst than he might have been by a small, yapping dog about his ankles. "You are not."

"Did you send that thug to try and scare me?" Sasha yelled at him. Koenyg was heir to the throne and renowned throughout Lenayin for cold, emotionless calculation. But he was still her brother, and Damon's brother, and Sofy's. She might not have expected any better of his actions toward herself, but if he was capable of this toward her, then he could do it to her other siblings just as easily.

"You should apologise to His Holiness," Koenyg continued. "He is rightly unaccustomed to such indignities. He is also the spiritual leader of all the Verenthane faith in Lenayin. That includes you."

Oh, and there it was. Koenyg the plotter. Dared she declare her true allegiances? Kessligh had warned her often enough that if she did, assorted northerners, nobles, bishops and fanatics would demand her head.

Sasha glared at him. Koenyg met her gaze calmly. A face much unlike Krystoff's—solid, where Krystoff had been lean; trimmed and presentable, where Krystoff had often been wild. Occupying chambers that had once been Krystoff's. They should still be his, Sasha thought bitterly. They *would* still be his, had not Krystoff offended so many of those same northerners, nobles, bishops and fanatics. Krystoff had fought them, but Koenyg sat at his private dining table and had drinks with them.

Would you wield the axe yourself, brother, she wondered bitterly. If the time came to dispose of me, like they once disposed of him?

"Did you send Martyn Ansyn to try and scare me?" she demanded once more.

"First, apologise to His Holiness."

Sasha glared. "I'll do nothing of the sort."

Koenyg shrugged. "Then we have nothing to talk about."

To Sasha's right, the curtains to Koenyg's bedchambers were abruptly pulled back and there stood Princess Wyna. She wore white, the colours of northern mourning, her light hair pulled back severely from her face. She was pretty, perhaps, in the way that a simple sculpture might be pretty, or a painting. The beauty of form, with high cheekbones and pale green eyes. But there was no beauty of warmth, or happiness.

"My children are saying their midday prayers," she informed them coldly. "Whatever this business of yours, it should not be so loud to disturb the mourning rituals beneath a woman's own roof."

"My apologies, my sweet," said Koenyg. "I do try to keep a civil tone at all times. My sister is challenged in this regard."

Wyna's pale eyes fixed on Sasha. Weeks it now was since Lord Rashyd Telgar had died, and still Wyna mourned for her father.

"Sister," Wyna said to Sasha coolly. "How do you fare?"

"Well enough today," Sasha said darkly. "It's tomorrow that concerns me."

"Tomorrow concerns us all," said Wyna. She walked primly to her husband's side, her white dress swishing. "I could not help but overhear through the curtain. Has my loyal servant Yuan Martyn been causing you some concern, dear sister?"

"Yuan Martyn has been causing the king's justice some concern," Sasha replied.

Wyna slipped her hand around Koenyg's elbow. "You seem very concerned for justice toward that mindless barbarian," said Wyna with a slight frown. "Pray tell me, where is the justice for my dear departed father whom he murdered?"

Sasha's eyes narrowed. You did send him, you ice-cold bitch. Wyna's gaze was as hard as glass. "If the king's justice does not extend to all Lenayin," Sasha replied, "even to mindless barbarians, then what possible use is that justice at all?"

"Mama?" came a boy's voice from the curtains. Sasha looked, and saw four-year-old Dany Lenayin standing in the doorway by the drawn curtain. "I said my prayers, Mama."

"Of course you did," said Koenyg, walking to the boy with arms out-stretched. Dany went to him and Koenyg scooped up his son, holding him effortlessly seated in the crook of one arm. "Dany, say hello to your Auntie Sashandra."

Dany had already said hello to his Auntie Sashandra upon her first arrival in Baen-Tar, but he turned and looked anyway. He was a pale boy, with dark hair like his father, but the features were mostly his mother's. Something about the pallid complexion, and the thin set of his lips, reminded Sasha abruptly of . . . Usyn, she realised. The boy looked like his Uncle Usyn. Gods and spirits forfend that he actually grew up to *be* like Usyn.

"I saw you playing lagand yesterday," said Dany. His eyes and voice were too calm for a boy his age.

"And I saw you in the stands," Sasha replied.

"You play very well," said Dany. "Not as well as my papa, though."

Sasha's lips twitched. "On the contrary, I thought I played somewhat better than your papa."

Dany looked at his father. "She's not very ladylike, is she, Papa? Nor very polite."

"Auntie Sashandra was very close to your late Uncle Krystoff," Koenyg explained to his son. "She's very much like Uncle Krystoff was."

"Uncle Krystoff was a very strange man, wasn't he, Papa?"

"No one truly knows *what* Uncle Krystoff was, Dany," said Koenyg. There was a darkness in his eyes as they met with his sister's. An old anger, never entirely quenched. "He remains a mystery to many, even to this day. Some say he was not truly a Verenthane."

"If he was not a Verenthane, Papa, then what was he?"

Sasha stared at the boy. It scared her that he could so innocently ask such a question. What indeed? What was a Lenay, if not a Verenthane? It was almost as though the wild, ancient half of traditional Lenayin had been erased from these people's memory entirely.

A memory struck her—leaping onto Krystoff's bed one morning to wake him. He'd wrestled her over, kicking and squealing, and tried to bite her on the neck. And over there, by the ornate wooden cabinets of glasses and plates, he'd shown her how a wondrous serrin invention—a looking glass—could burn a hole in an old piece of cloth when the sun fell through the open window just right. And back in the front room, he'd carried her in circles on his back, responding to her tugs on his ears, or her heels on his thighs, as a horse would to a rider's reins or stirrups. Once, she'd made a mistake, told him to go when she meant stop, and he'd careened straight into the wall. They'd fallen to the floor together, laughing.

Now, Koenyg and his Hadryn wife slept in his bed, and entertained by his table, and hung gaudy pictures of Verenthane saints on his walls. And it hit her, suddenly—the great, terrible injustice of it all. If he'd lived, she might not have become what she was today. But if he'd lived . . . well, there would not burn this endless pain in her heart, that burned all the more terribly every time she set eyes upon Koenyg.

"He may not have been a Verenthane," Sasha told Koenyg, coldly. "He may not have been always polite, and he may not have been always sensible. But he was my brother. Gods know what *you* are."

She turned and strode out, leaving the stone and their memories in her wake.

The foul mood stayed with her all the way down to the Great Hall, along gloomy hallways and flagstone floors. Memories of Krystoff. Her father, Koenyg, Kessligh, Damon, Sofy, herself . . . they all remembered a different Krystoff, a Krystoff shaped as much by their own personal needs and desires as by any truthful recollection. She'd needed Krystoff for her soulmate. Her father had needed an heir. Koenyg, a competitor to overcome. Kessligh, an uma. To Damon, he'd been yet another overbearing elder brother to measure up to. Perhaps only Sofy could claim any objectivity where Krystoff was concerned. Sofy, who was the most objective person on most things, it seemed.

So how did Sofy do it? Perhaps, it occurred to her, it was because Sofy was not selfish. Sofy did not harbour any great ambitions for herself and did not impose her self-importance upon others.

People saw what they wanted to see, Kessligh always said. They saw the world in terms that would paint themselves in the best possible light and excuse all their flaws, preferably by blaming them on someone else. The Nasi-Keth taught men and women not to be perfect, but merely to know themselves and to know their own wants and desires. Knowing that, a person might begin to understand his or her own prejudices and assumptions, and act against them. Kessligh had never claimed to be perfect, he merely claimed to make an effort. So what about me, Sasha wondered. What do I want? Was she so self-centred that she'd never be able to see the truth? How could she ever know anyone around her if she wasn't even sure of herself? Hells, she didn't even know if she was Verenthane, Goeren-yai or Nasi-Keth. Her own brother had challenged her to declare herself, and she didn't know what to say. Even after the duel at Halleryn, she still did not know. She knew what her heart said. But, in her life, to be ruled entirely by her heart would be suicide.

The day did not improve. After lunch, she did what she usually did when her mood was foul and visited the stables. Horses, she'd discovered, spoke a quiet, foreign language of posture and emotion. After a while immersed in it, she found her very human concerns beginning to fade. This visit, however, she discovered that Peg's right hind hoof was developing a crack about a horseshoe nail, and the shoe would need replacing.

The blacksmith's shop occupied a large, covered area to the stable's rear, facing directly onto the inside of the looming city wall. There were several blacksmiths, in fact, and they were clearly busy, their furnaces roaring, hammers clanging and new, glowing red horseshoes and nails being added to respective piles. Many horses occupied the hay-strewn floor, some worked upon by their riders, others waiting their turn. Sasha found Peg a spot at a water trough, found some tools and went to work.

Peg hated blacksmiths and holding his huge leg still was no easy thing. The nails came out with difficulty. The heat from the fires was intense, and the day was warming, so she removed her bandoleer and sword, then the jacket and long-sleeved outershirt. The short-sleeved undershirt was too loose at the waist and hung out when she bent, so she gathered the hem into two tight fistfuls and tied them in a knot beneath her breastbone, leaving her midriff bare.

She was starting on the third nail when she heard female voices coming along the row of horses, raised above the clamour of hammers. Baen-Tar ladies came to the stables often enough to admire the horses. There were male voices too—of course, she thought dryly, a true lady would require an escort. Peg tried to move his leg once more and she gripped it firmly between her knees.

"A little patience, please?" she asked him loudly, repositioning the nail. Peg snorted.

"Oh, look at that big black!" she heard then from the approaching ladies. "Isn't he gorgeous!"

Great, that was all she needed. She got the nail head in and started hammering. The hammer was heavy, but gave no real trouble to a swordfighter—as always, it was a question of rhythm, balance and timing. No sooner had the nail gone all the way in than there was a female voice directly behind her, coming from Peg's front.

"Excuse me? Rider? Could you tell me this horse's name and his owner?"

Sasha sighed, dropped the hoof and hammer, and turned to face them. "His name's Peglyrion," she said shortly. "I'm his owner."

The young ladies before her gasped in shock. They wore dresses of the Torovan fashion, one predominant colour with embroidered trimmings offset with an opposing-coloured sash tied at the waist. Some wore their hair done up with curls and combs, others straight and long down their backs. There were five immediately present, and one in particular, in a red gown with green sash and silver jewellery, was staring at her with contemptuous disbelief.

"You!" exclaimed Alythia. The sisters locked stares. "Good lords, Sashandra, you really have no shame at all, do you? Look at you! You're dressed like a . . . like a . . ."

"Like a woman trying to shoe her horse?" Sasha offered.

"Like a disgrace! Have you no respect for local sensibilities?"

"None," Sasha said bluntly. "Now, are you just going to stand there and hurl insults, or can I get back to my horse?"

One of the ladies murmured something to her companions, who giggled. They eyed Sasha's bare, sweaty arms and hard stomach with scandalised disbelief.

Alythia's dark eyes blazed. "Have you any idea of the number of people you've managed to offend?" she exclaimed. "To say nothing of Father, disgracing his name in this . . . this *appalling* fashion . . ."

"Father is both man and king enough to speak for himself," Sasha said darkly, "he does not need you to do his complaining for him." Sometimes Alythia worked her temper to boiling. But today, somehow, she just couldn't be bothered. It was all too predictable, too tiresome and far, far too silly. "Alythia, I'm really not interested. Enjoy your little day's outing, try not to step in anything foul . . ."

She was about to turn her back when a new figure appeared, escorting another lady. The man wore a dark jacket with bright silver embroidery, and pants that puffed out at the thighs before tapering to tight, slender calves and boots. He wore a slim sword at the hip with a fancy silver handguard, and a wide-brimmed hat upon his head . . . with a feather in it, no less. His goatee was neatly trimmed, and dark curls fell about his neck. Several other men in similar dress followed, each escorting another lady.

Bacosh, Sasha realised. Irritation at her prissy sister quickly vanished.

"Ah," said the man, seeing Sasha. "This must be the Lady Sashandra. Princess Alythia, would you mind ever so much for a formal introduction? I have heard . . . so many things . . . about your sister." The accent was very smooth and melodious, and ever so charming. The dark eyes, however, felt . . . cold. The smile, Sasha thought, did not touch those eyes. An older man, perhaps nearer to fifty than forty, though well-hidden beneath makeup and hair dye.

"Certainly, Duke Stefhan," Alythia said primly. "Sashandra, this is Duke Stefhan of the Larosa province of the Bacosh. Duke Stefhan, Sashandra Lenayin, my sister."

The duke stepped past the water trough and reached for Sasha's hand. Sasha seriously considered withholding it. But that was needless provocation. They were only formalities. She extended her hand and repressed a shudder as the duke grasped it lightly and placed it to his lips. His grip lingered, unpleasantly. Possessively.

"M'Lady Sashandra," said the duke. "Your fame precedes you. Even in my nation, we have heard tales of your exploits."

"In my nation too, we have heard tales of yours," Sasha said coldly.

The duke smiled. "They say that you fight like the serrin ladies. If any serrin can truly be said to resemble a lady." With a flashing smile at the ladies present, who laughed obligingly.

"After your armies are through with them," Sasha replied, "I doubt they could be said to resemble anything."

That provoked the first response from the duke's eyes yet—a slight widening beneath the hat's brim. A flash of recognition. "How true," he replied. Slyly, almost mockingly. "But do not feel too sorry for them, my Lady. They have no souls, you know." And he lowered his voice, with a glance behind, as if concerned someone back there would overhear. "That is why they try to steal our souls, you know. They lack their own."

It took every measure of Sasha's fragile restraint to keep her from smashing his smug, arrogant face with her fist. He knew which Larosa exploits she referred to. He found it amusing. Torture, rape and mass slaughter. And her father and Koenyg wanted Lenayin to go to war, and fight for men like this, against the serrin? Even in retaliation, the serrin had only ever killed soldiers and those who commanded them. *All* of those soldiers, it was true . . . but then who could blame them?

"Have a care, Duke Stefhan," Sasha said quietly. "You must still return home, through Goeren-yai lands. Many Goeren-yai think highly of the serrin. And some Lenay Verenthanes also accuse the Goeren-yai of lacking souls . . . Perhaps, were you to see what they do to men who attack their friends, you might understand why." And she smiled, dangerously. "Perhaps you shall. Should someone who knows your route send word to them."

The duke's smile disappeared completely. And he nodded, warily. "So. It is true what they say, of your loyalties and tempers both."

"You've yet to see my temper, Duke Stefhan. Pray that this should remain the case."

"Sasha?" came a new, familiar voice. Sasha looked and saw Sofy now come into view, escorted on the arm of one of the Larosa men. Sasha stared, disbelievingly. Sofy's return stare was accusatory. Sofy would not need the present situation explained to her—she could read body language like a book. "Sasha, what are you doing?"

Sasha gestured her forward, sharply. Sofy abandoned her companion's arm with a gracious apology and made her way between the drinking troughs, Duke Stefhan extending a courteous hand to help her through. Sasha took Sofy's arm with a dangerous glare at the duke and dragged her away to the smithy's wall.

"What are you doing with these bastards?" she hissed at her sister, above the continuing clang of hammer on metal. The heat from the fires was intense. "These are the Larosa, Sofy! I've told you about them!"

"Sasha, just once could you meet some new people without starting a fight?" Sofy shook her arm clear of Sasha's grasp, indignantly. "Duke Stefhan is an intelligent and cultured man, if you'd only give him a . . ."

"The man's a murdering villain, like all the Larosa ruling classes!"

"How do you know?" Sofy snapped. "You've only just met the man!"

"You don't care what they do to the serrin, is that it?" Staring at Sofy angrily. Sofy was supposed to be too smart for this. She couldn't believe that fancy clothes and a funny accent were all it took to dance past her sister's usually excellent judgment. "You don't care about the night raiding parties across the Saalshen–Bacosh border, about the abductions and massacres . . ."

"Oh, how dare you?" Sofy was really angry now. "How dare you say that I don't care? Of course I care, Sasha, but don't you see? You simply cannot continue to just tar everyone with one brush, I mean, the Larosa can't *all* be like that! There's so much *culture* in Larosa, Sasha, and the other Bacosh provinces . . ."

"So what?" Sasha fumed. "There's a lot of culture in Cherrovan too, and a lot of it's wonderful, but I'll be damned if I'm going to walk arm in arm with a Blood Tribe Warlord!"

"Not everything's a conflict, Sasha!" Sofy was pleading now. "You're so used to fighting, your whole life. You fought father, and you fought your minders and the holy scholars, and then you fought with Alythia, and then Kessligh and Krystoff taught you swordwork, and then after Krystoff died you fought against the Cherrovan . . ." She grasped Sasha's arms, lightly. "You have to stop *judging* people, Sasha! You did it with Damon, and you do it still with father and Koenyg . . . and if you keep on doing it, you'll find nothing but conflict your entire life!"

"And you have to stop assuming that everyone is gentle and kind until proven otherwise," Sasha retorted. "You're a good-natured person, Sofy, and evil people will take advantage of that if you let them. I've *seen* the real world. I've lived out there in it, and I've seen what people do to each other. If you truly believe that good tailors and a knowledge of artwork can excuse a man of crimes that heinous, then you're just another pampered, ignorant little palace girl."

Sofy stared at her, eyes wide. And swallowed hard, fighting back emotion. "Well, *that's* mature," she huffed. "When someone doesn't agree with you, just call them names, as if that solves anything. And you're supposed to be older than me." She turned to sweep away with her nose in the air, pausing briefly to give Sasha's person a disdainful look. "And seriously, Sasha . . . put something decent on. Even the tolerance of Baen-Tar Verenthanes has its limits, you know."

Sasha watched her leave, broodingly. Alythia gave Sasha a smug look and put a comforting hand on Sofy's shoulder, welcoming her back into the fold as they moved off. Duke Stefhan bowed, mockingly, and followed. Sasha looked about with hands on hips, searching for something she could throw.

Across by the nearest furnace, a Goeren-yai blacksmith dipped a red-hot horseshoe into a bucket of water, which hissed. His arms were huge, rippling with muscle beneath entwining tattoos. He looked at Sasha, beneath long, tangled, sweaty hair. And looked her up and down, lingeringly.

"Don't worry, lassie," he said. "Those clothes look plenty fine by me." And winked at her, cheerfully. Sasha gave him a reproachful look. The blacksmith chortled, withdrew his horseshoe, and resumed hammering. Sasha sighed in exasperation . . . Goeren-yai men were such idiots, sometimes. Rude, cheerful, irreverent, fearless idiots. And she nearly laughed. Spirits, how she loved them. She stretched, wincingly, for the man's benefit. He grinned, still hammering, evidently with only one eye on his work.

Sasha walked to stroke Peg's nose, an apology for taking so long. "This is why I like horses," she told him tiredly, feeding him a piece of fruit from her pocket. "Relationships are so simple, so uncomplicated." Peg seemed far more interested in the snack than her conversation. "I mean, I *know* you don't like me."

Peg snorted, and thrust his nose into her hands, searching for more food. Nudged at her pockets, breathing great, horse-smelling breaths all over her. Sasha smiled, and hugged him.

Thirteen

I T WAS COLD IN THE LIBRARY. Sasha sat on her stool before the wide, wood desk, and wrapped herself more tightly with her cloak. The lamp on the table flickered a wan light upon the page before her and a coal brazier gave some warmth to her back. Across the surrounding benches, several figures sat hunched, likewise with braziers and lamps—all men, some scribbling on parchment with a quill tip.

At either end of the vast floor, shelves lay dark and gloomy, groaning beneath their weight of parchment. Books were more trouble than they were worth, she'd often thought in her youth. Only living with Kessligh, scrolling through ancient serrin writings during long evenings before a crackling log fire, had she discovered their wonders.

"It was a female who came before the court, and she wore a sword at her back like a man, and did move and speak with the authority of a man. Her eyes were a demon blue, and all her soldiers wore a most ungodly aspect."

Before her lay the writings of a Torovan archivist who had lived in the Larosa court two centuries before. Here lay an eyewitness account of the Larosa court following the disappearance of King Leyvaan's Bacosh army in the hills and forests of Saalshen, and the subsequent occupation of the three Bacosh provinces now known as the Saalshen Bacosh by the serrin.

"The demon said her name was Maldereld, and that by her hand and others were King Leyvaan and his entire force of twenty thousand slain. Lord Sharis was enraged, and would have struck the demon down where she stood."

Why he did not, the text did not say. Perhaps it had something to do with most of the Larosa army having been killed with Leyvaan the Fool, Sasha thought sourly. Larosa had been defenceless, at Saalshen's mercy. Why the serrin had only occupied the three closest of the nine Bacosh provinces, she did not know. They could have spread further and made an empire. But then, maybe that was human thinking. The serrin had little interest in empires. The Saalshen Bacosh now made a wall, behind which Saalshen had been protected for two centuries since.

Echoing footsteps made her turn, with a reach for her sword hung across the chairback. A shadowed figure with one arm in a sling emerged from the doorway, and paused, scanning the room. Sasha straightened, pushing back her hood so that the lamp lit her face . . . the figure looked her way, then came quickly over between the tables.

Closer, the face resolved itself as Jaryd's, his expression urgent. "M'Lady," he whispered, "please come quickly. I ride on Prince Damon's business."

"Ride?" Sasha frowned . . . Jaryd did appear to be dressed for riding. "Ride where?"

"Please come, I'll explain on the way." And he leaned closer to whisper in her ear. "It concerns the Udalyn, M'Lady."

Sasha stared at him. Then she got up and blew out her lamp. She followed Jaryd between the tables, ignoring the cloaked, hooded stares of men at their tables.

Outside in the cold night, it was only a short walk to the stables. Torches gave the road a dim, patchy light, with the odd, passing shadow of another walker.

"M'Lady," said Jaryd, "I looked all over! Why were you not at the Rathynal feast with everyone else?"

"To avoid 'everyone else,'" Sasha said shortly. "They'd have made me wear a dress, for one thing."

Jaryd gave her a bemused look. "Would that be so terrible?"

"Would you wear one?" Sasha retorted. Jaryd blinked. "There you are. Should you even be walking around?"

"It's my arm that's broken, M'Lady, not my leg," Jaryd said testily. "I dislike sitting still."

"I felt the same, once. Then I discovered books."

Jaryd made a face. "Books are no friends of mine. Princess Sofy was missing you," he added. "She fears you're avoiding her."

That hurt. Sasha gazed at the lighted windows of a streetside building, biting her lip. She saw so little of Sofy. But . . . "I'm not avoiding her, I'm avoiding her new friends. I don't want to kill any of them. Or rather, I think I do want to kill some of them. But not in front of Sofy."

"You have my sympathies there," Jaryd said darkly. "That lot need a good belting. But the ladies love them."

"It's difficult enough to defend your gender, most of the time," Sasha told him wryly. "I'll not even try to defend mine. What's your urgency?"

"There is a rumour of refugees," said Jaryd in a low voice, with a cautious glance about the gloomy street.

Sasha stared at him. "Refugees from the valley? How has word come?"

"We don't know, M'Lady. We think they were seen upon the road. It seems a messenger was sent to Prince Koenyg at speed and now he has deployed men of Ranash and Banneryd upon the Baen-Tar perimeter this night."

"And now he sends loyal Verenthanes out to intercept," Sasha muttered. "You said 'we.' Is Damon . . . ?"

"Prince Damon has quietly asked some of the Falcon Guard, M'Lady," Jaryd murmured. "We feel we might find the refugees first if they arrive tonight, yet Prince Damon is required at the feast, and the usual routes through which one might move a person undetected into the city are watched by Prince Koenyg's spies . . ."

"Damon intends to smuggle a Udalyn into the city?" Damon, undermining Koenyg's authority beneath his very nose? She was amazed. "To what purpose?"

"M'Lady, Prince Damon wonders if the king is aware of all that transpires. He says . . . he says that while the king is in agreement with these policies in principle, he does not follow their implementation in detail.

"Prince Koenyg has done this before, M'Lady . . . two years ago, you might recall that a Goeren-yai village in Yethulyn fell beneath the thrall of a headman who proclaimed himself possessed by a great spirit and declared his village an independent kingdom."

"Father sent Koenyg, and Koenyg had the leaders killed and the entire village burned to the ground," Sasha replied.

"And the king, Prince Damon says, was most displeased to learn of Prince Koenyg's methods," Jaryd added. "He said the execution was just, but to punish the entire village was unnecessary. He sent gold and dispatched tradesmen to help in the rebuilding."

"And Damon thinks father is not aware that Koenyg may be encouraging a Hadryn attack on the Udalyn?"

"M'Lady, the king spends much of his days in temple. He prays and he reads from the holy texts. His directions are broad, Prince Damon says, yet he trusts Prince Koenyg to implement the detail of those orders."

Sasha nodded, thinking hard. The road wound about the armoury and the training hall now. On the right, the great city wall loomed dark and bleak in the night. "He should know," Sasha muttered. "How could he not know?"

"Prince Damon feels that perhaps if the king were presented with a refugee from the Udalyn, an eyewitness who might sway the king's compassion . . ." Jaryd took a deep breath.

Sasha gave him a hard look. "And why are you doing this? You don't need to help. Spirits, you're in enough trouble already."

"Trouble frightens me no more than it frightens you," Jaryd said stubbornly. Sasha shook her head in faint disbelief. In Lenayin, Goeren-yai men weren't the only ones with rocks for heads.

At the base of the Baen-Tar cliff, Sasha and Jaryd headed left and broke free into the paddocks and low stone walls of the rolling Baen-Tar farmlands. Many men were awake, she saw as they rode between the tents, rough-shaven and sleepy by the flickering light of torches. Here, a small cluster of men talked before an officer's tent. There, a pair of soldiers held six horses saddled and ready in case of sudden need. Sentries stood watch along the road, yet Jaryd took the fore, letting the front of his cloak fall open to reveal the full uniform of the Falcon Guard and mail armour beneath. Spirits knew how long it'd taken him to drag that on, considering his arm. No man challenged them. But something, it seemed, had aroused the soldiers.

Sasha took the first available right-hand turn, attempting to gain some sense of the placement of units. Here in the midslope, the soldiers seemed mostly from Yethulyn and Fyden provinces. Nearer to the town, it had been Valhanan. Now, as they rode a winding farmtrail downslope, the tents appeared largely of southern Isfayen. Jaryd pointed further downslope still, where a cluster of tents sat lonely within an isolated field, flanked by several large trees and neighbouring cottages. The camp was alive with the light of fires.

"I see Lord Krayliss is awake," Jaryd said. "Doubtless gnashing his teeth over not being invited to the Rathynal feast."

"Aye," Sasha said wearily. "Another chance to make trouble missed. The tragedy is that he and Usyn deserved each other. It should have been him and Usyn in that circle before the walls, winner takes all. Instead, we've only dragged the problem down here to infect Baen-Tar and leave the Udalyn undefended."

Jaryd took a torch from his saddle webbing, and they both paused while he gave it one-handed to Sasha to light with a metal flint. The night seemed all too silent, here on the lower slopes, away from the noise of men and horses in camp. Ahead, there was rough land and forest. Not a place to ride at night if one could avoid it.

At the bottom of the hill, the forest surrounded them. Sasha held the torch high and the light danced upon the trees, casting crazy shadows across the undergrowth. Once, Sasha fancied she saw a gleam of eyes from a branch—an owl, most likely. The trail climbed and fell across rocky folds, yet

Jaryd seemed sure of the way. When the trail divided, he took the less-travelled route, bushes thrashing against their horses' legs.

Then, ahead, there came a new light through the trees. Two, in fact. Jaryd saw, and reined to a halt. Peg fretted, ears flicking in the cold as riders approached. Sasha counted five horses . . . and a smaller pony, trailing behind on a halter. Jaryd called in a tongue Sasha did not recognise and received a like reply. And then, in the brightening light of three torches, she could see the green of Tyree beneath the riders' cloaks.

"My Lord," greeted a rider. Beneath the hood, Sasha recognised Sergeant Garys. He peered within the shadow of her own hood . . . and his eyes widened a little. Garys half bowed in the saddle. "M'Lady Sashandra. Two Udalyn, M'Lady. One of Jurellyn's scouts has escorted them this far but turned back as soon as he handed them over. Said he had to get back to Jurellyn."

Only then did Sasha see the small cloaked figure astride the saddle of another man, his shape lost against the soldier's bulk and shadow. A young face peered from within the hood, fearful. Now she understood where the pony had come from.

"Damn," she muttered, nudging Peg alongside Sergeant Garys. She handed him both rein and torch, and climbed down, giving Peg a reassuring stroke on the nose lest he yank the sergeant from his saddle. Then she walked briskly to the other soldier's side and threw back her hood. She reached up to put a hand on the child's arm. A boy, she saw, looking exhausted and dirty besides the fear. But he seemed to know how to sit on a saddle. If he'd come all the way from the Udalyn Valley, he must surely know. "Lad," she said gently. "Friend. Do not be frightened. These are good men. Where are you from?"

The fear remained in the boy's eyes. And incomprehension. "Doesn't seem to speak much Lenay," the soldier said with a concerned frown, looking down at the boy on his lap.

"Edu," Sasha muttered. "Of course." She gave the surrounding soldiers a wry glance. "I don't suppose anyone here speaks any Edu?" The men exchanged looks. "I thought not."

Edu, the tongue of the Udalyn. So accustomed had she become to the notion that most Lenays would speak at least a little Lenay. But that was a recent event, since the coming of King Soros. Lenayin had been a land of a thousand valleys and, it was said, a thousand tongues. King Soros had brought the warring clans together beneath the Verenthane banner . . . but not the Udalyn. A century of isolation. And now the boy spoke no language anyone here could speak. One look into his wide, frightened eyes and Sasha realised that she was gazing into the youthful face of antiquity.

"Damn it," she said to herself, trying to think. "Tullamayne wrote in Edu, yet all we know is translation. There must be something . . ."

From another horse, there came a plaintive, wailing cry. *Two* Udalyn, Garys had said. Sasha ran to the other horse and found in that rider's lap a young girl, of no more than six or seven. She looked just as bedraggled, weary and dirty as the boy . . . and now, utterly exhausted and terrified, amidst armoured strangers who did not speak her tongue, she was panicking. The soldier upon whose saddle she rode, a burly Goeren-yai with a thick beard, tried to restrain her thrashing. The wails grew louder.

"Oh, here, here!" Sasha said, reaching up to the girl as the rider gave evident thought to clasping a gloved hand over her mouth—there were northern riders out in the dark as well. The girl looked down through her sobs and saw Sasha. She held out both arms, instinctively. Sasha pulled her from the saddle and held her, as the girl clutched to her and sobbed upon her cloak.

"Rysha!" the boy now called out, alarmed. "Rysha, *elmat ulyn* Rysha!" He struggled clear of his soldier's arms, leaped to the ground with considerable agility and ran to her. Sasha put the little girl down and the boy grabbed her, and hugged her close. There was a desperation in that embrace. A closeness in the way the girl enfolded herself to him. A blaze of protective temper in the boy's eyes, a warning look.

"Oh, I see," Sasha said quietly. She squatted before them with effortless balance. And she extended a careful finger, pointing to the boy. "Brother?" she said slowly, eyebrows raised. Shifted the finger to the girl. "Sister?"

The boy frowned at her, warily. Then nodded. "Sister," he said, with heavy accent.

"Rysha?" Sasha asked. "Is that her name? Rysha?" Another nod. "That's a pretty name." With no hope that he understood. But it was important to keep talking. Silence, with children, was never friendly. "How old are you? Years? Summers?"

Incomprehension. Most Lenay tongues shared many words. Often, when meeting a nonspeaker, one could simply list relevant words until finding one that worked. Not this time, it seemed. She pointed to herself, then flashed ten fingers, twice. Then pointed to him, questioningly. Realisation, this time. He pointed to himself and flashed ten fingers, once. And to his sister, then seven fingers.

"And what is your name?" Sasha asked him. Pointed to his sister. "Rysha, and . . . ?"

"Daryd," said the boy, with more than a hint of pride. "Daryd Yuvenar."

"Greetings, Daryd Yuvenar," Sasha said with a smile. "My name is Sashandra Lenayin." A pause as he seemed to recognise that, frowning.

"Princess Sashandra Lenayin," Sasha added, carefully. Only too well aware of the men who surrounded, watching and listening.

Daryd's frown became a wide-eyed stare. Comprehension at surely the only human woman he'd ever met who wore her hair short with a tri-braid and dressed in pants with a blade at her back. "Synnich-ahn!" he exclaimed. "*Tel edan yl* Synnich-ahn!"

Dear spirits, not that again. Sasha put a hand firmly on his shoulder. Even little Rysha was staring at her now, teary but wide-eyed. There was a yellow flower in her hair of a kind Sasha had never seen before, now tattered and half dead. "Daryd Yuvenar. Udalyn?"

Daryd nodded vigorously. "Udalyn. *Ren adlyn* father! King Torvaal! *Vyl heryt ais on shyl* Torvaal!" Pointing to his own two eyes, desperately.

Sasha let out a hard breath. That was obvious enough. "Aye," she said, nodding softly. "I think we can arrange that." She gave the boy's shoulder a squeeze. "Brave kids. All this way to plead with the king. You could have stopped anywhere, but you didn't." Didn't trust anyone, she supposed. A century of isolation might do that. And they had been escorted, Garys had said, by one of Jurellyn's scouts; Jurellyn, who had blazed the trail for the Falcon Guard upon the road to Taneryn. Damon had left him behind to watch Usyn's movements and now Jurellyn thought the situation desperate enough to send these two straight for the king.

She heaved herself to her feet. "Well," she said tiredly to the surrounding men, "I don't speak any Edu to get a story from these two. But there is one who might."

The floor of Lord Krayliss's tent was spread with deerskin, alternately soft and coarse as Sasha shifted her weight where she sat. Lord Krayliss sat on a bundle of rolled skins at the end of his bed, a hard fist supporting his bearded chin. Before him sat Daryd and Rysha, eating hot soup and bread before the central tent pole that was impaled deep into the earth. Several senior Taneryn men sat about the tent, all rumpled long hair, tattoos and rings, in traditional stitched leathers and weave. For all Sasha's discomfort, it did occur to her that the scene might be straight from centuries past, when rulers called themselves chieftains instead of lords, and the ancient ways were the ways of all Lenayin. Only Jaryd, seated uncomfortably at her side, spoiled the scene's ancient purity.

Krayliss attempted questions of the children as they ate. Both were clearly frightened of the big, bearish man, but the warmth of both tent and food appeared to calm them considerably. Both, however, continued to cast anxious glances at Sasha, to which she would smile and nod encouragement, whilst trying to follow the broken snatches of conversation.

None of the Taneryn men spoke Edu with any fluency, yet the two dominant tongues of Taneryn were Dyal and Taasti, and both had many words in common with the old Udalyn tongue. Krayliss, to Sasha's moderate amazement, remained both patient and calm. When Daryd (who did most of the talking) did not understand, Krayliss simply invited his fellow yuans to try. What evolved was a three, and sometimes even four or five, tongued conversation, as men attempted various combinations, guesses, or even bits of Cherrovan, to ask questions or interpret puzzling replies. All the Taneryn men gazed at the children with evident fascination, and addressed themselves to the linguistic task with as much enthusiasm as Sasha had ever seen a bunch of hard-headed Goeren-yai warriors address anything so intellectually demanding. A pity there were no serrin present, she thought. They would have been utterly intrigued.

Finally, Krayliss straightened on his bundled seat, frowning heavily. It suited his face entirely. "They are from Ymoth," he said heavily. Sasha nodded, having gathered that much already. "Usyn's armies attacked. Thousands of men on horse, the boy says. They flew banners of the Hadryn clans. The spirits made sure these two were found by one of your brother's scouts, who guided them here. That was eight days ago."

"Then Usyn's army headed straight for Ymoth after leaving Halleryn," said one of the yuans, darkly. "No doubt he planned this treachery from the beginning."

"The Udalyn should never have resettled Ymoth," Krayliss rumbled. "It is not far from the valley mouth, amidst fertile lands. Surely it must have tempted them. But the word of protection from successive Verenthane kings has lulled their instincts for survival. Ymoth is too exposed, and the Udalyn too few in strength and weapons to defend it from Hadryn heavy cavalry. I fear the Udalyn have lost valuable forces defending Ymoth. Now, their defences will be fewer. There is no time to lose."

"The Udalyn have strong defences," said Sasha. "Further up the valley, the sides are sheer. And then there are the walls."

"And I say," said Krayliss, with a hardening tone, "that there is no time to lose!"

Sasha met his gaze firmly. "I agree. We should take at least one child to the king. We need to persuade him that the Hadryn must be stopped."

"I have no faith in the farsight and mercy of Verenthane kings," Krayliss muttered.

"The farsight and mercy of Verenthane kings has been the only thing keeping the Udalyn alive the past hundred years," Sasha replied.

Krayliss's eyes blazed. "The Goeren-yai are not weaklings! We can defend our own! We need merely a leader. The spirits show providence that we should all be gathered together so."

Sasha felt her gut tighten in cold anticipation. Krayliss believed someone must lead the Goeren-yai to save the Udalyn, if the king would not. And, of course, he intended that person to be him. *That* was what he gained by agreeing to leave Halleryn and come to Baen-Tar to face the king's justice. Here, at Rathynal, he would have a far greater audience. There were thousands of Goeren-yai soldiers encamped here before the walls of Baen-Tar. All Krayliss thought they needed was suitable motivation.

"The Udalyn have defended themselves for a century against overwhelming odds," Sasha said coldly. "There should be no rush into a crisis because we were too impatient to make a proper appeal to the king."

"The king shall wait until all are dead and the Udalyn are no more," Krayliss replied, his fist clenched.

"Should you desire my support, Lord Krayliss," Sasha said icily, "then we shall do things my way. Otherwise, you shall not have it."

Krayliss glowered. "When I need your help, girlie, I'll damn well . . ."

"Am I the lady of the Synnich or not?" Sasha said sharply.

About the tent, some men made the spirit sign. Krayliss bit his tongue with difficulty. Daryd and Rysha sat watching with wide eyes. Sasha saw that they clasped hands. "M'Lady," said one man, seriously, and with deference. "What action do you suggest?"

Krayliss's scowl grew deeper. "The king," Sasha told the man, coolly. "He is our best chance. Any other course would risk tearing Lenayin apart. We should not lose faith in our Verenthane brothers. Master Jaryd risked much to find these two children, as did many of the Falcon Guard's Verenthane soldiers. Should we ride to save the Udalyn, Verenthanes should ride with us. Lenayin must remain whole. Should a purely Goeren-yai army attack the Verenthane north, all Verenthanes shall rise against it and all shall be lost."

"And should the king not see reason?" Krayliss said darkly. "What then would M'Lady of the Synnich intend?"

Sasha exhaled a long breath, her gaze settling upon the two dirty, frightened children before her. "Let us hope," she said quietly, "that it does not come to that."

Fourteen

ONE OF KRAYLISS'S MEN ARRIVED the next morning as Sasha went about giving Peg a groom and wash. With the Taneryn man was little Daryd.

"Best you take him now, M'Lady," said the man, a lean Goeren-yai with his hair in many braids, but with no spirit-mask. He seemed edgy as he pushed aside the stall gate, casting a final glance each way up the hall. "We're being watched. The lad drew no special mention through the gates, we said he was M'Lord's nephew, but surely someone would notice that we don't talk to him, or that he doesn't listen."

"Aye," Sasha said, placing a hand on the boy's shoulder. "We'll just hope no one wants to question the feral princess. It would be a first, in Baen-Tar."

The Taneryn man gave a wry smile and departed. There was to be a formal welcome to the provinces at Soros Square that morning, with Rathynal proper to start the next day. Things happened slowly in Lenayin, where great meetings were concerned. A holdover, Sasha had heard it said, from the times when Rathynals had taken weeks simply because of all the multiple translations that were required for the discussions.

Sasha took the faintly bewildered, anxious boy to the back of the stable, from where she withdrew a cloth package from the straw beneath Peg's drinking trough. She unwrapped the bundle, to reveal good clothes of about the correct size for a ten-year-old lad. Perhaps Koenyg had been right to reduce access to Goeren-yai servants and staff. These had been delivered by one of Sofy's staff, and only too willing to help, when Sasha had asked. Whether Sofy herself knew, Sasha did not know.

"Here," she said, laying out the clothes. Daryd, however, was staring up at Peg with disbelief and wonder. The Udalyn, of course, would ride traditional dussieh, with perhaps only a handful of lowlands breeds. And, even for a lowlands warhorse, Peg was enormous.

"Big," Daryd said, greatly impressed. So that was one word in common with Edu. Or perhaps he'd learned it just now from the Taneryn.

"Very big," Sasha agreed. "His name is Peg." And when that drew confusion, "Sasha," pointing at herself. "Daryd," pointing at him. "Peg."

Daryd's eyes widened. "Peg?" he asked. "Peglyrion?"

Sasha blinked at him, surprised . . . until she realised that that, too, was most likely a northern tale in origin. She'd named Peg for the northern star that formed the sword hilt in the constellation of Hyathon the Warrior. That was an old legend, far predating even Tullamayne—Hyathon had named his sword Peglyrion, for the child stolen from him by the dark spirits.

"Peglyrion," Sasha murmured. "Son of Hyathon." As if hearing his name mentioned, Peg lifted his great black nose from his trough, and stretched toward Daryd . . . Sasha put a hand on the boy's shoulder, but Daryd did not flinch. Extended his hand for Peg to sniff. Peg, of course, was fine with children. In his experience, children meant treats. And Daryd, who had surely never seen an animal even half Peg's size before, was remarkably brave.

"Peglyrion," Daryd breathed, as Peg snuffled curiously at his fingers. Sasha ruffled the boy's hair.

"We've a little time yet," she said. "Dress first, then you can help me groom him."

Sasha and Daryd attracted little attention as they walked the back lanes of Baen-Tar. Daryd stared up at the stone walls around him as they walked, his stride a little awkward in his new, leather boots. His new clothes fitted him well enough and with his longish, light brown hair brushed into some kind of order, he looked very much the makings of a handsome young man. He found everything extremely strange, that much was clear. Yet if he was greatly frightened, it did not show, and he walked with the air of someone with important business. It was the first that Sasha had seen of the vaunted Udalyn spirit. She was not disappointed.

They arrived at the end of a lane and directly opposite loomed the palace, three storeys of grand, arching windows, and intricate stonework. Sasha cautioned Daryd to remain in the shadow, while she peered each way about the corner . . . there was street traffic, mostly groundsmen or tradesmen, and the clattering of a mule-drawn cart. Opposite and to the right were the great, rounded steps leading up to the main entrance. Further still, on this side of the road, were the even grander, square steps of the Saint Ambellion Temple.

Sasha pulled up the hood on her cloak—it was not a cold day, with sunlight spilling between broken clouds, but it would not look too suspicious given the gusting wind. She gestured to Daryd to leave his hood down. He, after all, was not the one who would be recognised. She then took a deep breath, grasped the boy's hand and walked around the corner.

Ahead, several Royal Guardsmen had stopped to talk in the middle of the road. None looked at her or the boy as they passed. From ahead, out of sight beyond where the road bent about the great temple onto Soros Square, there came the ringing of trumpets and the echo of drums. An audible cheer from a large gathering. There were no nobles on the streets because they were all at the ceremonies. It was well, then, that she did not look too important . . .

She ascended the great temple stairs, scanning up from within her hood to see the four guardsmen at the entrance, two halberds and two swords. Above, Ambellion's four great spires towered against the fast-moving clouds. Daryd nearly tripped on the stairs to see that sight . . . and Sasha suffered a flash of memory, as a little girl, spinning on the steps whilst staring upward, for that glorious vertigo of motion and dizziness . . . The tallest structures in Lenayin, they were, pronouncing Verenthane glory to the lands for many folds around.

The near guardsman was Goeren-yai and she stopped before him. "I wish to see the king," she said evenly.

"Sorry, lad, there's no admittance outside of service. You'll have to wait." Sasha pulled her hood back a little and lifted her gaze so that the soldier could see his mistake. He frowned . . . and blinked. Very few men of Baen-Tar knew her face by sight, there were no portraits of *her* adorning the palace walls. But then, there was only one woman in Baen-Tar who dressed and wore her hair as she did . . .

"Daughter to father," she said firmly, "I must see the king." The guardsman blinked again. Sasha took advantage, grasping Daryd's hand and walking past. The temple's huge doors towered overhead, left partly open to admit one at a time. Sasha went through, Daryd following behind, and progressed straight across the atrium. Guards here stood alert on the stone floor, many-coloured windows spilling light upon vases of blue ralama flowers. Flanking the main doorway ahead, two statues loomed—Saint Ambellion on the right, in flowing robes with a blessing palm upraised, and King Soros on the left, tall and armoured, with a Verenthane star emblazoned on the pommel of his sword.

The main doors were open and the central aisle between pews stretched invitingly ahead. For a moment, Sasha dared to believe that it might indeed be that easy. Then she heard a rattling footstep as a soldier came through the gap behind. "M'Lady! M'Lady, stop!"

From beneath the statues, guards sprang to life, blocking the way with hands on hilts. Others closed in on her side, and the guards from outside closed at her back. Sasha turned to face the man behind, but that man looked over her head. "Lieutenant," he said. "Sashandra Lenayin, she claims."

Sasha turned again, this time taking Daryd about with her. The lieutenant stared down at her, eyes narrowed beneath his gleaming helm. Sasha pulled back her hood and met his gaze. "M'Lady," said the lieutenant. "The king is at prayer."

"I know," said Sasha.

"It is a serious thing to disturb the king at prayer." The lieutenant's face was free of tattoos, but his hair seemed to have a little length beneath the helm. A single gold ring hung in his left ear. Her hope flared. It was not a great display by any means, but she knew from experience that one should never judge the depths of a man's feelings by the nature of his appearance. "With what emergency would you disturb the king's holy contemplation?"

"This boy," said Sasha, placing her hand upon Daryd's shoulder. The lieutenant's gaze dropped to regard Daryd. Daryd stared upwards, unflinchingly. A good, common lad might drop his gaze, confronted by a man of rank. Daryd's stare was defiant. "He is Udalyn."

The lieutenant's eyes flashed back to Sasha's, with sharp alarm. She could sense the disquiet her words had caused, in the stiffening poise of the guardsmen. Breathing seemed to cease. "Udalyn," said the lieutenant.

"A refugee," said Sasha. "From Ymoth. The Hadryn attacked it barely eight days ago. I would speak with my father, Lieutenant. The boy rode without halt from Hadryn lands day and night for that purpose. He's earned it."

"Lieutenant," said one man, in a low, alarmed voice, "we should alert Prince Koenyg." The lieutenant stared at him, displeasure in his eyes. Beyond him, Sasha caught a glimpse of a priest advancing up the long central aisle, to check on the commotion. The lieutenant seemed unconvinced. He stared back down at Daryd, convictions battling in his eyes.

"Daryd," said Sasha to the boy, urgently. "Speak, Daryd." And gestured to her mouth. Daryd spoke, proudly, in a high, clear voice. Complete sentences, precise and formal. The high, stone atrium echoed with foreign Edu vowels, unheard in this place since its construction. For a moment, Sasha fancied that the grim stone statue of her great-grandfather Soros might have flinched for shame.

The lieutenant squatted opposite Daryd and stared the boy in the face. Daryd completed his little speech and stared back, eyes blazing. And the lieutenant, for the briefest moment, appeared to battle against some powerful emotion.

"Go," he said then to Sasha. "The king's daughter has privileges much unused. Make it brief."

"But sir!" gasped a soldier. The lieutenant gave him a sharp glare and rose. Sasha fancied that his eyes were a little moist.

"Brief, I say," he snapped. Sasha grabbed Daryd's hand and edged quickly past. The priest approaching down the aisle changed directions as she marched by, hurrying to keep up.

"M'Lady Sashandra," he said, cool yet urgent at her right shoulder, "the king is in private chambers. His meditations are deep, he is not to be disturbed."

"So stop me," Sasha retorted, striding fast, little Daryd half-running to keep up.

"M'Lady," said the priest in worried exasperation. His robes were black and plain, and the top of his head was shaved bald, where the rest of his hair was short and straight. A large golden star bounced from a chain about his neck as he strode. He refrained from touching her. Priests and women, Sasha thought sourly. In her particular case, the dislike was mutual.

The temple aisle was long. Many wooden pews crossed the floor beneath an impossibly high ceiling. Coloured windows rowed the walls high above, the morning sun spearing low, angled rays across the stone. The light indeed seemed heavenly, and the temple air hushed and serene. Sasha had not chosen the ways of the Verenthanes, yet even she could feel the awed magnificence in every silent step across the floor. At her side, Daryd stared upward and about in silent incredulity. He made the spirit sign repeatedly. Sasha hoped the priest did not see.

Ahead, an altar rose on a broad stone platform with carved railings. Above were draped two vast curtains of crimson with gold trim upon which there was embroidered the great wooden staff of Saint Ambellion that he had used to walk from Torovan to Lenayin more than three centuries before, and then across all of Lenayin, preaching to those who would listen. Few indeed, it would have been back then, in pagan, Cherrovan-ruled Lenayin.

It was only then that she caught sight of a dark figure kneeling upon the raised space behind the altar, hidden from the central aisle by a lectern. He knelt on a cushion before a pedestal, upon which hung a Verenthane star on a gold chain. Across the wall behind was a huge wooden star, inlaid with gold and silver, and set into the very stone of the wall.

Sasha stopped as the priest scurried about the steps and whispered reverently in the kneeling figure's ear. The figure wore a communion shroud on his head, like a black, silken handkerchief, blocking out the physical world, so that he could focus entirely upon the spiritual. Sasha felt her heart gallop in gathering alarm and dismay. She had not known that her father wore the shroud at prayer. Such things were for the especially devout, and the penitent and fallible.

Torvaal rose, slowly, removed the cloth from his head, and gave it to the priest. Then he backed from the pedestal, head bowed, and straightened, arching his neck as if to stretch stiff muscles, gazing up at the huge, eight-pointed Verenthane star upon the wall above.

"Daughter," he said, and his voice was clear in the hushed temple air, although he had not spoken loudly. His tone held no anger, only calm. That, at least, was a relief. "You have come to me."

The priest gestured urgently for Sasha to approach. She did so, clutching Daryd's hand as she rounded the altar steps. She recalled blue blossoms behind the priest at the altar from childhood services. Now there was the neck chain and star. She wondered at the significance.

"My Lord," she addressed her father, and sank to one knee. Daryd did likewise, shooting her sideways looks to see that he did it properly. Clutched in her own, she could feel his hand trembling.

"Rise, daughter," said Torvaal. There was a calmness to his tone that had been absent on previous occasions. He seemed almost . . . content. Sasha's hopes rose dramatically. "How long has it been since you last ventured into this place?"

"A long time, Father." Torvaal had not yet looked at her. He gazed instead upward, his expression distant. His black beard, she saw in profile, had been recently trimmed. "Twelve years, I would think. Krystoff's funeral."

Her father drew in a long, deep breath. Sasha wondered if she'd said the wrong thing. "Yes," Torvaal said quietly. "Yes, that would be the time. The last time that Kessligh, too, was here."

"Aye, my Lord," said Sasha. "It would be."

"It is beautiful, is it not?" Torvaal asked. "Such tranquillity."

The priest, Sasha noted, had melted away. They were alone in the great temple, herself and her father. And Daryd, who understood barely a word. She had not been in such a circumstance with him perhaps ever, in her entire life. Suddenly, her mouth felt dry. "Very beautiful, my Lord."

A faint smile seemed to tug at Torvaal's lips. "Such manners. Whenever one of your sisters comes to me in search of some great favour, I hear much the same tone." Sasha blinked. It was almost humour. She was astonished. "What would you ask of me, daughter mine?"

"That you consider the plight of this boy, my Lord." Torvaal looked at her for the first time. His eyes narrowed slightly, as if the sight surprised him. Well, perhaps it did.

His gaze slipped down to consider the boy. "He is Udalyn, my Lord," said Sasha.

Torvaal nodded. "I know," he said, with a faint weariness. "I heard you from the entrance. Not for nothing do I wear the shroud. The gods are infallible, Sashandra. Yet the more I have attempted communion with their light, the more I recognise my own failings. Even with the shroud, I cannot find peace. The noise of the world penetrates my ears, and the silent enlightenment of heaven eludes me yet."

"Then you know that Ymoth has fallen, father!" Sasha was unable to keep the urgency from her voice. "Usyn Telgar leads the armies of Hadryn against the Udalyn, against all the instruction of Baen-Tar for the past hundred years! The boy's name is Daryd and he does not know whether his parents are alive or dead! He rode to Baen-Tar to plead with you for their lives, Father, and the lives of his people! Will you order them saved?"

Torvaal took a deep breath. He turned and gazed up at the great Verenthane star upon the wall, gloved hands clasped behind his back. "Such decisions," he said then, with heavy finality, "are no longer in my hands."

Sasha stared, incredulous. "Why? You are king! All of Lenayin answers to you!"

The king gave a faint shake of his head. "Daughter, you do not understand."

"Enlighten me." Her temper was slipping once more. She knew it was most unwise, yet she could not stop it.

"The gods have chosen," Torvaal said simply. "The wisdom of the gods is infinite. Once, I had thought that the signs pointed toward Saalshen and the Nasi-Keth. Now, I see that those were not signs, but merely my own delusion. Now, I see clearly that the signs point toward the great brotherhood of Verenthane. It is the gods' will."

"It's *your* will!" Sasha retorted, and took a deep breath, gathering herself. "Father. Father, please. Kessligh always told me of your justice. You know that the Udalyn Valley is the stitch that holds the tapestry of Lenayin together. If that stitch is undone, the tapestry shall unravel entirely. You *know* this!"

"You are young," said Torvaal, with hard finality. "Krystoff was your brother, and your love for him was strong. You saw him through a child's eyes—you still do. You never saw the gods' intent, daughter. You believed your own eyes, and trusted your own judgment, never realising how it could lead you so far astray.

"Krystoff was the king's heir, just as I was my father's. To be the heir is a sacred thing. I was anointed myself, here in this temple, as a child. The archbishop blessed me with the holy water before a gathering of lords from across Lenayin. In that, my fate was bound to the will of the gods. My father's rule was fair and just, and the gods smiled upon him. When your grandfather died, I became king. It was the gods' will, Sashandra. Such is indisputable.

"Yes, I ruled. I did what I felt was just. I did my best to please the fates." Torvaal reached with one black-gloved hand to the gold Verenthane star upon the pedestal. There was a sadness on his face. "And yet I failed. My heir was taken from me. Kessligh, Lenayin's saviour from heaven, left my service. And he took my daughter. Sorrows, the old texts say, always come in threes. Bad omens too. The gods' judgment is irrevocable. I must bow to it."

He looked at Sasha. The sadness vanished, replaced by cool formality, like a mask. "I am guilty of vanity, daughter. I had a great plan for Lenayin. Yet great plans are for the gods alone, and now, I must pay penance. Koenyg has shown great gifts of command. The north favours him and our lords and captains admire his leadership. The gods intend for Lenayin a new direction, Sashandra. Had they not, they would not have taken Krystoff from me. With Koenyg at my right hand, I shall follow it."

Sasha stared at him, mouth open in disbelief. Suddenly, the temple air seemed cold. A flash of memory struck her . . . Krystoff's chambers, filled with morning light from the windows. He had promised her a horse ride, and she'd burst in without knocking as the servants had learned to, and sent a half-naked lady-in-waiting scurrying for the covers. Krystoff, topless and muscular, had leaped from the bed and ushered her into the adjoining room. Sasha recalled his replies to her confusion, the winsome, faintly exasperated smile at her questions that told her she'd stumbled onto some peculiarly adult thing and was out of her depth. And she recalled the gold Verenthane star against his bare chest.

And she stared, now, at the chain and star upon the pedestal. It had been his. She'd rarely seen him wear it. He'd always worn the little bracelet of beads that she'd made for him, in one of the few craft lessons she'd ever paid attention to. And he'd always worn the stylised belt-knife that a visiting serrin, a friend of Kessligh's from Petrodor, had once presented him with. But rarely the Verenthane star, except on formal occasions. Or, perhaps, when bedding Verenthane maidens who needed convincing that the sin would not send them straight to the fires of Loth.

Looking at her father, Sasha felt an emotion beyond her immediate shock, or her more familiar anger. It was pity. Torvaal had lost an heir. He grieved for the loss in the terms of what it had cost him, as a father, as a king, and as a servant of the gods. He recalled Krystoff by this symbol, and placed it in such a position of prominence within the greatest temple in Lenayin. He prayed before it every day, seeking penance for perceived sins.

And yet, this symbol was not Krystoff. Not truly. Not according to one who had known him as she had. The star, to Krystoff, had been like all the formal clothes he had disliked wearing, or all the painfully self-important people he was obliged to greet, and be nice to, whilst muttering rude things about them when none save his delighted little sister could hear. It was pomp and ceremony, and badges of office, all the things that Krystoff had either despised, or found tiresome at best. If one had wished a more fitting tribute to Krystoff, one might have inaugurated a lagand festival in his name . . . or an annual dance, where dashing young men might pursue the pretty, available girls with a gleam in their eye. This star upon the pedestal was merely a father's projection of his own beliefs and desires.

Sasha's eyes prickled. For a father to grieve for his son was sad. For that father to do so without ever truly knowing who his son had been was tragic.

"And so Lenayin shall be torn to pieces," she said tightly, "because the king has lost his nerve."

A dark fire lit in Torvaal's eyes. Fearsome, in a way that another man's anger might not have affected her. Whether that was because he was her king, or her father, she could not guess. "The gods have entrusted in me a great responsibility, daughter," he said coldly. "As king I represent their will upon this land. Your insults cause me little care, for I am humble. Yet to insult the gods' will is sacrilege. I shall not allow it, and if you think the gods' justice shall be less for one of my own flesh and blood, you shall be sadly mistaken."

From the far end of the temple, there came voices and the approach of heavy footsteps. Soldiers, Sasha knew without looking. Her time had run out. Politeness had not worked. Pleading had not. And her fury was escaping its bounds.

"You hide behind your gods like a coward behind his shield," Sasha snarled. Torvaal's eyes snapped wide, as if he'd been physically struck. "The responsibility is *yours*, father! *You* were chosen! *You* are the heir to the legacy of great-grandfather Soros! You cannot merely abdicate from your true beliefs when your conviction fails and your grief grows too strong! You fear committing a crime against the gods, well I'll show you a crime—you *know* this is wrong, you *know* what the outcome shall be, and still you do nothing!"

Torvaal seemed to tremble. She'd never seen him so angry. For a moment, she thought he might strike her . . . or try to. Then he turned and strode about the altar's far side to meet the guardsmen who approached down the aisle. Sasha followed him, clutching Daryd, who was staring up at her, and at the approaching soldiers, in increasing alarm.

"Take custody of the boy," Torvaal told the first soldier who arrived. "Treat him well. Take him to Prince Koenyg, and be discreet."

The soldier and his partner advanced, at least ten more in their wake. The senior of the two was Goeren-yai. "You stop right there or by the Synnich I'll make you regret it," Sasha snarled. The man stopped, frozen in his tracks. His junior, although Verenthane by appearance, seemed greatly unnerved by his senior's reaction and also halted, a hand on his sword hilt.

Torvaal rounded on her in fury. "How dare you speak that name in this place!" he demanded, his voice trembling.

"Why?" Sasha demanded. "It is a name known to fully half of your people, and probably more! Your people, Father! Why are their names and words unfit for speech in the halls of Lenay power?"

"You presume to speak of things about which you have no comprehension!"

"I comprehend that you are the leader of your people! I comprehend that the Goeren-yai desire leadership! And what do you give them? An army of Hadryn fanatics to slaughter their kin and lay waste to the most admired, most loved soul of their ancient beliefs! As well rip out their heart and stamp on it! You proclaim to be the leader of all the Lenay people? Well lead!"

"*Neis*, Sashandra!" It was Daryd, tugging urgently on her arm. His eyes, pleading up at her, were full of fear. "*Neis! Neis!*" That word was common enough in the northern tongues. He had wanted her to win her father over, not to declare war on him. He turned to stare up at the stunned, motionless soldiers. At the king, churning with silent rage. He ran toward the king, a guardsman quickly leaping between, but Daryd threw himself onto his knees and pressed his forehead to the stones. He spoke no words, perhaps knowing by now their futility. There was only his one, last gesture. Total obeisance. Total desperation.

Torvaal edged the guardsman aside and stared down at the boy huddled at his feet. Emotions battled within his dark eyes. More emotion than Sasha could recall seeing from him in her entire life. For a moment, she thought he might speak to the boy. Might kneel down and raise him to his feet, in a kindly gesture.

"Take him," the king said instead, quietly. "Be gentle." The guardsman knelt and raised Daryd to his feet. The boy turned to Sasha before he could be led away. Sasha saw tears in his eyes.

"Rysha," he begged her. "Rysha." Sasha nodded, helplessly. Her right hand itched for the sword on her shoulder, but that would do no good here. She stood where she was and watched as a pair of guardsmen escorted the Udalyn lad up the temple aisle, toward the doors.

"You," Torvaal said darkly to Sasha, "are confined to quarters. The Nasi-Keth shall be without a representative this first day of Rathynal. Be thankful that your punishment is so light."

Sasha regarded him coldly for a moment. Then she bowed, lingeringly, with something less than polite intent. "My father's mercy is renowned throughout the land," she said icily. She stalked off, a guardsman joining her on each arm. "Don't bother," she told them. "I'm quite sure I know the way."

"What?" roared Lord Krayliss. "You think to bring this *charge* against me now, and call it justice!"

He rose to his feet, a hand to the hilt of his sword. About the circle of lords others also rose, officers and soldiers interposing, sword hands at the ready. At Damon's side, Myklas also made to rise, but Damon restrained him with a hand, and gave him a warning look. Koenyg stood before the king's throne imposing in his cloak of royal black. Behind, and up the length of the great hall, nobles and soldiers from each of Lenayin's eleven provinces also rose, smelling a fight.

"Lord Krayliss," Koenyg announced coldly, his voice loud enough that all could hear. "You were brought to Baen-Tar by Prince Damon on the understanding that you were placing yourself within the protection of the king's law! Your violations of the king's law are profound for all to see. You do not deny that you slew Great Lord Rashyd Telgar of Hadryn. The king deems it fit for you to be judged before a council of lords this Rathynal, as the king wishes the people of Lenayin to observe the justice of *all* Lenayin, and not merely the justice of its king. Do you wish to object to the king's law, and would you also reject its protections from the rightful revenge of the new Great Lord Usyn?"

"Object?" Lord Krayliss bellowed. "I agreed to be judged by your Verenthane law on the condition of the presence of Sashandra Lenayin! And now you wish to conduct this justice without her presence?"

At Koenyg's back, King Torvaal sat upon his throne and watched, his eyes impassive.

"The Lady Sashandra has acted against the express wishes of the king," Koenyg replied, "and has consorted with troublemakers. She forfeits her right to be present at the first day of Rathynal as the Nasi-Keth's representative."

"Oh aye, how convenient!" Krayliss turned to confront the crowd, with an expansive, theatrical gesture. "This is what we get to replace the good Prince Krystoff! Never was there a law or an honourable agreement that this man could not find a way to sneak around like a filthy, cheating coward!"

A roar of outrage followed and swords about the circle of lords were half drawn. Men yelled for the Lord of Taneryn's head on the spot. Behind the Taneryn flag that hung above Krayliss's chair, ten of Krayliss's senior men placed hands near their swords, a wild-haired, disreputable corner of an otherwise impeccably groomed gathering. Koenyg raised both hands, unmoved. The circle's fury, and that of the seated gathering behind, subsided.

Krayliss's eyes gleamed with triumph. He thought he'd won, Damon reckoned. Submit Sashandra to the trial, and risk revealing the truth of her Goeren-yai sympathies . . . or withhold her, thus breaking her agreement. That was the dilemma he had presented to the king and Koenyg. Now, he was the aggrieved lord, having suffered a great injustice at the hands of the Verenthane king. His stage was set.

"Look at you all!" Krayliss snarled at the furious men standing about the circle. "Verenthane pets! Do any of you know the wishes of the Goeren-yai of your provinces, the ones as whose lords you pompously style yourselves? Do any of you care to guess what shall happen to you when they hear of this outrage?" He strutted forward, bristling with self-righteous rage. "So brave you look, surrounded by your Verenthane cronies, and your inbred, sister-buggering uncles and cousins . . ."

Lord Kumaryn of Valhanan gave a roar of rage and drew his sword clear with a ring that echoed the clear length of the hall.

"HOLD!" Koenyg yelled, pulling his own sword clear.

Red-faced, Lord Kumaryn glared at his prince, gulping air like a stranded fish. "Highness!" he protested. "A man can only take so much!"

"A man can take all of this and more if his prince commands it!" Koenyg retorted. "And he shall!"

"How long will your bravery last, Lord Kumaryn?" Lord Krayliss roared at him. "You think your honour in tatters now? What of the honour you have stolen from your people? Will you be so defiant when all those neglected thousands arrive on the doorstep of your great Cryliss mansion, weapons raised in anger, and demand restitution for all the honour of which you have deprived them?"

"The Goeren-yai do not follow you!" Kumaryn yelled, trembling with rage. "All through the villages of Valhanan, they call you a fool, and a troublemaker!"

"And you think they will follow *you*?" Krayliss retorted. "All the way to Larosa to murder serrin children while they sleep? And what's this?" With feigned disbelief, staring about the circle of lords. "I count only ten flags! Even a pagan Goeren-yai has enough education to know that there are eleven provinces in Lenayin!"

He put a hand to his chest, in mock disbelief. "Where are the Hadryn? Where indeed, I wonder! I'll tell you where! They're off murdering the Udalyn in their valley! Just last night I received two small Udalyn children into my refuge! They had come from Ymoth, where the Hadryn had pillaged and burned! And how is it that the Hadryn feel so emboldened, we all wonder, when the Verenthane kings of Lenayin have always forbidden them in the past?

"They struck a deal with the king, didn't they?" He levelled a hard finger at Torvaal's throne. "I see you hiding back there, little king! You cannot hide behind your heir forever! You needed the north's support for your lowlands war and so now they have free rein to slaughter whomever they want, don't they? Lady Sashandra brought a child to you this morning to beg for the lives of the Udalyn, didn't she? And you were so *offended* that anyone should *dare* to care enough for the lives of a bunch of shaggy-headed *pagans* that you barred her in her room, and thought to spring this trial upon the last remaining pagan lord in her absence!"

"If you wish to make complaint against the king's rule," Torvaal said heavily from his throne, "then there are formal ways and means of doing so."

"No longer!" Krayliss thundered, with a thrust of his finger. "The time of rule by Verenthane kings is over! No more do we play by your corrupted and honourless rules! I declare Taneryn is no longer within the Kingdom of Lenayin! The last, free corner of Lenayin is free from the Verenthane yoke once and for all! I reject this Rathynal, I reject this city, and I reject *you*, Master Torvaal! Men of Taneryn, arise, we are leaving! And let it be known that any Goeren-yai from any province who wishes to ride in haste and save our brother Udalyn from annihilation, we shall welcome you with open arms!"

And with that, Lord Krayliss of Taneryn and his contingent of nobles and warriors strode for the hall's central aisle, and made for the great doors at the end.

"Let them leave!" Koenyg called, standing still upon the centre of the vast eight-pointed star splayed in tile across the hall's floor. Above soared the great palace dome, its ceiling alive with a mural—King Soros upon a white steed, leading his army of holy warriors to victory over the Cherrovan. Pagan Cherrovan fleeing his holy light, while pagan Lenays fall to one knee, in awe and gratitude. "They are but a crazed few from a dying breed. Let them leave."

Damon stared at his brother's cloaked back in disbelief. "I don't believe you just said that," he muttered, so that none but Myklas could overhear.

Myklas frowned. "It's true, isn't it?"

"A lot of men are about to die needlessly," Damon said quietly. He unclenched his fist from the armrest of the chair with difficulty, watching the last of the Taneryn contingent file out, with contemptuous glares at the watching Verenthanes on all sides. "Sasha was right, brother. Damn her for a pain in the neck, but she was right all along."

Sasha performed taka-dans with a naked blade until the light had crawled across Sofy's bed and fell now upon her own. With that and other exercises had she occupied herself all the morning, locked into Sofy's chambers. She heard the door being unlatched and then Sofy's maid Anyse appeared, a meal tray in her hands. Anyse paused, startled, to see the concluding strokes of Sasha's taka-dan. Sasha sheathed the blade in one smooth motion and the maid smiled nervously, then hurried to place the tray upon Sofy's writing desk by the windows.

Turning back to Sasha, she made a hurried curtsy, apparently wishing permission to speak. Sasha nodded. Anyse's freckled face was earnest. "M'Lady," she said in a low voice so that the guards beyond the door could not hear, "Princess Sofy sends her greetings."

Sasha frowned. "Is she having fun with her Larosan friends?"

"She is concerned for you, M'Lady. She sends word that she is seeking to know where the young boy is being held."

Anyse glanced furtively toward the doorway. "I was sent to give you a message. Lord Krayliss has caused a commotion at Rathynal. He accused the king of betraying the Udalyn, and all but issued a call to arms. He stormed out of the hall before he could be removed and has returned to his encampment upon the fields."

Sasha took a deep breath and stared toward the windows. She was not particularly surprised. Events were set in motion. Opportunists would seek to capitalise. Now, it had truly begun. "Thank you," she said quietly. "I am glad to know."

Anyse turned as if to go, hesitating even as she did. Sasha saw the indecision and gestured for the maid to speak. "M'Lady . . . what of the Udalyn?" Anyse whispered, with great apprehension.

Sasha frowned. "Would you follow Lord Krayliss?"

"No . . . no, M'Lady." A vehement shake of the head. "Not by choice. But . . . the Udalyn, M'Lady . . ."

"I know," Sasha said darkly. "Something shall be done, you can count on it. But Lord Krayliss is not the man to do it."

"Aye," Anyse replied, fear battling with relief and uncertainty in her eyes. "Aye, M'Lady." Another pause before she left. "Please be safe," she offered, and fled. Sasha took a deep breath. Surely Koenyg knew Sofy had Goeren-yai on her staff. Anyse amongst them. Surely he knew better than to try to persuade Sofy to have them replaced. And better still than to try and command it. Sofy was not an enemy a wise man would wish to make. But Sasha was equally sure that Koenyg knew who the Goeren-yai staff were and would have them watched. Any move she made now, after that visit, would surely be fraught with risk. Yet was there any choice?

She sat down to eat her meal, for her stomach was rumbling at the smell. Below through the windows, there were children running in the courtyard with squeals and cries as they played, leaping and rolling upon the grass. Rysha, she thought as she ate the soup and tore off a piece of bread. Daryd's last word, and last concern, as the soldiers had led him away. Rysha was at Krayliss's camp. She could not stay there—Krayliss's camp had just become the least safe location in Baen-Tar. Sasha had promised Daryd his sister would be cared for. And, besides, she needed to talk to Krayliss before any new calamity occurred.

Completing her meal, she stripped her bed of its sheets and began knotting them together. The problem with Baen-Tar Verenthanes, she thought as she worked, was that they were all so unimaginative. A man or woman born into such a world had duties to perform, and formalities to follow. They would think and reason as they did.

And so, even now that she was a trained Nasi-Keth warrior with a sword at her back, the good Verenthanes of Baen-Tar would assume that any princess ordered by her father to remain in chambers would stay there. She was little seen in Baen-Tar these days after all, and the guards only knew tales of her wildness from her childhood. There were two such guards at the door, with no view of the window, and she knew there would be no one in the courtyard below. She'd checked the moment she'd been quartered in Sofy's chambers.

She ran much of the way to the stables, darting through back roads and lanes wherever possible, slowing to a walk when there were people about, for fear of attracting attention. But the line of sheets trailing from the window of Sofy's chambers had doubtless been seen by now. She could only hope that the speed with which a message would reach Koenyg would not be as fast as she was.

The confusion of activity on the first day of Rathynal about the stables was a blessing and she passed unnoticed in her long cloak amidst the stablehands, junior nobles and soldiers. Peg seemed pleased to see her and offered no complaint as she saddled him in haste. She rode at civilised speed up the road toward the gates, passing yet more inbound traffic.

She announced herself to the guards at the main gate, hood thrown back, and received only frowning looks and a gesture to proceed.

Low cloud scudded above the hills as she rode toward the Baen-Tar cliff, grey and ominous, the farther, steeper hills shrouded in mist. Descending the cut, she saw a gathering of horse and men upon the eastern slope. They were barely dots on the paddocks, but there seemed a predominance of black to their uniform—a colour favoured by the northern provinces in battle.

"Damn," she muttered to herself, as a chill seized her heart. She had moved as fast as she could, but Koenyg had been faster.

She urged Peg into a fast trot down the rock-paved incline. Then they were at the bottom, and she kicked with her heels, pulling Peg off the road and onto the grass, where he accelerated into a joyful gallop.

She headed for a road which cut between walled paddocks toward the nearest tents. Peg saw her intention, and she let him choose his own angle of approach, hurdling a drainage ditch and then thundering onto the earth road between paddocks. She took the bends between low stone walls at speed, cold wind stinging her eyes as she tried to peer ahead and guess the best route between walls and encampments of tents, men, horses and carts. Upslope and around, she reckoned, going the long way about.

She leapt a fence as the road turned, racing across a paddock, sheep scattering in a bounding, woolly sea as she turned downhill, headed for the camp's outer edges. Leaping several walls, she then jumped a gate to rejoin another road. Peg wove through several more bends, cutting corners that flashed by with speed that few horses could have hoped to match. And then they were coming onto the lower slopes, where the paddocks fell away more sharply toward the forest below.

Sasha turned right along a narrow trail, wondering if any of the encamped soldiers would take note of the big black horse, and alert others . . . but she could not see any men about the nearest tents. Peg cantered as fast as the winding trail would allow, past a rickety farmer's shack and a pair of work-worn men tending plowed rows of vegetables . . . and there, against the wood-walled town houses ahead, was the Taneryn encampment, isolated in its field. A line of riders in black emerged from the town's streets ahead. Banners whipped on the wind, too distant yet for her to see, but it was obvious her time was short.

The trail straightened enough for her to get a good run at the next wall. Peg sailed over, and then it was a mad gallop across the paddocks, clearing several more walls and scattering livestock, before jumping a final wall and landing on the road she and Jaryd had ridden the other night. It forked where she recalled and then it lay before her, the Taneryn tents on the slope, the Taneryn banner flying atop a tent pole, cart horses grazing and tethered near their carts. Upslope, a dark line had formed. Mounted soldiers and banners—a red sword upon a black background. Ranash, Hadryn's northern neighbour. An opposing line was moving to confront them, a ragged assembly of Taneryn men and horses.

The gate leading onto the paddock's lower slope was open, and Sasha swerved Peg through it, racing uphill toward a large vertyn tree below the encampment. She hauled Peg to a halt, dismounted and threw his reins over a broken branch stump—there was no time for a full tether, but also little chance that Peg would wander anywhere except to find her. She removed her cloak, stuffed it into one saddlebag and ran for the nearest tents.

A Taneryn man came running across to intercept her—a guard facing the lower slope, watching for an ambush from behind. It was unlikely, Sasha knew—all cavalry sought the heights and it was the Taneryn, held fast to defend their encampment, who conceded those. The man's eyes widened as he saw who it was and his blade dropped.

Sasha ran to him. "The little Udalyn girl!" she demanded. "Where is she?"

"I . . . M'Lord Krayliss's tent, I would think . . ."

And Sasha was off, running between tents, trying to recall the way from the other night, though it had been very dark then and now it all looked different. She dodged guide ropes and steel pegs, with abandoned saddles and saddlebags suggesting a surprised, hasty departure. She found the central fireplace with cooking utensils lying about . . . There! The big tent beyond, its centre pole somewhat taller than the others.

She ran to the main flaps and pulled them aside. Within were familiar rugs upon the grassy floor, but no little Rysha. Sasha backed out, staring about in frustration. Where would they have taken her? She dared not call out, for the Ranash troops would be close enough to hear. To be placed in Krayliss's camp, at such a time, would be most unfortunate.

She ran to the nearest tent and looked within, but found nothing. Then the next, working her way upslope. She paused within one tent, lay flat on the ground and lifted the canvas. A line of Taneryn men confronted a larger, mounted force upslope.

To the front of the Ranash lines sat a man astride a big, grey charger. The bearer at his back carried the royal banner of purple and green, and six Royal Guardsmen held position at his flanks. Koenyg, Sasha realised, with little surprise. He wore battle leathers over a chain vest, as did the rest, a blade at his hip. And he was speaking, loudly, although his words were dimmed from this angle by the tailwind. Sasha strained her ears.

". . . by Royal decree!" her eldest brother was shouting. "The order has been passed! Royal sovereignty has been challenged and a retraction is demanded! Should the Lord Krayliss, Great Lord of Taneryn, fail to retract, then he shall be considered in open rebellion against the crown!"

Sasha ran her eyes along the mounted Ranash line. Red and black, their horses large, their shoulders broad beneath chainmail of northern forging. Grim-faced men, some with trimmed beards beneath their helms, but mostly clean shaven. Perhaps half bore shields, unlike the Midlands–Lenay custom. The northern heavy cavalry, renowned through all Lenayin and beyond. The shield of Lenayin, and the bane of Cherrovan.

Sasha felt her skin crawl, to see her brother, the heir to the throne of Lenayin, seated astride before such a formation. Doubtless he did not trust a mixed Verenthane and Goeren-yai formation to perform such a task. And so the king-in-waiting would lead a puritan Verenthane force to crush the last of the Goeren-yai lords, in full view of the other provincial contingents. Her heart was pounding. She had to find Rysha, yet somehow, she could not tear herself from the scene before her.

Lord Krayliss rode out upon a warhorse—one of Taneryn's few, no doubt, for most of their mounts were skinny dussieh. The wind gusted at his long, tangled hair, and swirled at his beard. He rode erect in the saddle, a cloak over hard-stitched leathers, and paused, alone on the hillslope. Beyond, Sasha could see the distant figures of yet more soldiers clustering in rows before their tents to watch. Very faintly, she heard distant yells, and then a trumpet, officers in those neighbouring camps attempting to form their men into orderly ranks. They feared a rebellion. They feared the Goeren-yai in their midst would break ranks and come racing downhill with blades drawn to save the last of the old chieftains from certain doom. Koenyg played games with Krayliss for the fate of Lenayin. The civil war could start here, upon this hillside, this chill and cloudy afternoon. The division of provinces and towns into warring factions, Verenthane against Goeren-yai, neighbour against neighbour. The end of a nation.

Lord Krayliss halted his mount and stood in the saddle. "And so it comes to this!" he bellowed, his voice carrying further and louder than Koenyg's had. "The heir to the throne, and his pet band of Verenthane murderers! You accuse me of rebellion! You accuse the Goeren-yai of disloyalty! Well, I shall tell you, Prince Koenyg, that the crown of Lenayin has never found such loyal, honourable servants as we men of the ancient ways!

"And what do we get for all our years of loyal service?" His voice lifted to a furious roar as he faced the watching ranks of mixed Verenthane and Goeren-yai soldiers upon the upper paddocks. "The massacre of the Udalyn! Yes, I receive battered and desperate survivors even now as the bloody Hadryn campaign through the ancient valley! And then, good Prince, you wish us to wage war upon the serrin, who have always been friends to the Goeren-yai! And all this, while you rape our culture, ignore our customs, send priests from your temples to convert impoverished villagers and then blame us for the troubles and anger it causes!

"It all ends here! We, the rightful men of Lenayin, demand justice! The honour of the ancient ways has for a century been dragged through the mud, stamped upon by each and every Verenthane boot in the land! The honour of the Goeren-yai demands that it ends, or that we must die fighting for what is ours!"

He clenched his fist in the air, and a roar went up from the Taneryn line. Perhaps fifty men, mostly mounted. Naked blades were brandished against the cloudy afternoon sky and chants of open defiance carried on the wind. It seemed that time had stopped. Such open defiance to the crown, from a provincial great lord, had been unknown in Lenayin for a hundred years. It did not seem real—that the moment should finally arrive.

Koenyg gave a signal and a Ranash captain galloped behind his line, shouting orders in a northern tongue. Blades were drawn, broad and sharp, clutched in gloved fists. The Ranash line numbered at least a hundred, in two ranks with more in reserve. They held position with the discipline of regimented drill. Whatever the wild-haired, brazen ferocity of the Taneryn line, it now appeared fragile indeed.

Krayliss, Sasha noted, had not moved. He stared upslope toward the tents and the half-assembled formations of provincial soldiers who stood watching. One of Krayliss's men rode to his side, appearing to beg him to fall back. Krayliss ignored him and stood once more in his saddle.

"Men of the ancient ways!" he roared toward the watching soldiers. "You serve with Verenthanes, but you do not belong to them! You belong to the spirits! You belong to the untamed hills, wild and free! Will you allow the Udalyn to be slaughtered? Will you watch your honour battered and stabbed until it crumbles into dust?"

A yell from the Ranash captain and the outer flanks wheeled, creating more space along the formation, the inner riders moving outward, dressing the line.

"What do you wait for?" Krayliss yelled. To Sasha's ears, it seemed as if a new, alien emotion had entered the great chieftain's voice. Desperation. He ripped his great blade from its sheath and thrust it skyward, glinting dully against the darkening clouds. "Fight!" he roared. "Fight, and claim what is yours!"

From the soldiers upon the upper fields, there came no reply. No restive murmuring, no chants or yells of fury, or of sympathy. Just a restless, disbelieving silence. Men stood, and waited. Krayliss stared in disbelief. His blade dropped. A yell from the Ranash captain and the northern line advanced, rising quickly to a canter.

Sasha dropped the canvas and ran for the tent exit as a roar went up from behind. "Rysha!" she yelled at the top of her lungs as hooves thundered, and then there were Taneryn horses wheeling back amidst the tents at speed. Horses thundered past, dussieh and then larger, weapons brandished, swords clashing as Sasha crouched behind a tent, awaiting an opening in the forest of hooves. A horse crashed through the tent, mount and rider falling as the tent pole broke, and Sasha scrambled backwards, then threw herself rolling as another came straight at her.

Then she ran, darting and dodging as best she could, as the world became a confusion of screaming men and horse, slashing blades and falling bodies. Horses tripped on guide ropes, fallen men were trampled by friend and foe alike, or slashed hard at the mounts of riders to bring down both beast and man in a thrashing, bloody heap. Sasha darted, dove, scrambled and crawled her way through the chaos, headed downslope as instinct drove her toward Peg and possibly the forest at the base of the hill . . . a Taneryn man was cut from his horse before her with an expert slash from passing cavalry, and fell in a spray of blood. Sasha ran for the riderless dussieh, grabbing a stirrup as the terrified animal tried to run, then hurdling astride.

The small horse wheeled in confusion, Sasha spurring hard until it lurched downslope, weaving between tents and tripping on bodies of fallen animals and riders . . . a pair of Ranash cavalry came across in front, Sasha reining desperately backwards, then sought the way those two had come, to wrongfoot and dash for the clear space . . . A dismounted man in black and red appeared suddenly in front, slashing low for the dussieh's legs. It fell with a shriek as Sasha barely managed to leap with her feet clear of the stirrups.

She hit the ground and rolled, coming to her feet, her sword in hand as the Ranash man came at her. She flicked his downward smash aside with a twist of wrists and elbows, then slashed his stomach and spun clear to remove his head as he doubled over. The first two riders were coming back, and she ran, dodging to avoid a rushing Taneryn, hurdling another's bloody corpse as yet another stumbled screaming nearby, his arm severed and spurting blood, until a passing cavalryman cut him down.

She dove behind a collapsed tent, gasping for breath, huddling close to the canvas for cover. Something moved beneath the canvas and whimpered. Sasha pulled it aside in horror . . . and found Rysha, staring with wide, terrified eyes. Sasha grabbed her with her free arm and held her. The little girl clung to her, too frightened even to scream or cry. I got you into this, Sasha thought. What have I done?

Beyond the edge of the encampment, horses wheeled and riders fought. She watched as Taneryn warriors were cut down, outnumbered, outmanoeuvred and overpowered. There were Ranash cavalry everywhere. If she could just find another riderless horse—if she could just break clear and make for the trees—a little dussieh would be more nimble through the forest than a great warhorse . . .

Only now there were dismounted cavalry moving in, searching through the tents, examining bodies. One drove his blade into a fallen Taneryn to be sure. Sasha felt a surge of fury, rivalling the fear.

"Hide," she said to Rysha, pulling the collapsed canvas more fully over her. Then she rose and stepped toward the approaching Ranash, having now no other choice.

They saw her, and one in particular had the lead. "Hello hello!" he said with cocksure delight, twirling his blade. His clean-shaven face was blood-spattered beneath his helm. "What have we here? The queen viper herself in the viper's nest? I'll have you for a nice trophy, my pretty. Goeren-yai princess indeed . . ."

He lunged and swung. Sasha faded, parried and split his head like a melon, helm and all. Another roared fury and leaped, Sasha parrying whilst spinning aside and into a third attacker. She defended once whilst falling to a crouch, and took his leg while rolling. She came up fast, crossed the next overhead defence into a vicious, diagonal slice of rotating shoulders and wrists, taking the second man across shoulder and face, then driving the sword point through the chest of the fallen man whose leg she'd taken, all in one motion.

Hooves thundered, and running footsteps approached from all angles. It had been seen. Dismounted men came running, weapons ready, their eyes wide, noting her identity and the corpses upon the blood-soaked ground beneath her boots. They encircled, warily, blades at the ready.

Sasha swivelled from one to the next, trying to watch all ways at once. The three at her feet, it occurred to her, had been easy. The next attack would be trouble—these would not take her so casually. But, even so, she fancied herself a slight chance. At the very least she would add to this pile at her feet.

This, she realised, was how it felt to be great. Not merely good, as many Lenay soldiers could claim, but truly great, as only one like Kessligh, or a warrior of Saalshen, might know. To feel confidence, where others might know despair. To know that the smallest error meant death, yet to remain unwavering. To see, in a vague and general way, that she was most likely doomed . . . and yet to stay calm, seeking an outlet, searching for the opening. To know that this, more than anything, was what she was, and what she was meant for. Despair was pointless. This was not her death. This was her life.

Shouts from behind, then, as several more horses came close, their riders dismounting. Then a Ranash man was pushed aside and Koenyg stood in his place, staring with disbelief.

"You!" he said. There was blood on his weapon, and more on clothes. But then, it had never been like Koenyg to order men into battle and not to partake himself.

"I came to rescue the little Udalyn girl," Sasha told him, past the lethal, bloody edge of her weapon. It had cut through northern chainmail, yet bore barely a mark. Neither did her voice, which was cool and steady.

"Which little Udalyn girl?" Koenyg asked flatly. There was hostility on his broad face. And suspicion.

"The sister of the boy I brought to father," said Sasha. "She is under the tent behind me. Look gently, she is frightened and harmless."

Koenyg nodded curtly to a man behind her and there came the sound of canvas being moved. Then a frightened cry from a little girl's mouth.

"It's all right, Rysha!" Sasha called, not turning to look. Neither did she abandon her ready posture. "Rysha, be still! My brother is an honourable man. He would not harm a little girl." With a dark stare at Koenyg, challenging him to prove her words true.

"You are in league with Lord Krayliss," Koenyg observed, just as darkly.

"I am not," Sasha said coldly. "I rode down here to rescue Rysha from your attack . . ."

"You left her here," Koenyg said bitterly. "You brought the boy here too. Only Taneryn men could make sense of the Edu tongue. He helped you. You are collaborators against the crown, each as guilty as the other."

Sasha felt a blaze of fury. Koenyg had often spoken of loyalty between members of Verenthane families, and now showed her none at all. Damn him. "If you wish to pass such hasty sentence," she said icily, "then best you come to administer it yourself."

"No," Koenyg said grimly. "You shall face the trial that Lord Krayliss was to have had. It is not the prince's place to deliver that justice which is the king's to dispense."

"Traitor," came the mutter from the men surrounding. "Pagan whore!" And, "Kill the pagan traitor!"

"Others have tried," Sasha said to that last, with an evil, sideways look. Braced and poised, awaiting an attack. "I stand on their bodies." There was disbelief, and fear, mingling with the smell of blood and the thunder and screams of final pursuits across the hillside. Some men of Ranash uttered oaths and made holy gestures, furious yet somehow constrained. The men of the north had never believed the stories of the svaalverd. Now, they saw the evidence. Sasha recognised the fear on their faces—it was the fear of the supernatural, the ungodly, the unVerenthane. And she did not mind at all.

A crossbowman appeared at Koenyg's side and levelled that wicked contraption at Sasha's chest. There was contempt on Koenyg's face, his jaw set. "You shall relinquish your weapons and surrender yourself to justice," he told her. "Do not be foolish. Your sister would never forgive you."

Sofy, he meant. Sasha lowered her blade, slowly, and looked her brother in the eye. "It's not me who should be worried about that," she said quietly. "When this is all over, brother, I fear few left alive in Lenayin shall forgive you."

Fifteen

"**I** DEMAND THAT YOU LET ME SEE MY BROTHER!" Sofy stared up at the impassive Royal Guardsman and tried very hard not to cry.

"I'm sorry, Your Highness," said the armoured and helmed Verenthane man, as firm as a rock before the door to Koenyg's chambers. "He is in audience. My instructions were explicit."

"Princess, please," Anyse said earnestly, tugging at Sofy's sleeve. "The sergeant is only doing his duty . . ."

"He threw my sister in a dungeon!" Sofy exclaimed on the verge of tears. "I want to know why!"

"Highness." Anyse's tug was firmer. "Let us leave, there are other people you can ask . . ."

The city was in chaos, all soldiers called to full alert, rows of archers standing upon the great wall while cavalry mounted in the stables and made rows before the main gates. Rumour was that the Taneryn contingent had been slaughtered, though details were unclear. The circumstance surrounding Sasha was even less clear. If not for Sofy's carefully cultivated lines of gossip amongst friendly palace staff, she doubted she would have discovered Sasha's plight at all.

Koenyg was keeping it quiet. Now Damon had fumed to her, moments before mounting his horse and riding out on guard as his brother ordered, that Koenyg had known how Krayliss would react to the threat of a trial without Sasha's presence, and had been ready for it. Koenyg, the master warrior, played games to destroy his opponents. Now that game included Sasha's life.

"Who is he meeting with?" Sofy asked the sergeant, struggling for composure.

"I'm sorry, Your Highness, I cannot say."

Sasha would know what to do, Sofy thought with a surge of frustration. Gods, she was so tired of being treated like a child. People ignored her, and patronised her, and told her to go elsewhere. Everyone except Sasha . . . and Damon.

She tossed her head back, and gave the sergeant a stare. "Do you have a sister, Sergeant?"

"I do, Highness."

"Do you love her?"

"Very much, Highness."

"Will you not let me in?"

"I love my prince too, Your Highness," the sergeant said simply.

Sofy sniffed. "One day, Sergeant, I fear you may come to question that ordering of priorities. Pray that you choose wisely."

She moved off down the stone hall, Anyse hurrying at her side. "Highness, we should really be making our way back to your Rathynal guests, they'll be wondering where you are . . ."

"Let them wonder," Sofy said shortly. They descended the grand staircase to the royal quarters, Sofy noting that the guard had been doubled. Instead of making her way onward to the great hall, she turned left, back toward Koenyg's quarters. A smaller, service corridor ran along the east palace wall, its windows overlooking Fortress Road and up to Saint Ambellion Temple beyond, all aflurry with commotion and soldiers.

"Highness," Anyse dared to ask, "where are you going?" Ahead, the corridor ended at an open kitchen door. A servant passed through, carrying porcelain plates on a tray. "Highness?" Sofy paused by one door, glanced up and down the corridor, then opened the latch and slid inside, beckoning Anyse to follow. "Those are the servants' stores!"

Sofy grabbed her impatiently by the arm and dragged her inside. She left the door ajar to let in some light, for the room was pitch black and musty.

"Anyse," said Sofy, "do you know where the servants' uniforms are? I want one."

Anyse stared at her. "Highness?"

"You heard me."

"You . . . you want to dress as a . . . ?" Sofy nodded.

Anyse looked aghast. "Absolutely not!"

"I'm going whether you help me or not," Sofy said firmly. "Do you want me to get caught?"

"I'll go!" Anyse said desperately. "I'll spy for you, I'll listen to what they're . . ."

"No!"

Anyse blinked in astonishment to see such anger in the younger woman's eyes.

"I need to hear myself, there's no telling if you'll understand all that's said. Now can you find me a uniform, I don't know where they're stored."

"Highness, no!" Desperately. "Sofy! It's too dangerous!"

"Do you think Koenyg would execute *me?*" Sofy said with disbelief.

"He thinks you're Sashandra's friend!"

"I am Sashandra's friend," Sofy said firmly. "And if you truly are mine, you'll help me."

The hem of the brown dress was low enough to obscure the fancy leather boots that were surely too good for any servant girl. No one looked at her as she entered Koenyg's personal kitchen. Cooks tended to pots atop metal ovens, firewood stacked high to one side. Another chopped and sliced on the main bench, while the head cook gave forceful instructions.

At the kitchen's far corner, a staircase wound upward. A servant descended that staircase now, placing empty entrée plates and glasses on a bench, picking up the empty water bucket and hurrying out, not sparing Sofy a glance as he passed. Sofy ducked her head, the servant's bonnet feeling most unusual tied beneath her chin and atop the bundled hair that Anyse had helped to arrange.

There was liquor waiting on a tray, arranged with six small glasses, and Sofy went straight to it. Barely had her hands grasped the tray when the head cook saw her.

"You girl! Just what the hells do you think you're doing?"

Sofy's heart skipped a beat. She turned, hands folded demurely, and lowered her gaze in the head cook's direction. "I . . . I was told to take these up to . . ."

"Where are your wits, girl? The whisky is for later. They've barely finished their tea yet. Take the wine, girl, the wine!" Pointing to a large decanter and glasses upon the central benches.

Sofy arranged the glasses and decanter on a tray, trying to keep her hands from trembling, and made her way up the stairs. No one stopped her. She felt a surge of relief and triumph. It was hardly bravery of Sasha's standard, but it was a bravery all the same. She nearly grinned with excitement.

The staircase spiralled once, then arrived at a curtain pulled across the entrance to Koenyg's quarters . . . Sofy had seen it before, but never from this side. She paused, excitement giving way to nervous concentration, straining her ears to make out the voices from the rooms beyond. Men's voices, clear and reasonably loud . . . but not immediately close. Another relief. They were in the main room, adjoining the dining room.

Well . . . she had to risk it. She backed through the curtain and into the dining room. A long table was set for lunch, six places ready with plates and cutlery. The windows to the right fronted directly onto Saint Ambellion Temple, with a view of Soros Square further to its north.

Sofy walked as quietly as she could to the table, trying desperately to recall how she'd seen the servants themselves do it, so as not to attract attention. She kept her back to the main room, where men stood and talked with cups in hand. She could hear Koenyg's voice as she unloaded the tray, but she was concentrating too hard on not dropping a glass to hear what he said. She heard an answering voice, with a familiar accent—lovely, flowing vowels and soft consonants. The Larosa. Sofy was surprised. Koenyg had just ridden into battle against the representatives of a province of Lenayin, and the first people he talked to were the Larosa?

She walked around the table, setting glasses before each plate . . . and glanced furtively into the next room. She could see four of the six men, and a servant with a tea tray, hovering inconspicuously. She recognised Koenyg, in formal clothes, his hair wet in the manner of one recently bathed. He appeared utterly unruffled. Another man she recognised was Archbishop Dalryn, black robed and fuzzy headed.

"One greatly doubts the risks to be quite so grave as some would make out," the archbishop was saying, in ponderous, thoughtful tones. "The pagans of Lenayin are truly pagan, yet they are also Lenay, and they obey their king. Obedience to the king is honourable to them and I must admit that, however godless, the pagans are greatly honourable. In their own way."

Sofy took up her tray and moved back toward the curtained exit. Beside that exit, however, the door to Koenyg's bed chambers was similarly curtained. Sofy took a deep breath, risked a glance over her shoulder . . . and slipped behind the bed chamber curtains. She waited, her heart pounding. She did not know what would happen if she were caught. Certainly it would be difficult to feign innocence.

She strained her ears to hear, but the conversation was mixed and it was difficult to pick out individual strands. Something drew her gaze back to Koenyg's broad bed in the centre of his room. Silver chainmail lay spread across the skin blankets, and heavy, leather gloves with steel knuckles. One had blood on it. Sofy stared.

And nearly jumped as voices came suddenly near, silencing a startled gasp before it could quite escape her lips. "I assure you that this was not entirely unforeseen," came the archbishop's voice. He seemed to be standing by the near end of the table. And he was not speaking so loud as the others. Perhaps this conversation was meant to be private. "The prince is truly a man of steel. Where another man might have faltered before such threats as Lord Krayliss made, Prince Koenyg has endeavoured to turn a difficult situation into an opportunity. And now, it seems, the Taneryn problem has been dealt with once and for all."

"I am most impressed, Your Grace," came Duke Stefhan's voice, silky smooth and ever so gracious. "And yet, one is still disquieted. My king was assured, in forging this alliance, that the clans of Lenayin no longer fought. It is disturbing to us to see our great ally so divided."

"I assure you, Duke Stefhan, these divisions are merely temporary. All bold new directions are accompanied by a temporary tumult, are they not? King Torvaal's mind is decided on the alliance, and he could not have an abler lieutenant than Prince Koenyg. I trust that you are not having second thoughts, my good Duke?"

"But of course not, Your Grace." The duke's footsteps came closer. Sofy stared down at the short gap between the bottom of the dividing curtain and the floor, wondered abruptly if the men might see her boots beneath. She backed up several steps, gingerly.

"Just . . ." and the duke sighed. "Please, Your Grace." The voice turned away from her. "I know that you are a proud Lenay. I mean no offence. But I also know that you are a true Verenthane, and a man of great culture and knowledge. I tell you only that it is no easy thing, Your Grace, for a proud people like the Larosa, and for the broader alliance of the free Bacosh peoples, to come to a land like . . . like Lenayin, for assistance."

"I quite understand, Duke Stefhan," said the archbishop. "Lenayin is a fair land, but we cannot possibly hope to match the measure of sophistication and artistry of a great people such as the Larosa." Sofy blinked in startlement. The archbishop truly believed *that*?

"I'm so pleased you understand," said Duke Stefhan, with the air of a man ever-so-relieved not to have been misunderstood.

"Dear Duke," said Dalryn laughingly, "of course I understand! Baen-Tar is but a small island of aspiring civilisation in a sea of barbarity! We try, my Duke. The holy fathers try so hard to bring civilisation to the masses, and in the larger townships I am pleased to say that we make progress. But the rural folk resist so, and they are fierce in their savagery. The king will simply not allow us to take stronger measures of persuasion, no matter how often we may ask it of him."

The duke laughed appreciatively. Sofy felt suddenly cold.

"Oh, I do have dreams, my Duke," Dalryn continued, with the weary amusement of a man confronted with a long and endless task. "I dream that perhaps, in several centuries from now, Lenayin may aspire to become even half of the great, civilised kingdom that Larosa presently is. But I understand that it must pain you to be forced to seek such an alliance, and on such terms. How could it not?"

"Your Grace is most civilised, and most understanding," said Duke Stefhan. "Your dreams for your kingdom are worthy. Indeed, my people say that is the truest calling of a Verenthane to pursue the greatest and most noble tasks, even if they may take many lifetimes to complete. We in the free Bacosh now endeavour toward such a grand task—firstly, to reunify the Bacosh, and secondly, to rid ourselves of the threats and barbarism of pagans and demons alike.

"One must deal firmly, Your Grace!" There came the smacking sound of a fist driven into an open palm. "The gods' word is final and the gods' word is law. The gods do not negotiate with their lessers. The threat must be removed. And one day it shall, by any means at our disposal. If Lenayin is to become the great civilisation of your dreams, Your Grace, you should learn this lesson. Be strong with the pagans—force is all they understand."

The cold in Sofy's veins grew worse. Her stomach tightened, and she felt ill. She stuck a knuckle in her mouth and bit to refocus her mind. She couldn't believe she'd been so *stupid*! Sasha had been right all along.

The archbishop made an appreciative noise. "And the girl, Duke Stefhan? You have been spending quite some time with her the last few days. Is she adequate?"

"She is pretty enough, one supposes," the duke said regretfully. "Our heir will not be offended by her looks at least. But she is so simple, Your Grace. Simple, childish and headstrong, with none of the sophistication of a cultured Larosan lady."

"But one must make allowances, Duke Stefhan. Her upbringing was not the equivalent of the royal Larosan court. And she is the youngest daughter, and spoiled."

Time seemed to stop. Sofy could not deny what her ears were hearing, even though her dazed and horrified mind refused to accept it. She stood paralysed, clutching the silver tray with numb fingers.

"This is true, Your Grace . . . but again, please understand that it shall be a sacrifice to the dignity of the heir. To marry such a girl, for the sake of an alliance, shall be distasteful."

"The Larosa require the services of the army of Lenayin," the archbishop replied, somewhat sternly. "Lenayin may be uncivilised, my Duke, but when held in tight rein beneath Verenthane command, the pagans can certainly fight . . . and, I might add, our Verenthane soldiers are perhaps unmatched in human lands."

"I do not doubt it, Your Grace."

"And Lenayin requires the alliance to bring them fully into the brother-hood of Verenthane kingdoms. Remember that it is not merely your Larosan king that you serve, Duke Stefhan—it is the gods. The gods shall be strengthened in Lenayin by this alliance, and the holy Bacosh shall be freed from pagans and demons alike and the holy Bacosh throne shall be restored to its former glory. Such a great destiny is worthy of some small personal sac-rifices, don't you think? And if the girl displeases the Larosan heir too greatly . . . well, he needn't actually *bed* with her, need he? I'm certain that, in a civilised kingdom such as your own . . . other arrangements could be found?"

Jaryd stood atop the great Baen-Tar walls by the main gate, watching the steady flow of Rathynal traffic. All entering the city, be they farmers on their carts, or townsfolk afoot, or nobility on horses, were being thoroughly searched by wary soldiers with drawn weapons—northerners, Jaryd saw, looking down on them.

"They're searching for weapons?" Jaryd asked Captain Tyrun, who stood on the wall beside him, looking grim. "Who would be foolish enough to smuggle weapons into the city at such a time?"

"Not weapons," said Tyrun, with a shake of his head. "Messages. Or maybe poisons."

"Even if there were Goeren-yai who'd take revenge for Lord Krayliss," Jaryd countered, "I couldn't imagine them being so subtle. Goeren-yai take revenge by chopping necks with swords. Anything else is dishonourable." His arm throbbed in its sling, and he felt naked beside his men's chainmail, which was too much effort to don because of the injury. He worried for Sasha, too. His men reported seeing her leave on her big black horse, and there were no reports of her return. He hoped she hadn't done anything stupid. But then, knowing Sashandra Lenayin, that seemed a futile hope.

Jaryd exhaled hard. "With Krayliss gone, what'll happen to Taneryn? Who'll be the great lord?"

"Uncertain," said Tyrun. "If I were a suspicious man, I'd guess they intended to decide that at this Rathynal. Only they thought we'd kill Krayliss when we went north and they'd just have to decide who to replace him with. Prince Damon only delayed things a bit."

"Won't Taneryn get to decide their own great lord?"

"Seriously?" Tyrun frowned at his commander in a way that made Jaryd feel about ten years old. "How many provinces get to decide their great lord? The Goeren-yai are a majority in maybe seven out of eleven provinces, and how many Goeren-yai great lords are there? Only noble lords can decide to raise a great lord from their midst if there is no natural heir; commonfolk have no voice. Krayliss's family survived this long because the chieftains of Taneryn have always held great power and Krayliss's great-grandfather fought hard against the Cherrovan, but refused to convert. He was the only one."

"Krayliss has sons . . ." Jaryd ventured.

"Huh," Tyrun snorted. "There's an old law, Sylden Sarach; it means 'judgment of clans' in some old tongue or other, I forget. Old Corporal Cadyth was telling me about it. Under the old ways, a chieftain's entire family could be dissolved if his peers deemed that family's honour stained beyond repair."

"Dissolved?"

"Aye, dissolved. The family heads executed, the children adopted into other families. King Soros kept that law, though it's never been used since. Mighty useful now, I'll reckon. They'll find a way to get the whole family out of the way, find one of Krayliss's enemies in Taneryn—and he has plenty— who's willing to convert, and there's your new great lord."

"You talk as though you don't approve."

Captain Tyrun shrugged. "Approve, disapprove . . . I am a humble company captain from lowly stock. My father was a stable hand and my sister married a miller. I do as the Great Lord of Tyree commands."

"And what of the king's commands?" Jaryd ventured.

"Usually that's the same thing." Tyrun gave his young apprentice a stern, sideways stare. "Pray that it should remain so."

"Master Jaryd! Master Jaryd!" Jaryd turned to find a young man in lordly clothes and chain mail emerging from the gate guardhouse, evidently out of breath from having climbed the stairs fast.

"Rhyst!" Jaryd welcomed the lordling with surprise, as he pushed past the other soldiers on the wall. "I had not spotted you lately. Captain Tyrun, have you met Master Rhyst Angyvar? He's the second son of Lord Ignys Angyvar, he and I were sparring partners as lads, among other things."

"Master Rhyst," Tyrun acknowledged, with a short bow.

"What brings you?" Jaryd added, unable to keep the edge from his voice. In all the days he'd been back in Baen-Tar, Rhyst had not so much as said hello.

"Word that you are required urgently at your father's bedside," the lordling replied. His young face wore the anxiety of bad news. "Your father has taken grievously ill, Jaryd. It doesn't look good, I'm sorry."

Jaryd stared, his heart thumping unpleasantly hard in his chest. Now? Of all the times, his father had to pick *now*?

"Best you go, lad," Tyrun said, with as close to a gentle tone as Jaryd had ever heard him use. "We'll hold the wall for your return."

Jaryd nodded and followed his old friend back to the guardhouse. His guardsmen looked at him as he passed; the nearest ones, who had overheard, with sympathy and concern.

"I'm sorry I did not visit when you were injured," Rhyst said anxiously as they strode across the vast, paved expanse of Soros Square. "I wished to, but . . . well, it's Rathynal. You know how it is, my mother introduces me to girl after girl, and my uncles invite me to feast after feast . . . I swear I never knew how many relatives and marriage prospects I had until now."

"That's okay." Jaryd gazed at the statue of the Angel of Mercy, looming in the square's centre ahead, wings unfurled. Where is your mercy today, angel? For Lord Krayliss, the people of Taneryn, or for me? "What do the healers say is the problem?"

"He has a fever and the sweats. He is incoherent and his pulse is far too rapid and faint."

"Do the lords gather?" Jaryd asked through gritted teeth.

"They do. My father among them . . . he sent me to bring you."

The day felt somehow surreal. As they moved together up the main palace steps, Jaryd noticed one of the Royal Guardsmen on duty by the grand doors staring at him. Another did also, then snapped his gaze forward when Jaryd looked at him. Evidently things were bad if the duty guardsmen were staring.

Glancing sideways at Rhyst, he noted the young man biting his lip as he walked. Of course he was anxious, escorting the great-lord-in-waiting to his dying father's bedside. But still . . . "Is there something else amiss?" he asked. One of the lords making trouble, he thought darkly. Even now, at such a time, they would not be able to restrain themselves.

"Something else?" Rhyst asked. "No, nothing else." Something about his manner felt odd. The young man's tone and expression were neutral, tinged with anxiety and concern for the situation . . . and yet. Jaryd recalled an old memory—Rhyst the popular, good-looking boy with the golden tongue. Rhyst had been his friend to his face, but then, later on, he'd overheard him making snide remarks about the "dunce of Tyree" to the other noble children, to much amusement from all.

Up the end of the Great Hall, rows of chairs were arranged beneath the great mural dome high above. There, Lord Krayliss had made his grand pronouncement and led his men from the hall in the uproar. There, he had signed his death warrant.

Jaryd noticed a man approaching from the left, aged and bald and dressed in the rough work clothes of a groundsman. He was glancing around nervously and heading straight toward them. Jaryd frowned. The man wore rings in his ears and his sharp, weathered face bore the faded marks of the Goeren-yai quill.

"My Lord," he called hoarsely, looking straight at Jaryd. "My Lord, please, don't go upstairs."

Jaryd sensed Rhyst stiffen with alarm. "Get away, stupid old fool!" he snapped, grasping Jaryd's good right arm to pull him past. A pair of young nobles appeared further down at a run. They stopped, stared about, then spotted the old man, Jaryd and Rhyst. They started running toward them.

"Don't go upstairs?" Jaryd asked incredulously, pulling against Rhyst's grip on his arm. "Why not? What in all the hells is going on?"

"Stop that old man!" yelled one of the approaching nobles. "He's armed! He means to kill Master Jaryd!"

"Kill me?" Jaryd had time to think in disbelief as Rhyst pulled his sword. "He could barely wield a hoe, let alone a blade." He shoved Rhyst aside and pulled his own sword. "What's going on?" he demanded of the old man as the running men came closer.

"Master," the old man rasped, with little apparent fear, "they killed your brother. I saw it with my own eyes . . ."

"Silence you!" Rhyst shouted, brandishing his weapon, but Jaryd stepped into his way. He could not speak. He stared at Rhyst, whose eyes were now wary, perhaps fearful. The running men arrived, slowing to a jog, then a walk.

"They took the boy from his class in the garden courtyard," the old man continued. "I tend the gardens there, I saw them grab him. But the boy was fast, he had a little blade—a knife, so long," he indicated with his hands, "a silver ornament on the hilt. He stabbed one man, and that man lost his temper and killed him."

Tarryn. He was talking about Tarryn. No. Tarryn could not be dead. Not his little brother. How could anyone kill Tarryn? Just the other day, Sasha had kissed his cheek and called him a darling. Everyone liked Tarryn . . . of course everyone liked Tarryn, who could possibly want to kill . . .

Rhyst, he realised, was just staring at him, not denying a thing. The tip of his tongue protruded from one corner of his mouth, anxiety now battling fear in his eyes. Jaryd recognised the expression—Rhyst had worn it when sparring against him as a boy, deciding whether or not to attack.

"Put the sword down," one of the new arrivals said and Jaryd saw their swords were also drawn. The old man wisely backed away. "Put it down and we'll talk about . . ."

Jaryd lunged and swung, one-handed, clashing the man's sword from his hand. The man cursed, leaping backward, and Jaryd swung at the other, who parried twice, desperately, as Jaryd retreated for a side hallway. Rhyst circled and tried to come at him from the side, then backed up quickly as Jaryd swung at him, fear in his eyes. Even one-handed, still they feared him. They always had. Maybe that was why . . . perhaps that was why they . . .

Jaryd turned and ran. His arm shrieked in agony, but he didn't care. He raced past several nobles and servants in the side hall. Footsteps pursued, voices echoed off the high ceiling, a general alarm being raised. Royal Guardsmen appeared ahead, weapons drawn, and Jaryd turned up a staircase, taking steps three at a time. He should not be going up, the thought occurred to him. On the ground floor or below, he might escape. But he continued up the flights regardless.

The sling slowed his ascent and his nearest pursuer was nearly upon him. Jaryd stopped abruptly, lunged back and swung. Rhyst partly deflected the blow, yet caught the blade to the face anyhow and fell to the flagstones screaming. The next pursuer stopped to attend him and Jaryd ran onward. He realised he was crying, tears wetting his face as he ran, and not from the pain in his arm. Tarryn was dead. They'd killed his little brother. It was a pain too big to be borne by one man. It needed to be shared. He would share it with them all. They too would feel this pain. All of them.

He reached the grand staircase to the palace's top floor without quite knowing how he'd reached it. There were men he recognised on the staircase, their figures outlined against the grand, two-storey windows. Their blades were drawn in response to the commotion approaching from below.

Jaryd charged up the stairs with a roar, forcing one into a stumbling retreat. The man lost balance and fell, Jaryd leaping over him to swing at the next, who backed away, parrying furiously. Then a third, whose defence crumbled beneath Jaryd's furious stroke, clutched his arm as Jaryd's blade bit deep. Agony slashed Jaryd's left thigh . . . the first fallen man had slashed from a downstairs crouch, and now the second took the chance to charge. Jaryd smashed his swing aside in fury and his counterslash sent him spinning to flop down the stone stairs in a bloody tangle of limbs.

Jaryd staggered up the rest of the stairs, dragging his uncooperative leg. His left arm had somehow torn free of its sling, the bandaged forearm screaming, a pain now dimmed by his leg. Beside the pain in his heart, both were as nothing.

Ahead, the hall to his father's chambers was filled with Tyree nobility, weapons drawn and eyes staring in disbelief. Jaryd charged them all, with no more regrets than that his bloody leg and broken arm would prevent him from showing them his best. Blades clashed and he drove back one man, then another, as men retreated before him, fear on their faces. The next man did not retreat and Jaryd split his belly all over the hall flagstones. They were all around him then, some approaching from behind, and he spun wildly in circles, swinging at all who dared his reach, grunting and yelling like an animal. He wounded another, then barely defended a lunge that slammed his parry back onto his chest and threw him sideways into the wall. He hit his arm, screamed, then fell against the wall, jolting his leg. The world went blank for a moment.

Then his head cleared and he tried to rise . . . too late, a blow struck the blade from his hand and then a kick found his leg. Shouts and yells echoed as he fell to the flagstones and blows rained down. A kick knocked him insensible, and then someone had a fistful of his hair and there was a blade at his throat. The cut did not come. He could hear voices, but not the words. There was an argument, and more yelling. He wished they'd hurry up and do it. Tarryn would be alone and frightened before the Verenthane gods. His big brother should be with him.

Soon, little mite, he thought. Soon. He could feel Tarryn near him, a warm, laughing presence. Comforting. Little mischief maker. He nearly smiled through bruised, bloodied lips. Why were they taking so long?

The cell was as cold, and as miserable, as Sasha had imagined it would be during her illicit childhood wanderings through this place. She sat on the bed—a wooden bench covered by an old, rotting blanket—and tried to be calm. There was a lamp flickering somewhere up the hall, flame dancing upon old, dark stone.

Her captors had allowed her to keep her cloak, yet it was barely enough against the chill. Her wrists throbbed where the bonds had pulled tight, and still the red marks remained. They had placed a hood over her head and wrapped her in the cloak, then loaded her onto a cart with other prisoners. The cart had then clattered up the central road of Baen-Tar—she knew because of the cobbles beneath the wheels and the jeering of locals, some pelting rotten fruit and a few stones. Hood and cloak ensured that no one knew her identity, or even that she was female. This secret, like others, would be smothered for a little while at least. How long that would last, and what the reaction would be when certain persons found out, she could not guess.

Her empty dinner tray sat upon the bed alongside. Plain bread and water, it had been. Perhaps they had expected a princess to protest, or to stick up her nose at such fare. In truth, she'd suffered worse upon the road chasing Cherrovan incursions. The tray sat empty, with barely a crumb remaining to tempt the rats. Or at least, she might have expected rats. But now, as she listened, she could hear only silence.

This, she guessed, was the oldest and most deserted of the old castle quarter. The dungeons remained the only part of the old castle still serving their original purpose. The old chieftains of Baen-Tar had made much use of their dungeons. Cherrovan overlords had ruled from here, and the chiefs of Clan Faddyn as well—as her own family had been known before the Liberation when Soros Faddyn changed his name to Lenayin to inspire the uprising against the Cherrovan. That Lenayin was now a better place could be seen by the number of empty cells stretching along vast underground halls of stone. The cold stone of Castle Faddyn's dungeons echoed with memories of bloody wars and ancient feuds long forgotten by most. Now, even the rats did not venture down here. A place so rarely occupied would offer nothing to eat.

There echoed the clank of a metal gate—the warden come to take the dinner tray, Sasha guessed. A light approached down the hall, casting new shadows in the gloom . . . and then—a surprise as the figure holding the lamp appeared, wrapped in a cloak with a long dress that swept the flagstone at her heels. Long hair framed an anxious face, eyes searching through the bars. Sofy.

She saw Sasha and ran the last few steps to grasp the bars opposite. Sasha climbed to her feet, slowly, not wishing a great scene. But she was very pleased to see her sister all the same, and delighted by her audacity. She only wished that Sofy's eyes would not shine so with moisture at the sight of her sister locked in this cold, dark cell below the ground.

"I'm well," Sasha said gently, answering the unasked question. Sofy seemed to be holding back tears with effort. Sasha grasped her slim hand through the bars, with what she hoped was reassurance. "I was not hurt."

"I heard you were with Krayliss," Sofy said, voice hushed and eyes wide. "Anyse told me she'd heard you joined with Krayliss to smuggle a pair of Udalyn children into the city to meet father! Is that true?"

Sasha nodded. "Father did not listen, Sofy. He took Daryd, the Udalyn boy, and confined me to quarters. Your maid sent word that Krayliss had all but declared rebellion and I suspected Koenyg might seize that chance. I tried to save the Udalyn girl, Rysha . . . and I nearly got away. She's alive, last I saw, but I was too late all the same."

Sofy's eyes were incredulous. "But Sasha . . . you could have sent someone else! One of my maids would have carried a message! No one would have wanted the little Udalyn girl in danger . . ."

"I got her into it," Sasha said stubbornly. "It was my idea to use Krayliss's camp as a hiding place for her. It was my responsibility, and I could not be certain any message would be sent in time. It was faster to do it myself . . . and even then, I was too late. Had I not gone, Rysha would probably be dead."

"But Sasha, what a risk to take! Do you realise how much the Goeren-yai look to you? You are a great hope, Sasha, for so many of them . . ."

"And what would you know about the desires of the Goeren-yai?" Sasha snapped, in a flash of temper.

"I was talking with Anyse," Sofy said reproachfully, wiping at her eyes. "She hears all the gossip about Baen-Tar from all the Goeren-yai staff and soldiers. They talk of you, Sasha. I think that it's largely because of you, and your known dislike of Krayliss, that none chose to follow him on the field today."

Krayliss on his horse. The final, desperate plea across the fields. The raised sword, slowly dropping. Utterly unexpected, a lump raised in her throat for the tragedy of Lord Krayliss. It must have shattered him. A man who, above all else, desperately wished to be loved by his people. In the end, they had not returned that love. He had been selfish, brutish, bloodthirsty and, worst of all, he had misjudged the desires of the people whose hearts he had claimed to know better than any other. And yet, in that final moment of despair, he earned her pity. She knew what it was like to feel so utterly alone.

"Don't make me regret it," Sasha muttered. "I won't kick the man's corpse while it's still warm."

Sofy blinked. "He's not dead, Sasha." Sasha frowned in surprise. "He lives, though not for long. They erect a stand upon Soros Square even now. Tonight, there will be executions. All the Taneryn party who survived, including Krayliss. Perhaps ten, I think."

"He was taken *alive*?" That was even worse. At the very least, Krayliss would have wished martyrdom. For all his bluster, she could not believe he had shown cowardice. His bravery, at least, had surely been genuine.

"His horse fell," Sofy explained. "Or at least, that's what I heard. He lost consciousness. But he dies tonight. Koenyg was very firm." There was an edge to Sofy's tone, faintly cold and somewhat sarcastic. Disdain, Sasha recognised it. Disdain for the barbarities of what some men called justice.

"He attempted rebellion, Sofy," Sasha said quietly. "He deserves death. Such is the law."

"And does Master Jaryd deserve death?"

"Jaryd?" Sasha asked with a frown. "What did Jaryd . . . ?"

"The lords of Tyree invoked an old law," Sofy said breathlessly. "Jaryd's father died, and rather than accept Jaryd as the new great lord, they invoked this law and . . . and they dissolved Family Nyvar, Sasha! Dissolved it!"

"Sylden Sarach," Sasha murmured, horrified. "That . . . that's an old pagan barbarity, how could a bunch of Verenthanes use . . . ? What happened? Where is Jaryd?"

"In a dungeon, somewhere near here . . . I couldn't get in to see him, Sasha, the dungeon guards turned a blind eye to me visiting my sister, and one of them's Goeren-yai anyhow. But there's a couple of Tyree lordlings doing guard duty down by Jaryd's cell, I don't think they trust the guards here." Sofy clutched the bars more tightly, her face fearful. "Sasha . . . they killed Jaryd's brother! Just a little boy, Tarryn Nyvar, they tried to take him, they tried to take the whole family, all the direct relations . . . but the boy stabbed his abductor and they killed him, right in the palace! It's so awful, those Tyree fools made such a mess of it, Sasha! And I always said it was so stupid to arm little boys with short blades, whatever the traditions say . . ."

Sasha was not listening. She felt paralysed. She remembered the little boy with freckles and sandy hair who'd sat on Jaryd's bed and chatted with a cheerful sparkle in his eyes. Sylden Sarach. An old Goeren-yai tradition, mostly abandoned now amongst the followers of the ancient ways. In disputes between chieftains over the line of succession, there was always the question of inheritance. Kill the father and the sons would grow up seeking revenge. Yet killing children was not honourable. Better to dissolve the family and adopt the children into friendly families, so that revenge would be all the more difficult for them when they came of age.

There were grand old stories about it, of heroes with torn loyalties, boys becoming men determined to avenge their dead fathers, only to find themselves in conflict with their adopted families. How could a bunch of noble Verenthanes invoke an old pagan law that the pagans themselves had long abandoned? The sheer, bloody-minded cynicism shocked her. And worse, her brother, and therefore her father, had most likely condoned it, given that it happened under their roof and their protection.

"What did Jaryd do?" she asked Sofy quietly, past the lump in her throat.

"An old Goeren-yai groundsman saw the murder!" Sofy whispered, as if scared the cold stones would overhear. "He found and told Jaryd before they could lead him into a trap and Jaryd went berserk! He killed the heir to Family Wyshal, whom I gather used to be an old friend of his . . . and he killed another man I don't know, and wounded three more before they overpowered him! I think Damon was there, I haven't been able to find out exactly, but someone found out what was happening and stopped them from killing Jaryd . . . some maids said it was Damon, but others disagree, and I can't find Damon anywhere! Sasha, I'm really scared . . . you don't think he'd be in any trouble, do you?"

"I don't know," Sasha said quietly. "But if the Great Lord of Tyree is suddenly dead, that's very convenient."

"Yes I know, isn't it just!" Sofy exclaimed, nodding vigorously. "The healers said he should have lasted several more moons at least!"

"The lords of Tyree must have asked Koenyg and father for permission," Sasha said heavily. She put both hands in her hair, as if to try and hold her thoughts in order with that pressure alone. "They caved in. Or they agreed. Just like they agreed to let the Hadryn attack the Udalyn, and like Koenyg arranged to have Krayliss killed. The king finally needs the great lords for something, and the great lords demand all their dues paid at once, a full, accumulated century of them . . . all save the Great Lord of Tyree, who suddenly became a liability, thanks to his stubborn, brave, naive fool of a son."

She turned away and stared at the bleak wall of her cell. All for a stupid holy war for a faith half of Lenayin didn't even belong to. And all because her poor, beloved pagans really *were* a squabbling rabble, just like the nobles claimed. Poor Jaryd. Poor, brave fool. Even if he'd known what was coming, would he have changed his course? Perhaps . . . but also, perhaps not. Crazy man. He was almost Goeren-yai in that. A stubbornness almost worthy of Krayliss. Or Krystoff. Or herself. All these crazy Lenays, all bent on self-destruction, and all for what? Why did they do it? Why hadn't any of them changed course when they'd had the chance?

Maybe this was what Kessligh had tried to tell her. Had struggled to drum into her thick skull, from the moment it was hard enough for him to rattle with a stanch. Beliefs are dangerous, Sasha. Be very careful what you believe in. Kessligh was gone now, headed for Petrodor. She'd cursed him for a disloyal traitor. But look at her now. Look at Krayliss. Look at Krystoff. Look at Jaryd. They'd all had the choice between pragmatism and ideals. Kessligh had taken the pragmatic option, whatever the emotional pain it cost him. She'd done what she'd always done and led with her heart instead of her head . . . and had ended up here.

Was this the culmination of Kessligh's last great lesson? He'd struggled to contain Krystoff's wilder impulses, but her crazy brother had alienated the north and the hardline Verenthanes, and lost his life for it. Had Krystoff in his last moments realised how he'd been betrayed, when the Cherrovan warparty had thundered down from the hills in far greater numbers than Hadryn information had led him to believe? Would she finally realise the truth of this lesson also, after the sentence at her trial had been passed, and the axe was finally about to drop? At least, she thought despairingly, she'd be in plentiful company. But that was no comfort at all.

"I hate him," said Sofy, with sudden venom. "I hate Koenyg. It's all a game to him, like a lagand contest. He wants to win, he doesn't care who gets killed."

"Father is king," Sasha reminded her. Sofy's vehemence surprised her. She wasn't sure she could remember Sofy ever saying that she hated anyone, let alone family. "The responsibility is his."

"You've seen him!" Sofy protested, anger in her dark eyes. "He's like a man lost in a storm, in a world he does not comprehend any more! When he had eyes to see for himself, when the world made sense to him, he held the reins like a true king and everyone bowed to his wisdom. But now he's a blind man, groping for support in the dark, and Koenyg is the one holding his right arm. Of course father should be wiser and stronger, but the fault is Koenyg's! Koenyg should guide better, he shouldn't be so . . . so . . . ."

To Sasha's consternation, Sofy's anger began to crumple into tears. She clutched her sister's hand more tightly through the bars with increasing concern. "Sofy? Sofy, what's wrong? What did Koenyg do?"

Sofy looked away, a hand to her mouth, trying to stop her lip from trembling. She took a shuddering breath. "I found out . . ." she began, and lost control of her voice once more. Tears flowed down her cheeks.

Sasha's concern turned to dawning fear. Koenyg had devious plans that involved Sofy? "What did you find out, Sofy?"

Sofy gasped, trying to gain control. She managed it finally, wiping her cheeks. "I found out the real reason why the Larosa are here," she said weakly. Her eyes focused on their clasped hands. "I . . . I overheard . . . or no, I didn't overhear, I spied. I heard them talking . . . oh, Sasha, I'm so sorry I snapped at you before. You were right about the Larosa—Duke Stefhan is a lying, conniving, murderous . . . ."

Sasha tightened her grip on Sofy's hands. "What did you find out?"

"They . . . they were talking about some girl, like two men sizing up a cow before the slaughter, and . . . and talking about marriage, and at first I thought they must be speaking of Alythia, since she's the one getting married . . . but then they made reference to this girl being the youngest, and they said how immature she is, and how stupid, and how absolutely foul it would be for the heir of the Larosan king to marry her . . . ."

Sasha stared in dawning horror, as it all, suddenly, made sense. "Oh no," was all she could say.

Sofy saw her expression, and the control crumpled once more. "Koenyg wants me to marry a bloody-handed tyrant, Sasha," she burst out all at once, "and Father must have agreed to it, and I'm still only eighteen, and I'm so scared because I don't want to go!"

She sobbed uncontrollably, her head bowed against the bars. Sasha tried to hold her with her hands through the bars, but it was impossible. She felt utterly, desolately cold. She had killed Lenays upon the fields before Baen-Tar and found little regret for it. Now, she felt entirely certain that if one of them had been her brother Koenyg, her regret would have been even less. Damn him to the deepest and hottest of his precious Verenthane hells. For the next time they met upon the field of battle with blades drawn, surely only one of them would walk away alive.

She awoke with a start, lying on the hard boards, and stared at the light that danced across the stone ceiling. The dream had been of Krystoff. She'd fallen off her pony. He'd been laughing at her. She'd tried to climb back on, but the pony had somehow become Peg and was far too tall for her little legs to reach the stirrup. Krystoff had galloped off, and somehow she'd managed to get up and gallop after him. And had found herself in a broad, wide valley with steep sides, cultivated lands and a wide, beautiful river that gleamed beneath the light of a full, silver moon.

From further up the hall, there came a scuffing, echoing noise. Then a clank of keys and muttering voices. Sasha sat up quickly, feet to the floor. The keys rattled some more, then the squeal of the gate opening. Several pairs of feet approached. She had no idea what time of night it was, or even if it was still night. But there would only be more than one guard if she were being moved from her cell.

Three men appeared, and none of them looked like guards. The leader held a flickering lamp which failed to illuminate his face beneath the shadowing hood. He handed the lamp to his companion and fumbled with a ring of keys, as his two companions took wary stances on either side. They appeared to be armed beneath their cloaks, and looked to be expecting trouble.

Sasha got to her feet in alarm, feeling naked without her weapons. A vigilante group come to murder her? Northerners seeking revenge? But how would they get through the guards without her having heard the sounds of battle?

"Who are you?" she asked, thinking furiously.

The leader, to her further surprise, appeared to be struggling to find the right key. He tried one, then another, muttering to himself when they did not fit. As his head bowed, some long hair spilled from within the hood. Not a northerner, then. "Patience, Princess, patience," he said, evidently through gritted teeth. The voice seemed familiar.

Finally, a key fit, and turned with a squeal of rusted mechanism. He took the lamp back from his companion, pushed the prison gate inward and threw back his hood. Long, partly braided red hair fell clear in the light, and familiar, roughened features . . . and Sasha blinked.

"Teriyan?" she exclaimed. Her old friend grinned, appearing to find her astonishment amusing. "What the hells are you up to?"

"Insurrection," he said shortly, and stood aside. "Come, let's go." Sasha stood frozen where she was. "Come on!" Teriyan said impatiently. "I'll explain on the way, there's no time to waste gawking."

Sasha went, having little other choice, and Teriyan placed a hand on her back and ushered her up the hall. The other two men followed. "What's going on?" Sasha demanded, keeping her voice low as they passed empty cell after cold, empty cell.

"Goeren-yai in these parts are having a little disagreement with your father," Teriyan said, in a similarly low voice. "It's all organised, nothing for you to worry about."

Somehow, Sasha did not find that reassuring in the slightest. "What kind of disagreement?" she retorted. "Organised by whom?" They climbed several steps and stepped through the open metal gate. Teriyan paused to lock it again behind them. The lamp threw wavering light up the length of the dank, gloomy hallway ahead, and revealed it deserted.

"A few friends," Teriyan said vaguely.

"How did you get past the guards?" Sasha demanded, growing angry at the lack of information. She rounded to face him as they strode, but he grabbed her arm and pulled her onward. "What are you up to?"

"Don't the serrin say patience is a virtue?" Teriyan retorted. "Why don't you show a little and shut up for a moment?"

"Great," Sasha exclaimed beneath her breath. "The next time you say that you'll explain on the way, don't wonder why I won't believe you."

They climbed a longer flight of stone steps and emerged into a guard-room holding another six cloaked figures. Seated on the floor in one corner, tied and gagged, were four prison guards. Not very many, it occurred to her. One of the cloaked figures approached to hand her her weapons.

"Andreyis?" she recognised, as there was more light to penetrate the shadows here. The young man looked extremely apprehensive. Sasha took her blade, secure in its scabbard, and shrugged off her cloak to begin fastening it to the bandoleer at her back. "What's going on?"

Andreyis looked to Teriyan and back in confusion. "He didn't tell you?"

"No damn time, I tell you," Teriyan growled. He, and all the men, seemed to be expecting discovery at any moment. "She'll just want to argue, let's move fast and argue later."

"I'll stand here and argue about what you're not telling me!" Sasha exclaimed, finishing with her scabbard and bending to strap the knife to her ankle. "I'm not going anywhere until I know what kind of hare-brained scheme you've gone and hatched without my . . ."

"There," Teriyan said to Andreyis in exasperation, "I told you, didn't I?"

"We're riding to the Udalyn!" Andreyis said breathlessly. "We're riding to save them from the Hadryn!"

Sasha stared at him, aghast. "Just like that?"

"No, not just like that!" Teriyan said sharply. "You think we're stupid? It's been planned, girl! The only thing we didn't count on was you being stupid enough to get caught in Koenyg's damn charge . . ."

"Planned? What's been planned? How many men?"

"Lots," Teriyan said grimly.

Sasha stared, her head spinning. How could this have happened without her knowledge? How could Teriyan be involved? He was a leather worker and town senior in Baerlyn, what in the world would he have to do with some Goeren-yai plot to rescue the Udalyn?

She looked at Andreyis. He nodded, anxiously. "Lots of men, Sasha," he confirmed. "The Falcon Guard, for starters. They said if we got Master Jaryd out, they'd come."

There was a flickering light emerging from another passageway, and then three men appeared, two Goeren-yai flanking a limping wreck that had once been a handsome lordling. Jaryd had no sling for his arm, the left forearm bound only with dirty bandages enfolding a pair of short splints. His torn pants revealed bloody bandages about his left thigh. His face was mottled with bruising, one eye entirely closed, his lips swollen and covered with dried blood and grime. His hair was a mess and there was a bloody sword in his hand.

Teriyan stared at the sword, then at Jaryd's two rescuers. "What the hells happened?" he said sharply.

The rescuers looked uncomfortable. "There were two Tyree lordlings posted guard. We overpowered them. We . . . he asked for a sword, we didn't think he'd just . . ."

"Oh great," Teriyan said in exasperation. "So what was a great and right-eous rescue is now the murder of innocent Tyree lordlings! That'll help. Both of them?"

"Just one," Jaryd rasped. Sasha did not recognise the voice. His good eye was cold, emotionless. "Mykel Mellat. I told him I'd kill him. He didn't believe me. He thought it was funny. Isn't laughing now, is he?"

"Now look, Master Verenthane," Teriyan growled, "I only agreed to drag you out of this place because your guardsmen demanded it and we need 'em. You're going to put that damn sword away and shut your damn mouth, and . . ."

Jaryd raised his blade at Teriyan, an awkward, one-armed, one-legged stance. "I'm not taking orders from you. Understand?"

Teriyan snorted, not even bothering to draw his own blade. "What are you going to do, hop after me?"

Sasha stepped between them. "Jaryd." Staring past the point of his blade. "I'm sorry about Tarryn. I lost a brother too. I know what it's like."

"Your brother was a prince, in armour, on a horse, with a blade in his hand. Mine was a little boy with a knife." There was emotion in his good eye now, and his speech, past swollen lips, was thick with fury. "I'm not going on your damn crusade. I've men to kill."

"In that condition."

"Aye," Jaryd muttered, lowering the blade. "In this condition."

"You're Commander of the Falcon Guard," Sasha said harshly. "They've asked for you to lead them. Had they not, you would not be free."

"I resign."

"Then you have no honour."

Jaryd's good eye blazed. "They murdered my little brother! Men I called my friends! Men I grew up with, who professed their loyalty and friendship to my face! And you accuse *me* of dishonour?"

"To meet dishonour with dishonour is to wash down a meal of corruption with a mouthful of ashes." The Goeren-yai men present had heard that line before. Jaryd, Sasha suspected, had not. "That's a quote from Tullamayne, the greatest Goeren-yai storyteller."

"I know who Tullamayne is." Sullenly.

"He was Udalyn," Sasha continued, forcefully. "We ride to save the Udalyn, before they are wiped out entirely. Imagine thousands of tragedies, Jaryd, each as great as you losing Tarryn. Many thousands. Your men asked for you, men who are vastly more experienced and who could probably manage very well without you. Didn't they?"

She looked askance at Teriyan. Teriyan nodded. "They say that with your father dead," he said, "you're the Great Lord of Tyree. They won't accept whoever the lords appoint, not after what they did. They won't be a party to that dishonour. That's what they said, even the Verenthanes."

Jaryd stared at the flagstones. Dirty hair fell about his brow, his battered face shadowed in the flickering lamplight. "If it's revenge you want," Sasha continued, "think about how many more of them you could kill if you waited until you were healthy. With patience, your revenge could be greater."

"You think you'll survive this?" Jaryd said bitterly. "Who'll join you? The Goeren-yai have never united for anything. You'll be smashed, and me with you. Better that I kill who I can now, before they realise I've escaped."

"And alert them to that fact before we're away?" Teriyan retorted. "I'll put you back in your cell first."

Jaryd stared at the flagstones for a moment. Then he snorted, with no real emotion. "Fine. Have it your way."

"Sword away," Teriyan commanded. "Hood up, keep your head down, and not a sound." Jaryd did so, without concern. Little seemed to bother him, not death, nor slaughter. Sasha feared for him.

They were walking from the dungeons when Sasha realised that somehow, she'd begun arguing for precisely the thing she had been arguing against. Lead an army to the Udalyn Valley? Her? In defiance of her father, to say nothing of Koenyg? But then . . . her mind began to accelerate, like a lazy horse building to a canter. What forces would Koenyg have if the Falcon Guard and some of the Black Hammers had left? Nearly half of the Hammers were Goeren-yai . . . and half the Royal Guard, also. Would some of the Royal Guard come? Would many of *their* Verenthane comrades? Was it even imaginable that she, the hot-tempered, troublemaking little girl in Krystoff's shadow, would for a time at least be commanding a greater army than the king or Koenyg would have available? From dreaming in her prison cell to this. It was overwhelming.

"Why in all the hells didn't anyone tell me?" she fumed in sudden temper, as she struggled to grasp this new reality. The dank passage from the guardhouse gave way to stairs, long and winding. She took them slowly, lest Jaryd be left behind. "What am I, just a piece to be moved upon some low-lands board game?"

"You," Teriyan said firmly, and with the edge of a man about to lose patience, "were our last hope of *not* having to do this. Do you think for a moment that any man here would willingly ride against the king's orders? We hoped you could persuade him. You needed to be convinced it was the only option for that to have any chance of working. We're all sorry if you feel deceived, but damn it, girl, it was the only way! Now, do you want to save the Udalyn or not?"

Sasha stared at him. Familiar features, a face from her childhood, since the age of eight, anyhow. A man she'd grown up with. He did not belong here, in this world. Certainly Andreyis did not. They were from her other world, with Kessligh, out in the Lenay wilds. Or perhaps, it occurred to her, it was she who didn't belong here. Confusion threatened.

Could she turn her back on them now? Tell them it was foolish? That she would not lead a Goeren-yai army in what could certainly become the opening battle of a civil war? If she did nothing, and the Udalyn were destroyed, there would be civil war regardless . . . only worse. Fighting to save a people from annihilation was an achievable goal, with a near-term end in sight. Fighting to avenge an annihilated people was not so much a goal as a state of mind, and could drag on for centuries. She could not allow it. Sometimes, Kessligh had told her more than once, you just have to act. If you wish for your every action to be entirely reasonable and thought out, you shall wish in vain. When action is required, act. Inaction, in such a situation, is always the wrong answer.

"You and I," she said, with a firm jab at Teriyan's chest as they climbed, "are going to have to improve our communication."

Even above ground the old castle was dark, dank and full of shadows. Bare stone passed silently underfoot—it was difficult to believe that such a desolate, soulless place had ever been a seat of power in Lenayin.

They passed through an abandoned guardhouse and out into the yard beyond. Carts were lined beneath what had once been a primitive stable, and men were hauling crates of produce from their trays. Above, the old inner walls loomed barely half as high as the grand outer walls, the stonework worn and weathered in places.

The Goeren-yai men walked calmly across the courtyard, soldiers with their hoods down, several hauling full wineskins in prominent view to prevent suspicion—it was well known that officers would send their men on unofficial "requisitional visits" to the castle storage rooms. Men loading carts, hauling crates or tending horses paid this new procession little heed as they headed toward the side exit that had been cut in the old stone for more direct access to the barracks and stables. Sasha walked with her hood up, and no great alarm in that, for the night was cold. Behind, she could hear Jaryd's occasional grunt of pain, but he made reasonable pace despite the limp. Two guards on the small exit waved them through with great nonchalance, and Sasha was not surprised to see both were Goeren-yai.

The street beyond was narrow and appeared empty save for a startled stray cat. Beyond the old inner walls, she could hear the echoing rumble of drums and the shouting of voices. Sasha threw a questioning glance up at Teriyan.

"Soros Square," he said grimly. "Lord Krayliss dies a glorious death."

Sasha recalled the execution stand . . . she'd snuck away, once, to see what her minders had insisted no little girl had any business seeing. For once, they'd been right.

"Nothing glorious in that death," she said quietly. "In battle, at least you have the mercy of being surprised. Isn't it a little late for an execution?" It was after midnight, she'd gathered.

"It took the carpenters this long to erect the platform," Teriyan replied, peering into the gloom as he strode, a hand on the hilt of his blade beneath the cloak. "No matter, it creates a diversion for us, in that, his death proves far more useful for the Goeren-yai than his life."

It sounded a particularly callous thing to say, even for Teriyan. "You set him up for this," Sasha said bluntly.

Teriyan grunted. "He set himself up. We needed him out of the way, and we needed a diversion . . ." he shrugged. "He gets his martyrdom, we get a blind space in which to organise, and most of brother Koenyg's loyal guards are busy expecting trouble at the execution. As if we'll all rise up in protest over that fool getting the axe. Koenyg sees everything, but understands nothing. We're heading north."

Organise? The Goeren-yai? Sasha stared up at his rangy height, her suspicion mounting. Teriyan had been most insistent in accompanying her on this trip. Teriyan, who had many friends and contacts amongst Goeren-yai all over Lenayin. Any Baerlyn man could have accompanied her, but Teriyan had insisted it should be him. "How long have you been plotting?" she asked, her jaw tight.

Teriyan threw her a serious look. "Look, Sasha . . . you didn't think the concerned folk across Lenayin wouldn't have *someone* keeping an eye on you all these years? Why do you think you haven't had crowds of the curious and the worshipful come clustering about the ranch or the Steltsyn all days? They needed word on what you were up to. I gave it. Nothing more."

But it had gained him status, evidently. "Kessligh knew about this?" she asked tightly.

Teriyan shrugged. "A little. Never seemed real interested, truthfully. Certainly he appreciated anything keeping the crowds away." Sasha felt her head spin as several new pieces fell into place. Kessligh's displeasure with her occasional long nights in the Steltsyn. Teriyan, on one occasion, sheltering her from the overly nosy questions of one particular out-of-towner. He'd had his curiosity answered later, it seemed.

"You didn't tell me," she muttered.

"Sasha . . ."

"Damn it, I'd have understood! I'm not stupid, I knew that you and the others deflected some attention from me . . . but you were using me, weren't you? Planning a bloody uprising, just like Koenyg suspected . . ."

"Oh aye, and how safe would that have been, to tell you everything?" Teriyan retorted. "Your brother Koenyg sending his damn spies through the

Steltsyn every few weeks . . . we learned to spot them, you know, even if you never did. Those merchants, traders, wandering minstrels, even some of the damn pilgrimage priests, all fishing for stories about you."

"They weren't *all* working for Koenyg," Sasha said disbelievingly. She felt suddenly uncomfortable. Could they have been? "Travellers gossip, it's not like every traveller who asks questions is pocketing Koenyg's gold."

"And that's been the difference between the two of us for the last twelve years," Teriyan said firmly. "You could afford to think that, up on your hill with your legendary warrior to watch over you. The rest of us learned to be suspicious. There's a whole stack of rumours and stories about you moving about the towns at any given time, Sasha. You don't think Koenyg wasn't listening to all of them? You don't think that at the first suspicion you were going to be a threat to the lords, by giving the Goeren-yai someone to rally around, he wouldn't have come down on Baerlyn like an avalanche?"

"He'd never have dared," Sasha retorted, eyeing a shadowy figure moving on the dark road ahead. "Any move against me or Kessligh would have achieved exactly what he didn't want—angry mobs of Goeren-yai looking for blood."

"Aye, well maybe you could take that risk. Me, I've got family in Baerlyn, and I'm responsible for all the other families too." He too watched the dark figure ahead. It vanished down an alley. "The lords thought you more of a risk than Koenyg did, they were twisting his arm all the time . . . shit, you saw what Kumaryn tried. They know that if the Goeren-yai ever got worked up, the lords' heads would be the first on the block—most Goeren-yai respect the king, but we've got no time for lords.

"So we kept feeding them all this nonsense about Krayliss, and how he was so popular. I did it myself a few times, just made up some pile of manure about the brave deeds of Lord Krayliss to tell some traveller when he was near face-down in his ale. He spreads it to the next town, and people talk, and the next thing you know, Prince Koenyg's hearing talk of great, heroic stories about Lord Krayliss spreading through Valhanan. Better yet, Lord Krayliss hears them too, and like any fool who thinks the stars circle his arse, he believes the people love him. Soon enough, he believes it so much he picks a fight with Hadryn, kills Great Lord Rashyd, and threatens the king with Goeren-yai rebellion. So while all the nobility's got their frilly lace knickers in a twist over Krayliss, they ignore you completely . . . or almost. Worked a treat, huh?"

Sasha stared at him incredulously. "They ignore me? You . . . you make it sound as if . . . as if I'm some kind of . . . I don't know . . ."

"Goeren-yai hero?" Teriyan peered down the dark alley into which the figure had entered. Within, there were only shadows. He shrugged. "Maybe. All I knew was better you than Krayliss. Some of us saw this day coming,

Sasha. A day when we'd need someone the Goeren-yai could look up to. Prince Koenyg never really believed it could be you, not truly . . . Goeren-yai never had women leaders before, it seemed a stretch. And who knows, he might yet be right. We'll see."

"I'm not a damn leader!" Sasha hissed at him. "I'm not some piece on your board game to be moved about at your leisure . . ."

"Kessligh didn't teach you nothing, did he?" Teriyan gave her a contemptuous stare. "We're all just pieces on some damn board game, girl. Either you play, or you get played. You choose. You're my friend, and I'm sorry you feel betrayed. But my first loyalty is to my people. I was hoping that'd be your first loyalty too."

"M'Lady," said another man moving up on her side as they rounded a tight bend between stone walls. From a high window, a baby squalled. "I have some men moving to recover the Udalyn children. The Princess Sofy assisted us in finding them in the palace. Should we bring them?"

Sasha looked up at him—way up, for this man was even taller than Teriyan. Goeren-yai, despite lacking the spirit-mask, like Teriyan. And recently familiar, somehow . . . her eyes widened, recalling the Royal Guard lieutenant who had let her into the Saint Ambellion Temple with Daryd.

"Is it a good idea to bring children?" she asked warily. "Surely they'll be safe enough here?"

"There's no telling that," Teriyan said darkly. They were approaching the Soros Library now, its archways looming on the left above dark, clustered rooftops. "They're proof of bad things happening in the valley, someone might decide them more conveniently disposed of. Besides, we may have use of someone who knows Udalyn lands from the inside—the boy may not speak Lenay, but he can draw maps. In an assault, that could save lives."

"They are Udalyn children, M'Lady," the lieutenant added. "The hardship shall not trouble them."

Sasha did not like the idea of taking children on such a ride. This, she realised, was one of those command decisions that she had always wondered if she would have the strength to make for herself. Many more would surely follow. She was no longer poised upon the point of no return. That point was now behind her. The realisation made her dizzy, with fear, excitement and a dozen other things that she had no name for.

"See to the children," she told the lieutenant. "Perhaps try to find the pony they arrived on, it shall make the journey easier for them."

"Aye, M'Lady," said the lieutenant, and made straight for the side road past the library, vanishing quickly in the night.

"His name's Alyn, Koenyg tossed him from the guard," Teriyan said in a

288

low voice. "Koenyg's done that quite a bit lately. Gained us a whole bag of recruits, he has."

Cut from the Royal Guard for letting someone into the temple to visit the king. The disgrace would lie heavily on the man's shoulders, Sasha knew, whatever the circumstances. A man so desperate to reclaim his honour might do crazy, reckless things. And she wondered how many more people would lose far more than just their honour because of decisions she would make now, or tomorrow, or in the days after that.

The stables were less active than on previous occasions, yet still busy enough for cover. "Be fast," Teriyan said in a low voice to the group, "word will reach Koenyg soon enough, the executions will only distract him for so long."

Sasha saddled fast and rejoined the group in front of the stables. As they approached the guards at the main gate, Soros Square became visible. Great fires lit the four corners about a large, raised platform, swarmed about by as large a mass of people Sasha could ever recall having seen. Light and shadow flung far and wide across the grand arches and towers of surrounding buildings, and the jagged lines of pikemen's ceremonial staffs made a sharp, teeth-like row against the glare of flame.

About the crowd's perimeter there were many soldiers, and even more upon the platform itself. Before the platform, there was raised a large Verenthane star on a tall pole. It loomed over proceedings like a watchful guardian, invoking the name of its gods upon all that occurred within its shadow. The symbolism both chilled her and filled her with exasperated rage. Koenyg had no clue. Perhaps Lord Krayliss did deserve this fate, and perhaps the majority of Goeren-yai would not grieve for him. But to take his head beneath the shadow of a Verenthane star? One could not have conceived a greater provocation if one's intention was to *start* a rebellion.

"Identify yourselves!" called a guard from the gate, evidently a little bored with his job and far more interested in the spectacle upon the square. The crowd on the platform was clearing now and the drums increased their pace. Of the victims, Sasha's vantage did not provide a good view.

"I know them," said another guard as the column arrived. "Let them through." A Goeren-yai man, Sasha saw as Peg sensed her tension and danced sideways a little.

"Hells no!" demanded the first man with typical Lenay bluntness. "Identity of all present, then pass!"

"I said I know them!" countered the Goeren-yai as his comrade turned to stare at him in amazement. The protocols were well known.

"Are you completely bloody stupid, y'daft Valhanan goose?"

"My name's Blossom," Teriyan said, all hard-faced aggression. "And so's my comrades'."

"Aye," said the next man, "mine too."

"And mine."

Horses jostled the guard, who stared around in amazement. Some of his comrades came over, heavily armed, yet not overly alarmed. There were at least twenty—Rayen men this night, of the Black Hammers company, not Falcon Guard, or it would have been just too damn easy. The first guard looked as though he suspected some kind of joke. All Lenay men loved jokes, particularly those that made another man look stupid.

"Oh aye, Blossom and Blossom . . ." he nodded up at them. "Suits you both, I must say. Would someone tell me what the bloody hells is going on?"

"Listen you," Teriyan told him gruffly, "we got a Goeren-yai lord getting axed on the stage yonder, I suggest you don't give us any crap just now, understand?"

"Aye," the guard said, suddenly all sober seriousness. "Aye, I hear you, friend. I don't like it much myself, but I've a job to do, don't I?"

"Aye," Teriyan said bitterly. "Jolly Prince Koenyg did a fair job on us today too, didn't he? You take your damn job, and stick it up your arse. We're leaving."

He slammed heels to his horse's sides, the other men following, then Sasha and Andreyis racing after as the guards swore, reached for weapons, yelled in protest . . . and yet did nothing to stop them. Then they were running at a canter along the paved road toward the Baen-Tar cliff, Sasha praying that there would be no whistle of arrowfire from the ramparts in pursuit as guards yelled that instruction up from the ground. None came and the group slowed as they approached the sharp drop-off and the view of hillside lights below.

It had been a masterful performance by Teriyan, Sasha realised as they descended. He had played the disgruntled, hot-headed Goeren-yai warrior to the hilt . . . and in truth, it had probably taken very little acting. Even a Verenthane guard had reason to agree that such a Goeren-yai hothead might be justifiably unhappy. In Lenayin, it was unwise to stand between a man who felt his honour slighted, and where he wished to go. Even more, such righteous furies were respected, as were the men who wielded them . . . so long as the cause was felt by all to be just. Teriyan had made the poor guards feel ashamed of their duty, inflicting yet another indignity upon a very angry, very righteous warrior. The incident would no doubt be reported immediately . . . but at least they were clear of the walls without a peppering of arrow shafts. Given events in the square, she guessed no one had had the heart to fire.

They arrived at the paddocks to a confusion of manoeuvres in the dark. A distance wide of the tents, horsemen were gathering amidst a dance of torchlight and far-flung shadow. Already there were several hundred and, even as Sasha arrived upslope of the gathering, many more were crossing from the tent city to join them. From amongst the tents, there carried the sound of shouting argument and the alarmed demands of officers. Some men went running and some horsemen went tearing off toward Baen-Tar, doubtless to inform Koenyg. There was little time.

"If we're going to move," Sasha said, "we'd best move now before the Ranash and Banneryd mobilise." Her heart was thumping with unpleasant anticipation as she surveyed this scene of armed men and horses by torchlight. In the confusion of shadows and light, it did not seem real.

"They'd not dare attack a force so strong, surely?" Andreyis ventured, staring wide-eyed and breathless at the scene. Sasha forced herself to calm—if she were alarmed, how would Andreyis feel?

"Not directly," Teriyan said grimly, "and not so long as we have such greater numbers. But they'll harass us all the way to the Hadryn border."

"Aye," Sasha agreed. Another cluster of horses was cantering across, perhaps sixty strong. Behind them another formed, men waiting for their comrades to saddle up. Bewildered arguments raged, visible in the camp light. Evidently many Verenthane men hadn't known it was coming. Sasha was further astonished. She'd never suspected any Lenay soldier could keep so large a secret so well. "We'll wait a moment longer. We don't want to leave a trail of stragglers for the Ranash."

"Sashandra Lenayin!" cried a restless voice from the midst of the assembled horsemen. "We were promised Sashandra Lenayin!"

A chorus of loud agreement rose from many others. "Is she present?" yelled another. "If not, we'll ride on Baen-Tar itself to free her!" Another rousing reply, filled with anger. More than five hundred horse stamped, jostled and snorted in the torchlight, feeding off their riders' mood. Sasha sensed that things might finally be approaching a boil. They'd been patient for so long. They'd watched the Taneryn contingent slaughtered on the lower slopes, and yet done nothing. Now, they felt their time had arrived. The men of the ancient ways would not be denied.

Sasha found Teriyan glaring at her. "Go!" he urged, with a hard nod of his head. Sasha felt as if frozen, unable to move. Real fear gripped her, worse than the fear of bloodthirsty northerners or Cherrovan intent on spilling her blood. Those, she was trained to deal with. This turned her whole world upside down. It was one thing to threaten rebellion, quite another to actually, finally arrive at the moment of partaking.

Kessligh, she thought despairingly, her heart thudding hard against her ribs. He'd been right, once again. She truly hadn't understood where her casual passions might take her. A daughter of Lenayin, riding forth before a rebellious band of Goeren-yai and declaring intentions entirely at odds with her father's will.

Quite unexpectedly, a line from an old serrin verse came to mind. "That was the river. This is the sea." She'd never seen the sea. The many rivers of Lenayin flowed into it, eventually, on their long, winding journey into the lowlands. A body of water so vast was unimaginable to her. And yet it existed, irrespective of her ignorance. Somewhere out there—vast, deep and blue.

Suddenly, she felt calmer. The destination was out there, whether she knew its nature or not. Surely it existed, just like the sea. It was only she who was uncertain. The destination would take care of itself.

She touched her heels to Peg's sides, urging him to a walk. He broke into a canter instead and she pulled on the reins, slowing her reluctant, impatient friend to a sideways, head-tossing prance. The men's shouts died away, eyes settling upon her, many with frowning curiosity, seeing her for the first time. Spirits knew what they'd expected from the tales spun about her. She pushed the hood from her head to at least offer that much proof. From behind, there came the thunder of yet more horses approaching, swelling their ranks further. Perhaps she should wait for them all to arrive . . . but then, she might never start.

"Men of Lenayin!" she called. Her voice did not sound right, and she wondered if it carried across all those gathered. And the words themselves were a stale, dull form of address, surely? Although it was certainly better than "fellow Goeren-yai" . . . and suddenly, new words formed in her head. "Some will say this is a rebellion!" she plowed on, before the inspiration could desert her. "Some will say that we ride against the king! They will say that we seek to set Lenayin at war with itself, and set Verenthane and Goeren-yai at each other's throats! But they will be wrong!

"We ride to save Lenayin from ruin! Lenayin must be saved from the hatred and bigotry of the north, or wherever it should arise! Lord Krayliss offered you a vision of a kingdom of the Goeren-yai, free from Verenthanes, serrin and lowlanders. I offer you no such vision! The Lenayin I offer you is a Lenayin of peace, not of hatred! Even now, there are Verenthane brothers among us who ride not for division, nor for hatred, but for all Lenayin, united together in friendship!

"I welcome my Verenthane brothers! I remind all who ride here that wherever my heart may lie, my blood is Verenthane and I love my family yet! Should any man who rides here tonight do so for hatred, or should he consider all Verenthanes to be the enemy, then I would tell that man that he is not welcome in this party! If he wishes to ride tonight for love—for love of the Udalyn, for love of tolerance and friendship between all Lenays, and for the love of a united Lenayin beneath a single king, then I say come with me, and none of us shall suffer in silence any more! What do you say?"

The answering roar astonished her in its power. Men clenched their fists in the air, or thrust their swords skyward, shouting with visceral passion. Sasha felt a flush of power through her body, chills tingling both hot and cold, her heart pounding in her ears. As if suddenly, in that moment, she could have taken on the combined Hadryn armies single-handedly and won. She fought the urge to grin like an idiot. A girl could get used to this.

"Form up!" she heard a yell as the cheering died . . . and looked to find Captain Tyrun of the Falcon Guard coming across the line at a canter, raised in his stirrups. "Form up, share the torches. We've distance to cover before the sun rises!"

Sasha set off after him, heading downhill as mounted soldiers wheeled and yelled, finding comrades and superiors in the darkness. She, Tyrun, Andreyis and Teriyan positioned themselves at the fore, watching the confusion and hoping there were not too many injuries before they even began to move.

"Where's Jaryd?" she thought to ask Tyrun.

"I put a few good men with him," Tyrun replied, surveying the scene with unreadable eyes. "To make sure he stays in the saddle, and to show the rest of the guardsmen that he's here. How do you judge his condition?"

"His body's a mess," Sasha said shortly. "But that's not the worst of it."

Tyrun nodded shortly. "He's a strong young man, his body will heal. About the other wounds, time will tell."

Sasha stared at the torch-lit, surging mass of horses and did some fast sums in her head. Eleven provinces at Rathynal. Roughly five hundred people per contingent. Half of those were nobles, including ladies and children. The other half soldiers—about two hundred and fifty per contingent. Maybe half of *those*, from every province but the three northern ones, were Goeren-yai. Which made . . . maybe nine hundred men? It certainly *looked* close to a thousand, but it was dark and there was no way to tell for sure. Had *every* Goeren-yai soldier come? And what of the Baen-Tar garrison companies?

"All the Falcon Guard have come?" she asked Captain Tyrun.

"Aye," said Tyrun. Verenthanes too, that meant. Tyrun was here himself, after all. That was another five hundred.

"And the Black Hammers, do you know?" she pressed.

"Uncertain. Captain Akyrman will not come, but many of his Goeren-yai will. Some of those said their Verenthane friends may follow later, once they realise what's happened."

"We'll have a straggling tail on this army no matter what we do," Sasha observed glumly.

"Aye," Tyrun agreed. "No helping it. Best hope they ride fast."

"Royal Guard?"

"A few. Perhaps two hundred. Leaving Baen-Tar undefended is a big thing, even lots of Goeren-yai won't do it."

Sasha nodded, biting her lip. Say two hundred . . . and two fifty from the Black Hammers, and five hundred Falcon Guard . . . She blinked in astonishment. "We're nearly two thousand strong?"

"Aye," said Tyrun. "Looks like." From back toward the tent city, there was more shouting and a chaos of galloping horses, milling men and bewildered officers. A pair of men on horses came across in front, close enough for Sasha to overhear their cries to the column.

"Where the bloody hell are you lot off to?"

"Udalyn Valley! Want to come?"

"To fight for the Udalyn? But I'm Verenthane!"

"So's he!" Some laughter above the thunder of hooves and jangling harnesses.

"Yeah, I'm Verenthane!"

"So why're you going?"

"My friends are going! What unit you from?"

"Fyden Wildcats! You?"

"Yethulyn Bears! You like the Hadryn?"

"Hells no!"

"Well, come and have a bloody fight then!"

The cheers and cajoling continued, the two Verenthanes paralleling the column downhill into the dark.

Sasha shook her head in disbelief. "Damn it," she muttered to Tyrun. "I've absolutely no idea what I'm doing."

"I'm used to that," said Tyrun, with the faintest smile beneath his bushy moustache.

They galloped to the lead of the column, then turned downhill toward the nearest open gate out of a paddock and onto the road. The column followed, a great, creaking, thudding mass of horse and armour, the light of many torches casting crazy shadows across the hillside.

Before long, several Royal Guardsmen, led by Lieutenant Alyn, cantered past to take the vanguard . . . one, Sasha saw, flying the royal purple and green. The banners of the Falcon Guard and the Black Hammers were also flying. The dark treeline approached and then enfolded them in the flickering, dancing shadow of firelight on trunks and leaves. From somewhere behind came a haunting blast of trumpet, once, and then again.

"Ranash," said Tyrun, his moustache twisting as he considered its import. There followed an answering call with different notes. "And that one is Banneryd. They are forming."

"How many do you think?" Sasha asked.

"The Ranash took a few losses against the Taneryn, but not many. Before, they were two hundred strong. Banneryd are not so many—only a hundred twenty.

"So few," Sasha remarked, thinking hard.

"Banneryd's Great Lord Cyan did not come for Rathynal," said Tyrun. "Some say he was otherwise preoccupied with the Hadryn . . . probably that's where the other Banneryd and Ranash soldiers are too. In the Udalyn Valley with the Hadryn."

Sasha rubbed her brow. "Why did no one notice Great Lord Cyan's absence until now?" she asked.

Tyrun shrugged. "Rathynal is just beginning. We thought perhaps he was late."

"So we shall have at least three hundred and twenty horsemen chasing us shortly," Sasha summarised.

"Aye," Tyrun agreed, as matter-of-fact as a farmer discussing the season's crop. It was a great relief to have such a wise, steady presence at her side. "And certainly more, once the king sends his summons. Neysh will likely respond with full companies, as Great Lord Parabys owes Prince Koenyg his place after family tumults there. And he's not the only one. Prince Koenyg crafts allegiances well. I'd guess he could have nearly a thousand men under arms within two days. Add to that the nobility themselves . . . perhaps a third are in good condition to fight."

"No more than a quarter," Sasha disagreed, sourly. "Some didn't come equipped and there's little camping gear on their horses. They were expecting lordly accommodation, not a war party. They're also short on armour and half can't fight well anyhow."

Tyrun might have smiled in the dancing shadows. "Aye," was all he said. He seemed a man who reserved judgment, whenever possible. No doubt one learned to reserve one's opinions, faced with the open disapproval of nobles who resented one's humble origins.

"So maybe five hundred nobles who can fight. But that's two days' head start for us," Sasha reasoned.

"Less," said Tyrun with certainty. "Prince Koenyg can gather some men on the move."

Sasha nodded, thinking hard. Speed was key, that much was obvious. It would be the kind of manoeuvring Kessligh had done so masterfully during the Great War, thirty years before—fast thrusts of mounted warriors across rugged terrain. They were, she knew, awfully large boots to fill.

"I'd guess, M'Lady," Tyrun continued, "that the northern units may form a skirmish party, or several skirmish parties, to delay our progress north. Our flanks should be careful and watch for ambush."

"If we're too defensive, we'll never get there in time," Sasha muttered. "The Udalyn's wall is strong, but the Hadryn have siege weapons. That, and I'd like to hit them hard before they have time to prepare for us at the valley mouth. If we're quick, we can trap them inside before they know we're coming."

"Aye, M'Lady," said Tyrun, with the first hint of satisfaction in his tone. Sasha gave him a curious look.

"Why are you here, Captain? For all I know, this could end with all our necks joining Lord Krayliss on the block. No one would have thought less of you had you declined to ride."

"A majority of my men voted to come," Tyrun said simply. "The Falcon Guard has a tradition of majority votes. So I came."

Sasha was surprised. She had expected to hear something about noble causes and compassion for his Goeren-yai brothers.

"I hope they don't expect further votes in the midst of battle," she said warily.

Tyrun shook his head. "That's not how it works, M'Lady. One vote, for any suicidal stupidity, then all must follow orders."

"Your own Tyree lords may have your head even if the king doesn't," Sasha added.

"Master Jaryd is the Great Lord of Tyree," Tyrun said flatly.

"The other lords claim otherwise."

"They raise the taxes to pay our wages," Tyrun said dryly, "and to forge our weapons, tend our horses and upkeep our barracks. Those, they own. Our honour, they do not. When this is over, they can disband the entire company if they wish, but I'd like to see them try and find replacements when word spreads of what they did to Family Nyvar. This is a day of infamy for Tyree, M'Lady. But it shall not be a day of infamy for the Falcon Guard."

It was said with the same dry calculation with which Captain Tyrun said everything . . . and yet, Sasha could not help but think that it was the most impassioned thing she'd yet heard the man say.

"Well," she said after a moment, "I'm glad you're here. I'm going to need some assistance, Tyrun. Kessligh taught me much, but . . . I haven't done this before."

"Aye, M'Lady," said Tyrun.

To ride at night through any part of Lenayin was no easy thing, for roads were rarely straight and level, and torchlight was of limited service after the setting of the moon. Thankfully there was plenty of oil for the torches and the wind was not too strong to weaken the flame. It swirled, however, cold and occasionally misty, threatening rain.

These and other thoughts crowded Sasha's mind. Before, on such rides, she could relax in the confidence that Kessligh would make the right decisions, now she worried and fretted. The sensation was most unpleasant, made worse by lack of sleep. How did anyone learn to handle such pressures as effortlessly as Kessligh had managed? She could not imagine.

Shortly, the road emerged from the forest onto the outlying Baen-Tar farmland, where the land lay relatively flat between rugged hillsides. The stone walls of farmhouses glowed dimly in the passing of many torches, displaying shutters firmly latched against the dark. It seemed unreal to be riding such a path at night. Torchlight did not reach the surrounding hills, merely caressing the lower fringes of their forested slopes. Above, the ridgelines were almost invisible against the black sky, featureless save for moving patches of stars through the cloud.

A new horse moved up on her right and Sasha recognised Andreyis's face beneath his hood.

"That was a good speech," he said, his voice barely carrying above the plodding hooves, creaking harness and sputtering wind. He sounded anxious. "You always said you never liked speeches."

"I can assure you I didn't like that one." She gazed at the distant, dancing shadow of a farmhouse and wondered if its occupants would cheer or curse them, were they roused from their sleep. Then she looked at her old friend in sudden concern. This was a war party and Andreyis had not yet passed the Wakening. "We'll have to find you some mail."

"You're not wearing any," Andreyis retorted.

"Slows me down. If I lose my speed and balance, I've no advantage left. Safer not to wear any." It troubled her, Andreyis being there. He was from her peaceful life on the hillside with her horses. Of course he'd always trained for warfare, as all Lenay men did, but she'd never thought to be present when he first put those skills to the test. And she'd *certainly* never thought to be in command. It scared her worse than anything had scared her so far in this night's young rebellion.

"Sasha, I'm . . . I just . . . wanted to say that I'm sorry." Andreyis looked even more anxious now. As if concerned, in a way that he rarely had been before, of arousing her temper. "Teriyan said you were angry at him. I knew that he was telling other Goeren-yai about you, but he told me not to say anything, and so did my father . . ."

"What did he say?" Sasha asked. "Teriyan, I mean?"

"He . . ." Andreyis took a deep breath, and glanced aside. "Folks were curious, Sasha. I mean, I've forgotten the number of times some out-of-towner stopped by the house on some business and wanted to ask me only about you. I always told them I only worked at the ranch, that I didn't know you real well . . . you know, just to shut them up. But they all gossiped, and that gossip went all across Lenayin."

"I know," Sasha said quietly. "I know they gossiped. I know they wanted a royal Goeren-yai. There was lots of talk that Krystoff was the first. Some said that the spirits had taken him, and turned his heart to the ancient ways. When he died, and I left to live with Kessligh, many felt that spirit had passed on to me. The Taneryn say it's the will of the Synnich. Everyone has their own little legend or prophecy. Doubtless if I die, they'll invent some new one."

"Sasha, don't blame Teriyan. He wasn't spying on you, he never told any personal details or anything . . ."

"Little enough he knows of my personal life," Sasha snorted.

"Aye, well . . ." Andreyis fidgeted with a handful of rein. "But someone had to talk to them. Goeren-yai from all over Lenayin were fascinated, Sasha. They'd all have turned up on your doorstep if Teriyan and Jaegar hadn't done some talking. It's not easy for them sometimes, you know, having you and Kessligh in town. I mean . . . I get told all the time, how Baerlyn ceased to be a normal town when you two arrived. Most are pleased, don't get me wrong . . . but it's just different, that's all."

"You didn't talk to any gossip mongers?" Sasha asked him with a firm gaze.

Andreyis blinked. "And tell them what? That you shave your legs with a hunting knife and candle wax?" Sasha bit back a grin and tried hard to look annoyed. Unsuccessfully, because Andreyis saw and smiled, exasperatedly. "I don't know what these idiots want, Sasha. Teriyan does. They want to know signs, you know . . . that you can quote some Tullamayne, that you make the spirit sign, that you wear the tri-braid and prefer wine to ale. Some holy folks think they can read the spirits' will in little things . . . I don't know, what colour socks you wear. Stupid stuff. Teriyan doesn't like it either, but they tell folks this stuff so Baerlyn doesn't become some damn pilgrimage town for crazy Goeren-yai hoping to catch a glimpse. It keeps them satisfied so they don't have to come and find out for themselves. Which wouldn't have made Prince Koenyg real happy, I'd guess."

Sasha breathed a deep, dark breath. "It's honeycomb wax," she said on an impulse. "Candle wax hurts too much."

Andreyis gave a snort of laughter. "Some people think you're a tomboy, but I know better. You're still just a pampered princess underneath, with all your girlie things in your washing stall . . ."

"I happen to dislike body hair in the wrong places!" Sasha retorted. "What's wrong with that?"

"I counted *nine* different soaps and oils," Andreyis countered accusingly.

"I take my luxuries where I can get them."

"Exactly."

"Did Teriyan tell them that too?" Sasha asked, with a lingering sideways look.

"How could he have? I didn't tell him. Besides, he was trying to *protect* you from that kind of prying, Sasha. People were going to pry anyway, you being who you are. Teriyan and Jaegar just tried to manage it, that's all."

Sasha sighed, heavily. Ahead, the vanguard's torches lit a wavering, ghostly line across the paddocks—a treeline, where the forest closed in once more. "Alythia accused me of trying desperately to fit in where none would willingly accept me," she said sombrely. And laughed bitterly. "Isn't that just like a sister, to know just where to stick the needle so it hurts the most? I just wanted to fit in, Andrey. I wanted friends and a place to belong. I didn't want to be a burden, or a . . . a pilgrimage attraction. Just a person, you know?"

Andreyis smiled at her, with friendly exasperation. "Sasha . . . you don't understand, do you? Look behind you." She looked over her shoulder. A vast column of horses, torchlit across the dark, rolling fields. Cloaked and armoured men in their hundreds. "You did fit in. The Goeren-yai are following you, Sasha. Teriyan spread word about you and men liked what they heard. They always have, even in Baerlyn folks think you can walk on clouds . . ."

"Don't be ridiculous!" Sasha said incredulously. Thinking of all the ribbings she'd received at the hands of Baerlyn men and women alike, the good-humoured slander, the teasing about her hair and how she showered far more affection on horses than young men, and how all those same young men were too frightened to flirt with her . . .

"I'm not being ridiculous!" Andreyis protested. "We don't do hero worship real well, Sasha . . . Goeren-yai men are proud, they don't bow at the feet of others easily. I'm your friend, Sasha. I've wrestled you down the hillside and rubbed dirt in your hair. But I'm not riding here tonight just because you're my friend. I'm riding here because I'm Goeren-yai and the Goeren-yai need a leader. They've chosen that leader to be you. And I couldn't think of anyone I'd rather follow."

Sasha gazed at him, a cold gust of wind threatening to remove the hood from her head. Tears prickled her eyes, and she reached and grasped Andreyis's hand with her own. "I don't know if I deserve that trust, Andrey," she said quietly. "I'm a spoilt, self-centred brat."

Andreyis grinned. "Aye, you are." Sasha laughed. Silly of her to have expected any other reply. "But you care for people. And you don't think yourself better than others, despite your talents. Lord Krayliss did neither. Which is why they follow you, and not him."

Sixteen

AT DAWN THEY CAME TO THE VARYSH RIVER, which marked the boundary between Baen-Tar and Valhanan. Water levels were low, typical of late summer, and Sasha rode to the far bank with barely a splash to wet her boots. Soldiers dismounted along both banks to lead their horses over the rocks and gravel of the exposed riverbed to drink.

Sasha was relieved to find that men had rations, for she had none. Her vanguard shared some bread and fruit with her as she stood and flexed her legs, watching Peg graze amidst the thick bushes that overgrew the riverbank. Birds choroused against the pale overcast sky, as hooves clattered on rock and men conversed in various tongues, weapons and armour clinking as they sat and ate, or briefly washed.

Finishing her breakfast, Sasha walked to a better vantage on the water's edge. So many men and horses. They lined the river as far as she could see to the upstream and downstream bends. Line company men, Lenayin's best equipped and most fearsome warriors. Not necessarily the best trained, nor even the highest standard, given the lifelong training that even simple farmers received. But these were the men she needed, more than common villagers. These men had *horses*.

Still, she reflected, she would have to get someone to count heads, just for certainty, and see if the number came anywhere near the two thousand of her earlier estimation. Lieutenant Alyn and the vanguard had followed her to the water's edge, she saw. They made a rough, informal line, separating her from the surrounding men and horses. It made her uncomfortable, as did many of the looks that came her way from the surrounding, mostly Goeren-yai soldiers. Some gazed in amazement, others in simple curiosity. Yet others were unreadable. Men of Lenayin were not easily impressed, she knew. And Kessligh had told her often that respect, in Lenayin, was no one's birthright. She took some comfort in Andreyis's words the previous night and yet she remained unconvinced. Many of these men needed no convincing of the rightness of their cause, but it would take plenty more than a pretty speech to convince many of them of *her*, no matter who her uman.

Some men performed taka-dans—as all soldiers would try to do them at least once a day, under any circumstances. Sasha settled for her stretching regimen—taka-dans could wait for a little more privacy. A soldier in Falcon Guard uniform approached, hair braided and ears ringed. He gained permission from Lieutenant Alyn, then squatted before Sasha, who sat upon a flattish rock with legs splayed, grasping one boot with both hands.

"Another thirty-five have joined from neighbouring villages, M'Lady," he told her. "Others are spreading the word, there is talk of hundreds more arriving shortly. It would be many more, but for the shortage of horses. Some are saying they will walk to the valley."

"And arrive ten days late," Sasha replied. "If they can find us, so can our enemies. It calls for watchful scouts, we don't want to mistake one for the other."

"Aye, M'Lady, we have men who know the region well. They are watchful."

He left, replaced by Tyrun and Lieutenant Alyn as she finished her stretching. "Advice," she asked the sharp-featured captain as they stood by the flowing water. "How do we stop this formation from turning into a rabble? Already we're becoming strung out across entire folds. If we simply keep adding new arrivals to the rear, they'll become easy pickings for ambush or charge from behind. These new arrivals are just villagers, they may be formidable warriors alone, but their equipment is not so good and their understanding of mass tactics even less."

"And we haven't trained together," Lieutenant Alyn added, looking about the riverbanks in concern, biting at his lip. "I served in the Yethulyn Bears before I joined the Royal Guard—it took me months to learn the different ways the Royal Guard fight. Understanding of tactics changes from region to region and unit to unit—some men will charge an ambush, others will dismount to fight on foot, others may try to outflank. We're only going to add new militia soldiers as we continue, how can we know how these new additions will behave? To say nothing of this great fruit salad of units we've accumulated."

Tyrun finished chewing a bite of fruit and spat out the pips. "At least you youngsters ask the right questions. Now you need to learn that not every question has an answer. To both of you, I say simply that we do the best we can. M'Lady, I regret to inform you that we *are* a rabble. No helping it. If we get hit in midcolumn on the march, we'll get split. I've instructed ranks along the line to circle and enfold, if any such hit us . . . but you know the difficulty of anything so rapid in this terrain.

"On the bright side, this is the easy bit. Making this rabble work against thousands of Hadryn and probably Banneryd heavy cavalry, especially if they get wind of us and have time to prepare . . . that'll be the test."

A man was running along the bank, feet slipping on stones in his haste. Lieutenant Alyn moved to intercept, but Tyrun barked a command and he was let through. "M'Lady!" he said, full of haste and alarm, but no apparent fear. It was not an attack, then. He seemed instead . . . bewildered. "M'Lady, we found someone on the road behind, following us. The scout did not know what to do . . . he thought . . . he thought perhaps it was best to come to you."

Sasha frowned at him, then looked beyond to where several soldiers were accompanying a somewhat scrawny dussieh pony along the riverbank. Upon the saddle sat a most unmartial figure, small and swathed in an oversized cloak. One soldier led the pony, while others moved alongside, and yet more stopped what they were doing and stared. Sasha began walking, her guard moving with her . . . and then, with a sickening twist of fear in her stomach, she broke into a run.

The soldier with the pony's halter stopped as she arrived, and another assisted the slim, shivering figure from the saddle, as carefully as handling eggshells. A dress was visible, briefly, beneath the cloak. Sasha grabbed the girl by the shoulders, pulled back the hood and stared disbelievingly at the young, pale, teeth-chattering face within. Sofy.

"Oh no," was all she could think to say. If Koenyg had been inclined to spare her neck before, he certainly wouldn't now.

"Sasha!" Tears filled Sofy's eyes, part exhaustion, part fear, and partly at the sight of her sister's horrified expression. "Sasha, I w . . . was scared! K . . . Koenyg was going to m . . . make me spend more time with those t . . . tyrants . . . and . . ."

Sasha grabbed Sofy's hands in her own gloved ones and held one to her cheek. "Hells, you're freezing!" She pulled aside the cloak, revealing nothing more than a palace dress beneath, its shiny green fabric muddied about the hem. "You rode all through the night in just this? It gets *cold* away from your warm fireplaces at night, Sofy, even in summer! What were you thinking?"

"Sasha?" Sofy pleaded. "Sasha, don't be angry with me! I . . . I didn't know what else to do . . . !"

Sasha put both hands to her head, half turning with the strengthening urge to scream, or to break something. More men were clustering about. "Princess Sofy!" she heard them saying urgently, one to the other. It spread through their ranks with concern and surprise. This was *just* what she needed . . .

"There . . . there was a big confusion after the executions . . ." Sofy continued, her voice shaking, ". . . men running around, saying . . . saying there w . . . was rebellion and that you'd escaped. E . . . even the gate guards weren't paying attention. Suddenly, there were people rushing everywhere . . . I took the horse from the stable and I just rode! I rode like you showed me, Sasha, those times before! I just . . . I just had to get out before . . ."

"You're going back!" Sasha rounded on her. Sofy stared at her in shock. "You can't stay here, Sofy! This is an army! People are going to get killed, do you understand that?"

Past her temper, Sasha half expected Sofy to collapse into helpless tears. "I'm not marrying that pig!" Sofy screamed instead. "I'm not! I won't marry a man who kills serrin children and calls it sport! I'd rather die!"

A hushed, incredulous silence settled over those near, as those further away scrambled to see or hear better. The sisters' stares locked, Sasha completely at a loss, Sofy tear-streaked and desperately furious, her slim shoulders heaving.

"Can't send her back now, M'Lady," said Tyrun in a low voice from Sasha's side. "We'll have northerners in pursuit, scouts skirmishing, village recruits on the trail, no doubt all tangling and making a mess. It's amazing she got this far without challenge. You send her back alone and she's likely dead by mistake. And we can't spare her an escort."

"Oh dear lords," Sasha muttered. Her temper boiled, desperate for release. She was angry at everyone—at every Goeren-yai soldier in the column for plotting without telling her, for expecting so much from her, for thrusting her into such a position without so much as a "Do you mind?". And at Koenyg for being a dangerous fool, at her father for his blind worship, at Kessligh for leaving her, at Sofy for needing her and at herself for . . . "Oh dear spirits, just stop!" she thought to herself, furiously. There were men watching, men whose lives now depended to no small degree upon the decisions she made. Back in Baerlyn, arguing with Kessligh, she might have been able to afford losing her temper. Here, she could not.

"I can ride," Sofy said in a small voice, fidgeting with some uncharacteristically tangled hair. "I think I'm quite good at it. I didn't fall off even once. I won't get in anyone's way."

"If you ride in this column, Sofy, you *are* in the way," Sasha retorted. "Everyone's in everyone else's way, that's what riding in formation *is*."

"She'll be fine," said Andreyis from one side, gallantly. "She can ride with me." Sofy gazed at him. Wiped at her tears, ducking her head shyly.

Sasha gave the young man a harsh look. "And what are you going to wear?" she asked Sofy. "You can't wear that dress . . . look, no wonder you nearly froze, you must have been riding with it up over your knees! I've a spare shirt and that's it, and I'll bet none of the men have anything your size . . ."

"M'Lady," volunteered a Black Hammers lieutenant Sasha did not know, "I believe we can find something among the men. We've got a few smaller lads, and even a soldier knows how to tailor in an emergency. If you were to leave the princess in my care, I believe we could find her something suitable."

Andreyis glared at the man. Sasha threw her hands up in exasperation. "Fine," she said, realising that she had no other choice. Which was seeming very much the way of things, lately. "You do that."

The lieutenant gallantly offered Sofy his arm. Sofy took it meekly. "But I could . . ." Andreyis protested, but Teriyan laid a hand on his shoulder, restraining him. The lieutenant gave the younger, plain-dressed man a cool look over Sofy's head as he led her away. There were other soldiers, mostly officers, practically queuing to be of assistance. Andreyis fumed.

Just wonderful, Sasha thought—the fate of Lenayin in the balance and the young men thought it more important to lock horns like rutting stags in the spring. She spun on her heel and made for her previous place on the bank, her guard moving behind. Teriyan leaped quickly to her side, his stride long, but his footing not quite as precise upon the broken, shifting rocks.

"You could go a bit easy on the girl," he suggested. "She didn't mean any harm, she just . . ."

"Spirits save me from people who don't mean any harm," Sasha snapped, leaping fast across a slippery boulder in hopes of losing him. A crash of boots on loose rock told her it hadn't worked.

"And do you want to know *why* she did such a stupid, desperate thing, riding all this way in the dark when she barely knows one end of a horse from another?"

"Not particularly, no," Sasha snapped.

"Because she needs you," Teriyan said firmly. "I'd never met the girl until now, but you read me some of the less private bits from her letters before, and Lynette tells me some more . . ." Memories of the Steltsyn Star, warm before the fireplace with a mug of ale, reading some delightful palace scandal from Sofy's latest letter that she knew her friends would love to hear. "You think of her as the smartest girl in Baen-Tar, and perhaps she is at that. But Sasha, she worships the ground you walk on, just as much as you ever did with Prince Krystoff. And now when she gets into the worst possible trouble, she comes running all this way to see *you*. Not Daddy the king, not brother Damon, not her palace friends and fellow girlies . . . you, Sasha. She needs you."

Sasha stopped on the riverbank, hands to her head, and stared agonisedly across the water. Wind gusted at the riverside trees. Above the eastern hills, the broken edges of cloud glowed golden in the dawn light. Perhaps the rain would hold off after all.

"Why can't people just look after themselves?" she said plaintively to no one in particular. "Why do I always end up getting caught in other people's problems?"

"If you really think that," Teriyan said sharply, "then you're even more arrogant than I thought." Sasha rounded on him, disbelievingly. "You, who spent your early years latched onto brother Krystoff like a foal to its teet, and your later ones just as much so upon Kessligh. That man gave his life to you when most people would have given their right arm for him to even say hello, and what thanks do you give *him* for it? You're a smart, strong girl, and you've more talent for swordsmanship in your little finger than most of us have in total . . . but you've a hell of a lot to learn about responsibility. The spirits grant each of us responsibilities over others. When they need our help, we give it. All I see from you right now is complaints and selfishness."

"I'd accept that dressing down from a friend," Sasha said coldly. "But from someone who lied to me, who was spying on me in secret, and has been setting up this whole campaign, with me to lead it, and never a word to *me* . . ." She took a deep breath, trying to keep from shaking. She'd nearly lost it completely, in full view of everyone. It had been that close. "From that person, I'll not hear *anything* lest I ask for it. Is that clear?"

"Ah . . ." Teriyan gave a contemptuous wave, turning his back as if to dismiss her in disgust. But he paused, and looked back at her. "I'm not perfect, and I'll bet I've made mistakes, with you, with Lynie, with Kessligh and everyone else. But everything I've done, Sasha, I've done with the good of other people in mind. You have a long, hard think about it, and you ask yourself if you can honestly say the same thing."

Damon rode across the chaos of the Rathynal tent city in the cold light of dawn, rubbing the sleep from his eyes. The once orderly, sprawling camp now looked as though a great wind had sprung up in the night and come howling across the slope, leaving a trail of destruction in its wake. Some tents were collapsed and belongings were strewn upon the ground. Mustering squares for horses now held only half their proper number and cartloads of fodder were stripped of feed. Soldiers wandered aimlessly, some talking in small groups, some sitting by lonely campfires and sipping tea.

Damon caught snatches of conversation as he rode past, some angry, some exasperated, some forlorn. There was not a Goeren-yai man to be seen. At Damon's side, Myklas rode with a bewildered expression. Myklas had never found the bickering of lords interesting before. A sixteen-year-old prince in Baen-Tar, Damon knew all too well, could lead a sheltered life, safe within the illusion that all Lenays shared the same values, paid homage to their superiors and would die for the same causes, if needs be. Damon had been eased from that illusion slowly, one small step into the freezing water at a time. Myklas had been thrown for a headlong plunge and his eyes now registered the chilling shock.

In a field beside the road, a group of soldiers gathered about a morning campfire. Damon recognised the flag atop a near tent—a battlehorn on a scarlet background, the Fyden Silver Horns. Damon called ahead to his Royal Guard escort and rode into the field. Morose, unshaven faces looked up as he approached.

Damon and Myklas dismounted and handed reins to the guardsmen. "Highness," said a Fyden sergeant, with no real enthusiasm. Of the six men present, this man was the senior ranked.

"What happened?" Damon asked. It was a question he'd asked numerous soldiers this morning. It was plenty clear what had happened. It was not a simple description of events he was seeking.

The sergeant shrugged. "Damn mess, Your Highness," he said, in a guttural western accent. "They leave, all my Goeren-yai. Many friends. Damn mess." His Lenay was not good . . . it rarely was, in the west. Nearby, an officer was shouting, trying to rally scattered men.

"How many of the Silver Horns contingent remain?"

The sergeant made a face. "Half. Maybe less. Some Verenthanes go. Lieutenant Byron go. Maybe I should have go too."

"Highness . . ." a man-at-arms ventured, cautiously, "we go . . . go chase? Chase our men?"

"They're traitors," Damon said flatly. Koenyg had been most insistent on that point. Insistent, loud and angry.

The westerners looked most unhappy at that. "Not traitors, Highness," said another. "Good men."

Another man said something in a western tongue, which got an angry retort from his comrade. Voices were raised, back and forth. Evidently the issue was not universally agreed.

Damon was not surprised. He glanced up at the Royal Guardsman astride his horse—a Goeren-yai man, one of the few Royal Guard Goeren-yai who'd remained. The man's face was impassive. Despite Koenyg's attempts to dismiss a number of Goeren-yai Royal Guards, Damon had insisted as many remain as possible. Koenyg had already had a list compiled, it seemed, and had spent half the dark hours summoning, ordering and shouting, trying to sort out the loyal from the disloyal. Even when it became apparent that some Verenthanes, too, had abandoned their posts, he only dismissed Goeren-yai guardsmen.

Then had come news that some other Goeren-yai guardsmen, infuriated by the dismissals, had taken leave to ride hard after the traitors and more were joining them. Some northern cavalrymen had intercepted them, with sporadic battles erupting by torchlight across the fields and into the forest below. That tally was twenty dead from both sides, with rumours spreading fast of how the Banneryd cavalry had executed several wounded guardsmen, not helping matters at all. The desertions had only ended after a furious row between Captain Myles of the Royal Guard and Koenyg, during which (it was said) Koenyg had threatened to dismiss Captain Myles as well, to which Myles had countered that all the Royal Guard would desert if he did so.

It had been a long, exhausting, bloody, rumour-filled night, and the day did not promise any better. Already there were reports of murders amongst the few Goeren-yai of Baen-Tar town, the finger of suspicion pointed immediately at the northern soldiers accommodating there. The rest of the Goeren-yai community were sheltering in the houses of Verenthane friends, fearing for their lives. The only positive Damon could see was that the soldiers themselves, with the predictable exception of the northerners, had not been killing each other. From the look of this lot, he reckoned that Koenyg would have his work cut out for him if he expected them to go tearing off in pursuit of their friends any time soon.

"Not bad men," the Fyden sergeant insisted now. "Good men. Verenthanes . . ." he shrugged, helplessly. "Verenthanes kill Lord Krayliss, kill Taneryn men, go Sashandra Lenayin to dungeon, now attack Udalyn." Another helpless shrug. "If I Goeren-yai, maybe I traitor too."

"Why don't you go and fight with them then?" Myklas said with irritation. "If you feel so sorry for them."

"Maybe I do," said the sergeant, with a dark glower at the youngest prince. "Maybe I start now. Boy."

Damon put a hand on Myklas's shoulder, pulling him back. "Thank you, Sergeant," he said, keeping his voice even. "You have every right to be angry. None of us like this situation."

"Aye," the sergeant muttered. He spat into the fire. "Aye, Prince Damon."

"You just back down to him?" Myklas said incredulously as they rode back along the road between paddock walls. "Who's the prince here, you or him?"

"Every Lenay man is a prince," Damon said darkly, casting his gaze across the desolate scene. "We don't rule by divine right, Myk, we rule on tolerance. They tolerate us, not the other way around. It's always been this way."

"Yeah, well, maybe it's time it changed," Myklas said angrily.

"Don't be a stupid little shit," Damon said coldly. "If you'd kept spitting in that sergeant's eye, he'd have cut your fucking head off, *Prince* Myklas, and devils take the consequences. In the last hundred years we nobles have begun to forget this fact and now we're paying for it."

"You're *defending* them?" Myklas said incredulously. "You're defending what they've done? What Sasha's done?"

"I'll tell you this, little brother," Damon said starkly, "thank the *gods* Sasha's leading this. The reason we aren't knee-deep in blood right now is Sasha. I've been reading a lot of history lately, the kinds of things our wonderful holy scholars never taught us and don't want us to read. Pagan history, before the Liberation. We've forgotten what honourable Lenays do when they've become sick of being kicked in the balls. So long as that column has Sasha at its head, she might keep it from becoming a bloody nightmare across the whole kingdom. But if something happens to her, it could be the end of Lenayin as a single kingdom, and sure as *hells* the end of Lenayin as a Verenthane kingdom. If it truly ever was."

Across an open stretch of lower slope, past isolated trees and water catchments that shone the dull silver of the overcast morning, rode the king. There were royal banners of purple and green, and a horde of Royal Guards astride some of the finest horses of any Lenay stable. The king wore black, tall and straight in the saddle astride a fine dappled grey. Soldiers across the slope stared as he passed and some cheered. Behind him, a host of nobility also rode, several hundred in number. The colours of their clothes seemed incongruous, a sea of courtly reds, blues, greens and golds across the dark green fields. Most, Damon suspected, had not changed from the previous day's finery. Last night, no one had slept.

"Look at them," Damon muttered, reining to a halt on the rise, with a good view over the royal procession along the lower slope. "Too scared to venture amongst their own soldiers except in force. They're more keen to lick the king's heels than they are to question their own men."

"Still, it's good to see Father out on a horse," Myklas said uncertainly. "It's been a long time." He paused. "In fact, I can't think of the last time."

Some of the nobles *were* riding amongst their own soldiers, whatever Damon's disdain. A small group of them came galloping across a near field, a flash of green Tyree colours amidst white canvas tents.

"Prince Damon!" called the handsome man with the square jaw and cool eyes who led them. They reined up opposite the low stone wall that separated the road from the field. Six men. Of the followers, Damon recognised Lord Redyk, but not the others, who were younger. Family, most likely. Loyal swords in uncertain times.

"Lord Arastyn!" Damon said coldly. "What can I do for you?"

"*Great* Lord Arastyn," Lord Redyk corrected, his face flushed red against his white whiskers.

"Your men don't think so," Damon observed. "Lost them all, have you?" Lord Redyk turned even redder. Lord Arastyn's dark eyes were cold. The Tyree contingent to ride to Baen-Tar had been one of the smallest. The Falcon Guard were already garrisoning Baen-Tar, so only a token fifty extra soldiers had accompanied Tyree's lords and ladies on the road. Those soldiers had been handpicked, almost all of them Verenthane. Now, all were missing. Loyalty to one's faith was important in Lenayin, but for many, loyalty to one's province was more. The Tyree soldiers had left no doubt who *they* thought were the traitors to the proud name of Tyree.

"Your great-grandfather, King Soros, decreed that the provincial lords shall rule their provinces directly," Lord Redyk growled. "We have so decreed. Lord Arastyn is now the Great Lord of Tyree, and the family name of Nyvar is erased, dishonoured beyond repair. It is done, and none other can unsay it!"

"Words are easy, sitting alone on your horse when all your men have deserted," Damon replied. "There is an old Goeren-yai tale of the mad chieftain Shymel, who left his clan to go and live on a mountain top and declared himself ruler of all the stars and the moon. Some say he is still there, ignored by all, an irrelevant speck on his peak. No one cared, my lords. Certainly not his clan, who did not miss him, and the stars and the moon least of all."

Lord Arastyn raised a hand, forestalling Lord Redyk's angry reply. Arastyn had always been loyal to Family Nyvar, his eldest son was to wed Jaryd's sister, and he had been a close friend to the late Great Lord Aystin Nyvar. Damon stared closely at the man. Had his loyalty been a lie? Or had he chosen this path simply to save his own skin, and the skins of his family? Some rumours said that his fellow lords had chosen him to be the successor because it would look less suspicious for a friend of the dying great lord to take his place. Surely such an old, loyal friend could not have ordered the destruction of Family Nyvar?

"The king has asked for an explanation of events," said Lord Arastyn, in calm, measured tones. "You were present, Your Highness, at the folly of the traitor and murderer Jaryd Nyvar. Your answers will be required."

Damon could barely restrain his anger. "You killed his little brother," he retorted. "Dare you call him a murderer?"

"Our actions were within the king's law," Arastyn replied, with stony calm. "An accident occurred. The boy was foolish. It is regrettable, yet the fact remains that Jaryd Nyvar's actions were traitorous, and they were murder. You were unwise to prevent us from killing him, Prince Damon. Your own actions shall be considered before the king's justice. Best that you consider your own position."

"How can a man be a murderer when he charges thirty armed nobles all alone?" Myklas asked suddenly. "Were the men he killed unarmed?"

"It was against the king's law," Arastyn insisted, "and therefore murder."

"Sounds like a damn brave man to me," said Myklas. Lord Redyk looked uncomfortable. Lord Arastyn seemed to grind his teeth. Damon nearly smiled. Myklas had that damnably annoying habit of saying what he thought. Usually that was no problem, because usually he didn't think much.

"I shall answer my father's enquiries as I see fit," Damon told the lords, coldly. "Appeals and treaties shall not sway me. I have better things to worry about than Tyree's succession, my lords. Good day."

"Pack of cowards," Myklas observed once the Tyree lords had departed and the princes were riding downhill toward the king's column. "I'm glad you saved Jaryd Nyvar, he is a good fighter and I can't see what he did wrong."

"Toward the throne, nothing," said Damon. "Toward his peers in Tyree, everything. But tell me this . . . back there, you said that Fyden sergeant should shut up and respect his superiors because nobility is always right. And now you think the Tyree lords are a pack of cowards. How can both be true?"

Myklas thought about it for a moment. A gust of cold wind caught at his typically unkempt brown hair. He had a face that would always remain young, Damon suspected, even when his body was grown. Sofy said that Myklas's greatest ambition was to remain a kid forever. People liked him because he was usually positive and had a simple, good-humoured and relaxed view of things. Damon often wondered what sort of man he'd become when he discovered that such an attitude would only take him so far.

"Why does everything have to be so complicated?" Myklas wondered aloud, finally.

"You can ask that question all you like," Damon said grimly, "and it won't make the world any less complicated. We can only accept that it is, and go from there."

"You're enjoying this," Myklas observed, watching his elder brother with a glint of mischief. "Crises suit you, all dark and foreboding."

"Shut up or I'll belt you," Damon snorted.

Soldiers were staring at the king's procession. If the king had emerged from within the Baen-Tar walls, surely things were bad. A short distance to one side, Damon saw Koenyg, all in black astride his chestnut stallion. He was involved in an angry exchange of waving hands and pointing. The nobles who were the targets of his rage remained stonily unimpressed. Finally Koenyg reined about in exasperation and rode away, his Royal Guards in pursuit.

He spotted Damon and Myklas descending the slope along the paddock road and turned uphill to meet them. He arrived at Damon's side with a thunder of hooves and an angry scowl.

"Can you believe it?" he exclaimed to his brothers. "Father insists we ride at once. I tried to explain to him that it would be better to wait for Lord Parabys to reach us, take the time to prepare and then depart together . . . but suddenly Father fancies himself a commander!"

"He is king," Damon pointed out, with less sympathy than he might.

"He's not ridden into action since the Great War!" Koenyg scoffed. He seemed, Damon observed, highly agitated. "This is my responsibility, I am Commander of Armies and protector of the realm. I can handle this."

"Like you handled the Goeren-yai?" Damon nearly asked. He refrained with difficulty, and despised himself for it. "Sofy is missing," he said instead, his jaw tight.

Koenyg gave him a dark stare, controlling his unsettled stallion with a yank of the rein. Damon's mare tossed her head. "You haven't found her yet?" Koenyg asked accusingly.

"She's not here," Damon retorted. "There are horses missing, there was chaos at the gate, there were guards away from their posts . . . she could easily have ridden out."

"She barely knows how to ride!"

"Sasha's shown her."

"Bloody Sasha," Koenyg said between gritted teeth. "As if it weren't enough to have *one* sister for a traitor, now she corrupts the other."

"Maybe she wouldn't have felt the urge if you hadn't betrothed her to that perfumed Larosan shitheap." Koenyg stared at him. "Yes, I know."

"Who told you?" Darkly.

"None of your damn business. It was your idea, wasn't it?"

"Not mine." Shortly, and more defensively than Damon might have expected. Koenyg was rarely defensive about anything. "Archbishop Dalryn's. And Father's."

"Father's?" Disbelievingly.

"Yes, Father's," Koenyg snapped. "As you said, he's the king. I'm a soldier. I think we should ally with the lowlands Verenthane brotherhood because I see the military possibilities. I don't arrange marriages. Dalryn took the idea to Father, and Father approved."

"And you went along with it," Damon accused him. "Why keep it secret? Is this how all Lenayin will be ruled from now on? You, Father and Dalryn, making decisions for the kingdom that are so unpopular amongst the people you don't dare even tell them?"

"You speak for the people now?" Koenyg said dangerously. "You sound just like Sasha."

"You ignored Sasha," Damon jabbed back, a forefinger extended, "and you ignored the Goeren-yai, and they brought all your precious plans crashing down around your ears. Ignore me if you like, and ignore Sofy and ignore all the people you've infuriated—that's your choice. But if this is what you and Father call leadership, I fear for Lenayin, because the kingdom can't take much more of this!"

For a brief moment, Damon thought Koenyg might strike him. One hard fist balled on the reins and his dark eyes blazed with anger. Then he snorted contemptuously and rode his prancing stallion ahead and across, cutting them off. "This is what happens when you spend all your time with girls," Koenyg said to Myklas, loudly enough that the guardsmen and soldiers nearby could hear. "You start to believe that men will love you just by smiling prettily and complimenting their shoes."

He dug in his heels, leapt the adjoining paddock fence and raced across the fields, weaving between abandoned tents as he went, his guardsmen in pursuit.

"I hope he falls and breaks his neck," Damon muttered as he and Myklas continued down the slope toward their father and his entourage.

"No you don't," Myklas replied, watching him with wary eyes. Damon matched his gaze. Whatever Myklas had hoped to see there, he didn't find it. "I hope Sofy comes back soon," Myklas sighed. "Last I saw Alythia, she was screaming that 'that mangy bitch Sasha' had ruined her wedding and that her husband would arrive in the midst of this chaos and there wouldn't be a proper reception to greet him. Sofy's the binding that holds this family together, everyone says so. Without her, we'll all kill each other."

"Only now she's being married off to foreigners," Damon muttered. "Maybe Father and Dalryn want us to kill each other."

"No offence, Damon," Myklas said with typical matter-of-factness, "but if it ever comes to that, my copper's on Koenyg."

The rebel column rode onward in the brightening morning, two abreast along the road and sometimes three, then thinning to single file in parts where the forest closed in, or the road climbed steeply to clear a ridge. Sasha noticed that the vanguard appeared to have doubled to as many as ten riders, in addition to several scouts who made brief, random appearances to declare what lay ahead, before galloping off once more. Sasha suspected that the increase was due to Sofy, who now rode several places behind Sasha, at Jaryd's side. Royalty always demanded extra protection in the mind of any loyal officer. Sasha considered sending Sofy further back in the column, but decided against it. Any ambush would likely strike midcolumn or to the rear. The column's lead, shielded by the vanguard and forewarned by ranging scouts, was probably the safest place of all.

Jaryd rode in constant pain, his face pale and grim. He had eaten and drunk, but had not spoken. A soldier who knew healing had cleaned his wounds and rewrapped his bandages. The leg wound was a flesh wound, he'd said, but it was not infected and would heal well enough in time. Sasha wished she had a moment to ride at Jaryd's side and talk to him, but the road required her attention. Besides, she would occasionally hear Sofy's light attempts at conversation, and the stony silence that followed.

For a while, the weather closed in with light rain and a gusting, swirling wind that tore at the treetops and scattered the road with falling leaves and needles. But then, just as Sasha began to fear that the road would become a muddy bog for those further back in the column, the rain ended and sunlight speared through lighter, scattered cloud. Craggy, sheer faces of rock climbed clear of the trees in places, looming above the road. At times, Sasha consulted with Captain Tyrun about possible ambush spots, but the scouts' reports remained positive, and the residents of one village turned out to greet them with cheers, ten mounted warriors to join the column, and some fresh provisions, which Sasha directed to the men further back. Food, at least, was one thing she would not have to worry about.

Approaching midday, the road was noticeably beginning to climb. Ascending the winding incline of a thickly wooded valley, Tyrun fell back to consult with some of his officers. Shortly, his place was taken by a small, wiry horse, ridden by a pair of children. Daryd and Rysha, Sasha realised with amazement. The Udalyn boy looked up at her—a long way up, from his little dussieh pony—and gave a clenched-fist salute, as might one warrior to another on the road. He looked quite cheerful, loose brown hair falling about his face, his hunting knife worn at one hip like a sword. Rysha's gaze was more serious, yet her posture on the back of her brother's saddle was comfortable, as if she had ridden this way many times before. She still wore the same, mangled yellow flower in her hair, now mostly dead.

"Where in the world did you two come from?" Sasha exclaimed, registering only blank stares from the siblings. "Lieutenant Alyn!" she called to the rider ahead. "Have the children been with us this entire time?"

"Aye, M'Lady," the Royal Guard lieutenant replied. "Princess Sofy's maid helped them from their palace room. The lad's a good rider and his sister can stay ahorse well at a gallop. I thought it best for them to ride at the front where they have protection, and can possibly give directions when we draw closer to the valley."

Sasha gazed down at the children. Daryd was marvelling at Peg's glossy black flanks. "Big," he said, his one Lenay word. And grinned. "Big horse."

Two words. He looked very pleased with himself. Sasha found herself smiling. "Big horse," she agreed. And pointed to their pony. "Little horse." And repeated that, making big, then little sizes with her hands. Comprehension dawned on Daryd's face.

"Big horse Peglyrion," he said, pointing to Peg. "Little horse Essey," pointing to the pony. "My *dasser* horse." Dass, in Sasha's limited Taasti, meant father. Probably Edu was similar.

"Ah, your father's horse. Father."

"Fa-ther," Daryd repeated. "Father." His eyes were suddenly sad. Fearful. At his back, Rysha gave a whimper and reached forward to take her brother's hand. Daryd clutched it hard. Their family had lived in Ymoth, Sasha recalled, the town before the valley mouth. Krayliss had been right—when the Hadryn attacked, Ymoth would have been the first to fall.

Something growing to one side of the road caught Sasha's eye. Blue ralama flowers, growing in a little clump. She dismounted quickly, picked the flowers, and bounced back up from stirrup to saddle as fast as twelve years on horseback had taught her. She arranged the little bunch of flowers whilst riding with her hands free, as Daryd and Rysha stared in amazement at that feat of horsemanship. When the bunch was tidy, she grasped the saddlehorn in her left hand and leaned far out on one stirrup to present the flowers to Rysha.

Rysha took them, blinking in wonderment. Sasha pointed to her hair, encouragingly. Rysha took out the mangled yellow flower and looked at it sorrowfully. Daryd suggested something to her in Edu. Rysha was displeased and complained. She tucked the dead flower into the front pocket of her coarse-weave dress, and considered the ralama flowers more closely. Counted their bright blue petals.

"Verenthane," she pronounced.

Sasha blinked. Verenthane? And then she recalled the great, eight-pointed patterned windows in the Saint Ambellion Temple. And, of course, the eight-pointed Verenthane stars worn about the neck of every devout follower. Eight petals on a ralama blossom. Lucky in Goeren-yai tradition, but holy for Verenthanes. Another point of commonality between the twin faiths of Lenayin.

"Lucky flower," she said to Rysha.

"Flower?" Rysha said with a frown. It stood to reason that Rysha understood that word first. But lucky?

"Hmm," said Sasha, thinking hard. Then it occurred to her. She pointed to Peg, looking at Daryd. "Peglyrion," she said and pointed to the sky. She dotted the sky with her forefinger to represent stars, like the Peglyrion stars in the sword pommel of Hyathon the Warrior.

"Ah!" said Daryd and told Rysha, "*Esi*."

"*Esi*," Sasha repeated. "Stars."

"Stars," Daryd echoed. Sasha then pointed up once more at the imaginary stars and made the spirit sign to her forehead. The universal Goeren-yai sign for luck. All Goeren-yai believed that stars were lucky and that the star spirits could bless a person's fortunes if one appealed to them. Daryd grinned his understanding.

"Lucky," Sasha explained.

"Lucky," Daryd agreed, nodding vigorously.

"Lucky flowers," Sasha concluded, pointing again to Rysha's ralama blossoms. Even Rysha smiled this time and marvelled anew at the pretty blue colour. It never ceased to amaze Sasha how people could usually manage to make themselves understood, even with no words in common, with just a little imagination and patience. "Pretty flowers," she added, deciding to push her luck.

"Pretty?"

"Pretty." Sasha indicated Peg's flowing, muscular curves and put a hand to her heart, with an expression on her face as if the most handsome man in all the world had just stepped naked into her chambers one evening. Rysha recognised that expression well before her brother and laughed.

"*Gadi!*" she exclaimed. "*Gadi tethlan* "pretty"! Pretty flowers!" It was the first time Sasha had seen Rysha look happy.

"Pretty Rysha," Sasha countered.

Rysha blushed shyly. "Pretty Sashandra," she replied.

Around a bend in the climbing road ahead, a scout emerged at a canter, slowing now to a walk as he sighted the column. Sasha turned in her saddle. "Sofy? Is Sofy riding back there? Tell her to come forward, I've a task for her."

There was a moment of commotion behind. Someone offered an instruction . . . "Just tap him lightly with your heels, Highness. Not too hard, he'll understand."

A second dussieh pony approached and Sasha pulled Peg right to the road verge, where the hill climbed more steeply. There was barely room here for Peg and the two dussieh. Sofy's horse came between Peg and Essey, and Sasha blinked in astonishment.

Seated in the saddle was a girl who looked remarkably like, and yet most unlike, Sasha's younger sister. Sofy wore a sheepskin jacket and a thick, plain undershirt, tucked into a pair of pants secured firmly about her narrow waist with a belt. There were riding gloves on her hands, soft-skin boots on her feet and her shining brown hair was tied in a simple ponytail at the back.

"Where in the world did you get those clothes?" Sasha asked.

"Some of the Tyree soldiers had bought good clothes for their younger brothers in Baen-Tar," said Sofy, in a very subdued tone. "They were very kind to lend me these."

Sasha stared for a moment at this most incongruous of sights—a princess of Lenayin with her hair tied back, in pants, jacket and boots, astride a horse in the Lenayin wilds. And she realised, suddenly, what a shock the first sight of *her* in such clothes must have been for her family, on her first return visit to Baen-Tar as Kessligh's uma. And she'd cut her hair short, too. And worn a sword on her back, and other weapons besides.

"Hello!" Sofy said cheerfully to the Udalyn children.

"Hello, Princess Sofy," said Daryd, echoed by Rysha. So they'd learned who the new arrival was, then. Both children bowed in the saddle.

Sofy laughed. "Oh, aren't you lovely? And Rysha, what pretty flowers. Pretty flowers!" Pointing.

Rysha nodded and smiled. "Pretty flowers," she agreed.

"Sofy," said Sasha, eyeing the scout requiring her attention. "I've an important task for you. You'll not be merely a passenger on this ride."

Sofy nodded nervously. "Yes?"

"Look after the children," Sasha told her. "See them fed, make sure they don't wander, maybe even learn a little Edu since you're so good with tongues. Can you do that?"

"Yes, of course!" Sofy looked relieved. It wasn't so much a task, Sasha knew, as something she'd have done anyway. But doubtless she was happy to have *some* responsibility. "I'd love to."

Sasha touched her heels to Peg's sides and rode forward to the scout. Behind, she heard Sofy resuming the conversation with the children.

By the time the scout had departed, the climbing, winding road had arrived at an open shoulder, overlooking the forested valley below. The wind blew briskly, but no longer as cold. Crumpled hills stretched into the distance, the flanks of Mount Tvay barely visible in distant mist. Sunlight splashed golden patches through the clouds, drifting slowly over forested ridges and valleys, interspersed with veils of misting rain. Ahead, the ridge onto which the road ascended fell sharply in a line of ragged cliffs, sheer rock plunging into thick trees below. Above the cliffs, riding the updrafts, an eagle soared.

"Oh, my lords!" Sasha heard Sofy exclaim, and turned in her saddle to see the youngest Princess of Lenayin gazing openmouthed at the scene, a hand to her chest. "My land is so beautiful!" Her eyes were shining.

"Pretty," Daryd agreed. "Pretty land."

As the column took a brief pause along a stream to water the horses, the first trouble broke out. Sasha ran along the forested streamside, dodging about horses and men as they pressed for space between the trees and waterside rushes, several of her vanguard in pursuit. Ahead, she could hear angry yells and threats, at alarming volume, and men along the stream craned their heads to look.

Sasha pushed her way past the last few horses and found two distinct groups of men in confrontation, each gathered behind their respective leaders. Both groups were Goeren-yai, but one was Falcon Guard soldiers and the other was villagers. Each was shouting in a tongue other than Lenay, yet familiar. Blades were not yet drawn, but hands were threatening on the hilts of swords.

Sasha stepped between the loudest, expecting them to stop. The men kept yelling, leaning around the new, inconvenient obstacle, jabbing sharp, accusing fingers. "Shut up!" she yelled at them. The men simply shouted louder, ignoring her. Sasha drew her blade and whistled the edge past one man's nose, then another, sending them stumbling backward. The men of her vanguard half drew their blades in case of retaliation, but none came, and the shouting paused.

"What's this about?" Sasha demanded into that brief silence. Men on both sides stared at her, and at each other, fuming. "Speak, or I'll banish you from this column and give your damn horses to someone who can ride without fighting his brothers! What's this about?"

She stared hard at a Falcon Guard corporal who seemed prominent in the argument. "I'm Jysu, M'Lady," the man said, as if that explained everything. "My friends here are Jysu." Gesturing to his fellow guardsmen. "We ride together in the guard. These men are Karyd." Pointing at the villagers.

Sasha blinked at him, waiting for the rest of the explanation. Nothing more came. "And?" she demanded. "So what?"

"The clans of Jysu and Karyd have blood feud!" a villager announced angrily. He was an older man, at least sixty, with wild white hair about his otherwise bald head, yet he had strength. The expression beneath his spirit mask was ferocious. "Just two years ago two brothers from the Jysu headman's family killed a Karyd boy in a manner without honour! We came just now to join the great battle to save the Udalyn, but men of Karyd shall not ride with murderers!"

"The boy declared immediate challenge!" a guardsman retorted. "Our lad was within his rights!"

"And what about the murder of Yuan Arsyn's brother just a year before?" another soldier shouted. A yell came back in the other tongue, and then the shouting and yelling resumed, as loud as before.

They were in eastern Tyree now, Sasha realised, with exasperation. Tyree had clans that united some villages together and thrust others apart. Another of the manifold confusions that were the Goeren-yai, and baffled so many foreigners.

A yell cut them short. Sasha turned and found Jaryd limping to the fore. Beside the obvious pain on his face, his eyes were cold and distant. Only anger gave them animation now, a deadly light that was chilling to behold. Men quietened, watching him. Jaryd stopped between the old villager and his Falcon Guard corporal, and said something, darkly, in another tongue. Everyone watched. There was no reply. Jaryd repeated it.

The corporal replied, shortly, with deference. Jaryd turned his stare on the villager. The villager snarled something in return and Sasha caught the words *"qualy kayat,"* meaning "many gods" in central tongues. Verenthanes. And not, by the villager's tone of voice, pleasantly meant.

Jaryd hit him, a right fist to the face. The man stumbled and fell, and his comrades drew their blades with a rush of steel. The Falcon Guards did the same. Everyone did, save Jaryd. Jaryd stared at the nearest man's blade and walked straight at him, unarmed, and only one-handed. Walked until the tip of that man's blade pressed directly at his throat. His eyes dared him to thrust. The villager backed away.

Jaryd turned on the other men and advanced, daring them also to kill the unarmed cripple. Those men also refrained. The elder villager watched, now seated on the ground, wiping the blood from his lip. His eyes, however, held a new respect.

Jaryd crouched before the man and repeated his question, quietly. The villager answered, warily. Jaryd drew a dagger from his belt and held the point to his own cheek. He drew the point down, cutting slowly, his expression never changing, his eyes never leaving the elder man's. Blood trickled. Jaryd sheathed the blade and wiped some blood on his fingers. Tasted it. Then wiped some more and held that hand for the villager.

The villager wiped some of Jaryd's blood onto his own fingers, and also tasted it. Sasha watched with heart-thumping amazement. She had not suspected Jaryd would know the ways of the ancient blood bond. Some old Goeren-yai traditions survived amongst Verenthanes in some parts of Lenayin, perhaps this was one such, in Tyree.

Jaryd stood and repeated the bloody tasting with the Falcon Guard corporal. Then he tasted a little more himself and spat upon the ground between the two sides. With a final, cold glare at them both, he limped off. The shouting did not resume. Neither did the two sides cross to embrace each other. Instead, they hung their heads and seemed reluctant to speak or act. The awkward silence lingered for a moment. Then, very quietly, the two sides began to disperse.

"What just happened?" Sasha asked Teriyan as the men on all sides retreated to their horses and prepared for the road ahead.

"When blood speaks, do you listen?" said Teriyan, watching Jaryd's slow departure through narrow, thoughtful eyes.

"Huh?"

Teriyan shook his head. "It's an old phrase . . . less common in Valhanan, probably why you haven't heard it. That's what Jaryd said. 'When blood speaks, do you listen?'"

"I don't understand." It pained her to say it. She'd thought she understood the Goeren-yai so well.

"Clan conflicts are driven by blood," Teriyan explained. "Blood between the warriors and the victims, and blood between the victims and their killers. One creates bonds, the other needs revenge. These men were fighting over someone else's kin, killed years ago. Jaryd lost his little brother, just yesterday. His claim to blood is superior. He shamed them. To continue their lesser squabble would dishonour Tarryn's spirit and bring bad luck upon them all."

"I wonder how he knew that saying?" Sasha wondered aloud. "Have you heard of Verenthanes saying it?"

Teriyan shook his head, with the intense thoughtfulness he always wore on matters of importance to Goeren-yai. "No," he said. "Not that I know. It's a puzzle."

More villagers arrived once the column recommenced, offering food, good wishes, seven more warriors and the assurance that neither they nor their neighbouring woodsmen had seen any northern forces passing near. There were many narrow horsetrails, however, that a smaller force could utilise if it wished. Sasha herself began to wish they could move onto a smaller trail themselves, where their passage would not be so obvious. But most such trails became churned after the fiftieth horse had passed over, to say nothing of the two thousand, five hundred and fiftieth (as one corporal had ridden up to inform her they had now become, much to her astonishment). And if it began raining, many of the routes up steep inclines would turn to impassable mudslides by midcolumn . . . No. One kept to the roads with a large force, Kessligh had always told her. And one went cross-country through Lenay forests only at the direst necessity, and only then for short distances.

Nearing evening, as they rode a flatter, rolling stretch of land, there came cries and yells from back in the column. Horses wheeled as weapons came out, Sasha holding Peg steady with difficulty with her own blade in hand, staring back over the confused, milling column behind. The vanguard closed about in tight, protective formation. Sasha could see soldiers spurring their mounts to leave the road, seeking paths to doubleback through the trees and bypass the chaotic blockage of jammed horses. Above the crashing hooves, shouting men and whinnying animals, she could hear the distant yells and clashing steel of battle. But it was too far back amidst the trees for her to see.

"Best you stay put, M'Lady," Tyrun advised, reading her expression all too easily. "By the time you get there it'll be gone, and the longer you're away from the head of the column, the longer it'll take to reform behind you once more. Command means relying on others to be your eyes. You can't see everything yourself."

And so Sasha sat where she was, listening to the battle, watching what she could see of men manoeuvring across the road whilst those nearest maintained their protective circle. Tyrun merely sat, grimly twitching his moustache. Sofy looked pale and wide-eyed with the children alongside . . . and Jaryd, Sasha saw thankfully, stood his horse nearby, ready to grab the rein should some panic strike. Of Teriyan, or Andreyis, she saw no sign.

The battle sounds faded as quickly as they had begun and soon a long-haired Falcon Guard corporal came thundering up the road at speed, several men at his rear. "Captain, M'Lady!" he announced as he reined to a halt. "Perhaps twenty horse, Ranash men, we think. They flee, and there is some pursuit, but we must not be delayed. We have four dead, three wounded . . . of theirs, I am ashamed to report two and one. We are dishonoured."

"It was always going to be thus," Tyrun said bluntly. "They have the advantage in such attacks and numbers count for nothing. Have the wounded head for the last village if they can, with a minimal escort. Have them try to keep off the road, if they can find a trail . . . the northerners wish to delay us, they cannot waste time on stragglers."

The corporal nodded. "I feel the wounded shall reject the escort, sir. They do not wish to drain our force of strength before the valley."

"As they will."

"And the wounded Ranash prisoner?" asked the corporal.

"If he cooperates, treat him with honour and send him with our wounded. If he does not, kill him."

"Aye, Captain." The corporal saluted, wheeled about and galloped back the way he'd come.

Sofy stared at the captain, with wide-eyed astonishment. "It is dishonourable for a wartime captive not to cooperate," Jaryd answered her unasked question, flatly. "Should he not cooperate, he forgoes honour, and thus deserves none from us."

Sofy bit her lip and said nothing. Sasha knew exactly what her sister would think of such logic, yet admired her for holding her tongue. Despite the pale face, in fact, she had handled the whole situation far better than Sasha would have expected.

"If I were in their position," Sasha said to Tyrun, "I'd try again, perhaps just after we've reformed. Keep us offbalance and slow."

"Aye," Tyrun agreed, surveying the surrounding forest. "But they may not have a choice. They rode hard to make that position and now the terrain works against them—they have to ride twice as hard to make a new position, while we travel in a much straighter line."

"Even so," Sasha replied, "if that was just twenty . . . and we might have three hundred immediately chasing? We could guess that there are many groups of ambushers. They've broken us up, chased us off the road . . . if we suffer six or seven of these a day, it will delay us considerably. And they can afford to exhaust their horses—their goals are near term, simply to buy time for the Hadryn in the valley. We have to retain enough strength to fight once we get there."

"Aye," Tyrun agreed once more, sombrely. "We shall have a three-quarter moon tonight at least, which we did not see last night since we began so late. I'd recommend we use some of it before making camp."

"We'd best make it a short camp," Sasha agreed, biting her lip.

Tyrun shrugged. "As you say, M'Lady, we're no good to the Udalyn if we arrive staggering like the walking dead. Horses especially. We'll ride for several spans of the moon, then camp until dawn. Horses are less resilient than men—if strained greatly, they can break."

"*Duul*," said Daryd, drawing a half circle in the dirt with his knife. "Wall," Sasha had gathered that meant. About the fire, Teriyan, Andreyis and Sofy watched as the markings on the earth increased to form a map of the town of Ymoth. "*Duul as tarachai*," jabbing at where the half circle ended, and made a wavy line with his knife where the rest of the circle would have been.

"Uncompleted," Sofy surmised. "They only have half a wall."

"Aye, but it's facing the right way—onto the fields," said Teriyan, fire-light turning his long red hair to dancing orange. He pointed with a long stick to the town's unprotected side. "These are hills, yes?"

Daryd frowned. "Oh, hold on," said Sofy, as if searching her memory. "I know that one . . . um . . . *fen*, that's right. This *fen?*" With a motion of her hands, outlining a hill.

Daryd nodded vigorously. "*Ennas fen, sa. Fen, fen, fen*," indicating with his knife all the way alongside the dual marks that described the banks of the mighty Yumynis River.

"Can't attack from behind," Sasha observed. "We'll have to come along the fields. An open charge."

"Why would they only have half a wall?" Andreyis wondered.

"Krayliss said the Udalyn only moved back into Ymoth recently," said Sasha. "It must have lain abandoned for nearly a century, too far from the valley to be safe for the Udalyn, but too close to the Udalyn to be safe for Hadryn to occupy. The lands there are fertile, it must have been tempting. But now, it seems they could not defend it."

They gazed at Daryd's little map in the firelight. About them was a much grimmer camp than Sasha had seen before. Men made no laughter and song about their fires and little conversation. Mostly they ate, or tended to kit or weapons, or saw to their horses, now haltered to trees in small groups wherever wild grass grew. All had drunk at the last stream crossed, and now the camp lay strewn along a winding ridgeline, easily defensible from either end, and most certainly from the steep slopes to either side.

After some further discussion, Sofy excused herself to go and sit at the neighbouring fire where Jaryd sat with his leg stretched out with Captain Tyrun and some other senior officers. Sasha saw her sit beside Jaryd, who barely registered her arrival. Sofy had been talking to Jaryd on and off along the ride, and Jaryd, unable to wield a sword and hold the reins at the same time, and thus unable to fight from the front of the Falcon Guard, had seemed to appoint himself her protector. Daryd then excused himself to go and check on Essey, whom he was clearly very attached to. Rysha remained behind, content to gaze into the fire with her big brown eyes, wrapped in a man's cloak a good four times too large. Sofy, Sasha noted, was walking somewhat gingerly. Her saddle soreness was surely terrible, Sofy had only sat ahorse a handful of times before in her life. But she did not complain.

"Ah, you'll have to be faster than that, lad," said Teriyan to Andreyis, eyeing Jaryd and Sofy. "That blue-blood boy, he's a slick one. Have the ladies eating out of his hand in no time . . . you'll have to make your move faster if a skinny village lad's to have any chance at all . . ."

"Shut up," Andreyis told him in irritation, staring into the fire. Teriyan raised his eyebrows in characteristic mirth. "She's a Verenthane princess, I wasn't thinking that at all."

Sasha repressed a smile. "Ah aye," Teriyan said slyly, "I'm sure that fleeting vision of a crown on your head at the grand wedding never even happened, not for a moment . . ."

Andreyis glared at him. "Teriyan," Sasha reprimanded. "Leave him alone."

Teriyan chortled. Rysha was humming the notes to a song, uncomprehending of the conversation. She looked exhausted, her eyelids flickering. Sasha recalled the comb she'd put into her pocket with forethought. She brought it out and gestured to Rysha. Rysha came without question, gathering her enormous cloak so as not to trip, and sat cross-legged before Sasha. It pleased her that the little girl with whom she could barely communicate, and who had every reason to be frightened of foreigners, showed such complete trust.

"I hope they're worth it," Andreyis said glumly. Broke a twig and tossed it on the flames. "The Udalyn, I mean."

Sasha frowned at him. "Do you doubt it?" she asked, taking the ralama flowers from Rysha's hair and handing them to her.

"Well, no one's ever met one, have they?" Her young friend seemed suddenly gloomy, gazing at the fire. "An adult, anyhow. What if they're all bastards?"

"You think bastards could have raised a little girl like Rysha? Or a boy like Daryd?"

Andreyis shrugged. "I don't know. Maybe. Half of Baerlyn thinks my father's a bastard, but I turned out okay." And, "Don't say anything," when he saw the cheap shot forming on her lips.

"All of the stories about the Udalyn suggest otherwise," Sasha said firmly. Freed from its three wooden pins, Rysha's brown hair fell in folded tangles. The comb was deer bone, finely carved and strong. Rysha winced as it caught at a tangle, still humming softly. "They've an eye for fine craftsmanship and a love of green things. Tharyn Askar was not only a great warrior, it's said he grew sunflowers."

"Oh aye, that's a real recommendation," Andreyis replied, poking the coals with another stick. "They're just stories, anyhow. Old Cranyk tells stories of the scores of Cherrovan warriors he's slain, and the great size of the bucks he's hunted . . ."

"To say nothing of the size of his cock," Teriyan added.

Andreyis nodded sagely. "Exactly. A shrivelled little thing, I'm sure. Who can tell which stories are true? People love to love the Udalyn. When people want to love something that much, they'll believe it whether it's true or not. Especially when it's useful to them. Look at the capital Krayliss got from everyone loving the Udalyn."

Sasha sighed, thinking as she worked. The comb caught at a hard tangle and Rysha complained in Edu. "I don't know, Andreyis," Sasha said tiredly, taking a handful of hair below the tangle and yanking hard. It wasn't so different from combing horses, really. "Kessligh says you can believe in everything, or you can believe in nothing, but neither path will grant more truth than the other. All we can do is trust our sense. My sense tells me the Udalyn deserve to be saved. I might be wrong, but . . ." she shrugged. "We'll find out when we get there."

Teriyan made a face. "It's irrelevant anyhow," he said.

Sasha paused her brushing to frown at him. "You think?"

"Whether people are right to love the Udalyn or not, it's irrelevant," Teriyan said with certainty. "The fact of the matter is they do, for better or ill. And if the Udalyn were to all be slain, people would be angry enough to do all sorts of nasty things to the people they deemed responsible for many generations to come. We either stop that, or we don't. Arguing over whether it's all sensible or not is like arguing whether it's sensible for rain to fall, or the seasons to change. They just do. Deal with it."

Rysha patted Sasha's knee impatiently. Sasha resumed brushing, with a final, incredulous look at Teriyan. "Aye, well that's high-minded idealism, isn't it?"

"It's survival," Teriyan said firmly. "Hard to be a Goeren-yai romantic when there's no Goeren-yai left. And equally hard to be a Lenay patriot when Lenayin's been split to pieces."

"Aye," Sasha conceded, reluctantly.

"Aye!" Rysha agreed loudly. Another Lenay word. And she giggled when they all looked at her. Teriyan grinned at her, and winked. Rysha considered her handful of flowers, coyly.

Sasha lost patience with an especially nasty little tangle, and quietly removed a knife from her belt so Rysha could not see, and cut it. Rysha hummed her tune, oblivious, as she had doubtless sat and hummed many times before, as her mother, sister or cousin had performed this task for her. The tune sounded strangely familiar. Sasha wondered if the Udalyn sang the same songs and knew the same tales that she'd come to love growing up in Baerlyn.

Soon Daryd returned, and Rysha began to doze. Sasha decided she'd best let Daryd tell the officers what he'd told her. She gave Rysha to Teriyan and the girl snuggled sleepily against the big man's side. Teriyan put an arm around her and gazed into the flames, reminding Sasha of many evenings at the Steltsyn with Lynette's head resting against him.

A Wildcats lieutenant made a space for her and Daryd upon a fireside log. Jaryd sat alongside on his saddle, his left leg outstretched, Sofy beside him. Conversation halted and Sasha encouraged Daryd to show them his map of Ymoth, drawing in the dirt by the fire with his knife. Men asked questions, gazing thoughtfully at the map. Jaryd only stared at Daryd, with more expression in his eyes than Sasha had seen since Baen-Tar.

Daryd was of a similar age to Tarryn, Sasha realised. Perhaps a little taller than the boy she remembered sitting on Jaryd's bedside. And a little leaner, with light brown hair instead of sandy, and no freckles. But, in the flickering orange firelight, it seemed that memory conspired with shadows to contrive a similarity. Tears wet Jaryd's eyes, then rolled down the inflamed, red wound on his cheek.

At first, none noticed but Sasha and Sofy. Sofy looked anguished, but Sasha shook her head faintly. It would not do for a man in grief to receive comfort from a woman before his peers. Such comfort was for children, not for men, and Sofy seemed to know it. Then the other men noticed, one after another, and conversation faded. Men stared silently into the flames and continued sharpening weapons, or sipping drinks, or mending gear, as they had been before. Jaryd's tears caused no awkwardness, no embarrassment, not even as he struggled to contain the sobs that threatened to rack his body. The officers simply waited, with quiet respect, for the moment of grieving to pass.

Daryd looked wary and concerned, aware that this matter somehow concerned him, yet uncertain of how. As Jaryd breathed more deeply, recovering his control, Daryd knelt before him, pulled his knife from its sheath and offered it to him, hilt first. Jaryd simply gazed, faintly incredulous.

He took Daryd's knife with his good hand and considered the blade. "A Udalyn knife?" he asked, hoarsely. There were decorations on the pommel, Sasha saw in the firelight, intricate spiral patterns.

Daryd seemed to understand. "Udalyn," he confirmed. "I warrior." Pointing to himself. "Fight for you." Sasha was astonished. Either Daryd was a remarkably fast learner, or Sofy a remarkably good teacher. Or both. Perhaps he'd been practising that line all afternoon, awaiting the opportunity.

Jaryd flipped the knife several times, testing its weight. Then handed it back to Daryd. "It's a good knife, warrior Daryd," he sighed. And ruffled the boy's hair. "But I'll be damned if you're going to fight. You can wait in the back with the princess, and I'll see you delivered safely back to your mother and father. If it's the only good thing to come out of this whole mess, maybe that'll make it worthwhile."

Seventeen

BY MIDMORNING, THE ATTACKS HAD BEGUN. The first struck midcolumn, from the west this time, causing confusion in the middle ranks. The second, shortly after, hit the rear, creating yet more delays as men doubled back to help and the entire column came to a forced halt for fear of dividing. Sasha was sitting astride, waiting for everyone to reform, when a scout arrived from further ahead, and informed them that he'd found the bodies of a travelling party from a nearby village—six men, all Goeren-yai, all no doubt riding to join the cause. More such were arriving constantly— as many as eight hundred men, the officers now estimated. For sheer strength, the column was in good shape. But now, they lost time. Word would be heading to the Hadryn in the valley as fast as horseback could take it. The more time the young Lord Usyn had to prepare for their arrival, the worse it would be.

Approaching midday, the road arrived at the foot of a gentle incline and began to ascend at an angle. The trees were all pine, tall and widely spaced, with little undergrowth between. Both Sasha and Captain Tyrun exchanged glances as the vanguard peered through the forest shadows and Lieutenant Alyn yelled orders for outriders to fan ahead.

"No choice," Sasha muttered. "We can't afford to lose time finding a better line."

"Aye, M'Lady," Tyrun acknowledged. And yelled to the rear, "Double the vanguard! Riders from the rear and upslope to the flanks! Cover the approach and wait for the entire column to pass!"

Riders thundered past, heading upslope and weaving between trees, their horses finding plenty of room to run upon the broad, brown carpet of needles. Barely had the riders begun to fade amongst the furthest trees when there came the distant yet distinctive buzz of crossbow fire. Yells followed, echoed by Captain Tyrun's and more up and down the column; blades rang out all at once as hooves came thundering in a great mass.

"Stay with her!" Sasha yelled to Jaryd, pointing at her ashen-faced sister and the children alongside, then pounded her heels into Peg's sides, joining others heading upslope at speed. Then she could see them, heavy horse coming line-abreast down through the trees, flashes of black and blue uniform, the colours of Banneryd. It was a cavalry nightmare, heavy horse with the full advantage of height behind them, holding their line in descent with all the proficiency one might expect of northern riders.

The outermost of the upslope guard were hit and upended like saplings before a spring river flood, men cut from horses, animals shrieking as they tumbled, hooves flailing the air. The defensive line roared, men desperately trying to form a strong line, some astride dussieh that had no business challenging that formidable downhill rush head on. They charged together with a horrific crash of bodies, blades, armour and flesh. Horses collided, riders catapulted through the air, bodies fell cleaved from the saddle in a bloody spray.

The line disintegrated, and then the northerners were through, still spurring hard, though there were wide gaps in their ranks, some men fallen, others entangled and seeking a less direct path. Sasha headed straight for one such hole . . . the nearest man saw her—a clutch of rein, a change of direction, massive hooves pounding the turf as he sought to bring his momentum to bear. Another horse might have struggled, but Peg accelerated with an explosive burst of raw muscle, with no regard for the slope. That closing speed seemed to surprise her opponent, who swung a fraction late, and Sasha, swaying away and under his stroke as she had learned playing lagand, slashed his arm in passing.

Then she wheeled, racing back down the hill, despairing even now of getting close enough as the Banneryd line hurtled onward . . . and directly in line ahead, with heart in mouth, she saw a little knot of riders with Jaryd shielding Sofy's pony with his larger horse. But riders further back in the column were arriving now, pouring in from the left and flying between the trees, blocking the approach toward Sofy's position.

The Banneryd line wheeled right, those riders furthest left making sharp turns across the oncoming line, slashing blows at those who came close enough. Sasha's previous target, riding fast with his arm clutched to his chest, managed to get his signals confused and slammed into a tree with a horrendous crash.

The Banneryd line then raced across the road, ahead of Sofy's position, continuing downhill, their formation now more line-astern than abreast as the left flank fell in behind the right, fighting off pursuers who tried to cut them from behind. A northerner fell, then another cut a Goeren-yai from his horse . . . Sasha saw she had a line on that one, aiming to a single point ahead of him through the racing trees. He hurtled across the road, her following, and as great as his speed was, Peglyrion on a downhill run, with a weight as little as hers on his back, was quite possibly the fastest horse in Lenayin. She was on him from the left before he even saw her, and she cut him left-handed from the saddle.

She was too fast, in fact, for she overtook another on his left. He saw her, blade in hand, and she knew that was not a fair contest on horseback . . . whipped a short blade from her belt and threw . . . *thud!* It impaled itself in an intervening tree trunk. Which was enough, she decided, and pulled hard on Peg's reins. The other rider thundered onward, the entire Banneryd line racing downhill where the trees became thicker. Sasha circled in a wide turn, heading back upslope . . . and realised she'd outdistanced nearly everyone. Only now were several pursuit riders thundering by, hot on the Banneryd's tracks, more to harass and make sure they did not come back than to seriously challenge.

Sasha held Peg to a calmer trot back up the slope, plucked her knife from the tree trunk in passing, and spared the fallen northerner a cold glance. He'd tumbled into the base of a tree, head mostly but not entirely severed . . . a weak, left-handed backhand it had been, glancing off the armoured shoulder. Sasha knew she would never be half the swordsman in a saddle she was on two legs. But then, she fancied her horsemanship against even the dreaded northern cavalry, especially on Peg.

A flash of light upon the needles nearby caught her eye. A Verenthane star, its chain severed, spattered in blood. She recalled the similar star and chain upon the pedestal in the Saint Ambellion Temple. Krystoff's star. And she shivered, making the spirit sign with her sword hand still wrapped around the hilt.

On the road the scene was of semiorganised confusion. Sofy, the Udalyn children, Jaryd and Captain Tyrun marked the head of the column, and what was left of the vanguard formed ahead. Other men collected bodies, tended to wounded and yelled at wandering warriors to get back in formation.

Sasha rode straight to Sofy and Jaryd . . . Sofy seemed ready to cry with relief. "You're well?" Sasha asked her in concern.

Sofy nodded, attempting composure. From the look on her face, it seemed likely to be the hardest thing she'd ever done. "I'm fine," she said hoarsely, blinking furiously at the tears in her eyes. "We were well protected."

"Peglyrion fast!" Daryd remarked, handling his nervous horse steady with skill. He looked shaken, but remarkably calm in spite of it. This was a boy who had seen killing before, Sasha judged. Rysha clung to him tightly, but made no complaint. With her face mostly hidden against her brother's back, it was unlikely she'd seen much.

Sasha faced Jaryd, steadying Peg's head toss and stamp with a reflexive yank as she wheeled him about. Breathing hard yet barely sweating, Peg seemed content enough to obey. "Thank you," she said to him. "I saw what you did."

"I did as much as I could with this blasted arm," Jaryd muttered. He slid his bandaged and splinted left arm back into its sling with a grimace of pain—Sasha guessed he must have taken it out to grab Sofy's reins. Any soldier drilled in cavalry knew that the best chance to survive a downhill rush was to turn into it—the faster the closing speed, the less the attacker's chance of a precise swing. Jaryd had grabbed the reins of Sofy's pony and positioned himself as a shield, unmoving and obvious. Daryd had sensibly placed himself on their far side. Had the Banneryd charge reached him, Jaryd would have been killed . . . but Sofy and the children, shielded from that first strike, would have quite possibly been saved.

"Sofy could not hope for a better protector." Sasha touched heels to Peg's flanks and rode to where Tyrun was surveying the scene. She came to Tyrun's side, and the lieutenant he'd been talking with inclined his head in respect. "The honour of Kessligh Cronenverdt rides with you, M'Lady," he said, and rode off to survey the carnage upslope before she could reply.

"Your friend Teriyan warned me you'd try something stupid like that," Tyrun said bluntly.

"Like what?" Sasha snorted. "I was trained to fight and that's what I did."

"In this column," Tyrun replied, utterly unmoved, "you're far more than just another warrior."

"Men aren't riding for me," Sasha retorted. "They're riding to save the Udalyn."

"M'Lady, the only reason a good Verenthane like me is riding in this column is because you're leading it." Sasha frowned at him. "You're my guarantee that this will *not* be the first blow in a Goeren-yai–Verenthane civil war. You're a symbol to both, and you've ties and loyalties on both sides. If you die, this could become exactly what Lord Krayliss would have made it—a slaughter of Verenthanes by angry Goeren-yai, with horrors to follow across all the land. Please think of that the next time you feel the need to take some needless risk to add one more notch to your belt."

He made sense, Sasha noted. The problem, of course, was that her definition of risk was somewhat different to his. Which was arrogance, obviously . . . but she couldn't help what she was. And she didn't particularly feel like arguing about it now.

"I'll take it under advisement," she said.

Another man rode down the hill toward them. "Captain, M'Lady," said the man as he arrived—a Black Hammers corporal, Sasha saw. "Twenty-three of us, thirteen dead, ten wounded. Only nine of them, five and four. Several of our scouting parties ahead surprised some and report another twenty enemy dead. Plus they'll be running into hostile villagers as they move along the trails, which will end some more of them, or tie them up. There can't be more than two hundred still harassing us."

"And all of them fanatics," Tyrun said grimly. "They'll grind their horses' legs to bloody stubs before they give us any peace."

"We could divert men to harass them back?" Sasha suggested.

"M'Lady, I'd advise not," Tyrun replied. "Ambush tactics in this country only work when your opponent is much less nimble, and when you know where he's going. They have that edge with us, we don't have it with them. We'd arrive at the mouth of the valley in worse shape than if we simply press on and accept the losses."

Another horse arrived at a gallop, Teriyan's red hair flying out behind as he pulled up sharply. "That was bloody Tyrblanc in person," he announced grimly. The blade in his hand was unbloodied. Sasha knew he would be unhappy about that. "I might have had him if he hadn't come through so damn fast. Damn this terrain."

Sasha recalled the proud, bearded man with a wide girth who had competed against Tyree that day on the lagand field.

"Some Banneryd men consider ambush tactics dishonourable," said the corporal. "I've heard Captain Tyrblanc is one who prefers single combat."

"That doesn't mean he's not good at ambushes," Tyrun said grimly. "And for a Banneryd fanatic, honour only applies to contests between equals. Against pagans, they'd slit our throats in the night if they could."

Sasha saw a Royal Guardsman riding downhill toward the vanguard leading a riderless horse. The man's face was contorted with grief. The horse, Sasha recognised, was Lieutenant Alyn's. A lump rose in her throat. It had been her decision to press on along this road, regardless of the startlingly obvious ambush terrain ahead. Her decision, her responsibility. Alyn had been seeking to reclaim his honour, having been cut from the Royal Guard in disgrace. She hoped fervently that his spirit would consider this, a death in a good cause, to suffice.

"We continue as before," Sasha said quietly. "We came to save the Udalyn. If we must take losses so that we can serve them best, then so we shall. But if we keep getting hit with this regularity, the Hadryn's defences shall be so well set upon our arrival that we may not make it into the valley at all."

Captain Tyrun and the Black Hammers corporal departed. "Where's Andrey?" Sasha asked Teriyan, suddenly anxious.

"We're riding further back," Teriyan replied. "It won't do for M'Lady of the Synnich to have her favourite friends all around her—it looks bad to the other men. I came ahead a bit when I saw this damn slope up ahead . . . Andrey got caught a little behind."

"Aye," said Sasha, reading gratefully between the lines. "Well, see that the next time it happens, he gets caught a little behind once more."

"Aye to that," Teriyan agreed. His eyes swept across the hillsides, the wounded men, the fallen horses, the screams of pain. "Damn tough business," he muttered, and stared at her hard. "How are you doing?"

He'd never have asked the question of a man, Sasha thought resentfully. She took a deep breath. "Good for now. But I'll be happier when we get to the valley."

Teriyan nodded, and slapped her on the shoulder. "There's a reason I never accepted a soldier's post," he said. "I knew they'd make me an officer, I had it offered to me often enough. I'm brave enough, but I never wanted to make those decisions. You've a damn sight more courage than I have, girl. Hang in there."

He tapped his heels to his mount's sides and moved off through the confusion to find Andreyis. "You had a choice," Sasha murmured to herself, staring up the winding, climbing road ahead through the trees. "I didn't."

Captain Tyrblanc of the Banneryd Black Storm sat on his saddle, and sharpened his blade upon his lap. The moon was high, three-quarters visible and baleful through the branches. It caused his weapon to gleam, catching on the notch midlength, a bothersome breach of purity. The whetstone clicked passing over it, interrupting the smooth, whistling song of stone on steel. He'd caught it upon the helm of a Royal Guard lieutenant in the charge.

His lips twisted in disdain. Royal Guards. The most overrated soldiers in Lenayin. No northerner had ever sought recruitment in the Royal Guard. That would mean service alongside pagans. Far better to seek glory in the great companies, their names stained in the blood of countless enemies, their ranks free from the defilement of the unworthy. And now, as if further proof were required, there were Royal Guards riding with the traitor-bitch herself.

A rabble if ever he'd seen one. Goat herders from Tyree. Mother-coddled whelps from Rayen. Barbarian animals from Valhanan, home to the traitor-bitch. It had been a pleasure to kill them. He prayed for many more such opportunities. The odds were overwhelming and he knew that he and his men would most likely meet their deaths upon this road to Hadryn. It mattered not. The gods were waiting for them, and they would be honoured in the heavens as heroes. But he would send many pagans down to burn in the fires of Loth in the process and, for now, the certainty of death only made his own glory burn all the brighter.

Two of his men approached, shadows amidst the trees. About the perimeter, men watched from the bushes, invisible to Tyrblanc's eye. The traitors had scouts who could doubtless track his men to this point, particularly given the moon. They would shift camp later, before the moon set behind the hills.

The two men sat opposite, collapsing heavily with stifled groans. The smell of unwashed bodies came clear to Tyrblanc's nostrils. Mail chafed at the shoulders, unmoved since this pursuit had begun. One man removed his helm, and Tyrblanc recognised Corporal Veln in the moon shadow.

"The horses are nearly spent," Veln said in Haryt, primary tongue of the Banneryd. "There's grass enough, but they need ruffage for true strength. I've searched for polovyn root but we never camp in the right spot."

Tyrblanc shrugged, still sharpening his blade. "Only a few more days. We've more horses than men now. We can afford to lose a few horses."

Veln gave him a hard, tired look. "In a great rush to get to paradise, are you, Captain?"

Tyrblanc grinned. "Always," he said. Veln restrained a hardened smile. Such was the humour of northern men, where death was ever present. "What's the matter, Corporal? Lost your nerve?"

"One kills more of the enemy whilst one is alive," Veln replied calmly, unruffled by his captain's teasing. A cloud was passing across the moon, dimming its silvery light to gloom amidst the trees. "We are tired, Captain, but should we not press the advantage at night? Surely we could kill more with surprise in the dark?"

Tyrblanc shook his head. "Our object is not to kill them, youngster . . . although it is a pleasant consequence. Our object is to slow them. Why attack them while they're not moving? They move a little by moonlight, but their numbers are great, they must slow for water and food for the horses. It grows difficult for them to hold such a large formation together.

"And also, at night, the advantage is always with the defender. The defender knows his ground, and knows his position upon it. It is the attacker who becomes confused, moving amidst alien defences. I remember it once, attacking a Cherrovan camp by moonlight . . . we lost all formation, lost even sense of direction, and nearly lost our entire company. We'd be more sensible to use the night for sleep, so we are rested for better fighting tomorrow. Attacking at night is for fools."

"Not always," said a cool female voice not more than five strides away. The men spun in disbelief . . . something whistled through the air and Veln's companion fell with a gurgling cry, clutching a knife in his throat. From another direction came a whistling arrow and a scream.

"To arms!" Tyrblanc yelled, to the answering shouts of men, steel ringing through the cold night air as blades came out. Tyrblanc ran in the direction from which the knife had come, sword in hand . . . there were bushes, man-height and indistinct in the gloom. He circled them, stumbling on an unseen root . . . steel clashed further downhill, then the distinct impact of a blade on mail, only this sound was different. A sharp, ringing *crack!* as if metal were fracturing.

Tyrblanc sensed movement behind and spun in time to see one of his men double over as a blade slashed him open, then a horrendous spurt of blood as the head was severed. A shadow danced past the falling body, as light and lithe as smoke on the wind. Tyrblanc charged down the slope toward it, and the shadow flitted one way through the trees, then another. Ahead, another Banneryd man stood with wide stance, eyes darting as he searched for that shadow . . . then lurched forward with a *thump!*, face first with an arrow between his shoulder blades.

Another arrowshot thumped and whistled in the dark. Tyrblanc threw himself flat, but it was another man who screamed and fell. Tyrblanc rose behind a tree, staring about desperately as men ran, and tripped, and yelled for lost comrades. The shadow he had been pursuing was nowhere to be seen. Then Corporal Veln arrived, running downhill, his fear evident despite the gloom. Tyrblanc realised his own heart was galloping, that his hands were shaking, and that bile rose in the back of his throat, threatening to choke him.

"Captain!" Veln cried, sliding on one knee to crouch beside him, as if expecting the shadows to strike him dead at any moment. "Captain, they are demons! Demons of Loth! I s-saw the eyes of one . . . th-the-they burned like fires!"

Tyrblanc muttered a prayer and made the holy sign with a free hand. Death was one thing, death at the hands of evil spirits was another. Steel clashed again, this time upslope, and the gurgling choke of a man swiftly killed.

"To me!" Tyrblanc yelled. "Rally to me! Rally to me and make defence!" Several men came running—one fell, Tyrblanc thought dead but then he scrambled back up, having only tripped . . . only to fall once more immediately, this time impaled with an arrow. More men came, backing up or running straight, spinning and staring in all directions at once, some swinging at shadows. Another fell to the archer, hands clawing the air . . . Tyrblanc reckoned he knew the direction this time—downslope, and to the left. Once he had some strength, they would charge that archer, and at least gain a chance against the swordsmen . . .

Shadows leaped from upslope and down, men yelled warning but were cut down even as the cries left their lips. One man fell near, and Tyrblanc saw the demon clearly for the first time—small, fast and certain, a shine of blue eyes in a pale face. Veln leapt at it with a cry, weapon slashing . . . the shadow flicked him aside with a clash of steel, cut off his arm and slashed him open through the middle in three blindingly fast, athletic strikes. Men fell to Tyrblanc's left and fell to his right, amid agonised screams and sprays of jetting blood. An arrowshot thudded close behind and another man slumped stiffly to the ground. And then, there was stillness.

But not silence. A man was sobbing, fallen to his knees nearby. Opposing him, one of the shadow demons approached. "Please!" cried the man. "Please don't kill me! Don't take my soul! I beg of you, not my soul! Not the damnation . . . oh lords, please save me, save me . . ." The words trailed into prayer, fast and stumbling over terrified sobs and gasps for air.

Tyrblanc realised that he was standing fixed to the spot, as if paralysed. He should kill the sobbing man for his cowardice. But then, how was he still alive? His men were all dead, and he still stood. Somehow, he had not attacked, but rather stood and watched in stunned disbelief. Shame flooded him. He wanted to die . . . and yet, did not dare to in such evil company. He could not kill the sobbing man, for the sobbing man, somewhere deep in his heart, was himself.

The demon confronting the sobbing man spoke . . . a male voice, in a tongue of lilting, alien tones. It sounded like a question. A female voice answered . . . Tyrblanc spun, and found her slender form poised behind him, a bloodstained blade in her hands. Her clothes seemed plain, and a black cloth was folded over her head, covering her hair. The eyes, however, gleamed a terrible, ungodly bronze.

The demon asked the question again. The bronze-eyed she-demon answered shortly, as though in mild exasperation. The he-demon struck, a sword hilt to the face of the sobbing man. The silence that followed was merciful. And yet not . . . for now, where there had been the conversation of men, and the activity of a night's camp, there was deathly silence.

A new movement downslope caught Tyrblanc's eye—a male figure, holding a huge bow, advancing past the bodies of his victims on silent feet. There was no uncertainty in the way he surveyed the surrounding night, an arrow nocked to the string. He did not stare about in bewilderment as a human man might. It was almost as though he could see his surroundings as clearly as daylight.

The moon chose that moment to break clear of the cloud and lit the forest silver. The hillside about Tyrblanc's boots flowed red with blood. The sightless eyes of his comrades stared aghast at the trees or the ground. Men known to him by name. Men of honour. Men of long friendship and service, to earthly masters and to gods alike. It did not seem real that this could be their fate. How had the gods allowed such a thing?

"You present me with a puzzle, Captain," the approaching he-demon said then, in faultless, barely accented Lenay. "Should I show you mercy, when you and your kind would never grant any to me or my kind should our positions be reversed?"

They were serrin, Tyrblanc knew. Rarely if ever seen in the north. But he cared not what scholars, lowlanders and local pagans might call them. A demon was a demon, by any other name. They were not human, they were unnatural and they had no gods. Death was too good for them.

"I would not beg for your mercy were it the only thing between me and eternal damnation!" Tyrblanc snarled. The sword was still in his hand. It trembled, so tight was his grip.

"Believe me, Captain," the he-demon said, with a narrowing of brilliant green eyes as he stopped and leaned upon his enormous bow, "your begging or otherwise shall have no bearing upon my decision. Reason may sway me. My pride is serrin. I do not require you to beg."

"We should let him go," said the bronze-eyed she-demon, coming to stand alongside. Her hair was short and her posture lithe. "He can tell the others what happened. It should be a warning."

The he-demon inclined his head in her direction, as if conceding that reason. "We should kill him, and this one," said the other demon who had knocked the sobbing soldier unconscious. "They fear us. They fear for their souls should they die at our hands. Allowing one to survive will lessen that fear. We should make it absolute." And the demon with the bow inclined his head to him, also. He turned his burning gaze upon the one who stood at Tyrblanc's back.

Tyrblanc turned around, slowly. The small one who had killed Veln, he realised, was also a female. Her eyes, fixed upon the carnage about Tyrblanc's feet, were troubled. Sad, even.

"Should all the rivers run red with blood," she said quietly, "and all the forests turn to ash and coal. Should black rain fall, and the spawning salmon gasp its last breath, and the green wren no longer sing its joy to the sun, where then, good friends, should our glory lie?"

Tyrblanc stared in disbelief. It was Tullamayne the she-demon quoted. Tullamayne the Udalyn, from the days before the Udalyn were corrupted by false prophets, and disgraced their name to eternal damnation by betraying the true and rightful gods. Tullamayne, who seemed so often, and so sadly, to predict his own people's coming betrayal, and their coming demise. How could one so evil speak the words of Tullamayne with such sad conviction? How did the gods not strike her down where she stood?

The green-eyed demon gazed at his companion. His brilliant eyes, for the faintest moment, seemed not filled with evil or terror, but . . . sadness. "Aisha says to spare you," he said to Tyrblanc. "Aisha reminds me that not all men of the north have always been so filled with fear and rage. Remember, Captain, that the words of an Udalyn saved your life. The words of a people you seek to destroy. Think of them, and think of us, and be grateful. And perhaps tell your fellow haters, so that they too might understand the true meaning of mercy."

"I reject your mercy," Tyrblanc spat.

"Mercy," pressed the he-demon, in quiet, deadly tones, "is confronting the thing that would destroy your people and letting it live. There are many of my people who no longer consider themselves capable of such mercy. You are fortunate, this beautiful night, to have encountered me instead." His hand whipped to one shoulder and pulled clear a blade to hold the point unwavering before the captain's throat. "Strike, if you will, and defy my mercy. Or drop your blade, and accept it. Precious it is, as are all things so rare. The days of serrin mercy, I fear, shall soon be a thing of the past."

The following day was free from attacks. Sasha allowed herself the luxury of considering familiar lands, and feeling some joy to be back so close to home ground. This was the road to Cryliss, Valhanan's capital, and less than a half-day's ride from Baerlyn to the northwest. There was a form to the hills, a certain colour upon exposed upthrusts of granite on the high ridges, a certain pattern to the trees that seemed familiar. Mount Tvay loomed in a much more familiar proportion whenever a rise took them high enough to see, and the northern Marashyn Ranges were more clearly visible through the distant mist. Another day, she thought, and they would be at Cryliss. As close as she would get to home this journey.

At midmorning a scout came galloping toward them with news of an unexpected arrival. A short distance further, on the edge of the forest, she saw four riders ahorse, amidst a large collection of riderless warhorses. The riders' hoods were thrown back and the steel blue hair of one gleamed in the slanting sun . . . another was red-brown, another light blonde, and another dark grey. The serrin had come.

The vanguard passed the clustered horses and Sasha signalled to Captain Tyrun. The call to halt echoed up the length of the column, fading in the distance as the great, rattling, snorting mass came to a stop. The serrin rider with dark grey hair rode forward on a lovely chestnut horse whose breeding Sasha could not immediately identify—a rare thing, for her. He had a long bow, unstrung along the horse's side, and wore a sword at his shoulder in the manner of all his companions.

"Greetings M'Lady Sashandra Lenayin and Captain Tyrun Adysh," he called, reining up before them. The vanguard, mostly Goeren-yai men, showed little of the caution that would normally be warranted by such an approach through their midst. "My name is Errollyn and I travel with three companions. I have brought you a gift."

Sasha blinked in astonishment. The serrin—Errollyn—was as wonderfully handsome as one came to expect of serrin. His hair was the thick, dark grey of looming thunderclouds on a bright day, and his eyes were a brilliant, almost luminescent green. His accent was negligible, and his manner as calm as one who knew himself to be among friends.

"How do you know our names?" Tyrun replied, somewhat suspiciously. Sasha gave the captain a wary look . . . probably he had had less experience with serrin than she. Serrin knew lots of things. "What brings you to this road?"

"You are Captain Tyrun because your helmet crest identifies you as captain and your uniform is of the Falcon Guard, and there is only one of those." Errollyn's tone suggested either amusement, or sarcasm, or perhaps something else entirely. With serrin, one was never entirely certain. "And if she's not Sashandra Lenayin," with a nod at Sasha, "then I'm a donkey's backside."

Sasha grinned. It was an unusual turn of phrase for a serrin. Colloquial, almost. Most serrin could think of far prettier things to say than *that*. But Errollyn smiled mischievously in reply to her grin. It changed his face, and the effect was very nice indeed.

"This *is* a pleasant gift," she said, looking about at the horses. All were saddled and with saddlebags. Her humour faded to see that some bore the obvious markings of Banneryd upon the leather. "Banneryd horses?" she asked the serrin.

"Black Storm, yes," Errollyn confirmed.

Sasha felt a cold tingle slowly working its way up her spine. "And their riders?"

"Indisposed," said Errollyn, coolly. His meaning was clear. At Sasha's side, Tyrun's hand made the Verenthane holy sign.

Sasha completed a fast count, arriving at nineteen horses. Even dismounted, the Banneryd Black Storm were formidable soldiers. Four serrin had done this in the night. Serrin, she knew, could see quite well in the dark.

"Which way do you ride, Master Errollyn?" Sasha asked.

Errollyn looked faintly surprised. "With you, of course. If you shall have us."

Have them? Sasha exchanged looks with Tyrun. Tyrun's expression suggested that he was content to leave the decision up to her.

"Let's get these horses rounded up and brought into the column!" Sasha called. "There will be willing soldiers without horses along the way, our serrin friends have now brought nineteen of them a ride!"

There was a cheer, and a sergeant moved to take charge. "Ride with me, Master Errollyn," said Sasha, and Errollyn inclined his head gracefully as the vanguard recommenced.

Sasha glanced at Errollyn's companions as they passed—there were two women and a man, all as unearthly strange in appearance as Errollyn. The other man was tall and wore a patterned headband to keep in place hair the colour of rust. The taller of the women had short, steel-blue hair and deep bronze eyes—common colours for serrin, but startlingly strange to any human not familiar with such people. The other woman was little, with mid-length blonde hair, cheerful round cheeks and laughing blue eyes. Her eyes were not as shockingly bright as the others and her face possessed fewer of those subtle little angles of cheek and jaw that typically combined, with serrin, to create a strangeness both intimidating and attractive at the same time. Sasha guessed that she might be from the Saalshen Bacosh, where human and serrin blood had mixed in many families.

All three serrin smiled or bowed to her in passing, then slipped into the column behind her where Jaryd, Sofy and Daryd reined back a little to let them in. The thunder of hooves resumed in full, an endless, drumming rhythm, heading north.

"So explain this to me," Sasha asked curiously. "Why are you here?"

"For the same reason you are here," Errollyn said plainly. "To save the Udalyn."

Sasha frowned at him. "You are from Petrodor?" Errollyn nodded. It seemed logical—many serrin served Saalshen in Petrodor. "It's a thirty-day journey to Petrodor in the best weather, I did not know the Udalyn were threatened until a few days ago. Word would have taken a full month to reach you, and another month for you to reach here."

Errollyn smiled. Beneath a thick, slightly shaggy fringe, his deep green eyes flickered with amusement. Those eyes seemed to glow, with startling colour, as if with some inner light of their own. He reminded Sasha somehow of a wolf—handsome, broad-shouldered and intelligent . . . but just a little bit scruffy.

"You are familiar with the tales of Leyvaan the Fool?" he asked her.

"The ones that everyone is familiar with, certainly."

"When his army invaded Saalshen, two centuries ago, he took us completely by surprise. Many villages were destroyed, their inhabitants slaughtered, because ever naive in the ways of humans, we did not see them coming. Saalshen is vast, more so than Lenayin, and much of its terrain is rugged, with roads that are slow in even good weather. It can take months to spread word from one side to the other. And yet, within a quarter-moon of the invasion, serrin forces from all over Saalshen were massing in the hills beyond the plain. Did you never wonder how they knew where to come?"

Sasha frowned. Beyond the approaching treeline, open fields glowed green in the midmorning sun. "The lay of the land in Saalshen is not well known to any humans, even the Nasi-Keth," she replied. "Without knowing that, we can't begin to speculate."

"They knew to come," said Errollyn, "as I knew to come."

Sasha waited a moment, before realising there was no more. "And how was that?" she pressed.

Errollyn's smile grew broader. He seemed quite young . . . although that was frequently deceptive with serrin. "We are serrinim. We know."

She looked at him for a long moment. The trees ended and they broke into the mottled sunshine of the paddocks. They were riding through green pastures in the shelter of a small valley.

"Right," said Sasha, blandly. "If you won't tell me how, at least tell me why. Why should the serrinim wish the Udalyn saved?"

Errollyn took a deep breath, his amusement fading. He gazed ahead, past the vanguard, up the length of the lovely green valley. "I never said they did," he replied. "I wish the Udalyn saved. I and my *esvaderlin*."

A group, that meant, in Saalsi. Of some indeterminate significance that doubtless changed depending on the context. Saalsi was by far the least precise and most infuriating language Sasha knew. And also by far the most poetic, subtle and beautiful.

"Why?" Sasha pressed, determined to get at least one straight answer.

Errollyn raised an eyebrow at her. "Why do *you* wish them saved?"

Sasha snorted. "You know, just once in my life, I'd like to meet a serrin who didn't answer every question with a question."

Errollyn laughed. "All the world is a question in search of an answer, and in truth, the truest answers are themselves only questions." Sasha's gaze was decidedly unimpressed. Errollyn repressed another laugh with difficulty. "I apologise. Human humour isn't what it used to be."

He was teasing her, she realised. "Serrin humour neither," she retorted with a glare.

Errollyn only seemed to find that more amusing. And he sighed, calming himself with difficulty. "I can't imagine anything more tragic than to lose an entire people," he said sombrely. "An entire culture. My *esvaderlin* feel likewise. Aisha loves the writings of Tullamayne . . . she's the little one with the blonde hair and blue eyes."

Sasha glanced about in her saddle. The woman with the short blue hair was talking to Sofy, with great animation on both sides. Behind them, little Aisha had introduced herself to Daryd and Rysha, and the conversation there involved many hand signals . . . although, given the serrin skill with tongues, Sasha would not have been surprised if Aisha spoke fluent Edu by the time they reached the valley. Nearer, the tall man spoke with Jaryd, pointing to irrigation along the valley sides, and asking curious questions that Sasha was uncertain Jaryd would know how to answer. Sociable serrin— in love with words and endlessly fascinated by new things.

"The tall one is Terel," Errollyn added. "The other woman is Tassi. We all decided to come. We are only four, but we see better than you by night and we fight with the svaalverd. I had thought that all assistance would be welcomed, however small."

"It is," Sasha assured him. "You sound disappointed at your numbers."

"Aye," said Errollyn, a little tiredly. "I had hoped for more. But the serrinim of Petrodor are hard pressed, with war brewing in the Bacosh and many things afoot. We were forbidden to bring even this many. Yet we came."

Sasha blinked. "You disobeyed an order not to come?"

"Order," said Errollyn, as if tasting the word. And shook his head. "Not an order. These concepts don't translate well from our tongue to yours. Rhillian was unhappy, but she did not order. She cannot. I am not within her *ra'shi*, I have my own. My concerns are not always hers. These three friends followed me, for reasons of their own."

"This Rhillian," Sasha ventured. "I've heard she had much *ra'shi*, amongst the serrinim. Is she your friend?"

"Yes," said Errollyn. "And no. Her intentions are kind, yet her methods are not approved by all. She is my friend in that I have good feelings for her and she for me. And yet she is not my friend, for we argue and I will not obey her every instruction as many have resolved to do."

Sasha took a deep breath. Sinking into serrin-thought was like climbing into a hot bath—best done slowly, one bit of skin at a time. "You have *ra'shi* of your own, then?" she asked.

"Everyone has *ra'shi*," Errollyn said vaguely, his eyes upon a little farming cottage ahead. Some figures were running from the valley's far slope toward the cottage, waving. "On this question, mine agrees with my *esvaderlin* and disagrees with Rhillian's." He gave her a sideways glance. "You're thinking of human leadership . . . *ra'shi* is not the same. Serrin do not appoint themselves leaders, nor is the loyalty of others within an individual's *ra'shi*, the same as the men in this column might have for you, or for Captain Tyrun. It is more . . . more a . . . a mutual consent of those within one *ra'shi* to appoint one who shall lead, on this matter, and for this time, at least. Does that make sense?"

Sasha grinned. "No." Errollyn sighed. "But you're serrin. I forgive you."

Eighteen

CRYLISS, CAPITAL OF VALHANAN, WAS A MESS. Rumours had spread in advance of a great, bloodthirsty Goeren-yai force advancing from Baen-Tar. With Great Lord Kumaryn and his fellow nobles mostly away at Rathynal, the remaining Cryliss nobility had panicked. Some had gathered belongings and fled for the hills, while others had attacked the few Goeren-yai who lived on the city outskirts.

Some cityfolk came out to greet the army as it marched into the city, followed by perhaps a hundred honourable Verenthanes who made a line across the main road, prepared to lay down their lives if the army did not have honourable intentions. A short talk with Captain Tyrun and several of the column's other Verenthanes convinced them to disperse, and even to organise supplies and spread word that the rumours of rape and pillage were lies.

At the Yethl River running through the city's heart, the column paused for a drink and some food. The toll amongst the Cryliss Goeren-yai was not as bad as first feared—four confirmed dead, but plenty of friendly Verenthanes had protected the others. The names of the murderers had been taken, some said coldly, and an officer of the king would be sought for justice.

It was not long before Andreyis arrived, insisting that there were some people Sasha should meet. He led the way along the riverbank, past more soldiers and horses than Sasha had ever seen in her life. Hooves churned the green grass as group after group led their animals to drink. She could barely see more than ten strides in any direction past the press of animal bodies and the forest of legs, but Andreyis seemed to know where to go. Sasha found herself watching the horses as she went, judging their character with a practised eye . . . perhaps half were lowland breeds and the other half either dussieh or part-dussieh.

The character of the column had changed. Now, instead of being predominantly line company troops, they were an army of many townsmen and villagers. Formidable warriors all, their skills forged in the many training halls of Lenayin. As cavalry, they were less impressive—a horse was a great expense and few could own one. Amongst those who did own horses, dedicated cavalry training was of uneven standard.

Andreyis found the Baerlyn contingent further from the river, their horses feeding from one of the hay piles some Cryliss Goeren-yai farmers had deposited across the fields. Jaegar was there, in laughing conversation with several men from another village, and looking the happiest Sasha had seen him in years. He hugged her tight enough to give her fear for her ribs, much to the awe of the other men. Then she clasped forearms with Byorn of the training hall, and his friend Madyn, and cheerful Illys the wood craftsman who played a mean reed pipe . . . and then others were coming, and she realised that there were far more men in the Baerlyn contingent than she'd have expected.

A familiar whinny caught her attention, and she looked at the horses to see a very familiar, white-starred face looking her way. "Chersey!" she exclaimed, and ran to the mare, who greeted her with a friendly nuzzle. Another shoved past Chersey with a loud, friendly greeting . . . "Ussey!" She hugged the young gelding about the neck and, looking wildly about, realised that all her horses were here. The stables of the ranch had been emptied.

Of course they'd emptied the stables, the more horses available, the more men who could join the column. But her horses were a part of her memories of home, happy, safe and comforting . . .

"Don't worry, girl," Jaegar said with a gruff grin, as Chersey nudged her in the stomach and Ussey blew in her face, "we'll look after your blasted horses."

Sasha gave him a helpless, protesting look . . . it was shameful—she should have been more worried for the lives of her Baerlyn friends. And she was, dreadfully so . . . and yet, this was different. From the look on Jaegar's face, however, she knew that he understood.

There came a cry from her left, then, and she was only half surprised when a slim tangle of red-haired curls came sprinting her way and threw herself into Sasha's embrace. Sasha gave the men an exasperated look over Lynette's head, and many of them found interest in things elsewhere, or scratched their heads, looking uncomfortable.

"What were we going to tell her?" Byorn protested. "You left her in charge of the horses, and her father's the only one who can control her anyhow . . ."

"Oh, they're all so pathetic on horses, Sasha!" Lynette shot back, disentangling herself. Her pale, freckled face was strong with determination. "And Ussey here gets nervous in crowds and needs to have a friend in sight, and Dass has a sore hoof that needs watching on a long trip, and none of this lot knows what to do because they've little enough experience riding anyhow . . ."

"She's been good," Jaegar admitted, ruffling Lynette's hair. "Bossy, but useful. She's been riding up and down our little column, talking with each man, telling them each horse's personality, how to ride them, then how to groom and care for them properly on each break. They're not *such* complete novices on horses," with a wry glance at Lynette, "those men like me who own them have shared plenty of times of drill and practice. But the deal was she'd come as far as Cryliss. And no further."

Lynette gave Sasha a desperate look. "Sasha, you'll need someone to look after the other horses too . . . I'm good at that, I could help!"

"I'm sorry, Lynie," said Sasha, shaking her head. "No."

"But why not?"

"You're not a soldier. You can't fight. If this were a foot campaign, then maybe, but there's no safe rear for noncombatants in a mounted campaign. The fighting could come from anywhere, you could be in it, and I can't spare anyone to protect you. I don't doubt you would be useful, but no."

"But Princess Sofy's going!" Lynette protested. "She can't fight either!"

Sasha stared at the men, who again looked uncomfortable. How had *that* news spread ahead of the column so fast? Perhaps it hadn't, she realised. Perhaps it had spread just now, shortly after arriving in Cryliss.

"And I'd drop Sofy in Cryliss if I could," Sasha said sternly. "But having ridden with us this far, she's now a target. I don't wish to insult Cryliss Verenthanes, I'm sure most of them are honourable, but I've no telling which are which on such short notice, and I can't be sure she'd be safe here. She stays with us because I deem it safer, but already she costs us several good men to watch over her. I can't spare several more to defend you, and if left alone, you can't defend yourself. Absolutely not."

"I wish I'd learned svaalverd," Lynette muttered, looking at the ground. "Then I could have come."

"Maybe one day the Nasi-Keth will spread from Petrodor," Sasha suggested. Lynette blinked at her. "Then you could have an uman like me, if you wish. There's no limit on age."

"One day," Lynette agreed, wistfully.

Sasha smiled at her. "But not today."

Two days north from Cryliss, the Shudyn Divide marked the beginning of the Aralya Range that separated much of the populated north from the rest of Lenayin. The Shudyn Divide was a ragged, uneven, rocky mountain face with many ridgeline ascents that looked both promising and treacherous in turn. The column now numbered nearly four and a half thousand, as a large group of Taneryn militia and most of the Taneryn Red Swords company had arrived the previous evening, with promises of more to come. If the column had been strung out before, it would now become much more so, toiling up the mountain rise.

By midmorning, the ride had indeed become a hard slog, riders dismounting in places to walk their struggling animals up a particularly steep or loose stretch. The road became little more than a narrow, rocky horse trail, flanked increasingly by sheer drops that revealed a magnificent yet alarming view. Many times during the climb, Sasha turned in her saddle to look back down and marvel at the endless line of men and horses, nose-to-tail in her wake. By midday the column head had cleared the worst of the sheer cliffs and, while the trail remained steep, they were enfolded once more by pine trees. But then, within the space of a thousand strides, the weather changed.

At first it rained, then it blew hard and strong, bending the trees and snapping no few within range. Soft earth turned to slippery mud and riders tried to hold their mounts to grass or loose gravel; Sasha heard many curses and calls of warning or alarm from further down the slope. Then the mist closed in, enfolding the column until it was difficult to see more than five or six horses in any direction. They stopped for a lunchtime rest, men feeding hay or oats they had brought with them from Cryliss to horses who had little grazing room upon the narrow, precarious trailside. Water at least remained no problem, as the trail crossed small runoff streams frequently.

Shortly after lunch, the trail became level and wound its way along one side of a rift known as Galryd's Pass, for Galryd the Bloody had used it frequently, legend told, to wreak havoc upon Valhanan and beyond. It was reputed to be spectacular, but Sasha saw little through the mist, and was forced to imagine the great, looming peaks presently towering to either side. Far better than a view, it made for some of the easiest riding since Baen-Tar, and the horses moved with a relief that spoke of their assurance that their riders were not entirely crazy, to have chosen such a route. But then, all too soon, came the descent.

"I'd thought when we were climbing," Sofy quipped, "that I'd like downhills much more than uphills. Now I see I like neither." Amidst slippery rocks and poor visibility, most riders spent more time dismounted than astride.

Daryd had to urge exhausted little Rysha to walk, lest Essey slip and topple her onto the rocks. He stepped carefully from loose, slippery rock to rock, Essey's reins in one hand, his sister's hand in the other. Seeing him, Sasha felt the most intense admiration. Daryd had not complained once, and his first thoughts were always for Rysha. And Rysha, the cautious, less adventurous one, had perhaps been even braver.

Halfway down the mountainside, the slope eased enough to allow riders back in the saddle and the column emerged below the grey, misting ceiling. The sight was breathtaking, with vast, tree-covered mountainsides plunging from the clouds. Branches dripped and small rivulets of water carved lines across the trail. There were thick tangles of broadleaf amongst the pine that Sasha did not know the names of, and vines that crept up the bark of pines and sprouted little blue flowers. Strange birds sung in the treetops, their cries echoing across the foothills. She was in Hadryn, where she had only been twice before, when several two-thousand-plus Cherrovan incursions had outflanked the Hadryn cavalry and threatened Valhanan. Before her, glistening through a break in the trees, was the curling bend of the River Yumynis, flowing from the heart of the Udalyn Valley.

Men stood in the stirrups to gain a better view, marvelling at a scene most had only heard described in tales. Some pointed, others muttered oaths, and some made the spirit sign. Daryd exclaimed something loudly to Rysha, who cried out in delight. Captain Tyrun fell back to ride at Sasha's side as the path became barely wide enough for two.

"Ymoth," he said, pointing through the trees toward a dark patch amidst the foothills. Sasha peered, straining her eyes. The Yumynis curled about before them, to the east it opened into Lake Tullamayne, which glinted dully beneath the overcast sky, flanked by mountains. That way was the Taneryn border, where more mountains rose. Beyond those mountains, Halleryn. So little distance had the Hadryn had to come.

About the western bank of the river's bend, the land rose in foothills that stretched from the base of the Shudyn Divide all the way to the valley mouth beyond, where they reared up once more to form steep, imposing sides. Another sharp range rose to form the valley's eastern flank, spreading from that narrow point as they progressed northwards, high ridges of treeless rock, linked in places by a dipping, sweeping spine that looked sharp enough to cut leather, swathed in cloud. Down below, nestled in the foothills upon the outer, western bend of the river, lay the town of Ymoth. Sasha caught a brief sight of green pasture along the riverbank, and a bridge. So beautiful, from this height. She had little faith it would remain so, once they were closer.

"What do you guess we are facing?" Sasha asked.

"It depends on how quickly their messengers moved," Tyrun said grimly. "Far slower than ours, certainly—among the villages, messengers and horses can be swapped, and ridden through night and day in all directions. Any northern messenger has had to avoid the villages, has received no change of horse and has had little sleep. It's possible we are less than a day behind such a message."

"And then the question is 'What will Usyn do?'" Sasha replied.

Tyrun nodded, a ginger hand on the reins as they turned a downward corner, avoiding slippery rocks. "We could assume he learned this morning. In that case, had he moved immediately, his forces could be gathered at Ymoth now . . . if hidden in those woods, we could not see them from here."

Sasha made a face. "That's a big force to move so fast. They'll have been encamped before the Udalyn Wall for a siege. Camps can tend to become permanent, and forces who do not believe themselves threatened are not prepared to move quickly . . . and they're not known as 'heavy horse' for nothing. The wall is at the valley's far end, and the valley is no short hike. Also, I'd not have thought it in the Hadryn's nature to hide in the woods. Heavy cavalry likes open space—I'd think he'd meet us on those fields beside the river. If he's here, we'll see him."

Tyrun gave her a wary glance. "M'Lady is an optimist." In a tone that suggested a learned distrust of such things, especially from youngsters.

Sasha shrugged. "Then I'll give you true optimism. I think Usyn is a crazed fool bent on avenging his father's death. I think he'll resist any request from his commanders to pack up and move away. At the least, that could gain us some time. When he does move to meet us, he'll also leave behind a portion of his force to keep the Udalyn contained behind their wall. He'll think to deal with us, then return to his siege. But he will not be at full strength when we meet him."

"Perhaps the Udalyn have already fallen, M'Lady," Tyrun said darkly. "Perhaps the valley wall is breached. The north has siege weapons . . . Hadryn in particular, one suspects, having dreamed of this campaign for some time. If that is so, we shall face the entire Hadryn force all at once."

"The valley wall stands firm," Sasha replied. "I'm sure of it." Tyrun just looked at her, even more warily than before. "It must," she corrected herself, with a resigned smile. "Otherwise, we'll have come all this way for nothing."

"Must move fast!" called Captain Akryd of the Taneryn Red Swords from behind, having ridden past Sofy and Jaryd. "If we waste time scouting, that bastard Usyn will arrive in force! Certainly we can't camp overnight. It's now or never."

Tyrun made a face, wrinkling up his moustache. Then he nodded. "We go immediately, no waiting." And spared Sasha a faintly amused look. "Otherwise, we'll have come all this way for nothing."

It began to dawn on Sasha what that would mean. A full charge into rolling terrain with plenty of ambush opportunities, without knowing what it was they were facing. She took a deep breath. "All right!" she announced, loudly enough to include Captain Akryd behind them. Akryd, she reckoned, would have been selected by Krayliss himself, as great lords typically selected the commanders of provincial companies. She hoped he wouldn't do anything stupid. "If it's not Usyn himself, it'll probably be Banneryd forces, largely those diverted from their path to Halleryn. At least one line company of heavy horse, more likely two, plus an awful lot of infantry militia."

"I'd bet on close to a thousand horse, maybe two thousand infantry at minimum," Tyrun agreed. Defender's advantage being roughly four-to-one, as Lenayin commanders traditionally insisted . . . they'd need nearly twelve thousand. They had less than half that. Damn. Even without the Hadryn, it didn't look good. With them, it would be a massacre.

"How strongly defended do you think the Ymoth wall will be?" Sasha asked Tyrun.

"Maybe some archers!" he replied. "No more than that. They'd be stupid to waste men on the wall, cavalry can't climb walls! They'll defend the flanks to stop us going around to the incomplete side of the wall. If they don't come out to fight, we'll have to go in and get them man to man. Ordinarily we could bypass Ymoth entirely, but if we tried it, we'd have no idea how strong a force remains inside to harass our rear when we head for the valley."

Sasha shook her head. "No bypassing—we're trying to trap the Hadryn inside the valley, we can't afford to get trapped ourselves. If I were them I'd put infantry on defensible ridgelines with trees for cover all about the exposed side of Ymoth. We can't ride around that uphill side, it's too rugged. We'll need two thrusts, one to hit the near side from the river, and one to flank around the town and hit the other. That second thrust will have to pass along the riverbank and head back upslope . . . straight into an uphill ambush. We'll stagger it, a forward force to spring the trap then double back, the later one to hit them hard."

"The girl knows her cavalry charges!" Akryd said with amusement. "What size the reserve?"

"Make it two hundred," Tyrun replied. "Can't spare any more than that. M'Lady and I'll take the far flank—she can spring the trap, I'll break it. Yuan Akryd, you can lead the near-side assault. Don't stop for anything."

"I shan't!" said Akryd, most cheerfully. "Sounds like a plan. I'll see you both inside!" And with that, he reined off the trail and stopped, waiting for his officers further back in the column to catch up to receive his orders. Sasha found herself somewhat unsettled.

"Aren't we supposed to plan a little more than that?" she asked dubiously. "Before the battle of Baen-Tar, Kessligh planned for nearly a full day."

"This is a cavalry charge," Tyrun replied, with a wry, twisting smile. "When you throw a melon off a cliff, do you plan to see which way it splatters?"

Sasha did not consider herself comforted.

Tyrun dropped back to talk to his officers, and Sasha allowed Jaryd to ride up alongside. "Did you hear that?" she asked. A part of her felt uneasy excluding Jaryd from the initial planning—in name at least, he was the Commander of the Falcon Guard. It was impossible to tell if Jaryd felt neglected. Lately, it had been impossible to tell if Jaryd felt anything.

"Princess Sofy and I shall stay with the reserve," he said grimly. "I shan't be much use in a charge."

"When the reserve is committed to the fight, stay with them," Sasha insisted. "Holding back on your own will only make you a lonely target."

"Sasha?" Sofy called from behind, anxiously. "Sasha, don't hold him back on my account. I'm okay, really . . . I think I'm getting quite good at riding."

"Damn it, Sofy," Sasha called over her shoulder, "I'm not doing this as a favour! You're far more a princess of Lenayin than I'll ever be, and you're valuable. I'll not risk an important asset of Lenayin if I can help it."

Sofy stared at her, managing to look both crestfallen and angry at the same time.

As the trail wound though the lower foothills, Sasha found herself alone at the head of the column. She shouted for the vanguard to raise a canter where the trail allowed. They rushed along winding trails, flanked by thick undergrowth, the vanguard lowering their banners to avoid catching them upon low branches. A scout joined them, accelerating to ride at Sasha's side, his little dussieh frothing white with sweat as its little legs pumped to keep pace, the wild-bearded woodsman on its back assuring her that there was open space ahead and no sign of ambush.

The column burst onto open fields, green grass wet upon steep, folded hillsides. Fences crossed the grass and small farmhouses perched beside water catchments. Sasha couldn't see any livestock as they thundered along the ridgeline road. That was a bad sign. Ahead, the Yumynis River glinted dully as it swept about in a giant bend. A glance over her shoulder showed an endless stream of mounted soldiers pouring from the treeline. She held the column to a comfortable canter with little fear of tiring the horses on such an easy downward slope.

The treeline continued downhill on the right, where dark shelves of rock thrust through the green grass. Beyond, the Shudyn Ridge towered like an almighty black wall supporting the grey ceiling of sky. A galloping horseman caught her eye, racing parallel to the treeline. A scout—they often flanked forward from a cavalry thrust, searching the hidden folds of land for ambush. And yet, the horseman swung across and headed for them at speed. Several of the vanguard fell back, riding on Sasha's right as a shield, but the approaching rider bore no visible weapons and held a hand aloft in a sign of recognition.

"M'Lady, I don't recognise him," said one of the vanguard, squinting as they rode. "He's not one of our scouts." The man's dussieh came racing up the slope at an angle toward them . . . and Sasha could see the man's face.

"That's all right!" she replied, with a leap of high spirits. "I do!" She stood in her stirrups and waved him in. "Greetings, Jurellyn! Funny seeing you here!"

"Funny?" yelled the scout as he closed the gap. "It's hysterical! Where the hells've you been, damn fool of a girl?"

Sasha threw back her head and laughed. Jurellyn leaped the stone wall beside the trail and joined her side with a skidding of hooves. The trail was turning northward, dropping into a shallow fold that blocked all view of the river. Upon the opposing slope, Sasha saw a farmhouse in charcoal ruins, the damage far too old to raise smoke.

She extended a hand and Jurellyn grasped it hard. He looked much the same as she'd last seen him upon the road to Halleryn—ragged and weather-beaten, a shaven jaw his only visible concession to civilisation. His rumpled clothes bore perhaps several more stains than she recalled, but it appeared as if the intervening weeks since Damon had sent him from the Falcon Guard to spy on Lord Usyn's army had caused him little concern. Certainly his horse seemed none the worse for wear, running gamely at Peg's side with barely a sweat to show.

"I've got good news and bad news!" he said to her above the thunder of hooves.

"Bad news first!"

"The Banneryd Holy Swords hold Ymoth, you're looking at nine hundred horse minimum, maybe two thousand infantry!"

"I already guessed that!" Sasha retorted. "What's the good news?"

"Usyn ain't here!" With a gleam in his eyes. "I know the Banneryd got wind of you coming, they've been scrambling about the place all morning setting up defences . . . but Usyn's still in the valley!"

"I could kiss you!" Sasha yelled back.

"Promises, promises! This road's fine—they'll see you maybe three folds from Ymoth so they won't have much time to prepare! There's open ground from there, you can form up okay—make it fast past the town, there's archers on the walls! And watch the damn bridge! I haven't been able to get across for two days, but there's Hadryn towns not too far east and my men saw riders heading across the bridge at speed this morning!"

Sasha nodded . . . from those villages would come the same men who ravaged Perys.

"Do the Udalyn still stand?" she asked Jurellyn, as they rose over the depression.

"No way to tell! Usyn's still in there . . ." Jurellyn shrugged. "I see you brought the kids with you!"

Sasha blinked at him. He'd sent them, she recalled. "If you thought perhaps the king still had a heart, it didn't work!"

Jurellyn shook his head. "Brother Damon's idea! I never had much faith in it!" They cleared the rise and could see the river once more. The lower fields were close, but Ymoth remained hidden behind a ridge. "I'll scout forward, maybe try and cross the bridge when you go! Luck!"

He waved and spurred his wiry horse to a gallop, raising clods of earth in his wake as he raced down the trail, then leaped a wall to ride toward the further treeline.

The formation seemed to take forever to arrive. Men poured down from the last rise of the foothills, officers on horseback yelling and pointing grandly with their swords, directing each group to their position. Sasha simply held Peg to his place behind the vanguard before the bank of a stream that cut through the paddocks into the Yumynis. The ruins of a farmhouse lay nearby, its charred timbers wet with recent rain. The senseless destruction sickened her and awoke her fury. It must have been such a beautiful residence, by a stream near a wide river, nestled amid green pastures and flanked by mountains.

Across the pastures behind, a great mass of men on horse now gathered. Sasha stared across their ranks in utter disbelief. Thousands of horses. They snorted, stamped, tossed heads and whinnied. Their lines were ragged, their size, colour and breeding uneven, and the men on their backs ranged from armoured cavalrymen to wild-haired, tattooed villagers to a smattering of clean-cut and shaven Verenthane townsmen. A rabble, Tyrun had rightly said. But a very angry, very determined rabble. A very *large* rabble. Sasha had never seen such mustered soldiery before in her life. The very ground seemed to sag beneath their accumulated weight.

Tyrun came galloping along the front line, raising a cheer as he went. He peeled off and stopped at Sasha's side. "They know what they're doing," he said, eyes squinted within his silver helm. "We've got them in teams of roughly ten, we try to keep the villages together where possible. This lot's yours . . ." pointing across the vast swathe of men directly before her, "the bunch behind them will be mine . . ." pointing over their heads to an even larger mass gathered there, "and Captain Akryd has that lot over there . . ." pointing furthest from the river, where at least two thousand horse were gathered in rough, shifting ranks.

"Your Baerlyners are with Captain Akryd," Tyrun continued, answering her unasked question. "I'm sorry they can't ride with you, but our organisation isn't quite that good, and contingents end up wherever they end up."

Sasha waved a hand. "That's okay. No favouritism." And it was better, perhaps, that their fates were entirely out of her hands. It would stop her from being distracted. Teriyan. Jaegar. Andreyis. Fear clutched her heart at the thought of her young friend. "Dear spirits look after him," she thought. "Help him remember what he was taught."

Some horses were grazing and some men had briefly dismounted to relieve themselves on the grass before the charge. Sasha herself had already done so, within the ruined farmhouse for privacy. The whole thing was surreal. Behind the great mass, Sasha could see some smaller ranks holding reluctantly back. Sofy would be there, with Jaryd at her side. Pray that they were not needed.

"What's the count now?" she asked, trying to keep her voice level. Her heart was starting to race, like a startled horse that wished to rip clear of her chest and go galloping off across the fields.

"Five thousand two hundred and change," Tyrun replied. "There's more behind, scattered in groups all across the Shudyn Divide." Even as he spoke, Sasha spied some latecomers pelting toward the rear, frantic not to miss the action. She could almost see their disappointment when an officer directed them toward the reserve. "We would be stronger every moment we wait, but the afternoon grows late already and the cloud will make the dark come sooner."

Sasha shook her head. "No waiting. As soon as you're ready." Any longer and her own racing heart would kill her.

"A gesture from the commander is customary," said Tyrun, indicating the waiting ranks behind. Clearly he read the look on her face, for he shrugged, apologetically. "Not to do so could be considered a bad omen."

Sasha reined Peg about in frustration, dug in her heels and raced uphill to what she considered would be the centre of that vast front line. Then she stopped, pulled the sword from over her shoulder, stood in the stirrups and held it aloft.

"LENAYIN!" she yelled. The answering roar gave her the worst goosebumps of her life, so loud it seemed it might blow her from the saddle. Thousands of blades speared the air and thousands of voices yelled, again and again. She turned and galloped back to her vanguard, still waving the blade. As she approached, Tyrun gave the signal and the whole front line began to move. The Battle of Ymoth was underway. Exactly *which* battle of Ymoth, whether the fifth, or the fifteenth, or the fiftieth, Sasha was far from certain.

Peg splashed through the stream, Sasha holding him to a canter up the far bank as the front line reached the stream unevenly. The water dissolved in a frothing mass of hooves and Sasha spared a long look behind, seeing that Tyrun had pulled aside for her own formation to pass and headed now for the greater mass of horse still waiting behind. The last of her riders cleared the stream and she lifted Peg's speed to a gentle run. The way ahead lay relatively flat along the riverbank. Tall poplars lined the river and upon the river's far side were fields and fields of wheat and oats.

The first fence was wooden and high, but Peg cleared it with ease. Sasha swung in her saddle to see the front line do the same, even the smallest dussieh having little difficulty. Her spirits lifted a little more—one more concern out of the way. Her vanguard spread out, still in front, clearing her view. Ymoth itself remained largely out of sight behind the one remaining ridge, blocking a view of those lower foothills where it cut across the riverside fields. She cleared another fence and saw the bridge emerging ahead, past intervening poplars. The ridge approached, and then Captain Akryd's left flank seemed to lift, accelerating to clear the rise and the fence that ran along it.

The river curled gently to the right, and suddenly, there was Ymoth. There was indeed a wall—perhaps only half the height of the walls of Halleryn, but a stone wall all the same. Within, and rising as the foothills rose, she could see the town itself—a mass of thatched roofs clustered for protection behind that stone. Surprisingly, there seemed to be little damage. Ymoth had not been raised to the ground. Perhaps the Hadryn had proved less barbaric than she'd feared.

The rear of the town rose considerably higher than its river-facing wall and dwellings seemed to blend into the tree-covered folds. Still Sasha could see no opposition. But the assault could be seen now and defenders would be preparing. Make them rush.

She gave a yell, and a wave of her sword, and Peg accelerated to a full gallop. An answering yell came from a thousand throats behind and the thunder of hooves became an earth-shaking roar. Sasha cleared the next fence, a ruined farmhouse flashed by, and she purposely slowed Peg with several gentle tugs lest he outdistance the vanguard.

She could see archers on the walls now, as Captain Akryd's flank began to divide from her own, headed for those nearside slopes and trees. Then she saw movement within the trees, an emerging line of archers, bows at the ready. Behind them, holding the flattest uphill ridges, were lines of infantry, the front ranks bristling with spears.

She tore her vision away from that impending collision, for the bridge was approaching and the Ymoth wall opposite on the left. The left flank would be engaging now, but she could not hear a thing above the pounding roar. Archers upon the Ymoth wall stood, drew and fired . . . Sasha could not help but spare the flying shafts a sideways eye as they fell behind. If they hit anyone, she did not turn to see.

She focused all her attention instead upon the left turn she had to make ahead, away from the river and up to Ymoth's far flank . . . not too tight, she urged herself, crouched low on Peg's heaving back. The entire formation would follow the line she set. Too tight, and they would stretch and scatter. Not tight enough, and they would still be turning when the reverse came, followed by confusion and collisions. The wall flew past on the left, the river poplars on the right, archers loosing soundless arrows from the parapets—everything was soundless but the charge . . .

She switched the sword to her left hand and held it out, beginning the left sweep as the wall ended. About they curled, racing hard as the ground began to rise, thundering toward the ragged treeline where the horses would surely begin to slow against the steepening incline . . . And there they were, suddenly a cascade of cavalry bursting from the trees ahead, plunging down the slope toward them. Banneryd cavalry, she could see the red and black banners, and the gleam of heavy mail, their yells now audible from the fore, testament alone to their number.

Sasha waved her sword in a wide circle, swinging Peg wide to the right as the right flank swung and the rear also turned. She could feel Peg's surprise, fighting the rein, thinking the direction lay ahead . . . Sasha pulled tighter as the main body began to swing, the huge mass of mounted soldiers somehow managing to avoid collision as they circled and doubled back on themselves. There was some jostling, some bunching up, some riders spurring wider circles to clear the congestion . . . Sasha threw a glance back over her shoulder and saw the Banneryd cavalry descending upon them in a huge, triple-ranked line, bristling with swords as they hurtled downhill. This was going to be close.

She found herself at the rear-left flank, riding hard amidst her vanguard and stragglers, closest to the river as her ragged formation fled before her. Clods of earth flew and pelted about like rain, the grass torn black by hooves. On the slope, Banneryd cavalry were cutting closer to the Ymoth wall, flying at great speed as their ranks divided, individual riders backing their horses to catch their fleeing quarry. Suddenly there was an armourless rider in her vision, dark grey hair flying, riding no hands with a huge bow drawn across his body, aiming back behind his right shoulder. Errollyn, and surely an impossible shot amidst the lurching confusion, the raining debris and the fact that she'd picked him for a right-hander, not a left . . . he fired, and a Banneryd rider fell with the shaft precisely through his unarmoured neck. If Sasha hadn't seen it with her own eyes, she'd never have believed it possible. Errollyn drew another arrow from his hip quiver, balanced the bow upon his horse's neck as they cleared another fence, straightened, drew, and fired all in one motion. Another Banneryd rider fell, clutching his neck.

The front Banneryd riders were closing on several straggling dussieh, yelling furiously, swords brandished in eager anticipation. So intent were they that they did not pause to ponder why their quarry, which had approached in such a wide formation, now allowed themselves to stretch in a narrow line close to the river. Nor did they look at the archers on the walls, no longer shooting but waving frantically, gesturing to something ahead that they could see, but their riders could not. Those closest to the wall did see, their view ahead clear. Perhaps they yelled warning, but in the roar of the charge, little could be heard.

Captain Tyrun's main formation tore past Sasha's retreating feint with a howling battle cry, a massed blur of horses and flashing swords by Sasha's right, smashed into the unsuspecting Banneryd pursuit. Behind them, Sasha's formation was now wheeling, doubling back for a second time. Some of those Banneryd in closest pursuit broke off immediately to help their brethren. Others continued, intent on the kill . . . Sasha wove to the right, trying to catch one on the blindside, only for Errollyn to shoot him off his horse. A rider with steel-blue hair beheaded another in passing, and then there were horses on all sides crisscrossing, weaving and reversing madly.

Sasha barely missed colliding with one of her own, spurred Peg fast around one falling, rolling horse and saw a Banneryd rider cut two of her men from their saddles in quick succession. Another came thundering at her and she spurred Peg onto his backhand, thinking to duck and cut low . . . an arrow buzzed from nowhere and upended that man too from his horse. There was confusion, beasts and men rolling underfoot, screams and yells, whinnies and clashing steel. Ahead, a Banneryd rider fought a Goeren-yai saddle-to-saddle . . . the northerner parried and slashed with superior skill, spurring his horse at a vital moment and killing the Goeren-yai with a reverse cut.

And lost his head a moment later as the blue-haired rider reappeared, then reined around to gesture madly at Sasha. "This way!" the serrin named Tassi yelled. It seemed as good a direction as any, so Sasha followed as Tassi plunged ahead, weaving between battling riders . . . and there suddenly was tall Terel, intervening in one contest to cut another Banneryd from his saddle. Sasha slashed at another in passing, but was parried, and galloped on regardless.

Abruptly, she was clear, following Terel and Tassi across an open paddock near the river. They leaped a fence, Sasha looking about to find Errollyn directly behind (how long had he been *there*?), three of her vanguard riders close behind him, and here now on the left was little blonde Aisha, a bloody blade in her hand, watching that great, sprawling mass of men and horses for possible threats. Four Banneryd riders came tearing directly at them, angling across in front to intercept Tassi's lead. Tassi pointed her sword at them, as a galloping rider might casually indicate a troublesome rock to her trailing comrades.

Errollyn shot the leader, the other three swerving about him as he came off, bounced, then dragged with a foot in the stirrups. Aisha then dashed toward them in a burst of speed, as Terel turned more sharply from the lead. One of the three was already separated from his comrades, and now conceded Terel's superior angle, reining wider . . . and directly into Aisha's path, slashing as she cut past behind, the Banneryd clutching a half-severed arm. The other two raced at Tassi. Errollyn shot one through the side and Tassi cut behind the other, galloping up on his far side, then swerving away when he tried to backhand at her head. Both cleared the next fence, and the surviving Banneryd tried to close once more on Tassi . . . and did not see little Aisha now racing up on his blind side, until it cost him his head. Sasha passed the Banneryd with the wounded arm as he tried to pull aside, but her vanguard were not so merciful, and killed him in passing.

They cleared another fence and then cut between a riverside farmhouse and the riverbank poplars, leaves whipping at Sasha's face. Upon the left, what remained of the Banneryd main force was falling back, spurring madly up the slope down which they'd charged. Archers fired sporadically from the walls, fearing to hit their own men. Others were breaking clear of the fight— great, untouched ranks of men, galloping wide for space in which to pursue the fleeing northerners, and Sasha's heart soared to see so many unscathed. Her plan trap had worked.

Tassi slowed a little to let Sasha catch up, and they curved away from the river toward the slope. Peg was tiring now, his black flanks frothing white with sweat, but at full gallop he still closed the gap to Tassi's horse in little time. One of Sasha's vanguard still had his royal banner flying and Sasha turned to wave him forward. Already, others of her men were seeing, pointing and then yelling to companions, urging them to follow.

"We must stay close on their heels!" Errollyn yelled as he came alongside. "It will hinder their archers if our lead arrives amidst their stragglers!"

Some racing riders gained on the fleeing Banneryd, and hacked them from the saddle. A group of northerners peeled away, spurring desperately for the rocky treeline and some safety . . . Errollyn calmly shot one from his saddle and reloaded with the air of a man picking off straw targets. The victim's comrades wheeled about in panic to see such accuracy . . . Errollyn shot another with a thud that fairly catapulted the man from his saddle, and the remaining pair were slashed and hacked by six racing Goeren-yai as they pelted past. Sasha could not resist sparing Errollyn an incredulous look. He hadn't missed yet . . . or not that she'd seen. Perhaps he couldn't.

The incline culminated in an uneven line of pines. Within those pines, beyond the racing horses ahead, Sasha could see a row of sharpened stakes driven into the ground—a typical defence against cavalry. Archers were firing through those stakes as the first men of the column arrived . . . some fell, others reined about in panic, but fire was sporadic as Banneryd and rebel horsemen mixed, the retreating with the advancing. Dussieh riders spurred their little mounts straight for the rifts in the treeline where water runoff made a rocky cleft and the line of spikes faltered. Further to the right flank, Sasha saw a line of such horsemen racing for the stream there, splashing through shallow water to run upon the rocky stream bed, where surely no great warhorse could hold his footing.

A tangled mass of horses reeled amidst trees and spikes—Banneryd cavalry now trapped against their own defences and fighting for their lives, rebel cavalry seeking a way through, others dismounting to hack at the wooden stakes and make a path while dodging the thrusts of Banneryd infantry spears from the other side. In several places, Sasha saw defences had been left open for the Banneryd cavalry to retreat, and those now dissolved into a mass of fighting, hacking men and thrashing horses, as massed infantry tried to prevent any breakthrough whilst admitting their own through the gap.

She, the serrin and her three men of the vanguard wove past milling, circling horsemen, dodging past the first trees and wincing at the occasional hiss of arrowfire. Past the row of stakes, Sasha caught glimpses of dussieh riders now behind the lines, wheeling and hacking at infantry, who broke formation to face the new threat at their rear . . . the defenders had not bet on the agility of little dussieh while planning their defences. More were streaming up a narrow rift ahead, an incredible sight, as long-haired Goeren-yai spurred their wiry little animals across rocks, steep sides and tangled undergrowth.

Sasha pointed with her sword, and saw Errollyn nod. They wheeled downslope for a run-up as the two stakes nearest the rift came down . . . other horsemen were already spurring toward it, yelling as they went, as those waiting jostled for position to make their own charge. Sasha yelled for them to make way, and men did so, looking around in startlement as they realised who it was. Sasha dug in her heels and sent Peg racing, the serrin close behind. She saw infantry on her left fighting madly to close the gap, more rebels circling back to stop them, a dussieh going down screaming under spear and sword thrust . . .

Peg hurtled up the slope and rushed over the broken defensive stumps, Sasha then turned him left amidst the trees in a wide circle, realising immediately that the best way to defend the breach was to outflank the men trying to close it and cut them to pieces. From this side of the stakes, she could see the mass of infantry building against perhaps thirty of her horsemen, who wheeled and circled, swinging furiously as the foot soldiers tried to overwhelm them, bringing down several. She accelerated to top speed, weaving narrowly past the sides of trees . . . an arrow felled one infantryman in front, the others scattering as the massive black warhorse crashed through. Sasha slashed from side to side, more in hope of creating confusion than clean kills, reining Peg about before the stakes, lashing and kicking. Then the serrin were in amongst it, all save Errollyn, who held back and felled any infantryman who threatened a blindside swing at his comrades.

A horn was blowing somewhere above the screaming, yelling and crashing, and then the infantry were falling back, attempting to maintain some kind of order, officers screaming at those who panicked and tried to run. They retreated along the line of pikes, dodging behind trees to avoid cavalry attacks—they had shields, a most un-Lenay device amongst foot soldiers, and they used them to form an armoured perimeter where they could.

Sasha spurred Peg into another run, headed upslope once more through the trees, searching for any sign of a second defensive line that might fall upon them from beyond . . . there seemed to be none. It seemed that three thousand men were not enough to hold Ymoth without its wall complete—these sloping flanks were too wide to allow a sufficiently strong first line, plus a secondary line. The defenders had gambled on a strong first line, and lost.

She'd won, the astonishing thought occurred to her in that instant. Bad defensive strategy, perhaps . . . fortuitous offensive strategy, certainly. But a victory, all the same. Yet men were still dying. She had to end it fast.

"Get to the town!" she yelled at the top of her voice, waving her sword for attention. She reined up a little as her vanguard flagbearer caught up, attracting attention once more . . . and hopefully not from surviving Banneryd archers. "Get to Ymoth! To Ymoth! Take the town!"

She raced through the trees as fast as she dared, other horsemen now breaking away from their engagements to follow—and that trickle became a flood. Rocks and undergrowth confused their passage in places, breaking the smooth carpet of pine needles. Finally, the land fell away into a sloping shoulder where the trees became thin, with ferns and bush holding thickly to the slopes. At the bottom of the shallow valley ran a stream. Downstream, where the valley sides diminished, was another row of stakes, manned by a defensive line of infantry in a wide half circle. *Here* was the second line, encircling Ymoth where the stone wall would have continued if the Udalyn had had a few more years to complete it. The fallback line, for disasters such as this. If the Banneryd had no place to fall back to, they were surely finished.

Already there were dussieh riders pouring off the slope and along the little valley side, pelting at a pace that no warhorse rider would have dared along sloping ground. Archers fired, and several fell, or had horses shot from beneath them, plunging head-over-saddle into the turf, but the others wove past undeterred. Ragged, running infantry were rushing to the fallback line from left and right flanks, some staggering and wounded, sliding through the gaps between stakes . . . and Sasha's eyes widened as she realised that those gaps, although tight enough to deter a warhorse, were barely enough to stop a dussieh.

Dussieh riders attacked the gaps between those sharpened points fearlessly, tearing into the thin defensive lines, cutting men down, then charging past the first houses of upslope Ymoth to hit the opposite defences from behind. Infantry abandoned the second line perimeter to intercept, creating space for other approaching riders to dismount and begin hacking through the stakes. And now, from the opposing side, riders of Captain Akryd's assault were pouring down the slope. Stakes came down in several places and warhorses and dussieh charged through, their riders swinging at any foot soldier foolish enough to try and stop them.

Sasha splashed along the streamside at a trot, watching the rout unfold and searching for her own way through, when Errollyn partially blocked her way. "No Sashandra," he said, holding a hand out. "You've done enough. You'll only present some beaten Banneryd crossbowman with a grand target with which to redeem his honour. Your men know what to do, let them do it."

Banneryd infantry still trying to reach the cover of town buildings were cut down as they ran, bodies tumbling bloodily down the stream-side slope. Further back along the flanks, the sounds of fighting continued, although drowned by the thunder of hooves and the triumphant yells of riders. Yet more riders poured through the ever-widening gaps in the defenses, an endless stream of mounted soldiery racing into Ymoth. Errollyn was right, Sasha realised. She was the commander. Now she had to know what the casualties were upon Captain Akryd's flank. The battle for Ymoth may have been won, but there was a long way to go yet.

She urged Peg up the opposing slope, staying wide of the oncoming rush of horsemen heading the other way. Soon enough Captain Akryd himself came toward her at a canter, several of his personal guard at his flanks.

"Well," he said cheerfully as he reined up beside her, "that's the first one down!" Sasha suffered a surge of relief to know that she was not the only one thinking ahead. Akryd was gasping for air, and his horse frothed foam from the mouth with each snorting breath, but he seemed healthy. One of his men clutched at a gashed leg, his companion now manoeuvring alongside to try and stop the bleeding. "Did you ever see such a poor defensive spacing?" Akryd continued, eyes alive with the light of recent battle. "Stupid northern fools, if they'd spaced their damn stakes they might have had a chance! We must have rushed them to a frenzy, getting here so soon!"

"What do you think you lost?" Sasha asked grimly above the ongoing thunder of hooves. Over by the stakes on this flank, past the onrush of horses, she could see little groups of infantry surrendering. Northerners rarely surrendered, or so the stories had it. In truth, it had been a long time since a large enough battle had tested that theory. A battle against someone other than the Cherrovan, who rarely *took* prisoners, making the whole question irrelevant.

Akryd exhaled hard, his expression darkening immediately. "Oh . . . damn it, hundreds. There was a second line, they fell on us once the dussieh broke through, a lot of them fell . . ." Sasha's heart sank in dismay. So there *had* been a second line upon the southern flank, just not on the northern one—they'd had cavalry instead, as she'd suspected, waiting on the blindside of their approach. Those first brave dussieh riders to penetrate the line must have been wiped out. "We got through eventually, but . . . at least three hundred, M'Lady. Spirits know how many smaller wounds."

Three hundred on one flank. At least that many on her own, either dead or unable to fight further. Many horses. Dear spirits, it was a lot. A wonderful victory, the analytical side of her mind knew. But . . . it seemed like a lot. It seemed like far, far too many.

"M'Lady?" said Akryd. Possibly he was unsettled by the look on her face. She straightened herself with an effort, and tried to think rationally. "What do you instruct?"

"Get into the town. Absolutely no pillage, I forbid it."

"Aye, M'Lady, I doubt it'll be a problem, but I'll see to it."

"I want to know what's become of the inhabitants. I want senior officers rounded up alive. Then I want a complete reassembly as soon as possible, I want horses cared for as a matter of urgency, I know they're exhausted but we simply don't know when the next fight will come. We must be ready."

"Aye, M'Lady," Akryd agreed, finding no argument with that.

"And someone find Tyrun!" Sasha added as he made to move off. "I wish to speak with him at the earliest. I'll assess the casualties over here and see what can be done for the wounded."

"Aye, M'Lady." Akryd rode off without further comment, and Sasha pressed her heels to Peg's heaving sides once more, asking for no more than a walk. He gave her a trot regardless, and she patted his sweaty neck.

Banneryd prisoners were being marched from the trees down onto the fields, flanked by mounted warriors. Bodies lay strewn beneath the trees— mainly Banneryd, but not entirely. A horse kicked feebly in a pool of blood . . . Sasha rode past, unable to persuade herself to do more, but Tassi dismounted briefly, drawing her sword. All the serrin rode silently, surveying the carnage with expressionless stares. This was foreign in Saalshen, this violence—at least since the invasion of King Leyvaan. Probably it was the first time any of them had seen its like, on this scale. Well . . . they weren't the only ones. She felt utterly numb now that the blood-pumping fury had left her. For the first time in her life, she was not entirely certain of her own emotional state. It scared her.

She rode Peg through a gap in the row of defensive stakes, the earth torn by the charge of hundreds of hooves. Here were more slain men and horses, mostly arrow-struck. Some horses still kicked and struggled, pitifully, but this time Tassi remained mounted. This, perhaps, was too much for even the most disciplined serrin warrior. Riderless horses wandered, while others were held in groups by soldiers. Quite a few soldiers were tending to the wounded and searching along the grassy hillside for those still living, checking each fallen body in turn. The reserve, Sasha realised, recognising several—they had followed behind and halted here where they were most needed.

She saw one man, a Verenthane, with short hair and an eight-pointed medallion upon his chest, kneeling by a fallen comrade. He was weeping. His comrade's long hair fell about the man's legs, the motionless head in his lap, sightless eyes gazing skyward from within a spirit-mask of intricate dark curls.

Then Sasha saw a horse she recognised and rode across the slope toward where several soldiers had gathered three wounded so far, and were attempting to aid them. Others carried a fourth even now, an arrow in his stomach, and resisting strangled screams at the pain. Jaryd was assisting as best he could, one-armed. A slim girl in pants and a jacket knelt by another man who was struggling to breathe, a shaft in his chest. She clutched his hand tightly in her own, whilst trying to pour water from a skin into his mouth, waiting for those treating the next man in line to find time to move on.

Without a word, the serrin dismounted and began unstrapping saddle-bags for their medicines. "Sofy?" Sasha said hoarsely, still in her saddle. From within the walls of Ymoth, there came now the sounds of battle, cries and clashing steel. The smell of blood was everywhere, and the sweat of horses. Sofy did not look up. "Sofy, I'd rather you weren't here. There could be a counterattack any moment, this is still hostile land and you're right on the field they'll come from."

Sofy looked up. Her face was pale, her brown hair windblown and tangled. Blood specked her cheek. Her eyes, strangled with emotion, also burned with something deeper, and far, far harder than Sasha had ever seen before. "Go and win the war, Sasha," the youngest princess of Lenayin said quietly. Her voice quavered, but only a little. "Go and give orders elsewhere. I'm busy."

Nineteen

"RYSHA, YOU HAVE TO STAY WITH ESSEY! It's dangerous!" Daryd had left Essey in the grassy enclosure within the walls, now crowded with other horses. Everywhere there were foreign soldiers, shouting orders, mustering horses by the enclosure's stream for a drink, searching for feed. There were clusters of prisoners, stacks of weapons and armour, and the occasional dead body—although mostly the fighting had not spread this deeply into town.

"I want to see Mama and Papa!" Rysha shouted at him, very upset.

"Rysha, no!" Daryd was so frustrated, and so scared. How could he explain to a little girl? How could he make her see without terrifying her? "Look, there's bad men all through the town, it's not safe for you! Stay here with Essey where there are good men to look after you . . ."

"No, no, no!" Rysha yelled, her eyes tearing up. "I want to see Mama and Papa! I'll go without you, I will!"

Daryd knew it was no idle threat—cautious Rysha did not make threats unless she meant it. He gritted his teeth. "Okay . . . come on."

He took her hand and ducked through the timber fence. The town looked so achingly familiar . . . and yet so different. Timber houses, and some stone ones, to either side of narrow, paved streets. Many gardens were damaged, fences destroyed, fruit trees stripped of their bounty. Some houses were missing windows . . . and he saw with shock as they rounded a corner that where Yuan Wenys's house had stood, there now lay a crumbled, charred ruin.

Rysha gasped. "Yuan Wenys is going to be so angry!" Daryd pulled her aside as some soldiers came running up the path. Down some steps, Daryd saw a pair of boots sticking out from the bushes surrounding the house of Yuan Fershyn. He pulled Rysha on quickly, but Rysha spared the body barely a glance. "Daryd, where is Yuan Wenys?"

"I don't know, Rysha." Daryd tried to keep the fear from his voice. "I think he'll be in the valley, Mama and Papa too."

"Why can't they be here?" Rysha protested, as if about to cry once more. "I want to see them now!"

Oh please, please, please don't let them be here, Daryd wished at the spirits, harder than he had ever wished anything before in his life. Please let them have escaped.

The stream that ran through the heart of Ymoth was crowded with soldiers, some walking, some resting, some drinking from waterskins. Daryd wondered why they weren't drinking from the stream like Papa always did when he returned from the training hall across the little bridge. Grasping Rysha's hand more tightly, he half ran along the streamside, past the front verandahs of familiar wooden houses, past Mrs. Karnysh's berry bushes, past the old tree that leaned out over the stream. The swinging rope still dangled above the water. He'd thought he was so brave the first time he'd swung on that rope. But now he realised that he hadn't truly known what bravery was.

And then it was there, their house by the stream bend with a good view over the main wall, and a glimpse of the wide Yumynis beyond. The fruit trees were bare, but the yard seemed intact . . . Rysha dragged at him, desperately, but he refused to release her hand. There were a pair of soldiers sitting on the verandah, helmets in hand, looking sweaty and tired.

"Mama!" Rysha cried as they leapt the stair and pushed in the front door. "Mama! Papa!" The front room was a mess, the table overturned, chairs broken. Mama's kitchen pots were smashed, the contents of shelves strewn across the floor. Papa's swords were missing from their wall rack, however, and most of the pots and pans were too. Mama and Papa must have taken them, Daryd thought with a surge of unspeakable relief. They must have taken what they could and headed for the valley. The men would have defended the bridge and bought time for the women and children. More warriors would have come from the valley to help—he'd heard his father talking about it with other men before, all the plans they'd made in case of attack. Surely that was where they all were now.

They searched the rest of the house and the rear yard, but found only ransacked rooms and torn vegetable plots. When they returned to the main room, Rysha was in speechless tears. "I *told* you, Rysha, they've gone to the wall!" Daryd insisted. "They'll be safe there. It's *good* they're not here, it wasn't safe here."

He looked up, realising the two soldiers had followed them into the main room. One was Goeren-yai, with long hair and tattoos, the other short-haired with a Verenthane medallion. Both looked concerned. The Verenthane asked him a question, indicating the house around them. "This is your house?" he seemed to be asking.

"Aye, this is our house," Daryd replied, helplessly. Had all the other villagers escaped also? All his aunts and uncles, nephews and nieces? Smyt the blacksmith? Agry the farmer's son, who was a bit funny in the head, and his right arm didn't work properly, but who was always cheerful and smiling when Daryd went to market to buy vegetables for Mama's cooking? Old Mrs. Calwyn and her many rabbits? He didn't know, he just didn't know . . .

The two soldiers exchanged grim looks. The Goeren-yai said something else, beckoning Daryd to come. Something in his manner was very serious and his gesture was not that of an adult to a child, but more the invitation of one man to another. The Verenthane soldier came and scooped up Rysha, who cried on his shoulder, having lost all fear of Verenthanes somewhere along the ride, especially after long days in the company of Princess Sofy. Daryd went with the Goeren-yai soldier, who led him from the house, the other man following close behind with Rysha.

They walked downstream, past soldiers and the broken debris that had been the streamside market stall. The stream, Daryd noticed, was red. Men must have died in the water, further uphill. When they reached the main gate in the defensive wall, Daryd could barely recognise it. The training hall, which had stood beside the gate, was a pile of ash and charred timbers. The big trees that had surrounded the hall, and shaded it beneath wide branches on a summer's day, were strangely scarred, the bark torn in a series of half-circular cuts. And there were big iron nails driven into the trunks, with chains dangling from them.

On the other side of the gate, also against the big wall, the stables and adjoining barn still stood. Some soldiers had gathered there, standing about some limp things on the ground. Daryd's soldier escort led him that way. Some of the other soldiers saw, and stood aside for him.

They were bodies, Daryd saw. Mostly naked, dirty and bloody. He stood over the nearest, barely recognising it as a person. It had tattoos and dirty, long hair. Suddenly he recognised the grass-spirit tattoo spiralling up the right arm. It was Farmer Tangryn. Or rather, it had been Farmer Tangryn. Farmer Tangryn had been a strong man, but the corpse's ribs were showing. And he didn't smell. There were scars on his wrists where they'd bound him. And a stab wound through the ribs. Probably they'd killed all the prisoners as soon as the attack began.

Daryd was amazed at how calm he was. Everything seemed surreal. All the soldiers were looking at him with grim expectation. They knew what this was. Well, Daryd thought, so did he. He'd heard the stories of the Catastrophe, since as far back as he could remember. He knew what the Hadryn did to Udalyn prisoners.

There were five other bodies. Three he could not recognise. Two were Mrs. Castyl, who lived nearer the upper slope, and old Yuan Angy, who still liked to spear fish in the river shallows on a warm day, despite his years. No more, it seemed.

Daryd turned back toward the pile of ashes that had been the training hall. Men were sifting through the rubble, poking with swords. Even now, a man found something metal and examined it—a ring, Daryd thought. He stepped across to a comrade and dropped the ring in an upturned helmet that man carried. Soon another man found something else and did the same. Then another man found a further object and picked it up, reverently. He carried it from the ashes, as his fellow searchers made spirit signs or holy signs, and placed it on the ground, where it formed the latest in a long line of similar objects. Human skulls. There were at least twenty. The northerners hadn't just burned the training hall, they'd put people in it first.

Still . . . Ymoth and its surrounding region had close to two thousand. This here was just twenty-five people, maybe thirty. Surely most of them had escaped. Surely these were just the unlucky few who had been caught in the wrong place at the wrong time. His gaze shifted back to the big tree. He knew what the scars were now—whip marks. His people would have been chained to that tree, tortured and mutilated, until . . . until what? What could they have told their torturers? There was no great wealth hidden around Ymoth. As for the valley's defences, well . . . they hadn't changed much since the last time the Hadryn attacked a hundred years ago. What could the northerners possibly have gained by doing such things to his people?

Soldiers pushed a man forward, arms twisted behind his back. The prisoner had the blond hair of many northerners—a man in his thirties, but no company soldier. He wore good, arm-length chain mail, heavy boots and hard leather leggings, but his surcoat bore the crest of a noble house. A nobleman. Daryd had heard of them, too. Strange ways, the Verenthanes had, to place one man above another by birth. Master Jaryd was a nobleman too, he'd gathered. But Master Jaryd would never give the orders that this man had given.

The soldiers yelled questions at the nobleman and hit him, pointing to the bodies. The northerner snarled in contempt. Said something, shortly, and spat near the bodies. One of the soldiers raised his weapon in fury, but another stopped him. Took his own sword and offered it to Daryd. Daryd looked at the sword. At the cold, hateful northern face. At the bodies on the ground and the ashpile by the wall.

Then he strode forward, ignoring the offered sword, and drew his knife instead. Soldiers forced the northerner to his knees. Daryd stepped to one side, as he'd once seen Udalyn warriors do to a captured Hadryn raider. Then he cut the man's throat with a single, hard slash. Blood spurted and flowed.

Soldiers held the man up, then let him collapse. He kicked and spluttered, then went limp.

Daryd stared down at the corpse. It had been so easy. He'd always imagined it would be harder than that. He felt no elation, no surge of satisfied revenge. Yet he felt no regret, either. If there were more northerners present, he'd have killed them too. He'd seen what they'd done to his people, and he now knew for certain what it would mean, in this battle, for his people to lose. Killing was easy. Living, it seemed, was the hard part.

He wiped his knife on the back of his victim, and sheathed it. Men regarded him with hard, thoughtful eyes. When he walked to the ashpile, to view the remains of villagers he'd once known, no man moved to accompany him, or guide him, or pat him on the head. His Wakening remained many years away, yet his blade had tasted the blood of enemies. He was not yet a man, but today, Daryd Yuvenar was no longer a child.

Captain Tyrun was dead. Sasha stood in the central courtyard of Ymoth. Tyrun's body lay upon a low stone dais, hands folded on his breast, wrapped in his cloak to hide the drenching blood. A crowd of men had gathered and a light, misting rain fell from a bleak and weary sky. From the surrounding town, there carried the yells and instructions of men searching from house to house. But here, there was silence.

A Verenthane corporal from the Falcon Guard, who was learned in the ways of the temple, performed the Verenthane rites. Tyrun had been carried directly to this place from before the Ymoth wall, and this assembly had gathered fast, lacking any time for delay. He had been killed, men said, in the opening moments of the charge, when the formation he had been leading had plowed into the Banneryd flank. Tyrun had cut down one man, fended a second, then been struck by a third. It had happened so fast, a stunned sergeant had said. Northern cavalry were superbly skilled, even in such dire circumstances. Many men of those forward ranks had been lost before the Banneryd had been driven back.

At Sasha's side, Jaryd stood impassive and pale. Men of the Falcon Guard, in particular, appeared shocked. Sasha worried for them. And worried for the entire campaign, to have lost its true commander so early. She was the figurehead, perhaps, but this victory was surely Tyrun's. Without him keeping things together, and offering sage advice, she'd have been hopelessly lost from the first. But she dared not suggest such a thing, lest the men lose hope. She dared not shed a tear, lest the men recall that she was, after all, just a girl, whoever her absent uman might be.

The Verenthane corporal completed his rites, and stepped back. Then from the crowd came Jaegar—still alive, Sasha had discovered to her immense relief, as were all her Baerlyn friends. They had been in the rear half of Captain Akryd's attack and had escaped the initial casualties with barely a scratch. The luck of it all stunned her. Some villages had lost numerous men by simply being in the wrong place at the wrong time. Others were unscathed. It was outrageously unfair. And she recalled, suddenly, Kessligh's tired derision of her occasional statements of moral certitude. "Nothing's fair," he'd told her. "Fairness is an invention of ours. One day, you'll understand that."

Jaegar was stripped to the waist. Tattoos spiralled down his enormous chest and made rippling patterns upon the six outstanding segments of his stomach. He swaggered to stand behind Tyrun's body, a sword in his right hand, a knife in his left. His hair hung free of its braid, flowing loose upon massive shoulders. The right side of his face—the side clear of tattoos—was streaked with three red lines, beside which his tri-braid hung. Not only Chieftain of Baerlyn, Jaegar was Umchyl—spirit talker—for the town and its regions.

Now, Jaegar extended his arms, surveying the crowd with the stern, wide eyes of power. "Umchyl!" the Goeren-yai chanted. "Umchyl! Umchyl!" The arms extended out, then back, and Jaegar thumped himself on the shoulders, wrists crossed at the heart, with the hilts of his blades. Once, twice, and fortunate-three times.

"This day shall mark the passing of many great warriors!" Jaegar announced, in the slow, lilting chant of ceremonial Lenay. He stared about at the crowd, blades extended, muscles and tattoos rippling. He looked like a god. Sasha found herself staring, spellbound. "One shall be appointed to lead them to the next world! Who here shall bear witness?"

"Umchyl! Umchyl! Umchyl!"

"This, our brother, was named Tyrun! He was born to the town of Banyth, in the province of Tyree! His was a wife, and his were three children! He did serve his family with honour, and his was the honour brought to his town, and his people! He was brought before his spirits by his father, and his spirits were the gods of Verenthane! To those spirits did he present his soul, and they did find him worthy!"

"Wor-thy! Wor-thy! Wor-thy!" Sasha found herself joining in. This, she had heard before.

"We are gathered today upon the ground of a great victory! The great peoples of Lenayin have joined together and brought honour in their unity!

The great gods of Verenthane are strong! The great spirits of the Goeren-yai are strong! But together are they strongest, and most honourable! We are gathered today before the loyal men of Verenthane . . ." and here Jaegar's sword pointed to Jaryd, "and before the brave men of the Goeren-yai . . . !" and his blade swept across the vast crowd behind, "and before the wise ones of Saalshen . . ." as the blade pointed to Sasha's left, where the four serrin stood entranced upon the edge of the dark stone, "and before the dark power of the ancient Synnich!"

The blade pointed at Sasha. A hiss escaped the lips of the Goeren-yai, and the rustling murmur of many spirit signs being made. Sasha stared back at Jaegar. She didn't quite believe he'd done that to her in front of all these people. Surely Jaegar had never thought of her in that way. Had he?

"Let them be joined in the sky as they are on the earth! Tyrun of Banyth shall lead and the fallen of Ymoth shall follow, Goeren-yai and Verenthane together, as brothers! Who shall bear witness to this journey?"

A wordless cheer followed, full of passion, fists thrust in the air. Repeated, twice, and then the crowd began to disperse. Horses were being watered in large groups down by the river, surviving barns and warehouses were being searched for any remaining feed, and as the afternoon darkened toward evening, there were many things yet to do. But they walked now with a greater purpose in their step than they had approached this gathering, having learned of Tyrun's death.

Jaegar was putting his undershirt back on, his mailshirt spread at his feet. Sasha walked up to him. "I wish you hadn't done that," she murmured. The bit about the Synnich, she meant.

"Would you deny it?" Jaegar replied, eyebrows raised. Sasha looked at her feet, unable to answer that. Daring not to, lest men who put their faith in her overhear and lose hope. And . . . and . . . for some other reason, too, that she could not truly define. "Besides," Jaegar continued, bending to gather his mail, "they needed to hear it. Now more than ever." He held the shirt up, effortlessly despite its considerable weight, and slid it on.

Sasha turned then to look for Jaryd, and found him standing by Tyrun's body. She walked over and put a hand on his arm. "Come," she said softly. "You are Commander of the Falcon Guard now, for true and proper. It will not do for your men to see you grieving."

"Yet I grieve all the same," said Jaryd. His voice was tight as he gazed down at Tyrun's impassive, silent face. "I am not half the commander he was. I was guarding the princess. I did not lead in this battle. I did not lead in any battle."

"You are wounded," Sasha replied, trying to be reasonable. "You cannot be expected to . . ."

"Nothing can be expected of me," Jaryd said bitterly. "I am nothing. I was angry at my family's so-called friends for stripping me of everything that I had. Now, I wonder if I ever truly was anything. Perhaps father knew best when he called me worthless. Perhaps Family Nyvar could never truly have amounted to anything with me at its head. The only thing I was ever good at was riding and fighting, and now when the last people left in the world whom I love require my assistance, I can't even do that."

"Captain Tyrun is dead, and you take the opportunity to feel sorry for yourself," Sasha said angrily. She felt for Jaryd's suffering, but she simply didn't have time for this now. "You look around you, Jaryd. You look hard. Many families have ended here, and more tragedies unfolded than I care to count. These men fight for something bigger than themselves or their families. If you can't feel that, if you can't understand what it was that Tyrun died for, then maybe you'd be better elsewhere."

Jaryd stared at her, his jaw tight, his stare as hard as stone. "If my services are not required," he said coldly, "then I shall leave."

"Your services?" Sasha replied, incredulously. "What do you believe in, Jaryd? Why be here, if not for a cause?"

"I believe in nothing. My family is no more, and my brother is dead. All the ideals of Verenthane brotherhood and Lenay honour I had been taught to believe are lies."

"Then why *are* you still here? Why come this far at all?"

Jaryd looked down at Tyrun. The lateness of the day cast all colour, all life, all joy to shadow. The light, falling mist gathered at the tips of his lank hair as it fell about his face. "The Falcon Guard are all I have left," Jaryd said quietly. "Yet with this arm, I cannot serve them."

"Then just be here to pick up their wounded when they fall!" Sasha retorted. "Jaryd, you're . . . you're such an arrogant, pigheaded . . . *man*!" It was, for the moment, the worst insult she could think of. "You're so accustomed to the glory, and the place in the lead, that you can't see the honour in following. Just *be* there! That's what old Cranyk in Baerlyn told me, he said it was the greatest lesson he had to teach about life. Just turn up!"

Her vanguard were waiting for her, and her officers were moving further downhill into the town. From somewhere in the town, a cry went up. "Usyn's coming! Usyn's coming!" And not before time, either. Sasha placed a final, gentle hand on Jaryd's arm and departed after them in haste. Master Jaryd, of the family once known as Nyvar, stood over the body of his captain in the misting rain. He stood with his weight on one leg, a dark sentinel amidst the sudden confusion of shouts, yells and hasty preparations. If he noticed, or feared, he gave no sign.

Sasha, Captain Akryd and other officers, either from the line companies or appointed from amongst village chiefs, gathered on the field beyond the main gate of Ymoth's wall. Men were leading horses back from the river in great groups as others ran to retrieve them. The air was filled with yells of instruction and question, galloping hooves and the urgent whinnying of horses who knew that something more was afoot. The fields nearby remained littered with dead, mostly Banneryd, as men continued even now to reclaim the bodies of comrades, and check to see if any still lived. Already the grey sky had grown dim with the approach of evening, and Sasha thanked the spirits that it was late summer still and the days remained long.

"The road comes like thus," Jurellyn was saying, drawing a line with his sword on a patch of bare turf amidst the grass, "upon the other side of the river. It's not far, as you can see. He'll be here by nightfall. My best guess is that he has six thousand in the valley—half cavalry, half infantry. This column seems also half-and-half, cavalry to the front and rear, infantry in the middle. But being stretched so long upon the road, we could not see the column's end, so we have no means of guessing their number."

"Well," said Captain Akryd, with a thoughtful glance across the Ymoth wall and the fields about, "these defences will serve us better than they did the Banneryd. Usyn won't have dussieh riding with him, he'll be unable to exploit the gaps in the line. We've received another several hundred men riding over the Shudyn Divide just since the attack commenced. Usyn won't attack at night and we can still sneak riders from the Shudyn through the back woods and into the town. Half the Goeren-yai with horses across central Lenayin are coming to our aid. Most upon the Shudyn will ride through the night, knowing the battle has commenced ahead. By dawn, we could number nearly five thousand, despite our losses. Defender's advantage shall be with us. Usyn may have six thousand, and cavalry of a greater quality, but ours are entirely cavalry, and we have the defence. He shall not overrun us."

Conversation flowed, terse and urgent. Men discussed possible deployments, weak spots and guard posts from which to observe Usyn's forces through the night. Sasha stared at Jurellyn's lines in the bare turf, thinking furiously. Then stared up, gazing north up the Yumynis River toward the valley mouth looming beneath the darkening sky.

Defender's advantage. Cavalry shock. Such were the established norms of Lenay warfare. Kessligh employed all such terms . . . and then, in the next breath, disparaged them. It had frustrated her, listening to his lessons. He was always so contradictory. Nothing he'd told her was ever guaranteed, and written in stone. But now . . . dussieh racing through the narrow folds in the defensive line. Charging through the spaces between sharpened stakes. The Banneryd line, once so impenetrable, had been outflanked. The cavalry, at one moment charging downhill with advantage behind them, the next, blindsided, outnumbered, broken and overwhelmed.

An advantage was not always an advantage. A weakness was not always weak. What had Kessligh told her? She recalled a training session beneath the vertyn tree. She couldn't have been any more than twelve, as the stanch had felt huge in her hands. Kessligh had spent much of the lesson demonstrating to her the variations on the low right-quarter defence. The combinations were seemingly endless, depending on the nature of the attack and what one wished to do next, one, two, three or even more moves into the future. But there were ground rules, basic principles that all combinations had in common. He had drilled her on them, endlessly and, slowly, she'd found her selection and execution improving.

Then he'd asked her to attack him so he could demonstrate how one could improvise when one had mastered the fundamentals. After several exchanges, she'd thought of an attack that was particularly cunning and involved a feint she'd seen Kessligh himself use against men at the Baerlyn training hall. Kessligh had responded with a defence-to-offence combination that had been like nothing he'd previously been demonstrating and had knocked her firmly on her backside. She had protested—not so much at the rough treatment, for at that age she'd still been so utterly in awe of Kessligh's swordwork that even a beating could be a delight—but that he'd just spent all that time with her teaching her exactly why she shouldn't be doing it like *that*.

He'd given her one of his rare, wry yet genuinely amused smiles. "I never thought I'd see the day when you, of all people, would complain of someone *else* not playing by the rules," he'd told her, yanking her effortlessly to her feet. "That's why I teach you these rules. It's not so you can follow them religiously. It's so that one day, you'll learn when, and how, they can be broken."

"This land here," she asked Jurellyn, pointing to an area of road not far north of Ymoth toward the valley. "What is this like?"

"Some fields of ripe grain and some fallow." Jurellyn was looking at her intently, his eyes narrowed. Jurellyn had known Kessligh from the Great War. Perhaps he guessed at her thoughts. Some of the other men were breaking off their discussions to listen.

"Could we ride on them?" Sasha asked. "A large force, in a charge?"

Jurellyn nodded. "Not easily, the fallow ground is a little rough and the grain fields are near what should be harvest. There are fences nearly hidden. But yes, it's possible."

"M'Lady, no," Akryd said firmly, and with some alarm. "We've good defences here and it'll shortly be dark. That's maybe three thousand Hadryn heavy cavalry out there—they like the open ground, each of them is possibly twice the quality of our average cavalryman, they'd just love to meet us away from these walls where they can do what they do best. Absolutely no, we should stay put."

"We have no archers," Sasha replied, fixing him with a hard stare. She was not certain where this sudden burst of conviction had come from. But it was there, nonetheless. "A defence without archers is like a feast without ale—utterly pointless. The Hadryn will reach our defences in perfect order and shall do to us what they will. We shall lose all initiative and will become their playthings, free to toy with as they please until my dear brother arrives, whereupon we can all get down on our knees and beg him to save us from this siege."

"M'Lady . . ." Akryd began in exasperation, but Sasha cut him off.

"Furthermore, their infantry is strong and well drilled, and they *can* mount an infantry assault through the wooded foothills, although slowly, as we could not do with cavalry. We would be forced to divert large numbers of soldiers away from our forward defences, leaving them pitifully thin, and we just saw what happens here when the flanks are stretched so badly." There were some thoughtful nods from some men at that. She could see them thinking, picturing. Others looked unconvinced. "An attack in the open is not what Usyn expects . . ."

"With good reason!" Akryd retorted, with no little sarcasm.

". . . but he is all strung out upon the road and he has no formation." Sasha finished, determinedly. Some of the thoughtful looks had become intent. She had those with her, at least. "We'll spring the trap, and he won't have time to form up his flanks! What's more, he's an arrogant little snot, he believes in the tales of the Hadryn cavalry's invincibility just as much as some others do . . ." with a pointed stare at Akryd, who was now beginning to look angry, "and I'm convinced the Udalyn have not yet fallen or he would have been here already. Some of his forces will have remained behind to keep the Udalyn trapped behind their wall so that he can return to finish them later. I'm betting he won't even be at full strength. After all, we're just a pagan, or pagan-loving, rabble of limp-wristed southerners led by a girl. What threat could we possibly be?"

That got a grim laugh from some. "He'd not have needed to leave many behind," said one of those, "he's only guarding one gate in the Udalyn wall."

Sasha shrugged. "Aye. Maybe a few hundred horse and some archers, that would block one gate, given the Udalyn only have dussieh and aren't much renowned for cavalry anyway. The Udalyn might overwhelm them with a full-scale breakout, but I'll bet they've guessed what's happened, now they've seen Usyn turn tail and leave, and will wait for the result. They'll hope that Usyn will lose men in this fight, leaving him unable to breach the wall. Better yet, if we win and drive him back into the valley, he's stuck with a wall at his back and a huge mob of angry Udalyn behind it."

Some of the men were nodding now, openly. "It's what Kessligh would have done," Jurellyn opined. "Don't give them a break, keep it moving all the time."

"He could retreat east if beaten," another said doubtfully. "Rather than into the valley."

"That land's impossible," Jurellyn answered. "These ridges run down from the Nyfaal Range here that forms the valley's eastern ridge . . ." he demonstrated with his sword, more lines in the dirt, "all the way out to here. To escape the valley with any kind of a force, one must follow the river. The key to the river is Ymoth, and we hold it."

"M'Lady," Akryd tried one last time, "we've no time to plan an ambush. Usyn is nearly upon us, and . . ."

Sasha jabbed at a spot upon the line that marked the riverbank. "Here," she said. "Jurellyn, this bank is wooded, yes?"

"Aye, M'Lady. Mostly broadleaf, nearest the river. Plenty of under-growth, not good for riding warhorses, certainly not in numbers. But dussieh could ride there. I have. You could put . . . oh, hundreds there. Maybe a thousand. Wouldn't see them from the road."

"We'll do that," she said with certainty. "Every dussieh in the ranks. They'll cut the line in half, we'll smash them head-on. Agreed?" Looking about the group. Some voiced their assent, loudly. Others murmured it, reluctantly. Several remained silent. Akryd was one. "Agreed?" Sasha repeated, looking at him firmly.

"Aye," Akryd sighed, with the air of a man doomed to an unpleasant fate. "Aye, M'Lady. We will at that."

Twenty

SASHA SAT ASTRIDE HER HORSE in the middle of the road that wound along the right bank of the Yumynis River. The sky was dull with early twilight, yet somewhere beyond the western mountains, there seemed to be a break in the clouds. Beyond Ymoth, peaks glowed yellow on their far sides, as if silhouetted with light. Low-angled rays fell upon the mouth of the Udalyn Valley ahead, and those craggy slopes seemed to glow.

To either side of the road lay vast fields of grain with pale green stalks and golden heads. They rippled in the light wind, moving swathes of colour in the glow from the further mountains. To her left, the Yumynis flowed wide and gentle, rugged forests encroaching upon its rocky left bank where the foothills came directly down to the river. Poplar and willow continued to line the banks and Sasha wondered if they had been planted long ago by human hand and maintained all this time.

Ahead, majestic upon the riverbank, was an exquisite pagoda of beautiful arches, apparently well maintained. Talleryn symbols climbed the supporting posts, a foreign, strange script whose shapes seemed to repeat through the form of the structure itself. This was a culture enlightened, yet almost lost. This, surely, was worth fighting for.

Behind her, across the fields of grain, stretched the forward rank of an army. Warhorses waited now more calmly than before, greatly tired from the day's exertions. Many nibbled at the grain as they waited. Soon, much of these unharvested fields would be destroyed. A necessary sacrifice, she hoped. To the rear, a new reserve was gathered, and once again Sofy was with them. Sasha had considered leaving her at Ymoth . . . but again, Ymoth was badly exposed to raids from Hadryn villagers to the east, its garrison held by fewer than a hundred men. Thankfully, Usyn's forces had brought with them plenty of chain and manacles, enough to bind most of the Banneryd who had surrendered. Two new men protected Sofy in the reserve. Where Jaryd was, no one knew.

Peg shifted tiredly beneath her and tossed his head, with somewhat less than his usual vigour. Those men tasked with caring for the horses had managed to get him a drink, some feed, and a very basic wash to remove the dried froth and sweat, but nothing more. She leaned forward now and rubbed his neck.

"I'm sorry," she told him, to the backward, attentive twist of one ear. "I know you're tired. Just a little more. One more charge, Peglyrion, son of Hyathon the Warrior. Then you can rest."

There was a gentle rise in the fields ahead. Beyond it, she could hear the distant roll of many hooves, drawing slowly near. Usyn was marching fast, wishing to make camp before the walls of Ymoth prior to nightfall. Surely he'd had scouts enough to tell him that Ymoth had fallen. Jurellyn's latest report had said that his line was much wider than the road, and trampled much of the grain on either side . . . but still, not a combat-ready formation. Jurellyn's men had killed several Hadryn scouts just recently and it was unlikely Usyn knew of her latest move. In scouts, at least, Sasha knew that her column possessed a clear advantage, both in number and talent. Usyn sacrificed caution for haste and gambled that they wouldn't dare attack the Hadryn heavy horse on open ground. This had to work. Surely it would.

She felt strangely calm, unlike before the previous charge. Fatalistic, perhaps. Maybe that should have worried her—in all the great tales of doomed heroes in battle, all had accepted their fate before the end and faced it without fear. Sasha gazed at the mountains that flanked the valley mouth ahead, all alight in a golden glow, and felt that surely there was something here at work that was not of any merely human plane.

"Are you there?" she thought toward the valley. "The valley of the Udalyn is said to be the home of many great Lenay spirits. Where is my Synnich spirit hiding? They call me the Synnich, but I cannot hear you. Speak to me."

Riders moved up on her sides—her four surviving vanguard riders from the first charge, plus two new ones. Or no, she realised, looking around—four new ones. There riding up behind, were Errollyn, Terel, Tassi and Aisha. Errollyn stopped at her side. He too gazed at the golden valley beyond. His handsome face was serene.

"You don't need to come, you know," Sasha told him.

Errollyn smiled, and gave a faint shrug. "We chose to," he said simply. "We," Errollyn had said, with complete certainty. Sasha recalled the battle just past. The effortless coordination, the serrin guiding their horses in unison. Tassi distracting one Banneryd's attention, while Aisha killed him from the other side. "And we were appointed by the others. They saw we protected you in the last battle, and wished us to do the same in this one. We accepted the honour."

"Can you tell each other's thoughts?" Sasha asked, feeling suddenly curious. It seemed a good time to ask. Suddenly, she wished she had asked a great many more questions than she had. Of many people, and many things.

Errollyn spared her a curious, green-eyed glance. "A question of debate, amongst the serrinim," he conceded. "The *vel'ennar* is not what you suggest. And yet, in some ways, perhaps it is." The *vel'ennar*. Another Saalsi term for which there was no direct translation into any human tongue Sasha was aware of. The "single spirit," perhaps. Or maybe the "great soul." Something singular, and yet divided. And so like the serrin, to take seemingly contradictory concepts and twine them together to make a whole.

Sasha snorted in amusement. "I bet I couldn't get a straight answer from a serrin on his deathbed."

Errollyn's smile spread wide. Stunningly. "The world is not simple," he said coyly. "To value the chaos is to value life."

"Difficult people," Sasha teased.

Errollyn shrugged. "We cannot help but be what we are, any more than humans can."

"I am glad of it," Sasha said softly. "The world would be a far poorer place without the serrinim. It has occurred to me very slowly, over the last few days, just what some of these people see in me. The Goeren-yai *and* the Verenthanes. Tyrun insisted that I was the only person to lead this column. Teriyan too, and others. At first I was angry. I thought *surely* they could find someone else. But I've thought about it, and I concede I can't think of anyone."

Errollyn's gaze was intensely curious. His stare held a force that only a serrin could wield. "Why do you think?" he asked.

"To be a leader of both the faiths is difficult, I suppose," said Sasha. "In this land, with our history. We are a divided land, if not by faith then by language and region. I think I understand better now why Kessligh had such faith in Lenay royalty, and in my father despite his flaws. Royalty is of no particular province, but of all Lenayin, and is, as such, a uniting force, not a dividing one. But then, royalty cannot unite everyone, especially when it is so strongly Verenthane, and does not treat the Goeren-yai fairly."

"But you are neither Verenthane nor Goeren-yai," Errollyn completed for her. He turned his gaze to the golden, sunlit mountains, as if drinking in their splendour. "Such was always the intention of the Nasi-Keth. To find a third way. That is you, Sashandra. I am certain Kessligh was aware of this. Perhaps it worried him. He always considered Petrodor and the Bacosh as the centre of all the world's troubles, the questions to which he wished to contribute. He went to Lenayin, in part, to find an uma untainted by Petrodor thinking and prejudices.

"But it seems he could not so easily separate the uma from her own world, and bring her into his. And that is the dilemma of us all, in the end. The dilemma of overlapping worlds. Each of our worlds is unique. Only where they come into contact with the worlds of others do they join, and find points of commonality."

Sasha frowned at him. "You know much about Kessligh," she observed.

Errollyn shrugged. "He is a son of the Petrodor docks. His once-neighbours still boast of the little boy who used to play in this yard, or practise swordwork in that alley. People talk of him often, and the latest news of his doings in the barbarian kingdom. They wonder as to his uma. She is reputed to be both wild and beautiful."

Sasha managed a faint smile. "Well," she said, with mock elegant decorum. "I suppose one out of two will do."

"No," Errollyn replied, also smiling, "you are beautiful too." Sasha scowled at him. Then smiled more broadly. How easy it was to talk to this serrin. Most serrin were nice, but many remained somewhat aloof, for all their charms. There was nothing aloof about Errollyn. For a serrin, he was blunt, direct and . . . "Did you dream of this valley?" he asked, before she could complete the thought.

Sasha blinked. "Dream? How can I dream of a place I've never visited?"

"A wide and open valley, with a river along the bottom. And a full moon in the sky, lighting all to silver." Sasha stared at him. He was . . . he was describing her dream . . . the dream she'd nearly forgotten, that she'd dismissed each time she'd awoken with it fresh in her memory . . . Errollyn's bright green eyes burned into her like nothing human. "You asked of the *vel'ennar*," he said softly, as the rolling approach of hooves beyond the rise ahead grew louder. "I am *du'janah*, a special uniqueness among serrin. The *vel'ennar* and I have a unique relationship. We serrin admire your Goeren-yai for a reason. In this land, we know where to come, and when. The spirits speak. Listen now. Your Synnich calls to you. You are almost home."

From hidden amongst the wheat further ahead, a signal came. Behind, the shouts of officers echoed across the formation. Swords came out. Sasha stared at Errollyn, small hairs prickling at the back of her neck.

Errollyn rested his bow upon his saddlehorn, and the swords of her vanguard and the other serrin also came out. "You are Goeren-yai, but you do not truly believe," he said. "Believe now. It is time."

From behind, there came a cheer, rippling slowly across the front rank. Sasha turned to look and saw Jaryd riding to their fore, both arms free and a sword in his right hand. He seemed to be steering his big chestnut mare with his heels and gentle tugs on the rein alone . . . but there was no way he could possibly handle the reins while wielding the sword. He'd come out here to die, Sasha realised. And she recalled what she'd said to him, standing by Tyrun's body, and regretted it.

But there was no time for regrets, she realised. By the end of this day, there would be more than enough regret to go around.

Sasha drew her sword. From behind, she could hear the blades coming out, a great, rasping ring. There was no need for a speech now. The battle had been underway since Ymoth. Now, they finished it. A man stood from the grain to the left and held an arm aloft. Sasha raised her blade and then dropped it. Peg snorted as she tapped her heels, and broke into a trot, then a canter. She held to the road, as behind, the great line of horses cut through the fields of grain, approaching the first fence.

They leaped it, and then the ridge ahead was fading and a huge, winding column of horseback warriors appeared, perhaps eight abreast on either side of the road. Black Hadryn banners flew against the golden mountains from which they'd come. Horns sounded and yells from ahead, rearward ranks accelerating to spill across the fields from the road, moving up to broaden the lines.

Sasha thumped Peg hard with her heels and yanked him into the grain— a difficult ride for a dussieh, perhaps, but the heads of the grain barely came past Peg's knees, and all of the column behind her were warhorses. Peg hurtled across the flat ground, the serrin and her vanguard to her sides, as behind, a great wall of charging animals decimated the golden fields beneath their tearing hooves. Sasha held Peg's speed enough to allow the line to catch up, timing the impending collision with a practised eye.

There came another roar as a mass of dussieh erupted from the riverside forest ahead and charged into the Hadryn column. Many of those Hadryn galloping up to the front now turned at this new attack, the great mass wheeling like a flock of birds against the sky. The ambush had been sprung. Still the Hadryn front line did not charge, holding back as more riders poured onto their flanks, widening the line . . . but now, the charging rebel line began to split, riders following Sasha's path to envelop the Hadryn column about the sides.

At the last moment, the Hadryn charged with a yell, the rebel line now closing directly on Sasha's heels, and overtaking her to either side in places . . . An arrow whistled past Sasha's ear from behind and skewered a Hadryn's shoulder directly ahead. The impact spun him half-about in the saddle, hauling his horse sideways, colliding with the next horse in line, and making that one rear aside. Sasha raced straight for the gap . . . and saw in the corner of her vision something dark and lithe racing alongside. It materialised into

Tassi, who leaned from her saddle with expert horsemanship to duck the other rider's blow whilst tearing him across the side with her blade.

Horses flashed by on either side, blades clashed, and riders fell in bloody impacts. Lightweight and unarmoured like the serrin, Sasha half fell from the saddle to go beneath one onrushing blow, then came up in time to swing and collect another across his shield, then ducked instinctively below a third as Peg shied away, probably saving her life as her head nearly hit the passing rider's knee.

And then, they were clear, and racing along the column's side—the Hadryn were too spaced out, trying to fan across the flanks but leaving huge gaps through their midst in the process. Rebel riders were thundering in much greater numbers, tearing along the roadside, diving between gaps in the ranks, slashing at Hadryn riders who defended valiantly one, two and then three blows with shield and sword, only to fall to the fourth and fifth as they flashed by. Errollyn was suddenly alongside, wheeling his horse back and forth for space, then finding a gap within which to load, draw and fire at startling speed, and send another Hadryn tumbling from the saddle. One came across his front unavoidably—Errollyn tore a short blade from a saddle-sheath, dodged and deflected that man's blow, then simply sheathed the blade and resumed his hunt for targets.

Sasha alerted Peg to the next approaching fence with her customary little tug of rein and tap of stirrups . . . and again there seemed to be a black shadow racing at her side. She leaped the fence, and the black shadow appeared to swing right, urgently. Sasha followed, cutting behind the flanks of Errollyn's horse . . . and saw the hidden tree stump amidst the grain flash by to the left, directly where she would have ridden into it. She waved her sword and pointed to alert those behind, who would in turn alert the next.

To the right, one of the vanguard riders clashed a defending Hadryn across the shield, distracting him enough for Terel to hack him blindsided from the saddle. And then they were amongst the dussieh riders, racing circles around the surviving Hadryn in that part of the line, where desperately outnumbered northerners had had no chance to form up. Sasha raced back toward the road and saw right-flank riders were doing the same upon the other side. The forward half of the Hadryn cavalry were encircled. Back at the roadside, she wheeled about and galloped back the way she'd come.

The Hadryn were now in a mess, and the bodies on the road and in the fields were mostly uniformed in black. Men fought and struggled desperately, some now wounded, as passing rebels hacked them from all sides. Sasha cut a backhand low across one wounded man's side, then crossed another man's front as if meaning to engage him—with his attention drawn and defences raised at her, the next rider behind killed him from the blindside. Riderless horses tore past in crazed panic and Sasha realised that there simply weren't enough Hadryn left along the road to make it worth continuing the charge.

She held up her blade and reined Peg to a halt. Wheeled him about to survey her surroundings—there were many Hadryn riders racing back toward their main column. Many were fanning wide, small figures against the east-ward forest, or the western forest that bordered the river, far off across the fields. It was possible, she realised, that quite a lot had escaped that way, real-ising they'd been overrun.

She stood in her stirrups and waved her sword for attention. "Form up!" she yelled. "Form up!" Then a vanguard rider was alongside with his royal banner, waving it madly. Sasha brought Peg to a trot along the road, as offi-cers yelled, and weapons were waved, and men brought their horses wheeling across the fields, abandoning their pursuit of the fleeing Hadryn to reform the line in her wake. Many now were dussieh riders, and more were racing away from the main Hadryn column, having no wish to face that countercharge alone. If the middle and rear portions of the Hadryn column had merely come racing to their comrades' aid, then the Hadryn were finished. If, however, they had shown patience as their comrades were slaughtered, and had taken the time to form a second line, then the battle would be far from over.

Looking about, Sasha saw Errollyn unstringing his bow and sliding it back beneath his leg—the top half bore a deep cut, and clearly would not take the weight of a full draw. He pulled his blade instead. Nearby also were Tassi and Terel. She could not see Aisha, but had no time to worry about that now. Ahead, the remaining riders were clearing—the dussieh riders toward Sasha's line, the Hadryn back toward the north. There was indeed a Hadryn line forming . . . yet it was disorganised and chaotic, stretching wide across the fields and fractured in places. It was blocked by wheeling mobs of riders and appeared to be mostly comprised of infantry in the middle. Here was a chance, but it was quickly fading. They had to form up fast. Too long, and the Hadryn defensive line would become an impenetrable wall of armoured men and cavalry, against which her exhausted, lighter cavalry would dash themselves like waves upon a cliff.

She stood in her stirrups and half turned. "Through the centre!" she yelled. "Get those infantry! Split them down the middle and they'll run like sheep!"

Officers repeated the order, and yells echoed further out toward the flanks. Sasha waited for three repeats, and charged. Peg heaved himself tiredly into a gallop, great limbs now heavy where they had once been sprightly. There was fear in his every sinew, his eyes rolling, his ears far back

. . . and yet he ran straight toward that shield-fronted line that bristled with sharp things that cut, simply because she asked him to. Sasha loved him as much at that moment as she had ever loved anything.

A sudden burst of wind tore across the fields, whipping the grain ahead of the racing line. It howled into the Hadryn, as horses whinnied and reared, and the front ranks of infantry hid their heads behind their shields to keep the swirling debris of hoof-torn grain from their eyes. The Hadryn cavalry tried to charge, uneven and ragged. The infantry stood firm, crouched behind their shields. Suddenly the air was full of whistling arrowfire, men and horses to the flanks and rear falling. The shields raced closer, a wall like any fence, and Peg simply leapt, straight over their heads.

He came down in their midst, men trying to scatter, hooves plowing into bodies as soldiers were flung spinning like tops on all sides, others diving flat for cover . . . Peg lost balance as he tried to gather, front legs flailing as he hit another several men, Sasha riding the saddle down with a desperate grip. He hit and rolled with incredible force, Sasha felt herself flying, colliding with something hard, then rolling instinctively with arms over her head as the forest of hooves descended upon her with an earth-shaking roar. Hooves struck near, steel met steel, and then flesh, a body falling, spattering her with blood.

She risked a look up as the rear of her formation cut through what infantry remained standing. She could not see Peg—a relief, since he was not lying dead or wounded, but a concern, as she was now more or less alone, and afoot, with enemy all around. She stumbled to her feet, gasping at the pain of her left shoulder. There were bodies lying about, some still moving, limbs broken from impacts, or mail torn by blades. Some were running, trying to reform in small groups, others picking themselves up off the ground, as the battle continued all around.

An infantryman came at her from the side—shield and spear. She saw the unusual combination with disdain, knocking the thrust aside and reversing for the wielder's head. The shield intervened, but her serrin steel cut halfway through the wood, meeting the helm with force enough to knock him over. Her shoulder blazed with pain, but another two were coming at her . . . a straggling dussieh rider cut one down from behind, reining about as he realised who was in trouble. Sasha feinted the remaining man, danced back as he slashed at her, took his sword arm on the down stroke, and tore him open with the reverse.

There were horses racing through now, hurdling bodies, Hadryn and rebels in mutual pursuit. Terel came galloping, sending an infantryman spinning with a flashing blade, a Falcon Guardsman riding wide to guard his approach. Sasha switched the blade to her left hand, indicating she wished him on the right—but Terel pointed urgently behind her. She spun and saw a pair of Hadryn cavalrymen charging straight for her.

She feinted left, then dove right across the leader's path, rolling under his whistling blade as he somehow made that backhand reverse with amazing skill . . . and came to a crouch directly in the second rider's line. She swung, falling backward as blade met blade in defence . . . the shock nearly tore the weapon from her hands, no sooner falling than Terel met that man in full charge and fairly cut him in half. Sasha stumbled to her feet, her shoulder screaming, the blade strangely light in her hand, which she put down to the jarring numbness of impact . . . until she realised that her blade had shattered midway from the hilt.

She threw the hilt away as Terel came back, grabbed his hand with her good arm and swung up behind him. He galloped immediately for the rear, heading away from the fighting, swerving to avoid some intervening clashes as Sasha clutched to his middle and fought the urge to try and steer. Dear spirits, she *hated* being a passenger.

"Where's my horse?" she yelled at Terel. "Where's Peg?" Terel did not bother to reply to a question he had no hope of answering. The guardsman raced protectively to one side and Sasha hunted around for Errollyn, but could not find him. That scared her. No Errollyn, no Aisha. She heard a new round of bloodthirsty yelling and then some of the reserve was charging back the other way—perhaps a hundred horse, and desperate to get into the action.

Terel stopped in the middle of a field of grain, his horse heaving desperately for air. The racket of battle continued behind, but now, there were horns blowing. The Hadryn retreat. They were pulling back.

"They need to stop," Sasha gasped, realising suddenly that she was shaking all over. "We . . . we need to tell them! Someone tell them, pull back! We must preserve strength!"

"I'll tell them," the guardsman said grimly and galloped his poor, frothing horse back toward the fray. Sasha felt Terel's muscles twitch, the reflex to follow.

"Go help him," she said. "I'll get off."

"No," said Terel, putting a hand on her leg. "Stay. I can't leave you here alone."

They must have been winning, Sasha reckoned, because there were officers backing off and watching the battle with the confidence of soldiers seeing their enemies flee. The guardsman arrived beside those officers and pointed back toward Sasha. One put a horn to his lips and blew the reform. Horns duelled in the darkening sky, and the cries and yells of men also began to change pitch, seeking now to instruct and organise.

Sasha turned in the saddle and surveyed the scene behind. The fields of grain, once soft and level, were now torn and flattened like the coat of some animal ravaged by a terrible disease. Some bodies lay visible, and some horses struggled terribly against a fate they had not deserved. Some men were walking, or limping, searching for comrades, or simply away from where they'd been. Two Goeren-yai guarded a Hadryn rider with wary blades, to the Hadryn's apparent disinterest, as he listened in stunned silence to the trumpets.

The remnants of the reserve were riding across the fields now, dismounting as they found wounded. Sasha tapped Terel on the shoulder and pointed. He reined his horse about with no dissent, and rode that way.

Soon a dussieh rider came racing toward them, two Falcon Guardsmen on warhorses close behind—one apparently Verenthane, the other clearly Goeren-yai. Sasha blinked as she realised that the owner of that fast-moving little horse was none other than Sofy, her brown hair flying out behind. She slowed and circled to Sasha and Terel's side with remarkable judgment.

"Sasha!" Sofy stared up at her in alarm. "Where's Peg? Are you injured?"

"I fell," Sasha replied. Her voice was strained and hoarse. She barely recognised it. "There are many missing whom I hope to find again."

"Terel," Sofy said urgently, "you'd better come this way." And she was off again, galloping ahead through the twisted wreckage of grain, men and horses. One of Sofy's guards gave Sasha an apologetic shrug before galloping off in her wake. Terel managed to get his mount to a canter, but seemed not to have the heart for more. They followed Sofy across the corpse-strewn fields where the lead of the Hadryn column had been so totally enveloped and annihilated. They reached a spot near a fence, now far more exposed with the surrounding grain all beaten down.

There, Sofy stopped beside a fallen horse. Alongside knelt Aisha, holding a body in her lap. Terel dismounted quickly and ran to her side. Sasha followed, and her knees gave way as she hit the ground. She rolled and came up covered in wheat chaff, too exhausted to care. She staggered to Aisha's side and found that the body was Tassi, bloody and limp, her strange, bronze eyes gazing sightlessly at the overcast sky. Tears rolled down Aisha's cheeks from her pale blue eyes, and blood trickled from a cut on her temple. Serrin blood was red, Sasha saw, just like a human's. Some Verenthanes rumoured otherwise. Sasha would much rather have remained ignorant of that truth.

Aisha gazed up at her. She looked too young, and too pretty, for such a scene. Like a little girl. Sasha's breath caught in her throat. "Her mother had travelled to Lenayin many times," the serrin girl said softly, cradling her friend's body. "She fought in the Great War, with Kessligh."

"Kessligh told me that many serrin did," Sasha said quietly.

"Not as many as should have," said Aisha, gazing down at Tassi's lifeless face. "Even then, the serrinim were withdrawing inwards. Tassi thought it a terrible thing. She'd been to Lenayin twice. She loved this place. She did not understand why some amongst us thought the Goeren-yai less important. She feared the serrinim were becoming selfish. Tassi was never selfish."

"I can see," Sasha agreed, tears blurring her eyes.

"The serrinim are changing," Terel said quietly, kneeling at Aisha's side, and placing a hand on her shoulder. "Those of us who still care pick the hardest fights, and our numbers decrease. Now, we are fewer still."

At Sasha's side, Sofy's gaze was pale and sober. Sasha reached and grasped her sister's hand.

Jaryd awoke. He hurt. He hurt very badly. That was good. It meant he was still alive. Snapped stalks of wheat pressed against his cheek. It seemed strange that he should feel that discomfort above all the other pain. He could smell horses. And leather. And sweat. And blood. That latter smell stuck in the memory with the force of an axe thrown into a tree. Quivering, it triggered other memories. Tarryn. Father.

Galyndry. Galyndry? He hadn't thought much about his sisters. Galyndry was to be married anyhow. She'd be fine. Family Nyvar meant naught to her once she married. Delya was already married. No big thing. Wyndal, though . . . Wyndal was fifteen. He was still in Tyree, not everyone could go to Rathynal. Wyndal had always been quiet, he wouldn't make a fuss when he found out. Who would own their land now? And who would adopt Wyndal? Maybe Family Shaty would adopt him, at least then he could be with Delya.

His mind was wandering. That wasn't good. Everyone always said his mind wandered too much. Focus, Jaryd. You'll never make a great lord of Tyree if you don't learn to concentrate. Fool. Gods, he was a fool. He'd never thought a family so fragile. It had always been such a grand thing, full of uncles and aunts, cousins . . . In truth, it had never been more than him, father, and his siblings. Everyone else had another allegiance. Family? What did family matter to those people? As much as honour, perhaps. Or loyalty.

He tried to move his left arm. The pain of it nearly made him pass out. He moved his right instead and rolled heavily onto his back. His ribs hurt. Surely he'd broken some. He knew the feeling well enough. He could hear horses, distant shouts and trumpets. He tried opening his eyes. That was an anticlimax. There was no rush of blinding light, for the sky above was darkening. Soon it would be black. Best that he discovered where he was, and who had won, before all light disappeared entirely.

He levered himself upright. That hurt like hell. He was reminded of countless times he'd fallen from his horse playing lagand and awoken to find people looking down on him. Only now, he seemed to be alone.

Gasping, he got his good arm down for balance and sat up. Still he could see nothing . . . except that there was a dead horse lying beside him, partly obscured by the grain. Enough grain still stood to block all other view. The horse, at least, was not his. That was something.

He recalled charging into the Hadryn lines. He'd had no hope of steering, nor of wielding a shield. Nor of using his left hand as a pivot on the saddlehorn for leverage to duck, dodge and lean. His only defence had been attack. He'd struck one sword that would have killed him had he not . . . and then . . . he winced, trying to recall. His head hurt, along with everything else. His helm had fallen off. He could not see it in the grain about him. A horse galloped nearby and he had no idea if it belonged to friend or foe.

A pain stabbed at his right side, worse than the others. Jaryd put his hand there and found a tear in the heavy mail. His fingers came away bloody. He recalled banners . . . yes, he'd seen banners ahead, near the road. He'd charged at them. There had been some very good Hadryn warriors there, black and silver with big shields. Guarding someone. They'd seen him coming, and . . . but try as he might, he could not recall any more than that.

He staggered slowly, agonisingly, to his feet. The mail seemed impossibly heavy and his right shoulder guard was slashed in two. He could feel the bruise on his shoulder beneath. How the hells was he still alive? Far off toward the valley was a huge mass of riders, a dark and silver line against the fading gold of the fields. Behind them were scattered many stragglers, picking amongst the fields. If Sasha had lost, Jaryd realised, the armies would be south instead, toward Ymoth. They must have won.

Dark shapes littered the torn and mangled fields. Dead men, and the occasional horse. He staggered around the dead horse, but could not find its rider. Another dead man lay near, a Falcon Guardsman. Jaryd bent, painfully, and took up the man's sword. The face was not one he recognised.

Some instinct convinced him to walk east, away from the river, toward the broken folds of forested land that ran down from the mountains. The stiffening wound on his left leg throbbed painfully . . . Jaryd guessed he'd probably torn the muscle once more.

In the gloom ahead, faded of colour, he saw the shape of a banner, leaning on the body of a dead horse. He limped over and found a tangled mess of bodies, Hadryn and not. One of the Hadryn was gasping, trying to live, propped against the dead horse's side. Most of his entrails were in his lap. A sergeant in Yethulyn Bears colours lay with his head split open. Jaryd limped past them, searching the bodies with his eyes. The desperate story of their fight revealed itself in their final, fallen forms. Here a desperate, heroic defence. There a defiant charge. Men had fallen from their horses and fought on the ground. One of the dead Hadryn had deep bite marks through his hand and glove, the familiar curve of human teeth. Desperate fighting indeed.

Another dead horse, a dappled grey. This one, Jaryd saw as he limped around the dead animal's head, had a rider trapped beneath it, caught by the right leg. The horse's head was half severed by a single blow. The horse must have fallen hard and taken its rider down with it, even harder. The rider had that look, splayed on his right side, an arm outstretched, twisted and half conscious. Like a man who had fallen from a great height onto hard ground. His clothes were lordly, over his mail, with decorated stitching on his leather gloves and silver embroidery on his belt.

Banners. He'd charged this way, seeking banners. Lordly banners. Jaryd took another two steps. The half-conscious man seemed to register the boots before him and looked up, his helm askew. "Help me!" demanded a thin, anguished voice. "Help me, I'm hurt!"

A northern accent. A familiar, petulant tone. Now he remembered. "There's many hurt, Lord Usyn," said Jaryd, hoarsely. "Help yourself."

Usyn stared up at him. Perhaps the darkening overcast remained bright enough for silhouette, because the Great Lord of Hadryn's eyes seemed to widen with recognition. "Jaryd Nyvar!" He sounded almost relieved. "Master Jaryd, you must . . . you must help me up. My father was on good terms with your own. You are heir to the great lordship of Tyree. Great lords should always conduct themselves with honour, even in battle."

"And with what honour have you conducted this battle, Lord Usyn?" Jaryd asked. In the distance, trumpets blared again. "I saw the bodies in Ymoth. You attempt the slaughter of an entire Lenay people, and you speak to me of honour?" The fury was with him again. They were all the same, these nobles. His so-called peers and comrades. Everything he'd ever aspired to be, it was all a lie.

"You would stand there and snarl at me, while I lie wounded?" Usyn looked about, desperately, and found his sword on the ground nearby. He snatched it, and tried wriggling free from the horse's weight . . . and nearly screamed. "Have you . . ." he gasped, desperately. "Have you no honour?"

"My father and brother are dead," Jaryd said tonelessly. "Family Nyvar is no more. We were betrayed. If that is the honour of Verenthane nobility, then no, Lord Usyn, I have no honour. I reject your honour. I am a man already dead, and I have no fear of anything any longer."

"You would kill me?" Usyn asked. There was fear in his voice, a high, thin quaver. "Like this? Defenceless? I am not your enemy! Why . . . why do you ride with these . . . these people! You have the blood of the chosen in your veins! The nobility of Lenayin! The masters of the land!"

"The nobility of Lenayin slew a ten-year-old boy for daring to be frightened. Your honour is horseshit. Or worse. At least horseshit has uses."

"I didn't do it!" Usyn screamed. "I didn't kill your damn brother! You can't . . . you can't accuse me of . . ."

"Of vanity? Of power lust? Of murder? Of massacres and hatred? I know only too well what you are, and what you've done, Usyn. I know because I was once of your kind. I've been so stupid, and so blind, that I didn't realise what they'd do until it was too late. For that, I deserve death. And if I do, I'm quite certain you deserve worse. Look about you."

Some men were groaning, amidst the tangles of wheat. A little further, someone was sobbing. Torchlights now moved across the fields, riders searching for wounded.

Usyn was crying, Jaryd saw with surprise. He'd thought him many things, but not a coward. Yet it did not surprise him too greatly. They were all hypocrites and fakes, all the nobility.

"I just . . ." Usyn sobbed, his face contorted, ". . . wanted to be worthy of my father! I . . . I wanted to be a great lord of Hadryn! I wanted him to be proud of me, and . . . and I want to see my sister again, and . . ."

He lashed his blade in sudden fury at Jaryd's leg. Jaryd leaped back, with the barest moment to spare, and hurled his sword point first for Usyn's throat. It struck, and Usyn died with a horrid gurgling, drowning fast in his own spurting blood.

Jaryd turned away, unable to face the sight. He put his good hand to his head and stared across the battlefield, to where the tips of the northern mountains continued to glow, long after the light had fled the land below.

In a clump of wheat nearby, he heard a man coughing. He walked and found it was a Goeren-yai villager, with a bloodied face and a sword thrust through his side. Not deep, though. He might yet live. Jaryd sheathed his borrowed sword and managed to haul the man upright with one arm, long enough to dump him over one shoulder. Then he stood, muscles, ribs and leg shrieking protest, and began limping toward the river.

Dusk was falling as the army reformed behind a defensive line. No counter-attack came, and masses of riders began falling back to rest their horses and water them at the river. Others searched for fallen comrades. Sofy helped with the wounded, and Sasha joined her, being horseless for the moment.

The wounds were terrible. Soldiers bound bloody gashes with rolls of coarse cloth, stripping spare shirts for further bandages. Men bore terrible, disfiguring injury with a courage that defied words, biting back screams. Goeren-yai recited spirit chants, and Verenthanes holy verses. Others acted as healers, administering herbs and pastes for wounds as were available. Others brought full waterskins from the river. Men died upon the ruined fields of grain. Others lived, and suffered.

When Errollyn arrived Sasha felt horribly guilty at the relief she felt to be summoned away from that patch of bloody, hellish ground. She climbed up behind him, leaving Sofy to attend the wounded amidst the lines of flaming torches men were planting in the ground to ward the approaching night. Her little sister moved from man to man, holding each hand in turn, assuring those in delirium that it was indeed the Princess Sofy who attended them, and that they would not die alone. Errollyn then touched heels to his horse, asking nothing more than a walk of the weary animal, heading for the masses of horses by the river.

Sasha rested her cheek wearily against his back. "I thought perhaps I'd lost you," she murmured.

"And I you," Errollyn replied. Torchlight lit the fields, sentries standing with light aflame, guiding the way. "I didn't see you fall, there was too much happening." Sasha felt him heave a deep breath. "I hope to never have to do anything like that again."

A Lenay man would never admit to fear. It did not surprise her that Errollyn would. He was so . . . straightforward. For a serrin, anyhow.

"Take this sword," he said then. "We cannot have a commander without a sword."

He pulled a serrin blade in its scabbard from a binding alongside his saddle and handed it to her. Sasha pulled the blade a short way from its sheath and examined the edge. It was every bit the deadly, unblemished edge that her old blade had been. Even without fully drawing it, she could see that its balance would be perfect.

"Whose is it?" Sasha asked.

"It's Tassi's," said Errollyn.

"But . . . oh no, I couldn't just take her . . ."

"Aisha insists she would wish you to have it," said Errollyn.

"Me? Why? These things are expensive, Errollyn. It should be passed on to her family, and then on to their children . . ."

"Not so expensive in Saalshen," Errollyn corrected. "Only here. That steelwork is not a technique we share with humans. In Saalshen, it's no rarer than any other blade."

"But even so . . ."

"You don't understand," Errollyn told her. "Tassi rode all this way because she had some hope that there were old and ancient ways amongst humans that were worth saving. She had hope that humanity itself was worth saving, and that in the saving, there would be good for serrin as much as humans. If the uma of Kessligh Cronenverdt, the greatest Nasi-Keth of Lenayin, does not represent that hope, then no one does. Tassi gave her life for that hope. Allow her blade to continue to serve, even as she cannot."

Sasha gazed at it for a long moment. "If you wish to return it to her family one day," Errollyn added, "you may do so in person. But I suspect they shall tell you exactly what I have."

Sasha undid her own empty scabbard and replaced it with Tassi's. Her shoulder hurt—more wrenched than damaged, she thought. She'd been lucky. Unbelievably lucky, when she recalled her blade breaking. If that had happened a moment earlier, she'd be most likely dead. Serrin steel was not supposed to break. But her blade had been old, she knew. Everything broke sometime.

She found Peg amongst the horses by the riverside, drinking knee-deep in the flowing waters of the Yumynis. He whinnied as she dismounted, and came to the riverbank to greet her. Sasha stroked his nose and hugged his neck. Errollyn had found him wandering, sniffing fallen riders, searching for her. But he had recognised Errollyn and Errollyn's horse, and allowed himself to be led to the riverbank. Sasha took off her boots and waded into the cold water to give him as much of a rubdown as she could, without daring to remove his saddle lest some emergency happen.

Two of her vanguard riders were also present, haggard but desperately apologetic for having lost her in the confusion. Sasha waved their apologies away, commended them on their valour and asked after the missing two. One was dead, she heard, and the other wounded, but expected to live. She could not internalise so much suffering so quickly. She found her mind wandering to thoughts of Kessligh, his reactions when faced with memories of the Great War, and his occasional, unbridgeable distance. All this time, she'd been living with a stranger. Only now was she coming to understand him.

She was leading Peg ashore amidst the mass of riverside activity in the torchlight, when Captain Akryd arrived and embraced her.

"You were right," he said apologetically. She could see his face properly for the first time with his helm removed. It was a homely face, round and ruddy, with only the tracings of spirit symbols about one brow and temple. The face of a farmer, or a husband, or a good father. "Forgive my opposition, M'Lady. We'd have suffered far worse than this had we stayed in Ymoth, with the outcome yet uncertain. This has been a glorious victory, and it is truly yours."

"No," Sasha said quietly. "It's theirs." Nodding to the men about, particularly back to where the wounded and the dead lay.

"Aye, M'Lady. We found Lord Usyn slain on the battlefield. Several senior lords, also. Hadryn is severely wounded, no wonder they retreat in such disorder."

Sasha blinked. Usyn dead. Just like that. She did not know who would be in command now. He had a younger brother, she recalled . . . but too young to be on this ride. The great Hadryn army was leaderless. "They'll fall back into the valley now," she said quietly. "They'll know we have suffered losses, and will delay. They'll know that Prince Koenyg will ride behind us and they'll hope to hold out long enough for Koenyg to rescue them."

"Aye." Akryd nodded. "They have little other choice. Does M'Lady wish to make camp here?"

Sasha shook her head. "This is too exposed to the rear. The moon rises. We'll ride tonight, force the Hadryn far up the valley. We can rest when we're camped."

Akryd bowed. "I shall make arrangements."

Approaching midnight, and the clouds had cleared. The moon burned in the sky above the Udalyn Valley like a small silver sun. To either side, the valley sides loomed, bathed in moonlight, their broad slopes patched with fields and forest, grain and paddocks. Little cottages watched over their respective lands, some high on the furthest slopes, others nestled on the banks of the river, or hidden amongst folds in the valleyside. The Yumynis flowed broad and straight down the valley centre, flanked by green pasture and fields of grain. Its waters gleamed silver in the moonlight, and the entire majestic valley seemed to wait, and watch, with hushed anticipation.

Sasha rode near the head of the column, along a road that lifted slightly on the sloping right bank of the river, and felt her skin prickle uncontrollably beneath her clothes. The air seemed warm as a gentle southerly breeze blew from behind their backs. She had never been here before, and yet it felt as familiar as the Baerlyn Valley.

She felt herself filled with longing. She wanted to call up Andreyis from the column behind, and talk with him as they once had talked—as children on the hillside by the ranch, eating fruit from one of Madyn's orchards, and talking about horses, or swordwork, or the doings of other Baerlyn children, and how stupid they all were. But Andreyis had survived his first battle with glory, a rider from the rear had told her, and now rode with his comrades as an equal for the first time.

Now she felt more apart from that idyllic childhood world than ever. Kessligh, the towering pillar of those years, had become someone far different than she'd realised. Andreyis was no longer a boy, but a warrior, blooded in battle. Baerlyn had lost Dobyn the drummer, whose wonderful rhythms would no longer fill the Steltsyn Star on a rowdy evening, and Tesseryl the farmer, who would no longer share fresh mountain olive and goat curd with his neighbours. Farmer Lyndan, from whom Kessligh had often bought chickens, had lost a hand—a common enough injury in cavalry exchanges. But he'd been in good spirits, declaring that he and Geldon the baker could now compare stumps, and that chickens required no more than five fingers anyhow. Nothing was as it had been, and there was no going back.

Ahead, Sasha realised that someone was singing. It was a low, gentle voice, barely audible above the plodding of hooves and the shifting of harness. But it was beautiful, and strange, of lilting melody and haunting melancholy. The singer did not seem to wish to bring attention to herself, yet all murmured conversation behind ceased as men listened to the song. It was Aisha, Sasha realised, and her voice was fair indeed.

She seemed to sense, then, that the attention was on her, and sang louder. Clear notes drifted on the moonlit air, high against the soaring valley sides. Sasha could not make out the exact words, but it seemed that she sang of a lost friend, of suffering seen and partaken in, and of beloved lands, family and friends far away. The gentle swaying of Sasha's saddle seemed in time to the ceaseless murmur of the never-ending river, and the vast, beautiful silence of the fields, farms and cottages. She found herself thinking of all the strands in her life that had brought her to this point—of Krystoff and Kessligh, of Torvaal and her mother. And those more recent faces—Sofy, Damon, her friends in Baerlyn, and Andreyis and Lynette in particular. Jaryd. Captain Tyrun. Of friends made upon the road, and then lost forever.

Tears prickled at her eyes. To her side, she saw that Sofy too rode with tears in her eyes. And yet, for all her sadness, she rode with a newfound confidence, straight-backed and certain in the saddle. Whatever the tears, her eyes never stopped wandering as she gazed about at this legendary sight in wonder. Sasha extended a hand down to her. Sofy looked up, clasped her sister's hand, and smiled.

Twenty-one

Sasha awoke to the disorientation of a comfortable bed and blankets. She looked across the little room and found Sofy's bed empty. Daylight streamed through the window and, with it, the sounds of camp from the lower slopes—whinnying horses and soldiers at early muster. Somewhere distant, she fancied she could hear the yells and grunts of morning drill as soldiers trained upon an available patch of ground. Beyond that, drumming from the Udalyn wall. Sometimes it seemed that they'd never stop. Surely they'd be getting tired, after two days and nights without pause.

She blinked at the ceiling, massaging her aching shoulder, and trying to clear her head from sleep. It was the third morning after the victories of Ymoth and the Yumynis Plain. The previous evening, the king himself had arrived at the head of an army of nearly six thousand. Torvaal, at least, was taking no chances. The banners last evening had suggested that Koenyg was with him, and probably Damon as well, but the light had been poor and the royal messenger had not bothered to clarify. She was to meet with the king this morning. The very thought was enough to make her wish she could roll over and go back to sleep.

The little room had a stone-paved floor covered by a thick rug. The beds were of simple wooden frame. The room, and the entire cottage, had a simple dignity that appealed to her.

From beyond the window, she could hear Sofy humming a tune in the garden. The splash of water from a pail. An inaudible question from one of the guards . . . although Sasha could guess. A cheerful reply, and the splash of more water being gathered, then poured. Sasha smiled. Sofy would give the entire guard contingent green thumbs soon enough. Kessligh would approve.

Sasha stretched aching limbs, careful of her shoulder, and then began to dress in clean clothes she'd washed the day before, and dried before the fire that night. She'd washed herself too, in the warm water, and what a luxury that had been. Once dressed, she straightened out the bed and made a spirit sign to the house spirit for watching over her and her sister while they slept

. . . not that she truly believed in such things, but because she suspected the Udalyn who owned this house might, and it was considered bad luck to leave such things neglected for any period.

Stepping into the main room, she found that the interior guard had already started a fire in the central pit and was boiling some water.

"Hello!" said the guard with a bright smile. "Would you like some tea?" Sasha blinked. It was Andreyis.

"I'd love some," she replied with a sleepy grin, trying to brush her hair back into place with both hands as she walked over. "How did you grab this duty?"

Andreyis grinned even more broadly, and looked smug. "The honour is being given to all those of outstanding service. The men chose me to represent Baerlyn." And he shrugged, stirring the tea with a wooden spoon. "I know they're just being nice. And I don't think any of them really fancied the morning shift."

Sasha considered him as she blinked sleep from her eyes. Was it her imagination, or did he wear the sword at his hip with greater confidence now? And had he even filled out a little within his jacket?

Andreyis poured the tea—it was strong, as he knew she liked it. They talked of the men and the horses. It had been another delight to discover that of her beloved horses, only one had been left behind at Ymoth, and that only for a strained hind leg.

Teriyan had embraced her upon first seeing her after the battles, and had called her a "bloody genius," professing that he'd expected half of them to wind up dead even if things went well. "If you hadn't seen straight through that snotty little bastard, we'd have met them on even terms and lost five times as many men! You saved an incredible number of men, Sasha! We're all damn proud of you, and Kessligh will be too when he hears of it!" Which had made Sasha feel at least a little better, about Dobyn and Tesseryl in particular . . . but not enough.

Halfway through tea, the front door opened and Sofy entered, carrying an empty bucket that held gardening tools, her hands smeared in rich, black dirt. "Good morning!" she said brightly, depositing the bucket on the table.

"Highness," said Andreyis, and bowed.

"Oh, stop that!" Sofy reprimanded with a slap at his arm. "Sasha, I've already told him that he's like an old friend, but he keeps bowing."

"It is my honour and privilege," said Andreyis, with a faintly mischievous confidence.

"I wish you'd bow like that to me occasionally," Sasha offered past her cup.

"Not bloody likely," Andreyis retorted with a grin. Sasha and Sofy laughed.

Many had seemed to expect Sofy to trade pants and jacket for her dress and resume princessly ways once some semblance of civilisation had been restored. Certainly any number of young soldiers remained ready and eager to wait upon her every need. And yet Sofy remained in the clothes she'd ridden in, alternating between those and some others she'd borrowed from the cottage, seeming to belong to a boy of younger years. When asked, she'd simply smiled and said, "There will be plenty of time for dresses later, I'm sure."

Much of the past two days, she'd spent watering and tending to the gardens, accumulating dirt stains on clothes and face, and becoming sweaty in the warm midday sun. Sasha was sure that "happy" hardly described Sofy's mood. But it was equally plain that whatever unhappiness there was, the gardening was a part of the cure.

Sasha went outside to sit on the wooden bench before the lower garden and survey the scene as she ate some breakfast. Sunlight fell upon the valley's far slope, although this, the eastern side, remained in shadow. Snowcaps upon the further mountains gleamed in the light, and the terraced fields, cottages, orchards and trails along the valley's western side shone in serene, golden detail.

Across the valley floor below camped her army . . . if one could call it a camp. There were no tents, of course, although men were sharing empty accommodation on rotating shifts. There were many, many hundreds of horses across the green fields to either side of the Yumynis, and many thousands more back to the south. They were more than seven thousand, now, and more had continued to appear up until the king's arrival last evening. Even now, she could see perhaps three hundred horse to either side of the river, formed and ready, in case of action. At night, that number doubled, and shifts were constantly rotated. But the moon had been full and the Hadryn had not risked such overwhelming odds.

Further north, the Hadryn camp appeared strangely orderly by contrast, white tents lined in neat rows across the fields. Black banners flew, and catapults stood at intervals along the line, their long arms drooping as the morning shadow crept across the valley floor. Men could be seen exercising and drilling, others moving about the tents, tending to fires and breakfast. Horses grazed on the grass, and opposing formations of infantry and cavalry remained also on permanent watch—their numbers roughly similar to what opposed them. A thousand remaining cavalry, it had been estimated, and another two thousand infantry. Not nearly enough to break through the force that had trapped them.

Beyond the Hadryn, where the grassy fields turned to rising rock, and the valley sides began to draw together in steep, precipitous sides, a stone wall spanned the valley from side to side, its ends buried into near-vertical cliff. Blue and gold banners hung along the wall, the colours of the Udalyn, and warriors could be seen moving upon the battlements. There was a large single wooden gate on this side of the river, a smaller one upon the far side. Most amazingly of all, the Yumynis River spewed through a narrow cleft in that rock, a roaring spray of white foam. The Udalyn had moved the river, a long time ago. The wall's foundations spanned a dry, rocky depression where the river had evidently once flowed. They must have carved this steep, narrow cut themselves, diverted the waters into it, then built the wall over it. The scale of it amazed her.

Several Udalyn warriors had climbed across the steep cliffs and around the wall by moonlight to tell those who could understand their broken Taasti that there were caves at the valley's end. Thousands of people were hiding there, having left their land before the advancing Hadryn wave, driving most of their livestock before them. Food for people and animals was constantly stockpiled in those caves, and the Udalyn were a long way from hungry yet.

The wall was another matter, cracked and crumbling beneath the constant pounding of Hadryn artillery. In several places, the wall had collapsed entirely. The Hadryn had made four breaches, the Udalyn said, and then tried an attack. Even with four separate points of attack, their men had taken heavy casualties from arrowfire as they'd scrambled up the unstable mounds of stone, and had then met ferocious resistance at the top. The Hadryn had dismantled houses and fence walls in their thirst for ammunition, and many of their catapults had required repair. From her seat, Sasha could see new, developing breaches in the wall, where the sheer face was crumbling and leaning, and artillery stones were piled high at the base. Another two days, perhaps, and there would have been seven breaches. The Hadryn had been making more ladders too, using wood from the forests around Ymoth.

Even the most confident Udalyn had admitted that would have been the end. They had been somewhat surprised to be rescued. Like Lord Krayliss, it seemed that they too had lost all faith in the mercy of Verenthane kings. Sasha wondered if despite their isolation, they'd somehow managed to know something others had not.

Sofy joined her on the bench with a cup of water, but no food. "You've eaten?" Sasha asked her about a mouthful.

"It's late," Sofy said with mild amusement. "You keep missing breakfast."

Sasha restrained another yawn, and stretched her legs. "I haven't slept this well in years," she conceded.

"Father will ask about me," Sofy said then. Gazing out across the Udalyn wall, and the opposing armies. The sound of drums drifted on the golden air. The Udalyn messengers had been disappointed that she refused to countenance wiping out those Hadryn who remained. They'd offered to coordinate an attack, pouring from their gate into the Hadryn's rear as Sasha attacked from the front. From the sound of the drumming, however, it did not seem as if they'd allowed their disappointment to get in the way of a good celebration. "He'll want to ask about the marriage."

Sasha chewed for a moment as the porridge seemed to lose its taste in her mouth. "What do you want me to say?" she asked.

Sofy sighed, and adjusted her ponytail. It seemed to Sasha that she might have even had it cut a little. Barely seven days ago, such a decision would have been monumental. "Say that I'll do it," Sofy said quietly. "Say that I'll marry that bastard. If it's what Father and Koenyg have truly decided."

Sasha said nothing. She wanted to protest. Badly. But then . . . She placed a hand on Sofy's arm and gazed at her closely. "Are you certain? I have some bargaining power here, Sofy. We have much of the Hadryn army trapped, Father's most loyal supporters. Several of his closest northern lords also. Father and Koenyg will need such men if they wish to join the war in the lowlands."

Sofy met her gaze, in sombre earnest. "I know," she replied. "I know you have bargaining power, Sasha. And that's just why you can't waste it on me. I've . . . I've been doing a lot of thinking. This is just . . ." and she waved a hand at the view before them. "The things that I've seen in the last few days just make everything look different to what it did before. I mean, when I heard the word 'marriage' . . . my head was so full of all the things Alythia has been fretting about, wedding preparations and ceremonies and whether or not she'd like her in-laws.

"But it's so much more than that, isn't it?" She shook her head in disbelief. "Seriously, I can't believe I've been so selfish. All these men who live and die by the decisions people like us make. All of their families, deprived of fathers, brothers and sons. You've led a rebellion, Sasha. You've trapped the Hadryn, but now Father's forces have *us* trapped. You'll need all your bargaining power to gain clemency for these men, for the sake of their families. You'll need it to ensure the Udalyn are safer in future. Lenayin cannot remain so divided, or all this bloodshed will be just the beginning, won't it?

"You can't put that at risk for me. When I found out Koenyg's plans I thought it was the worst thing in the world that could possibly happen to me. But now, to think that I might be responsible in some way for *more* of what I saw on those battlefields . . ." Sofy shook her head, adamantly. "It's the least I can do, Sasha. If I need to marry someone I dislike to help keep Lenayin whole, it shall be a vastly smaller sacrifice than the alternative. I won't be the first to suffer such a fate. I'll survive."

Sasha held Sofy's hand, tightly. There was no sign of tears in her sister's eyes. It was clear that she had given this much thought, and had arrived at some kind of peace with it. Past the sadness, Sasha felt a pride so intense she thought she might burst. "Koenyg might have changed his mind, Sofy," she said gently. "Father too. Their plans haven't worked out anything like they'd anticipated."

Sofy gave a sad smile and shook her head. "You don't know Koenyg or Father as well as I do. These preparations are far advanced. Lenayin would lose face to back out now. In Koenyg's eyes, to lose face is to die. And Father . . . has not changed his mind on anything since Krystoff died."

"We can hope," Sasha offered.

Sofy squeezed her hand tightly. "We can hope," she agreed.

After breakfast, Sasha rode to the cottage her father's men had selected, further back along the valley. Ahead and to the rear rode the men of her vanguard who had protected her through both battles, and now sat astride with the hard-edged pride of those who had earned great honour and respect amongst their peers. Directly at Sasha's rear rode Jaryd, in the full colours and armour of Commander of the Falcon Guard, and Captain Akryd, likewise resplendent as Captain of the Red Swords.

It was midmorning and the sun was threatening to break clear of the ridges above, sunlight now falling golden upon most of the valley floor. Encamped across the valley floor and up either sloping side massed the king's army.

She gazed across the trees and fields along the terraced slopes as they rode, marvelling at the wide variety of crops, the ingenuity of downhill irrigation ditches and the profusion of trees that kept the soil stable. Here and there were talleryn posts, engraved with the curling script of Edu writings. Colourful flags flew like streamers above long terraces of grain . . . to keep the birds off, Sasha guessed. And they were beautiful, swirling in the valley breeze. Along fence posts there were wind chimes, making gentle music of the breeze.

Soon the small column of riders came upon a cottage, with many horses tethered by a bend, guarded by soldiers. Flags flapped, the royal flag most prominently of all. The lead rider halted them short of the other horses, and they dismounted.

Jaryd and Akryd walked with her along the road toward the path that led up to the cottage, as the vanguardsmen remained behind.

A Verenthane Royal Guard lieutenant stopped the trio at the base of those steps, resplendent in full colours and gleaming helm. "M'Lady," he said, with a very faint bow. "You must surrender your weapons to enter the king's presence."

Sasha eyed the horses tethered further up the road. They were splendid indeed, and several were of various shades of white or grey, a colour favoured by breeders from the royal stables. "No Lenay commander yet has come to parley between armies without weapons," she replied to the lieutenant.

"M'Lady, it is the king," the lieutenant replied sternly. "You must disarm."

Sasha repressed a snort of disgust, and gave a signal to her companions. Together, they turned about and began to walk back to their horses. "M'Lady!" From behind there were footsteps and mutterings of consternation. The three were halfway back to the horses when there came another call from behind. "M'Lady, we have reconsidered!"

Sasha stopped, turned about, and gave the gathering of soldiers a very displeased look. "Told you it would work," she murmured from the side of her mouth at Jaryd, as they began their walk back.

"M'Lady is truly insightful," Jaryd muttered. Sasha gave him a worried look. Probably it was not a good idea to have him here. But then, such talks required the presence of the most senior and, with Tyrun dead, that meant Jaryd. Lord or peasant, he was still Commander of the Falcon Guard.

Sasha allowed Jaryd to take the lead up the stairs. There were flowerpots at the cottage entrance, where several more Royal Guards stood at attention. Several long-stemmed flowers were bent. Sasha stepped across to them, with a disapproving cluck of the tongue at the guardsmen.

"We are guests in these houses, gentlemen," she said sternly, straightening the flowers. "Kindly look after their property as you would your own. Or else the house spirits will become upset with the mess, and haunt your sleep."

And with that, she walked inside, satisfied with the disquiet on several faces at that last remark. Even Verenthanes could become superstitious of Goeren-yai spirits, in the land of the Udalyn.

The house was plain and simple like the many others that dotted the valley. Men stood about a dining table and turned to observe the new entrants. Sasha saw her father, slim and dark in a black cloak against the morning's chill. He wore mail beneath, with leather shoulder guards and heavy boots. Sasha's gaze lingered. She could not recall the last time she'd seen her father in mail, with a sword at his side. A childhood parade, perhaps.

Koenyg, of course, was similarly attired. A king in waiting. Damon leaned against the far wall, a cup in hand. While the others looked grim, Damon's expression was sour. From his posture and expression, and his place at the back of the room, Sasha guessed that he did not feel himself to be in good company. She hoped he'd been making a pain of himself.

Of the others, well . . . here was Great Lord Kumaryn, stiff as a poker. Spirits knew why anyone thought him important enough to include in this gathering. And there was Great Lord Rydysh of Ranash no less. Also present was Lord Arastyn of Tyree . . . no, Sasha corrected herself, *Great* Lord Arastyn of Tyree. His handsome gaze, fixed on Jaryd, held a curious, expressionless intensity.

The last two great lords were Lord Faras of Isfayen and Lord Parabys of Neysh. The south, Sasha thought darkly. The other large piece of the Verenthane puzzle. The south had harboured Verenthanes long before they became popular in the rest of Lenayin.

"My Lords," Sasha said by way of greeting. She did not, she was surprised to realise, feel particularly anxious. There were nearly seven thousand men under her command. Her forces could be destroyed if attacked, but the catastrophe would not be hers alone. Hers was a position of power. However her father and Koenyg might desire it, she would not grovel or plead. "We are all known to each other, I'm sure. Shall we sit?"

King Torvaal gazed at her for a long moment. Everyone awaited his command. Koenyg, Sasha noted, seemed to be grinding his teeth. As Commander of Armies, and protector of the realm, surely it grated to be outranked in such a setting. Even by his king. The tension in the air felt different than she'd expected. Men held their tongues and their tempers. They stood with a faintly awkward manner, as if uncertain of their standing. King Torvaal had not needed to ride forth from Baen-Tar and deal with a military matter for quite some time. Since the Great War, in fact, when he'd been barely more than a lad. No doubt the lords wondered if the king was truly up to the task.

Well. Sasha wondered herself.

"Sofy is with you?" Torvaal asked.

"Concerned, were you?" Sasha nearly remarked, but refrained. "She is," she said instead.

"Did she discover the wedding plans?" Sombrely.

Sasha stared at him for a long moment. "You don't sound surprised."

"It was necessary," said Torvaal, closing his eyes briefly. "It remains necessary." The eyes opened and fixed on her directly, with more than their usual impassivity. Brooding. "The marriage remains as arranged. It shall proceed because Lenayin requires it. On this point I shall brook no argument."

"Sofy tells me she no longer objects," Sasha replied. "You make no decisions for her. She goes of her own free will." At the back of the room, Damon stared at his boots. Great Lord Rydysh of Ranash looked severely agitated.

Torvaal indicated to the table. There were only two chairs set, one on either side. Sasha nodded and stepped to her seat, waiting first for the king to sit. Then sat, directly opposite her father. It occurred to her, looking at him now, that they had never sat together like this before. Krystoff, Koenyg or Damon might have chanced a moment with their father, but the girls did not warrant such attention.

The old anger resurfaced, cold and hard. Tempered now, by the circumstances, but real enough. He'd ignored her before, all her views, values and opinions. Now, finally, she would not be ignored.

There was a pitcher of water and two cups on the table. Torvaal took the pitcher himself, and poured into both cups. Raised his cup to his lips, inviting her with his eyes to do likewise. "Don't drink it, M'Lady," said Jaryd from behind. "There's poisons that can be put on the cup, not in the water."

Torvaal stared up at the young man with genuine anger. "Master Jaryd," he said coldly, "I would never poison my own daughter."

"Then you'd be the only man amongst you who could say that for truth, Highness," Jaryd said darkly.

"You have no standing here, Jaryd," Lord Arastyn told him, very coolly. "You are a traitor to Tyree. Family Nyvar is no more, all its properties and titles are barren. I have no idea why Sashandra brought you, you are less than a landless peasant."

Sasha hoped Captain Akryd would restrain Jaryd before he tried anything stupid. But she made certain that her chair remained a suitable distance from the table, her feet braced upon the floor, rehearsing in her mind a fast grab for her blade.

"I am Commander of the Falcon Guard," Jaryd replied. There was no apparent tension in his voice, which only made it all the more ominous.

"And I just told you that you are not," Arastyn replied.

"The men of the Falcon Guard tell me I am," said Jaryd. "There are men of the Tyree White Talons who say so as well, and will tell any others of the commonfolk in Tyree who care to listen. How long will the noble families of Tyree survive should both their vaunted companies and most of the commonfolk, Verenthane and Goeren-yai, decide that you have outlived your usefulness?"

"Your Highness," Lord Rydysh broke in angrily, in heavily accented Lenay, "this is madness! You bargain with traitors! Look, this whelp threatens insurrection even now!"

"Any enemy of the Tyree nobility is an enemy of the Valhanan nobility too," Lord Kumaryn added, ominously, looking hard at Jaryd. "Should our noble friends in Tyree be threatened, all of Valhanan shall ride to their aid."

"All of Valhanan wouldn't ride to your funeral, Kumaryn," Jaryd retorted. "You don't speak for all of Valhanan any more than I speak for all of Saalshen."

"Silence!" Torvaal shouted. From either side of the table, the lords glared at Jaryd and Akryd. Behind them, Damon took another sip from his cup, apparently disgusted. "I shall not have arrogant fools destroy these talks before they have even begun."

"Talks!" Lord Rydysh snorted. "She's your daughter! Bring her to heel like a true Verenthane lord, show her her place with the back of your hand!"

"You watch your mouth with the king!" Koenyg snarled, turning on the northern great lord.

"Bah!" Lord Rydysh waved a dismissive hand. "Southerners have no balls. Your Highness, I tell you again—let me raise my forces and we'll ride through these traitors like a scythe through wheat!"

"She has seven thousand to command," Lord Parabys of Neysh came to his king's defence. "Don't be a damn fool, man."

"Seven thousand and the Udalyn," Sasha told them. "They've barely any cavalry, but taken all together it's a good ten thousand warriors. One move against me and all Hadryn's remaining force shall be destroyed between us. We'll give them as much mercy as they gave the Udalyn. That'll be most of Hadryn's standing soldiery gone. And almost all of their lords, I believe."

"You unutterable fool!" exclaimed Lord Kumaryn, horrified. "You are not merely a traitor, but an enemy of Lenayin! The Hadryn are the shield of the north! You would destroy the very protection that saves Lenayin from Cherrovan domination!"

"I'm not playing dice for a few coppers here!" Sasha retorted, allowing her voice to rise in volume. "I know exactly what I'm up against." With a hard stare at Lord Rydysh. "You have all lost the Goeren-yai. Not all of them, but an awful lot. That's neither my fault, nor my doing—I was recruited, plucked from my dungeon without any foreknowledge of what had been planned. This uprising was *their* choice, not mine.

"You've made a mess, my Lords. You've ignored the wishes of the very people whose welfare is supposed to be utmost in your hearts, and now you pay the price. They will *not* just lie down and let you ride over the top of them. If you fight them, they will fight back, and you know by now that there's an awful lot of them. It's your choice, my Lords. I'm perfectly happy for it all to stop right here. But the terms must be favourable. Unfavourable terms have already roused them to fight once. Assuredly they could do so again."

"No terms!" snarled Lord Rydysh, utterly unimpressed. "No terms with pagan traitors! Not on northern soil! We would rather die!"

"Perhaps that's just as well," Sasha said coldly. "We've already killed two of the three northern great lords this ride. Why don't we make it a clean sweep?"

Lord Rydysh glared at her, his narrow, dark eyes blazing fury. No one had realised that Great Lord Cyan of Banneryd had been amongst the defenders of Ymoth. He'd partaken in the cavalry defence and died within a few strides of Captain Tyrun before the Ymoth walls. Word had reached Sasha just ahead of King Torvaal's arrival, when someone from the Ymoth burial detail had realised just who the corpse had been.

Sasha gave Lord Rydysh a nasty little smile. "It hasn't been a wonderful month for northern great lords, has it? Three in thirty days. Your gods must love you dearly, to be claiming you all so fast."

"You speak of the deaths of Lenayin's finest as though it gave you pleasure!" Kumaryn exclaimed.

"Lenayin's finest picked their fight with me and with the Goeren-yai long ago," Sasha replied, unimpressed. "Their fight, their consequences, their problem. Not mine."

"You speak as though all the Goeren-yai worship you," said Great Lord Faras of Isfayen, contemptuously. "The Goeren-yai of Isfayen have barely heard your name. It is the same in most of the west and the south. The north despises you, and there are few Goeren-yai of consequence in Baen-Tar.

"In truth, all that follow you can be drawn from Valhanan, Tyree and Taneryn. You may stand now with seven thousand beneath you, but should the other great lords call their forces down upon you, seven thousand would seem as a sapling before the forest. The Goeren-yai of Isfayen shall not weep for you."

Sasha knew that he spoke the truth. The Goeren-yai of the western provinces of Yethulyn, Fyden and Isfayen practised ancient beliefs tending toward a mysticism that very few easterners pretended to understand. All had been traditionally hostile toward foreigners, and so had had little contact with either serrin or fellow Lenays over the centuries, except through conquest and bloody battles. They had participated in the Great War sparingly, preferring to let the easterners and northerners bleed against the invading

Cherrovan army. Kessligh was no legend worth the speaking in the west, and the Nasi-Keth just another bunch of odd foreigners. Company soldiers had ridden with her, those having been in Baen-Tar, and having seen and heard of injustice firsthand, and company soldiers tended to be more well travelled than most. But for the most part, she would find no love in the west, and probably not in the south, either. Neither would the serrin.

"You may speak the truth," said Captain Akryd at her back, long-haired and grim, his thumbs tucked into his swordbelt. "It matters not. She has Taneryn, she has Valhanan and she has much of Tyree. I speak for Taneryn in Lord Krayliss's absence. Not many of us cared for that pompous goat. But we care for the Udalyn, and we reject the rule of Verenthane lords."

His eyes fixed hard on his king. "You are not King Soros, Your Highness," he continued. "You have not come to liberate us from anything, and we don't owe you any more than a fistful of horseshit. Should you find a leader amongst the Taneryn to elevate to a lordship, we'll kill him. Should you send priests to convert our poor pagan souls, we'll kill them. Should you send a Verenthane lord from the outside to rule over us, we'll kill him. Should you send armies to enforce any of these rules, we'll fight them until there's not a Taneryn man left alive."

"That is acceptable!" Lord Rydysh spat. "Your Highness, please accept this pagan's challenge."

"We are not here to bargain for the fate of Taneryn," Koenyg told Captain Akryd, unable to hold his tongue any longer. "We discuss the fate of the Udalyn, and the fate of the Hadryn army, and that's all!"

"It's the same thing!" Sasha retorted in exasperation. "You don't understand a thing, Koenyg. You never did." Her eldest brother glared at her. "The Goeren-yai of Taneryn, Valhanan and Tyree are angry as all hells. Angry enough to defy a king they've otherwise always respected. And they do still respect you, Father." Meeting Torvaal's impassive stare across the table. "Don't they, Captain?"

"Aye, M'Lady," Akryd echoed. "Never had no quarrel with the king. The king brings peace and trade. It's the lords we've had a full stomach of."

"We're here to discuss terms for a peace," Sasha said firmly. "Terms acceptable enough to allow angry men who've ridden against the king's wishes to go back home and care for their families. If you don't understand why they're so angry, then you'll never be able to offer those terms. They only ask you to listen, Father. Listen to them, as you've been listening to the lords. The lords would have you believe that they are the only voice in the land. These men tell you differently. Only if you listen to *all* the voices of Lenayin can there be peace.

"Lords' rule might work well in the lowlands, but Lenayin is *different*. Lowlands peasants live their whole lives doing what their lords tell them. It doesn't work here, and it's time all you lowland-lovers learned it! Lenays have *never* liked being told what to do! They'd rather fight. Even the poorest Lenay farmer is a formidable warrior. You've been kicking the hornets' nest for far too long, my Lords, and finally the hornets are swarming. I only tell you what you need to know to let them go back to their nests and leave you alone. But if you refuse to listen, there will be nothing in Lenayin's future but blood and tears. Even in Isfayen," she added, with a glare toward Lord Faras, "where the Goeren-yai may not give a holy damnation about me. You try and put them under the feudal yoke, there'll be enough blood on the hills of Isfayen to make the rivers of Raani run red for a month."

"Name your terms," Torvaal said suddenly. Sasha stared at him, completely off guard. Blinked, trying to gather her thoughts. Behind their king, the lords were seething, but they dared not interrupt once the king had made his request. She had to get this right.

"Safe passage for all these men," she said finally. "Reinstatement of all those who may have lost title, rank or pay—with no punishments." Torvaal simply listened, his black-gloved fingers interlaced on the tabletop. "The Udalyn shall be granted royal protection. Royal soldiers shall hold open the Udalyn pass into Valhanan. The Udalyn shall be allowed to trade, to move back and forth, and to become a part of broader Lenayin. Royal soldiers shall ensure the safety of any moving along the pass."

"Impossible!" Lord Rydysh snapped. "The Hadryn shall never agree! Royal soldiers on Hadryn soil is a violation of the sanctity of lords' rights, an insult to Hadryn pride, and is against the letter of the king's law as written by King Soros!"

"King Soros is dead," Sasha replied, looking only at her father. "King Torvaal rules now." Perhaps there was a flicker of response in her father's dark eyes. Or maybe she imagined it. It was unclear why the Hadryn had not sent a representative to these talks. Perhaps, with Usyn dead, they had not reached agreement on who led them. Or they found the prospect of talks with their female vanquisher too shameful to bear. Even so, Sasha suspected something more was at play. Where matters of power were in question between lords, it was always safest to assume intrigue.

"Continue," her father said simply.

"No additional powers shall be granted to the great lords, nor to the nobility in general—no new taxes, no new rules of justice, no more authority over the priesthood, nothing." There were, predictably, cries of outrage. Sasha ignored them. So, for the moment, did the king.

"Continue," said Torvaal, once the outbursts had faded. Could it be that there was a faintly different expression now upon his face? It seemed to Sasha that there was . . . perhaps a wry acknowledgement of a common exasperation between them—the lords. And, just maybe, a hint of . . . no, not pride. Respect. An acknowledgement that perhaps father and daughter, as little as they knew each other, were alike in one respect—in stubbornness, and determination, and an utter disdain for the disapproval of others.

"The Taneryn shall be free to choose their own succession to Lord Krayliss," Sasha continued. "I understand from Captain Akryd that Krayliss's eldest son now claims the title of great lord, but under the ancient ways, such claims can be challenged. I understand that none of Krayliss's sons are particularly respected in Taneryn, and a challenge may be forthcoming. Whatever the result, the Verenthane great lords, and the king, should respect the result."

"The ancient ways have never truly recognised great lords, however Krayliss styled himself," Torvaal stated, with grim curiosity. "How can the laws of the ancient ways determine the outcome of a modern, and some would claim Verenthane, invention?"

Sasha blinked at him. It was the question of a knowledgeable man. She was astonished. And, just as quickly, she doubted herself. How well did she know her father truly? And how often had Kessligh insisted, against her own disbelief, that all through Krystoff's life, King Torvaal had been a fair and just man with the Goeren-yai? Things had only changed when Krystoff had died, he'd told her. When the sheer weight of protest from Lenayin's Verenthane leaders had shifted the path of the future, and convinced the king that his previous vision for the kingdom had been ungodly after all. Her father's knowledge of the ancient ways was not dead, it seemed. Merely dormant.

"The ancient ways are flexible," Captain Akryd spoke up. "Taneryn has its own Rathynals, where chiefs and village seniors gather to discuss matters of the province. We shall arrange another. The old ways accept much that is new, Your Highness, even if Lord Krayliss did not. Not all in Taneryn are like him."

"Might you stand for the Great Lordship of Taneryn yourself, Captain Akryd?" the king asked shrewdly. "Lord Krayliss spoke often of saving the Udalyn, but it is you who stand here today."

Sasha resisted the urge to turn around and look. Behind, she heard a creak of mail and leather as Akryd shrugged. "Perhaps," he answered.

Torvaal considered him with narrowed eyes. Pressed his lips thin and gazed out of the cottage windows across the sunlit expanse of valley. "It is beautiful here," he conceded. "The Udalyn have cared for their valley for many centuries. It seems that the gods have plans for this to continue."

"Your Highness!" Lord Rydysh exclaimed angrily. "The gods put men in the world to do their bidding and fight their battles! One does not simply give up the battle as lost because of setbacks! At least we must demand that the Udalyn convert! This is Verenthane land, surrounded by Verenthane peoples! To ask the two to continue to coexist would be folly!"

"They do everywhere else in Lenayin," the king said mildly. "Why not here?"

"This is the north!" Lord Rydysh seethed. "We value our independence. These lands are ours. We do things our way, Your Highness. King Soros decreed that it would be so."

"King Soros is dead," said the king. "I rule now." Lord Rydysh glared at him, grinding his teeth. Koenyg looked uncomfortable and uncertain. For twelve years, the powerful men of Lenayin had taken the king's lack of involvement in such matters for granted.

Watching him, Sasha felt her heart thumping with a new, hopeful urgency. Dared she hope? Dared anyone hope that the old king had finally returned?

"The Hadryn have been defeated on their home soil, Lord Rydysh," Torvaal said. "The gods have chosen. The victor is clear."

King Torvaal turned to Sasha. "Your terms are acceptable." There was a deathly stillness. Sasha could see the lords thinking furiously. She wondered how long any decree, even the king's, could survive against all the forces pushing the other way.

"I, however," Torvaal continued, "have terms of my own."

Sasha nodded. "Name them."

"All men who rode on this adventure shall once again declare their fealty to the throne, upon their honour. Only then shall they receive their pardon."

"Of course," Sasha agreed. "They never *left* your service, Father. They fight unjust lords and bigotry, not the king."

"It gives me little comfort to preside as a neutral over a Lenay civil war," Torvaal said somewhat testily. "Sofy shall return to me, and quickly."

"Aye," said Sasha. "She will when she's ready." Her father's stare darkened at that. "Father, this is her first breath of freedom in eighteen years! Give the girl a little time."

"Two days," Torvaal said firmly. "She keeps the company of rough men and soldiers. People will talk. It will not do."

"She tends our wounded," Sasha corrected, dryly. "She assists those in need."

"Two days," Torvaal repeated.

Sasha sighed. "Aye, Your Highness."

"Master Jaryd shall present himself to his Tyree lords for judgment."

"Not a bloody chance," Sasha said grimly.

"Sashandra," said her father, with the beginnings of temper, "the powers of a king in Lenayin are limited. The lords rule within their provinces, up to the point where those rights come into conflict with the king's law. A king has no say in a fight between provincial lords. This is an internal matter for Tyree. It must be settled."

"What's to settle?" Sasha retorted, glaring at Lord Arastyn standing over by a window. "Family Nyvar is no more. You are Great Lord of Tyree now, Arastyn. Why do you need Jaryd?"

"Tyree law is Tyree law," Arastyn said stonily. "It is immutable."

"Aye, well we're not *in* Tyree!" Sasha snapped. "I have seven thousand under my command, and I make the rules for men beneath my command. You want him, you come and get him."

"Your Highness," Arastyn said to Torvaal, "she is unreasonable." Torvaal gave him a look that suggested him a fool to have expected anything else.

"Who'll you get to come and take me?" Jaryd said from Sasha's back. His tone was flat, edged with darkness. "The Falcon Guard? They stand with me. You are powerless, Arastyn. A powerless coward. All the power and wealth of the Tyree nobility, and you're afraid of one man who does not respect your laws.

"Well, damn right I don't respect your laws. I challenge those laws. I challenge *you,* Arastyn. I challenge you to a duel. If you want me dead, you'll have to kill me yourself."

"Master Jaryd," Arastyn said, with dry contempt, "even a fool like you should know our laws better than to think a landless nothing like you can challenge his superior to a duel."

"Verenthane law, aye," said Jaryd. "But not Goeren-yai."

Arastyn stared at him, uncomprehendingly. "Goeren-yai? Master Jaryd, you are a Verenthane."

"Aye," said Jaryd, reaching beneath his collar, "well, not anymore." He pulled free his Verenthane star, snapped the silver chain about his neck with a sharp tug, and threw it at Arastyn's feet. "I reject your gods. I reject your law. From this moment, I follow the ancient ways. And I challenge you to mortal combat, Lord Arastyn, for the Great Lordship of Tyree, and the death of my brother and father."

About the room, men stared in disbelief. "You . . ." Arastyn began, and floundered, speechless.

"You can't do that!" exclaimed Lord Parabys, horrified.

"Good gods, man!" said Lord Kumaryn. "What of your soul?"

"Arastyn took that when he killed my brother," Jaryd snarled. "If the gods shall not allow me my revenge, then I rest my claim with the ancient spirits instead."

Koenyg snorted in profound frustration, and flicked a gloved hand through his hair. "Where's a priest when we need one?" he muttered.

King Torvaal frowned hard at Jaryd. Evidently thinking. When *was* the last time a Verenthane noble had converted, Sasha wondered past her astonishment? If it had ever happened, she couldn't recall it. Plenty of senior Goeren-yai had converted the *other* way to please King Soros . . . but this? She couldn't recall it happening even amongst poor, common Verenthanes.

Lord Arastyn fingered his own neck chain uncomfortably. He seemed a naturally calm and sensible man. A trustworthy man, with an inoffensive, handsome face. Exactly the kind of person, Kessligh insisted in his more cynical moments, from whom one should expect the worst treachery. "Even if such a thing were possible," Arastyn said defensively, "you are still a man of Tyree. You are subject to our laws and punishments."

"And as Goeren-yai," Sasha added, "he is entitled to redeem a slight upon his honour, no matter how high the rank of the man he challenges."

"After his trial," Arastyn said stubbornly.

"Before," Sasha insisted, shaking her head. Nice try, slippery worm. "He can't challenge after you've cut his head off."

"Actually," said Captain Akryd, conversationally, "this is the kind of thing a Goeren-yai man's immediate headman or chieftain should decide. Duels must be conducted according to the proper protocol."

"Pagan madness!" Lord Rydysh snarled, and strode from the cottage with a disgusted wave of his arm. He exited with a slam of the rear door.

"Who would be Master Jaryd's immediate superior?" asked the king, as if Lord Rydysh had never spoken, nor stormed out in rage. "Given his . . . circumstance?"

"Your Highness!" Lord Parabys exclaimed. "You're not seriously considering *allowing* this . . . this . . ."

"I'm not a priest, but I don't see how a man can be instructed by others on what he does or does not believe," said the king, looking at Akryd. "How about your poor bloody daughter?" Sasha nearly asked, but didn't. "Captain Akryd, humour my curiosity."

"Well, Your Highness," said Akryd, "I believe since Master Jaryd is not born into a Goeren-yai community, and has no village headman to speak for him, his senior commander in military matters should suffice for a judgment."

"As the senior military Goeren-yai," Torvaal observed, "that would be you."

"Aye, Highness," said Akryd, somewhat smugly. "It seems a quandary, does it not? One law for Verenthanes, another for Goeren-yai."

"One of the great quandaries of Lenayin," the king agreed. "Especially considering the Goeren-yai *have* no written law, and will not accept one. There is only tradition."

"One reason, perhaps, why Goeren-yai and Verenthane do not frequently live together," said Akryd. "These squabbles can be confusing."

"And one reason why certain Verenthanes would like nothing better than to see the Goeren-yai destroyed completely," Sasha said darkly, with a stare at the lords.

"There is no solution," said Akryd with a shrug. "Lord Arastyn need not comply with Master Jaryd's demand, yet the opposite is also true. It is the sort of matter on which a king could intervene as judge, Your Highness, but as you have already stated, kings cannot intervene on provincial matters."

"Hmm," said Torvaal. Another man, Sasha knew, might have raved at "pagan madness" just as Lord Rydysh had. But her father was actually considering the problem, no matter how it bothered his Verenthane soul. This was why Kessligh had served the man so unswervingly for nearly twenty years. King Torvaal, cold as stone and about as impassive, was one of the fairest men in Lenayin.

"Your Highness," Lord Arastyn said stonily, "Master Jaryd must face Tyree justice. This is imperative. We have enough great lords present for an appeal to be lodged, should you not allow Tyree's rightful justice."

"Any more out of you," Sasha told him, with darkening temper, "and I'll challenge you myself. I *am* Verenthane and such *is* my right, since you've made no finding of law or any other of your pointless horseshit against me. Unless you fancy yourself more than an equal to the departed Farys Varan with a blade, I'd suggest you shut your mouth."

"You would require fair cause to challenge the Great Lord of Tyree," Arastyn bit out, with barely restrained frustration and anger. "Your father would have to decide if your challenge was valid, and there is no fair cause that you could offer that would . . ."

"Fair cause!" Sasha said loudly, placing both hands flat to the table as if preparing to rise. "I am the uma of Kessligh Cronenverdt, the daughter of King Torvaal Lenayin, the saviour of the Udalyn people, and you're *making me angry!*"

Arastyn swallowed. There were great lords who would have accepted her challenge, not because they were fools, but because they were brave, and honourable, and Lenay. Lord Arastyn, Sasha was sourly noting, seemed to have dubious claims to all three.

"A personal insult seems a very fair cause," Damon offered from the back of the room. He was considering his cup, offhandedly. "You're trying to kill a friend of hers, Lord Arastyn. And a friend of mine. I think you'd best quit while you've still a head on your shoulders."

Arastyn gave a bow. "I must discuss with my fellow Tyree lords," he said. "If I can be excused . . ." He left without waiting for confirmation, following the path that Lord Rydysh had taken out the back door.

Sasha ran her gaze along the remaining lords. "We're losing them fast this morning," she remarked. "I wonder who shall be next?"

"I have one more term to state," said the king.

"Only one? Name it."

"You yourself shall be banished from Lenayin for the rest of your life."

Sasha gazed at him. Her father's expression held no remorse, and no pity. From Koenyg, she saw cold satisfaction, as if there were at least one good thing to have come from these events. She was not surprised. She knew the trouble that her continued presence in Lenayin would cause the lords, and therefore her father. But it hurt all the same.

"Absolutely not!" Captain Akryd exclaimed. "There can be no question. The men shall not accept."

"The lords call for your head," Torvaal said, looking only at Sasha. "By the king's law, I can pardon the soldiers of a rebellion. But the law demands death for its leader. I offer you mercy."

"No deal!" said Akryd, angrily. "You assume too much, Your Highness! We are the victors in this fight, not you!"

"For how long?" Koenyg retorted, standing grim-faced near his father's side, thick arms folded across his mailed chest. "Every Lenay region or province to rise up against the Cherrovan always won its initial encounters. But once the Cherrovan brought their full weight of force to bear, the uprising was crushed. The throne has not even begun to bring its full weight of force to bear. We had hoped such drastic measures would not prove necessary."

"Oh aye, your mercy and forbearance are well known throughout Lenayin, Prince Koenyg!" Akryd retorted sarcastically. Sasha held up her hand to silence him.

"It's all right, Akryd," she said quietly. "I knew that this would happen. My father has no choice. Maintaining a balance of power in Lenayin is difficult at the best of times. My presence here, having led this rebellion, now threatens that balance."

"That's the point!" Akryd exclaimed, striding to the side of the table so he could look down on her. "M'Lady, you rode for the Goeren-yai!"

"I rode for Lenayin," Sasha corrected solemnly, looking up at him.

The long-haired, plain-faced Taneryn man shook his head in frustration. "What's the difference? We had to choose a leader, and it was between you and Krayliss! We chose you and now you would abandon us?"

Sasha sighed, tiredly. "Please, Akryd, just . . . just think. This isn't about us and them. It's about Lenayin. Far more than I stand for the Goeren-yai, I stand for Lenayin. The nobles view a united Goeren-yai as a threat to everything they've worked for. They will attack us. They will attack me, more precisely. I will need protection. All the Goeren-yai flock to my defence, and the next thing you know, that's a civil war. The king has no power without the support of the lords. He must support them, or there is no king in Lenayin. No king in Lenayin, and we're back to where we were beneath the Cherrovan heel, a bloody rabble, and a united kingdom no longer."

"You're . . . you're saying a united Goeren-yai would be *bad* for Lenayin?" Akryd looked disbelieving. "What were we riding for, if not for that?"

"The Goeren-yai are *not* united," Sasha said firmly. "Lord Faras is right in that. The west and the south are mostly not with us. They are strangers to us. It's not the right time, Akryd. Now is not the moment to make such a stand."

"When then?" Akryd showed no sign of retreat. His eyes were angry, and he showed no qualm in displaying such disunity before the watching eyes of the Verenthane lords. One of Lord Krayliss's men, Sasha reminded herself. A passionate man, willing to fight, whatever the cost. Reckon that into any future Lenayin, should he or a man like him become the new Great Lord of Taneryn. "When would be the right time, if not now?"

Sasha returned her gaze to her father. "Lenayin marches to war," she said. "War in a foreign land, far from home. Our leaders feel we have allies there. They feel we shall be amongst friends, fighting for the Larosa, and the other, Verenthane Bacosh. I feel otherwise. I believe that our leaders are fools to believe appeals to Verenthane brotherhood, as if a common faith can patch over the profound differences that exist between peoples from far away lands. I believe our Bacosh friends will stab Lenayin in the back at the first opportunity, and leave us to bleed and die. Kingdoms are built in such ventures. Men from all over Lenayin will march and serve side-by-side, as they have never done before in all their long history. I wonder if the leaders of Lenayin shall emerge from such a campaign with the same sense of where Lenayin's future lies as they hold today. Many things can change on the road to war."

The many faces opposing her were wary. Even Koenyg's gaze showed a new, dawning respect, to accompany the anger. She'd been thinking on it, on and off, all the ride north. They could send her away from Lenayin. But they could not stop what she had started.

"I'll not fight our serrin friends in any lowlands war!" Akryd declared. "Should the call come, I'll refuse!"

"No you won't," Sasha said firmly. "You won't because I tell you you won't. Lenayin must stand together, Akryd. Goeren-yai and Verenthane, and all the provinces as one. You will march with the rest, when the call comes. Someone has to keep an eye on our brave and wise leaders. Someone has to make certain they don't sell Lenayin down the river for a handful of coppers and a holy blessing. That someone shall be you."

Understanding dawned on Akryd's face. He stared at her. Then gazed at the lords. And drew himself up, slowly, with a disdainful stare. "Aye, M'Lady," he said coldly. "I understand. We'll watch them. Perhaps it's time, after all, for the Goeren-yai of the south, east and west to all get to know each other better. Perhaps we can come to an understanding."

"You mangy bitch," Koenyg fumed beneath his breath.

Sasha gave him a slow smile. "You worry about your own hide, brother. You can throw me out of Lenayin, but I was heading that way anyhow. In fact, I think we all are."

Fires burned before the Udalyn wall and the sweet night air mingled with woodsmoke and the smell of cooking, laughter, ale and song. Sasha sat beside one particular campfire, a cup of wine in her hand, and watched the celebrations. The Hadryn had left—taking artillery, tents and every last sign of habitation with them. Now, men of the column rejoiced at that, and the news that they would be pardoned their disobedience to the king by the king himself, and that their families would suffer no hardship by their actions.

The Udalyn had emerged from behind their wall for the first time in numbers, amid scenes of wild celebration. Goeren-yai had embraced and, Sasha was pleased to see, her column's Verenthane warriors were also greeted with enthusiasm. Many of the Udalyn seemed astonished, in fact, to see so many Verenthanes in the column's ranks. The Udalyn's Chief Askar was thrilled and humbled to find that so many Lenay Verenthanes would shed their blood for the Udalyn. He did not hate Verenthanes, he said. Only Hadryn.

Sasha watched now as men about neighbouring campfires ate, sang, danced, or attempted broken conversation with Udalyn men, often through a chain of interpreters who made increasingly less sense the more ales they downed. There was much fascination that the Udalyn did not look particularly different from other Goeren-yai. More beads and patterned clothes, perhaps, but otherwise they might have been Tyree or Valhanan Goeren-yai to look at. There was more blond hair and red hair, however, and more blue eyes. Goeren-yai they were, but the Udalyn were northerners too.

Somewhere amidst the crowd, Daryd and Rysha sat by a separate fire, surrounded by parents, siblings and extended family, who pressed them for telling after telling of the things they'd seen—Baen-Tar, the Saint Ambellion Temple, Tyree and Valhanan, King Torvaal and the battles of Ymoth and Yumynis Plain. Sasha had received the impression that were it not for her own presence, the Yuvenar Family might not have believed the tale. She'd been pulled to that fireside by Aisha, who'd thought it something she should see—the Udalyn children back with their family, all of whom seemed to be accounted for. Rysha had sat curled in her mother's lap, and Daryd upon a stone by the fireside. Sasha had seen immediately that their mother would as gladly have clutched Daryd close for the entire night as she did to Rysha, but there was something in Daryd's manner now that forbade it. The men, too, watched and listened to the boy with a quiet, thoughtful respect.

Upon seeing Sasha, Rysha had leaped from her mother's lap with a cry and run to her. Sasha had picked her up, hugged her, then carried her back to the fireside, where she'd given Daryd a more respectful kiss on the cheek. The Udalyn boy had at least had the good grace to blush. Introductions had followed, to the astonishment of all the family when they realised who she was. Aisha, Sasha discovered with incredulity, was now partly fluent in Edu, from her time riding with the children, and these last few days in the valley. Barely a week to learn a new language. Even for serrin, it hardly seemed possible.

Aisha had shrugged. "Well, I know Cherrovan," she'd explained. "Did you know that Cherrovan is actually the root tongue for much of the northern Lenay tongues? If you know Cherrovan, Lenay and Lisani, you can work out the rest pretty fast."

"You know Lisani too?" Sasha had asked, aghast. Lisani was the most prominent western tongue, named as such for its origins from the great Lisan Empire beyond the western Morovian Mountains. The mountains were nearly impassable, and contact between Lenayin and the unfriendly Lisan was rare.

"Actually," said Aisha, "Lenay Lisani is very different from the actual Lisani of the Lisan Empire. Some serrin scholars speculate it actually came from Kazeri, from Kazerak to the south. Others insist it is entirely indigenous to western Lenayin. I have some ideas of my own, I'd love to travel there in more peaceful times."

"You speak Kazeri too?" Sasha had sighed, resignedly.

"Of course!" Aisha had been scandalised. "How can one speculate as to the origins of Lenay Lisani without knowing Kazeri?"

"How indeed." Sasha had found it a little depressing, in truth, to be confronted by a foreign people who knew far more about Lenayin than she ever would. Terel had told her afterward that Aisha spoke seventeen languages, not including her native Saalsi dialects. She was now intent on making that eighteen, in the days they had left in the valley.

"That's inhuman," Sasha had made the mistake of remarking.

"Indeed," Terel had replied, with an amused flash of bright red-brown eyes. And Sasha had realised that she'd only stated the obvious.

She'd left Family Yuvenar together at their fireplace, pleased that at least one family had found an entirely happy ending. And had dared to wonder if her own family could ever dream of such a future.

She wondered now, sitting with Sofy and Errollyn by their own little fireplace. Teriyan and Andreyis were off carousing with the rest of the Baerlyn gang. A part of her wanted to be with them, but she knew it would be wrong. She was the leader. She could not favour one group of soldiers with her presence without offending the others.

"Where's Aisha and Terel?" she asked Errollyn, watching the surrounding commotion. There was a lot of music, much of it poorly played, but the dancing was of a higher quality. Udalyn and other Lenay men, having no other means of communication, resorted to songs, dances and friendly contests of strength or knife-throwing. And, of course, that age-old contest of thick-headed men who ought to know better—drinking.

"Terel found an old lady who carves wooden figures in a traditional Udalyn style," said Errollyn. The firelight lit his eyes to a bright, flickering green that was like nothing human. He sat on an old stump, elbows on knees, gazing at the fire with a cup in his hand. "Terel's a master with wood. I believe she's giving him a tour of her cottage, it's just nearby. Aisha is no doubt off talking to every Udalyn she can. Working on her accent."

"I saw her," Sofy said, nodding. The cup in her hand was half empty— the first cup of wine Sofy had tasted in her life. She looked a little unsteady, but Sasha was not about to stop her sister's one night of rebellion just yet. "She was attracting quite a crowd. All very gentlemanly, I was pleased to see. And plenty of Udalyn women around to make certain their husbands did not wander."

"She deserves a distraction or two," Errollyn said quietly. "She misses Tassi. She does not relish the long ride back to Petrodor without her."

Saalshen's trading interests in Petrodor were huge, Sasha knew. Kessligh said that Saalshen's wealth had built Petrodor and turned it from a little fishing village to the most wealthy city in all Rhodia. She did not pretend to understand the complex web of power and relationships between the various competing families that dominated the Petrodor trade, the trading interests of Saalshen, the mainland feudal lords, the dockside poor with their strong ties to the Nasi-Keth, and, of course, the hugely powerful Verenthane priesthood. But she was determined to learn as much as she could from Errollyn before she arrived in Petrodor herself. A three-week journey to a foreign land where she had never travelled before. A part of her looked forward to it. And a part of her dreaded it, for fear that she would truly never see her homeland or her people again.

"I'd love to see Petrodor," Sofy sighed. "It's not fair that I have to travel all the way to the Bacosh, but I won't get to see anything interesting along the way."

"Oh, untrue," Errollyn said with a smile. "If your column takes the most direct route from Baen-Tar, you will travel through Vonnersen and see the riverside capital of Lanos. The crown palace there has sheer walls that rise a hundred armspans from the riverside, and towers that loom well above even that. And I hear that Telesia is a lovely place, where the highlands fade into low, and the land is rolling meadows with a thousand kinds of flower and a hundred kinds of grapevine."

"I don't think they'll travel through Vonnersen," Sasha replied. "When Sofy's wedding party goes, it'll be as part of the marching Lenay army. Vonnersen won't want that army marching through their lands. They've had bad experiences with Lenay armies in the past. And Telesia will want them crossing furthest from their cities too."

Errollyn shrugged. "Well, southern Torovan is very pretty," he offered. "And you'll travel through northern Bacosh, where there are some fantastic castles and palaces."

"Such a long way," Sofy said quietly. She sipped again at her wine. "Still, it shall be spring. I have a winter yet to last through."

"I'll be there, Sofy," Sasha assured her. "Somehow, I'll be there. You shan't be married without me, I swear it."

When Sofy looked at her, her eyes seemed to shine in the firelight. "You shouldn't make promises you don't know if you can keep," she replied. "I'll be fine. My father shall be there to marry me off. And some of my brothers, at least."

Sasha shook her head. "Kessligh insists that Petrodor is the key to preventing this conflict. I'm still uncertain. I have a feeling that I'll be finding my way across to the Bacosh at some point. I think we all will, whether we like it or not."

Sofy smiled. Then smothered a laugh behind her hand. "Oh dear," she half giggled. Sasha and Errollyn exchanged glances. "I'm sorry," said Sofy, recovering herself. "It must be the wine. I just recalled that Alythia's wedding party should be arriving in Baen-Tar from Petrodor just now. Only no one's there! How beastly of me to find that funny. The poor girl, she must be distraught. How embarrassing for her."

"Another reason for her to hate me," said Sasha with a shrug. "I'm sure that'll suit her well enough."

"She'll learn," Sofy sighed, considering the contents of her cup.

"What?" Sasha pressed, with a sly smile. "No haughty defence of Princess Alythia?"

Sofy smiled. "It's not that. It's just that . . . well, I was feeling so sorry for myself for a while as I was gardening here . . . you know, wishing for the innocent little girl that I was, and wondering if I could ever be her again. But then I realised that no one can. This valley is different today. It'll never be what it was, and the Udalyn will never be what they were—and for the better, I hope. And it occurred to me that not only is it inevitable that people can't always get their own way, it's good. Usyn didn't get his own way. The Tyree lords didn't. And if they can't, then it should be no surprise that I can't, either. And neither will Alythia."

"Nor I," Sasha agreed sadly.

"Nor any of us," said Errollyn.

Sasha gazed at him for a long moment. She could not, at this moment, be with her Baerlyn friends. Kessligh had gone to Petrodor. The old foundations that had once underpinned her life had all shifted, and now there was a new path before her. She had served Lenayin as best she could in this one, desperate act. Now, she would follow her uman to Petrodor. She was Nasi-Keth, and Petrodor was a stronghold not only for them, but for the serrin as well. She gazed at Errollyn, and wondered if this future she glimpsed was really so strange and unpredictable after all. The serrin had always been an enormous part of her life, through Kessligh, and the svaalverd, and the many teachings of the Nasi-Keth. Kessligh thought she had not given those teachings, and that heritage, the respect that it had deserved. Perhaps now it was time to put old grievances to bed. Time, as the old Valhanan saying went, to put the shoe on the right foot for a change.

"So, Master Errollyn," she said. "*Ras'el malhrahn tilosse?*" How do you see the road?

Errollyn smiled. "*Way'un ei,*" he said. Steep. No . . . more than steep. *Ei,* the active tense of *ei'lehn,* the root word for "curl," as a girl's hair might curl, or a dying leaf. Saalsi words came often in two parts, which came together and came apart to make new meanings, and hint at many more. Steep and winding, but with a hint of beauty in the treachery. "*Leh bel'eraine mahd'se fal svain'ah si.*" But the view has such beauty. Or no . . . not beauty. Enlightenment? *Svainerlai* was an old form of "beautiful," meaning something ancient and beautiful, but the *ah* probably came from *ahshti,* a related word that meant, very roughly, "to gain enlightenment from beauty." And so . . .

She shook her head in faint amazement. The grammar was appallingly vague, by human standards. But then, humans were empirical. Serrin made imprecision into an artform. Serrin words. Serrin thoughts. Serrin worlds. One door closed, another opened.

"What are you saying?" Sofy pressed with intrigue. "Oh please, don't talk Saalsi without me! I need to know what you're saying!"

"You need to know what *everyone's* saying," Sasha told her. "The Princess of Gossip. It's an addiction."

"Something old and wise and extremely dirty," Errollyn told the younger girl.

"Don't tease me," Sofy sniffed, with a haughty angle to her slim jaw. "I'm very frightening when I'm angry."

"Finish your wine," Sasha told her with a smile. "The night's only young yet. Father may get you back, but he won't get you back so pure and innocent as he'd like."

Sparks swirled and climbed into the night sky from the fire, mingling with the sparks of many surrounding campfires. Sasha watched them rise into one of the few constellations bright enough to brave the light of the rising moon. Hyathon the Warrior, with his belt, sword and helm. The hero of Lenayin, clear in the night sky above the Valley of the Udalyn—brave, proud and free.

About the Author

JOEL SHEPHERD was born in Adelaide in 1974. He has studied Film and Television, International Relations, has interned on Capitol Hill in Washington, and traveled widely in Asia. His first trilogy, the Cassandra Kresnov Series, consists of *Crossover*, *Breakaway*, and *Killswitch*.

Also by Joel Shepherd